The
Dakota Series

TRILOGY

The Dakota Series

TRILOGY

LINDA BYLER

Good Books

New York, New York

The characters and events in this book are the creation of the author,
and any resemblance to actual persons or events is coincidental.

THE DAKOTA SERIES TRILOGY

Copyright © 2020 by Linda Byler

All rights reserved. No part of this book may be reproduced in any manner
without the express written consent of the publisher, except in the case of brief
excerpts in critical reviews or articles. All inquiries should be addressed to Good
Books, 307 West 36th Street, 11th Floor, New York, NY 10018.

Good Books books may be purchased in bulk at special discounts for sales
promotion, corporate gifts, fund-raising, or educational purposes. Special
editions can also be created to specifications. For details, contact the Special Sales
Department, Good Books, 307 West 36th Street, 11th Floor, New York, NY 10018
or info@skyhorsepublishing.com.

Good Books is an imprint of Skyhorse Publishing, Inc.®,
a Delaware corporation.

Visit our website at www.goodbooks.com.

10 9 8 7 6 5 4 3 2 1

Library of Congress Cataloging-in-Publication Data is available on file.

ISBN: 978-1-68099-596-1
eBook ISBN: 978-1-68099-634-0

Cover design by Abigail Gehring
Cover photo: Getty Images

Printed in Canada

TABLE OF CONTENTS

THE HOMESTEAD

CHAPTER 1

As far as the eye could see, nothing but waving grass rustled in a wind that still carried a hint of winter. Brown and dry, it whispered the secrets that grew beneath its dying roots, as the sun coaxed tender green shoots of newborn grass from the snow-soaked earth.

If you looked closely, the beginning of a structure raised itself into the blue of the sky, thrust upward unfamiliarly, sharp and brown and out of place in the sea of grass, like the hull of a ship aground on the beach, the waves continuing their pounding as if the vessel had never been there.

Here, on the high prairie, the wind never ceased. Only before a storm did it become quiet, held back before it unleashed its power, multiplied by the calm, wreaking its havoc in the form of a deadly tornado or pelting hail driven by the storm's fury.

If you looked closer still, to the left you see faint wagon tracks that had crippled the waving grasses, crushing the brittle ones with each turn of the steel band that encircled the heavy wooden wheel, the plodding horses' hooves digging up the tender earth, erasing some of the weaker green shoots of grasses and delaying the stronger ones.

The trail curved away across the prairie until the distinct, sharp lines of the building jutted into your vision off to the right, marring the otherwise flat and serene landscape, the rough logs lashed and pegged firmly against the restless wind, and the steep pitch of a roof without lath or shingle.

The road turned down a small incline, rose slightly upward, and came to the mess of uprooted grasses, mud, and butchered logs dragged in from a place unseen. The whole scene was like a small wound on the immensity of the high prairie, smeared with wet salve. Off to the left stood a worn wagon, the dirty yellowed canvas straining against the ropes that lashed it to the bows bent into an upside-down U shape spanning one side of the wagon box to the other. It had once been a fine Conestoga wagon, but months on the road had aged it considerably.

It was the house that disturbed the blue of the sky and the waving grasses. Substantial in size, made of logs entirely, without a roof, windows, or doors, it was a structure being born nevertheless.

Two horses were tethered a distance from the wagon, the dusty harnesses slung across a steel-rimmed wheel. Granite buckets, the remains of a fire, an agate washtub and coffee pot, wooden troughs and crates, an assortment of stumps set around the campfire—all told of the human beings who traveled here to make a home in the vast and magnificent land, away from the East, from the congestion of religions and doctrines, and from brethren who bickered and fought among themselves like European starlings wearing their wide-brimmed black hats and broadfall trousers like an armor against evil worldly practices.

Mose Detweiler did not always know who was right and who was wrong. A simple, stalwart, dark-haired, sturdy man, he adhered to the doctrines of the Old Order Amish, the Christian sect founded in Switzerland by Jacob Ammann, who, in 1693, broke from the Mennonites over issues concerning excommunication and the practice of shunning.

By the twentieth century, most of the world's Amish lived in North America, their faith growing as they raised families according to their interpretation of scripture, and the rules and regulations written in the "*Mutterschprache*," — the mother tongue of the Swiss and German lands from where many Amish trace their ancestry.

The Great Depression of 1929 had hit Mose like a ton of bricks; it flattened him and took away his farm with its wonderful black loam soil of Lancaster County, Pennsylvania. Unable to make the mortgage, steep by all accounts (his father and older brother had warned), the bank that held it crumbled under the weight of a worthless dollar. Mose took to making moonshine illegally and selling it to bootleggers for a few dollars. After selling off most of the cattle and all of the sheep and pigs, what else could he do with the grain?

When the church discovered his secret, it excommunicated and shunned him. Shamed publicly, no longer able to hold up his head and look his brethren in the eye, he told his good wife, Sarah, that he was going West.

Her large brown eyes filled with the softness of tears, jewels of love and forgiveness. She said she would go, but not with ill feelings and certainly not with the curse of the ban. "You done wrong, Mose," she said softly, placing a hand on his solid shoulder as she looked into his brown eyes, watching them soften and become liquid with love. "Now make it right."

He hung his head, then, ashamed of his misdeed in the purity of her forgiveness. He went out, hitched up his horse and spoke to the bishop, repenting of his illegal work. He returned to the fold at peace.

So the family left, the shame of losing the farm riding with them on the high wooden seat. The many doctrines of the numerous Plain churches confused Mose, saddling him with a driving need to escape the noise and the cackling of a hen house with too many hens.

He wanted to continue in the doctrine his father had taught him, the simple belief that Jesus paid for his sins by His death on the cross. The Bible commanded a plain and peaceable way of life, and that was all. It seemed to Mose that everyone around him complicated matters, stirring controversy with the wooden paddle of heresy. He didn't understand the endless prattle caused by dissecting Bible verses and examining them under a microscope of ill-feeling and tightfistedness. When he couldn't breathe love among his brethren, choked on the fumes of a hundred different voices spouting as many different views, he drove away on his Conestoga wagon with the most blessed among women by his side. His Sarah. His jewel. His finest God-given possession. In the light of her love he became a better man, for he knew he was simple and didn't comprehend many of life's intricacies and the complexities of other men's outspoken knowledge.

It had always been so, even in school. Quiet and subdued, he fell behind in class, suffering misery at the teacher's rebuke and dissatisfaction with his many shortcomings. Somehow, though, he had won Sarah, a dark-haired, dark-eyed beauty from Honeybrook who placed her hand in his and never left him alone or insecure again. She was his rock, his helpmeet, and his best friend.

The journey was arduous, but they were a stoic family. Their oldest daughter, Hannah, was tall, thin, and had her mother's brown eyes and creamy skin. But there the likeness ended. Easily riled, her full mouth frequently pouted contemptuously, a fire in her eyes like brown sparks, the least provocation setting off the shooting flames. Her adolescence was fraught with prickly ill-humor and dissatisfaction with everything and everyone around her. At fourteen she was the bane of her patient mother's existence, the thorn in her father's side, but the delight of her brother Manasses, known as Manny or, in Hannah's silly chatter, simply "Man."

Manny was twelve, dark-haired, sturdy, tall, and winsome, with eyes that were completely without guile. He adored Hannah, loved his mother, and held his father in high esteem. He was content with whatever came his way, so when the children were told of the move west, he merely nodded his head and agreed. He didn't know what the West was, but he figured it would be all right, as long as his father thought so.

Hannah threw a royal fit until Mose sent her firmly to her room with no supper. As she laid on her bed listening to her stomach growl, she vowed never to become a vanilla pudding like her mother—no backbone, no will, no nothing. She did not want to leave Lancaster County no matter how poor they were. Her father could get a job at the harness shop or the butcher shop or any place. She wanted to stay here with her friends Rebecca, Annie, and Katie. What was out West besides nothing? She guessed they'd all be dead by the time they got to the Mississippi River, and if they weren't, they'd all be drowned shortly thereafter.

Eight-year-old Mary was dark-haired as well, but her wavy tresses were shot through with golden strands. Her eyes were light hazel, her skin pale with a dusting of earth-colored freckles as delicate as stardust. Mary was an astounding-looking child who skipped blithely through life, turning heads with her adorable smile. She carried her sheer unspoiled air of goodwill like an essence. At her young age, the West was a good place filled with bluebirds and colorful butterflies, fascinating bugs, and warm bunnies.

Mary persuaded six-year-old Eli, short, stocky, and dark-eyed with a thatch of thick black hair that always stood away from his cowlick like a mild explosion. He had inherited the same wild gene as his sister Hannah, so he was given to bursts of anger over slight irritations. Talkative, he voiced his childish opinions forcefully. As an infant he had yelled with colic day and night, aging his parents with relentless crying as his stomach churned with gas and indigestion, his feedings coming back up with the force of a water spigot. He fell down an entire flight of stairs at eight months, bumping his forehead until a blue-black

egg formed like a frightening growth. His cowlick stood straight
up and never laid back down.

Relatives cried, hugged, sized up the wagon, and shook their
heads. "Why don't you take the train?" one of them asked. But
Mose was determined and Sarah was submissive. Eager to see
the world, they trusted that the money would last and the Mississippi would be crossable. God would provide, and they'd be
on their way with His blessing.

And they were blessed.

They made good time with the heavy horses suited for travel,
the endurance bred into them. The hardest part was the cold
weather, when the snows blasted them with tiresome fury. When
a roaring campfire was not enough, they settled into a small
clapboard house for a few months before moving on.

Sarah's lovely face had become gaunt and pale. She was short
with the children, her hands riddled and crosshatched with chil-
blains. It was when she hid her eyes from her husband's searching gaze that he decided the cold and the monotony of days
on the wagon seat were too much. So they stopped in western
Indiana, in the forsaken little town of Salem, and took up residence in the other half of Mrs. Ida Ferguson's town house, built
in 1848 by her husband's own hands, may he rest in peace.
Hannah told Manny that Mr. Ferguson couldn't be resting too
peacefully the way he slapped this cheap house together, then
went and died and left his widow to stuff things like sheep's
wool in the cracks.

Ida was short and buxom, a white apron encircling the vast
circumference of her stomach. She wore it low and snug, leaving
her hips to sprout like two appendages on either side, a resting
place for her balled up fists, shoved snug by the weight of her
lumpy elbows, scattered with blue veins and purple moles. Her
nose was round and loose like a manatee, her mouth wobbly
with relaxed skin, her eyes pinpricks of brilliant blue that fired
good humor.

She put them up in the "harvesters' quarters," as she called the two rooms downstairs and two upstairs. It was drafty, the nails studded with frost like pristine mold, the rooms bare except for the minimum of necessities, the rough board floors scattered with bits and pieces of linoleum, frayed and cracked around the edges like a flapping, hazardous doily.

But there was a roof over their heads, and a rusty dysfunctional coal stove that was either red hot or barely producing heat, nothing in between. Their humble home was a source of comfort, a spot of warmth out of the wind and the constant smell of dirty wool, limp flannels, and unwashed bodies.

The first week in Salem, Sarah washed clothes in Ida's wringer washer and hung them on racks around the stove where they steamed with the good smell of lye soap and powdered detergent. She swept and scrubbed, lifted the derelict linoleum and swept underneath. She washed windows with vinegar water, ironed clothes, and soaked their white head coverings, which were now yellow and flattened from being stored in trunks and leather satchels.

They ate soup and fried meat, pots of oatmeal, and cornmeal pudding called corn pone. Sarah's cheeks were again pink, and her eyes soft and dark. She cleaned and cooked and slept in a bed with Mose by her side, like civilized folks, she said, not unkindly.

Ida visited every day, eyed Sarah's burgeoning figure, and asked how soon. Sarah's face flamed, and she kept her eyes downcast. "Not yet," she mumbled in a reply that barely made it past her lips. Ida watched her face, the spreading suffusion of color, patted her cheek, and said she hadn't meant to be nosy.

Hannah drew her eyebrows down and opened her mouth, but that was as far as it went. Her father kicked her beneath the table, his eyes sizzling with rebuke. These things were not spoken of, certainly not by a brash fourteen-year-old.

Ida missed all of this; her good humor rode on the wings of the blushing Sarah, so sweet, so grateful to have this house. Poor dear. What a journey! Why they had not taken the train was beyond her; but then, it was none of her business. She went home and baked them a molasses cake with crumb topping, opened a jar of preserved peaches, and took it over for their dessert. She sat on a chair by the stove and ate a large portion herself.

She cried when they left too soon, mopping her streaming eyes as she wished them Godspeed. She prayed fervently for Sarah every night before she went to bed.

The return of the cold, the flat monotony of the land, snatched the color from Sarah's face, turning her eyes dull and tired, like an unpolished rock. Her mouth was set in a straight line, her nose white and pinched, her eyes never leaving the brown, flapping haunches of the horses. It was only when spring arrived that she came back to life, the scent of new grass and south breezes filling her with hope.

Mose marveled at the land, the sheer, unbelievable magic of the empty space, immeasurable sky, and the distance from one line of cottonwoods to another. There was an occasional ranch, a cluster of houses, sometimes a small town, but mostly there was the endless sea of grass, the road before them, and the flat sky that turned from gray to blue and back to gray again.

Cold rains were the worst, draining their spirits, and sapping goodwill and energy. Roaring campfires dried out the worst of the discomfort, but dampness remained for days, leaving the children sneezing and coughing fitfully during the night.

Sarah wondered vaguely what would become of them out here in this wild, treeless land. Not one other Amish person to be with, to attend church with, to hold quiltings and hymn sings with, and no visitors to invite to your table. Would they all drift away, like miniscule seeds from a dandelion head, blown about by the winds of the world?

She watched her husband's smooth, untroubled face, thought of the small amount of dollars left in her cache, and wondered how they would survive. Must she go willingly, without question, hiding all her fears of the future? To second guess their decision now would serve no other purpose but to bring him down to the level of her pessimism.

Who would help her birth the baby? Who would know they had even arrived, let alone existed, needing help? Was there no kindly soul anywhere close? She felt her heart tightening, her stomach contracting, her pulse gaining speed. Her breathing became light and quick, and nausea rose in her throat.

"Mose." Her voice was quick and breathy.

He looked at her, shocked, his eyes widening. "Not already?"

"Oh, no. No. But, who will help when my time comes?"

Relieved, Mose laughed a genuine laugh filled with good spirits and calm. He put his arm around her shoulders and drew her against him, rubbing the palm of his hand up and down the sleeve of her coat. "Ach, my darling Sarah, don't worry. I'll find someone."

When they finally rolled to a stop one day in April on the small rise close to the line of cottonwoods and box elders, with a creek winding among them, full and wide, overflowing its banks in the wet springtime, it was like a miracle, a mirage, something you believed you saw but that would disappear before you had a chance to touch the bark of those trees or the rippling water.

They set up camp and walked the property lines. Mose got out the documents as if they were sacred, read them aloud slowly, mispronouncing the words, but Sarah knew what it meant. They would homestead these one hundred acres. At the end of five years, they would be the owners of this wild and foreign land. Sarah scratched the red rash on her forearm, squinted into the late afternoon, and stopped her rising panic as she turned her body from east to west, then north to south. *A trail, a roof, a rider, please God.*

Her face calm, unruffled, she walked to the wooden stake that sectioned off their acres and began to shake uncontrollably. Grateful for her long skirt and the fullness of the gathered fabric, she gripped each elbow in the palms of her hands and held them, crushing her arms against her stomach as tremors of the unknown shook her.

All around was only the untamed land and the enormous sky with a white cold sun lending its half light. The wind moaned and blew ceaselessly, ruffling the ends of the brown, dead grass, pushing the faraway trees into a crooked, swaying dance. Brown birds, the color of the grass, wheeled across the sky at breakneck speed, squawking a shrill, short note before disappearing into the restless grass. There were no crows or vultures, no deer, only the incessant calling of the numerous prairie hens. A gopher stood on its hind legs and gripped its front legs in front of itself like a reverent little minister beginning a soul-searching sermon.

The wind spoke to Sarah of longing in a restless attack of homesickness so real it felt physical, as if a giant hand gripped her heart and squeezed. She lowered her head as hot tears squeezed from her eyes, trembled on her lashes, and dripped onto her stomach. When she turned her head to one side, the tears splashed on the wooden stake. Some fell into the thick brown grass, anointing the soil of North Dakota, her home, her place to live for the rest of her days on earth.

It was Hannah who marched down to the creek bed and swung an axe alongside her father. Her fierce energy finally had a productive outlet after months of travel. Her eyes flashed with renewed interest. She hacked and whacked and rode one of the horses to pull the logs to the site where their house would be built, her smooth white legs exposed until Sarah ran gasping in horror with a pair of Manny's trousers and told her to wear them; they weren't completely savage just yet. Hannah looked at her mother with narrowed eyes, asking who there was to see. No use putting on the constricting trousers.

Sarah spoke levelly, without anger. "Put them on. Get down off that horse and put them on."

The flash of rebellion from Hannah's eyes staggered Sarah. What was this? Resolutely she went to the horse's bridle, faced Hannah's anger, and repeated her order without taking her eyes off her daughter's.

Hannah was the first to look away, followed by a slumping of her broad shoulders. One leg swung over, a quick slide, and she landed on her feet like a cat. Springing up, she took a few steps, grabbed the trousers from her mother's grasp, held the offending garment up, hiked up her skirts and stepped into them, holding her skirts with her chin as she buttoned the waistband. Lifting the broadfall, she buttoned it without speaking.

Sarah held onto the bridle and stroked the faithful horse, still working after all those miles. For the first time she thanked God for the isolation, her daughter displaying an utter lack of discretion.

Turning, Hannah stood back, gathered herself again, so cat-like, Sarah thought. Hannah leaped, slung a leg over, grasped the reins and turned her head. The horse wheeled in response to the jerked left rein and galloped off in a spray of mud and wet grass.

Sarah lifted a hand to her forehead to shade her eyes and watched Hannah go until she disappeared into a hollow. That was the thing about this flat land, the deception of it. It wasn't as flat as it appeared; only the grasses waving in the restless wind looked even. Sarah shuddered without knowing why. She returned to the camp by the Conestoga wagon and continued her ironing.

She had set up her ironing board between two stumps, so she lowered herself to sit and iron. The sadiron was no longer hot. She attached the handle, placed it on the red coals and loosened the handle to let it heat up. Mary looked up from the book she was reading, smiling sweetly at her mother before returning to her concentration.

Sarah sighed and watched the light playing on Mary's gold-streaked head. Why did she bother ironing? There was no one to see, no one to care whether their clothes were wrinkled or soiled, or if they wore none at all.

She snorted, a derisive sound, surprising herself. Oh, this was only the beginning of having to think differently, of stepping outside her well-structured life. No longer would she be able to wash on Monday, iron on Tuesday, plant and harvest and go to church and visit relatives and live among decent, God-fearing folks who lived together in unity. Well, mostly. How well she knew the unhappiness of her Mose, how the long and complicated talk of his peers bothered him, unsettled his simple way of life and his uncluttered thoughts. She knew too that he loved everyone and never thought ill of one person, in spite of not agreeing with him. Rufus Bontrager was the worst. Loud, obnoxious, cutting into other men's conversations to set them right with his own high opinion of himself, he rankled every-one's good humor. Mose always said he was loud, yes. And yes, a mite *grosfeelich*. But Rufus knew how to shoe a horse. He had a gentle hand in spite of his brute strength. When they lost their farm, he was the first to extend sympathy and shod both horses without charge.

Mose would never forget that act of kindness. And yet, he couldn't stay in Lancaster County. Ah, there was the mystery for Sarah. Would she ever understand his reasoning for going out and buying that still and making whiskey illegally to sell to disreputable men? The shame that followed, the women's unhid-den pity as they let her pass along the row of benches in church.

Fresh shame washed over her, remembrance as painful as daggers. Her Mose. In the end, though, she reasoned a sensible answer to herself, that desperate men did desperate things. Mose was just trying to save the farm and his good reputation. The hurt settled into her bones, evened out, faded, but stayed, like an arthritis only time could cure.

She missed going to church the most. The easy chatter of the women, the admiring of babies, young mothers bending to tie their little girls' head coverings, stashing their shawls and bonnets on tables or benches provided. Shaking hands, bending forward to give and receive the holy kiss, their traditional way of greeting one another. She could still feel the papery softness of Grandmother Miller's loose cheeks, the smell of starch from her covering, the wide strings beneath the soft, loose folds of her neck.

She lifted the sadiron and resumed ironing. A chill rushed up her spine as the grasses swayed and bent. The campfire hissed, crackled, threw sparks as the flames flared up by the wind.

Soon the chilly winds would stop. Soon the warm sun would win. Sarah became quiet inside herself knowing her time would be here then. They must find someone, somewhere. The quick panic that rose within her was successfully pushed back by her whispered prayers. She believed God was out here with them. She couldn't believe otherwise or she'd be swept away by her fear, her lack of trust in Mose, whom she had promised to obey, to love, to care for.

She put the ironing aside, shrugged on a light coat, and asked Mary if she would like to accompany her to the creek bed to watch her father cut down trees. Mary eagerly rose to her feet, grasping her mother's hand and looking up into her face as they set off down the path made by the horses dragging logs up from the creek.

Soon it would be time for their evening meal, the preparations still unfamiliar after all these months on the road. Sarah could never feel as efficient or in control as she had back in her own kitchen. Now she always reverted to soups or stews or cornmeal mush. A campfire was an unhandy thing in spite of the grate and the iron rod set up between two sturdy posts to hold the blackened kettle above the fire.

Sarah squeezed Mary's hand and smiled down at her. "Soon we'll have a house, Mary!"

"Yes, we will. Dat said we will."

Ah, to be young. To trust with that childish, doubt-free trust that erased every worry. Sarah only hoped—with a doubt-ridden hope speckled with fear—that they would have a house and beds to sleep in by the time the baby arrived.

She thought of Abraham and Laban's flocks of sheep. The Old Testament described them as pure white or speckled with color—the impure ones. If she put her faith beside her small daughter's, her own sheep would be the ones spangled heavily with the impurity of brown spots.

CHAPTER 2

THE WALK THROUGH THE HEAVY GRASS LEFT SARAH SURPRISINGLY breathless, considering they were headed slightly downhill. Mary chattered by her side, sometimes racing foolishly after small brown birds she had no chance of catching. Running back to Sarah, bent over, her tongue hanging like a winded puppy, she waved her arms up and down in exaggerated effort.

Sarah laughed, the sound almost frightening in its unnatural, hoarse explosion. Mary laughed with her without noticing any change in the sweet mother she knew and loved. For this, Sarah was deeply grateful. She had to do better, to find a place deep within herself and draw on this source for strength and courage. Lifting her head, Sarah vowed to rise above the most difficult situation without allowing Mose or the children to see her inner struggle. There was a word for that, a Dutch word, but she could not remember it.

They came to the group of trees where the grasses thinned and the wide creek wound its way among them. At the far end there were the patient horses, tethered to each other, heads hanging straight in the quiet repose of a sleeping animal. There were five logs, straight ones, cut and ready to be hauled to the house, a pile of twigs, thin branches and brush, and another tree laying along the creek. At one end, Mose lifted the axe and brought it down precisely into the whitish crevice where it had struck many times before. Hannah whacked away at another tree in short, swift strikes, her face red with exertion, working twice as hard as Mose but accomplishing little except wearing herself out.

Manny was hacking small branches off the fallen trees, dragging them to the brush pile and walking with a sense of newfound purpose, his old gray hat brim flopping over one eye, torn away from the crown, and his dark hair spilling out like extra stuffing.

He caught sight of his mother, waved and grinned and called out to them before continuing his work. Mose stopped, wiped his face and turned, his face creasing with pleasure at the sight of his lovely Sarah and Mary. Hannah stopped, scowled, turned her back, and resumed her senseless whacking.

Mose laid down his axe and stepped away from his work to greet them. Dressed in patched denim broadfall trousers, an old blue chambray work shirt, the sleeves rolled above his elbows, the muscular arms straining every seam, he never appeared more handsome to Sarah. Gladness lit up her face, evincing radiance from within. The light drew Mose and had drawn him since he was young. "Sarah! So you came to see what we're doing? Good for you. And my best Mary."

He laughed as he kissed Sarah's cheek, one arm about her waist, drawing her close. She smiled up at him, their souls united in their searching gaze, seeking, finding, content for all the ages, being together, bound by their love.

When did she first think of Eli? Who spoke of him first? Mary or Mose? Was it herself? She could only remember the yawning pit of realization that Eli was not here with Mose.

"I thought he was with you." She was never sure who said the words first but knew instantly that something was terribly wrong.

Sarah's hands went to her mouth. Her brown eyes searched her husband's face as if she could gain entry to a reassurance in the depth of his brown eyes. "Where is he?" she whispered hoarsely.

"Wasn't he with you at all this morning? This afternoon?" Mose's voice was quick, firm.

"No. No." Sarah shook her head and pointed a shaking finger at Mose. "I thought he was with you."

"He wanted to come with me but I told him no. He was to stay with you."

Sarah's first thought was to run. She wanted to flee the terrible specter of a missing child on this immense prairie with its hidden hollows and swells, the grass waist high in some places.

With the realization that Eli was lost—she could not run from this fact—came the knowledge of hope, of bare spots where he could gauge his surroundings. She became rational, pushed back the panic, searched Mose's eyes.

"He can't be too far. Did he not come with you at all?" she asked, her mouth becoming dry with her accelerated breathing. She licked her lips, tried to swallow.

"When I told him to stay, he was headed to the wagon. After that, I can't remember seeing him." His brown eyes filled with tears as his brow furrowed. He turned to the four directions, shading his eyes, searching the far-flung reaches of this strange and mysterious land.

Mary's eyes became troubled, large and round with concern. "Mam, he told me he was going rabbit hunting."

Sarah looked at Mary and grasped her shoulders with hands like claws, clamping down until she winced, shook herself away, and began crying.

"Tell me, where did he go?" Sarah ground out between clenched teeth.

Mary shrugged, sobbing now, her soft heart shattered by her mother. A kind of hysteria gripped her. Sarah began talking, moving away, moving back, babbling incoherently. The thought

of their Eli, so short and stocky and manly, reduced to shrill cries
of terror without knowing where he was and how he would find
his family—it was almost more than her heart could bear.

He was her child, her baby. For six years he had been the
youngest, the only one she had to cuddle and love, and now they
had brought this innocent child to this terrifying, grasping prairie, this strange restless, treeless land of no mercy. A great sea of
grass that was capable of swallowing children.

Mose came up with a plan. He told Hannah and Manny
to stay together and keep calling, never losing sight of the
treetops. Hannah listened to her father's words, her head bent to
keep her emotions hidden, before saying that the whole plan was
senseless on foot. Why not ride the horses? So Mose allowed it,
watching both of the older children mount their horses and ride
off up a small grade, the grass coming to their boot tops. Dimly
they heard them calling, "Eli! E—li!" as the prairie and the sky
swallowed them whole.

It was then that Sarah began sobbing—dry, harsh sounds of a
mother's despair when a child is lost. Mose turned to take her in
his arms, the sounds from her twisted face a form of torture to him.

"Don't, Sarah, my Sarah. Please don't. We'll find him. He's a
tough little chap. We won't let him die. You and Mary go back
to the house now and build a roaring fire. Maybe he'll see the
smoke and find his way home. I'll start walking in the direction
God lays on my heart. I'll see where He leads me by my prayers.
Now go, my precious Sarah, put your faith in God. He'll take us
through this valley."

He reached into his trouser pocket for a worn, wrinkled
square of cotton fabric, lifted her chin and wiped her cheeks
tenderly, searching the closed lids of her anguished eyes as if he
could see through them and find his Sarah beneath them. As
it was, the pain on her face became mirrored on his own. His
smooth, untroubled features were now drawn, as lines appeared
on his forehead and he became one with his heartbroken wife.

"Go now," he said gently, as he placed a kiss on her forehead. She stumbled away, the grasp of Mary's hand the only thing that kept her from falling. Mary was wide-eyed, serious, but too young to absorb the significance of a lost child in a strange land.

When Sarah looked up through streaming eyes that squinted painfully against the afternoon light, the prairie and the sky above appeared clouded in menace. The whole circumference of her world was ripe with portent.

They would not find six-year-old Eli. He had already been gone at least eight hours without returning, which meant he had gone too far to find his way back. These wide, harsh grating grasses never stopped their whispering, their rasping against each other. Their unstable movement deceived the eye with the appearance of sameness, and yet the height and depth was not similar at all. What if Eli stumbled onto a lowland, a swamp with mud underfoot and grasses above his head? He could wander for days in circles, never being found until it was too late.

The thought was too bitter, she could not tolerate the suffering of her small, squat son, the mighty one, the temper that flared like Hannah's. She kicked the red coals of the campfire, scattering the ashes, threw a handful of small wood pieces on top and watched it flare up. Dry-eyed with fear, she carried larger pieces of wood, rolling them expertly on top of the flames, watching the thick white smoke reach upward.

Oh, Eli, see this smoke. Look in this direction wherever you are. Taking a deep breath, she steadied herself, stood straight and searched the horizon, the far reaches of this endless land that contained nothing but grass. She shivered, hostility like goose bumps on her spine.

She had blindly followed Mose to this forsaken country, trusting his judgment, leaving her own will behind like clouds of dust curling from beneath those sturdy Conestoga wagon wheels. Here they were, cursed, *fer-flucht*. It was his disobedience to

God with that insanity, that whiskey stilling. God is not mocked. What a man soweth, thus must he reap.

Oh, but he had repented though. Yes, he had, and truly. What had the bishop said? Though your sins are scarlet, I will make them white as snow. Clean like sheep's wool. Who was to know God's ways?

She threw another chunk of wood on the fire and watched the thick smoke curl, lift off, spreading upward, and on up. Look down on my offering, Lord. Accept it graciously the way you did for Abel all those many years ago. Accept my desperation, Lord, and return my son to me.

The sun's light was dimming now as it began its ascent into the waving grass. A chill crept across Sarah's arms and she shivered again. Darkness would come, inevitably. A darkness so black it would crush her if Eli was not found. She bit down on her lower lip, her teeth beginning to chatter with the new fear of day's end. She would not sleep, ever, until they found Eli.

But darkness came and with it a separation from any source of human comfort. Her husband and two oldest children were gone, for all she knew they were lost too, never to return. She paced the perimeter of the camp, tried to scale the walls of the house for a view of the darkness around her. Anything except to sit by the wagon and the half-built house with Mary quietly watching her with hazel eyes and helplessness.

Sarah could not comfort her daughter; she could not comfort herself. She felt cold toward Mary, a strange removal of feeling. She did not want Mary to see her like this. She wanted only Eli. To see his black hair sprouting from his hat, his open, laughing mouth, his snapping brown eyes, so alive, so eager and full of ideas, so restless in all of his imaginings.

Mary's whimpering about hunger brought a deep shame, a scramble to set things right. A slice of cold corn pone, some beans warmed by the fire. Sarah sat with her while she ate, an arm around the thin little waist. She assured Mary they would bring Eli back, and told her to put on her warm nightdress. Sarah tucked the girl into her bed in the wagon, with difficulty now, but she managed. Since the hour was much later than her accustomed bedtime, Mary breathed lightly, tucked her hands beneath her cheek and fell asleep almost as soon as Sarah pulled up the heavy woolen blankets.

Alone now, Sarah began pacing again, her hands clutched tightly over her stomach, causing a weird, rocking gait, but there was no one to see, no one to care. She cried then, loud, agonized wails until she was spent. She lay down on a blanket by the fire. Fear and doubt mixed with her heroic efforts at prayer. She could not concentrate. Her anxiety scrambled every coherent word until she gave up and lay there prostrate on her bedroll, a mere speck in this alien, unforgiving land. I just am, she thought. I am only one person. God knows where I am, and He'll just have to take over. I can't pray, my bones have turned to ashes, and my strength is gone. I have no will. It's all right to give up, isn't it?

She thought of her own mother so far away, so unreachable, as if she no longer lived on the same earth but had spun off into the sky to some other world.

"*Shick dich*, Sarah."

How often had she heard the command as a child to behave herself? Yes, that was what she would do. She would accept the situation, give up her own will to God, and if He chose to take Eli to heaven, then so be it. At this thought, fresh tears squeezed from beneath her closed eyes, and she knew she wasn't close to accepting Eli's loss.

The night wore on, the half-moon lending its ghostly light, the stars blinking around it like silent listeners awaiting the outcome, offering their tiny pinpricks of light and comfort. The stars seemed close, a part of another world that looked out for people on earth, folks like her and Mose and the children, alone on the North Dakota prairie.

Sarah sat up, straining to see, to hear. There was only black night and silence. Even the wind had stilled. There was no swaying, no movement, no scurrying creatures. Only the silence laden with the knowledge that Eli had wandered off, that her husband and children were out there somewhere with the only two horses they owned, their only source of survival. That, the bags of seed, and the rain and the sun to coax them into germination.

She got up and tended to the fire once more. She thought it was useless to build it so fiercely if the dark sky swallowed the smoke without helping, the way the daylight would illuminate it. And yet she threw chunks of wood on the embers simply for the need to move, to do something.

She didn't know what time it was, too afraid of the time on the face of the clock in the wagon. One o'clock? Two? Would the time make a difference in her agonized waiting? Surely that was not a streak of dawn to the east. Please don't let it be the dawn. If they were out all night long and returned at daylight without Eli, she could see no way of being able to accept it, to comprehend with the settling of the horrible fact that her son was still missing.

She sat up. The earth spun, slanted on its axis, while a deep blackness engulfed her as the weakness spread through her limbs. Then—a smear of light on the prairie as if a star had fallen into the grass and shattered. There. Someone had extinguished it. A hand went to her chest to still her heart's pounding. Her eyes watered from intensely straining to see, to make the light appear. Perhaps it was only a giant lightning bug. No. There. There it was again.

She got to her feet, clumsily, whimpering now. It was a light. It was. It came on, closer. Voices. Real voices. Like a statue she stood, one hand clamped to still her heart, the other to her mouth to stop the trembling sounds that came from her throat.

There were horses. Ah, yes. There was Pete, with Mose. And Dan following with two riders. Hannah and Manasses. Manny. Somehow, this moment seemed too holy to call him Manny.

Was that a dark bundle across Mose's saddle? Sarah stood, straining to see, then took a few steps forward, her hand out-stretched, reaching, hoping.

The horses and riders stumbled into the circle of light, the flickering fire illuminating the spent horses and the slump of the weary riders' shoulders. Mose called out, a quick high cry, in a foreign tone of voice she had never heard before.

Ah, yes. There was a hefty bundle across Mose's lap. Now Sarah could see the outline of a gray and rumpled hat, the shape of her missing son, her husband's strong arms around him. They came to a stop. Sarah reached Mose before he had a chance to dismount, her hands grabbing, claw like, her arms outstretched, muffled sounds no one understood coming from her open mouth without stopping until Mose had lowered her son into her arms. He was half asleep, filthy dirty, his hair stuck to the brim of his hat. When Sarah crushed him to her chest and rained tearful kisses on his face, he began to protest, turning away, spluttering and waving his arms.

"Eli. Eli. Eli." Over and over Sarah said his name, unaware of Mose or the other children's vigil.

"I'm all right, Mam. Stop it!" Eli protested hoarsely.

The horses were taken away by a dry-eyed indignant Hannah muttering to herself, a reluctant Manny following, having rather enjoyed the theatrics of his brother's return.

Sarah collapsed on a stump by the fire, her energy drained away by the enormity of her relief, the deflation of loss replaced by a sense of wonder and the dawning realization that Almighty God had heard her pitiful doubt-filled cries and had taken mercy. She could barely stay on the stump, her arms like water now, liquid, without substance. And yet she gathered her son to her breast, the rough wool of his coat a luxury, the softest fur imaginable.

"Eli, where were you? Where?" she asked, both laughing and crying. Mose sank to his knees, his arms going around his wife and son, his brown eyes searching Sarah's face, lit only by the fading embers of the fire.

But Eli didn't answer. He had fallen asleep. They laughed then, her and Mose, with a sound of bell-like joy, an exultation. A miracle. Their son had been returned to them. Together, they undressed him, washed his grimy face and hands, put him to bed beside the still sleeping Mary. Then Mose told Sarah his story.

They had ridden in wide circles around the creek bed. Keeping the treetops as their center they circled farther and farther, always calling, until their throats were parched by their hoarse cries. Darkness fell and hope with it. Mose could not understand why he had no guidance, no inner light. He asked God over and over, he explained. Stumbling around the seemingly endless prairie, only the North Star lending its light to keep their bearings, the horses became too weary to go on. Hannah complained about the senseless riding without an idea where Eli may have gone. Manny wanted to go back, rest, and resume the search in the morning. Mose could not face Sarah with empty arms and crush her with disappointment. So they kept riding.

It was Mose that ran his horse into the strand of barbed wire. Pete stopped, then shied away from the cutting of the sharp barbs, almost unseating Mose, but a cry went up from Hannah who immediately recognized the significance of a fence. Follow it and they'd find folks, other human beings in this forsaken place. She meant godforsaken but couldn't say it, having had her mouth slapped for it earlier and sent to the back of the wagon to ride with the horse feed—like a sack of oats.

They rode and rode, always by sight of the fence looming to their left. Sometimes, the prairie rose gently; sometimes it dipped down, but never very far or very steeply.

They found the outbuildings first. Black silhouettes, stark and unwelcoming in the dark, star-pricked night. Cattle stood around the barn like dark ghostly humps. A raucous barking rattled Hannah badly. There had to be five or six of them, all wolves or half-wolf. She fell back, holding Dan until Mose rode ahead. By the sound of them, they'd slay the horses and have them for dessert.

On they rode, past the corner post, beside an old wagon parked in waist-high grass, the dogs appearing like a dark sea of moving bodies, roaring and growling, leaping but never touching. Hannah wanted to turn her horse and get out of there but Mose said no, not before they spoke to someone.

They didn't have long to wait. There was the slam of a door, a shout of command, and the dogs' barking was extinguished like magic. A figure appeared carrying a lantern with a small orange flame burning inside the glass chimney, surrounded by tin and held by a thin metal handle. The opposite hand carried a rifle, long and low, the dark figure revealed only from the waist down.

"State yer business. If'n yer cattle rustlers, I kin tell you right quick that if'n you don't leave this here propitty straightaway, ye'll be peppered wi' gunshot."

"No, no," Mose called out, his voice gravelly with exhaustion.

"Wal, what you here fer?"

"We lost our son, a little fellow named Eli. We're probably nine or ten miles away homesteading government land. Name's Mose Detweiler from Pennsylvania."

The bobbing lantern came to a halt, hoisted by one arm, it showed a grimy denim overcoat, a battered brown Stetson pulled low over a thin face, eyes barely visible, a moustache like a plastered-on chipmunk tail, a thin, scraggly gray beard, and a face like overcooked ponhaus. Silence spread through the night, thick and uncomfortable.

"Wal, I'd say we gotcher son. Little fellow, stocky on 'is feet, he is." Mose couldn't speak, afraid to show weakness in the face of this unknown character. He swallowed, felt the tears, and swallowed again.

The house was behind the barn, rising like an unkempt monster in a sea of mud. Lights glowed from the windows though, and somewhere was Eli. Somewhere behind those crooked walls with rectangular yellow eyes, perhaps his son would be safe and sound.

And he was. He didn't cry, only blinked and blinked again. The lean woman sitting beside him was stringy and mean-looking like her husband, as if all the years on this harsh land had honed them into this toughness. But she smiled, said "Howdy," and that was most important.

Their names were Hod and Abby Jenkins. Lived on this here place all our lives, spoken proudly. Had three sons. Hod out riding, he said, checkin' cows. Stumbled on the sleeping li'l guy. Scared 'im, so he did.

They would come visiting. There was a road, a pattern of dirt roads. They had missed them all. Ranches dotted this land now. Surprised they could still get a grant to homestead. They'd be over, they said.

Mose's voice was an endless stream of rich gold oil that poured into the loneliness of Sarah's soul. There were people! Dirt roads! Even if it was nine or ten miles, that was a jaunt compared to the months and months of weary travel they had just come through.

Sarah had not realized she felt so alone until she knew they had neighbors. Real human beings. Flesh and blood. Someone to talk to, share lives, stories, find out about weather, crops, what could be done, what was profitable and what wasn't.

Here she was, holding her beloved son, delivered to her by God's own hand, the promise of folks living around them. People who built fences and lived in houses would come visiting.

Sarah breathed deeply, her eyes taking in the sweep of dark prairie, the sky above them, dark and starlit, the moon wan and impotent now, sliding toward dawn. The chill of fear and foreboding left with Mose's words, replaced by a warmer, more welcoming atmosphere, an air of hope, a breeze of anticipation. Perhaps it would be possible to feel content here, flourish even. Who knew?

Suddenly bone weary, her head drooped, her arms fell away from her stomach, as she tried to get to her feet. Mose came to her rescue, then held her lightly, too weary to think of further conversation. Hannah and Manny returned, spoke a few words before retiring to their bedrolls, arranging themselves into a comfortable position before nodding off.

Mose and Sarah knelt by the wagon, side by side, bowed their heads in silent prayer as each one silently spoke their gratitude to God. They retired for the night, rolling the heavy sheep's wool blankets on the canvas, drawing down the sides that allowed them a small amount of privacy beneath the wagon, still grateful, and immeasurably drained of strength.

Mose snored almost immediately. Only a minute had elapsed before the comforting sound of his breathing told her he was asleep.

Oh, she was blessed. Blessed beyond anything she deserved. Blessed among women. She reached over and stroked her husband's shoulder, then drew closer for the warmth of him, and shivered once before slumber overtook her.

In the waning hours of night, prairie dogs slept in the rich soil of their tunnels dug beneath the heavy growth of prairie grass. Rabbits tucked their twitching brown noses into their forepaws and rested, their ears flat along their silky backs. The firelight died down until only a few red embers glowed into the dawn of a new day.

CHAPTER 3

IT WAS THE CRY OF A MEADOWLARK THAT WOKE SARAH, OR SOME other familiar bird from Pennsylvania, she thought, without being fully awake. The sun was already high in the sky, which made her throw back the blankets and leap to her feet, thinking of the washing and the cleaning.

It was only after she stood on her feet, her hair scraggly, her dress rumpled and mud stained, the cold spring air sharp on her face, that she remembered where she was, how she had gotten there, the whole scene before her eyes a reminder of the shadow of hopelessness that had threatened to envelop her and choke life's breath from her body.

Squaring her shoulders, she took a deep breath and winced as ragged pains shot across her ribs. Ah, yes. This too, to be dealt with. Well, Mose had found someone, as he promised he would, so they were not alone.

She poured water into the coffeepot, set it on the rack above the fire, poured some into an agate bowl, grabbed a bar of Castile soap, and began to wash. She combed her hair, winced at the snarls, then twisted them along the side of her head. Using the very tip of the comb, she drew a straight line down the center of her head, divided the dark hair and twisted each side into a long roll before coiling first one, then the other, to the back of her head. She inserted steel hairpins with a quick, practiced precision. Satisfied, she placed a black scarf on her head, tied it beneath the thick, dark coil, and then began to prepare breakfast.

She shook her head a bit, thinking of her *wasser bank* back home. The kitchen cupboards lined along one wall, the deep sink where she placed her dishpans, the spot where the drain cover allowed the dirty water to drain out, the days she spent there, baking and cooking, and the wood-filled cooking range with the smooth cast iron top she cleaned with a piece of emery board until it gleamed like a polished mirror.

No use thinking about that. All she wanted was a roof over her head and four sturdy walls that kept out the night sounds. She hoped for the cleanliness of a floor, even if it was made of rough wood.

Her heart leaped at the thought of the possibility of a frolic. Inviting all the neighbors for miles around to have a day of building, erecting a house or a barn in a few days, the whole place swarming with straw-hatted and suspendered men, like a new hive of worker bees.

The sun's light dulled, the light fading out as if night were falling. Astounded, she lifted her head and saw a gray bank of clouds building up in the west. It was only midmorning but something was brewing, like a pot of coffee that had been percolating too long.

Well, if it was going to rain, she had better alert Mose and try to stay dry somehow with a canvas stretched between poles for a makeshift shelter. She rubbed her back when she straightened and searched her surroundings, with no trace of her husband.

As she sliced the boiled, congealed cornmeal mush, Hannah rose, disheveled and mud splattered. She stretched as far as she could reach then eyed the fast disappearing sun, the half-finished house, the weak morning fire out in the open, her mother's back rubbing, and her burgeoning figure. She snorted, stamping one foot.

"Mam, you know a storm is brewing," she said, pulling out hairpins and running her fingers through her thick, black tresses, spreading them around her face and shoulders.

"Yes. I believe there is a storm coming." Sarah stopped slicing the mush and turned to look at her oldest daughter. "Up already? I thought you'd sleep later, having been up all night."

"Yeah, well, we found him. We have neighbors too. They definitely aren't like us. Not Amish, that's for sure."

Sarah eyed her sternly. "What do you mean?"

"Well, after the wolf pack stopped braying, he carried a rifle to greet us and meant to use it if we were cattle rustlers. What's a rustler?"

"I suppose a thief. What else?" Sarah answered. "Now get your hair combed, Hannah. Your father will be here soon."

Hannah obeyed, and Sarah turned back to frying mush. Sarah thought wistfully of the brown hens in the whitewashed chicken coop with the fenced-in yard surrounding it. Gathering the warm, brown eggs in the rubber-coated wire basket, washing them carefully, cracking them in the black cast iron skillet and watching the clear whites set to a white deliciousness surrounding the yellow yolk, like the sun in a pale patch of sky. She swallowed, her mouth watering for the taste of an egg. And freshly baked bread, yeast bread, white and so soft with the light brown buttery crust. She felt faint with hunger and longing then thought it may have only been the night's emotional chaos taking its toll on her well-being.

Fried cornmeal mush with a side of cooked navy beans; that was all they had. Hannah shook salt over her helping of beans, frowned as she scooped them into her mouth, and said she didn't care if she never saw another bean as long as she lived and that she was going to shoot a bunch of rabbits and prairie hens. At least they'd have meat and gravy.

Mose laughed outright and said she'd best help get the house finished. He looked worriedly at the changing color of the sky and asked Sarah if she needed a shelter before the rain came.

"Well, what do you think? Should we just stay in the wagon?" Hannah pursed her lips as she listened to her parents. Always asking Dat, always following, going along with what he thought best. It drove her crazy. Didn't Mam ever have a will of her own? Not a thought in her head, other than what Dat thought? Gee. She was never getting married if she was expected to give her husband everything, including the contents of her head.

Take this whole catastrophe. Plopping his family down in the middle of a gigantic haystack, no thought for where he would get lumber or glass windows or shingles, just slapping logs into the form of a house, as if he knew what he was doing. She could not imagine that log dwelling keeping out the rain or the cold, the way he was going at it.

Hannah knew her place, though. She knew she could not say everything she thought and that about three-fourths of her thoughts were like seeds on unproductive ground: they withered before they took root and turned into words. Manny told her she needed to keep more of them to herself. It was not necessary to say everything she thought.

Well, maybe so, but Dat was going to need help with that building unless he came up with a better plan. What was he going to use for a roof? She'd bet he hadn't thought that far, or perhaps he'd prayed that a roof would fall out of the sky and land on top of the walls.

Hannah scraped her plate clean, fishing the last bean from the side of her bowl. The sky turned gray, but a soft white gray, so perhaps the day would turn out cloudy, without sun, and no cold rain would fall.

Dat seemed in no hurry to accomplish anything, so Hannah wandered off to check on the horses. The wind was picking up. She noticed a sharp edge to every breeze, bending the grasses, ruffling them with gusts.

She lifted her eyes to the sky, taking in the shifting clouds. The now strange yellow light turned even the gray clouds a sickening color. Like vomit. The yellow light washed across the brown grass, turning it into a dark and sinister sea of ever-changing shadows.

It was late March, so surely this strange light and these churning, roiling clouds that erased the morning sun would not be the harbinger of snow. Or one of the Midwestern blizzards she had read about in her history book at the school she attended back home in Lampeter Township.

Hannah's large brown eyes took in the changing light, the bank of clouds. She wrapped her hands around her waist, her shoulders squared, wide and muscular on a tall, thin frame, her feet planted wide, leaning against the wind. She was defiance, strength, her unwashed hair in loose coils that stayed in spite of the growing gale.

As she stood and watched, the air took on a new chill in a few minutes. She shivered and wrapped her thin coat closer. Her calculating thoughts took stock of their situation. A sweep of prairie as far as she could see. The horses on their hobbles. The small pile of firewood, the fire out in the open, her mother bent over it. The only shelter, or some form of obstruction, was the four walls of the house, the stark rafters jutting into the sky, the Conestoga wagon with its worn flapping canvas.

Sitting ducks, that's what we are, she thought. Genuine sitting ducks. Greenhorns from the East who don't know anything about this high prairie and the weather that can wipe us all off the earth. Dat has so much faith. He'll just turn all soft and reverent, lift his face to the sky and place his trust in God alone, thinking He'll preserve us, and if our time is up, we'll go to our eternal home. Oh, I know how he thinks. Well, maybe I'm not willing to leave this earth quite yet.

With that, she stalked back to the camp and stood before Mose, who was eating his breakfast, hungrily slicing his cornmeal mush with his knife, a serene smile on his face, the welcoming light in his eyes as he watched Hannah's approach.

"Good morning, Hannah. Have you slept well?"

"Yes. Dat. Did you watch the sky this morning? Do you sense the wind?"

Mose finished chewing, swallowed, and then smiled. "Yes, Hannah, I did. I believe we're in for some hard rain."

"What about snow? It's only the end of March. We are not prepared to survive a winter blizzard, the way they arrive here in the West."

"Oh, I don't believe we'll have snow. The weather has favored us so far this spring. Our house will soon be finished."

Sarah sat on the stump, her plate balanced on her narrow lap, and looked from Hannah to Mose and back again. As usual, the decision was up to Mose. "I figure we'd better hitch up the horses and move out, find the Jenkins' place right quick. We can't survive snow and wind if it's a bad storm," Hannah said forcefully, spreading her arms, her hands palms up in a pleading gesture.

Mose finished scraping beans off his plate, deep in thought. He lifted his head to search the sky, watching the bank of gray building in the northwest. The sun was white, barely visible by the haze of yellowish gray smeared across it.

"Why don't we pray?" he finally asked.

"You can pray if you want, Dat, but I think we should get out of here. Now!"

"What about stretching the canvas across the rafters of the house? Could we quickly make a temporary roof? We'd have the four walls, such as they are," Mose said, his eyes searching his wife's.

"We could. But if this is a blizzard, how could we secure a canvas good enough to withstand the winds?"

Mose considered this, tugging at his long, dark beard. His eyes went to the clouds, and back to Hannah, his daughter, who was fast growing into an adversary, a presence he did not understand. A girl growing into a woman, outspoken with quick words and brute strength, the opposite of his soft, winsome wife and her quiet, accommodating demeanor, her willingness to let him lead in all things.

His first response to Hannah's plan was to reject it. A rebellion he did not understand welled up inside him. Who did this upstart think she was? His eyes went to the skies, back to the yellow brown of the moving prairie, ominous with the unnatural light that lay over the landscape like a threat.

He was still considering, mulling things over, when Hannah turned suddenly and pointed. Low on the horizon a dark, fast-moving blur that quickly came on, until they saw three riders bent low, their horses lathered, slick with sweat, their nostrils flaring red. They slid to a stop, breathing heavily, the riders flinging themselves off, the horses stretching their necks, tugging the reins from the riders' hands, then stood, intent on breathing.

It was Hod Jenkins and what Hannah assumed were two of his boys. In the harsh, yellow light he looked formidable with his dark, weathered face, his beard like frayed cloth, his clothes slick with grease and dirt. The boys were younger replicas of their father, tall and thin with angular features. Their hats were pulled low on their foreheads, their hair the color of the old tomcat back on the farm. Torn jeans and worn-out boots with crooked heels worn down from years of wear in all sorts of weather.

Hod wasted no time, minced no words. "Don't like the looks of this." He lifted a hand to the sky, a gnarled finger pointing in the sun's direction. "You better come with us. We don't have much time. I don't like the looks of this," he repeated.

Mose was at a loss for words. His gentle brown eyes worriedly searched the sky. Then his brow became smooth with his childish faith. Turning, he told the men he appreciated their concern and was thankful for good neighbors, but he believed the Lord would provide.

Hod let fly with a string of forceful words, telling Mose that he could think that if he wanted, but his thought of staying here unprotected on the high prairie was foolish. The temperature could plummet to a freezing low with strong winds and biting, icy snow. More folks than he could count had met their deaths, frozen less than a mile from home. "You don't mess around with Mother Nature, I'm tellin' you now," Hod finished.

Sarah stood, pulled her coat closer, shivered, and watched her husband. She could tell what he was thinking by the untroubled expression in his brown eyes. He wanted to stay and place his trust in God alone.

Manny came stumbling from his bedroll behind the wagon, his face alarmed at the presence of these men, their blowing horses, the dark sky and the sense of unease. He stood with his hair sticking up every which way, unwashed, his blue chambray shirt wrinkled from his night's sleep.

From the wagon, Mary and Eli's dark heads poked out from beneath the canvas, their faces alight, black eyes curious, without fear.

Hod waited, watched the sky, his boys' heads lowered, scuffing at the dirt with their boots, hands hooked in their jeans pockets.

But Mose was not stubborn or headstrong. He did not place trust in his own way. In the end he figured that Hod knew more about the weather in North Dakota than he did, being a newcomer and all. Yes, God did provide. God knew every sparrow that fell to the ground, but he also felt the wisdom of letting Hod advise him where the weather was concerned. And so he gave his consent.

Hold told them there was no time to waste. They had best get that wagon going as fast as possible. His clipped words were obeyed. Mose brought Pete and Dan and hitched them to the wagon. Sarah and the children stored their belongings beneath a canvas in a corner of the house. They packed extra clothing in a small trunk. Hod told them to leave the food; there would be plenty at his house.

The riders went on ahead, leading the way. Mose drove Pete and Dan, prancing, misbehaving, jerking at the traces, pulling left rather than right. Sarah sat on the wagon seat clutching Eli as his head bumped one way then another. Mose sawed at the reins and tried to control the team.

Sooner than he thought possible, Mose guided the horses onto a good dirt road. In spite of the line of grass growing in the middle, it was more than wheel tracks in trampled grass. It was a good road.

Hannah stood, clutching the back of the seat for support and watched Hod and his boys ride. She had never seen anyone ride like that. It was as if the rider was merely an appendage, part of the horse, like an extra leg, something attached. It was a sight to behold, this skill of sitting on a horse so easily, a grace that stirred her senses. If it was the last thing she did, she would learn to master the skill of riding a horse, not just bouncing along, her legs flopping like a sack of feed.

Hod kept watching the sky, then held up a hand to get their attention. "Storm's movin' in awful fast. We still got an hour to go. If'n I was you, I'd get them horses going right smart."

Mose nodded. He had felt the change in the atmosphere, felt the air hitting his face turn frigid, slamming into his chest as if the buttons weren't securely closed.

Pete and Dan, the faithful brown Standardbred and Hoflinger cross, felt the storm's approach, the static, the wind and cold increasing as they trotted.

Sarah grimaced, holding on to the metal rim attached to the side of the heavy wooden seat, the wood and steel wheels jarring even with a slow steady trot. Now at every dip or hole in the road the thick mud was like glue. The horses tugged unevenly and threw them all around like corks in a bucket. But with the lowering skies, it was better to stay quiet, grit her teeth and endure the torment to her heavy body.

She felt Hannah's sharp knuckles through the folds of her skirt. She turned and found her daughter braced against the seat, her eyes burning dark with excitement, the storm mirrored in the depth of her gaze, watching the riders, a half smile on her face. She was enjoying the whole bit—the riders, the frightening weather—as if it was a deliverance, elevating her above the drudgery of their trip and the endless hard work that followed. Ah, Hannah, how will we be able to keep you with that spirit within?

The light was fading fast. The bank of yellow gray was changing to solid gray that spread over the enormous sky and the prairie below. Mose saw the storm, recognizing a fraction of its fury. His eyes widened as he leaned forward, bringing both reins down on the backs of the tiring horses. Sarah looked at him sharply. To goad a jaded horse was just not her Mose.

Hod yelled at the moment Sarah felt the first spit of snow. The atmosphere lowered, crushed the breath from them, as if a giant hand swiped through the air and took all the oxygen with it.

Hod pulled his horse back until he was level with Mose, who was concentrating on keeping the wagon intact and on four wheels. If there was an accident now, they might not make it to the ranch at all.

"Use your whip, if you got one!" Hod roared. "We got another few miles, but she's comin' fast. Keep your eye peeled for my buildings. If they get wiped out, concentrate on that spot. Your life and your wife and kids might depend on it."

Mose spoke sharply. "Hannah, help your mother get in the back."

"I can't," Sarah cried. Before she could muster any resistance, Hannah's powerful grip seized her shoulders, clamped down like a vice, and flipped her over the low back like a cat.

Sarah cried out in fright. She grabbed an edge, anything within reach. It was the sturdy wooden trunk. She hung on like a drunk lost in his own dizzying world.

Mose was bringing the whip down on the terrified team, lunging and galloping, wild-eyed, the lather flying in white flecks into the howling wind. There was a gray whirling outside now. Through the small hole where the canvas was drawn together by a heavy ford, Sarah caught glimpses of a driving, slanted snow so thick it looked like the foam from the dishpan. She realized now they may never reach the Jenkins' ranch. She had heard of folks dying in a storm, disoriented, frozen to death. But in March? In early springtime?

She heard Mose yell, calling hoarsely and still goading the weary horses. Above the wagon's clatter, she heard a faint call like the bleating of a sheep.

On rattled the sound of flying hooves, creaking wood, flapping canvas, the children's whimpers, Mose's voice like a hoarse scream. Another sound above the wind's howling and the roar of the snow. Again, that sheep's bleating.

The wagon slowed. Sarah felt it turn and tilt at a crazy angle. Mose's voice rose again. Sarah hit her head on the trunk as the horses broke into another frenzied gallop. Hannah yelled out to Mose in a panicked voice, screaming, "Left, Dat. Left. Bear left. I saw something!"

Mose did not hear, intent on the lagging horses, coaxing only a bit more speed. With an impatient snort, Hannah heaved herself up over the seat, grabbed the left rein and hauled it in, using both arms, her feet sliding off the dashboard now coated with ice and snow.

Mose tried to gain a hold on the left rein, but Hannah shouldered him away. Straight ahead a black hulk rose through the storm. Mose cried out, his relief putting him back on the seat, giving Hannah both reins. She kept her feet positioned against the dash, squinted through the thick gray turbulence, the whirlwind of snow, ice, and wind, elements that had the power to bring death to all of them.

When she pulled the team to a stop, dim figures appeared out of the black wall, pushed aside a part of it, the smell of hay, straw, manure, and oats, all pungent sweet smells from the interior of a barn, mixed with the roaring wind.

Hannah jumped down off one side, Mose the other, their hands like frozen chunks of ice as they fumbled to loosen the traces. Someone pushed her aside. Someone else took her arm in a tight grip and pulled her into the barn. Another person appeared out of the gloom and told her to stay; they would bring in the rest.

Hannah was startled into obedience long enough to step aside and allow the steaming, panting horses to be led through the wide door. Foam, white lather, and sweat that had been rubbed against their skin by the chafing harness, dripped off their bodies. Their flanks quivered, their sides heaved.

Hod appeared carrying Eli, with Mary clinging to his hand. Manny led his mother through the door, white-faced, her lips twisted in pain. Mose was the last one in the door, his hat carrying a layer of snow, his face red with cold, his eyes still wide with the real danger his family had experienced.

The horses were cared for first, rubbed down with gunny sacks and given small amounts of water and hay. "No oats yet," Hod said stiffly. "It'll kill 'em, blowing the way they are." Mose nodded gratefully. He noticed the row of stalls, crude and makeshift but clean and mucked out, spread with fresh straw and plenty of hay, the watering trough clean.

"A' right folks. We need to get to the house and to do that, it'll take all the wits and common sense we got. We can't see more'n a few inches in front of our faces. Let's put the women folk between us." He turned, his gaunt, chiseled face taut with concern. "We ain't got no clothesline to hang on to, and this 'n's a humdinger. Biggest March storm I ever seed all my born days."

He called to his three sons, who stepped up in various stages of slouching, all tall, slim and crowned with the same battered wide-brimmed Stetsons rimmed with dirt and grease. "Clay, you're first. Your sense of direction's the best. Like a homing pigeon. See if you can get us to the house. Now, whatever you do, don't let go of the hand you're holding. If you slip and fall, yell as loud as you kin, a'right?"

He pushed Hannah forward. "Take this 'un, Hank. Take her other hand." And so Hannah found herself grasping two gloved hands. The rest of the family was strung out, children between adults.

"You best start yer prayin' early," Hod said, but good-natured. Mose nodded. "You know if we miss the house we could all freeze to death wandering the prairie in circles. That's a human condition, a natural thing, to go in circles when it feels like yer goin' in a straight line."

Hannah thought he was making a big deal out of nothing until they stepped out into an alien world that contained a fierce cold. The whirlpool of snow and wind sucked all the air from your lungs and left you floundering to get only a fraction of what you needed, like a catfish on the riverbank before it was put on a stringer.

The cold slammed into her, through her thin coat and heavy skirt. Her hands that had been cold before were numb within seconds. There was no use trying to see through the gray, whirling whiteness of snow and ice. It was like being blind, but not black—only moving particles of white.

They kept moving forward. No one fell and no one hindered Clay's steady progress. The snaking line of human beings were being introduced to forces of nature they had no idea even existed. The worst they had ever experienced was a heavy, crackling, sizzling thunderstorm in the fertile valley called Lancaster County.

There was a bump and a shout. Clay had hit the corner of the house. More shouts went up and were snatched away by the powerful wind. Clay felt his way along the side of the house and found the porch. He stepped up on the porch and would not relinquish his hold on Hannah's hand until every last person was grouped on the porch, all accounted for and standing on his or her own two feet.

Only then did Hod raise a fist and brought it down on the doorframe over and over, a rhythmic banging that must have frightened the lone occupant within, Hod's wife, Abby Jenkins. Within seconds, the door opened a mere crack and a wrinkled face framed in fuzzy gray curls appeared, checking to make sure it was her husband and sons.

"You don't need to break down the doorframe, Hod. Git the little ones in. Watcha waitin' fer? Summer?"

Hod stepped back, extended his arm and pushed them all through the door where they tumbled, numb with cold, fear, and a real sense of having been placed into a strange, distorted world where nothing made any sense. The sun had ceased to exist, and God had forgotten them, all alone out here in the bitter, unsheltered prairie country.

CHAPTER 4

As THE DAY WORE ON, THEY REALIZED THEIR MIRACULOUS DELIVERY. They had never imagined God could create a storm of such intensity, with such a roaring, battering wind that sucked the heat up the chimney in spite of a good stove filled with massive chunks of wood. The glass panes in the windows rattled and jingled, lashed by heavy gusts of ice particles that scoured the house continuously.

Abby Jenkins was calm and in control, her lean, weathered face as tough as good leather, the frizz of gray curls sprouting out of her head with no rhyme or reason, no part in the middle, cut just below her ears and left to fend for itself. She wore a house dress with a row of white buttons down the front, the fabric having been adorned with flowers at one time, but washed and faded to a light-colored material with faint squiggles of color and held together by small safety pins in place of its missing buttons.

Her apron of sturdy oxford cloth pleated around her thin waist; woolen socks were pulled up halfway to her knees from severely tied sturdy brown shoes.

First, she brought a wooden clothes rack to the stove and dried all the Detweiler's outerwear. Then she found seats for everyone, the long green sofa a luxury that Sarah sank into as she closed her eyes on waves of pain that rolled across her back.

She gritted her teeth and willed it away, clutching Eli on her lap. Mary snuggled beside her, the child's hazel eyes wide with concern.

Mose sat beside Mary, watching his wife's face when he could. He felt out of control because of a situation he had not foreseen and had not even known existed. A belittling sense of shame and a stifling humility settled around him. For the first time in his life he questioned God, as if he was a bit put out that God had dared put them through danger that made them beholden to heathen folk. Their language was abominable in spite of their attempts to curb it for their visitors' sakes. He was not one to speak of religion to others. You had to be careful throwing out holy words in case you might be casting your pearls to the swine. These people likely didn't have a faith or believe in God. They appeared reckless, and the words coming out of their mouths were simply wrong. A sin, that's all there was to it. The Bible admonished plainly to let your yea be yea, and your nay be nay, and anything *dorüber* was unnecessary.

Manny and Hannah watched wide-eyed as they took in the talk that flowed so easily between the father and his sons, Clay, Hank, and Ken. Clayton, Henry, and Kenneth, Hannah thought. Everyone appeared to have come from the same mold with almost identical slouches.

The house itself was surprisingly large and tidy for the plain appearance of the outside. A living room, complete with the large green sofa, a few rocking chairs, scattered rugs on a wooden floor gleaming with varnish, a few bureaus, dressers, and small cabinets with crocheted doilies. Most of all, the whole house had plaster walls that were painted just like the Amish homes back East.

The kitchen was substantial with a gigantic woodstove in the center, a long plank table, benches and various mismatched chairs. There were cabinets, a pantry, and a sink built into the simple cupboards that lined one wall.

Calendars hung above the table, from a feed store, granary, and a livestock market. Cast iron pans, blacker than night, hung from pegs on the wall, along with tin dippers and cups, saucepans, and an agate dishpan.

There was a bedroom downstairs for Hod and Abby and three upstairs, she said. There'd be no problem, her and Hod would move upstairs and she'd put clean sheets on the bed for Sarah and Mose. The kids could sleep on the floor. Hannah could have the couch in the living room. They'd make out and everyone would be fine.

And then she pulled an enormous blue roasting pan from the oven, took off the lid, and stirred the contents, releasing some mouth-watering scents Sarah couldn't identify. With easy movements she unhooked a frying pan, got down a tin of lard and slapped a sizable amount into the heating pan. She disappeared through the pantry door and emerged with a parcel wrapped in white paper. Unwrapping it, she lifted a large slab of meat, threw it in the pan, followed by a few more, then another.

Sarah had never seen anyone fry so much meat for one meal. These were the years of scarcity, the Great Depression, when meat was rationed. Even a small beefsteak was hard to come by. Sarah would fry a small amount, cutting it carefully into tiny pieces and stirring in milk to make gravy that barely tasted of meat at all. In spite of herself, her mouth watered. Sarah pulled herself up from the couch and offered to help, but Abby waved her away. "I'm used to doing for my menfolk. It'd make me right nervous havin' another woman in my kitchen. Clay, git the table set."

Clay moved forward into the lamplight, hatless, his dark yellow hair sticking to his forehead in clumps, his face as red as a sunset below his eyes. His heavy plaid shirt hung in folds on his loose, skinny frame, but he moved with an easy, unselfconscious grace, as if it had never occurred to him that he should care what anyone thought of his appearance.

His eyes were blue, narrow, and surrounded by skin weathered beyond his years. He had the most honest, frank gaze Hannah had ever seen, as if he didn't think bad of anyone and no one thought bad of him.

Hank was a bit shorter, wider in the face with the same lower level of red topped by that white ring where his hat hid his skin and hair from the elements. Odd-looking, but necessary, living on the prairie and working cattle.

Ken was the youngest, tall and thin with the identical phenomenon of red skin fading to that alarming, marble white. His face appeared youthful, unsullied by wind and weather. He caught Manny's eye more than once, grinned a lot, confident, swaggering, and like his brothers, unselfconscious.

Clay spread a long white tablecloth, and clattered dishes of various shapes and sizes. He splattered tumblers and silverware haphazardly around the table.

Abby turned. "There, we'll all fit. I'll sit beside Hod, then the kids can all slide along the bench there, and we're in business." She smiled her flickering smile that bunched her leathery skin into an accordion of creases as her blue eyes swept the room. "You must be starved, poor babies."

Sarah was dismayed to feel a swelling in her throat and the quick stab of tears. Surely she was stronger than this. But the truth was, she hurt all over, especially her lower back, and she was more than afraid of what it was. Ah, submission. So here she was, in an impossible situation, dependent on these kindly people, having no will or place of her own.

She felt Mose's eyes on her and turned to meet his worried gaze, assuring him with the light in her own dark eyes. I'll be fine.

When they were all seated, Hod spoke. "Now, it ain't our custom to do any prayin' before meals. But you folks has religion, I'm guessin', so you go right ahead if'n you wanna bless this here food."

Mose looked around the table and said, yes, they were used to praying before partaking of a meal, but always in silence, never speaking a prayer out loud. Hod nodded, said that was fine with him and bent his head. Everyone followed suit. Mose bowed his head, silently said his usual prayer, and waited for Hod to lift his head first. This was, after all, his home and his table, and by the customs of the Amish, it would be Hod who would end the prayer.

They sat and sat. Mose became uncomfortable, peeped at Hod, and was met by the top of his white, balding head. Thinking Hod must be more devout than he gave him credit for, Mose quickly lowered his head again.

Sarah cleared her throat and felt a blush of color suffuse her face as she thought how ridiculously long her husband was praying. Perhaps he was that grateful for their deliverance and the safety of this house.

There was a loud rustling, a cough and the clatter of silverware. Everyone lifted their heads, relieved. "I'm hungry. If none of you men will end the prayer, I will." It was Hannah who spoke. Sitting there in the lamplight without a smidgeon of shame, it was she who ended the prayer, so far out of her subservient place and quiet meekness that befitted women of the plain churches.

Mose was furious but quickly squelched his anger, gave a quick smile and a smooth "Why, Hannah. . . ." Sarah felt the beginning of a raucous laugh and pushed it back by lowering her eyes, her humility holding in her real emotions.

Hod looked at Hannah, really looked at her. His eyes shone. "Wal, Mose, I'll tell you right now. This young 'un's got some spunk. She'll make it." He nodded. "She'll make it out here, if'n no one else does."

Hannah gazed back at Hod, clearly pleased. She began to shovel an alarming amount of beans onto her plate followed by the crispy fried potatoes. Sarah couldn't help herself. She said, "Hannah, mind your manners. Perhaps there isn't plenty."

"What you talkin' about?" Abby spoke up. "They's always plenty at my table. I allowed for six extra. Let 'em eat. She's a growing girl." After that, the bowls were passed, enormous blue stoneware bowls of beans cooked with tomatoes and onion, ground beef and bacon, fried potatoes and thick slabs of steak fried in lard and liberally salted. There were baking powder biscuits, so thick and light, and homemade butter. Sarah told Abby she must teach her how to make biscuits like these.

No one said much of anything. They simply applied themselves to their heaping plates of food. Outside, the storm continued, screaming around the corners of the house, whistling between windowpanes and walls, roaring across the level land with no obstruction in its way save for an occasional house or barn, which were like matchsticks compared to the power unleashed on them.

Hod said they might lose a few cattle but they'd felt it in the air, ridden hard, had most of 'em in the shed or corral. "Nothin' to do about any of 'em now. They ain't dumb. They'll find a shelter somewhere, left on their own."

Mose shook his head, doubt filling his eyes. "I don't know about this country. I had no idea the weather could turn severe this quickly."

Hod snorted, but not unkindly. "You got a lot to learn. This country ain't for soft folks or whiney ones that complains. Reckon if'n you want to make this yer home, you best hear me out.

"Fer one thing, you need to get that plow in the ground. You need to finish that house and with just you and the kids, it ain't gonna happen. Your first year depends on the success of your wheat crop. You gotta get it in. Start a few calves and get your herd started. Me an' the boys'll be over. Get the house done."

"But . . . but . . ." Mose was at a loss for words. He shouldn't be needing all this help. It was not the way he had planned. He was from Lancaster County, Pennsylvania, the most fertile land in the East. He had planned on flourishing, raising corn and hay, and showing the West how it was done.

Already they had almost lost their lives, and here they were, dependent on these heathen who didn't pray before a meal, which told him they lived unthankful lives, and that was one of the seven worst sins. How could an Amish man of faith join with the man of the world? You cannot serve God and Mammon.

Mose pursed his lips and said, "Well, I do appreciate your offer, but I hadn't planned on growing wheat. I'm accustomed to our way of growing corn. And hay, of course."

Hod sat at the end of the table and stared open-mouthed at this young upstart. He thought, he won't last one year unless someone knocks some sense into that pious head. "Corn ain't much for this land," was what he said.

"Why not?" Mose countered.

"Wal, fer one thing, growin' season ain't too long. Fer another, it don't rain when it's s'posed to. Wheat comes up early and ripens early. You get it shocked and milled before too much drought rolls around."

Mose shook his head. "Hard work."

"You skeered of it, or what?" Hod asked, eyes flinty with irritation.

"No, no. Oh, no."

"Yer money's in them cows anyways. You got all the hay growin' wild. This here's ranch country."

Mose nodded. This was all news to him. He hadn't planned on this. He had nothing but seed corn, and it was going in the ground no matter what Mr. Jenkins said. And he would not have to know that he didn't have enough money for a few cows and a bull to start his herd. He hadn't thought about raising beef cows. He had traveled all this way to a government homestead cultivating the thought of corn and milk cows, pigs and hens. He had no idea it didn't rain very much, or that the money they had brought was disappearing at an alarming rate.

So, according to this man, his own well-thought-out plan was not going to work. He would talk it over with Sarah, his support.

Abby saw to it that each child was comfortable for the night and assured them the storm would likely blow itself out in the morning. She hauled out blankets and quilts from chests smelling of cedar, plumped pillows into flour sack pillowcases, and fussed over Mary's hair, saying wistfully it would have been awful nice to have a daughter.

"I'll be real nice to the boys' women if'n they ever show an interest. All's these men think of is cattle, the market, hay, and wheat. That's it." She laughed, still good-natured about her life in spite of living with these men.

"I got a few womenfolk neighbors. Now not between us, the way the men say. But there's Bessie. Bessie Apent. And Ruth. Ruth Jones. All married to ranchers, about five, six mile away. We'll get together every so often, exchange news and recipes. We listen to the radio and talk about what goes on in the world.

"Bessie's got four daughters. She'd love to marry 'em off to every one of mine. But I'll tell you, them girls is so fat and lazy, I dunno how she's ever gonna git 'em married off. She needs to git out and chase 'em around the corral a coupla times, melt some o' that lard off 'em. Big girls, not bad looking, but don't work hardly nothin'. Her husband runs the feed store in Pine. Pine's the town. Don't ask me why they named it Pine. They ain't any pine trees for hunnerts a' miles. Some say if Philip, that's Philip Apen, Bessie's husband, would get them girls to work, they'd have a right decent cattle ranch. But he has to hire help for whatever he does.

"Ruth Jones is a good friend. Salt of the earth she is. She'd give the shirt off her back. Has two daughters an' two sons. Names Lucille and Isabelle. They's awful nice girls. Work the cattle with their brothers. But seems like they don't have a hankerin' fer my boys. Somethin' about book reading and college. Want to go east to New York. I'll tell you right here, it ain't gonna work. Once this beg sky gits in yer blood, you never leave.

"New York City? They ain't gonna make it. Now you Amish. You don't marry outside a' yer religion, do you? What's *Amish* mean? Yer just plain down better than ordinary folk? I mean, same as them Catholic nuns dressin' themselves covered all over and not marryin' and stuff. Yer Hannah wouldn't marry outside her faith, is what I make it out to be."

Sarah answered her questions and explained about the Amish emigrating from Switzerland a long time ago for a place to practice their religion, how today there was a large group in Pennsylvania, but Mose wanted to see the West, so here they were. And no, normally girls did not marry outsiders. It would be a disobedience and a sadness to see their daughter overstepping the parental boundaries.

Abby nodded and shook her head wisely. She commented kindly, accepting Sarah into the realm of folks she kept in her heart. "We womenfolk, we have to stick together in the big country. It's all we got, an' if we can't get along, then the loss is ours, 'cause we all know we need each other. Stuff like, I'll give you my biscuit recipe, tell you how to make 'em, and you give me one a' yers. I ain't sure how Amish eat. You eat kosher, like them Jews? You fast and eat a bunch of purified fish and stuff? I'll tell you right now, there ain't no fish on the prairie. You eat hogs? Jews don't eat pork do they? If'n you don't, there's bacon in them beans we just ate. Hope you ain't left yer religion about my beans."

Sarah laughed outright. "No, no, Amish is different than Jewish, although we respect their religion. Jews are God's chosen people you know."

Abby narrowed her eyes. "You sure about that?"

Sarah laughed again, easily, and could see the suspicion of new and different cultures. Was it just Abby, or was it the West?

"Now that black shawl and bonnet you had on? You know yer gonna have to be careful where you go with that on. Folks'll take you for a witch. I mean it. We ain't used to that hereabouts. They'll not do you harm; they'll just keep about a mile between them and you. People get superstitious about ghosts and haunts and stuff, livin' alone the way we do. Might make us crazy in the head, probably."

"I won't go anywhere. Where would I be able to go? All I have is my family.

"Yeah, and looks like you got one on the way."

Sarah blushed and felt the swelling in her throat. "I do," she said softly.

"When's yer time?"

Sarah mumbled a date, then lowered her eyes. She mustered all her courage to meet Abby's eyes and asked softly if there was any help close by and how they should go about finding someone.

"Wal, there's Doc Elliot, but he's in Dorchester, thirty some miles away, which probably won't do you much good. I dunno. It's been awhile since I was in need of someone, so I'll ask around fer you."

"Thank you," Sarah whispered.

When she woke up in a stranger's bedroom, her children piled around her in dark bumps under someone else's quilts and pillows, she could not get her bearings or understand the dream that had awakened her. Someone was hitting her repeatedly until she woke covered in cold perspiration and a new knowledge of her fate.

Mose and Sarah's third daughter was born in the middle of a howling snowstorm out on the Hod Jenkins's ranch, on the high prairie of North Dakota on March 31.

They named her Abigail, for Abby, who had woken right up, got dressed, and taken matters in hand, Hod hovering by the woodstove and smoking so many cigarettes in the lean-to out back, he almost froze.

She was a tiny thing, born five weeks early by Sarah's calculations. Abby's face grimaced and twisted as she fought her tears, her soft heart touched by this squalling infant, so skinny and helpless, born too soon, frightened and cold.

"Ain't no different 'n them scrawny calves that comes early," she chortled, digging out some small blankets. She ripped up some of the boys' long underwear and slipped the soft fabric over the baby for a makeshift gown. She wrapped the red-faced, black-haired infant in two old baby blankets and put a cut-off sock on her head. She handed her back to Sarah after her bath, cooing and fussing, her eyes wet with tears. It didn't matter how hard she tried to look stern, nothing worked. So she blew her nose, wiped her eyes, closed the bedroom door and made breakfast with Hannah's help.

They cooked a huge pot of oatmeal, fried cornmeal mush, made up a batch of biscuits, set the enormous blue coffee pot to boiling, fried some bacon, and made a pot of bacon gravy to ladle over the biscuits. She called the men, who tumbled into the kitchen in various stages of fright and embarrassment.

Abby set everyone straight by telling them it was as right and natural as the calvin'. She brought out little Abby, as she proudly called her, to show her around. Hod's face was alight with happiness, as proud of the little one as if she were his.

"Little Abby," he chortled. "Wal, Darlin', you got yer daughter!" The three boys looked into the pile of quilts and asked if everyone started off that tiny or if it was only Amish babies. Clay said she didn't look a whole lot different than a tomato, and Ken thought she should be kept in a box behind the stove, the way premature calves were.

Mose was clearly humbled, reverent, going about his devotion to his wife and newborn daughter with a newfound zeal. How could he ever have doubted God's leading? Clearly, he had given himself up to Mr. Jenkins's urging. Here they all were, his wife delivered of the infant that had so troubled her.

Again, he had won favor in God's eyes by relinquishing his own will, and the rewards were amazing. And so he loved his wife with renewed emotion and opened his heart to his tiny daughter named Abigail. A rather fancy name, but it was found in the Bible so he knew it must be all right.

The storm weakened in the late morning hours. By dinnertime the roaring of the wind, that scouring, whistling sound that buzzed at loose shingles and played with loose boards, had turned to harmless gusts. The sun shone on a white world with drifts packed against buildings and piled around fences and trees. As far as anyone could see, the snow lay in waves where the force of the gale had sculpted it. The sun's light cast a blue and green aura on the beautiful prairie, washed clean of all the ominous shadows.

Hod and Abby generously allowed them to stay, saying that Sarah could not travel and had no place to go if she could. The snow wouldn't last long, they said.

And it didn't.

By Sunday the grass was showing. Bare spots sprang up in the high places. The children wanted to play outside. They got on everyone's nerves until Abby shooed them out. "Like a buncha spring heifers, that's what they are," she laughed.

Sarah told Abby many times that this was all too much for her and they could go home. She would be fine in the wagon. Hannah was old enough to help with the family. But Abby would hear none of it. She shouldered all the extra work with alacrity, her curls bouncing on her head and her leathery skin creased into constant smiles.

"This ain't no bother, an' you know it. At the end o' March, we're all house crazy, fit to be tied, I'm tellin' ya. Here you all blew in, givin' me someone else to think about other'n myself."

Hannah was unimpressed with the baby's arrival, deeply ashamed of being so needy and pathetic to these English people. What must they be thinking? Being part of a poor, pathetic family of greenhorns was not the way Hannah wanted to live her life. The whole episode was intolerable, and then Mam went and had that baby. She told Manny those boys probably thought they were all from the poorhouse somewhere. She didn't care that Dat made it sound as if he owned Lancaster County. Really? She knew very well what happened to the farm, the whiskey fiasco, everything. Here he was acting as if he had never done anything wrong in his entire life, and it simply wasn't the truth.

She became slavishly devoted to every move the three brothers made. How they shoveled snow and cleaned stalls. How they fed the livestock, saddled a horse, pulled on their boots, the way they wore their hats, their language, and above everything, the way they rode a horse as naturally and as easily as walking.

Manny was awestruck as well, except he felt as if they shouldn't imitate the way they talked. Dat had often warned against unnecessary words. Hannah shrugged her shoulders and said there was nothing wrong with it, not if their parents talked like that themselves. Maybe everyone talked like that out here in the West, away from ordinary civilization where people were packed together in cities and towns and worried a lot more what others thought of them.

"I'm never going back, Manny. These people suit me just fine. If we weren't so poor, I'd buy a saddle, a bridle, boots, and a hat, and I'd learn to ride and rope right along with them. You bet!"

Hod and Mose decided that Sarah would stay at the Jenkins' with the two youngest children, while Mose took the two oldest children in the wagon and drove Pete and Dan home through mud, defeated grass, and patches of snow. White geese flew far overhead, heading south, honking and whistling without ceasing. Hod said they were snow geese and would stop at Fall Lake. He'd have to take the whole family there sometime to see all the migrating birds.

The homestead was still there, the mud and the half-finished house, the logs and the sprawling trees in the creek bottom, the cache of food and belongings beneath the canvas.

Mose stood and surveyed the center of his domain and knew he could not finish the house without a loan. He had underestimated expenses for the months of travel, and now there was not enough for a decent roof, windows, and floors. There was not a person he knew for miles, except Hod, and he could not lower himself to ask him for a loan. He never spoke of finances, not even to his closest relatives, whom he thought would never know. But things got around.

They would manage. He'd learn how to make his own shingles. They could do without windows and a floor until the first corn crop was sold. They'd make do. Sarah would be willing, he knew. A virtuous woman, her worth was far above rubies. The truth, for sure. He never had to navigate life's path without her support. She would sweep her dirt floor, and if the roof leaked, she would set an agate dishpan under the leak and take it in stride.

Yes. He took a deep breath, filling his chest with appreciation of the good, moist air. The sun had risen in all its splendor. This was a land rich with the promise of wealth, with loamy soil and verdant grass, fair weather, and God's promises. He was a man blessed beyond measure.

And so he took his two horses, his two oldest children, his axe and his wedge, and went whistling to the creek bottom to fell more trees for the building of his house on his homestead.

CHAPTER 5

When Hod saw the log walls going up, he squinted, ran a hand over Mose's workmanship, and whistled softly. "It's a right good house you got here," he said.

Mose smiled his thanks, his eyes reflecting his goodwill. He nodded and said yes, he thought after those logs were chinked with mud, the house would outlive any of them.

"You got shingles or sheet metal for the roof? I'll tell you right now, the tin roof is the best in these here winds."

Mose stammered, his words didn't make much sense, saying he'd likely make his own, or something Hod didn't understand.

"You can't make yer own shingles. Not with these logs. Don't work. That's how come the folks here build sod houses."

Mose set his axe aside, pushed back his straw hat, and scratched his head. "Really?"

"Yep. These here trees in the bottom? They're too soft for shake shingles. Can't be done. I know. I'll take you to Dorchester, make a two day trip. We'll bring home the windows, doors, an' the roof."

Mose pondered Hod's kind offer, wishing there was enough cash in the box and ashamed to tell Hod there wasn't. He shoved his hands in his pockets, kicked at a clump of mud, then straightened, looked at Hod with the straightforward look that reminded him of a child, and asked if he could get credit at the lumberyard.

"You need credit? You don't have money to finish?"

"No."

"How were you figgerin'?"

"Well, I thought I'd make my own shingles and doors. We could do without windows until cold weather, then my first corn crop would be ready to sell, and I could pay for a floor and windows."

Hod said this wasn't Pennsylvania; he better not count on a crop the first year. This was the West, and anything that can go wrong usually does.

Nonplussed, Mose smiled. "Like what? What can go wrong?"

"Wal, about a hunnert different things. This country ain't fer the weak."

Quickly Mose defended himself. "Oh, I'm not weak."

"Obviously, yer not. These walls couldn'ta been easy."

"That's right!" Mose was pleased to receive Hod's praise and felt powerful, as if he could get through anything the Lord chose to test him with. Anything. Out here in this level, uncluttered land, free of other brethren, those bickering, complicated fellow men who robbed him of his peace, his self-confidence knew no bounds.

"You know I have a good wife. She won't complain about a dirt floor. I can't go into debt. It would worry me."

Hod considered this, stuck both hands in the back pockets of his jeans, flapped his elbows a few times, pushed back his hat, squinted at the straight rafters and thought this man may well be able to figure something out on his own. He knew, too, the futility of the projected corn crop. And he thought of Sarah and her baby daughter.

"I'll tell you what, Mose. I got some windows stacked along the back of one of my sheds. We'll paint and putty, replace the panes o' glass. But you have to have a roof. Whyn't I pay fer the tin, an' soon's you can, you pay me back? How's that fer a pretty decent plan?"

"Oh, I'll pay you back. I certainly will," Mose said gratefully.

"Sure you will." Hod stuck out a hand, and they shook with strength, an amiable light on Hod's leathery red face and an eager, guileless one on Mose's.

So it was agreed by the pact of a good handshake. They made the trip to Dorchester with the two sturdy horses, leaving Sarah in Abby's care, and Hannah and Manny to fend for themselves in the middle of the prairie's expanse until their father's return.

Left to roam free, they explored their world on foot, took their father's rifle and shot prairie hens and rabbits, blowing the heads clean off, delighting in their marksmanship.

They skinned the animals, taught themselves to clean them and cut them apart into decent sized sections. They fried them in a cast iron pan over a bed of coals, in lard and cornmeal sprinkled lavishly with salt. They ate well, delighted in their freedom, slept late, and forgot to say their prayers until Manny reminded Hannah they hadn't prayed once, not even before eating all that fried meat.

Hannah eyed her brother, shrugged her wide, angular shoulders and said that praying before every meal they ate wasn't so all-fired important as Dat let on. You could wait and pray at the end of the day, when you said your goodnight prayer, or the end of the week. Same thing, so long as God knew you were hungry and thankful. You could even wait until the end of the year, if you wanted to.

Manny narrowed his eyes, pondered his sister's words until he came to the conclusion that she had no fear of God. No *Gottes furcht*, and told her so. Mose and Sarah would have quaked in their shoes if they heard their daughter's brazen answer. Manny showed no surprise, just stripped meat off a delicate prairie hen bone with his teeth and flung it over his shoulder into the deep black shadows behind him before shaking his head, wise-like.

"You better watch your words, Hannah Detweiler. You'd put our father in his grave if he heard you say that."

"He didn't hear me."

"Well, watch what you say. You're disrespectful."

"You think? Oh, hush."

Hannah sat cross-legged, her elbows resting on her knees, her hands loose, perfectly imitating the Jenkins brothers when they sat watching one another rope a calf or train a horse. If she would have had a fence to sit on the top rail, boots on her feet to hook her heels over the lower rail, she would have done that too. Manny did the same, whether he was aware of it or not.

The brothers were a wonder. They could do anything. Anything they tried, with loose-jointed skill, an unhurried grace, ambling through difficult tasks as naturally as if they'd been doing it all their lives.

Which, Hannah supposed, they had.

Her awe of them bordered on reverence. Their easy gait, the language they used, the way they stuffed a wad of pungent smelling dark brown tobacco into the side of their mouths and left it there, spitting a majestic stream of brown tobacco juice unbelievable distances.

When Hannah compared her own tiresome existence with the lives of those boys, it didn't seem fair being a girl, and an Amish one at that, with parents who set all these careful guidelines, recited those endless verses and Psalms from the German Bible, instilling the words of wisdom and the fear of God in their children. They were taught well. Behave, honor your father and mother, live righteously in love and truth, keep the Sabbath, fear going to Hell and missing Heaven by one wrong deed—it all hung over Hannah's head like irritable black ravens she wished she could shoo away.

What was the use of going through life when it was all so boring, so pale, like milk pudding without sugar or cinnamon? Take Mam. She'd live the remainder of her life walking behind

Dat, her steps measured and careful, always obeying, always smiling into his kind eyes. They were always polite, always caring, always flat-out boring.

She was pretty sure Manny thought so too, although he was far too good-natured, too subservient, to say so. She doubted if he would ever stray very far from his parents' wishes, which were good and right.

A twinge of apprehension settled over her shoulders, as if this self-examination came with a price, and the cost was frightening her. So be it. Dat had no business packing her out here to the middle of nowhere, with not one other Amish soul around. Didn't he know in just over a year she'd be at the age when she'd begin her *rumschpringa*? Then what was expected of her? To have no company, no friends, and certainly no husband?

Manny's voice broke into her train of thought, derailing it precisely by his announcement that Clay asked him to help herd the cows to the corrals, as soon as they decided to do it.

"What?"

"You know, ride all over their land looking for cows and calves."

"Why not me?"

"You're a girl."

"What does that have to do with it?"

"A lot, actually. You're supposed to be in the house, helping Mam."

"She's taken care of, being with Abby."

"She's coming home, soon as this house gets done."

In answer, Hannah threw a few chunks of wood on the fire and flounced off to her bedroll in a huff. Manny watched her jerky movements, her stiff gait and elaborate thumping into her bedroll, and grinned. Here was a job for Dat. Good, kind-hearted Dat.

The Jenkins men descended on the Detweiler house, wielding hammers and nails, bringing tin, windows, and doors. They cut and sawed logs for the floor, working long days before beginning their ride home, often through the dark. Hannah stayed with the men, keeping the coffeepot filled and heating the stews and soups Abby sent along.

Hod showed them how to chink the logs with a mixture of cement and mud, which Hannah tackled with her usual aplomb, shouting at Manny if he took a break or watched the men too long.

Mose was effusive in his appreciation, pumping the men's hands, emotion making his eyes shine with a gleam close to tears, which made Hod uncomfortable, not being accustomed to flowery speeches. But he guessed Mose was thankful, so he shrugged his shoulders, went home, and told Abby he believed Mose was a little soft in the head.

They brought Sarah home to the new house, pale and wan, but with a new eagerness to begin life in a house, living like civilized folk. It was small compared to her house in the East, but it smelled fresh and clean and had a good wood floor that had been sanded and oiled. That was plenty good enough for her, as Mose knew it would be.

They had no furniture. There had not been room to bring anything except the sewing machine, the trunk, a few dishes, pots and pans, extra clothing, and bedding. There was no fireplace and no stove, so the cooking was done outside, the stones set up in a circle, closer to the house.

The first thing Mose built was a sturdy table made of planks, which he sanded smooth. One of Abby's tablecloths fit just perfect.

The breezes carried moist warmth, and the columbines began to bloom in the low places. A variety of birds moved across the sky of whispering grace. The air smelled different and infused a hope that had been elusive for Sarah.

Sometimes she stood at the doorway and watched Mose with the two horses and the plow, drawing a straight black line across the level prairie, tufts of grass sticking up like an old man's eyebrows. She thought of all that grass decomposing beneath the western soil, making possibilities seem like a certainty, a reality.

Then her heart soared, a song came from within her, and she felt a fresh will to continue, a desire to see what they could accomplish here, so far away from everything they had ever known.

In time, then, with the Jenkins' help, they had a decent place to live. The house was small, the furniture sparse, but there was a lift, a good solid space under the eaves for the children's sleeping quarters.

Sarah had brought her flannel comfort covers, leaving the sheep's wool at home, reserving space for other necessities. So she stuffed these serviceable covers with thick, dry prairie grass, and the children slept well. Manny and Eli at one end of the loft, Hannah and Mary at the other. It was a wondrous roof; the gray tin didn't allow one drop of rain inside. When there was a storm, the sound was like a barrage of ice pellets thrown against it, though it really only was raindrops of water. Hannah loved the sound of it and the safety of lying cozily under this new roof.

Sarah never complained that she had to cook outdoors. There was no fireplace and no money for a stove, but she was grateful for the house nevertheless. She sang as she swept the floor with her homemade broom of willow twigs. She praised the Lord all her days for the roof and the good walls surrounding her at night.

She cared tenderly for little Abby, who was a good baby, lying in her little bundle of blankets because there was no cradle or crib for her. Mary was in awe of her, sitting on the one luxury they had brought from the East—the cane bottom armless rocking chair. Hannah tickled her under her dimpled chin and watched her mere seconds before directing her interest elsewhere. Babies were a bother, and they smelled.

Abby Jenkins shared more of the crumbling squares of white lye soap with Sarah, so it wasn't that the baby's diapers weren't clean. Sarah watched her oldest daughter warily. Her eyes followed her as she went through the door, pushed back the tide of alarm that threatened her calm, and wondered what kind of girl would be so unaffected by the innocence of a small infant.

How had they managed to raise this unruly daughter, this distant person who showed increasing disinterest in all manner of spiritual teaching? When Mose read the German *Schrift*, she either tapped her foot as if she was irritated, or lifted her eyes to the ceiling while she strummed at her lips with two fingers, making a strange buzzing noise, which apparently Mose never heard, or if he did, he gave no indication of being distracted.

Sarah, however, was distracted. Always glad when devotions were over, she felt the stiffness leave her neck and shoulders, her breathing slow to normal. She could sense the lack of interest, but surely they would not need to raise a heathen in this wild and lonely country without sufficient people of religion to give her good company. How could they expect it of their children, wearing the white head covering if there was not another girl within a hundred-mile radius brought up in the doctrines of the Amish?

Sarah's way of dressing was very important to her. As long as she could wash, starch, and iron the large white head covering, she would wear it, and if it wore thin, she would patch it with fine and even stitches. Without it, she would feel unclean, exposed, naked. The head covering was instilled into her upbringing, infusing her life like a warm and fragrant tea, comforting, sustaining, a perfect guideline on how to live a godly life.

She thought of the Jenkinses often. Here was an uncouth and worldly family, one who had no religious principles. And yet, their kindness knew no restraint. It flowed from them, an unexamined virtue they were completely unaware of, brushing away any grateful words with an air of unease, as if praise was an unaccustomed visitor, a stranger who made them nervous.

The diapers Abby had given them came from a store of good quality flannel from her high walnut cupboard in the living room, a massive, ornate piece of furniture that made Sarah wonder about the Jenkins' background. Much too polite to ask about their past, Sarah had kept quiet and accepted the small favors, the tiny gowns adorned with old lace, the hand crocheted booties, yellowed with age, but wearable and comforting.

Abby's dry, weathered face had been a beacon of joy, the lines and wrinkles increasingly deepened as she smiled and laughed out loud with a coarse sound that came from her throat every time she held the tiny bundle. Until one day, a strange sound strangled the laughter. She sat back in the wooden rocker and gasped for air, trying to stop the sobs that began in the midst of her smiles.

"I had a little one once," she said suddenly, her voice raw with suppressed emotion. "I had myself a baby girl. As perfect as the rising sun and as welcome. We found her in her cradle, cold and still one frosty mornin'. Her life was not quite three months on, an' she was taken. I guess the Lord must have had need of her up there in His Heaven. I don't know. It still hurts after all these years. She was like a doll, my firstborn. Bitter, I was, for the longest time. But there ain't no use carryin' on if'n you can't have what you most want, so in time, it became a small pain instead of a big one. Clay came along then, and took a chunk of the pain away. Seems as if each baby that came along took some more of it with him. But now I remember back to how it all was."

She swiped at her eyes with the back of her hand, blew her nose with the square of muslin she always kept in her pocket, and shook her head. "Times come when it's hard to figger out the Lord. Why He does things the way He does. Not that I'm overly religious, mind you. Hod don't hold much with church going and prayin' an' stuff. But when you folks came along, it put me to mind of the time we used to go, singin' and prayin' and listenin' to the preacher yellin' about God and all kinds of them things."

She shook her head again, pondering. "I dunno."

Immediately Sarah's motherly heart took up the pain, understood Abby's ache, the longing she still felt, and she said softly, "The Lord giveth and He taketh away. The Bible is so clear about that. It was God's will."

"Yeah, well, I know. But I've come to doubt God, livin' out here in this place where you can't count on nothin'. The dust and the storms and the cold and the heat, when yer crops shrivel and the cows can't hardly find a thing to eat until their ribs is like bed slats under their dried out skin, it's enough to make a person wonder if there is a God, and if there is, if'n He cares about this here prairie an' the folks that live on it."

Sarah murmured, "Oh, but His mercy is unfailing. His goodness is always with the righteous."

For an instant, Abby's eyes flashed, as if Sarah had angered her, and just as quickly, it was gone. When she spoke again, she had changed the subject to the amount of dark hair that adorned little Abby's head, and after that she never mentioned God in Sarah's hearing.

Had she angered Abby? Sarah did feel God would bless them here in this verdant prairie if she lived righteously, submissive to Mose and the way he ordered their lives. Had God not provided even now? She had not been able to see her way through the birth of little Abby, and the building of the house. Everything had seemed insurmountable, like a steep, forbidding mountain that was impossible to climb. Oh, her faith in God had multiplied, abounded, her heart filled with strength to go on, for He surely provided, even in the darkest times.

On their journey, when the horses tired, the way looked long, stretching before them like an invisible question. God had provided. It was only her own doubts and fears that had hampered her faith. She wanted to tell Abby this, share her testimony of dependence on a much Higher Power, fill the woman's heart with God's abounding mercy. But she was afraid Abby would not be open to it and that it would only anger or provoke her. Perhaps she had seen too much.

Mose hitched the horses to the sturdy new plow and went out to a section of land he felt was the most fertile, where the soil was thick with black loam and decomposed grass. He set the plow and called to the faithful creatures.

They lunged into their collars. Mose hung on to the two wooden handles and together they plowed a long, dark ribbon of upturned soil, clumps of grass sticking up out if it like misplaced whiskers. After a few rounds in the hot, spring light of the sun, dark streaks of sweat marred the horses' flanks, their nostrils were distended, blowing out with the force of expelled breathing.

Mose stopped, flexed his shoulders, pushed back his straw hat and surveyed the upturned ribbon behind him. Here was good soil, no doubt. Here he would prosper, his crops a beacon of good management that came directly from his forefathers, generations of men who had tilled the land and sowed the seed that had been blessed by the God who was rich with mercy and unfailing goodness.

With each turn of the good earth, his heart rejoiced in the Lord. He knew the corn he would plant would stretch on either side of his buildings, a waving sea of green, the wide, rustling leaves eventually producing large yellow ears of corn to feed the hungry children and animals, an abundant food supply, coupled with the endless sea of grass that could be harvested for the horses.

He hoped to obtain a calf from the Jenkinses, if the Lord so willed it. He thought he might be able to barter a few days' wages for it, perhaps longer than that, a few weeks, possibly, for a bull calf and a small heifer to start his herd.

Mose smiled at the thought of Sarah's delight in milk, cream, and butter, a veritable luxury, and one he looked forward to with keen anticipation. Yes, life was worth living. Oh my, how much it was worth! Out here in this powerful land, where God's presence hovered across the waving sea of prairie grass, the air was pure and as sweet as the nectar of a honeysuckle vine, free of the foul breath of other men's opinions. His spirit soared on the wings of the small brown birds that raced across the sky in acrobatic rushes of reckless flight. Uncharted, freewheeling, but crafted by the Master's hand, Mose thought, as he squinted into the brilliant noonday sun.

On into the afternoon they toiled, man and beast, using every resource they were given, struggling on across the land, tearing up the hardened grasses by the roots, tossing them aside by the shining plow slicing into the moist earth.

In the evening, Sarah stood at the edge of the field, her eyes wide with wonder. The thin line of plowed soil had turned into a broad, dark band, the clumps of moist earth sheared cleanly, glistening in the late-day sun. The soil was moist and heavy with promise, a harbinger of things to come.

She breathed deeply, never tiring of the sensuous odor of freshly plowed soil. It spoke of Mose's labor, a good man doing what God had ordained from the beginning, that man labor by the sweat of his brow.

She pushed back the notion that there were obstacles, the clumps of grass still protruding from places where the soil was not fully turned over. Would there be sufficient rain? Hadn't Hod spoken of drought?

Sarah hunched her shoulders, wrapped a hand around each elbow and stood, her head bowed as she murmured her lowly prayer to her God. One day at a time, Lord, one drop of rain at a time. *Himmlischer Vater. Meine Herre und mein Gott.*

The harrow bounced cruelly across the sturdy clumps of grass, jerking the hames of the horses' collars, rubbing them raw, their skin oozing drops of blood that smeared with the white foam of their sweat, turning it pink as the flecks dropped from them.

The sun was high in the sky, hot and getting hotter. Mose was perspiring freely. His legs and feet ached from the agonizing jolts as he stood on the rusted old harrow he had borrowed from Hod.

The morning was well spent, but his work seemed fruitless. Discouraged, he stopped the team, watched the heaving sides of the horses, noticed the raw places beneath the harness and became alarmed, stepping quickly to their sides. He looked back and his heart sank within him.

How would he ever get a crop into the ground with this rusty harrow and two horses? This grass was far more than he had bargained for.

He thought of the sturdy Belgians, the powerful, lunging teams hitched four abreast, easily drawing well-constructed, well-equipped harrows and discs and plows across soil that was easily turned and easily crumbled beneath the steel equipment. The corn planters were so new and efficient.

For one moment this journey fell on his shoulders with the weight of a sack of grain. He felt the folly of it. Or was it folly? Perhaps he was only discouraged and tired. To be back on the home farm, though, was like an invisible thread that pulled steadily, waking up thoughts and memories long buried.

His mother, plump and happy, always smiled as she rang the dinner bell that called them in to her well-laid table. There was prosperity and happiness, so much food, such luxuries in the barn alone—cows, milk, butter, and cheese. There were hens in the henhouse laying eggs, clucking and cackling. His mouth watered thinking of two fried eggs with a side of scrapple after the hog butchering.

Suddenly, a longing to return seized him and shook him to the core. Just hitch up these horses and travel back home, resume life, swallow his pride, learn to listen to the arguments, and learn to appreciate other men's opinions.

His hands shook. Sweat poured freely from the agitation in his soul. He felt elated, ashamed, humbled, and uncertain.

What would Sarah say? Where did this thought come from, this seizing of his emotions? Only yesterday he had felt so certain of God's will leading them safely through adversity to the prairies of North Dakota. They were blessed indeed.

He wiped the sweat from his brow with fingers that fluttered, his mouth gone dry, his heart racing with a deep, unnamed fear. He looked up, expecting to see a black cloud covering the sun, turning the land gray and cold and barren. The thought of a flowing sea of green corn was replaced by a sick and colorless despair.

CHAPTER 6

Hannah snorted as she watched her father's pathetic progress, bouncing around on that ill-constructed harrow, the jaded horses plodding along. "Look at him, Manny. He is so determined to grow corn out here. There's an impossibility if you want to see one, and I mean it."

She had taken to hitching up the belt of her dress, imitating the way Hank and Clay tugged at their belts on their patched jeans. She stood with one leg crossed over the other, foot propped on the toe of her cracked and worn shoe. If she would have had belt loops, she would have hooked her thumbs into them. As it was, she balled her fists and pushed them against her narrow hips.

Manny stopped cutting branches from felled trees, shaded his eyes with his hand against his forehead, squinted, and nodded. "Horses are shot."

"I know. It's ridiculous. He'll kill them yet."

Manny shook his head and turned away. "He's our father," was all he said.

"Yeah, but he doesn't have too many good ideas. He never did. Do you know why we came out here to live? 'Cause he lost the farm and then tried to use up the leftover grain to make whiskey."

"He did not do any such thing, Hannah."

"Yes. Yes, he did, Manny. They kicked him out of the church. He had to join up again and do all that repentance stuff that sinners do. Then we left."

Manny drew himself up to his full height and addressed his sister in clipped tones. "I don't care what you say, Hannah. You lie. You say anything you feel like saying. You don't respect our father."

"Why should I? He's a dreamer. A loser. Not even Hod Jenkins can tell that man anything. Dat thinks Hod is a man of the world, so he doesn't amount to anything. He's not gonna listen to him. Hod knows he can't grow a decent crop of corn, not with those two spindly horses. And certainly not without bigger equipment. Hod's just humoring Dat, lending him that plow."

Manny stood, a man not yet formed, an ache in his youthful heart brought on by a young man's devotion to a godly father. He respected him, refused to believe in the hard, accusing words of his sister. She was the one with the problem, not his Dat.

The sun shone hot and bright, pressing down on his shoulders as he watched Mose slap the reins down on the horses' backs. They dutifully responded and clawed forward, their haunches lowered by the force of their efforts. He tried not to see the futility of his father's form bouncing around on top of the poorly built monstrosity on which he balanced. Beside him, he felt the prickly disapproval of his sister, but he said nothing when she snorted.

After that, they went back to work trimming branches from felled logs meant for the barn, tedious back-breaking work that kept them perspiring all morning. Hannah wanted that barn in the worst way, so her efforts were relentless, her energy unbounded. She was determined to have her own horse, a corral, to learn to rope and ride, and to drive cattle—all of it. She had a goal in mind and nothing would keep her from it. Nothing. If she had to build that barn with her own hands, then so be it.

Her dat was on the wrong track, so she figured it was up to her to keep things going if they were going to survive out here on the prairie. The only way she could see it work out was to employ Hod Jenkins and his boys, try and lay down her pride and accept whatever they saw as necessary. Otherwise, they'd never make it.

She straightened from her job, kicked a pile of branches, and watched as three riders approached from the south, their horses' heads lowered as they rode down the gentle incline toward the creek bottom. She swiped the back of a hand across her forehead and turned to watch.

How easily they sat astride their horses! If she never attained any other skill in life, it was all right if only she could learn to ride like that. It was an amazing feat, to become one with such a beautiful creature, to know its mind and become attuned to its instincts. To sit astride so high above the ground, to feel the wind and smell the endless fascination of the earth and the waving grass, the great nothingness of the landscape, knowing she was only a dot, a miniscule form in a vast, mostly unexplored region.

Who knew what lay twenty, thirty miles west? Or east? No doubt there were more ranches, folks like the Jenkinses, who ran cattle, some without fences to retain them. It was the way to make money, these cattle, tough, skinny creatures that plopped a calf on the still-frozen earth every spring, as regularly as the season changed.

You needed your own brand, though, the sign of ownership sizzled into their hairy flanks. Clay and Hank roped them with a swinging jute rope called a lariat. One arm swings a loop of it over his head with a muscular strength, a calculated grace that sends it over the running calf's neck. The horse immediately sensed his master's aim and stopped in seconds, haunches lowered, forefeet braced, as the rope twanged taut.

To Hannah, the taut lariat performed a song to her senses, like the strings of a guitar, the *verboten* musical instrument she

longed to hold, to cradle in her arms, the form and sheen of it
a thing of beauty, a vessel of sweetness that sang unbearable
notes unlike anything she had ever heard. Its notes could evoke
unnamed feelings of dissatisfaction, a glimpse into the unknown,
a beckoning world she knew nothing about, like a promise of
light and brightness at the end of a dark hallway.

She still hadn't reckoned it all out. It was like a jigsaw puzzle
with half the pieces missing. But she watched Clay sitting on
the top rail of the fence with the heels of those wonderful boots
caught on the lower rail, the guitar balanced against his long
legs, his hands plucking idly at the strings, as easily as brushing
his horse's mane. Watching him laughing, nodding, his light blue
eyes twinkling at his brothers who sang, their heads bobbing
with the movement of Clay's hands, brought all these questionable longings. Her heart quickened, making her sit up and take
notice of a world without the blackness of restraint and the laws
that ruled her life.

Sometimes, when she was with her mother, the sweetness of
her, the light around her an aura of goodness, she felt pulled by
a rope as strong as a lariat to be like her, to live out her days in
peace and contentment with whatever the Lord sent in her direction, plodding one step behind her husband. Just, well, taking it,
"it" being whatever he decided, like pulling up her roots from
Lancaster County and leaving her aging parents, severing the
ties with her family with the sharp blade of his will. A stone was
the only remnant of her past life that she kept, a stone where her
heart should have been.

Glassy eyed with numbness, a deep keening, a mournful
sound that stayed enclosed, tamped down with the strength of
her will, her mother had remained seated on that wooden seat
beneath the canopy of dirty white canvas.

Oh, Hannah had seen. She had felt every womanly sorrow
along with her mother, knowing that the waxy contours of her
face were the feelings so successfully banished, like her own.

Hannah figured they were here now, in this strange new world, so thinking back with yearning for the closeness of cousins, the kinship of grandparents and aunts and uncles, wasn't going to help a lick, so she may as well square her shoulders and get on with it, this living out here in this land full of nothing.

She looked up as the riders approached, watching the way they sat in their saddles, their limbs loose, relaxed, their hands idly holding the reins as if they weren't necessary for guiding or stopping their horses.

Hannah threw her axe, swiped at a thick strand of dark hair, and watched Hank's face, then Clay's. They both lifted their hats with that offhanded push they always applied, a gesture that puzzled Hannah. She thought perhaps it was a sign of good manners, like a handshake, only easier, but she wasn't sure about that. She smiled as her eyes met Clay's.

"Whatcha doin', Hannah?" Clay stopped his horse, threw a wrist across the saddle horn, put the other one on top and leaned forward slightly as he watched Hannah's face.

"We're cutting logs for the barn," she said, a smile playing around the corners of her mouth.

"You know you and him's gonna get hurt whacking them trees down," Clay said slowly.

"Him?"

"Your brother. You're nothing but kids. Your pa oughta be helpin' you some. Where's he at?"

Hannah shaded her eyes and pointed to the horses plodding methodically, their faithful noses almost touching the ground with exhaustion.

Clay's eyes narrowed into slits as he watched. His long, greasy blonde locks barely moved in the ever present wind, the cleft in his chin covered with blonde stubble, about a week's growth. His cheek twitched like a horse's hide when a fly bothered him, his jaw set. He shook his head.

"He's killin' them horses."

Hannah nodded.

"You know he ain't gonna grow no corn."

Hannah felt Manny behind her before she heard his voice, high and strident. "You don't know anything either, Clay Jenkins. You don't. God can bless my father and his corn crop."

Deeply ashamed, Hannah whirled to face her brother, eyebrows drawn, trying to shush him with her glare of warning.

Clay said slowly, "Well, that can all be, but looks as if he's gonna have hisself a job just keepin' them horses alive."

"God can do anything!" Manny spat out, his face white with childish rage and suppressed tears.

"I reckon."

Hank watched the plodding team, then turned his horse toward Hannah. "We come over to invite you and yer family to our round-up and neighborhood git-together in two weeks."

"Neighborhood? There are no neighbors," Hannah laughed.

Clay watched her face as she laughed, one of those laughs that came from deep within, that bubbled to the surface as clear and pretty as spring water in the Ozarks. He squinted, blinked, and kept watching as Hannah said that if there were neighbors, they sure were well hidden.

"Some of 'em are, some of 'em ain't. You get yer horses, we'll ride around and meet a few."

"Mam won't let me."

Manny nodded in agreement, eyeing the Jenkins brothers with distaste. He hitched up his trousers and told Hannah there was work to be done and the sooner they got to it, the better. Then he turned on his heel and picked up his axe, his posture and vehement chopping giving away his disapproval.

"S'wrong with him?" Hank asked.

Hannah shrugged.

She met Clay's pale blue gaze boldly, as if trying to make up for her brother's bad manners. Suddenly embarrassed for different reasons entirely, she scuffed the toe of her old leather shoe into the wood chips and trampled grass, lowering her head to focus on the mud and wood chips.

"Hey, it's okay," Clay said in that slow, soft way of speech that he had.

He looked off across the grass to the house, where Sarah appeared in stark relief against the dark logs, her posture bent over the outdoor fire as she tended the pot hanging on a tripod.

"Yer ma never got a stove?"

"Not yet."

"Why'd the old man build a house without a chimney or a fireplace?"

Confused, Hannah lifted dark eyes to their blue ones. "What old man?"

"Yer pa."

"He isn't old."

"Just our way of talkin'. The old man's my pa."

"Oh."

Hannah looked away. Hank and Clay swung their wrists to the left, laying the rein on the right side of their horses' necks, shifted in the saddle, and were off in mere seconds.

Sighing, Hannah turned, slowly picked up her axe, and resumed her work halfheartedly. They must all appear like beggars, pathetic losers without a clue how to go about making a living. And that, precisely, is what they were. A hot wave of shame swept through her, followed by a pride so icy it stung.

Why couldn't they have stayed in Lancaster, where they were the same as other folks? Hannah thought of riding around to meet the neighbors on one of the sturdy, all-purpose Haflingers, dressed in her plain Amish garb with the large white covering on her head, without a saddle and without boots. She felt a sense of loss so keen she shivered.

It was the loss of being able to hold up her head, to feel as if she was a normal, attractive person of means, someone who knew what was going on in the world around her. She felt displaced, blinded by the vast world of the treeless plain, where the winds blew constantly, and the clouds hung in the sky, uncaring, void of color or meaning.

Sarah tended to her bubbling stew, wiped the sweat from her streaming brow, then hurried back to the house to hush her crying baby. She smiled warmly as Mary dashed to reach baby Abigail before her mother did, lifting the swaddled infant and clumsily patting her back.

Sarah sank into the armless rocking chair, so grateful yet again that they had had the good foresight to bring it all the way from home. As she fed her baby, her eyes grazed the interior of her home and again she felt deeply grateful. A good floor made of wood, sturdy walls, windows, and a door, the four necessities of a decent home. Beds to sleep in, a loft for the children, may God be praised.

Mose would *sark* for a chimney, he would. He wanted to get that corn in the ground first. Oh, he was working so hard to get started farming. A crop of corn would be all they needed.

She thought with satisfaction of the stew bubbling on the fire—potatoes, carrots, a few prairie hens, wild onions, garlic, and salt. It was a stew hearty enough to stick to her men's ribs. Her men.

Manny was growing so fast into a sturdy little man. She was grateful too for the gift of potatoes and a bucket of carrots from Abby Jenkins. What a treat to be able to change the daily diet of cornmeal and prairie hens. And so Sarah rocked, the stew bubbled in the open air, Mary ran out to play with Eli, the great open space beckoning, the world for them an endlessly unexplored place.

Sarah cared for little Abby with an even greater appreciation than any of her previous babies. Hadn't God provided? Oh, He had, and so much more than she could have comprehended, were it not for the fact that she held this perfect little girl, dressed in warm clothing, all taken from Abby Jenkins' chest, where she had stored away the clothes of her baby who had died. There was much to be thankful for, much to consider in the ways of the Lord, indeed.

A shout broke through her reverie, a far away sound that shattered her peace, as if a mere pinprick of noise became a harbinger of alarm. Her rocking ceased. Slowly she lifted Abby, closed her dress and held stock still, listening.

There. Another shout!

In one swift movement she gathered Abby in her arms, moved to the pile of blankets in the corner and laid her gently on her stomach, covering her with her own small blanket. She stood at the door and surveyed the flat expanse before her, involuntarily searching for Mose.

Her heart sank within her as she saw Mose circling the horses—or the lone horse left standing. The other was a dark mound on the upturned soil.

Sarah ran, leaving Abby alone in the house, calling to Mary and Eli. When she reached her distraught husband, she took one look at his red, streaming face, the panic in his eyes. Throwing up her hands, she asked what she should do.

"Water!" shouted Mose, as he bent to untangle taut harness pieces. Sarah ran back to the house, her skirt billowing behind her, the wind in her face. Her thoughts were racing over what a dead horse would mean: one horse left over, and they could not go on. She could not think about that now.

Grabbing the water bucket, she lowered it into the wood rain barrel until it was full, hefted it out with all of her strength, and walked fast, water sloshing over her skirt, the sound of Abby's wails in her ears.

Mose watched her approach, ran to grab the bucket, lowered it by the heaving horse's head, tried to lift it, coaxed, spoke gently saying, "Here's water, Dan. Water. Drink some water."

Sarah bent to examine the horse's eye, the lids falling heavily. The horse was covered in white foam, his sides streaming, the rivulets of sweat joining the foam, creating small crevices, and staining the earth where it ran off. She grimaced, seeing the blood seeping into the white lather, staining it pink, the dry nostrils expanding and contracting rapidly with the unnaturally quick breaths that came in desperate spurts.

"He needs water, Sarah."

"I know."

"How can we get him to drink?"

Sarah shook her head. "Loosen Pete."

"I did. Can't you see? He's not attached. He wants to stay."

They stood helplessly as the horse continued the fast, raspy breathing. The sweat continued to stream from him as he struggled to inhale and exhale.

"Can we get him up, do you think?" Sarah asked.

Mose nodded, grabbed the bridle, chirped, tugged at the bit, and kept calling his name over and over. Sarah watched the noble, obedient horse try to lift his head, scramble to regain his footing, scraping one foreleg and then the other along the partially tilled soil before a deep groan escaped him. His head sank forward, his body shuddered into a solid heap, and his breathing slowed until he was still.

Mose called his name again, urgently, but there was no response. "Is he gone?" Mose asked Sarah, a look of blank bewilderment in his brown eyes.

"Yes, Mose. He just took his last breath. He must have become overheated." Sarah's hand went to Mose's shoulder, moved up and down, a gesture of comfort, the caress of caring.

Mose lowered his face, and then lifted it to stare at Sarah. Her eyes opened wide, shocked at the incomprehension in her husband's eyes. "But, I can't harrow without Dan."

"No, you can't."

Mose hesitated, shoved his hands deep into his trouser pockets. "But how will we go on?"

Alarmed, Sarah soothed him, saying God would provide, thinking God would provide by borrowing a horse from the Jenkins. Here was a case where they would evolve from God's testing and do the right thing by using common sense and the sound mind God had given them.

"But how will God provide?" Mose asked, as he brushed Sarah's hand away from his shoulder. Her hand fell away and for the first time ever she felt his reproach. Quick breathing beside her made her turn to see a white-faced Hannah, fists clenched, chest heaving, followed by an out-of-breath Manny, who came to a halt, peering down at the dead horse.

"So you really did kill this horse. I knew you would. You're nothing but a thickheaded farmer! Don't you know you can't raise a crop of corn in this soil without at least six horses and a plow twice the size of yours?" Hannah shouted, her white face reddening with the force of her fury.

Without hesitation Mose drew back his hand and smacked Hannah's face a glancing blow. "No daughter of mine will ever speak to me like that," he ground out.

Hannah's head snapped back, a red stain appeared on the side of her face and, for a moment, Sarah thought she would lower her head and take this as the chastening she deserved.

But in another moment, Hannah lifted her head, faced her father and spoke levelly, the words laced with a disrespect so potent it sickened Sarah. Hannah's eyes glittered and drew into narrow slashes of dark brown as she spoke.

"You killed that horse, Dat. You'll kill Pete, too, if you keep on. Didn't Hod tell you this is cattle country? Didn't he tell you? You won't be able to raise a crop of corn. You left Lancaster, Dat, now you're going to have to change your ways."

Mose stepped up to his daughter, his fists clenched, his jaw working. Sarah realized his intent and reached out to grab his arm and plead with him. "Come, Mose. Everyone is upset. Let's go to the house and eat our dinner. Bring Pete, Hannah. Manny, get the bucket."

They turned as one, this small band of people walking together leading the tired, sweating horse that remained across the level prairie with the grasses waving back and forth in the uninterrupted wind, each one carrying their own different loss and feelings of foreboding.

True to her word, Sarah calmly took up the stewpot, set it in the middle of the table, and got out the dishes they'd need. Hannah sliced a loaf of sourdough bread.

Manny put Pete on a tether after giving him small amounts of water and tried not to hear his weak, anxious nickering. Mose sat on a stump by the doorway, his head in his hands, his wide shoulders slumped forward with the crushing weight of his loss.

They all sat down together, bowed their heads, and prayed silently, although it was questionable whether Hannah prayed at all, the way she chewed at her lip and her eyes glittered like brass, the rebellion raging through her body. Manny and Eli bowed their heads low, squeezed their eyes shut, and said their prayers dutifully, not quite understanding what the death of a good horse entailed.

They all ate hungrily, sopping up the good, sustaining stew with slices of bread. Breakfast had been early and sparse, Sarah doling out the thin and watery cornmeal porridge.

The meal revived their spirits, and they kept up a conversation, a planning, of sorts. Mose took his rightful place as head of the house saying that God would provide another horse if they repented of their sins, lived righteously in godly fear, and prayed day and night. God had never let them down, and He wouldn't this time either.

Sarah bowed her head in submission, listening to her husband's words, wanting desperately to have a faith as great as his, although basic common sense knew there was only the Jenkinses and the begging—humble asking accompanied by the sense of failure—that remained. But she bowed her head anyway then looked up into his bright eyes, shining with a new and vibrant light. She smiled And said, "Yes, Mose, I do believe you are right. We will continue our work on the barn and see what the Lord has in store for us."

Happily and vigorously the children nodded, content to live in the realm of a father who based his whole life on his faith. Manny, especially, was filled with a deep sense of the celestial, his face glowing with an inner light.

To see Hannah's face, then, was a study in light and dark. Her cheek still flushed from her father's administration of discipline. Her face was shadowed with anger and ill feelings playing across it like puffy, wind-driven clouds.

"Hannah, what do you think?" Mose asked, appearing to make restitution for his harsh discipline earlier.

No answer.

"Hannah?"

Still no answer.

Sarah looked at her eldest daughter with pleading in her soft eyes, but Hannah's eyes were well-hidden by the heavy curtain of her upper lids.

"Hannah, you will speak to me when I ask you a question," Mose said with conviction.

She refused to answer, as before.

Sarah had begun to rise, a hand on the table to steady herself, her mouth open to speak, when Mose's chair fell backward and clattered to the floor with the force of his rising. The kindness and warm benevolence with which he faced the world was erased by a black anger, the likes of which Sarah had never seen.

He grabbed Hannah's shoulders and shook her, from behind, her head flopping like a fish, but only once. Hannah wriggled from his grasp, lunged through the door, and was gone before anyone had time to stop her. Sarah ran outside, calling her daughter's name, but she obeyed when Mose ordered her inside, saying she'd get over it. That girl needed her sails trimmed good and proper.

His words proved true. Hannah crept up to bed, avoiding the steps that creaked, thinking no one would hear. But Sarah lay wide awake, worrying and praying alternately until she heard Hannah's return, then wondered whether they were turning into uncouth heathens, same as the Jenkinses.

CHAPTER 7

As predicted, the miracle horse's arrival came in the form of Hod Jenkins and his boys, who rode over to confirm the announcement of the calf roping and neighborhood picnic.

They met Mose, who walked out of the house in the late afternoon, said he'd been resting, had a bit of a headache, blinking his eyes in the strong, hot sunlight. He scratched first one underarm and then the other and rolled up his shirt sleeves to reveal gray long-sleeved underwear. His hair was parted in sections, each chunk held together by a lack of washing. He yawned widely, revealing yellowed teeth caked with plaque.

Hod threw him a shrewd glance, figured this guy was going downhill without brakes, but said nothing, just threw himself off his horse, strode over to stand beside him, surveying the unfinished barn, the partially tilled field.

"Yer not up to par, then?"

"I beg your pardon?"

"Ain't feelin' good?"

"Well, yes. Just a bit of a headache."

Hod nodded, his eyes searching the man's circumstances. "Yer other horse run off?"

"No, he's dead."

Hod looked at Mose sharply. "He got colic?"

"No, I must have worked him too hard. He went down and never got back up. I don't know what was wrong with him."

"Yer horses gittin' only grain?"

Mose shook his head.

"So now what's yer plan?" Hod asked, shifting his toothpick to the opposite side of his mouth.

"The Lord will provide. He always does."

Hod chuckled, deep and friendly, the crow's feet around his eyes like fans crinkling out at the corners as his shoulders shook silently.

"Wal, neighbor Mose, if'n I was you, I wouldn't bet on a horse droppin' out of the sky, but whatever you fancy, I suppose."

They spoke of the coming roundup. Hod urged him to bring the family, and they left soon after. Hod took notice of all three of his boys trying to look for Hannah behind each other's backs and his chuckle increased to full blown mirth that he did nothing to hide. He just shook his head and knew the impossibility of all of it. Mose would have a fit. He chuckled again, shifted his toothpick, then looked to the left. His whole countenance changed to one of deep concern, then irritation.

"How's he gonna do that?" Clay asked, jerking his thumb in the direction of the field.

"His horse died."

"Yeah."

But, as was the custom, nothing more was said.

The bucket of carrots and the burlap bag of potatoes were stretched as far as they would go, the prairie hens Manny shot helping to round out the meals. But when Sarah found the bottom of the cornmeal barrel so close, she felt as if she could not take another day of her husband's alternating between headaches, reading his Bible, or disappearing into the bedroom to pray.

Hannah and Manny did their best to prepare logs for the barn, but progress was slow without their father's help, the logs becoming smaller and more misshapen. Every day Sarah kept up a positive outlook, swept her house, cared for the children, cooked the frugal meals, and encouraged her husband whenever he needed it, which, increasingly, bordered on the impossible.

When she looked back, the change in Mose was not slow in coming. Starting with the loss of the farm, the hard times when the animals' worth dropped so dramatically, the desperation without forethought of using up the leftover grain to make illegal liquor, the childishness afterward, and now this—yes, it was strange behavior.

To admit this to herself was frightening. How could she have escaped the fact that something was wrong with her husband? Should she try? Or should she accept it, unquestioning in her faith? She had no one but the belligerent Hannah, and they were barely on speaking terms.

When the cornmeal ran out, the last potato was eaten, and one wrinkled carrot remained, Sarah followed her husband into the bedroom when he went through the door to pray.

"Mose," she said.

"Do not disturb me, Sarah. I am entering holy ground."

"Mose, please listen. Our food is all gone. The children will be hungry in the morning. You must stop this. You must stop praying and fasting. You're only working yourself into a frenzy. Mose, we must do something about our plight."

"The only plight, my Sarah, is yours. When our faith falters, we have a plight, whereas we have heavenly peace when we trust in the Lord with all our hearts."

"But, Mose, listen to reason. God provides when we do what our minds can direct. If our food is all gone, we must find some. Don't you see?"

"No. My face is turned to God alone. Leave me."

Sarah knew now that she must be strong. She squelched the sob that tore at her throat and swallowed a hard lump as her eyes remained dry. The fright she kept at bay by moving about the house, caring for the children, putting them to bed, everything proceeding normally for their sakes.

It was the hunger in Manny's eyes that brought on the boldness. She stopped Hannah midstride, laid a firm hand on her arm, and waited until she met her eyes. Sarah spoke in firm, even tones.

"Hannah, you must ride out in the morning. We have one wrinkled carrot and a handful of flour. Neither one are enough to feed anyone breakfast. Your father is not well. I have no hope of being saved from starvation but you. Can you ride to the Jenkinses for help?

Hannah stared at her mother. "You mean he's crazy, or what?

"He's acting very strange is all I can say. I'm afraid it's been going on longer than we think."

"You mean I have to go and beg?"

"Yes, you must."

"Mam, I'm ashamed."

"I know, Hannah. I know. If you want me to go I will, except I'm not a good rider. We have only the one horse, and he's not in the best shape to pull the wagon alone."

Hannah's gaze flickered. Her shoulders lifted and then slumped. "What do we need?"

"Everything, Hannah. Everything."

And so, midmorning Hannah rode out on Pete, the former beautiful, well-groomed muscular horse that had been worked too hard and spent months without grain. That was fine for animals accustomed to a steady diet of prairie grass, but not for this well-fed, well-cared-for Eastern horse.

His hair was long and unkempt, although Hannah had done her best to brush out the worst of the dirt and tangles. His ribs were like a small train track, with his belly hanging down, loose, muscle loss evident from every side. Even his well-rounded haunches that had been taut and firm now quivered with deep vertical lines every time he took a step.

Hannah felt hot tears prick her eyelids. She steadied herself with a deep breath and a measured squaring of her shoulders. Here she was, then, riding out to beg for food, set plumb down in the middle of nowhere, with people spread out like chaff scattered in the wind. Miles and miles of nothing but grass, driven in seventeen different directions by each gust of wind.

Dat was out of his head, it appeared, and Mam was as scared as a chicken with a fox in the henhouse, fluttering around the house with a smile that wasn't real. Just the corners of her mouth lifted to keep everyone else calm and let them think everything was fine with Dat, who held his head and moaned. Nothing to eat, a dead horse, and a stalled corn crop. If they all got on the train in Bismarck and went back home, there would be hope. Grandparents and aunts and uncles would all ask the church to help them with a fresh start.

A cold fear swept through Hannah. This was the first time she was close to admitting defeat. But this ride to the Jenkinses had to be done. They could not survive on prairie hens and gophers. An occasional herd of antelope could be seen in the distance, but they moved swiftly, far away, a blur of brown and white, so that was out of the question.

She hoped she would not miss the road to the Jenkinses. She kicked her heels into Pete's side and was rewarded by flattened ears and the beginning of an easy lope. Her teeth rattled, her head was jarred on her shoulders, so she kicked him again, slapped the end of the reins against his neck, chirped, and urged him into a gallop.

Pete's hoof beats sounded dull and muffled on the track through the grass that served as a road. He soon tired, and reverted to his bumpy trot, then down to a slow walk.

Hannah sighed, loosened the reins and looked around. It was a bright May morning with blue skies flecked with thin white clouds, like a bride's veil, she thought. It was as if the brilliance of the sky was too bold, too bright, out of the *Ordnung*, and needed to be covered with a thin layer of white. Not that she'd ever be an English bride, having a worldly wedding and wearing a long white gown with a lot of her back bare for anyone to see.

Once, back home, she'd seen all those beautiful dresses in a Sears, Roebuck & Co catalog from 1931. She had pored over them for days, whenever her mother wasn't looking, eager to see how differently the lace draped around the tiny waists, down to the great swelling flow of the skirt just brushing the floor.

She smiled to herself, thinking of the Amish way. She had been to weddings. In awe of the solemnity of the occasion, the sober-faced row of ministers, the bearded bishop speaking about Ruth and Boaz (what kind of name was that?), and all the other love stories in the Bible. *Heiliche Schrift.* Holy Bible. All that seemed dim and faraway, like a tarnished memory, one that had too many days and too many miles between now and back then.

When her cousin Edna was married, her white Swiss organdy cape and apron was stiff and brand new, pinned up under her chin and close about her neck in modesty and *demut.* Her face was white and frozen, like a porcelain doll, as she sat erect and unmoving for the four-hour ceremony. When they (finally) stood in front of the bishop to say their vows, Edna looked as if she would fall over in a swoon, that's how scared she was. Well, Hannah had decided right then and there that she'd be scared into a faint too if she had to marry Samuel Stoltzfus!

He was thin as a stick and just as ugly. Mam had told her back then already to stop saying those things. It was brazen, loud-mouthed, and not spoken in Christian love. She guessed she should have sugared it down a little by saying only that he needed a few good home-cooked meals and that he wasn't handsome.

But it was true. Samuel was homely looking as all get out. Edna was no beauty, but she was a lot better looking than Samuel. She hoped they were happy in their little rental property. She should write to Edna. Dear Edna, we're starving and Dat's crazy!

She smiled to herself thinking of Mam's letters to her relatives, the eagerness in her voice when Abby offered her paper
and pen, stamps and envelopes. Like water to a dying person.

No doubt her letters spoke of only goodness—Abby's birth,
the new house (she wouldn't mention not having a chimney),
the Jenkins family's generosity. Oh, it would all be sweetness
and light—how Mose was tilling the soil, how Manny was
turning into a man, so strong and able to help Mose. It was
Mam's way, the Stoltzfus pride, the ability to squeeze every
drop of goodness out of the most horrid situation. Keeping
the moldy cheese curds of life to herself, letting others see only
what they could gather from the buttermilk that flowed from
her cloth.

Well, that didn't sit right with Hannah. You were who you
were, and if people didn't like it, then that was tough. Out here
on the prairie there was no one to worry about, no one who
cared what you wore or how you talked or if you were clean or
filthy dirty from a day's hard work.

She shaded her eyes with her hand and searched the surrounding area for signs of a barbed wire fence, a roof, or some
sign of civilization. She should soon be at the Jenkins' place.

She leaned forward, patted Pete's neck, and spoke to him,
telling him he was a good horse, it wasn't too far, and then he
could rest. On the horizon, she saw a darker blur against the
sky. She watched until she could see it was a spring wagon, or
buckboard, as they called them out here. It was pulled by a lone
horse. Who could it be, other than the Jenkinses?

Warily, she watched them approach, clouds of dust billowing behind the rattling buckboard, the horse trotting at a brisk
pace. She slowed Pete, waiting by the side of the road, thinking
perhaps they would want to speak to her.

Keenly aware of her poor horse, her dress, her white head
covering, wearing men's trousers, and riding bare back with no
shoes, Hannah kept her eyes lowered, overcome with shame.

"Whoa!" The rattling buckboard came to a halt, the black horse hitched to it prancing impatiently. The seat was high, which made the couple appear even larger than they were.

"How do!" yelled the red-faced, heavyset man on the right. Hannah nodded, smiled only for an instant.

"My, my, here we have a girl," the woman burst out, identically heavyset and rosy-hued.

Hannah thought fleetingly of two well-fed happy piglets, but banished the thought immediately, thinking of Mam and her admonishments.

"You from hereabouts," shouted the man, more a statement than a question.

"Yes."

"Where?"

Hannah turned and pointed back the way she had come. "I'm Hannah Detweiler. My father's name is Mose. We just arrived five, maybe six, months ago. We're from Pennsylvania."

"Ah, hah, homesteading are you?"

"Yes."

The woman's hair was braided, then wound about her head like a crown. She wore no head covering, and her dress was a brilliant hue of pink, mostly made up of pink flowers and green vines. There was a row of buttons down the front of her dress, also pink. Her face was about the same shade of pink as her buttons, with a pert little nose and two bright blue eyes. She was actually pretty, in a pink sort of way.

Her husband wore a hat that was not a Stetson, the way the Jenkins men wore. It had a soft, floppy brim, and it looked as if it was made of leather. His shirt was white, and he wore a leather vest that he had no hope of closing over his well-rounded stomach.

Hannah swallowed, thinking of all the good, rich food they must enjoy, being so well fed and amiable.

"Where are you off to?" asked the woman, leaning forward eagerly, her eyes searching Hannah's face.

"To the Jenkins' place."

"That far? Oh, we didn't tell you our names. My goodness gracious. We are Owen and Sylvia Klasserman. We live over thataway." She pointed a short, square finger to the east, the sleeve on her dress riding up to reveal a pink, flapping underarm.

"We must come look where you live. Detweiler, you said? We're always happy to have new neighbors. We've lived here for thirty-some years now. Arrived here at the turn of the century. We're from Sweden. Rode the whole way across the Atlantic when we were young, full of spit and looking for adventure. We sure got it, let me tell you. There ain't one speck of bad weather God forgot to send on these Dakota plains, I can tell you right now."

Hannah smiled now, revealing her white teeth.

"My, ain't you just the purtiest thing! Too bad my boys is all married." She narrowed her eyes, touched her own braid on top of her head, and asked if she was a nun, from the Catholics.

"No, we're from the Amish, in Lancaster County."

"What are they?" the man broke in, curiosity beaming bluely from beneath his hat brim.

Hannah shrugged. A deep sense of shame kept her mute. How to describe their way of dress? Their beliefs? They would laugh at her if she tried. Perhaps they weren't Christians, didn't even believe in Jesus or anything. She wished she didn't have to wear this covering anymore. It was just so strange looking, so out of place in a world where there was no one else just like you.

"Just people like you," Hannah muttered, hating the self-consciousness that welled up into a blush. She felt the warmth spreading across her cheeks.

"Ain't that the truth? Throw us all together in a pot and what you get is vegetable soup. All good, all together, a fine flavor."

Hannah swallowed, thinking of her mother's vegetable soup in the fall when she cleaned out the garden, cut and sliced, diced and chopped, cooked and stewed potatoes, tomatoes, lima beans, green beans, carrots, onions, celery, parsley—and flavored it with beef broth. It was so good with applesauce to cool it down.

"Wal, we best be on our way. We're on our way to the Apents. They got a steer down, so we'll help with the meat."

Hannah nodded and wondered who the Apents were and where they lived.

Owen picked up the reins, clucked to his horse, and with a wave of fluttering hands, the large black horse drew them away.

Hannah was hungry now, and thirsty. She hoped she'd soon be in sight of the Jenkins' buildings, or at least see a few cattle dotting the green grass, black dots on green fabric.

Someday, their own acreage would appear just like that. Branded cattle growing fat on the lush grass, a barn filled with hay in winter, the cattle driven to market, money in the bank. She'd already named the place the Bar S for Stoltzfus, her mother's maiden name. Right now it was the Bar Someday, a future planned, the biggest obstacle persuading her father and Manny, who was as obstinate as Dat.

She rode on, gratified to recognize the rolling of the land, the hollows and swells invisible from a distance but close to the Jenkinses. But as faithful Pete neared the outbuildings of the ranch, a sick feeling clenched her stomach. For a moment, she felt like throwing up. Where was her courage, her bluster, when she needed it?

Angrily she swiped at a bothersome horsefly and decided she'd best get this over with. No one else was going to do it. She hoped Clay would not be in the house, with his week's growth of blonde stubble on his cleft chin, his lazy blue eyes that watched her, as calm as pond water on a still day. Blue.

There was only Abby, her gray, curly hair flapping about her thin, wrinkled face, her eyes welcoming Hannah from beneath leathery lids. She was out in the yard hanging up the last of the day's washing, shaking out denim jeans with a flick of her skinny wrists, pegging them to the sagging wash line as if a strong gust of wind would take them away.

"Ya ride all the way over her by yerself then, did ya?" was her way of greeting Hannah.

Hannah dismounted off Pete's back in one easy motion, tried to throw the reins the way the boys did, but one caught on the horse's ears and she had to stand on her toes to pull it free.

"Yeah, I did."

"What brings you?"

"Well, my mother sent me. We're . . . well, we're out of food. The potatoes and carrots you brought are gone and my father— my father is acting strange. He doesn't seem to be . . . thinking the way he should. You know our horse died, his corn crop isn't going to get into the ground, and he's upset. We just need a bit of help until we can pay you back."

Abby kicked the wicker clothes basket against the wooden clothesline pole, untied the sack of clothespins from around her waist, and shook her head. She looked off across the shed roof, a scowl marking her face, drawing the lines taut, downward, as if a clamp scrunched up her cheeks. Her small blue eyes snapped.

"That man shouldn'ta brought you out here. This ain't no country for you folks. You best git back on home."

Hannah scuffed her bare toe into the dust, unable to meet her gaze. It was too sharp, too penetrating. "We can't," she said, finally.

"Why not?" Abby asked, her eyes watching Hannah like a hawk's.

Suddenly, Hannah hated Abby with a raw anger that shocked even her. Up came her face, her dark eyes blazing with a black glitter. "We don't have money to return, that's why!" she shouted. "You know we don't. You just want to hear me say it. We're poor, we're half-starved, and my father is slowly losing his mind. So how do you expect us to go back home?"

"Honey, here, here. I didn't mean it that way." Abby stepped forward as if to hug her, at least to protect her with an arm about her heaving shoulders.

But Hannah shrugged her off, turned and shouted, "Don't touch me. Go away and leave me alone."

She gathered up Pete's reins, draped them across his mane, grabbed a handful of hair and stood back, ready to fling herself on his back.

Abby's bony hands reached out, grabbed Hannah's arm, and tugged her away from Pete. He looked as if he didn't have the strength to return to the homestead.

"Look here, young lady. You ain't talkin' to your elders thataway. You best git yer wings clipped, or you ain't havin' no friends hereabouts."

"I don't care!" Hannah yelled.

Abby stepped right up and grabbed her arm in a grip like a clamp. "You better care," she shouted right back, "cause I can tell you, in this here country, you need folks to help you out sometimes."

Hannah said nothing, just stood by her horse's neck, a handful of his mane twisted in her grubby fist. She glared at Abby like a trapped animal.

"Let goa yer horse," Abby commanded. "Come on, let go. You best come on in and help me get dinner."

"No!"

"Fine. You and yer horse are so hungry and weak you'll drop halfway home. Suit yerself." With that, Abby walked away, picked up her clothes basket, and walked across the scrubby yard up onto the porch. She flung the empty basket on a metal chair and let herself into the house with a backward glance.

That made Hannah so mad she couldn't see straight. She leaped up on Pete's back, kicked her heels against his knobby sides, startling the horse into a clumsy lunge that unseated her and landed her by the corral fence with dust all over herself, the chickens squawking and flapping their wings as they dashed to safety behind the fence.

Thundering hooves rounded the corner of the barn. Three horses slid to a surprised stop, their riders grinning down at her. The spectacle of a young girl sitting in the dust, her riderless horse a few paces off, face suffused with anger, dark eyes popping and snapping—it was all hilarious to them. Not accustomed to young women, they laughed without restraint, not aware that their laughter was neither polite nor proper.

"That sorry old nag dump you?" Hank chortled.

"Slid right off, did you?" Ken asked with a wide grin.

Clay said nothing, just sat on his horse and looked down at her with that slow, easy light in his blue eyes.

Hannah fired a round of defensive words that hit them without making a ruffle in their denim shirts. Still laughing, they dismounted and walked toward the barn shaking their heads.

Except Clay, who walked over and offered her his hand. "Want up?"

"I can get up by myself." In one quick movement Hannah was on her feet and dusting herself off with rapid strokes of her hands. She straightened her head covering, tucked a few strands of hair beneath it, and glared at Clay.

"Yer lookin' awful puny. You folks gittin by?"

It was the way he said it that upset her most. Her glare and her defensiveness melted away as his kindness seeped through her belligerence. She swallowed and felt the prickle of hated tears, her face changing expressions like a soft, spring squall of warm rain.

She shook her head, swallowed again and whispered, "Barely."

Clay stepped closer. All she could see was his blue denim shirt front, the pockets with flaps buttoned down over them. She smelled the horse, the prairie grass, the wind, his tobacco, and a masculine scent that made her want to touch his shirt pocket and straighten the one corner that stood up as if blown by the wind.

She looked at the pocket, then dared to lift her eyes to his open collar, his tanned dusty neck, and the cleft in his chin. She had no nerve to meet his eyes. They were too blue, too slow and easy.

He saw the dark hair, thick and wavy, the eyebrows on the perfect brow, twin arcs of dark perfection. Her eyelashes lay on white cheeks, so thick and long it was ridiculous. He'd never seen anything like it. He was gripped by a longing to see the dark eyes beneath those unbelievably perfect eyelids, a longing that left him shaken and weak-kneed.

He hadn't expected this. He sure hadn't figured on any such feelings for this girl wearing that white head covering, her father like a prophet straight out of the Old Testament.

They were worlds apart.

Clay Jenkins knew plenty of girls. He knew too that he could have anyone he set his mind to. At twenty-two years old, he was up for grabs, in many of the local girls' minds. So far, he'd never met one he wanted to spend the rest of his life with, let alone marry one and raise a brood of children.

"Barely, you said?"

Hannah nodded. "My father isn't right. Something's wrong with the way he's acting. My mother isn't used to fending for herself. She does whatever Dat says. Our food is all gone. The garden doesn't look too promising. You know our horse died. We would go back home to Pennsylvania, but our money is all gone too.

"So I rode over for help. Mam made me come. She doesn't know what else to do. The children are hungry. We've been eating prairie hens, but it's not enough to keep hunger away."

Clay had never felt anything close to what he was feeling now. It wasn't pity, not even sympathy. Her words were pressed out from beneath a covering of pride. He saw the courage it took to speak about their situation, the force of her will, the desperation to help her family. He knew that she was the only one who could lead this group of well-meaning, misled Christians. He guessed that was what they called themselves—Christians. He couldn't seem to pronounce Amish correctly.

"But that doesn't mean we can't make it here on our own," Hannah continued. "We just need to borrow some food until we can pay it back, if that's all right with your parents anyway."

She stepped back and gripped her hands behind her back. She looked into his eyes, hers masked by her fierce determination to hang on to her pride. She looked too thin herself, with the faint blue shadows of hunger beneath her dark eyes.

"That bad, is it?" Clay asked, hating the way his breath caught as if he'd been running up a hill.

"It's pretty bad, yes."

"Did you talk to Ma?"

"Yes. She made me mad."

Clay laughed, wanting to take her hand but didn't. Hank and Ken followed them back to the house, sat with them at the dinner table waiting for Abby to dish up the potatoes and roast beef. Hod joined them, stomping onto the front porch with the force of a tractor, yelling to Abby that these cats had to go! There were about half a dozen too many around here!

Abby lifted her head from the hot oven door and told him if he touches them cats, she'd chase him off the ranch with her varmint-killing .22 rifle.

Hod laughed, removed his hat to reveal his white forehead that began after the red stopped, about halfway between his eyebrows and his hairline. Hannah looked at the boys' foreheads, and found them to be the same, only not as pronounced as Hod's.

Hannah took the heavy plate filled with boiled potatoes dotted with browned butter and chunks of beefsteak as large as her fist. She tried to eat slowly but found herself having to lift her head repeatedly and lay down her fork to keep from wolfing down her food like a dog, putting her face in her plate without bothering to use fork or spoon.

Clay watched her, the same unnameable feeling welling through his chest until he felt as if his heart was floating in moving water. Everything in the room spun before righting itself, and he figured he'd better watch himself. These feelings were far harder to handle than a bucking mustang or a wild steer.

CHAPTER 8

THE JENKINSES CARED FOR THE DETWEILERS, BRINGING MORE potatoes and onions and carrots, cold-packed beef in Mason jars, flour, baking powder and salt, cornmeal and coffee. They brought a milk cow and two calves.

Hod sat down with Mose and explained in detail that their only hope of carving out a life for themselves here in North Dakota was raising cattle. Abby told Sarah they may as well get on the train and go home, which didn't sit well with Mose at all.

He had, by this time, mostly given up on his fasting and praying, seemingly humbled that the Lord he knew so well had hidden His face from him for reasons he did not understand. He told Sarah in a quiet, subdued tone of voice that yea, though He slay me, I will trust in Him, just as the Bible tells me to do.

Sarah's heart swelled with love and something akin to worship. To have her Mose back with sound reasoning and peace of mind was more than she deserved. Surely now things would begin to look up.

The Jenkinses brought a horse, a contrary old nag they hitched to Pete in the harrow. At this, Pete threw a fit, crow hopping, shaking his head, and flattening his large ears. But Mose trained him well, and eventually, the team tilled the soil and planted the corn seeds in the ground.

They named him Mule. His ears were only a fraction smaller than a mule, and he beat every mule Mose had ever seen for crankiness. The most important thing was that he served his purpose well and Mose was thankful.

For a time, then, things progressed for the Detweilers. The barn was finished in due time, such as it was, built with logs and rusted tin patched in pieces. But it was free from the Jenkinses, so no one thought to complain.

The whole family helped drop the corn seeds, even six-year-old Eli. Mose drew a homemade tool with one horse that dug furrows, and everyone followed with the precious seeds, dropping them not too deep and not too shallow.

The days grew warmer. Puffy clouds hung in the sky like pieces of cotton stuck to the blue dome above them. The wind blew, but it was a warm, friendly wind, a playful breeze that tugged at the women's skirts as they bent over the soil and sent their white covering strings dancing, slapping them against their faces.

The large square of tilled soil by the house, flecked with clumps of stubborn prairie grass, they called the garden. It was, by all means, a primitive patch of half-tilled soil that swallowed the seeds, leaving Sarah with the feeling that if anything sprouted out of that wet, clumpy ground, it would be a miracle.

But it did. Little by little, the beans and potatoes and onions showed tender green plants shoving up from the earth, and Sarah's eyes filled with tears of gratitude. Such hope!

No matter that things had been hopeless, here was promise. Here was a sign from God above, who looked on them with benevolence, love, and mercy. His ways were so far above her own. All she needed to do was continue to trust, even when the way grew so hard there was no light at the end of a long and dismal tunnel.

Manny became an expert shot, killing prairie hens, which Sarah learned to skin expertly, eliminating the need to boil water and pluck feathers, a time consuming, tedious task. The small amount of meat on each one was sufficient to keep protein in their diet and with the bread baked with flour the Jenkinses had donated, Sarah stretched the potatoes and carrots as far as she could.

The roundup day arrived with Mose refusing to allow his family to attend, saying they had no fellowship with the world. They were a peculiar people, set apart to be holy unto the Lord. Sarah agreed, hiding her grudging heart, covering her longing for women's company with her head lowered in submission. She could see her husband's point, especially with regards to Hannah. She was so set in her ways, so determined and quick to mouth her opinions, like throwing rocks neither Sarah nor Mose could always dodge.

When she heard they would not be going to the roundup, she said her father was right; they were peculiar people, completely strange. They didn't fit in anywhere, like a boatload of slaves brought over from Africa, the ones she read about in school. All they were good for in the western country was being stared at, poked at, and made fun of.

Mose drew himself up, took a deep breath, and did not look on his daughter with anger or rebuke. But there was no kindness in his voice either. He told her if she didn't learn to curb her tongue and respect her elders, she would become a slave of the devil. Didn't she know the tongue was untamable and like a ship without a rudder unless she learned to master it—may God help her. Sarah stood by her husband, her gentle brown eyes filled with rebuke.

Hannah went out to the calves and changed their tethers, pulling up the long pegs driven into the ground, moving them to an area where grass was more abundant. She stood with her hands on her hips and decided there was no difference between her and the calves. She was pegged tight to her Amish heritage by her father's views, and there wasn't a soul around to pull up her peg and change her position either.

She noticed the ribs beneath the hair on the calves' sides, the way their necks appeared too thin, and decided this was no way to raise calves. She marched back into the house and approached her father without shame.

She told him what she thought, mincing no words. A calf tied by a rope to a peg in the ground was not the way things were done out here. Barbed wire was out of the question, the ever-present ghost of being poor hovering over them. So why didn't he brand these little calves and the one cow so they could roam? That's how it was done.

Mose listened to his daughter's voice and thought that here was a more daunting job than all the acreage he had been given by the United States government. Here was a challenge so steep it made the prairie appear bridled in comparison.

His own daughter.

She was beautiful by anyone's standards, with a head on her shoulders and a voice unafraid to be heard, opinions aired so freely and as naturally as the wind rushing past their house.

His head hurt. He gripped it with both hands and shook it back and forth like a wounded dog.

Hannah burst out, "Stop that!"

And still his head hurt.

The two oldest Jenkins boys rode over after Hannah asked them to acquire a branding iron for them. She named their homestead the Bar S, just the way she planned. She told Clay without preamble, leaving him scratching his head and wondering what other ideas were floating around in her mind.

"You know I'll have to go to town for that, don't you?" he asked.

"Why?"

"They have to make your brand if they don't have it."

"Who?"

"The horseshoe guy."

"Who's he?"

"Someone who makes horseshoes."

"How's that done?"

"You'll just have to come with me and see."

But Mose and Sarah were adamant. Absolutely not. Their daughter would not be riding into town in the Jenkins' old pickup truck with Clay at the wheel. To begin with, any form of automobile was the workings of the devil. Any contraption that ran by itself was devised by his cunning. God surely would not allow anything like that to be put on this earth—a machine breathing fire and brimstone, like an instrument from Hell itself.

No good would ever come of it. Mose trembled at the thought of those fire-breathing monsters rattling all over God's green earth, leaving plumes of black smoke, with leering, grinning, ungodly people at the wheel. His judgment was harsh, in black and white, labeling cars as evil; and that was that.

So Hannah stayed on the homestead, helped her mother with the washing, cooking, and cleaning, all the while fuming silently about the plight of the calves tied to their pegs. She washed sheets and pillowcases with a mad energy, rubbing them across the hated washboard as if she hoped it would bleed from her frenzied rubbing.

Sarah watched Hannah from the doorway, holding the baby in her arms, her face untroubled and still beautiful in spite of the long, arduous journey and the hardships she had endured since.

Hannah twisted a white sheet from the rinse water, her face grimacing in concentration, water sloshing down her dress front, the soggy garment now clinging to the womanly curves of her body. Going without an apron again. The *Ordnung* meant nothing to Hannah, of this Sarah was now convinced. The rules of the church were an unwelcome tether, a binding to authority that, to her, was unnecessary. A burden, a prickly collar she wore with disdain.

Suddenly irritated, Sarah called out, "Hannah, you're wet. What if someone came to visit and there you were, half-dressed?"

Hannah lowered her eyes and turned away without answering. "Come," Sarah said gently. "Put your apron on."

"Why would I put an apron on? There's no one coming to visit, and who cares?" Hannah spoke with resentment, her eyes black like coal.

"God cares," her mother said, this time a bit firmly.

"Who says?"

Oh, the impudence of her own daughter! Sarah was dumbfounded and had no ready answer. To quote the Bible to her would only cause more irritation. She must speak to Mose. Turning, she went inside, hefting Baby Abigail on her shoulder, her smooth face now gray with a certain weariness she could not explain. She would not stand in the doorway trading barbed remarks with her eldest. Tears pricked her eyelashes and a lump of despair formed in her throat.

"Yea, though I walk through the valley of the shadow of death, I will fear no evil." The comfort of this Psalm spoke gently to her as she laid Abby in her box in the corner. Yes, she would not be fearful of the evil that would constantly waylay her daughter. With that attitude, she was an easy target for the devil and his wiles. She would trust her God and leave it to Him. He had created Hannah and would care for her. She would be a devout mother, praying constantly and giving all her cares to God alone.

Why, then, instead of peace, did Sarah experience foreboding? An ominous black cloud seemed to raise its head on the horizon, and the wealth of waving summer grasses suddenly turned harsh, as if they whispered of an impending doom.

Sarah shivered and turned away from the window. It was time to begin the day's bread making. She lifted the lid of the agate kettle, where the sourdough starter was kept, took out a cupful, and replaced the lid before turning to the flour container, alarmed at the weight of it. So light. What would she do when the flour ran out? She knew they could not depend on the Jenkinses forever. Their assistance had been more than generous. How could they keep asking for more knowing there was no income?

The sun laid a square patch of heat and light on the oilcloth tabletop. Another sunny day. Every day the sun shone, the heat became more intense, the wind blew and blew and blew, unstoppable, never ceasing. Sarah wondered as she watched the tender green shoots of corn as the wind tossed about the leaves of the fledgling plant. The corn would need rain. The sun hiding behind gray clouds, raindrops beginning to fall, first a tiny, wet splash, then another, until the earth was moist and lovely. The rain smelled wonderful, an earthy aroma of moisture and promise and God's goodness. But each day, that seemed a thing of the past.

Surely God would send rain. Surely.

Sarah kept a calendar of her days, marked them off with a large X across the square. She kept a careful account of the weather in her diary, writing each day's work, the children's growth, ordinary goings on with a family of five. At home, in Lancaster County, she had always recorded where church services had been held, who gave the sermon, and the number of visitors present.

Her whole being seemed to fold in on itself, until she felt as if her very breathing became constricted, so sharp were the pangs of her homesickness, her longing to see her mother, her sisters, her grandparents. To be among them, one of the Stoltzfuses, a happy, well-adjusted *freundshaft*, a group of people so near and dear she could feel their presence, here, today, in this crude house made of logs in the middle of this unbelievable prairie.

Unbelievable, yes, it was. Living in this treeless, mountainless land, without neighbors or any roads of significance, without an income or a church to rescue them from the raw poverty in which they lived. What was her duty?

Should she always be submissive, when she felt in her bones that there'd be no corn crop, no money, only debt to the Jenkinses? Should she always trust Mose? Yes, that was the right choice. The Bible clearly stated this truth, the ministers expounded the women's path as followers of their husbands, calling him Lord, as Sarah had called Abraham and God had blessed him beyond all understanding.

So Sarah looked upon the stunted corn sprouts, watched sadly as the heat of the sun and the wind's ceaseless pounding tormented the brave growth they had planted with their own hands.

Two weeks without rain, then three. A month passed, with the sun rising in unfettered glory each morning, a giant, orange ball of pulsing heat, surrounded by a brassy blue sky that contained only wispy plumes of thin white clouds that hurried by, as if they were ashamed to be seen on this otherwise perfect day.

In spite of the constant heat, the corn must have dug its roots deeper into the earth, finding enough moisture to keep growing. Mose exulted in every healthy cornstalk. He fashioned sturdy hoes from straight tree limbs and sharp rocks, sent Manny and Mary to the cornfield to hoe thistles and other weeds that threatened to choke the corn.

They became deeply tanned, their dark hair bleached to a lighter hue, yet they never complained of the backbreaking work, obeying their father without question. Sarah always walked out to the cornfield with a tin pail with a lid on it, to bring them a cool drink of well water.

Hannah refused to hoe corn, in spite of her father's orders, or his threats. Mose and Sarah discussed this refusal and decided to leave it. As long as she performed her other duties, they saw no reason to bully her into submission. Her hatred would only intensify, they felt.

The sun shone on the little homestead, the rough-hewn log house and adjacent barn for which *shed* was perhaps a more fitting description. The buildings were not too far from being hovels, both for the human beings and their animals. The children played around these buildings, in chopped, scythed grass, trampled and dusty. A clothesline was strung between two sagging log poles, but it was serviceable, the clothes drying fast in the hot, dry wind.

Sarah still cooked outside on the fire surrounded by rocks taken from the creek bed, a tripod on each end, the blackened cast iron pot in between, the earth trampled around it by Sarah's bare feet as she bent over her cooking. Little Eli played with sticks and bark, made grass huts, and generally ran wild, often with Mary by his side, if she wasn't needed to watch Abby.

Their clothes became too small in time. Mary's dresses were snug across her chest, tight beneath her arms, and much too short, but the one remaining tuck had been left out, so there was nothing to do but wear short dresses. Sarah patched trousers again and again, until the denim fabric ran. The boys lived with ragged edged holes in the knees of their pants; they were like open mouths to Hannah, shouting of their shameful poverty.

The corn turned color, slowly, into a dry, olive green, the leaves curled into harsh tubes that mocked the whole family, rattling in the wind, tossed and twisted piteously. Sarah's gaze swept the endless blue sky. Mose returned to his headaches, gripping both sides as he swayed back and forth in abject misery.

Again, hunger became their constant companion. Too proud and too stubborn to ask for help, they survived on prairie hens, the few onions and scraggly carrots they pulled from the garden, the soil packed down, jagged with cracks where the dried earth had shrunken like a toothless old man.

One morning in July, Hannah ate one bite of prairie hen for her breakfast, laid down her fork, and announced in a tone as bitter as horseradish that she was riding into town to look for work.

Mose looked at his daughter, his eyes popped and snapped in the most uncharacteristic manner, and he told her she was doing no such thing as long as she was under his care.

Hannah shouted then, her voice raised so that the baby woke and began to cry. "Care! What care? Every one of us is starving, our clothes are wearing out, and you say we're under your care? I'm going, so don't even try to stop me. I'll get a job doing something, and I'll return home every Saturday evening with whatever I'm paid. I am not going to the Jenkinses ever again, to *beg*!" The last word was a shriek laced with anger.

Mose's eyes settled back into their sockets, and his heavy lids fell halfway and stopped. He spoke quietly, his words measured, his tone soothing.

"Well, my Hannah, if you feel the need to have more earthly goods than what the Lord has provided for us, then I suggest you take up the Bible and read about the lilies of the field, how Solomon in all his glory, a wealthy man, mind you, was not arrayed like one of these."

"I don't need earthly goods, Dat. We can't eat lilies, and Solomon's not here either. I'm hungry, that's what. So I'm going to do something about it."

"Which town, Hannah? Surely not to Dorchester?" Sarah asked.

"Of course not. To Pine. I'm going to Pine. But if I can't find work there, I may have to go to Dorchester."

"You may not have one of the horses," Mose spoke with authority.

Hannah snorted. "What would I do with a horse? If I perish of hunger, it'll just be me, you'll still have your horse."

Sarah gasped. "Won't you reconsider, Hannah?" she asked.

"Why would I? We're all going to starve out here on the prairie. We can't eat grass. The corn is shriveling up in the heat, and we just sit here like ducks waiting to be shot."

Manny's eyes flashed. "Dat knows what he's doing, Hannah. Why do you have to do something foolish?"

Mary and Eli began to cry in earnest, the usual breakfast harmony shattered by Hannah's announcement. They were too young to understand Hannah's undertaking, too young to know how their lives were rimmed with desperation. They only wanted Hannah to stay, to stop frightening her parents.

Mose spoke then, in tones dripping with patience and loving forbearance. "My Hannah."

Before he got any further, she shot up out of her chair, launched by her complete disdain of him. "Stop calling me that! I am not your Hannah. You don't own me the way you own Mam. You own her only because she allows it. Let me tell you, when I come back, you'll be in debt, trying to pay me back for providing for your family, a job you aren't able to do."

Before she left, she tied on a clean gray apron on top of her ill-fitting faded blue dress. Barefoot, her clean covering patched where the straight pins had torn the fabric, her face was like stone, hard with resolve, compacted with bitterness.

Sarah tried to hold her, grabbed at her arm, and tried to draw her into an embrace. But Hannah would have none of it, shrugging free of her mother's pitiful attempts at restraint.

Sarah began to weep, softly. "Just be careful, Hannah. Be wise. Don't let anyone persuade you to do wrong. Men are not always trustworthy. Here, take this."

She pressed a cold, gleaming half dollar into the palm of Hannah's hand, her fingers grappling for a hold on her beloved daughter's hand. "Please, please be careful. Remember that you were raised Amish. You cannot go out into the world without conscience. Keep your way of dress. Let no man seduce you.

Take your small prayer book, the German one, the one Mommy Detweiler gave you last year. Was it just last year?"

Sarah took a deep, ragged breath, wiped her eyes with her apron, her voice trembling when she told her not to allow anyone to give her a ride.

"Hannah, we are Amish. We are not of the world. We are forbidden to ride in cars. We must always bow our heads and pray before and after meals. Your head must be covered with your prayer covering. Remember the Lord Jesus, who died for you. When you feel the need to be baptized . . ." Here Sarah's voice dwindled to a whisper, then stopped.

"Then what, Mam? Huh? Then what?"

"Don't, Hannah." But she raised her eyes level with her sixteen year old daughter, saw the hard, unwavering truth in her dark, fiery eyes, shrank from it and tried to erase it by lifting a hand as if to ward off a blow.

"You expect me to travel a thousand miles back home to become a member of the Amish church? You know it's not possible. I won't spend the rest of my days alone because my Father chose to leave the only way of life I had ever known."

"We didn't leave a way of life, Hannah. We are still Amish, born and raised, keeping the faith."

"And how will I? How will I ever marry or have children of my own, with not one other Amish in these woebegone parts? Huh?"

Sarah began weeping softly again, a torn handkerchief held to her face, shaking her head from side to side, as if that move alone could dislodge this hard truth. Hadn't it hung between mother and daughter long enough? A gossamer veil, mocking their camaraderie, blown against one or the other repeatedly, an annoyance that couldn't be denied.

Here is where Sarah was torn. To be blindly submissive to a husband who had just not taken his children into consideration when he thought of making this move.

Had it been the correct way? Already she understood the way of a woman. Hannah was grown, and longed for the companionship that Sarah had also longed for and had found in good, gentle Mose.

But here was her own daughter, flesh of her flesh, heart of her heart. The urge to hold her was so strong it felt as if her arms were made of iron, too heavy to hang from her shoulders. She lifted tormented eyes to her daughter's.

"Hannah, I can't promise you that your life will be easy, if you choose to do this. Just make sure that you pray every morning and every evening. A young girl needs guidance from a personal relationship with Christ. *Mitt unser Herren Jesu Christus*, Hannah. Oh, that we could both be seated on the bench in a house in Lancaster, listening to our beloved Enos Lapp. Sometimes it feels as if I'll just break in two with homesickness, missing the ones I love."

Hannah's hard brown eyes misted over, like polished coal. She turned her back, her shoulders squared, before facing her mother.

"Here comes Dat, so I'll say this quickly. Don't worry about me. I'll make it on my own. And I'll pray, whenever I think about it."

There was no embrace, only the sight of her thin form in the faded blue dress, her covering strings slapping in the wind, walking away from the log house with the ring of stones and the smoke wafting away from it.

Sarah lifted a hand, lowered it. A fierce, possessive pride gripped her soul. She wanted to shout words of encouragement, knowing her daughter was capable of anything. Anything. She was young and beautiful and talented, smart as a whip and not afraid to speak her mind.

Sarah swiped at her streaming eyes, the vision of Hannah becoming a blur among the waving prairie grass. But there was a consolation now: her trust in Hannah she could acknowledge in secret. No one needed to know.

And when Mose mourned his daughter's absence, Sarah lifted devout eyes that effectively curtained the small spark of pride she tended well.

CHAPTER 9

THE DAY WAS HOT, SO BY MIDMORNING, HANNAH WAS WIPING HER face with a corner of her apron.

She was following the road to the town of Pine, consisting of a small group of crude buildings with a cattle auction, a feed store, a gas station, and, if she remembered correctly, a large general store and a café. Maybe more, she wasn't sure. She'd only been there once.

She gripped a small black valise that contained a change of clothes, her prayer book, a comb, and a toothbrush. The half dollar was in her pocket, a deep patch of fabric sewn to the front of her skirt. She had used a safety pin to secure the top of the pocket, so she wouldn't lose the most precious of all her meager possessions.

The road stretched before her, perfectly straight, on level ground, disappearing into a V on the horizon. Sometimes, grass grew along the middle; only the sides of the road were bare, gray, and dusty, the grass parched and brown. Heat shimmered across the plains, the light white hot against her eyes. She squinted, then closed her eyes for a moment and stumbled on a tuft of grass before opening them.

The light was unbearably bright. Or hadn't she slept much? Probably not, the way she'd tried to untangle everything during the night. She could see no way out of her family's desperate poverty, as long as Mose kept up that childish, undying optimism. It was almost pitiful, the way he assured himself constantly that God would send a miracle, a gift, and save them all. No matter that the hot winds blew and shriveled the corn, or that they were all skinny and hungry, every prairie hen shot to death for miles around.

And still he prayed.

You had to admire a man like that, she supposed. Admire him for his determination, if nothing else. Pity for her mother was like a dagger, only for an instant, before she steeled herself against these unwanted loopholes of emotion. She couldn't go all soft like this.

The soles of her feet were beginning to hurt. She was thirsty, but that couldn't be helped. Like a camel, she'd drank her fill at breakfast, hoping it would last all day.

Who would hire her? They were in the throes of the Great Depression, whatever that was. She'd heard her father and Uncle Levi discussing the United States currency, the closing of well-established banks, the crash of the stock market. She didn't actually know what the stock market was, but if it broke down, it must be important. She guessed that if wealthy people were in trouble, the poor would face some rough times, for sure. Well, it couldn't get any worse than their plight, that was another thing sure.

Even if those calves grew, they couldn't sell them. They were meant to be breeding stock, according to Hod. It could take five or ten years to build up a sizable herd. The corn was nothing but a loss. Which meant that someone had to get a job. Become gainfully employed. Do something that put a few dollars pure profit in your hand. Enough to buy flour and cornmeal and a bit of shortening.

Her mouth watered, thinking of biscuits and sausage gravy. Or fried mush and shoofly pie. When had she last eaten a piece of pie?

A speck in the distance took her mind off her hunger. The Klassermans again? Surely they weren't on their way home. They never had been true to their words, coming to visit them. Just as well. She would have been deeply ashamed to allow those well fed individuals to see how bad off they really were.

Yes, it was a wagon. Wait. No, it wasn't. It was an automobile; the dust rolling behind it was too dark to be purely dust.

Now she heard it, the *poppa-poppa-poppa* sound of the engine. The car slowed as it approached, the windshield splattered with dust and insects, gleaming underneath its layer of dust nevertheless. A deep shade of red. The center of the wheels were silver, the spokes like pinwheels.

Hannah stepped off to the side, allowing the car to pass, which it did not do. When it came to a stop, Hannah immediately observed that the driver was a young man, unaccompanied, which spelled caution in capital letters, plus an exclamation mark.

"Howdy, sister!" The voice was loud, brash, without restraint. The face was tanned, smooth, and boyish, the eyes as blue as Clay Jenkins's.

Hannah didn't say a word, just stood there by the side of the road with her covering strings blowing and her dark hair shining in the sun.

"You some kinda nun, or what?"

"I'm no nun."

"Well, you look like one. Where you going?"

"To Pine."

He put both hands on the steering wheel, leaned back, and whistled. "You got a ways to go."

"How far?"

"Eight, maybe nine miles."

"No, I don't."

"Hm. Huffy, are we?"

Hannah stalked off. She wasn't about to be ridiculed, called a nun, and then told a lie about the distance to Pine. Who did he think she was? She didn't bother looking back and wasn't surprised when she heard his approach from behind.

"Get in," he called.

"No."

"Why not? I'll take you to Pine. I'm going that way."

"You are now. You weren't to begin with."

He rolled his eyes and whistled.

She walked off. He followed her, slowly. "It's getting hotter. Get in. Come on. I'll be nice. There's nothing to be afraid of. Not with me. I wouldn't hurt a fly. I mean, flea."

Hannah walked on.

"Aren't you going to talk to me? You are a nun, I can tell."

"Just leave me alone. I can walk to where I'm going."

"Where you going?"

"To Pine."

"But where in Pine?"

"None of your business, you know."

"Come on, I'll give you a ride. Do you drive?"

Hannah said no and walked faster.

"What's your name? I'm Philip Apent. Phil, as everyone calls me. You can call me Phil."

Hannah stopped and glared at him, her dark eyes polished with impatience. "I'm not calling you anything. Now leave me alone!"

After he had roared off in a black cloud of exhaust, Hannah wished she would not have been so cautious, so obedient, so everlastingly conscious of her mother's words. The sun was hot enough to fry an egg on this dusty road. Her throat was parched, shriveled together like a hog's intestines on butchering day. Her feet were scratched and aching. Well, there was nothing to do but keep going and hope for the best.

The land was the same the whole way to Pine. Nothing but sky and level land and grass. Occasionally, the dry dusty smell changed to a more earthy one, which made her wonder if she was close to a creek or a water tank.

She saw the windmill first, then the town. A church spire. A grain bin. White buildings, gray ones. Now that she saw this group of homes and established businesses, an overwhelming shyness, a shrinking inside of her, made her stop and consider this bold venture.

Times were tough. This was the Great Depression. There were no jobs, no money, nothing much available. Hod Jenkins had spoken of his family's self-sufficiency, how fortunate they were to raise cattle, and own the ranch free of debt.

Who would hire her? Who could afford wages?

Her mouth dry, her knees week, her heart pounding in her chest, she approached the first building, the side of a white clap-board house with a foundation of fieldstone.

A white sign, faded and peeling, hung from an L-shaped wooden post that said, "Welcome to Pine."

Nothing seemed welcoming. A wide, dusty street, with wood-sided houses facing each other, like two sides of an argument, their false fronts held aloft by weathered gray braces that no one had bothered to paint. A hardware and feed store. Better not.

The café was next, a yellowed building that had been white at one time. A thin plywood sign above the door said, "The Waffle Café." A sparrow had built a nest in the bottom crevice of the sign, sending a spray of white offal over the screen door. The windows, two of them set side by side were so dusty on the outside you could not see if there was anyone inside behind the greasy pink curtains that were hung halfway up the frame on sagging rods. There was a yellowed sign in the window that said, "Waffles, 25¢. Everyday Special."

Hannah's mouth watered. Without hesitation, she opened the screen door and stepped inside, the bell above the door tinkling with the force of Manny's .22 caliber.

All heads turned in her direction. Bold, curious eyes, eyes accustomed to knowing everyone that stepped through that door.

Quickly, Hannah found an empty table, slid into it, her eyes lowered, her hands clasped on the table top. It took awhile until someone had the nerve to approach her. These prairie folks had probably never seen a woman or a girl wearing a head covering.

When someone did come over to her, Hannah assumed it was the owner, a buxom woman who was so tall she seemed to touch the ceiling. Dressed in a fiery red housedress, layered by a greasy white apron, her yellow hair stacked in a loose bun on top of her head, her lips painted the exact shade of red as her dress, she was as intimidating as a runaway horse.

"Hi, honey!" she boomed.

"Hello."

"What can I getcha?" Her eyes were kind. Curious, but kind. Hannah smiled up at her.

"I'll have a large glass of water, please. And a waffle."

"You want chicken gravy on your waffle?"

Hannah thought of prairie hens and shook her head no.

"Syrup? Butter?"

Hannah said yes, that would be fine.

When she brought the glass of water, there was ice in it, clinking invitingly. Hannah drank thirstily and asked for more.

The owner of the café was named Bess. Bess Jones, sister to Ruth Jones. Did she know Ruth Jones?

Hannah shook her head, then offered the information Bess wanted from her. She had walked to Pine. Mose Detweiler was her father, and she needed a job. She did not mention the hunger, the failed crop of corn, anything. Nothing about her dress either. Let them figure it out.

Bess sat opposite Hannah at the table with a thick white mug of coffee. She brought out a package of Lucky Strike cigarettes from her skirt pocket along with a silver lighter that was square and smooth. She expertly flipped up the lighter's top, ran her thumb along a small wheel, then put the cigarette in her mouth and lowered it to the small flame. She breathed out, spewing a cloud of smoke toward the ceiling, then hooked two fingers into the handle of her mug and swallowed her coffee.

Fascinated, Hannah watched every move. Her fingernails were long and red and mirror smooth. How could that be? How could she cook like that? Didn't it hurt, drawing all that smoke into her throat? That explained her deep voice. At first, she'd thought a man had spoken when Bess greeted her.

But the waffle was so good, the water so cold, the café cool and inviting. Bess had kind eyes, so she'd ignore the rest.

"So tell me, honey, how old are you?" Bess asked, squinting through yet another cloud of smoke. Reaching out, she drew a heavy ash tray toward her, tapping the quivering, gray ash into it.

"I'm sixteen."

"And you need a job?"

"I do, as soon as possible."

Bess looked at her sharply. "Why?"

"Well, we just arrived not too long ago. We lost our farm."

"Whaddaya mean, you lost your farm? You mean because of this awful depression, or what?"

"I guess. I don't know. We traveled from Lancaster County, in Pennsylvania."

"On the train?"

Hannah was tempted to nod her head. Who would know if she lied? She could save herself some humiliation. But she said, "No, we drove a team of horses and a covered wagon."

The waffle was gone in about five memorable bites, dripping with butter and syrup. She was still hungry, but it had to be enough. She picked up her water glass, swallowed.

"Real pioneers, are ya?" Bess asked, smiling broadly. She leaned back, tilted her head to survey the room and nodded in Hannah's direction.

"We got ourselves a pioneer girl." She laughed, a hoarse cackle, not unlike a crow. A few heads nodded and looked in her direction. One said, "Aw, Bess, give her a break."

"She don't need no break. She's a big girl. Ain't you? What did you say your name was?"

"I didn't say."

"Oh, well, you can tell me, honey. I'm your friend. You want another waffle?"

Hanna shook her head no, the fifty cent piece heavy in her pocket.

"Sure you do." She lifted her voice and yelled, "Mabel, another waffle, with a side of bacon." Turning to Hannah she asked, "So what did you say your name was?"

"Hannah. Hannah Detweiler."

Bess gave no answer, simply lit another cigarette, and watched her with squinty eyes. "You're hungry," she said finally.

Hannah nodded.

"So, if I give you a job, I can't pay you much. Times are lean. I don't need anyone, really. And I don't know what folks will say coming in here, with that thing on your head and all. It won't make 'em feel right."

Hannah considered this, thought of taking off her covering. She knew she would feel downright exposed, sinful, and rebellious. But if it fed her family, would it be all right in God's eyes?

Bess nodded in the covering's direction. "What are you? Jewish? Catholic?"

Hannah didn't want to say the word, knowing this woman would have never heard of the Amish, and how would she explain? But there was no way around it, so she said, "Amish."

"Never heard of 'em."

Hannah nodded, thanked the cook when she brought her waffle, then concentrated busily, spreading butter on the hot waffle, watching it melt and run into the squares of sweet dough, her mouth watering.

Bacon. When had she last had a slice of bacon? A few years ago. It was crispy, salty, and perfect. Her heart was soft toward this large, garrulous woman dressed in red. A woman of the world, and one to be avoided at all cost, she could hear her father say. But she had fed her and thought nothing of it.

"So, what can you do?" Bess asked now.

"Everything."

"Everything?" An eyebrow raised, followed by a burst of raucous laughter, a tap of a red fingernail on her cigarette. "Honey, you're a babe in the woods, is what you are. You'll be devoured by wolves, let me tell you."

Hannah looked up from cutting her waffle. "I can take care of myself."

She was met with another peal of hoarse laughter that seemed to ignite the few men lounging around the greasy tables, snorting and sniveling like mockingbirds.

Hannah popped the last bite of waffle in her mouth, chewed, pushed back her chair, and looked at Bess, her eyes two wet coals of anger. "Go ahead, make fun of me. Thanks for the waffles. You won't see me in your stinking café again. Plus, you better learn to take care of yourself, smoking the way you do."

With that, she walked out, the fifty cents still pinned securely in her pocket, leaving Bess with her mouth open. She didn't close it until the screen door slapped against its frame, leaving a small shower of dust in its wake.

Hannah was furious. She walked fast, her fists clenched, hating everyone in that dirty eating place. Filthy, cheap, smelly. Who did they think they were?

She walked past more houses, weedy alleys between them, littered with old boxes and tin cans, pieces of rope like dead, dusty snakes. The sidewalk was made of cement, but it was cracked and dirty, and some sections lifted up at the corners as if a miniature earthquake had rumbled underneath. Or prairie dogs.

To her left there was a large plate glass window with "Rocher's Hardware and Mercantile" printed across it in square capital letters, each one exactly alike. She stopped and considered the mercantile part. Ladies' stuff? Fabric, yarn, and house wares? Fueled by the waffles, her spirits high, she decided to enter the store and see what happened.

The door was heavy, wooden, also painted red, with a massive handle that ran horizontally along the middle. She pulled, then tugged back harder, before looking and reading the word "Push." To her acute embarrassment, a tall thin man wearing a white shirt stood inside grinning broadly at her.

"It won't open by pulling," he informed her, still smiling.

His head was so bald it shone like a pale, polished apple. A luxuriant moustache covered every inch of space between his nose and mouth, like a limp animal tail, but clipped and groomed to perfection. A pair of round, gold-rimmed spectacles hung on a string around his neck. His eyes were small and squinty looking, as if he needed the spectacles on his nose instead of hanging from his neck. Hannah didn't hesitate to tell him that the "Push" should be in larger letters.

"You think?" Well, maybe I'll have to see about that."

Hannah walked past him, her large, dark eyes taking in everything. Every shelf was piled with men's tools, pipes, copper tubing, rubber hoses, nails, screws, seeds, and fertilizer, just about anything they could have used at home.

One side of the store was stacked with fabric, bolt after bolt of gaily colored material—flowered, patterned, plaid. There was heavy denim for work pants, suspenders, buttons, thread, needles, pins, just about anything any woman would need to sew for her family, plus dishes, buckets, pots and pans, mops and brooms, towels and washcloths. The list was endless.

Hannah walked up and down the narrow aisles stuffed with goods and thought of her mother's patched stockings and aprons, the broken comb the whole family used. She nodded brusquely at curious customers, or kept her eyes lowered, intent on fingering an especially fine piece of cloth, riffling through buttons as if searching for a special one. She noticed the dust, the chewing gum stuck to the floor, cigarette butts tramped flat, bits of thread and dried grass, clumps of yellow earth, bits of newspaper. The buttons should be sorted by color and size to make it easier for the housewives to find a button to match a certain fabric. Same way with the dress material. Much better to stack it together by color—blue plaid, blue flowered, navy blue, sky blue.

She stood still, took in the lone electric bulb hanging from its greasy black rope like a malevolent eye, barely giving enough light to distinguish the blue from the green, much the same as the conglomeration of buttons.

Why didn't he add more of those light bulbs, clean them up a bit? She wasn't accustomed to electricity, but she bet it was much the same as a lamp chimney all smoked up.

She stepped aside to let an elderly lady pass, then walked up to the counter before she lost her nerve. "Mister?"

The man was taking down a dozen eggs in a wire basket, but he stopped and gave her his full attention, his eyes telling her he was in a hurry but wanted to hear what she needed.

"You need me to work for you. Your store needs to be cleaned well, and you need better light. I could rearrange your fabric, sort buttons, and clean windows. You could make many improvements in here."

The owner of Rocher's Hardware and Mercantile had been in business for close to thirty years. Out here on the plains, with folks scattered around for miles, none of them could afford to buy too much at any given time. So to survive, he'd learned to cut corners, keep his overhead down. His boys had both worked in the store until they went east to a college in Ohio, which left him scrambling to stay efficient, with this depression clamping a lid on any thoughts of bettering himself. His wife was, sadly, crippled with arthritis, her knees painfully swollen, her fingers becoming more twisted each year.

This odd girl, though, with that ungainly white thing on her head. "I would like to have you in my employ, but times are not good, as we all know. I couldn't pay you any wages to speak of."

Hannah answered immediately. "You wouldn't have to. All I'd need for a month or so for my beginning wages would be ten pounds of flour, ten of cornmeal, some salt, and a bit of sugar. Oh, and a ride home on Saturday evening, if it could be arranged. Plus, I'd need a place to stay."

"Harry!" The voice came from the back, loud and demanding, capable of turning the man immediately, as if the strident voice had strings attached to his hands and feet, puppet-like.

"Yes, dear." That quick, he was gone.

The bell above the door pealed. All the light coming through the door was darkened by a stout figure wearing a short sleeved dress, pulled in at the waist by a thin strip of fabric, which divided her effectively into two parts, a rounded upper and a more rounded bottom. Her face was as red as a sour cherry, and as shiny, her yellow hair in a braid on top of her head.

Mrs. Klasserman. She was followed by Mr. Klasserman, who was mopping his own florid, shining cheeks with a great red handkerchief as large as a pillowcase.

"My lands, it's hot," Mrs. Klasserman said. "When it gets this hot, there's a storm cooking out there somewhere. You mark my words."

She sailed past Hannah without showing any sign of recognition, then realized that Harry was not behind the counter, where he was supposed to be. The heat had put her in foul mood. She was in a great hurry and needed only twelve black buttons for her Sunday serge. She was not about to wait.

She blinked, her eyes adjusting to the dim interior. She saw Hannah, followed by a smile of recognition, saying her name, both the first and last one correctly.

"Are your folks well? Never thought we'd run into you way out here in Pine. We must come and visit now. I told Owen I'm ashamed to go anymore, not having taken the time to meet your folks."

Hannah smiled, acknowledged her kindness, and told them Harry had been called to the back by his wife. She was sure he'd be out as soon as possible and offered to help her locate the black buttons, which took only a few minutes, with Hannah pouring a whole scoop on the countertop for Mrs. Klasserman to search for herself. When Harry did not appear, Hannah found the card taped to the wall with a list of button prices. She decided on a fair amount for twelve black, steel buttons, collected the money, and scooped the buttons into a small paper bag she found. She handed the bag to Mrs. Klasserman, smiling and accepting her thanks with a polite, "You're welcome."

When Harry returned, Hannah stood by the counter with her hands clasped behind her back, radiant with the feeling of ownership and accomplishment the transaction had given her. She wanted this job. Harry Rocher had a sickly wife, and his store was an unusual hodgepodge of items thrown together with no one to arrange things in an inviting manner.

She watched his face and saw the gray weariness, the lines drawn deeply around his mouth, the twitch in the muscle of his cheek. She stepped up to the counter and said, "So, would you consider my offer? My family is homesteading, and my father is without money. If you would allow me to be in your employ, I'd make a difference. I could help your wife with the cooking if you have a place for me to sleep. I'll do my best in return for enough food to feed my family for a week. That's all."

Harry Rocher looked at her, this able-bodied, fresh-faced girl with flashing dark eyes and, no doubt, an assertive manner. He desperately needed help but could not afford to pay her. Quickly he calculated—ten pounds of the food she had mentioned would cost a few dollars. Perhaps he could throw in some lard and a partially opened sack of sugar that had turned hard. He thought of the widow Hennessy's oatcakes that hadn't sold. It would be a shame to feed them to the hogs. There was nothing wrong with them.

He looked at Hannah and knew how desperately poor some of these homesteaders were. He slowly nodded his head.

Chapter 10

THE NEW CHAPTER OF HANNAH'S LIFE THAT BEGAN WITH HER JOB AT Rocher's store would, in many ways, prepare her for the future God had planned for her.

Harry Rocher introduced Hannah to his wife, Doris, a slim woman who must have been pretty at one time. But, ravaged by a cruel disease, her hands were little more than pitiful claws that scrabbled to hold a comb or a glass of water. She was an unhappy woman, obviously despising the town of Pine and all its inhabitants. For more than thirty years, she had longed to return to the East, and three decades was an interminably long time to someone who would rather be elsewhere. It was her husband's will for them to live on the plains, but her love and loyalty also chained her to the prairie. Corroded by bitterness and dissatisfaction, she mostly kept to herself and spent her time reading or talking on the telephone to relatives back East. On good days, when the pain in her hands subsided a little, she wrote letters or played Solitaire.

She told Hannah to find her own way up the narrow staircase to the room on the left, Bob's room, but he wouldn't be home for at least nine months, perhaps a year. Harry followed her, opening windows in the stifling heat, turning back covers, running a hand across the dresser top, and shaking his head after examining his fingers.

"Everything, just everything, shouts neglect," he said quietly, so Doris would not hear. "Perhaps you are sent by God, an angel worker."

Hannah stopped short, astounded. Here was a man of the world, Dat would say, and he talked religion, just like Dat? Well, she could bet the fifty-cent piece in her pocket that he hadn't fasted and prayed and carried on the way Dat had. Likely he'd went about his life, patiently doing what he could, as best he knew how, balancing his work and the demands of his sickly wife.

Huh? Hard to think of herself as an angel worker. A few hours ago that Bess had called her . . . what was it? A waif? No, a babe in the woods, whatever she meant by that dumb saying. Well, an angel she was not, but she'd try hard to make a difference in this place. It appeared to have been much better at one time, especially this upstairs bedroom.

The furniture was made of good quality oak, just like at her aunt's house back home. The mirrored dresser was small, but had an ornate frame to hold the mirror, attached by dowels so that if you pulled it away from the wall, it swung forward or backward. The bed was a luxury Hannah couldn't even think about, having slept on ticks, those buttoned up covers filled with stinking dried hay. You could never get away from the feeling of being in a barn, sleeping in a haymow, but then, it was better than sleeping on the ground or a bare floor and waking up with your legs as stiff as a stovepipe.

She sat on the edge of the bed, marveling at its firmness and luxurious softness at the same time. Real pillows, clean white sheets. The walls were finished with a grayish white paper that had the texture of burlap. Ohio State pennants hung on the walls with framed black-and-white photographs of groups of boys kneeling or standing, wearing what looked like uniforms, a football in the foreground. She wondered which one was Bob, and what the name of their second son was.

There was a straight chair, a clothes rack, more pictures, a few dull brown rugs scattered on the floor, chintz curtains blowing in the hot breeze that sucked against the screen when the wind changed direction. Everything was dusty, the window screens, the sills, the curtains, the tops of every article and piece of furniture. She went over to the window and looked down, but could see only the rough side of another building not more than six feet away, plus weeds, tin cans, empty Coke bottles, and piles of what looked like horse manure scattered along the narrow alley.

There was no sense living in this squalor. The townspeople needed to get busy and do something about the appearance of this derelict little place. But first things first, she supposed. She'd go downstairs and get acquainted with Doris and her kitchen and see what Harry's plans were. She tingled all over with the anticipation of returning home with the flour and cornmeal, to see her mother's happiness and her brother Manny looking forward to a good meal. As often as he tried to disguise the hunger in his eyes, he would be rewarded with corn cakes and pan-baked biscuits. She ached to do anything to feed her family and lift their spirits, so alone out here on these plains.

As far as her father was concerned, she felt nothing except perhaps a mild disgust. He needed to take responsibility for the well-being of his family. It was hard to have respect for someone who walked around with his head in the clouds, dreaming of all the miracles waiting just beyond the horizon, in the time when God's provision would wondrously manifest itself. Oh, he didn't doubt that a black cloud would appear one day, move over the homestead, and soak that corn.

Hannah shrugged, shook off her reverie, went to the mirror, and looked at her reflection. Skinny. She was thin. Her eyes were huge, and her face looked thin too. Ah, well, hopefully she could eat here. Taking a deep breath, she turned and made her way down the steep, narrow staircase.

Doris looked up at her with a wan smile. "Harry says you can cook. It will be wonderful to have a bit of help in the kitchen. Are you acquainted with a stove?"

Hannah looked around the kitchen and saw the white appliances, the refrigerator, and what appeared to be a square white object with black coils on top. "A wood stove," Hannah answered.

Doris introduced Hannah to electricity and all its wonders. Wide-eyed, Hannah discovered a quart of ice-cold milk in the refrigerator, just where Doris said it would be. And you can keep butter and meat in there for days without spoiling, she explained. The stove became red hot at the flick of a button, the heat contained in the black coils.

Hannah learned to cook well with Doris hovering at her elbows, a certain delight now smoothing her unhappy features. For one thing, Hannah made Doris laugh. Her blunt, unapologetic way of viewing the world and its inhabitants, and the colorful way she described her family filled Doris's gray world with small rays of brilliant light, pinwheels of imagining, little bursts of unexpected humor that elevated her existence to a higher level of happiness. She could picture the drab homestead, the beautiful children (Hannah was a beauty), the submissive Sarah, the dreaming Mose. Doris knew Hod Jenkins and had seen Abby in the store, but didn't know them personally.

By the end of the week, the house had been cleaned to a spotless sheen, the floors swept and scrubbed, the windows washed, and the screens taken down and scrubbed with soap and water. Dust flew, and Doris held her breath as Hannah whipped about the house, rocking precious china dishes and lamps, shaking rugs with so much energy she was afraid they'd fall apart.

Hannah swept the store, but the rearranging would come later. She felt she was not acquainted with Harry as she should be before suggesting ways his goods could be better displayed and more appealing to women's eyes. There were so many changes to be made, so much to do in a week's time that Hannah plopped into bed bone-weary every night, wishing Manny could know what it was like to sleep on a mattress with a good soft pillow again.

On Saturday afternoon, then, Harry told her firmly that she could not walk home. His wife would accompany him, and they would drive her out to the homestead. For all Hannah's pluck, she found it extremely difficult to tell him her father would not want her to ride in a car.

Harry was bagging her flour and cornmeal, preparing a tin of lard, and gathering bits and pieces of leftover merchandise to give her. For a moment, he stopped what he was doing and asked, "And why not, do you think?"

"It's our religion."

"You can't carry these things the fifteen miles home. Not in this heat, and the day fading already."

"Does someone have a buggy? A horse?"

Harry shook his head and said, of course, but you'd kill a horse driving all those miles in this heat. So if she wanted to go home, she would have to ride in his car.

And so Hannah did. She sat in the back seat of the glistening black car, which shone in spite of an ever-present layer of dust. The seats were upholstered and springy, in a kind of smooth leather, although it seemed too slippery to be leather. She sat stiffly, her feet braced side by side, her knees held together by her fear, and watched steadily out the front windshield through a gap between Harry and Doris.

They rumbled away from town, picking up speed. The wind rushed in through the open window, lifting her white covering by its strings and tugging it away from her head. The pins that held it to her hair pulled horribly, so she grabbed her covering strings and tied them beneath her chin.

The speed was frightening. She had never moved across the earth like this. The level prairie moved by as if it was propelled by a large, unseen object. The car sputtered and clattered. Harry gripped the steering wheel with both hands, but never moved it much, neither right nor left.

The car slowed when Hannah gave directions, then slowed again, bumping over ruts and deep holes, grasses growing in over the track that served as a road. Doris tugged at the thin scarf she had tied over her coiffed hair, then closed her window, cranking a handle that raised or lowered it.

Dust rolled in through the opened windows. Harry sneezed, then cleared his throat. Black dots appeared on a rise to their left, which puzzled Hannah. Whose cattle were they? They had already passed the road that led to the Jenkinses' so perhaps there was another ranch they knew nothing about.

Nervous as they approached, Hannah slid forward, gripping the front seat with both hands, asking Harry to drop her off before they reached the homestead.

"I will not let you carry those parcels by yourself," Harry said, turning to look at her while the car kept moving by itself.

"We can't do that," Doris said matter of fact.

"My father will not be pleased. I'm afraid he won't be very kind or welcoming." Hannah faltered in her speech, ashamed of her father, ashamed even more of the conditions in which they lived. The crude barn, the unfinished house made of crooked logs, the campfire in the yard, and the ruined corn crop. Since she had spent a week in town, their glaring poverty, their poor management of trying to raise corn, the garden struggling through the grass that threatened to reclaim the tilled earth, the thin children with the too-short pants and dresses, patched and ragged, assaulted her. Yes, they were ragged. Yes, they were thin. All of this seemed to press Hannah down into the smooth surface of the seat, shrinking her to a small black blob, an unnoticed, unworthy piece of failed humanity that had no business living in town, eating the Rochers' good food, sleeping in a clean, comfortable bed, and acting as if she knew something about the store when, in truth, she was nobody. Raised surrounded by a secular community a thousand miles away, blindly following a delusional father with a broken wife by his side, she was now returning to the unpresentable situation they accepted as home.

A fierce pride, coupled with anger, rose up in Hannah. She hated being poor. She could not face her father or her mother. This feeling left her scrambling for a handhold, as if she was climbing a steep cliff and could not find a way to keep pulling herself up. It would be easier to stop trying, just let go of all of it, and fall. Tumble down, down, down until her body collided with the earth, folded in on itself, and perished. All of this went through her mind in a second, the knowledge of her station in life, the confrontation of who she was, where her roots lay, and from where her father had pulled them up to transplant them in this forsaken country.

Is this what her father meant by dying to self? All of that talk about being born again? You just fell off a cliff and gave up, figuring your life was no longer your own? She resisted fiercely, the thought of turning into her mother, going about her days with a song on her lips, no strength of her own, like a rubber band pulled this way and that, always depending on her husband, going through life without questioning anything.

As the homestead came into view, Hannah looked out of the window of the car and thought bitterly. This is where it got you, here in the middle of nowhere, starving, her head as empty as a stone. Well, it wasn't for her. She still had her wits about her.

As Hannah expected, her father was taken aback, to state it mildly. His eyes popped in his head when he saw the car approaching, his pain and disbelief evident when Hannah got out of the car, clutching the groceries to her chest like a peace offering, her face a mixture of bravery and confusion.

Harry stepped out, greeted Mose with a handshake, introduced himself, and told him they'd brought his daughter home. Doris remained seated, her face bland with hidden feelings, surveying the log house with careful, measured eyes.

Hannah tried to slip past her father, going around him from behind, but he turned and caught her with a sharp, "Hannah!"

She stopped and turned, her eyes bright and unflinching.

"I thought we told you not to ride in cars. You have openly disobeyed."

What was there to say to that? Hannah ground her teeth in anger. Now why couldn't Dat have waited to cut loose until after Harry and Doris had left instead of displaying his righteous little sermon here and now? "I brought food. I couldn't carry all of this." She thrust the heavy parcel out to show him what she had brought.

When her father's eyelids came down, and he spoke the inevitable, Hannah remained standing, clutching the cornmeal and flour as if his words could take it from her.

"I have prayed that God would send us a blessing, but I didn't think He would send it in the devil's machine. So I propose, Mister . . ." he faltered, forgetting Harry's name.

"Rocher," Harry supplied.

"Yes, Mr. Harry Rocher. Our religion doesn't hold with riding in cars, so I suggest that Hannah will not be in your employ in future. Also, the food you have so graciously brought, according to my way of thinking, has been tainted by riding in an automobile. So I would suggest that you put it back into the machine that brought you."

Hannah had never felt so helpless, or outraged. She opened her mouth to speak to her father, but could not utter a word. She could only stutter.

Her father smiled at her, then walked toward her to take the food she clung to, as if her very life depended on it. "Hand it over, Hannah."

"Dat," she began, feeling tears of rage and frustration prick her eyelids. "You need this flour and cornmeal. You can't do this to Mam and the children. We . . . you, are hungry."

At the thought of Sarah and the little ones, Hannah saw the flicker of reconsideration, felt his weakening, and she resolved to stand her ground. "You can't go on, Dat. We need to sit together and talk this over. I have a job now. I work for these people. They can't afford to pay me, but they can spare us some food."

"Very well, then. But you must not ride in the automobile." Turning to Harry, he said that Hannah would return on Monday by horse, which was their way. As for the food that had ridden in the *verboten* vehicle, there may be a time when common sense was involved, and this may be one of those times.

So Harry and Doris Rocher rode back to the town of Pine, without meeting Sarah, having caught only glimpses of the children, their curiosity riding home with them. Harry shook his head and told Doris he had never seen anyone quite as strange as that Mose Detweiler, but Hannah seemed normal enough.

For one evening, Doris forgot her own woes and talked in a lively manner, thinking up ways in which they could be useful in helping that family. Harry watched his wife's face, the expression in her eyes, the way she waved her hands for emphasis, and thought that a miracle had happened right here in their car in the middle of the high plains.

The evening meal was something to remember. Sarah worked the dough as if it was made of diamonds, each pat of her hands holding anticipation and gratitude. The children crowded around the bubbling cornmeal mush, sniffing, laughing, and clapping their hands. The smoke from the campfire made their eyes water. They coughed and scampered away only to return for more.

Hannah spread the tablecloth, brought out the dishes, poured the cold well water. Sarah warmed the prairie hen gravy. The bread baked over the fire in a covered skillet. The mush was thick and salty, filling their hungry stomachs with heaven-sent manna.

Sarah watched her family eat until they were full. Now they were happy, light-hearted children, their cheeks flushed with the warm food. She took pity on Mose, trying hard to contain himself, to eat without wolfing down the food, but his eyes gave away his glittering hunger from within.

Sarah knew the dull ache of an empty stomach herself. Nursing Abigail, she could not have gone on for many more days without a better supply of food. All week, she had considered asking Mose to hitch up the team and go to the Jenkinses' for help, although knowing he would not allow it. At night, when the baby cried, not satisfied, it seemed as if the corners of the dark room contained a black portent, a foreboding of unseen hardship, and her soul felt weak with trembling.

But she must be strong. She could see the despair in Mose's eyes, the way he plied his religion to keep it at bay, the futility of his constant vigil and his expectation of a miracle. There was a certain hope in the way he watched the half-grown corn wither and curl in the blazing sun and the increasingly hot winds. He built a barnyard for the cow and two calves, which brought Sarah to a weak belief that he may be willing to change, to take what Hod Jenkins kept telling him into consideration.

But tonight, with their stomachs full, Sarah did not want to bring unwanted worries to the table. Tonight, she would enjoy having Hannah back, relishing the new-found maturity she displayed by accepting the food as payment.

They talked while they washed dishes, Sarah listening to Hannah's expanded world with awe. She gave a small laugh, eyes wide as she listened, thankful for every scene her daughter allowed her to see. They giggled like schoolgirls, thinking what Mose would say about Bess. Then Sarah turned to Hannah and asked if she honestly would promise to stay out of the café. She believed Bess was kind, but likely the men that frequented the café would not be very good company.

More than ever, the crude house and barn seemed primitive to Hannah. It was pitiful in its raw state, as if unlearned children had decided to build stick structures. The logs were thin and crooked with yellow, cracking clay clapped between them, the roof gray and rusted brown in long streaks.

The outdoor cooking was the worst. Like Indians. Sarah did not seem to mind, but living the way they did chafed at Hannah's spirits, like ill-fitting boots rubbing blisters of shame. But she was here now, in the company of her family. So she would not let the state of their lives drive away the comfort of being with them.

They sat around the fire late into the evening, the logs burning down to embers, a soft glow encroaching in the west as darkness crept across the sky, pinpricks of stars poking their way through. At night, the wind slowed to a whisper. The grass stopped its constant tossing, as if knowing it was time to go to bed and rest while the world closed its wings and slept.

Eli and Mary sat close to Mose, leaning on his legs with their elbows, their eyelids drowsy, the heat of the fire putting them to sleep. Sarah held Baby Abigail, although she was sound asleep, loving the feel of the small, pliant form in her arms. Manny sat cross-legged, staring into the fire, his dark eyes hiding any form of emotion, his handsome face etched in stone.

Hannah watched her brother and wondered. What had occurred this past week while she was gone? Manny loved his father, stood by him, and defended him with his whole being, in spite of Dat's erratic behavior.

Hannah broke the silence by asking about the calves. Mose said he believed they were doing well. Hannah asked if they were still tethered on ropes.

"No, they are in the barnyard now."

"Always? Don't you let them out to graze?"

"No, we don't. We give them grass by the forkful." Sarah's eyes cautioned Hannah.

"You know, the Jenkinses' cows pretty much roam at will. They don't go far, and if they do, they are branded. Everyone knows whose cattle they are. We haven't branded ours yet."

Mose nodded.

"Clay has a brand made at the farrier. The Bar S for Stoltz-fus, Mam's maiden name."

Mose looked at Hannah in disbelief. "You took that on your-self, then, to name the homestead into a place called a ranch, the way our worldly neighbors have done? We are not of the world; we are a peculiar people, set apart. We are God's chosen, so we do things differently. Who gave Clay Jenkins the right to carry on with the name of our ranch, I mean, homestead?"

"I did."

"Without my permission?"

"Yes." Hannah hung her head, her gaze dropping to her hands in her lap.

"So, you are planning on turning this productive little home-stead, a humble place of abode blessed by God, into a ranch with a worldly name?"

"Dat, we have to. Don't you see? We have no choice. Look around you. The corn is withering on its roots. This is normal weather for early summer. They don't grow corn here. They raise cattle. The grass is abundant and it's free. The cattle grow fat and we sell them. That's how we survive. Until the herd is built up, we need to have a paying job to stay alive."

Mose pursed his lips. "The rain will come, Hannah."

"And what if it doesn't, Dat? Do you have any plans beyond the withered corn, already dying in the field?"

"God will provide."

And then Manny spoke in a deep voice, a man's voice, bring-ing Mose to attention. "Dat, I want to be an obedient son, and you know I always have been. But Hannah's right. Perhaps this is a test for our faith, a test of our will to survive these first years. Already we would have perished without the help of our worldly neighbors. We are no longer among our own people, so we need to accept advice and help from those around us. I met a man named Owen Klasserman when I was out riding, a heavyset man who speaks German. Their ranch is closer to us than the Jenkinses'. He says, too, that cattle is the way to make a living in the Dakotas."

A long speech for Manny. Mose listened to his son's words and considered them, Sarah could tell. With the respect he had for his son, his words meant more than if Hannah had spoken them. For a heartbeat she waited for her husband's reply and when none was forthcoming, she continued to wait, knowing Mose would think for a long time before he spoke.

She got up, put Abby to bed, and returned to find her husband waving his arms forcefully, speaking in loud tones. She stood in front of the house in the darkness with her arms crossed, watching the red glow of the fire and her husband's waving arms. As she listened, his voice seemed like rocks thrown on the roof, and a genuine dread gripped her.

"Who are you to be telling your own father?" he shouted.

Eli and Mary rose to their feet, fleeing from their father's rant to take refuge in Sarah's arms. Quietly she put them to bed and knelt with them to say their German prayer. She kissed them goodnight before returning to the fireside to sit with Mose, his speech now done. A cowed silence, rife with unspoken words, settled over them.

The fire glowed. Mose got up to add a stick of wood, sparks shooting upward to the magnificence of the vast night sky. Somewhere, a wolf howled its eerie call of the wild across the rustling night grasses, immediately followed by the high yipping of a coyote.

And then Sarah spoke in a voice filled with peace. "Children, I do believe your father and I can see that what you are saying is true. But it is hard for parents to accept the counsel of their children, knowing that we are older and wiser and have been here on earth longer than both of you. So, we should be the ones who guide and direct you. However, our situation borders on the desperate, and without the aid of our English neighbors, we will likely not survive. My whole heart yearns to return to Lancaster County, the land of my childhood, the home of our dear parents, and aunts and uncles. But that too is an impossibility with no money for train fare, and no resources to make the long journey with horses and wagon.

"Hannah, you are doing the one thing that for now will save us from starvation. Manny, you are right. We need to learn to adapt and accept help from those around us, whether they are people of faith or not."

Here Mose broke in. "Believers should not be yoked to unbelievers."

Sarah went on, "We are not yoked, my husband. We are here in a harsh land where folks need each other, and without that, we will surely perish. So we will continue allowing Hannah to work for the Rochers and try our best to grow the food we can, watering the garden and branding the calves, which looks to be a necessity. Then we will wait on the Lord, and see what He has for us in the future."

Chapter 11

On Sunday afternoon, Clay Jenkins appeared riding a black horse that still tugged at the bit in spite of having traveled the miles between them, carrying the branding iron he had picked up at the farrier's that week.

It was fortunate that Mose was asleep, that Hannah stood by the barnyard fence watching his arrival, painfully aware of her threadbare blue dress that was too tight across her shoulders, the torn black apron tied around her waist, her bare feet.

The welcoming light in his blue eyes, the way he lifted his old brown Stetson, and the blonde hair falling over his forehead put her at ease so that she smiled her welcome in return.

He proffered the iron. She stepped up to take it from him, lifted it carefully, examined the insignia on the bottom, and ran her fingers over it as if the shape of the cast iron was the shape of her future. She looked up at him, her dark eyes thanking him.

"I guess you know I can't pay you for this."

He nodded and said, "It's all right." Then, "Mind if I get down?"

"No."

He dismounted in one easy movement, then stood, so tall above her, and asked if she'd want to walk with him.

Hannah glanced at the house and noticed the lack of activity. She nodded her head, her heart pounding in fear of her father.

Clay knew he would be unwelcome, but was determined to take this chance when it presented itself.

They walked side by side, Clay leading the horse, down the grassy track that served as a driveway to the buildings.

The air was hot and windy, the sky a dome of blue heat, the grass waving restlessly, tossed by the constant current of air that tugged at her skirts, flapped the strings of her covering and loosened her dark hair from its restraints.

The horse blew from his nostrils, the way horses do, with a rumbling sound that made Hannah jump.

Clay laughed. "Thought it was your pa comin' up behind us?"

Hannah laughed that rich laugh that came from deep inside. Clay looked down at her and saw only the top of her head, the band of white that was her covering, and the dark hair blown loose by the wind.

She looked up then and caught his gaze. "He'd be yelling long before he got this close."

"He don't like me much."

"No."

"Well, what I came over for was to give you the branding iron, but also to see how you all are gittin' on. I can't see how you're livin' half decent with no food, and I don't believe money's plentiful around here. I guess to say it right, I'm plain worried about you."

Hannah sighed. She gazed off across the prairie and then stopped walking. Looking at Clay, really looking at him, she told him there was a time when her pride would not have allowed her to say how bad things actually were. But now, she'd have to.

Clay switched the reins to his other hand, tipped up his hat, and waited. With a proud lift of her chin, Hannah told him about going to town, relating the whole story in minute detail, to the filth in the alleyways, Bess at the café, the room she slept in at the Rochers', and Doris's unhappiness.

"I just want to be able to keep my family. The children are hungry." Defiance flashed from her dark eyes, carrying the knowledge of her father's disapproval.

Clay showed his disbelief. "Whyn't you ride over? You did once."

"I'm no beggar."

"But it wasn't begging. You did what you had to do."

"I know."

There was a silence, long enough that Clay was aware of her, so sharply aware of wanting to comfort Hannah and take away the unfair burden that had been laid on her too-young shoulders. She was tied to her father by her strict upbringing and would become her mother when she was married. He could see this plainly. Slowly, her spirit would change.

"So your mother wouldn't go against your father?"

"No. Well, not really. She did give us a little speech last night, although in her own timid way, which I suppose will help somewhere down the road. But in the meantime, the situation is real. Someone has to come up with a plan to put food on the table."

"Looks like you're doing it. Right plucky of you."

"You think?"

"Yeah."

"There was nothing else to do."

"So tell me, Hannah, when you get married, will you be like your mother?"

"Who would I marry? There are no Amish within hundreds of miles. I want to get married. I figured that out soon after we left home."

"You can't marry a normal person?" Clay asked seriously.

Hannah laughed. "You're saying you are normal and we aren't?"

"Something like that."

Hannah thought for awhile, then shook her head. "I'm still young. I don't know what would happen if I met someone and fell in love with him. If he wasn't Amish, my parents would never allow it, so I could never receive their blessing. That's a scary prospect. Besides, I don't know what love is, or how to fall in love. How does a person know when that's about to happen?"

Clay gave a short laugh. "I've been in and out of love 'bout a hunnert times."

"See what I mean? It didn't work for you. Probably never will for me."

Clay dropped the horse's reins and asked if she would sit for a spell, then bent to flatten some grass by the side of the road. Grateful to rest, Hannah sat facing him, her legs curled beneath her skirt, her dark eyes on his face as he removed his hat. His hair was so long she couldn't tell if he had the telltale blue-white forehead of every man on the plains.

He did have a nice face, she decided. The squint of his blue eyes, the straight nose that appeared to have been smashed once, or at least broken, the cleft in his chin, his smooth skin already had the makings of fine lines and fissures around his eyes from the unforgiving weather.

She did not let her gaze linger on his mouth for reasons she did not understand. Perhaps it was too perfect. She had never seen a mouth with that kind of perfection. It was unsettling, so she looked at his nose again, but that was too close to his eyes. So she settled on a region somewhere beyond his shoulder.

He told her that her family would need help getting along. Did she know that? She said yes, she did know that, but figured as long as she stayed on at the Rochers' store, she could supply sufficient food for all of them.

"What about your pa? Couldn't he find work someplace? Or your brother?" Clay asked, watching the way her eyes grew darker, thinking on things.

"Manny will have to, eventually. Even if it's for food, the way I'm doing."

"Your pa? He wouldn't work for wages?"

Hannah shrugged.

"You dread goin' back to town on Monday morning?"

"No, not really. I'll like it better once I know everyone."

"When's those boys comin' back from college?"

"Not now. Maybe in six months or a year. I don't know."

Clay said he'd never wanted to go to college. All he wanted to do was buy his own spread and raise cattle his whole life long. That was all he knew.

"Do you want to get married and have children?"

"Yeah. Probably, if I can."

"Why couldn't you?" Hannah asked.

Clay shrugged and thought, *because I can't have you. I would get married right quick, Hannah, if I knew I could have you.* But he didn't say it.

"Yeah, well, same for me, Clay. There's no one close, so I'll probably remain single and work to feed my family."

Suddenly she sat up straight, a fierce light of determination in her eyes. She told him she was going to learn how to rope and ride if it was the last thing she ever did!

Clay looked at the sun and told her there was time to ride home to his place and practice in the corral. Would she?

She couldn't go home and get one of the horses. Her father would never allow it, with Clay and on a Sunday.

"You always bring your pa wherever you go? Come on. You can ride with me."

Hannah felt the blush before it colored her face, then kept her eyes downcast, afraid to let him see how badly she wanted to do just that. She became so flustered, she could not think of an answer fast enough, so she started to laugh, which came out in a mixed-up sob, the hysterical sound of a young girl's heart.

Clay stepped closer, reached down, and pulled her to her feet, searching her face, not understanding what had caused the sound coming from her throat.

She yanked her hands out of his, stomped one foot, and told him to go away and leave her alone, accusing her of bringing her father when he wasn't even close, and if he was, she'd do exactly as she wanted anyway.

With that, she ran off toward home, her feet pounding the dry, hard earth, tears of rage and frustration welling up as she ran.

Clay called after her, then thought better of it. He gathered up the reins and made his way home, thinking the less he saw of Hannah Detweiler the better. But he knew too that he would look forward to their next encounter, which he planned for next week, when he would go to Rocher's Hardware for some bolts. Or nails. Or something.

Hannah rode the faithful Pete to work the following morning, beginning at daybreak with a parcel of cold mush in the pocket of the clean brown dress her mother allowed her to wear. It was a dress kept for church on Sundays, but since there was no church to attend, what was the point? She wore Manny's old pair of trousers underneath, for modesty.

She looked down at her mother from her seat on the horse in the half-light of dawn, when everything was still and as pristine as an angel's wing.

"Are you sure you'll be all right, Mam? You have enough to eat, enough to get by 'til Saturday?"

"Oh, yes, Hannah. With the prairie hens Manny shoots, I feel sure we'll have enough."

"Then I'll be off. Good-bye, Mam."

Sarah touched her daughter's knee, gave it a little tap of affection, and let her eyes tell Hannah how much she cared. She raised a hand, stepped back, and said, "Bye."

The day was sharp and cool, the prairie appearing like a dark ocean, the tips of grass waving like ripples of a current in a vast body of water. The sky was gray, tinged with the color of ice, the sun's advance below the horizon bringing a soft shade of pink, like a bunny's ear.

Hannah always thought the velvet pink of a rabbit's ear was the loveliest color she had ever seen. Someday, she might have a dress of that shade, if she worked hard enough.

Her cousin Samuel had a whole pile of rabbit hutches on the east side of their barn. He raised them to see at Easter, but since the Depression, no one wanted to waste their money on things that weren't necessary; a rabbit wasn't something you absolutely had to have. Someday, though, she would own a pale pink dress and a row of rabbit hutches painted white. She would clean the cages every day, give the rabbits fresh hay and cool water, get them out of their hutches and let them nibble on green grass and hop around on their long hind legs before replacing them in their cages. Perhaps rabbits couldn't survive the cold Dakota winters. Well, she'd put the hutches into the barn for the winter.

She wondered if Samuel's family lived in the same state of poverty as her family did. It probably was hard times to Samuel, but she'd bet their living conditions would be a rare luxury to them. To Mam anyway.

Her thoughts rambled along in the past, remembering times when she would have never imagined having the responsibilities that were on her shoulders now. They were like a hard, wooden yoke chafing her neck and bowing her into submission, she guessed. But she wasn't beaten yet.

The sun burst on the horizon, painting the sky in crimson, orange, and yellow. The sun's rays rode on the birdsong that came alive as the morning progressed. Chirps and liquid trills, short light chants, and shrill whistles, all the merry sounds from numerous birds flitting among the grass and racing across the sky in showers of dark-colored winged acrobats—but Hannah missed them completely, immersed as she was in her own thoughts.

When the town of Pine came into view, she slid off Pete's back, ashamed to be seen riding into people's scrutiny of the Amish girl who was forbidden to ride in cars. How many people in the town knew about her, now that the garrulous Bess had her in her teeth? She'd shake her like a dog, leaving her to pick up the pieces by herself, no doubt.

Well, in this town, her father did not follow her. She was her own person. She squared her shoulders and walked with her head up, leading the horse through the back lot in the small fenced-in area behind it, as Harry had instructed her. She made sure the stable was accessible, that there was water in the trough, and then removed the bridle, petting good old Pete with love and affection. She removed her trousers as quickly as possible and hung them on a nail beside the bridle. Taking a deep breath, she began her day in the other world, the realm of life that was lived among *auseriche leit*. Outside people. People of the world.

Doris greeted her, dark circles under her eyes and a tired, half-lidded expression. The kitchen was a mess! Harry's relatives had been here, Doris explained. They were quite the company, she said, leaving her with a mountain of dishes and never offering to help with them.

Hannah eyed the sink, laughed, and said that the mountain was still there all right, which made Doris smile. She kept smiling as Hannah emptied the sink, banging pots and pans, scraping dried food off casseroles and cast-iron pans, water splashing out of the sink and dribbling down the front of the cabinet, and soapsuds as high as her elbows. Her shoulders erect and her head bent forward, Hannah threw herself into a frenzied attack on the towers of dishes. In no time at all, the pile was gone — washed, rinsed, dried, and stacked neatly in the cupboards. The electric stove shone like a mirror.

Doris sat in her rocking chair, her feet propped on an upholstered footstool. She wore a clean yellow housedress covered with a sunny print of daisies. She had a simple crocheted afghan over her lap, the radio on the small dark table beside her spilling the morning news, an electric fan whirring from the opposite side.

Hannah remained in awe of electricity and its amazing ability to be carried on a wire stretched between poles for hundreds of miles, a substance you couldn't see contained in one wire. It sizzled into homes, turning them into well-lit dwellings with hot and cold water coming from a spigot by the mere turning of a handle, keeping refrigerators ice cold, and stoves red hot. A man's voice came from a wooden box called a radio, and a telephone on the wall transmitted your own voice to someone else through a wire, allowing you to hear the other person's voice as well.

She figured there had to be some smart people in this world, much smarter than herself, but that was all right. Being Amish, she'd never have a need for electricity. It was amazing, nevertheless, and she planned on enjoying every luxury as long as she was here in Pine working for the Rochers.

She told Doris her dress was lovely, like a field of flowers on a sunny day, which made Doris smile again, reaching up to fix her hair so that it fell just so over her ears.

"Now, what do you have for me to do today?" Hannah asked.

"Why don't we take this week to do all the housecleaning here in the house?" Doris replied, anxiously searching Hannah's face for signs of disapproval.

"Sure. That would be great. You just want me to do it the way I was taught by my mother?"

"Oh, yes. I'm sure the way you clean will be fine. I just have one request, and that is that you use the Murphy's oil soap for the furniture and floors."

"Right. Okay. I'll get started then."

Hannah turned on her heel and went up the stairs. Doris heard scraping and banging, bumps and footsteps, before Hannah ran down the stairs with an armload of sheets, quilts, and curtains. She carried them to the laundry room behind the kitchen, a sunny little alcove containing the wringer washer and rinsing tubs, a shelf with powdered soap, vinegar, bluing, and cakes of lye soap. Other shelves held cardboard boxes and the remains of geraniums planted in coffee cans that had died years ago. The shelves were littered with dead flies and bees, the windows were hazy with grease and dust, their curtains hanging haphazardly on bent rods and a film of spider webs like lace over everything.

Neglect, is what it is, thought Hannah. Here was a woman without enough spirit to even attempt to keep things up. Harry should take his wife home to the East if he took the teachings of the Bible seriously enough to give his life for his wife, as Christ loved the church. Or something like that.

That was her whole grievance with Dat. All of his pious show, his holiness, didn't amount to a hill of beans with her the way he brought Mam out here to live without a plan, and now look at all of us. Living like poor squatters, starving, corn dying in the field. Anger brought rebellion to the storm of her thoughts, stuffing quilts through the wringer with a vengeance.

Before lunchtime the clothesline was pegged full of flapping quilts, curtains, and sheets. Hannah was upstairs wiping down walls, polishing windows, and washing floors when she noticed her arms becoming weak. Dark spots floated in front of her eyes and the room began to tilt and spin. Quickly, she sat on the edge of the bed, then realized how hungry she was.

Should she ask Doris for lunch? Make it herself? Either way, she had to eat or she'd fall over in a faint. So she made her way down the stairs and found the kitchen empty. There was a note telling her that Doris went to her doctor's appointment and to help herself to food in the refrigerator.

She ate cold fried chicken, like a dog, she thought wryly, tearing at the tender meat that fell away from the bones. She ate mouthfuls of sweet pudding, slabs of cheese, crackers, and a dish of cold oatmeal. Because she was alone, she could lower her head and shovel the food into her mouth, acting like the starving person she was.

The nausea that rose up immediately after the gorging of food surprised her, and when she miserably retched up all of her lunch soon after, she wiped her mouth, sat down against the wall in the bathroom off the kitchen, and cried. She cried because she loathed herself for eating like a pig. She cried for the state of poverty her whole family was in. She cried mostly for being in this dingy, dusty little town, living with people she barely knew. And she cried because she was so angry at her father.

Why couldn't Dat go out and get a job? He was the one who was shirking his duty, going through life shining with religion, without seeing to the basic needs of his family.

And then she was done. She wiped her eyes, straightened her shoulders, and checked her appearance in the small cracked mirror on the medicine cabinet, just like the one they used to have at home.

She went back to work after slowly eating a slice of buttered bread and honey and was still cleaning when Doris returned. She wondered vaguely whether Harry had accompanied her to the doctor's office and who would have watched the store while he was gone.

Hannah cleaned all afternoon, then brought in the sweet smelling quilts and sheets, while Doris ironed the curtains with an electric iron that stayed hot. She never had to heat it the way they heated their sadirons over the fire at home.

The evening meal was reheated leftovers and Hannah ate slowly, savoring each bite of the delicious scalloped potatoes and corn and applesauce. She had a large slice of spice cake and more of the pudding. She felt full and satisfied. Her spirits lifted as she washed dishes and offered to help stock shelves in the store.

It was a joy and a pleasure to work in the unorganized, dusty store. She filled a bucket with soapy water and started in the back, where the sewing supplies and fabrics were kept, removing everything off the shelves, scrubbing, dusting, and rearranging.

Finally, she realized she was weary. Bone tired. Her shoulders ached, her lower back hurt, and her feet felt like lumps of iron. She pitched the dirty water out the back door, wrung out the rag with her hands, and called it a day.

She tumbled into her bed after washing up in the bathroom and fell asleep without remembering to pray. She slept a deep and restful sleep so that when she awoke, she was surprised to find herself disoriented, not realizing where she was.

The night of rest had done wonders for her outlook, and she thoroughly enjoyed her time finishing the upstairs cleaning. Doris said at lunchtime that she could have a break to eat her soup and bread and then sit down with her for a talk.

The kitchen tidied, the afternoon sun shone through the back windows as the fan whirred by her chair. Hannah appreciated the homey atmosphere, the way the chairs were situated side by side with the sofa along the opposite wall, the patterned rug in between. The rose-patterned wallpaper was in soft pink and a mellow green, which was duplicated in the pillows on each end of the couch.

The wide door between the kitchen and seating area allowed the sunny light to shine through, leaving a glow in a room that would have appeared darker without it.

At first, seated beside Doris, Hannah felt self-conscious, but only for a short time. The way Doris asked questions and the kindness with which she accepted Hannah's answers was encouraging. Often, Doris would shake her head and murmur an expression of pity or disbelief, but always politely, never making Hannah feel like the oddity she knew she was.

"So," Doris continued, "that covering on your head symbolizes submission to God first, then your husband. But you aren't married, so why do you wear it?"

Again, Hannah reminded her that there wasn't always a clear reason. It was a rule, called the *Ordnung*; it was part of their belief, the way they were born and raised into their culture. The head covering on girls likely portrayed their recognition of God, their obedience to the *Ordnung*, and their obedience to the verse in the Bible about women having their heads covered.

"But I cut my hair short without guilt, knowing that same verse says that if a woman's head is uncovered, let it be shorn. So how can that be?" Doris asked.

Hannah smiled, then laughed. "Well, to put it the way I see it, you were born to English parents . . ."

Doris interrupted, "Not English."

"I don't literally mean English people from England. We Amish call anyone who is not Plain, people like you and Harry, we call them English. Maybe that goes way back to the May-flower and the Puritans, I don't know."

"But you're not Puritans or Quakers."

"No. We're from Switzerland, from a group started by Jacob Ammann."

"Hmm. That's interesting. But what I have a hard time with is why would your father have brought his family so far out here to this . . . " Her voice trailed off, and she waved a disfigured hand weakly, then let it drop. "It's just such a big land full of nothing. Nothing. Dust and dirt and poor people living on ugly ranches, scrabbling to make a living, raising horrible cattle, and riding around on horses, shooting each other."

Hannah threw back her head and laughed, the deep laugh that affected everyone who heard it. Doris smiled, put a hand to her mouth, then laughed out loud, a sound no one ever heard from her. "I'm serious. I hate it."

Hannah stopped laughing and thought a minute before replying, "I don't hate this land. I rather like the emptiness of it, the wildness and the great big nothingness. I could live here for the rest of my life if our situation was different. We are dirt poor, which I'm sure you could tell when you drove me home."

Doris shook her head. "It's just so sad. And your father is such a strict man. Does he really feel the way he spoke?"

Hannah nodded. "Yes, he does, but he forced himself to take the food because he knows his family is starving."

"But he needs to change his mind. He needs to see that God is not so harsh and does not require such stringent rules."

Hannah nodded and again stayed quiet. So deeply were values ingrained in her conscience, she knew it was better not to speak too bitterly against her parents, no matter how often she rebelled. No, she did not believe such restrictions were required for herself or her mother, sisters, and brothers, and yet it seemed wrong to openly belittle her own father to a woman like Doris who was not born among the Amish.

She didn't know. She was only sixteen.

"Tell me, Hannah, as a young girl who is very acceptable to young men, I would think, will you marry someone of another belief?"

Hannah shook her head. "No, not if I obey my parents."

Doris looked bewildered, then shook her head. "But he brought you way out here! For what?"

All Hannah could think of was the poor management, the loss of the farm, the public shaming of being excommunicated for the distilling of his grains, the long, arduous journey to a land of poverty, and near starvation. What kept her from being honest, from going against her father and belittling him to this woman the way she often did alone, in her thoughts?

It would be so easy to abandon ship. To tell Doris how she actually felt. To convert to their faith and take off this covering that labeled her as odd and different. To wear sunny, daisy patterned dresses and cut her hair in a flattering style. Sometimes she hated her father and wanted to do something just like that to hurt him, to see him on his knees begging her to come home. So far, that kind of hardness was impossible for her to obtain, or to be comfortable with.

CHAPTER 12

Sᴀʀᴀʜ sᴛᴏᴏᴅ ɪɴ ᴛʜᴇ ᴅᴏᴏʀᴡᴀʏ ᴏꜰ ᴛʜᴇ ʜᴏᴜsᴇ, ᴛʜᴇ ʜᴏᴛ sᴜᴍᴍᴇʀ sun searing the dry dust at her feet, the sky spreading before her pulsing with a brassy light, the heat baking even the clouds into obscurity. The wind was strong today, moaning about the tin roof, rattling loose edges, the grass rattling and brittle, browned and bleached by the soaring temperatures and the constant hot wind.

She squinted, trying to see where the corn had been, but was hardly able to see where Mose had tilled the soil. The prairie reclaimed the land quickly, as if the tilling and growth of foreign plants had been an affront to it, the grass having been there for many centuries.

A calf bawled in the barnyard. Sarah turned to see Mose hoist an armload of hay across his crude fence, then stop to lift his soiled straw hat and wipe his brow. Manny was at work behind the barn using a scythe the Jenkinses had loaned them to cut grass for the winter's supply of hay.

Hod had insisted he'd come over with the tractor and the mower, but Mose would have none of it. He didn't even own a pitchfork, a fact he hoped to keep hidden from his neighbor. Mose just did not like accepting charity from worldly people, although there had been a time, when Abigail was born, he had been appreciative. Enough was enough. With Hannah working in town, they had become self-sufficient once more.

Sarah watched him taking turns with Manny at the scythe. It all seemed like such senseless hard work, with the horse standing in the shade of the barn. But if they had no mower, she guessed there was no alternative.

A wail from the baby made her turn, pick her up, and croon and cuddle. She sat down in the armless rocker to feed her, and quickly became sleepy, dozing off, waking and dozing again.

A cry from the barn woke her. Startled, she scrambled to close her dress front and hoist the baby to her shoulder for a quick burp, before going to the window. Oh, it was Hod and Abby!

Exhilaration filled her, like a drink of cold, sweet peppermint tea. Here was company. A woman to talk to, share details of their lives. Oh, how she missed the camaraderie of other women!

Abby sat on the spring wagon, her back straight as a stick, her green plaid sunbonnet tied so tightly below her chin, her face appeared pinched. Her dress was, or had been, a violet purple at one time, but had faded to a gray lavender, the row of purple buttons marching down the front like a colony of ants. Hod beside her, his Stetson pulled low, his clothes faded and worn, like Abby's, his face creased with dozens of deep lines and crevices, chiseled and molded by years of extreme weather.

Sarah called, "Get down, get down, Abby! Oh, I am surely glad to see you. Get yourself down and come on in!" She realized she was babbling, but didn't care.

Abby came striding across the dusty yard, glancing at the smoldering ashes in the fire ring made of stones, and greeted Sarah in her own inimitable way. "Sarah, you know, you folks will start a prairie fire, sure as I'm born. Why that lazy Mose don't get you a cook stove is beyond me. He coulda laid a fireplace."

"Well, Abby, it is certainly good to see you. I am so glad you came over. I've been wishing for another woman to talk to for so long."

"Where's Hannah?"

Sarah led Abby to the armless rocker, took the remaining chair herself, and balanced the baby on her shoulder. "She's in town working for the Rochers. I guess they own a store, the way she said."

"Is she being paid?"

Ashamed, Sarah lowered her eyes. "With food."

"Enough?"

"Yes, I believe so."

"What did she bring?"

And so Sarah told Abby the story of Hannah going to look for work, eliminating any distress, any hunger, and of her return, without mentioning Mose's reaction to the automobile that brought her. This was Sarah's way, to erase the desperation and heartache and replace it with sunny optimism. It was good, her glittering unshed tears a dead giveaway to how bad matters actually were.

When she had finished, Abby said curtly, "Well, you can keep talkin' but it's as plain as the nose on yer face, yer starving. There ain't nothin' to eat, lest you started chewin' hay."

Sarah laughed, a fine, tinkling laugh without humor. So near were the tears of their affliction to the surface that she bit her upper lip hard with her lower, her eyes wide, watching Abby's face. The dear, kind face, like an angel with wrinkles and well-washed clothing. She would never forget this woman as long as she lived.

"Hod come over to try and talk some sense into Mose. We're willing to loan you the money to go back East on the train, back to yer family. This weather, you know, is why. It'll turn into a drought, maybe the worst one we've ever seen. Hod says there's sun dogs and it don't rain; the storms aren't coming. The wind is from the southwest an' we ain't gittin no rain. He says the crick'll dry up right soon, an' he ain't sure how good the well is you got here.

"Thing is, you ain't got money in the bank, no cattle to speak of, and jobs is hard to come by. Hannah won't make enough to keep all of you goin', you know that."

Sarah nodded, bit her lower lip, and pondered her words. Finally, she spoke. "Abby, I would get on that train today, with your money. I would gather up my children and board that train, return to my family with nothing but pure joy, the greatest joy, Abby. But I know Mose will never return."

"He will have to. This kind of weather is nothing to mess with. There's always the fear of having no water for the cattle."

Sarah shook her head, her large eyes apprehensive. Hod and Mose came through the door, lifting their hats and wiping their foreheads exactly alike. The day was very warm, too warm to be operating a scythe, Hod said, clucking his tongue.

Mose smiled. He looked pale, a bit peaked. Sarah had dark circles under her eyes, her hands looked thin and claw-like.

Hod stated his case in forthright language. It was hot and dry. It would likely get hotter and drier. They were concerned for the Detweiler's welfare, willing to pay the train fare home.

Mose sat on the crude stump at the makeshift kitchen table, his head lowered, his hands between his knees, without watching Hod's face as he spoke.

Abby reached for the baby, crooned, and snuggled her as she smiled a beatific smile of contentment, holding this baby girl, the real live baby of her past. Sarah watched with tenderness.

When Mose looked up, Sarah recognized the steel behind the heavy lidded eyes. Hope dashed to the ground, smashed like fine china thrown with force. "I don't believe we'll take up your offer. I have no need to return to Lancaster County at this time."

Hod became agitated, his blue eyes opening wide beneath their busy gray brows, the wrinkles and lines around his mouth lengthening and deepening. "You're crazy, Mose!" he burst out. "You ain't gonna survive a few years of drought. You have nothing to go on. 'Less you git a job in town, and they're scarcer 'n all git out. Ain't nobody payin' good wages. Me and Abby, we can do what we can, but you got the children to think of and nothin' put by."

"We are, in fact, surviving well. Hannah, our daughter, is employed at Harry Rocher's store."

"For what? He can't pay her big wages."

"She brings home sufficient food, week by week."

"You need to get them calves out of the barnyard. Did you brand 'em yet?" Hod was almost shouting, veins sprouting blue on his neck.

"Not yet. I understand they roam quite a bit, and I only have the 320 acres. One claim."

"How'd you get a claim?"

When Mose told him about signing the paperwork and getting his government papers, Hod wondered if a word of it was true. For all he knew, these people were merely squatters the government would drive out if they weren't here legally. But he liked Mose. He genuinely liked the fellow, and gave him the benefit of the doubt, sitting there in his crude house.

"Another thing, Mose. You're gonna have to come up with some kind of indoor heat. You know that fire thing you got out there's gonna put the whole prairie to flame one o' these days."

Abby nodded vigorously, keeping time by patting the baby on her back with her gnarly fingers, like misshapen twigs.

"Well, here we do have a problem then. I have no means of procuring a stove. Nor do I have the resources for a fireplace."

"What d' you mean, no resources? What's that supposed to mean? Sure you have the resources. They ain't very big, them rocks in the crick, but you could build yourself a decent fireplace, you and the oldest boy."

"I have no cement."

Suddenly Abby burst forth, her words as if someone were pounding on piano keys. "Well, you sure don't have anything else, either. No money, no food, and no ambition to try and make life better for yer wife and five beautiful kids. You best listen to me and Hod whilst you have the chance. Get on home. You ain't cut out to be pioneers in this hard land. It ain't gonna deal kindly with any of you if we're reading the signs right."

A woman speaking in those tones was like a cheese grater on Mose's well-being, scraping and mangling the respect he held loosely for women to begin with.

"You are implying that I have no ambition," he stated, wounded.

"I sure am."

"Who, then, built these dwellings?"

"Why, I'll tell you who built 'em. Mostly your two kids, an' Hod, an' the boys, that's who. You was too busy readin' and prayin'.

Mose sighed as a sad smile crossed his features. "Well, neighbor Abigail, to all Christians, persecution must come. I forgive you for your misunderstanding of our circumstances. Many were the nights when I lay tossing and turning, pained by the soreness of my muscles."

Abby muttered something that sounded like, "Good for you," but no one was sure, so the conversation took a turn to other subjects of interest, including the rapid regrowth of the prairie grass after a field had been tilled.

Sarah sat in her chair, shocked and humiliated in turn. She knew there was far too much truth in Abby's words, but loyalty to her husband came easily. To admit Mose was making a mistake was like being pushed off the face of the earth to go spinning into a vast galaxy without gravity.

Her safety lay in obedience, one step behind her husband, her will given over. When he stopped, she stopped. When he moved on, so did she. When he climbed on the covered wagon for the western sojourn, she followed in body and spirit. She well knew their dire situation. She knew. But to rebel, take the children and return, was as unthinkable as just that, being pushed off the earth. Better to stay where she felt safe, at peace, her place secure in the realm of her husband's wishes.

"I would offer you a drink, but we have no tea or coffee," she said.

Hod assured her they didn't expect anything, and they soon took their leave as Eli and Mary watched wide-eyed, their mended, threadbare clothes another testimony to this family's hardship.

The following day Hod and Abby returned, driving a pickup truck with wooden sides flapping and rattling, the back loaded down with a kitchen stove with a rusty top and one leg missing, stovepipe and chimney blocks, and enough bags of cement to build a chimney.

Hod didn't waste many words, just told a gaping Mose and a tear-eyed Sarah that this thing had been settin' in the shed since they got an electric stove. Mose may as well roll up his sleeves and begin mixing cement because they were getting a chimney, before the whole prairie went up in flames.

Abby brought towels and sheets and pillowcases. She had a whole cardboard box of fabric, needles, dishes, and all the groceries she could spare, which was a sizable amount from her well-stocked pantry and cellar.

She brought two cupboards, one to set on top of the other, for kitchen space, and a table that suited well as a sink, the height perfect for washing dishes in a dishpan. She barked orders to the men, telling them where to set the stuff, busily carrying in boxes herself.

The three boys followed about an hour later on horseback, clattering up to the house on their foaming, wide-eyed mounts. Hod took to scolding, telling them it was far too hot to race them horses, but then he laughed. He'd been young once himself.

When the sun began its western descent, the Detweilers had a chimney and a cook stove. The cement was dry, and the stove was set up with a sturdy square of cement block replacing the missing leg. Abby helped sand down the rusted top, which they cleaned with ammonia water and lye soap.

They made steak and potatoes, with cabbage from Abby's garden. They ate slice after slice of custard pie, a delicacy that seemed impossibly delicious. Sarah's eyes shone as the children ate. Mose was effusive in his gratitude.

They sat together on the front porch, the yard strange without the fire ring. When they started a small fire in the cook stove, the smoke leaked out of the new stovepipe, setting Eli and Mary both to crying, thinking the only safe way to build a fire was outdoors until Sarah explained it to them. She was so glad to be rid of the outdoor cooking, now that she would not need to do it any longer.

Drinking coffee was a luxury both Mose and Sarah had almost forgotten. Abby taught Sarah the Western way of making coffee, with no fancy percolators or other gadgets. "You just throw a handful of coffee grounds into the water and keep it boiling awhile," she said, producing a cup of steaming hot bitter liquid that could easily have been stretched into two cups.

So the neighbors parted amicably, although Abby made a point of ignoring Mose, neither looking at nor speaking to him. Mose was all right with that. Having been raised in a family of nine sisters, nothing surprised him. It rankled him, though, to be called lazy. As far as he knew, he'd never shirked any manual labor a day in his life.

Mose and Sarah lay side by side on their tick filled with hay and talked as the crescent moon hung in the sky, surrounded by the kingdom of blinking stars. The heat hovered inside the house, but there was a cool breeze blowing through the open window.

"I feel as if we have been visited by a miracle," Mose said, his hands behind his head, his elbows sticking up like wings on either side of his head.

Afraid that her husband would resume his fasting and praying, Sarah quickly assured him that it was only the Jenkinses' generosity, their caring, that made it possible to live closer to normalcy. She added the fact that they should not live on more charitable donations. "Wouldn't it be better to make our own way?" she asked, timidly.

"Yes, yes, it would. I'm praying about it, asking for the Lord's leading. You may not think so, Sarah, but I am sincere. I believe I have overstepped my boundaries of faith, that point where it blurs a line with determination, and even where you start blending reality with unreality."

Sarah felt a love and gratitude well up inside and turned to stroke his chest and face, a caress of true love. "Oh, Mose, for some time now I've been afraid for you—almost afraid of you from time to time. You were so determined, so not your usual self."

"I can see it now, Sarah. I have blurred the lines, and my family has suffered the consequences. Hod's visit has brought up reality very sharply. Do you think a drought of that proportion can occur here? Years? Hod said years."

"I don't know. But we do have well water."

"The well is old. Remember? It was almost like an accidental caving in, the well was so easily dug. And who knows? If a long-term drought should occur, will we have water?"

"We'll see. Do the Jenkinses feel the winter will be dry too? Or does the snowfall replenish the moisture? We didn't think to ask."

There was a small space of restful silence, a moment when the breathing between them was a harmony of their hearts, a married couple who had both come through the fire that heats the dross to form a golden vessel, the purity and comfort of their union.

"Yes, for now, we are provided for, once again. But we will both continue to pray." Then, "Sarah, do you want to return home?"

"Oh, I do, Mose, I do. If it was only me, I would be on the train tomorrow. But I know you would not go willingly."

"As much as you want to go, I want to stay. The clamor and shifting for position, the greed and desire for the best farm, the best cattle, the constant overload of relatives and church members, the endless discussions of hay and corn and religious doctrine—I am seriously in fear of Lancaster County."

"But, Mose, perhaps it is only in you. No one else seems to mind it. They rather enjoy it as a way of life. Surely God is blessing that fruitful land and will multiply the heirs of farms for generations to come.

Mose shook his head from side to side. "Then I, alone, am a failure. A heretic, if you will. I have failed to keep the farm, failed to keep the *Ordnung*. I was abused by my brethren when I was only doing what was necessary to keep the farm. The distilling of grains. Who decided that it was worth being excommunicated?"

In his petulant tone Sarah heard the self-righteousness of the spoiled youngest son and thought, yes, he had failed in many ways. He was failing again. But did that give her the right to return without him? Oh, she could. Fiercely she knew that she could but never would. She was bound to him by the holy vows of matrimony. She had promised to care for him, for richer or for poorer, in sickness and in health. Yes, they were poor beyond anything she had ever imagined, her husband's mental health had been in serious decline, and could possibly still be, although his talk tonight was encouraging.

"The bishop, I suppose," she said, mildly, covering all her thoughts.

"One person?"

"No, Mose. You know these decisions are conferred."

"Not always."

So there it was, the impossibility of their return. Her husband harbored a sore bitterness toward the ministers of his church, a canker sore that rose on his skin, which might never burst and heal. His outward display of religion, keeping the *Ordnung* to the letter, his tight-lipped conservative manner, it was all a hooded cover-up for his own seething rebellion toward higher authority. Clearly, his choice to live in the middle of nowhere, surrounded by a level sea of grass, made perfect sense. It was the staking of his own claim to be free of his own failures. And he kept failing, but blindly.

When Mose took her in his arms and kissed her, the tears had already begun to flow. Later, when he lay softly snoring, she cried with the raw abandon of the brokenhearted, her face stuffed into the goose down pillow from home.

But in the morning there was a song in her heart and a light in her eye, seeing that Mose had started a small fire in the gleaming new stove that stood in the kitchen on three legs and a block of cement. She got down the cast-iron frying pan and fried mush with newfound pleasure, and gave herself up to her life on the plains as the slabs of mush sizzled and sputtered.

Every morning she thought of Hannah and prayed that she would stay true, unspotted from the world. She missed her fiery oldest daughter and the abandon with which she viewed the world. She wouldn't be a bit surprised if Hannah never stayed Amish. How could she? She was already too aware of Clay Jenkins. Would it matter to God if she had been brought out here to live by a father who would not conform?

In her heart, Sarah was thrilled by the budding romance, the way mothers are when their oldest daughters grow to the age where boys notice them. She had seen them leave together and didn't have the heart to call them back.

When Baby Abigail awoke, Mary tumbled down the stairs to reach her before her mother did. Sarah ran to playfully snatch her away, grabbing Mary's waist to set her aside. Mary screeched and reached out to smack her mother's arms. Sarah laughed and handed a delighted, cooing Abby to her sister, then set a pot of porridge to boil. There was coffee to be made too, a rare and wonderful treat.

To think of cutting and sewing fabric, turning it into new dresses and shirts, was beyond anything she could imagine. She felt so warmhearted toward Abby; somehow, she must think of some way to repay all she has done. Surely her kindness paralleled, even overrode, any kindness she had ever received from members of the close-knit community back home.

That day, the Klassermans arrived, driving their spring wagon up to the house and calling out in a blend of jovial voices. "Hey, ist anyone to home?"

Sarah rose from scrubbing the wooden kitchen floor, shocked to hear the strange voices, shocked to see they had company yet again, which was unusual. For a moment, she felt afraid, alone and unprotected the way she was.

So she was weak-kneed with relief to see the pink, portly pair seated cozily side by side on the high seat of the spring wagon, mopping their brows. The patient horse, as well fed as his owners, was already stretching out his neck for a nap.

Sarah walked to the spring wagon, leaving Mary with Abby. "Hello," she said, wondering.

"Vy, hello." They introduced themselves as Owen and Sylvia Klasserman, come over from "Chermany." Neighbors to the east and closer than the Jenkinses. They had met their daughter on horseback.

Sarah looked off behind the barn but saw no sign of Mose, then beckoned them to get down and come inside to visit.

They were happy to do just that, grunting and grabbing the steel rimmed wheel to heave themselves off their high perch. Sylvia laughed as she alighted, said that age and extra weight took its toll in getting on and off that wagon these days.

She had brought a German chocolate cake, a thing of magical flavor and texture. Sarah served it with cups of coffee, being careful to give Eli and Mary their share, their large eyes in awe of the wondrous cake.

Sylvia's round face looked crestfallen though as she looked around the primitive home. She tried to compliment the housekeeping, but through her eyes, accustomed to a house with papered walls, painted trim, and linoleum, it was a shame, a shame. The beautiful children. The tired yet beautiful mother. So little. These people had so little, and they had a pantry full and overflowing.

Sylvia held the baby. Owen eyed her fondly. "We'll come back often," he promised. He knew his wife's love of babies, never having had children of their own. But they enjoyed a loaded table, a good meal bringing them contentment.

Sylvia chortled and chuckled, holding the baby with an obvious sense of glee. "Oh, but Mrs. Detweiler, if you'll chust let me half the baby ven I come to visit, I will be the happiest voman on earth."

"Why, of course you must come. I often wish for the company of other women. I grew up in a close-knit family, with mothers and grandmothers and sisters and cousins nearby and everywhere."

"Where are you from?" Owen inquired, polishing off the last bit of cake, relishing even the last crumbs on his knife.

"We are from Pennsylvania, from Lancaster County, where a group of our people have settled. We were farmers who fell on hard times. The Depression had hit us hard, and we could not make our yearly mortgage. So my husband, Mose, wanted to try homesteading on 320 acres here."

"You haven't been here long, have you?"

"No, not quite a year yet."

"I see." Owen looked around at the misshapen logs, the slapdash chinking, which looked to be mostly clay from the creek bottom, and the peeling, rattling windows. Here was a winner, he thought. But he smiled at the children and asked about cattle, nodded his head in understanding when Sarah told him they had a start with a cow and two calves.

"You should do all right in about five years," Owen said.

Sylvia nodded. "It takes awhile. We started on 160 acres and own about a thousand now. We're running about 300 head of Black Angus cattle."

Sarah observed the buxom Sylvia and thought of her on a saddle, riding the range and throwing a rope. No, she decided, that that was an impossibility. "You are part of this operation?" she inquired politely.

Sylvia threw up one hand; the other was clamped to the baby's back. "Just the records. Only the bookkeeping, nothing else. Owen oversees the entire operation from horseback, though. He's a good rider and has a good horse. Seems in this area, that's what counts. A good horse."

"Do you raise any crops at all?" Sarah asked, curious.

"We grow oats for the horses, and I hear there's a few chaps trying winter wheat over the other side of Dorchester. I look for that crop to be taking aholt here, with sowing it in the fall and cutting it before the hot, dry weather begins. I think with tractors becoming more common, that will likely be the crop for profit, if any."

Talkative and amiable, the time flew till Mose came in for dinner, surprised to find a visitor's team tied to the fence.

He found the Klassermans very informative and helpful in the ways of the land. They agreed with the Jenkinses about the drought, about most things, actually. Politely they did not inquire about their income or lack of it. They just took their leave with polite goodbyes and promises to return.

The minute they were perched on the high wagon seat, Sylvia was making plans for the old davenport in the parlor, the table on the back porch, the blankets in the cedar chest she would never use, the canned pickles and red beets, all those whole tomatoes canned in wide-mouth jars none of us enjoy. The faster Sylvia talked, the faster Owen nodded his head, bringing down the reins on the horse frequently until they jostled and bounced over the rutted road at a frolicsome speed.

CHAPTER 13

Hannah fed her horse, stabled him in the small barn along the back alley, stroked his face, and told him to be patient; the week would be over before they knew it. He snuffled around in his box of oats, chewed, and lowered his head as if to assure Hannah he was fine as long as he was fed.

She turned to go outside when she heard voices coming from beside the barn, men walking along the back alley, carrying their lunch buckets, on their way to work, she supposed. She stepped back, allowing them to pass before making her way back to the house. That was the thing about living in town. There was no way you could avoid folks and their ordinary, everyday comings and goings, having to greet them amiably in spite of wanting to push them out of your way, just getting on with your life unhindered, the way they did out on the homestead.

For that is what it was, a homestead. A place called home, no matter how primitive or how far they sank into the endless crevice called poverty. She missed the wide open space, the purity of the endless wind, the rustling of the grass—everything.

But here she was, no closer to the one thing she yearned to do, which was rope cattle, learn to ride the plains with the Jenkins boys. She guessed if she ever wanted to do that, she had to stay alive, which meant she was stuck here in this dingy town to scrabble for food, like a possum looking for eggs in a henhouse.

With a sigh, she went into the house, to find Doris in her housecoat, yawning and pouring herself a cup of coffee, her hair flattened from her night's sleep. She seemed almost like a child, young and vulnerable, as if she needed care, someone to hold her and help her face the day that was dawning hot and bright and dusty.

Doris whimpered a good morning, then sank into the rocking chair with her coffee, drawing an orange patterned afghan across her lap. "This dust. This endless dust. I declare, it will be the death of me."

Hannah stopped, looked at her, and could not think of a word to say. So she shrugged her shoulders and said she never heard of anyone dying from breathing dust, but she guessed you could if you wanted to. Doris threw her a tired glance, wrapped her hands around her mug of coffee, and sighed deeply.

Hannah got out the cast-iron frying pan and scrambled eggs, made toast, and poured juice. She called Harry and told him breakfast was ready.

They sat down together, Harry bent his head with his hands clasped on the table top to pray audibly, in his own words, thanking the Father for his food, may it bless their bodies and so forth, a practice so new and strange it made Hannah want to hide under the table in shame. She had never heard anyone pray out loud, much less using their own words. Dat would always take the lead, lowering his hands beneath the table, bowing his head in silence, each family member learning at a young age to pray their prayer in private. The Amish all did that. Hannah had never questioned this, but now, she needed to know why all praying was done in silence. She'd ask Mam.

When his prayer was finished, Harry shoveled in his scrambled eggs, praised Hannah's toast, and asked her how she'd done it.

Hannah told him she'd fried it in the pan, with butter, the way they always did at home. Doris didn't eat eggs, the toast was a bit greasy with butter, so in the future, would she do hers dry?

Hannah washed the dishes in a fury. She had no patience with this whining, sickly woman. Doris needed to get out and do something, anything, other than sitting at the hair-dresser or pitying herself. She needed about a half dozen kids to care for, that's what.

She wiped the cast-iron pan and flopped it into the cupboard, stalked past Doris without saying a word, slapped the door open that led into the store, and set to work.

Customers came and went, spoke to Harry, picked up their purchases, the bell above the door ringing constantly. Hannah stayed in the back, by the low windows, arranging and rearranging, wiping down shelves until the water in her bucket turned black from the years-old dirt and dust.

When she came to the jumble of ribbon, thread, elastic, snaps and buttons and braids, pins, needles and pincushions, she stood back with her hands on her hips and surveyed the dusty mess. Lifting her hand to wipe at the beads of perspiration forming on her brow, she left a smudge of gray dirt across her forehead.

How could this man sell anything? Even if he was living in hard times, there was no sense in this. She marched up to the counter where he stood cleaning eggs from a wire basket, wiping each one methodically with a rag and stopping to examine an oversized lump of dirt stuck to a large brown one, before taking a fingernail to scratch it off, letting it fall on the countertop.

Hannah swiped it to the floor. "You know, Harry, this place is so dirty that I can't see how you stay in business, selling things that are covered in dust and soot and crap!" she said forcefully. "You blame Doris and her poor health, but I hope you know you don't try, either."

Harry looked at her. "Well, well, what is this? Why do you say this?"

"It's offensive, that's why. Trying to make a decent living is not easy for anyone right now, but the place could be more appealing if it was clean."

Harry put an egg in the carton, carefully, then said that if that's how she found things, then go ahead, go right ahead and clean and change whatever she thought best.

That was exactly what Hannah wanted to hear. She turned on her heel and marched smartly back to the hopeless jumble of sewing notions and began to blow the dust off each individual spool of ribbon and thread. She threw each one into a bin and was just starting to wipe down the shelves when Harry's voice caught her attention.

"She's in the back with the fabric," she heard him say.

Hannah was standing on a wooden crate, reaching up as far as she could, when someone called her name. She turned to find Clay Jenkins looking at her, almost level with her height. Her knees turned weak and her mouth became dry as the air around her.

"Hi." He smiled his lazy, relaxed smile and melted Hannah's resolve, just tipped it over like butter in a hot frying pan.

She was so glad to see him she could not keep her lips from parting into a smile of true gladness, a welcoming he understood. "What are you doing in town?" she whispered.

"Needed a bunch of staples."

"Staples?"

"Yeah, the kind to fix a wire fence."

"Oh." Flustered now, Hannah wasn't sure where they were kept. She looked past him as if to go around him and show him, wanting to impress him with her expertise as a salesperson.

"Hannah."

She looked at him.

He reached out a hand, touched her cheek where a smudge of gray dust had smeared across it. "You think you might need a ride home on Saturday afternoon?"

"I rode Pete here."

His eyebrows lifted and then settled back down. "So I can't give you a lift, then?"

"Not in the truck. Dat doesn't allow me to ride in one."

"If I came with the buckboard?"

"Buckboard?"

"You call it a spring wagon."

"Oh. Well, no, not if I have Pete. No. Guess it won't work."

"What about the food they give you as wages?"

"I'll strap it on, somehow. Pete is just like a pack mule." She smiled to assure him she'd be fine. She wanted him to leave her alone; at the same time, she wanted him to stay.

"Can you have off for an hour or so? We can go to the café and get a soda or something."

Immediately, the specter of the red, brassy Bess filled her head, and she lifted her startled eyes to Clay's achingly blue ones. "I can't. Harry needs me here to finish this."

"Do you mind if I ask him?"

"No, no. Don't ask. That's fine. I'm not hungry. Or thirsty."

He touched her shoulder. "Hannah, that's not why I asked you to go. I want to talk to you. Just sit across a table and look at you and listen to what you have to say."

"Clay, I can't be seen with you. Not here in town. My father will never allow us to . . ." She stopped.

"I didn't ask you to marry me, just to have a soda."

Humiliation and anger boiled up, turning her face dark and staining it a deep color of shame. "Clay Jenkins, you stop that. You just stop saying things like that, making me feel like a pathetic idiot. Leave me alone. Just get out of this store and don't come back. You have no right to talk to me like that."

And then, after that forceful speech that should have turned him on his heel and blown him out the door and down the street, he reached out and cupped her chin in his hand, smiled that smile that took all the strength from her legs, and said, quiet and low, but not in a whisper, "I'll see you around, Hannah."

He took his good old time leaving too, stopping at the front counter and talking to Harry while he cleaned that disgusting chicken dirt off those eggs.

The whole encounter was too humiliating. Hannah attacked the shelves with so much energy she knocked down five bolts of fabric that landed on her bucket of filthy water, almost upsetting it. By this time, Hannah declared it was one hundred degrees in the filthy store! She was already worn out and the day still stretched out like a long summer's drought.

He didn't have to leave so soon. She wanted him to stay so they could have an ordinary conversation the way normal people do. She wanted to talk about horses and roping cows, things that interested her. She didn't want him touching her cheek or her shoulder. Not her chin either, talking to her as if she was as old as Eli.

If this didn't stop, her future roping cows was fast going down the drain. She couldn't learn to rope and ride with all three of those boys if this was how things were going.

All week that same dark cloud called Clay Jenkins hung over her head, putting her in a prickly state of mind. The one good thing that came from his visit was her never-ending energy, banging and lifting, arranging articles in eye-catching displays and placing the new signs she made beside them. Customers began to notice and comment about Mr. Rocher's new arrangements. Old spools of trim and braid, dusted off and placed in a wicker basket with lace and yarn sported a sign that read, "Special 10¢," sat in the middle of the aisle on a walnut end table. Hannah dug out bolts of cloth that had been buried beneath more popular patterns. She cleaned and displayed them by draping a corner of the fabric loosely over the bolt so that the women could touch it and run it between their fingers to examine the texture more closely.

Talk began to flow. Beth Apent told Bess at the café, and Bess told Ruth Jones, who had come in for a waffle with chicken gravy. Harriet Ehrlichman sat on a barstool and listened as Bess told her what she'd heard about Harry Rocher's store. Harriet told Sylvia Klasserman when she came into town for some chicken feed.

Sylvia clapped her hands and said she knew Hannah and had been out to see her family. Then she lowered her voice and said it was pitiful, just pitiful the way that poor family lived. She held her hand to the side of her mouth and told Harriet how they'd traveled the whole way from Ohio—or was it Pennsylvania? Anyway, they didn't have a cent. That Harry likely paid her in peanuts, old tight-fisted thing. And that dusty wife of his was enough to drive you straight up a wall, not that it would be an easy feat, at her size. Harriet chuckled along with Sylvia and said they'd go down to the store next time Sylvia came to town.

On Saturday, the temperature shot up to 105 degrees, and the wind stilled until it became unbearably hot. Harry worried about Hannah riding home, but she assured him she'd wait until later in the day to start out, after the temperature had cooled to a more comfortable level.

He taught her how to run the cash register, so it got alarmingly late, well past six o'clock, before she had gathered all her provisions into a gunny sack and slung it across Pete's rump, well-tethered to the saddle that Pete was now proudly wearing. Harry allowed her to use it if she would always return it on Monday morning.

So Hannah set off for home, eyeing the sun's descent, planning to push Pete to arrive home before nightfall.

She was glad to be away from the buildings that seemed to stifle the breath from her. Away from the untidy lots filled with patches of red root and thistle, broken tin cans, and all kinds of refuse, just an accumulation of stuff people pitched out of moving automobiles or off horses hitched to faded old buckboards—and anything that carried folks to town.

Someone had thrown a feed sack filled with half-starved mewling kittens on the doorstep of Harry's store, which made Doris wrinkle her nose and call them rats. So Harry left them in the weedy, overgrown lot as well, saying the townkids would either rescue them or get rid of them, one or the other.

Hannah would have loved to take a cat home for Mary, but they could barely feed themselves, let alone a cat. Someday, she would bring a full-grown cat home, a good mouser, one that was self-sufficient, the way their barn cats had been back home.

Pete's head nodded, his heavy mane fell on either side of his neck, cream colored, thick and dusty, the way the top of a horse's neck always was. She rode comfortably, her bare feet resting on the wooden stirrups, heels down, the way the Jenkins boys had told her. She sat straight, the reins held low, but not loose. They had told her to do that too.

The heat hung over the flat land, like an oven that had been turned off but still retained the radiance of the coils in Doris's electric stove. The grass hung limp, baked, and defeated. The road stretched before her, the yellow brown of the dirt cracked in long, jagged tears where the ground had become steadily parched, drawing together, packed down and covered with dust.

A layer of dust covered everything everywhere. Every blade of grass, every rooftop, every living creature. It lined Hannah's nostrils, filling her mouth with a powdery taste, and it coated the gunny sack filled with the week's provisions for her family.

Every day the sky remained the same hot blue. Every day the sun rose, a huge, orange circle of untamed heat, the light blinding and brassy with the dry, unchanging fiery temperature.

They said this was common. Summers were always dry. But the grizzled old men wearing their slouched, greasy hats made of leather, the ones who came from Utah, the gold miners and trappers, some of them with slovenly, unkempt Indian women who came to town looking for trades—they all said there'd be a real drought this time, the likes they ain't seen in many years.

Fear shot through Hannah's stomach when she heard it, thinking of the sprouting cattle herd, the two horses, the weak, shallow well. How would anyone survive if there was no rain for years? They'd be forced to move. The cattle would die. Dat would resume his fasting and praying. Hannah shuddered, reached back to touch the sack of food, assuring herself of the next week's survival.

She watched the sun. The heat no longer shimmered across the prairie the way it had at midday. She shifted in her saddle and spoke to Pete to move him along. She couldn't goad him into a trot with the awkward pack on his back, so she'd have to keep him stepping. In the distance the sun had already slid lower in the sky.

She had a good feeling about the pack, or rather, its contents. The usual flour, sugar, and cornmeal, but this time there was more coffee, tinned milk, canned peas, a round of hard, yellow cheese, and a side of bacon covered in green mold that had been left hanging in the widow Layton's attic too long.

Layton had brought it into Harry and wondered if he'd trade it for a few necessities. He said yes, not having the heart to turn her away with that little flock of pale, wide-eyed children. How could he?

Hannah respected Harry for his choice, respected him even more when he wrapped it in brown butcher's paper and sent it home with her. As a last-minute kindness, he added a large sack of dried navy beans, so Hannah could hardly wait to present her mother with the beans and bacon.

She'd carefully cut away the mold, breathless and intent on each slice of her knife, knowing the salted meat would not be spoiled on the inside. She'd soak the beans overnight, add a bit of onion, simmer the soup on the back of the stove all day, and bake fresh bread with so much care, resulting in a meal that would be a spread of pure thanksgiving.

She came to the crossing where the road turned east, lifted the reins and urged Pete on, now watching the sun with a sense of agitation. Had she started out too late?

"Come on, Pete. Hurry up." Pete quickened his steps, his ears coming up and flicking back at the sound of her voice. If only she could made him break into a good, fast gallop she'd soon be home. She thought of loosening the pack and holding it across her lap, but that might be foolhardy with those tin cans flopping and banging around. Perhaps she should have accepted Clay's offer.

She urged Pete on again, felt the clapping of the gunny sack against her lags. The trousers were so thick and irritating, being alone and no one to see her riding, she decided to stop Pete and get rid of them. She pulled on the reins, slid off the saddle, and lifted her skirt to work on the buttons with one hand, holding on to Pete's reins with the other. She could soon tell that wouldn't work, so she dropped the reins and returned to loosening more buttons.

She didn't know old faithful Pete could take off like that. One second he was there; the next he'd dug his hind feet into the hard, dry soil and taken off in a flash, leaving Hannah with the unwieldy trousers half buttoned, standing in the middle of the road and yelling until she was hoarse.

Then she shed the trousers and began to run. She ran until the sweat rolled down the side of her face and the neckline of her dress was wringing wet. Her breath came in gasps of pain, but still she ran.

Twilight settled across the immense, level land, cooling the air. Hannah slowed to a walk, shaded her eyes for a sign of Pete, but there was none. He had vanished over the horizon, the gunny sack tied to the empty saddle and flapping wildly. With a sinking feeling, Hannah knew there was not even a slight possibility the sack would stay on.

There was nothing to do but keep walking and hope the sack would fall off on the road, food intact, so she could carry it home. But what if Pete took a shortcut, traveling straight across the prairie, dropping the sack in high grass where it would never be found?

That would mean they'd go begging to the Jenkinses again, or she would, since no one else took that task upon themselves.

She wouldn't go this time. Absolutely not. She would not go crawling back to Clay after refusing his offer of a ride home.

She calculated she still had five or six miles to go. Frustrated, she stood in the middle of the road and screamed, stamped her foot, and screamed again. There was no one to hear, no one to care, so why not? Here she stood, carrying the stupid pants that had caused all the trouble to begin with. She wanted to fling them into the tall, dry grass and leave them there.

With the twilight came the birds' evening calls, their wheeling across the cooling sky that was still misted with a rose color, the afterglow of the setting sun. The birds' songs made her feel a bit better, along with the pungent, earthy smell of the dry grass. The flat plains stretched away on every side, the grasses now appearing shadowed, unmoving, an immense expanse of nothing, yet everything. The sky, the air, the earth beneath, the sharp tang of the listless wind; it was everything to Hannah.

This was her home. A clean, unfettered place that spoke of freedom. The magnificence of being in a world that was so vast, so immense, dwarfed every care, every fussy little worry in her head. Here on the prairie, all the pressure, the tugging on her mind about ordinary things, simply evaporated.

So she set off with one foot in front of the other, and she walked. Darkness fell, the stars poked their blinking little faces through the dark night canvas of the sky. The moon appeared above her in a thin crescent.

The darkness deepened. Hannah thought she should be coming up on the creek bottom shortly, or at least be able to see the tops of the cottonwood trees. But still, just dark blobs in a dark world.

Was she still on the road? She guessed she must be, or else she'd be in tall grass, although this wasn't much of a road.

Ahead, a light flickered and went out. Hannah's breath quickened. Was she close to home? No, they had a chimney now, and a cook stove. It couldn't be Mam's cooking fire.

Hmm . . . There! There it was again. A fire. But who would build a fire in the middle of all this dry, blowing grass? Surely no one in their right mind.

Certain now that it was a fire, she moved slowly toward it and saw the hulking figures squatted before a ring of torn away grass with a crackling fire in the center.

She stopped. To walk up to two strange men in the dark of night would be unwise, that was sure. On the other hand, what if they had found her sack of food and were helping themselves to it, having a hearty meal with the only food that would mean her family's survival? Well then. She had only one choice, foolish or not.

She kept walking, then thought better of it and stopped. Perhaps if she got closer and listened to their speech, she could tell whether they were trustworthy or not. Her instinct told her to make a wide turn through the grass and slide silently through it, like a wraith, a ghost. They'd never know anyone had ever crossed their path.

But the food. What about the food? She hesitated, then began to walk until she was so close she could see the spit with the broiling animal roasting on the fire.

Two men. Hats like the trappers and gold miners.

"Hey!" Hannah called.

They turned toward her voice, their faces shadowed but illuminated on one side by the firelight. Their eyes appeared like slits in their faces, their noses were the only thing visible, protruding from faces covered in dark facial hair.

"Hey yourself."

Hannah stepped forward, the trousers bunched in her hand. "You didn't come on to a gunny sack filled with food, did you?"

Slowly, they both got to their feet and turned with their backs to the fire. They appeared completely black now, like menacing ghosts that had stepped straight out of some book her father would never let her read.

"Wal, what's comin' down th' road? A vision. A angel's come to visit."

"A crown on 'er haid," the other one remarked. Their voices were raspy with age and life, but not unkind.

"I'm Hannah Detweiler. My horse ran off when I was coming home from work. He had a sack tied onto his saddle."

"No ma'am. We ain't seen no horse. But we ain't been here that long. We is Peter Oomalong and Bradley Hopps. Jest travelers makin' our way. Some people call us tramps, or hobos, but we ain't either one. Just folks like other folks, makin' our way."

Hannah stepped past the fire, thanked them properly, and ran like the wind, stumbling over stubbles of dried grass, putting as much distance between them and herself as she possibly could. She calmed herself by walking again, straining her eyes to find the tops of trees, the creek bottom, anything for a sign of home.

Then suddenly, there it was—a pinprick of light that was the window of the house. She walked slowly now, savoring the new feeling of safety contained in the lighted window.

She found her family in tears, Mose and Sarah pacing the floor. Pete had returned, riderless, the food intact. The only thing that had gone wrong, the beans had spilled from the paper bag into the gunny sack, but they could be washed and used just the same.

Sarah held Hannah in her arms, and Hannah did not resist. Mose was reverent in his gratitude. Manny was pale-faced, but as brave as he was able to be. Hannah recounted her story, which left them shaking their heads in bewilderment.

"It just isn't like Pete. He's never done anything like that," Manny grinned, saying that the thought of Hannah taking off the trousers in the middle of the road must have scared him.

Sarah said there would be no more riding home from work, ever.

CHAPTER 14

THE DREADFUL NEWS OF SARAH'S MOTHER'S PASSING ARRIVED IN A letter from her sister. Hod had gone to town, brought back the letter and watched Sarah's still lovely face crumple and fall, her large dark eyes straining to contain the endless reservoir of tears that would follow. She would have fallen if Hod had not reached out to support her, which is how Mose found his wife weeping in his neighbor's arms.

Sarah would not be comforted, her grief like a great swelling of darkness in her body that shut off the light and life around her. Mose led her away from Hod to the armless rocking chair, knelt before her, and dried her tears. He spoke many words of comfort, quoted scripture in soft tones that Sarah failed to hear, so completely was she swallowed by her grief.

Hod stood, shifting awkwardly, cleared his throat before offering them money for the train fare.

"Do you want to go, Sarah?"

Sarah shook her head and whispered that she'd been buried weeks ago. Hod ground his teeth, the muscles in his cheek working. How could this man take his wife to a region such as this with none of their own kinfolk near? Obviously, the Amish were a close-knit group, like birds or animals, one kind stuck to their own. This Hod understood, and as time went on, their existence here, dependent on others, made no sense.

He sent Abby over with an agate roaster of beef stew and dumplings. Sarah was composed but fragile with the force of her grief. Hod sent Clay with the truck to fetch Hannah, saying the family needed her until Sarah was better, which Clay did, trying to hide the happiness he felt.

He had a hard time persuading Hannah to go with him. She stood like a statue, her arms crossed, and listened as he spoke of her grandmother's passing, her face white and resolute, not a tear in her eyes.

"I'm not going back in the truck. I told you. Before."

"Yes, you are. Your mother needs you."

"And what if Dat sees me pulling up to the house? Then what?"

"He ain't gonna do nothing."

"You don't think?"

"No. He's real worried about your Ma."

"She's not my ma. She's my Mam."

Clay didn't answer. He wanted to smack her the way she was acting, all hoity-toity and holier-than-thou. When he didn't answer, she didn't know how to take it, just watched after him when he strode out of the store.

He went out and sat in the truck, figured he'd wait about a half hour, and if she didn't get her royal self out, why then he'd just go back home without her.

Ten minutes passed, then twenty. He was just about to start the motor when she yanked the door of the truck so hard he thought she might pull it off the hinges. Still mad, he warned her not to pull on that door like that. She'd pull it right off.

"Oh, get over it," she answered rapidly.

Clay didn't say anything, just started the truck, turned the steering wheel and moved out into the street, reached down to shift gears when it was necessary. Keeping one hand on the wheel, he stared straight ahead with a deep scowl on his tanned face.

Hannah slouched back in the corner of the truck, as far away from Clay as possible, which was still much too close. She had never been able to study him in such close proximity, so she took her time, noticing the way his light hair hung down over the back of his gray shirt collar, the plane of his nose, the set of his jaw, the way his mouth turned down at the corners. He had pockets on his shirt, and wore jeans with a leather belt and a big silver buckle, which was way out of the Amish *Ordnung*, especially that silver clasp on his belt. Or whatever it was.

His hands were big, the fingers long and the backs covered in fine blonde hair. When Hannah had finished sizing him up, she crossed her arms and looked out of the window to her right, decided if he wasn't talking, then she wouldn't either.

The truck rattled and bounced over the cracks in the road. The hot wind puffed in through the window as the level land flew past, and nothing was said.

Finally, Hannah had to know why he was riled, and asked how they found out her grandmother had died.

"A letter." And that was all he said the remainder of the trip. Hannah flounced out of the pickup and slammed the door as hard as she had yanked it open, then fled into the house as the truck pulled away.

Well, be that way then, she thought, before she entered the house to find her mother quietly sitting in the armless rocking chair, holding Abby and weeping with soft little moans into her blanket.

Hannah stood before her, uncertain. "Mam," she said softly.

"Oh, you're here. They said you were coming. That's good." She lowered her head and laid it on top of Abby's blanket, the tears resuming with soft moaning sounds of devastation.

Unsure what to do, Hannah remained standing, awkwardly, her arms at her sides, thumbs tucked in her closed fingers, one bare foot propped on the other.

"Don't cry, Mam."

"I won't. Not much, anyway," came the muffled answer.

So Hannah went to work, trying not to compare this dwelling on the homestead with the one in town. Everything seemed so dull and brown and rough, especially the floor and the walls. She missed the sink and the cupboards and the clean, sanitary bathroom with everything in order. And here, well, this was her home, so she would have to accept it.

She cooked the simple evening meal of corncakes and beans, glad to see Manny's surprise when he spied her. The children were quiet, watching their mother's face as she picked at her food. Mose ate well, with concerned eyes lifting to his wife's face every minute.

Hannah decided enough was enough, with that awful, quiet ride home from Pine, and now this. It was like living in a tomb. No one laughed or spoke. The wind rustled the grass and blew in through the window as the children's spoons clanked against their plates. Dat cleared his throat or swallowed noisily, liquid sounds that rankled Hannah's ill humor to begin with.

Suddenly, she pushed away from the table and said she was going outside. She couldn't get away from that house fast enough. Blindly she ran, not caring where she went. Eventually, she flopped down on the grass and laid on her back, her breath coming in short, hot puffs. The sky loomed over her, a gigantic lid of heat that would not let her breathe.

So Mam's mother had died. She was dead to Mam the day they had left. She knew then that she'd never see her mother again. Or did she? Who could tell, plodding along behind Mose the way she had done. Her father, Mose. What a dreamer! Now, here he was, watching his wife's face with all that loving worry and concern, which wasn't worth the effort it took to lift those pious black eyebrows.

Hannah felt the old resentment rising up. She didn't care that she ought not to think these negative thoughts. If he could only lay down his self-righteous life and take Mam home to her family, his own life would be free from all of this concern. He knew how she struggled. He knew it. Then why stay here?

But to go back home would be strange too. They would be not only strangers in their own community, but, perhaps even worse, failures. He'd lost the farm. He'd lost everything. They'd all say that.

No, this was home. These 320 acres were their homestead, their own proof that they could make it. They could face every adversity, every drought, every storm, every winter, everything. Poverty wouldn't put them under, either. Poverty was the worst. In life, you needed certain things to survive. You needed food and clothing and money.

Well, they'd beat poverty too. They would. Somehow. With God's grace, Dat would say. And yes, she agreed fiercely, with her determination and God's grace. His *byshtant*. His standing by.

She pictured the squalid buildings, surrounded by acres of grass, with a God who stood as high as the sky, standing by, ready to defend them, His arms outstretched, His robe white, His countenance like lightning. No one had ever seen God, but He was there all right.

That was one thing she never doubted, the presence of God. From the time she was a wee toddler, she had known there was a Heavenly Being watching over her, the Good Man, *der Gute Mann*, as her parents had taught her. So now, when they needed Him, she believed He would bring them through these daunting obstacles.

She started by telling Hod to come over and show her how to brand their calves. Of course, it was Clay who showed up, by himself, which she figured would happen. She was glad he came; he owed her an apology.

She took good care to brush her hair, wash her face, and pinch her cheeks. Her dress was plain brown, faded, and worn thin, but that could not be helped.

She met him at the barnyard, smiled, and said that these calves needed to be branded, and the cow too. It was time they were turned loose. Someone was going to have to teach her how to rope.

Manny was summoned from the hayfield, followed by her father, who seemed amicable, offering to help wherever he could, which was nothing short of a miracle. Hannah eyed him warily, however, wondering what holy lesson he had up his sleeve this time. She knew he was suspicious of the Jenkins boys.

He set to work building a fire, though, and watched with a smile as Clay let Manny ride his horse and showed him how to coil and hold the rope. "It's in the wrist, I guess," he drawled, in that easy relaxed manner of his. "Let them out, Hannah," he said briskly.

So Hannah opened the barnyard gate, watching from the fence as the calves charged through it, their tails held out like broomsticks, kicking and bawling and acting as crazy as loons, in Clay's words.

"Ride after 'em. Run 'em down. Bring 'em back," he called to Manny. It was obvious the horse knew more than Manny did. He took off as if there were coiled springs in his legs, dodging along with the calves, leaving poor Manny clutching the saddle horn just to remain seated. He couldn't attempt staying in the saddle and twirling a rope at the same time, so he galloped back, the horse fighting the reins every step of the way.

"I can't do it," Manny said, his eyes alight.

"Takes practice."

"Your turn," Clay told Hannah.

It couldn't be that hard, she thought to herself, as she watched Manny dismount. She clapped his shoulder for reassurance, then climbed into the saddle without looking at Clay, hoping she knew enough to climb astride a horse without looking like a cow. She figured she'd better let the horse do the chasing because, like Manny, just staying on was all she could manage.

The calves lowered their heads and came bawling, only to veer away at the last minute, the horse turning with the calf, almost unseating her. Determined not to grab the saddle horn as the horse veered left, Hannah slipped right off in the opposite direction, landing hard in the dry grass, with a crunch, on her right shoulder.

The horse stopped.

She heard footsteps and saw Clay and Manny looming above her.

"You hurt?"

"I don't think so."

She sat up, felt her arms and gingerly stretched her legs, but everything seemed intact. She stood up, brushed off her skirt, and asked Manny if he wanted to try again.

He did, so she stood with Clay, watching Manny at his first attempt at roping. This time, he stayed on but accomplished nothing as far as the roping went. Breathless, he galloped back, his black eyes sparkling, his straw hat lying in the grass, his dark hair tousled. He was laughing.

"It's impossible to ride and swing a rope at the same time," he called. Clay laughed.

"You can practice on a fence post awhile. That's what I did."

Hannah mounted again and stayed on this time. But like Manny, she couldn't touch the rope, much less think of lifting it or throwing it over a calf.

Then Clay said he'd get the job done, and it was a breathtaking sight. It was as if he and his horse were one, both thinking the same thing before doing it—turning, stopping, galloping full speed from a standstill.

When he rode along the plunging calf, his wrist flicking the rope up and over his head, throwing it out with the ease of long hours of practice, the horse stopped, sat back on his haunches, pulling the rope taut and flinging the bawling calf to the ground. It was only a matter of minutes before the hot branding iron sizzled its way through the coarse, black coat into the calf's leathery skin, branding it forever with the Bar S brand.

The old cow was heavy, close to 1,800 pounds, Clay guessed. She had horns like thick tree limbs protruding on each side of her head. Red-eyed and belligerent, she stood in the grass, pawing at the dirt and raising clouds of brown dust.

"She don't like us, so everyone watch out. You don't mess around with this kind. They can be as bad as a bull any day."

Clay galloped off, swinging the rope. The cow charged, bellowing her anger, but the horse dodged easily, prancing like a bullfighter in the ring.

The dance between horse and enraged cow was something to see, like a poem someone put into motion. The horse's flanks were dark with sweat, and a splotch of moisture dampened the back of Clay's shirt.

The cow was tiring, so the rope slipped easily over one horn, but she shook the rope loose and took off in a wild plunge straight toward the fire and the branding iron—and Mose. He leapt toward the fence and got a leg up to step away from the bellowing cow. She charged for the fence and hooked one horn into his suspenders, flinging him to the ground. Clay yelled and goaded his horse. Hannah screamed, a hand on each side of her face as she watched the cow grind her horns into her father's flailing body. Repeatedly, the animal twisted and turned, her goal clearly to rid herself of this adversary that had disturbed her peace.

Clay rode up to the blindly enraged cow. He kicked at her and prodded her away from Mose, yelling all the while. Manny stood rooted in horror, his face contorted with the intensity of his feelings.

The cow lifted her head and came charging toward Clay and his horse, leaving Mose lying in the dust, a shadowy, dark figure behind the brittle, waving grass. Clay turned her into the barnyard and slammed the gate before they all rushed to Mose's inert form.

Manny screamed, "Dat! Dat!" before prostrating himself by his father's side, reaching out to touch his chest.

Clay knelt, his face as white as his shirt. "Mose. Mose. Can you hear me?"

Hannah lowered herself slowly, kneeling beside Clay, nausea welling up into her throat, horrified to see her father lying by the fence so bloodied and battered.

Clay laid a hand on Mose's chest, then threw his hat aside to put his ear to his torn and bloodied shirt front.

"Mose. Mose."

His eyes were open, his mouth in a grimace of pain. He was breathing in short, painful gasps. But he was breathing.

"Get yer Ma," Clay ordered. "I'll get the doctor."

Mose was whispering, struggling to breathe, the dust and dirt slowly stained dark by the blood seeping from his wounds. Manny stayed by his father's side as Hannah raced blindly for the house, calling, calling hoarsely for her mother, who raised eyes that were cloudy with mourning to absorb this bizarre thing Hannah was saying.

The children were told to stay in the house and watch Abby. Like an old woman, Sarah made her way slowly to her dying husband, held his hand, and told him she loved him one final time. At peace, Mose took his last breath, secure in God and his wife's love, the two things he valued far above any earthly possessions.

Hannah would never forget the picture of Sarah kneeling by Mose's side, her head on his battered chest, tears flowing. A heavenly light surrounding them in the gray dust, their union immortalized by his death, the only sound the waving of the grass—or the rustling of angels' wings. Who could be sure?

The song of the heavens was the angels who came to take his spirit home, the soul that often yearned for a home, for Mose often found the earth riddled with too many complexities, too many cares, and too many people he did not understand. A simple man, Mose was one who would find death a victory.

Sarah understood this, and she understood her husband. She truly knew him—his failures, his triumphs, his every breath.

When Clay returned with the doctor, all that remained was a small group of people dressed in plain, worn garments, with tears flowing, but an acceptance buoying their spirits with the power of a solid rock. Clay told Abby at home that he'd never seen anything like it.

Mose was carried to the house by strong men who arrived from town and from neighboring ranches, men the Detweilers did not know and had no idea they existed. In the middle of her numbing grief, Sarah wondered at the kindness of the *ausriche*, these worldly men with leathery faces and grizzled beards. They were like the Amish, come to help at a time when they were needed.

The yard filled with automobiles. Women dressed in flowered prints, bright plaids, some in trousers, wearing lipstick and coiffed hair like bonnets of curls, brought casseroles and fried chicken, cakes and pies. They gathered Sarah and Hannah into embraces of perfume and expensive talcum powders, left traces of red lipstick on dry cheeks, like rose-colored benedictions of concern.

Here, on the high plains, they had all known devastation and loneliness. Plain or worldly, hardship and loss were a way of life. So when the news of Mose Detweiler's death reached their ears, they knew what it would take.

The Amish relatives in Lancaster County were notified, a telephone call to the local police barracks in the city of Lancaster was sufficient.

With the heat so prevalent, a small group helped wash Mose's battered body, dressed him in his white Sunday shirt and trousers, and laid him tenderly in the rough casket Hod and the boys fashioned in a hurry.

Sarah moved as if in a gray dream filled with dark shadows of longing and despair. She did what was required, fed and cared for Abby, thanked the unknown flock of brightly dressed women for all their kindnesses, seeing them as through a mist of grief that blended all the bright colors back to gray.

It was only at night that she allowed herself the blessed relief of sobbing, howling into a pillow pressed tightly against her mouth. The loss of her mother had stripped her of the warmth of remembrance, leaving her scrabbling for a firm foot stone to step through the iciness of the unrelenting river of grief. The homesickness was one thing, worn like a collar around her neck that ceased to chafe with time. But never to see her mother again, never talk to her, was more than she could bravely carry.

And now her husband, Mose, the light of her life, the reason for her existence, the pillar of strength on which she leaned. Yes, he had weakened, but it was a test of faith that he had come through admirably. She couldn't see how she would survive without him.

She chose a plot not too far away. How could she have him buried on the flat prairie covered with blowing grass, the plain stone marker gone from her sight and her mind?

South of the house. Southeast, where the morning sun would find the gravestone and caress it with light. When she stood on the porch, she knew he would not be far away.

Owen Klasserman read the German scripture, words of promise and hope that Sarah could only hear through the noise of her shock and anguish. It was comforting, though, to hear the German read the way she had been brought up, sitting on a hard wooden bench in various homes, listening to the scriptures and the sermon in the German language.

Hod and Abby were there, and the boys, dressed in clean shirts and jeans, holding their hats awkwardly by their sides.

Owen and Sylvia, Harry and Doris Rocher, and a new pastor from the First Church of God in Pine, a tall, lanky fellow who spoke with so much kindness the tears rained down Sarah's face before she could begin to constrict her throat to hold them.

They lowered the casket into the dry earth and covered it as the dust whipped away on the hot wind. Manny had been a pillar of strength throughout the ordeal, but the cakes of hard soil hitting the wooden casket was a finality he could not contain. Miserably, he lowered his head and began the anguished sobbing of a boy, not yet a man, but no longer a boy.

Hannah stood, her eyes lowered, her mouth in a tight, grim line, showing no feeling, no emotion. She just wanted this whole ordeal to be over so she could begin her life, taking care of Sarah, and figuring out how they would proceed. Her thoughts spun, caught on irritation, dangled on pegs of grief, flying through her head propelled by remorse. If only she had been a better daughter. Half the time, she hadn't liked her father and had barely tolerated his pious attitude. Now he was gone, and there wasn't a thing she could do about it.

Wouldn't he have a fit, though? All the automobiles that had come to be at his funeral. All the worldly people who stood to bury him, with the relatives chugging along somewhere in a train between here and Ohio, probably. She'd bet they weren't too happy. Mose had gone off to North Dakota after his humiliation, and here he was dead.

Well, she wasn't going back, that was for sure. They couldn't drag her back with a logging chain. She simply wasn't going.

Hannah stood in her black dress with the cape pinned over her shoulders, the apron around her waist, barefoot, refusing to put her feet into those too-tight shoes or pull the prickling stockings over her legs. Her shoulders were wide and erect, her feet planted apart in a stance of firmness, a strong-minded figure, obstinate. Her chin was lifted high enough that folks took notice.

Here was a stubborn one, they thought. Here was one different from the rest. Beside her stood her mother, surrounded by the little ones, her shoulders rounded, bent forward with the weight of her heartache. The children were wide-eyed, observing the way Owen spoke, seeing the clods of dirt, wiping their eyes from the dust, without understanding very much at all.

Their beloved Dat had been ground into the earth by an enraged cow, but he went to Heaven to be with God and Jesus and all the angels. Yet here he was, being put beneath the earth on this great big prairie that would swallow him forever, and they'd forget where he was. So they clung to their remaining comfort, their mother's skirts, and Mary cried because she couldn't bear to see her father buried.

The sun blazed down on the small group surrounding the grave. The searing wind blew skirts and dust and grass, till they turned one final time and made their way back to the house.

The women who ministered to Sarah were dressed in black or gray on this day of Mose's funeral. As gentle as doves, their kindness like a healing balm, Sarah allowed them to heat the food, care for Abby, and sit beside her with a hand on her shoulder as they murmured words of comfort and encouragement.

Doris Rocher's face glowed with an inner light as she set casseroles, pies, and cakes on the table. There were not enough plates (this woman had so little) but they made do with bowls, allowing the men to eat first, then rinsed the dishes and set the table for the women.

The food was so delicious, so bracing, in this time of shock and unreality. Manny found comfort in the rich potato-and-cheese casserole, the home-cured ham and green beans, applesauce, cabbage slaw, and the mound of baked beans well-seasoned with bacon. Hannah piled her plate to overflowing, consumed every bit, spoonful by spoonful, then ate two slices of custard pie and a thick chunk of yellow cake sprinkled with sugar. Mentally, she calculated the days the food would last before they returned to their steady diet of cornmeal and beans.

The pastor was friendly, with smile crinkles at the corners of his eyes, round spectacles somewhere between the bridge and the tip of his nose, a ready smile, and hands that were made to comfort with a warm touch. He noticed the bare room, the primitive furnishings, the abject poverty that lived in this simple house with these plain people whose pillar of strength had been taken away by God's Hand.

He pulled up a chair and sat beside the grieving widow, who refused every attempt the women made to get her to eat. Didn't she want to taste the beans? The pie?

She would not. Her face as white as the puffy clouds in the sky outside, her large dark eyes deep wells of pain, she sat holding Abby as if holding the baby was her only link to reality.

She had borne so much, been brave in the face of so many obstacles, but this cruel taking of those most beloved to her had shattered her strength, drained her resolve, and rendered her as limp and pliable as a wet dish rag, unable to will herself off the armless rocker.

Abby Jenkins stayed all night. She sat beside Sarah and stroked the back of her hands, without uttering a word. She put the children to bed, swept the floor, cleaned the stove top, and sat with her suffering neighbor far into the night, before finally succumbing to drowsiness.

And Sarah sat alone, wondering how soon the Lord would allow her to join Mose. She was tired, tired of this life on the prairie, tired of the prowling poverty that threatened to pull her into its deadly, gnashing jaws, tired of Hannah's rebellion, tired of being alone.

There was no reason for her to go on.

CHAPTER 15

THE RELATIVES ARRIVED, A FLOCK OF FAMILIAR FACES CLAD IN BLACK. Wide black hats, large black bonnets, black dresses, trousers and vests, shoes and stockings. They arrived in two buckboards pulled by a team of sweating horses, this day as sweltering as each one before.

They removed their cardboard boxes, suitcases, and satchels, the black garments carrying a coat of gray dust.

Sarah stood in the doorway, dressed in black, thin and pale, the tears already streaming silently with no other display of emotion. There were firm handshakes, a deep searching of eyes, but no hugs. Only the common, traditional way of greeting.

Sarah's father. Older, broken, but the same tall man, not stooped, alive and vibrant, smiles tinged with sorrow, but no tears. Strong. This man was so strong, so able. Sarah found herself longing to stay with him, return to the fertile land of her childhood, take his strength for her own, and rest in it for the remainder of her days.

Two of her sisters, Fannie and Sadie. Tears flowed like water. Her brothers, brave and stalwart, their eyes blinking furiously to stop the tears. Her Aunt Eva and Uncle Henner. Ah, but they had aged. Brave to come all the way on the train.

Her father spoke first. "Ach, Sarah. So this is where you are. Isn't it something?"

Sarah managed a smile through her tears. "Yes, it is, Dat. It's very different."

"Here you are, and *der Herr* has seen fit to take Mose. Tell us about it. Tell us what happened, Sarah."

But it was Hannah who spoke, with help from Manny. The sisters, like magpies, like fussing house wrens, their hands over their hearts, gasping and exclaiming, broke in with voices filled with disbelief.

How could this be? How? What kind of animal did they raise out here on the prairie? To kill a man.

"Oh, but it's happened before," Sarah's brother Dan broke in, nodding. "Remember Kaiser Elam's Jacob?"

"Ah, yes. Yes. Forgot about him. That was a bull, though, wasn't it?" Fannie asked.

"No, a big cow. Just had a calf. They can be dangerous."

The hot sun chased them inside, seeking shade. The sisters were shocked at the living conditions, the aunt pitying, but they all tried to hide their feelings from Sarah, who seemed proud to show them the rough walls and dingy floors.

"We built the house together, Mose, Hannah, and Manny. We had help from the neighbors. Hod and Abby Jenkins and their boys," she explained.

Her father nodded, pleased to know they were not alone.

They talked for hours and ate the food leftover from the funeral. They renewed the old bonds, precious as fine gems. They exchanged news, mulled it over, exchanged it again, and the fine soup of happenings nourished Sarah's starved heart and gave her a spot of color in her thin, white face. She smiled and laughed and her eyes regained their sparkle.

Hannah watched her mother's transformation and fear struck her heart. She'd go back. She'd ride that train back home, Hannah knew it. Her breath quickened, her eyes dilated to a bitter black. Resolve welled up like dark oil and filled her mind. Every atom of her being resisted the idea of going back to Lancaster County, to plod the well-trod road of her forefathers, the jobs, teaching, working in the fields and gardens, being a *maud*, the girl who lived with other Amish families in time of need, when there was a new baby or housecleaning in spring or church services. Keeping up with everyone's expectations of a well–brought-up, obedient young Amish woman, following the same road as her mother.

She felt real nausea well up. She could not leave this land. These 320 acres were theirs. All they needed to do was stay here another nine years and the homestead would be all their own. Her and Mam and Manny and the little ones.

When Clay rode over that evening, her heart beat rapidly. Without a backward glance she raced out the back door and down to the barn, her eyes wide, her lips parted in greeting, motioning him to step behind the barn so no one would see. He led his horse in the direction she indicated, searching her agitated face.

"They're here. All of Mam's family. Well, not all of them, but a bunch. They can't see us. Mam will want to go back."

Clay looked at her, then whistled softly and shook his head. "You think she will?"

"Oh, Clay! You should see her. She's a different person. She's alive. She talks and smiles and even laughs. She's eating again. I know why. There's hope for her, thinking of returning."

"You'll have to go?"

"Of course. How could I stay?"

"Do you want to go?"

She shook her head from side to side, her brows lowered over her dark eyes, spots of color infusing her tanned cheeks.

"Why don't you want to go, Hannah?"

Suddenly confused, she looked away from him to the right, where the cottonwood treetops swayed in the wind. "I don't know. I just don't want to. I don't want to go back and be exactly what everyone else is. A *maud*, a teacher, then a wife, with a whole pile of babies, turning old and fat and, well, like Mam."

Clay's eyes lit up with merriment, then he laughed, a slow, easy sound that Hannah loved to hear. "You're something, Hannah."

She looked at him, and she should not have. His eyes were filled with so much longing, she knew it mirrored her own feelings, and this was not anything she could have prepared herself for. Swept away by the light in his eyes, she was captive, a willing prisoner, propelled forward into his waiting arms. He held her there against his wide chest, her cheek resting against the flap buttoned over his shirt pocket. She wanted to be held closer, to stay there forever while the rest of the world went away.

"Clay . . ."

"Shh. Don't talk, Hannah."

He bent his head and lifted her chin until her eyes found his, blazing with a new and fiery light. His kiss was soft and tender, his lips asking questions, claiming her love, then wondering if it was possible.

Hannah had never felt a man's lips on her own. Shocked, her first instinct was to step away, smack his face, and ask him how he dared. But the need to be close to him, closer still, was so overpowering that her own arms crept about his waist and drew him to her, the world turning liquid with stars and butterflies, and the sweet breezes and light.

"Hannah!" The voice tore through her spinning senses as she wrenched her arms away from Clay. She stepped back, a hand going to her mouth, her eyes wide with horror to find her Uncle Dan standing at the edge of the barn, his wide-brimmed hat squarely on his head, his brown eyes spitting indignation and outrage.

"*Voss geht au?*"

Hannah opened her mouth, but no sound came out of it. Clay regained his senses, cleared his throat. "I'm sorry. We just . . ."

"You just what? Hannah, come with me. I believe your mother will want to know this." Glaring, he looked at Hannah until she started to walk away from Clay. He reached out a hand, as if to keep her, then dropped it helplessly and stood rooted by his own sense of having overstepped his bounds.

Slowly, he gathered up the reins, swung into the saddle, and without a backward glance he rode away.

Hannah walked behind her uncle, her head bent, her eyes blazing into the grass at her feet, unprepared to meet the shame that would be showered on her. The discipline that would follow was unthinkable.

Why had she kissed Clay? What had compelled her? She knew any feelings for Clay Jenkins were an impossibility.

The time of sitting in the house with the posse of relatives was worse than if Uncle Dan would have blurted out the awful scene he had encountered behind the barn. She made small talk, her agitation making her face flush, then drain to a chalk white, her eyes black with shame and remorse.

Dan waited to tell Sarah until they had a moment alone, so Hannah lived through hours of fear and unknowing, before Sarah approached her on the porch, in the still of the night.

Hannah felt the soft presence of her mother before she could see her. The heat had evaporated into nightfall, the grass quieted, the moon rising in its perfect symmetry in the east, the vast night sky sprinkled with the stars that were still uncountable, as they had been for Abraham of the Bible.

"Hannah." When there was no answer, Sarah wasn't surprised, so she pressed on. "Dan told me about you and Clay."

"So?"

"Hannah, you must try to understand. It isn't allowed. He is not of our faith. He is a boy—a man—of the world. We are a Plain sect, set apart, living in a culture he would not understand.

It can't be love. You are too young to know your own heart. Our bodies sometimes betray us. Loneliness, fear of the future, a need for safety, these can all be mistaken for love. A young girl can be swept away by infatuation, a need that is nothing close to what God wants us to have, the real, spiritual kind of love that is lasting and by far the most important love, blessed by Him."

"I didn't say I loved him."

"Then why were you in his arms, Hannah? He was kissing you."

Hannah choked, hearing her mother say that word, almost like an obscenity. Her face flamed in the dark and she turned it away.

"Listen, *meine dochter*. Clay is very handsome. No doubt he has had plenty of experience with girls and knows every wile to captivate a young girl's heart. You were ripe to be falling for him with Mose, your father's, death. Please don't tell me it is nothing. The kiss meant something."

"You're going back, aren't you?"

"Don't change the subject."

"But you are going back." It was a statement, each word a stone thrown in Sarah's direction, stones she could not dodge.

"Yes, I am planning on returning."

"I knew it!" Hannah shouted.

"Shh! You'll wake everyone."

"I don't care. I don't care if they all wake up and come down the stairs to point fingers at me. You can go, Mam. Just go, you and nice, obedient Manny and the little ones. I'll stay right here. This is our home, this is where we belong. We built this house, and we will own all these 320 acres of land. Dat is in his grave, here. Here, Mam. Not in Lancaster County." She rose from her seat on the steps by the power of her passion.

"Hannah, listen to reason. We can't live here without Mose."

"And why can't we? He did nothing but fast and pray and dream and read his Bible. He didn't know a thing about making it on the prairie. He didn't know his foot from his elbow when it came right down to it. Look at the way he penned up those pitiful calves. He was so stubborn, so dumb."

Hannah drew back, but not fast enough to save herself from her mother's solid, open-palmed smack that hit her cheek, twisting her head sideways with its force, promptly followed by another, then a claw like grip on her shoulder, shaking her firmly until her head spun.

"Stop it! Stop saying those words, Hannah Detweiler. You are blaspheming against God and your poor, dead father," Sarah panted, her throat hoarse with pain and emotion.

Hannah didn't cry. She stood with blazing eyes that appeared like black, glistening pools in the moonlight, her fists clenched, her feet planted firmly.

"I don't care what you say. He was not the reason we got this far. It was all the help from the Jenkinses, and you know it. We'd all be dead, starved, lying like skeletons, our bones picked by buzzards, if it hadn't been for you and me. You were the one who sent me to the Jenkinses for food. I was the one who rode into town for food. He was off on a tangent, wishing God would help us. Wishing!"

Hannah was crying now, her face contorted, hot tears of shame and hurt and rebellion splashing down her cheeks.

"It was his faith, Hannah, his faith. He believed until the end, and will be rewarded in heaven."

"That may be so. But *we* did the work. We used our God-given talents and found food. Barely enough to keep us, but *we* did it."

Sarah sighed and sat back down on the porch steps, lowering her face into her hands. "How could our lives come to this? It all started with Dat's dreaming back in Lancaster County and losing the farm."

"It was the Depression. We're not the only ones who were unfortunate." There was nothing to say to this. It was uncontested truth.

Hannah said, "We're here, now. I'm not going back."

"Because of Clay Jenkins?"

"No."

"The homestead?"

"Yes."

"Then you're going back. You will have to obey. Please Hannah. It's your duty."

"You can't make me go with you," Hannah stated flatly.

"You can't stay here."

"Could Manny stay?

Sarah sighed. "He says he'll go back."

For a long moment they sat in silence, absorbing the night. Was anything ever as wondrous as the prairie at night? The moon was twice as brilliant, unfettered, shining with a blue-gold brilliance that washed the grass in tinted white shadows. The soft rustling was like a plucking of nature's guitar, a moving music of sighs and longings, the call of one melancholy heart to another. The boundless territory of nothingness, when a lone person could disappear into a small black dot, insignificant, unnoticed by the human eye, but much closer to God than ever before. He reigned absolute here on the plains, with nothing to come between a mortal and her Maker.

Together, mother and daughter breathed in the solitude and let it wash out the hopelessness, the anger and passion that goaded it, until their spirits became restful. Yet they did not speak, both realizing they had reached an impasse.

Hannah would refuse. Sarah would not allow it. There was no sleep for either one as they lay on the hard wooden floor by the kitchen stove until the old clock banged out the hour of morning.

Stiff, tired, and obstinate, Hannah dragged a comb through her hair, dressed, and left the house long before the relatives were awake.

There was no dew, not even a trace of moisture after months of no rain, so Sarah set out in her bare feet to check on the calves. They never strayed far, and she wanted to make sure the brands were not bleeding or infected.

She walked briskly, as fast as her skirts would allow, her eyes searching the dry grass for the telltale black calf backs rising above it. After she found them, she called, "Sook, sook, sook," gently, the way she used to call the calves in Lancaster. They allowed her to walk up to them and she rubbed the tops of their heads, ran a hand down their backs, parting the thick, black hair, till she came to the Bar S brand.

The Bar S—her own project, her own idea. The S standing for the heritage that was her mother's name. And here she was, faced with the awful prospect of following her remaining family away from this, away from everything she loved, all her hopes and dreams.

Her goal was to own a herd of cattle. A good bloodline, like the Jenkinses and the Klassermans. Decent buildings, a better well, horses in the stable, not horses like Pete and that leftover pile of bones the Jenkinses had sent over.

She'd work at the Rochers to support the family. Manny would have to get a job. After she became good at running the store, she'd demand wages. She'd put every nickel, dollar, penny, and dime in a jar until she could build up the herd. With the sale of the first calves, she'd dig a better well, and think about a windmill.

She could probably do better than the Jenkinses. They were all an easy going lot, in many ways. Especially Hank and Ken. Probably the reason she liked Clay best was that he came around most often and seemed to be the one with the most ambition.

Take all that junk lying around, which didn't seem to bother them a bit. Hannah figured her ranch would not look like that at all. Everything would be in its place. She'd plant trees and water them with water from the new well, the windmill pumping it up out of the ground.

At breakfast, she didn't talk and avoided the cold stares by remaining invisible. She ate coffee soup and fried mush, thinking what a treat coffee soup had turned out to be. Buttered bread sprinkled liberally with brown sugar, placed in a bowl with a cup of hot coffee poured over it. Aunt Eva had brought a can of tinned milk, which only made the coffee soup better.

She wasn't going to let anyone see her taking pleasure in her meal. She simply sat at the corner of the table and ate deliberately, spoonful after spoonful. Sarah seemed pale and edgy, but if anyone noticed, they said nothing. Hannah looked up once to find Uncle Dan's accusing eyes probing her face and felt her face flame before lowering her eyes.

Old goat.

It was her grandfather who opened the subject of returning, like lifting the lid off a beehive, the bees filling the room with their terrifying buzz. "So, we need how many tickets to return?"

An icy silence crept across the room. Fannie said he didn't have to know ahead of time, they could purchase the tickets at the station. Sadie said certainly not.

Uncle Dan said Fannie was right, everybody calm down.

"But everyone is agreed to go?"

"Yes, I believe so," Sarah said quietly, without looking at Hannah.

"We need to get the train in Dorchester, right?"

"How will we get there?" And so on.

First of all, the horses had to be taken to the Klassermans, who were closer than the Jenkinses. The cow and calves could be turned loose, they'd find their way to the water, and had plenty of grass. There was nothing to do about the stove and the beds and the table, although no one said what they were truly thinking, that they weren't worth a red cent anyhow.

Sarah worried about Abby Jenkins's dishes, her tablecloth and fabric, all things she had given them.

All around Hannah, plans swirled, buzzing in her ears, torment-ing her head like a fever. They, none of them, were considering her refusal. They forged straight ahead, pushing her along like that blade on the Jenkins's tractor, pushing a load of snow ahead of it.

It was now or never. Loudly, actually louder than she intended, Hannah blurted out, "You don't have to worry about anything. I'll be here to *fa-sark* everything. I don't intend on leaving the homestead. This land will be ours after nine years, and I don't plan on giving it up."

All eyes turned to her. Mouths hung open in disbelief.

"Ach, Hannah, stop chasing rainbows, you silly girl," her grandfather said.

"I'm serious. I have no plans of returning."

"But you must. You can't stay here. Surely you know that."

Hannah shook her head. "I can stay, if Manny will stay with me."

Sarah opened her mouth, then closed it. She met her daugh-ter's eyes, shivered at the light of determination, helpless before it. She began to cry, lowering her eyes, then her head, reaching into her apron for a handkerchief.

This angered Sarah's father and Uncle Dan. "Hannah, you are an *ungehorsam* daughter. Nothing good will come of this."

Hannah met their eyes, unflinching, unmoved.

"God is not mocked. What you sow, that shall you reap. You have already taken up with an *ausricha*, that despicable man you were with." This from Uncle Dan.

Audible gasps went around the room. Sarah slid down into her chair, flinched until her features looked folded.

"What man?" shouted Fannie.

"What do you mean?" barked Sadie.

"Hush. Everyone hush. I will not put up with this public shaming," said Uncle Dan piously. "It was nothing."

Hannah exhaled, grateful for his words. She sincerely hoped it was the end of that subject, or the way it was headed.

As luck would have it, the Jenkins family arrived that afternoon, the parents driving the rusted out pickup truck, the boys following on horseback, tanned and lithe, easygoing and full of laughter.

Hannah yearned for Clay. She yearned to be with him alone and be rid of this flock of people dressed in somber black, with their dire predictions and spouting the evil that would come to pass if she disobeyed.

Her mother's tears, though. They fell red hot on Hannah's conscience. That was the lone reason that Hannah finally admitted to herself that she simply could not do this to her mother. She knew if she stayed, her mother would not have a moment's rest if she traveled home to Lancaster County without her. So she, herself, would lay down her own will, the flesh, and stay with Hannah. She'd follow Hannah in much the same way she'd followed Mose, cowed by the will of another person, a sheep to the slaughter.

So she sought out Clay, made sure there was no one to see, and slipped behind the barn, away from prying, curious eyes. He asked her what the plans were.

"I have to go, Clay."

"You said you wouldn't go."

"I know. Oh, I know. But my mother won't go without me. She'll stay here, give up for my sake, and I'll be like my father. Someone she gives her life for, a person she follows, in spite of her own unhappiness. I can't make her do that."

Clay kicked at a clump of grass, his hands in his pockets. "What about us? Is that simply not possible?"

"What do you mean?"

"A future together? You know, getting' married an' all."

"I'd have to leave my faith, my family, and my life as I know it."

"Stay, Hannah." He clasped both of her hands in a grip of iron. Hannah winced. "Stay with me," he whispered brokenly.

All of her yearned toward him. She wanted to do just that. Stay here with him. Together they could have a prosperous ranch. Would their love be strong enough to bridge the divide between the two cultures?

Hannah saw herself take off her large white covering, let down her long dark hair, shed the plain, homemade dresses, and put on the gaily flowered shirtwaists, the flesh-colored stockings, and high-heeled shoes. Eventually, she'd wear jeans and shirts, go to dances, drink beer, and paint her lips as red as a cherry. She'd change over to a woman of the world and be like everyone else. Never again would she belong to her family, her relatives, in the true sense of the word.

She'd never joined the church, never taken vows, so she wouldn't be excommunicated. She'd just not be a part of it any longer.

She'd be like her cousin, Harvey, who had run off to join the army. They talked to him when he returned, but with a certain reserved, careful way of speaking, as mistrustful as a wild steer. He was a man of the world, especially because of joining the war effort—oh, doubly so. He was an apostate, a heretic, responsible for breaking his mother's heart, bringing his father to an early death. Some said there was no hope for his soul. He would burn in hell for all eternity for going against his father's wishes. Cursed is he who brings sorrow to his mother.

At the tender age of sixteen, Hannah grappled with all of this, confronted by a handsome young man who pleaded with her to stay with him in the land that she loved.

With a cry, a plea for help, she flung herself into his arms and clung to him, trying desperately to rid herself of her own conscience. Her *bessa-grissa*. The knowledge deep within that she knew better than to disobey her mother, caring nothing about her feelings of despair, living only for herself, selfish, unthinking, without natural love.

They had a few moments of stolen kisses, with Clay's tears mingling with her own, his arms around her like velvet, steel beneath the softness, their longing and denial a battle that had only begun.

"I'll go back, Clay," she whispered, brokenly. "I'll listen to my poor mother. But the rest of my life, I'll try and figure out a way to come back to you. I will. We can write. I have your address."

Clay groaned as he pulled her closer. This final time together was the worst kind of torment he had ever known. He had never fallen so hard for anyone. All the relaxed manner he had ever known could not have prepared him for the agony of their parting.

CHAPTER 16

THE TRAIN CHUGGED INTO THE STATION, PLUMES OF BLACK SMOKE rolling from the smoke stack as if the devil himself was in charge. Which he probably was, Hannah thought bitterly. Her black shoes and stockings pinched her feet and chafed at her heels. Her breath, sour with the morning's coffee soup, irritated her as much as the prickling at her waistline where her apron was pinned too tightly.

The mountain of suitcases and cardboard boxes was embarrassing. They looked like a bunch of immigrants from another country, everyone dressed in crow-like black. Aunt Eva looked like a crow, with that monstrous nose of hers. Probably the reason she never wore her spectacles was because they'd never fit on top of that nose. Her eyes were as sharp as a crow's eyes too; she saw right through you.

Manny sat beside her, his tanned face quiet, serene, his eyes darting everywhere, taking in the sights and sounds around him. He didn't speak to Hannah; he merely ignored her, knowing the mood she was in would not bide well with him.

Sarah could not hide her childlike wonder. The pure happiness of returning to the land of her youth, back to her childhood home, was almost more than she could grasp. Every click of the train wheels sang a song that traveled to her feet, through her body and into her heart. Home, home. I'm going home. Never more to roam. Never would she return, never.

She hardly slept and didn't mind the grimy soot that seemed to coat every available surface with black dust. Even the inside of her nostrils were stopped up; her tongue was dry with it and her teeth clacked together as if they were grinding eggshells. Tenderly, she held the baby and cared for Eli and Mary with a heart that bubbled over with joy and anticipation.

She felt as if she would never need to eat another meal. This unexpected homecoming was all the sustenance she needed. It was only at night, when the train slid through the darkness, that she closed her eyes and saw her husband's wracked body, the pitiful gasping for breath, the final moment when he had to let her go, that she shuddered, reliving the pain and the onslaught of grief that followed.

She would never be free of this and didn't want to be. She remembered Mose as a strong, healthy man, a lover of life, her heart's desire, a tender man who loved his wife and children beyond all reason.

They had a layover in Chicago. The children huddled around their mother with large, frightened eyes, taking in the enormity of this strange, bustling world of people, cars, trucks, and hissing locomotives. Hannah stood with Manny on the platform of the great station as they peered up, up, and up at buildings so tall they could not imagine them staying upright in a wind storm.

"But Hannah, what are these buildings made of?" Manny asked, breathless with wonder, his large dark eyes unable to absorb it all.

"I don't know. Steel? Cement? Who knows, Manny?"

"We didn't learn much about things like this in school, did we?"

"Not much."

Then, "Hannah, you didn't want to come back, did you?"

"No."

"Because of Clay?"

"No. The homestead."

"We can't go back without our father."

"Sure we can. I will, someday."

Manny watched his sister's face and knew she meant it. He smiled at her, his youthful face beginning to show signs of manhood.

Hannah touched his arm and grinned. "Don't worry, Manny. I won't go without you. I know you'll want to go when the time is right."

Their arrival in the city of Lancaster was uneventful, the train sliding smoothly into the station. Two of the uncles came to greet them and hustled them into wagons with teams of horses.

There was so much talk, so many greetings, so much formality and recounting of her father's death. Hannah was bone weary, completely sick of the fuss, the endless whirl of coming home, that she slouched down in the back of the wagon, drew up her knees and closed her eyes. She thought of Clay and his eyes when he pleaded with her to stay.

It was dark, late in the evening, when the horses trotted into the driveway that led to Sarah's father's house. A sprawling house built of gray limestone, with wooden additions, a black slate roof and a wire fence around the yard, it was everything Hannah remembered.

Sarah cried with the joy of being at home, a place she didn't think she would ever see again. Empty and cold without her mother, carrying the loss of her husband like heavy armor, the room seemed to fold in on her chest and squeezed the breath from her body.

Her father sensed the immense upheaval in his daughter's spirit and took the children to their rooms, showed them where to wash, and produced the suitcases that held their nightclothes, leaving Sarah to lay her arms on the tabletop, her shoulders heaving with sobs. There was too much grief, too much to absorb, the awful pit of her grief yawning before her, the joy of coming home lifting her to new heights, only to return to her grief by the kitchen of her childhood without her precious mother.

She became aware of her father standing beside her, quietly waiting until her sobs subsided. He handed her a folded white handkerchief. "Will you be all right, Sarah, through all of this?"

Her swollen eyes still leaking tears, biting her lip to regain her composure, she nodded, then wiped her eyes and blew her nose. "It's just so empty without Mam," she wailed, on a fresh note of despair.

"Yes, it is that. It will never be the same. But we are not put on this earth to stay. Our home is not here, and the Lord truly does give and He taketh away. Her time was up, in spite of those who are left behind missing her so badly."

"As was Mose's time," she whispered.

"Ya. Oh ya, Sarah. I'm so glad you accept that. It is the truth. We can never blame ourselves or circumstances for a death. God cuts the *goldicha fauda*, the golden thread of our existence, and that is that."

So with a calm heart and a weary body, Sarah went to *die goot schtup*, the guest bedroom, the room with sheets that smelled of dried lavender, quilts that smelled faintly of moth balls, green window blinds, and freshly starched white curtains that were hung halfway up the ornate trim work, which was varnished to a high gloss.

The kerosene lamp illuminated the old oak sideboard that had been her grandmother Stoltzfus's bonnet cupboard. The gilt mirror hung above it, and the old, hand-embroidered family record. Even the pitcher and water glasses with painted fruit. It was all here, just the way she remembered.

She washed in the basin provided by her father, slipped into her old nightdress, and lay between the smooth, cool sheets on

the firm mattress she had once been used to. Never in her life
had she experienced such luxury, almost sinful comfort. Clean,
soft, and smelling of lavender, Sarah pressed the palm of her
hand into the pillow beside her head—empty.

So this is what widowhood was. An empty pillow beside her,
only the memory of Mose's dark head remaining. A fresh wave
of longing seized her, the grief and sorrow pressing her into the
mattress.

*Ah, dear God, dear God, how can I bear up under the weight
of this loss?* Silently she prayed, silently she cried gulping sobs.
She simply could not sleep alone. She threw back the covers,
tiptoed across the room and down the hallway to the children's
room, found Abby and lifted her soft, sweet body into her arms,
then laid her in the bed beside her, becoming sleepy in an instant,
her arms wrapped tenderly around her precious baby.

She would need to care for her children, was her last thought
before a blessed slumber overtook her.

Sarah awoke to find the sun's rays poking between the green
blind and the window frame. Cows lowed in the barnyard, and
the birds twittered and chirped their morning song in the oak
branches outside her window.

The sounds of home. She really was home. She dressed quietly, leaving Abby asleep, then tiptoed down the stairs to the
empty kitchen to comb her hair and wash her face.

The sun's early rays that lit the kitchen illuminated the cupboards and dry sink, the basin by the kettle house door, and the
old woodstove that contained live red coals, even in summer.
The homemade rag rugs scattered across the linoleum looked
worn and muddy, the floor itself scuffed and dull. The windows
were greasy and unwashed.

Well, here was her work. Here she would live with her children, do for her father the tasks left undone in her mother's
absence. Filled with a new sense of purpose, Sarah drew a deep

breath, then began to open doors and drawers, searching for food, knowing her father and two younger brothers would be hungry after the milking.

A disgruntled Hannah took all the light out of the kitchen. Belligerent, refusing to comb her hair, she sat on the sofa, yawning, stretching, doing anything she could to ruffle Sarah's good humor.

Finally, exasperated, Sarah turned with her hands on her hips. "Hannah, if you won't try to cooperate, then return to your bedroom until you can face the day in a better state of mind."

"What state of mind do you think I should be in? Huh? I hate Lancaster County. I don't want to live here with our doddy. I'm not going to milk those stinking cows, either."

"Go to your room, Hannah. Go." Sarah's voice was icy with disapproval.

Hannah didn't go. She didn't want to return to that stuffy upstairs bedroom smelling of mothballs and feet. Someone's feet smelled like spoiled cheese, the kind that had green mold growing over the rind. So she sat on the davenport that perpetually smelled of cows, glared at her mother, then shuffled off to comb her hair.

Sarah's hands shook as she measured oatmeal into the boiling, salted water. So this is how things would be. How could she have tricked herself into thinking Hannah would give in? A sense of unease followed her to the henhouse, where she lifted the wire basket from the peg on the wall, reached under the brooding brown hens to find the perfect eggs underneath.

An egg. A real miracle. How long since she had had an egg for her breakfast? Likely the eggs would be rationed, the way they always were. Only one apiece. There was too much money to be made by selling them at the market, or peddling them to the neighbors. Oatmeal, coffee soup, and fried mush were much cheaper and filled stomachs sufficiently.

But these eggs were glorious orbs of deliciousness. Her mouth watered, in spite of herself. A golden yolk in the middle of perfectly cooked white, a slice of firm, spongy homemade bread fried in butter, torn into pieces and dipped into it, was a rare treat she had often longed for in their crude house on the Dakota plains.

Now, on this perfect day, with birdsong trilling and whistling around her, the oak and maple trees like a benediction from God alone, the deep green of the mowed lawn, the irises and gladioli, the marigolds and petunias in a border along the stone house—so much beauty around her she could scarcely take it all in. The brilliant yellow of one marigold was a miracle in itself.

She paused to admire the perfect red of the flowering quince bush and breathed deeply of the pungent pine boughs. She picked up a pinecone from the carpet of pine needles on the ground and held it to her cheek, rolling it in both hands to release the scent.

Today, she would visit old neighbors, laugh and talk and weep. She would renew old bonds, revel in friendship, become alive to the sounds and sights of her world, her senses filled with the compassion and love of her beloved church members.

Hannah would come around. She would learn to like the hustle and bustle, the friendship of other girls her age. So strong was her longing to stay, she resolved fiercely to make Hannah become obedient, to force her to comply. Why couldn't she be like the other children? With God's help, she would nip this blossoming rebellion in the bud before it bloomed into a scarlet life of sin. She had come this far, and she would complete the journey to fit back into the mold.

Her father and two brothers, Elam and Ben, walked into the kettle house, the room where the laundry and washing up were done, a smile on their faces, sniffing the tantalizing aroma of fried bread and eggs, the steaming coffee for coffee soup.

"Good morning!" Sarah trilled.

Hannah, perched on the edge of the davenport like a displeased crow, glared at her mother's happiness.

Her father returned her greeting warmly. Elam and Ben nodded and smiled. "It's so nice to come into the kitchen with breakfast waiting. It makes me miss Bena more than ever." Her father ducked his head to hide the emotion he felt so strongly.

Breakfast was a happy affair, the children tumbling sleepily down the stairs, Mary carrying a waving and smiling Abby, Manny sheepish for having overslept on his first morning.

Her father smiled at the one egg apiece rule that she had remembered. "Eggs are dear, especially now in these hard times. Most folks can't afford the laying mash, so the hens don't produce the way they should. We get over a dollar a dozen in town."

Hannah shoveled her egg into her mouth, spoke with her mouth full, "I'd kill the chickens and eat them. Fried chicken is better than eggs."

Elam and Ben both looked at her sharply. Sarah's heart sank, the delicious breakfast like sawdust in her mouth. Blinking rapidly to repel the tears that constantly lurked so close to the surface, she rose to dish up the creamy oatmeal.

To her relief, her father smiled slowly, challenging Hannah. "And why would you do that?"

"I said, fried chicken is better than eggs."

"But after the chickens were all eaten, you would have neither one."

"So. I hate chickens."

Sarah stared at her daughter, astounded at this flagrant display of rebellion. She had not spoken one suitable word all morning. A tightness in Sarah's chest accelerated her breathing. She opened her mouth to speak harshly to Hannah but was stopped by her father's eyes.

"Why is that, Hannah?"

"They're stupid. Pecking and flogging, *mishting* all over everything."

Elam and Ben threw back their heads simultaneously, howling with laughter. "You have to agree, Dat," they chortled.

Her father laughed along with the boys, then told Hannah if that was the case, they'd try and keep her out of the henhouse, which evoked a reluctant smile from her. And so it went.

Every day was a rediscovery of joy, renewing old acquaintances, working on the home place, doing for Dat and the boys. Her sisters were regular visitors, flocking into the yard like garrulous birds, dressed in greens and purples and blues.

But Hannah constantly chafed at the restraints that held her. She felt suffocated by the towering trees, the still and stifling air, the barn hovering over the house, rearing its head like an overprotective guard. Sometimes she felt as if she should lean all her weight against it, move it away. It was built too close to the house, in her opinion.

The smell of manure clung to everything. It was spread on the fields with a rattling contraption drawn by horses. It clung to the cows' tails and there were piles of it in the barnyard. It permeated every denim coat and pair of rubber boots that stood on the woven rug inside the door.

Thunderstorms and rain showers were frequent, loading down the unmoving air with dense humidity that drew sweat until it ran down her face. Her dress back was soaked with it as she bent over picking lima beans and string beans, tomatoes and cucumbers.

The only bright spot in her restricted, clamped-down world was her unmarried uncles, Ben and Elam. Hannah made them laugh. She was always surprising them. Girls her age did not talk the way she did. She viewed the world through thorny glasses, unafraid to voice an opinion, no matter how colorful or prickly.

The aunts supplied the Swiss organdy fabric for a new white cape and apron and a new covering so she could attend church services. New shoes and dresses materialized for all the girls so they could be seen as decent, hiding any signs of the poverty in which they had lived.

Hannah forgot how itchy that stiff Swiss organdy was. She grumbled and complained; she couldn't get the pins in straight, her hair wasn't rolled right, and her bob on the back of her head was too loose. "I don't know why we have to roll our hair along the side of our heads. Whoever invented that was just plain ignorant."

Sarah peered around Mary, who stood in front of her mother. She was pinning the white organdy apron around Mary's narrow waist, looking pretty herself in a purple dress with a black cape and apron pinned perfectly.

That was the thing about being Amish, Hannah thought. There were so many ways of being neat and just as many of being sloppy. The *leblein* sewn on the back of each dress—the small piece of fabric sewn to the waistline—was where the sides of the apron had to be pinned to with precision, so it would hang straight and even on each side.

Same way with the pleats pinned on the shoulder of the cape: perfectly aligned down the back, the neckline in front not too low (that projected *hochmut*, or "loose morals") or too high and certainly not crooked.

The hemline of the apron should be aligned with the hemline of the dress, the double row of deep pleats in the back, below the *leblein* as straight as a pole. It was all about neatness, modesty, precision, and if it came right down to it, perhaps a tinge of fashion as well.

The fancy girls' head coverings were smaller, their hair combed in loose waves. Dresses could be shorter or belts on aprons wider. Anything tight or form-fitting was considered risqué, but some girls tried to get away with it, creeping out of the side or back doors before their fathers caught sight of them.

So Hannah went to church services for the first time in many months, in a district that was not her own (they had lived close to the town of Intercourse), in a foul mood, dissatisfied with her appearance, without knowing a single person.

She rode with Elam, Ben, and Manny. Twenty-one-year-old Elam and twenty-year-old Ben were dark-haired, dark-eyed young men. Good-humored and easygoing, they enjoyed life on the farm, their social activities, horses, and girls. Both of them could have had almost anyone they chose from the flock of young ladies they hauled to and from hymn singings and Saturday night barn parties called hoedowns.

Elam, especially, at the age of twenty-one, was considered quite a *ketch*, the girls clamoring for his attention in their covert glances and witty remarks.

None of the youth drove a buggy with a top on it, as was the custom at the time of the Great Depression. They only bought a *doch-veggly*, literally translated as a roof wagon, after they married, if they could afford one. If not, they continued traveling in the courting buggy, a one-seated buggy with a lidded box in the back, a rubber blanket to pull up over the people seated on the lone seat fastened to a hook with a leather strap. A sturdy black umbrella was poked down along the side, where it was within easy reach, in case of rain or snow.

When there were three or four individuals to take, the driver merely plopped himself on someone's lap, and they rode in layers.

This morning, Hannah and Manny were seated, with Elam and Ben perched comfortably on their laps. It was a fine morning, already uncomfortably warm, the sun an orange ball of heat, the air moist with humidity.

The horse was black with four white feet, a long blaze of white down the length of his face, his neck arched like a show horse, his small curved ears turned forward. There were white porcelain rings on the harness, which were there only for show, although usually the young boys would try to pass it off as a necessity. The buggy was gleaming after its wash with buckets of soapy water, the spokes of the wheels throwing off sparkles in the sunlight.

"You may as well own a car," Hannah blurted out.

"What?" Elam was incredulous.

"Why do you say that?" Ben asked, pretending innocence.

"Your horse and buggy is all about *hochmut*. You can't tell me you don't have loads of pride in this horse. I bet it's the fanciest horse in Lancaster."

"God made this horse. We are not out of the *Ordnung*," said Elam, testily defending himself. He did have pride, but to be told it to his face was a different thing entirely.

"God doesn't make cars. Men do," Ben agreed.

"Puh. Men can't do a thing unless God gives them the knowledge. We're supposed to have cars or God wouldn't allow it."

"Perhaps their knowledge is of the devil."

"Oh, now you sound like Dat."

"Hannah, your father is in his grave, may he rest in peace. You should not be talking like this."

"I don't care what you say. You still sound like him. I can't stand the way Amish people speak about anything they reject. Just because they can't have it doesn't make it wrong for everybody else."

Elam and Ben both shrugged, held their peace. She spoke the truth, and they knew it. Each man's conscience had to account for himself and not another person, especially those who were *ausriche*.

Unapologetic, Hannah rode to church, figuring those two needed to get off the tower of their own goodness, get back down, and live like the rest of the world. Life pinched your backside sometimes. It sure did.

Here she was, then, pushed into this strange room with a gaggle of girls dressed in a colorful display of Sunday finery, the white capes and aprons like a mist of purity. They were all shapes and sizes, dark-haired, blonde, some with facial pimples, others with clear skin, large noses, small perfect ones, bad teeth, and beautiful smiles.

Hannah shook hands, a twisted half-smile of self-consciousness plastered on her stiff features. Her hair was rolled too loosely, resulting in *shtrubles*, loose hair that floated free, the first mark of a sloppy, ill-kempt girl. Her cape was pinned wrong too, the pleats down the back crooked, one sticking out the side, the other plunging straight down the opposite shoulder. Her stockings were too heavy. *Who would have made her wear those hideous stockings?* the observant girls wondered.

Some of them knew who she was, had heard of Mose and Sarah Detweiler and their ill-timed voyage to the West.

The room quieted as they examined this tall, dark-haired girl with the unfriendly expression, the too-dark eyes that threw their own glances back at them making them uncomfortable. The silence became strained; a few ill-timed and out-of-place giggles erupted. No one welcomed her. Most of them were simply at a loss in the face of Hannah's belligerence, if you could call it that.

Everyone was relieved when the lady of the house came to tell them it was time to be seated. They filed in after her. The girls were accustomed to being seated strictly by their age, but no one was brave enough to ask Hannah how old she was.

Hannah stood watching as one by one they formed a line and walked out the door on their way to the barn. A small girl who looked no older than twelve called out, "Wait!" She pointed to Hannah. A heavy-set girl, her wide face friendly, stepped back and motioned Hannah forward with a wave of her hand.

She fell into line then, wondering if it was all right for a sixteen year old to be seated with the school-aged ones. Nothing to do for it now. A deep dislike for the girls her own age, for Lancaster County, for tradition, and for everything about this day, this church, and her own life settled about her shoulders like the ill-fitting white cape she wore.

She wanted her own Sunday on the prairie back in North Dakota, where she was free to roam, to ride horses, and to watch the calves; to contemplate the grass blowing every which way by wind that smelled of clean, dark earth and dried plants; to reflect on gophers and prairie hens and wet mud and trickling water in the creek bottom, where dragonflies perched on weeds and the breeze rustled the cottonwood leaves like a song; and thinking, most of all, that Clay Jenkins might ride over, which he sometimes did.

Hannah missed him with an acute sense of absence that was always brought back to earth by their impossible situation. Sometimes, she wondered to herself if his love would be deep enough that he would become Amish, follow her culture, and submit to the *Ordnung's* ways. And quickly she knew he wouldn't.

To imagine Clay perched on a courting buggy, driving along the well-kept roads of Lancaster County, the thick green corn growing like a forest on either side; a life of order, hard work, and restrictions was a joke, and she knew it with a sense of hopelessness.

He was as free and unfettered as the wind, his life revolving around a wide space of choices without demands. A whole other lifestyle. A heap of old boards and tin and automobile parts, wheels and unkempt weeds around the barn, broken fences patched with barbed wire and dry boards the cows would easily break through again—none of it mattered to the Jenkinses. If the fence wasn't repaired immediately, it posed no real problem. The cows and calves that broke through would be rounded up sometime, and, if not, the Jenkins men enjoyed chasing and roping them on horseback.

This glaring difference was like a slap of reality, sitting on the hard bench, a head taller than any of the girls around her. It was bad enough being so tall without having to be seated in a row of much younger girls.

Well, she knew one thing: she was going back.

CHAPTER 17

THE REMAINDER OF THE CHURCH SERVICE PASSED IN A HAZE OF remembering. The need to get away from this stifling, bustling colony of relatives and friends she was sort of acquainted with consumed Hannah. Perhaps she could manage to act like everyone else—friendly, bland, saying just the right thing at just the right moment—enough so that everyone would approve of the widow Detweiler's oldest daughter.

What a nice young woman, they'd say.

What was *nice*? By whose measure were you *nice*? Which words and actions came under *nice*? It was a high ceiling to measure up to, that was sure. The whole world of being proper, well brought up, soft spoken, and sweet, was a world in which she simply wasn't interested. She wanted to live a life that was real—to herself and her own dreams and expectations, not someone else's.

Her mother, though. That was the one bond she could hardly bring herself to break. To tell her outright that she was not staying here but returning to North Dakota was almost more than she could think about. Sarah wouldn't agree, but to keep Hannah, Sarah might offer to follow her back to the homestead, like the willing servant she was.

Hannah didn't help sing. The swells of the German plainsong around her brought an unexpected lump in her throat, a surprising and unwanted emotion. After services, she slouched in a corner of the room, without taking part in the conversation, her glowering expression keeping everyone at bay.

No one spoke to her while she sat at the table to eat the *schnitz boy*, jam, and bread and butter, pickles and sour red beets, so she didn't bother waiting on tables or helping with the dishes.

Visibly relieved when Manny came to ask her if she was ready to go, she rode away from the church service with pleasure.

Elam asked if she wanted to go along to the hymn singing that evening.

"No!" Hannah shouted.

"Whoa," Ben laughed.

"I don't know anyone, no one talks to me, so why would I?"

"The West has changed you, Hannah."

"You didn't know me before I left, so how would you know?" Hannah was bristling with enough anger to repel any advances on her good humor, unknowingly separating herself from anyone in the courting buggy.

"Yeah, maybe so," Elam replied quietly, leaving a silence to settle around the open-seated buggy the remainder of the ride home.

Hannah locked herself in the guest room and wrote a letter to the Jenkinses, not just to Clay. No use him getting all kinds of ideas about her missing him, which she didn't.

"Dear folks . . ."

That didn't sound right so she erased "folks" and wrote "friends." Better. In North Dakota your folks were your family, and there was no sense in letting Clay think she was part of the family, which she wasn't.

"How are you?" Should she include "all"? If she wrote, "How are you all," they might think she was trying to write or speak the way they did, with their *y'alls* and their *fers*.

She erased the whole question.

"We're here in Lancaster County at my mother's home place. The barn is much too close to the house, everyone knows everyone else's business, and the relatives are like a large gaggle of geese. They all look the same, except some are older than others."

Here she paused, wondering if she should tell Clay about her plans. Perhaps she shouldn't, since the plans for how she expected to go about it weren't solid yet. But they would be. She just couldn't be sure how she planned to go about it.

"The corn here in Pennsylvania looks like a never-ending forest of upright stalks with huge yellow ears. It rains regularly. If North Dakota had some way of watering the fields, my father's idea might have worked. But you can't grow corn without water. Doesn't rain out there.

"I can't ride horses here. My grandfather would be shocked. Girls just put on their neat dresses and capes and aprons and ride around in dumb buggies and say exactly the right thing in the right tone of voice, which I suppose I'll have to learn." (Let Clay think she was not coming back. That would be good for him.)

Midway through her letter writing, there was a firm knock on the door, followed by, "Hannah!"

"What?"

"Go along to the singin'. You know Rebecca Lapp."

"Is she there?"

"Usually."

"I don't have anything to wear."

"Yes, you do. What's wrong with what you wore to church?"

Silence.

"Come on, Hannah. You have an hour to get ready."

"Who else is going?"

"Open the door."

Hannah slipped the paper and pencil into a drawer, then unlocked the door, peering around it to find Ben in the dim light of the long hallway.

"What?"

"I think you should try being part of our group. Give *rumschpringa* a fair chance. Come on. You shouldn't lock yourself away from the world we live in. You can't go back, not for your mother's sake, Hannah."

"No one talks to me."

"Not with that expression on your face."

"What expression?"

"You know. Mad. You're plain mad."

"No, I'm not."

"Come on. I'm leaving at seven. Get ready."

With that, he left, but Hannah could tell he genuinely wanted her company, which was something, wasn't it? But still . . .

Torn, Hannah wallowed in indecision. It would be so much easier to return to the West if she could alienate herself successfully. Why try and enter the world of *rumschpringa*? What was in it for her? She didn't need the company of other young girls, did she? They talked about stupid things that held absolutely no interest for her. They giggled and laughed and simpered about things she didn't think were one bit funny. They were just plain dumb.

She didn't like the way they all had the same goal. Getting married. Finding a suitable young man and getting married. It was considered the highest honor, the ultimate destination.

Hannah couldn't understand that very well. She wanted to get back to the homestead, learn to rope and ride, install a windmill and a tank, run the best herd of cows for miles around. Her and Manny.

It was all right, this bit of excitement with Clay. He was someone to talk to and admire. But what she wanted from him was certainly not marriage. She wanted his experience, his knowledge of the West, the cows, all of it. This kissing thing wasn't anything. She had no plans of falling in love, which was a term that hung on the edges of idiocy.

What all that love thing entailed, she had no idea. She wasn't about to be trapped, like a groundhog in the steel-toothed jaws of a rusty old trap like Manny used to set on the edge of the cornfields. Anyone who was smart could plainly see what marriage brought. Look at Mam. She had no life. She gave her life to her husband, and to God, and look where she landed. No, this thing of giving your whole life and will to a man—incompetent creatures, half of them—was for the birds.

Then for a fleeting instant, she heard her mother's beautiful voice and saw her happy, serene face as she sang to Abby in the crude house, rocking in the armless rocking chair that had ridden in the covered wagon, the whole way out there. Was there a peace, an underlying happiness that blossomed like a rare and beautiful flower after you did the unthinkable—surrendered your own will?

Hannah's own will, getting out of life what she wanted, was what made her happy, so there. She wasn't like Mam.

She did get dressed, then, in her own haphazard, slipshod way, her dark hair sliding out the back of her covering, loose strands on her forehead, her apron crooked, too low in the back, too tight.

She kept the brick wall of belligerence firmly around herself. She thought that if Ben wanted to drag her to the singing, he wasn't going to be rewarded with a different person.

The home where the hymn singing was held was a typical Amish farm, with a white house and barn, a cow stable, corn crib, outbuildings that housed chickens and pigs, and some horse-drawn farm equipment. Dusk was falling, enveloping the farm's perfection in a glow of sunset, before the mist of twilight set in.

The thought of being married, gardening, milking cows, having a dozen children, living in this congested valley of rich soil and expectations, set Hannah's teeth on edge.

"Now what am I supposed to do?" she asked Ben, after he had pulled up to the farm, surrounded by other open seated buggies and horses being led to the forebay of the barn. Groups of young men stood around wearing colorful, long-sleeved shirts with black vests and trousers, black hats set at rakish angles, pretending they didn't know she sat in Ben Stoltzfus's buggy like an oddity.

Ben hopped off the buggy, told her to go into the house and look for someone she knew. Rebecca Lapp would likely be there.

Wishing she hadn't come, or could go sit in a cornfield until this dreadful singing was over, she climbed off the buggy, walked across the driveway and up the sidewalk to the house, carrying herself as if the chip on her shoulder was more important than anything else.

It didn't get any easier once she was inside. The kettle house was lined with girls of every description, the only difference being the absence of white capes and aprons, which were worn only to church. Now they all wore capes that matched their dresses, with black belted aprons around their waists. A colorful gaggle of hopeful geese, she thought.

A dark-haired girl stepped forward, proffered her hand, gripped Hannah's, and said, "Welcome. Are you Mose Detweiler's daughter?"

Hannah nodded, her reserve masking any relief she may have felt.

"I'm Katie Esh. We used to be in the same church when you still lived here in Lancaster. Remember Simon Eshes?"

Hannah nodded.

"I'm sorry to hear about your father?" The sentence was spoken as a question.

Probably wonders if I'm sorry he died, knowing he failed at farming and then did something as despicable as that whiskey thing with the leftover grain.

"Yeah, well, things happen." She didn't need to know more than that. The poverty, the homestead, the crude house, was all hundreds of miles away, hidden from their scrutiny, so that was the end of the conversation.

Rebecca Lapp found her and set up a hysterical giggle of greeting that chafed Hannah like an ill-fitting shoe. Held to Rebecca by duty and good manners, they exchanged news of the past year, insipid words like dandelion fluff blown on a stiff breeze.

What did Hannah care about her job picking produce on their farm? If she wanted to break her back picking strawberries and beans under the hot sun in the humidity of Lancaster County, it was none of Hannah's business, or her interest. So that conversation melted away as well.

Relieved to be sitting at the long table made of church benches on wooden racks built for that purpose, opening the thick, black *Ausbund*, the book of old German hymns written by their ancestors in the prison in Switzerland, in Passau, to be exact, where they were imprisoned for their Christian faith.

That's what happened to history, Hannah thought. Way back then, the Amish were persecuted, hunted for their beliefs, and thrown into prison for believing on the Lord Jesus. They were real Christians, saintly in their martyrdom, tortured and burned at the stake, their passage into Heaven secured by their unshakable longsuffering faith.

Now, through many reprints of this very same book, these songs remained in use at every hymn singing, every church service, still honored and loved. But so much had changed since then.

Prosperity in America had directed the Amish down a new path of farming, building, other thriving businesses, and the *Ausbund* was no longer understood and revered the way it was hundreds of years ago. As is the way of all people, one slowly gets off track from the devotion of these writers, composing in dank prisons. God was everything then. God was all they had.

Very nearly, Hannah could identify with their forefathers. Her family surely hadn't had much more, there in North Dakota.

Plus, her father had held true faith and a real belief that God would look after—*fa-sark*—them all.

Had God done that? Had her father given his life for his faith? Or was the generosity of the Jenkinses and the Rochers the only thing that pulled them through? Was everyone too blind to see the real part of life?

The sacks of flour, cornmeal, and the other provisions she toted home from the town of Pine were real; they didn't fall from the sky like manna for the children of Israel. They were given by the generosity of an English person, an *ausricha*. Her father had eaten the corn pone like a starved person, lifting the spoon rapidly, convinced his fasting and prayer had secured it. Pensive, her lips in a tight line, without joining the singing, Hannah sat along the table with dozens of other girls, like a mystery.

The young men filed in, hatless now, their hair combed very carefully, parted in the middle, hanging loosely halfway down over their ears, cut round in the back. The collars of their purple, green, and blue shirts were closed according to the rules set for men's clothing. Their rich baritones enhanced the girls' voices, until the room was filled with a beautiful cadence.

Later, the wild boys filed in, seated themselves along the benches in the back against the wall. Their hair was combed up over their ears, bangs fluffed and combed sideways, shirt collars hanging open, a few in short sleeves. They slouched against the wall, talking to each other, laughing, openly having a great time, disregarding the watchful eyes of the gray-bearded elders in their presence.

They didn't hold Hannah's interest. She was curious, watching them with dark eyes that smoldered, her thoughts miles from this room, in North Dakota. Tall and upright, her wide shoulders in their usual position of defiance, her mouth closed and not singing, she bided her time, filling her thoughts with subjects that mattered.

The first youth that led the pack of *ungehorsam*—young men—was much older than the rest, Hannah could tell. He was scruffy looking, as if he hadn't shaved well. His hair was dark as midnight, as were his eyes. Big eyes, with lowered black brows and no smile. While the others carried on with their pinching and punching, he brooded.

Hannah noticed this all without a trace of interest, merely observing in passing his unhappy face.

His name was Jeremiah Riehl, and he was twenty-three years old this past March. His father could see no other alternative than to ask him to leave, not being able to raise a family of nine boys with his rebellious example like poison, spreading it around without fear of parental authority.

Like a weed in a field of young rye grass, he was torn out and disposed of, his father white-faced and grim, his mother dry-eyed and staunch, like a post shoring up his father's decision. A well-meaning relative took him in and regretted it later. The boy had no scruples, no conscience. He ran with the town boys, got drunk, drove a car, returned to his relative's house to eat and sleep and sneer in his face.

But years of patience paid off. The relative's wife wrote Bible verses on scented stationery, left them on his nightstand, loved him unconditionally, and saw through the veneer of evil rebellion. Here was a hurting child; here was a soft-hearted boy who sought his parents' approval in strange ways that neither understood.

The soft heart was coated with the steel of nonconformity and the need for vengeance. His saving grace was the relative's interest in good horses, the gift of a fine thoroughbred, presented with eyes blinking back tears, received with surprise, and resulting in the first chip in the coat of steel surrounding his heart.

By the age of twenty-two, he was known as Jerry, the horse dealer. He bought and sold horses trucked into Lancaster County and bred his own line of Standardbred road horses for the Amish and riding horses for the English.

He developed a keen eye for good horseflesh, inheriting his sense of business from his father and the drive to succeed from his steel-willed mother, who managed the house and surrounding gardens with an iron hand. Cuffed and pinched from the time he was a toddler in diapers, belted by his father for every misstep, his soft heart bruised, then broke, then covered itself with hard rebellion, taking a long and difficult journey beset with wrong choices.

Here he was, then, tempered by his difficult past, seeing in front of him the only girl who had ever held his glance.

He blinked, blinked again. His heart rate picked up considerably, his hands became sweaty, his breath shallow. Pride lowered his eyes, caution kept them glued to the thick book in his hand.

Eventually, he looked up. Like a wild, unkempt mustang she was. Untamed, her free spirit evident in the set of her shoulders, the set of her mouth. She was more than beautiful. She was like a vision. Her eyes were huge, set in her small, heart-shaped face. A perfect mouth. So different from the other girls, with that hair.

Who was she? Where had she come from?

When the other girls began their ridiculous water drinking and giggling, passing around hard candies and chewing gum, she merely sat without a trace or sign of interest. Obviously unhappy, she was like a tethered, untamed horse, pawing at the ground, resenting the halter and rope that held her to the singing table.

How long did the singing keep going? He had no idea. His whole world stopped, held by the vision of this mysterious girl in front of him. When his group of young men rose to leave the room, for the first time in his life he wanted to stay.

If he left, she might not be there when he returned. He had to know who she was. Always the last one to return for the remainder of the singing, he had to stay, talking, laughing, spending time outside, away from the parents and more obedient ones.

To hide the fact that he was eager to return, he was the last one in, now seated much farther away. When the cookies and popcorn were served, she rose from her seat on the bench and made her way to the door with Rebecca Lapp.

Tall. She was much taller than Rebecca. She moved like a princess, her head held high, gliding, not walking. She didn't speak to anyone. Quiet. She was a quiet girl.

Jerry did his best to hide his interest, now much more than a spark. A flame had begun, and he was swayed by his lack of power in the face of it. Inwardly he writhed helplessly as the sight of her hammered painfully at his efficiently armored heart. All of his failure and inability to please accosted him like a river of molten steel, ready to replace any sign of breaking away the coating that was already secured.

The cookies and popcorn passed through his hands unnoticed. "S' wrong with you, Jerry. Aren't you hungry?" Laughing, Jerry grabbed a cookie and bit off half of it. Oatmeal, like sawdust in his dry mouth.

She returned. He choked on the crumbling cookie. Laughter and backslapping. He looked up in time to see those large, black eyes on his own red, spluttering face, holding so much disapproval.

Then her eyes slid away with a lowering of her eyelids, an unconscious natural look that set his heart to its accelerated racing, as if it was not a part of him but a mere projection of his weakness.

So he stood in a dark corner of the yard and watched. It was Ben Stoltzfus who came to claim her for the ride home. His girlfriend from another county? There were Amish in Berks County, where they had originally settled when they emigrated from Switzerland.

Nonchalantly, on the outside, every sense honed for a response, Jerry dropped the question. "Ben after a woman?" He had to repeat himself, before anyone heard, the boisterous crowd rife with Sunday evening shenanigans, as usual.

"Naw, that's his niece."

Words like ambrosia. A sweet nectar sipped from the cup of promise. "Really? That's his niece?" He could have slapped little Amos when he snorted about all that happiness about only a niece. What was up with that?

So, he was more observant, but spoke nothing afterward. He watched Ben back his horse into the shafts, the tall girl holding them aloft, expertly lowering them, quickly fastening traces and britching. Ben said, "Better watch it, Hannah. He rears when he's riled up."

Hannah. That was her name.

"Want me to hold him?" Her voice was low, almost like a youth. Low and husky.

"Afraid you can't get in."

"I'll be all right."

And sure enough, the nervous horse rocked on prancing legs, gathered himself on his hind legs, ready to rear and come up on those muscular hind quarters to paw at the air with his front feet. But the girl was too quick. Without fear, she yanked down on the bit and said, "Hey. Oh, no you don't." She stood her ground like a soldier.

Jerry knew expert horsemanship when he saw it. His chest felt constricted, choked with emotion.

The horse stood, recognizing her fearless command.

"Get in!" Ben called.

"I will when I'm ready. He needs to learn to stand." By this time a crowd had gathered. Hannah was oblivious. She held firm to the bit, stroked the horse's white blaze, and murmured something.

Someone called out, "He's not a dog! He'll come up the minute you stop that, you know."

She never bothered answering. Jerry watched as she slowly loosened her hold on the bit and said, "Whoa," firmly, then walked to the buggy step and climbed in without hurrying.

Ben lifted the reins, and in a flying leap they were off in a spray of gravel, the light courting buggy swaying, fishtailing, righting itself before disappearing into the dark night.

They rode through the warm summer night at a fast clip, the humid air turning Hannah's *schtrubles* into curls, moistening her skin, and ruining the crisp white organdy of her covering.

Ben whistled, enjoying the fast trot of one of his best horses, thinking of a perfect time to ask Rebecca Lapp for their first date. He already planned on Hannah helping him out, which was the real reason he had urged her to go to the singing with him in the first place.

"My covering is ruined," Hannah lamented.

"The other girls wear bonnets. That protects them from the damp night air."

"I hate bonnets. They smash your covering worse than the night air."

"Really? I wouldn't know."

"I guess not. You don't normally wear one."

They laughed. Ben thought she had an attractive laugh, deep and genuine. Too bad no one hardly ever heard it.

Then Ben said, "Hey, go along to Stephen Zook's on Saturday evening. There's a hoedown in their barn."

Hannah's voice caught, faltered. "I don't know. I don't know how to play."

"You don't have to. You can sit and watch."

Hannah shook her head. "Probably not. You know I don't have much interest here. I will be going back to the homestead as soon as I can. I have no intention of letting those 320 acres go to waste."

"But Hannah, you have to think reasonably. Your mother will never want to go back. How can you think of going, with or without her? Give up those acres of land. You can't do it."

"Manny and I could."

"How?"

"Cattle. A windmill. Horses. Ben, the land is free! Think of it. Free! All it takes is a bit of guts to get started. Once those cattle get going, we'll be rich. Acres and acres of free grass. You know we don't have a penny. If we stay here, we'll be sponging off grandfather for the rest of our lives. Or I'll be slaving in produce fields, teaching school to a bunch of snot-nosed little kids who don't listen to the teacher. I don't want to get married like everyone else. I'd be tied to housework and diapers for the rest of my life. Besides, what if I end up with a genuine loser and have to live the way my mother always has?

"I'm going back, Ben, and no one will stop me. I'm different than most of the girls you know, so get over it."

CHAPTER 18

Hannah's grandfather approached her about getting a job. In September, picking was at its peak, and she could make good money picking tomatoes and lima beans at Uncle Henry's. He was concerned that Sarah didn't have enough to do, her grieving turning her into a thin, sorrowful person.

"It seems as if you do the biggest share of the work, which gives her too much time to sit and think. I don't believe this is good. Everyone has to move on, forget about themselves. Hard work is a good cure for grief. It is as the Lord intended. Besides, you need to think of footing some of your own expenses soon. It doesn't sit too well with the other children that I am your sole provider."

Hannah felt an instant surge of rebellion. "Oh, they don't think you should provide for your widowed daughter, do they? Well, then, I suppose I'd better get to work, huh?"

"Yes." Her grandfather failed to take the hint of sarcasm in Hannah's voice, merely accepted her response as a willingness to comply, went peacefully on his way with the two brown mules and the wagon, back to loading corn for silo filling, the heat of the day marking his straw hat with a darker rim of perspiration around the crown, where the black band was tied with a knot.

Safely out of her grandfather's hearing, Hannah let loose with a volley of rebellious words like bullets pinging across the kitchen.

Sarah's face was pale, tired, and weary, despite a temporary bright spot of color on each cheek from the heat of the cook stove, where she was boiling tomato juice to make ketchup. Glass jars lined the countertop, scalded and sparkling clean. Mary was playing with Abby on the green marbled linoleum, pulling a small wooden duck by a string, the orange feet flapping rhythmically with each step. Abby laughed and waved her arms, then fell to one side, where she rolled, happily grabbing her bare feet. Mary giggled, then went to blow kisses on her little round belly.

Manny and Eli were helping the silo fillers, driving teams of horses while the men hoisted the heavy bundles of corn.

"Hannah, watch what you say."

"Why? No one can hear me. They're all just afraid Doddy is going to spend his money on us instead of stashing it away at the bank so that when he dies, they all get a nice check. Their inheritance. Greedy, greedy. Well, I have news for them. I'm not picking produce. I won't break my back so they can have more inheritance."

Sarah wiped the back of her hand across her forehead, then turned to sink onto a kitchen chair, hitching up her skirts only a bit, just enough to cool herself a little while remaining chaste.

"Hannah, you make me so tired. Why can't you do this for us? I know my sisters are right."

"What?" Hannah shrieked.

Sarah lifted confused eyes to her daughter's angry ones. "We can't be like a leech to my father's money."

"What about the church? Isn't that what alms are for? To keep the widows and orphans? The poor? Well, we qualify under poor and certainly widowed, so there you go."

"Hannah, listen to reason now. As long as we are able-bodied, we deserve to be employed, to make our own way. You can do this for us. Your father provided for us when he was alive, now it's your turn."

Without glancing at Hannah, she rose to her feet to stir the bubbling tomatoes on the hot stovetop.

"Well, Mam, if I have to be the breadwinner, then I'll do it my way. I'll make money all right, but it will not be here. I'm going back to the homestead, me and Manny."

Sarah gasped, a hand went to her chest. "You can't!"

"And why can't I?"

"You just can't, Hannah. We almost starved. The winter is coming."

"So? We have firewood."

"You know I don't ever want to leave Lancaster, my family, my church. My heart is here with my loved ones."

Hannah threw her argument like a knife. "What about Dat lying alone under the prairie sod? What about 320 acres of prime grassland to fatten cattle?"

Sarah moaned softly, began to weep, making small mewling sounds that failed to break Hannah's resolve.

Why couldn't her mother brace up and be her own person? Simpering through life depending on everyone else's judgment rankled Hannah, spreading thistles into her own fiery ambition, irritating her to the point of anger. "I'll work in the fields but Doddy Stoltzfus is not getting all my money. Some of it is mine. I'll save it for my train ticket. Mine and Manny's."

Up came her mother's face, followed by the sound of honking into her handkerchief. "Yours and Manny's? What makes you think he'll go with you? He's not like you. If I ask him to stay, he'll obey me."

Hannah had no answer to that. Sarah looked at the clock, gasped, and sent Hannah down to the cellar for potatoes. The silo fillers would be hungry, twelve men who had not eaten since their early breakfast.

Hannah washed and peeled potatoes, cut them in chunks, and put them on to boil, adding a stick of wood to the cook stove. "It's hot enough to fry an egg on the table," she grumbled.

"Be quiet. Hurry up and quit complaining," Sarah said roughly.

Hannah threw her an unapologetic look and fried the chunks of pork in lard, added salt and pepper, while her mother grated cabbage for pepper slaw. They boiled long yellow ears of corn, cooked navy beans that had been soaking all night and seasoned them with bacon and molasses, tomato juice and pepper. They sliced the red and succulent tomatoes in thick circles, and piled homemade bread on ironstone trays, with deep yellow churned butter and raspberry jam, in addition to applesauce and small green pickles.

For dessert there was chocolate cake, ground cherry pie, cornstarch pudding, and freshly sliced peaches sprinkled with sugar. Tall glasses of sweetened meadow tea acquired a sheen of moisture along the outside of each glass, the humidity soaking everything, man and beast alike.

Sarah wrinkled her nose as the men filed into the kettle house to wash up precisely on the dot of twelve o'clock. From noon until one o'clock, the men refueled themselves and their sweating horses.

"They stink!" Hannah hissed to her mother.

"Hush, they'll hear you."

She thought Ben and Elam's foot odor was unbearable. The smell was like cleaning the cow stable on a rainy day. She grimaced as she watched the long hair and ratty beards being sloshed with soapy water and dried on one towel for all twelve of them, their thin, short-sleeved shirts sticking to their backs with perspiration and dust. Ruddy faced and muscular, these husky men were used to manual labor, heat, and humidity, eagerly facing whatever came their way.

Silo filling was an event, a neighborhood get-together. Each farmer had his own silo, his own cornfields, but the work went

so much better with a group, many horses and mules, the camaraderie of their neighbors a boost to everyone. Showing off their
strength and tirelessness, they encountered plenty of friendly
jokes and ribbing, especially the one who was perhaps a bit over
confident.

Hannah served them with a minimum amount of breathing,
especially when she refilled glasses of tea or retrieved empty
serving dishes. She had a good notion to pinch a clothespin on
her nose, but she was sure her grandfather would be mortified.
Didn't these men ever bathe? They should be thrown into the
watering trough.

Chewing with alacrity, talking around mouthfuls of mashed
potatoes and gravy, wiping their hands on the tablecloth or,
some of them, on their shirt fronts—it was the worst display of
manners she'd ever seen.

Was this how the Jenkins men ate? She hadn't had too many
instances to remember. She knew Harry Rocher did not talk
around his food or wipe his hands on the tablecloth. But he was
English, and they were fancier in their eating habits. Likely she
had been accustomed to this behavior her whole life long; now
grown up and having seen some of the world, she had a new
perspective on scenes like this. She had no plans of becoming
anyone's wife, ever, so her worry about cleanliness and table
manners was unnecessary.

She wondered if the Jenkinses had received her letter. Would
Abby be the only person to write back? Or would Clay send her
a letter? And if he did, what would she make of it? There was
an ocean of culture separating them. No matter how hard she
tried to make it go away, to minimize its length and depth, it
was there, inaccessible, uncrossable, without a deep and abiding pain that would cut into her mother's already grief-battered
heart. There was no easy way out.

She served the chocolate cake and pudding, followed by
the ground cherry pie, amid yells of approval, yellow-toothed

smiles, gulps of tea thrown down throats with heads tilted back, and calls for more coffee.

Ephraim Hershberger watched the daughter of Mose Detweiler and thought someone had their hands full with that one. Her expression was enough to pickle red beets, sour enough to curdle milk. She probably didn't want to live under her grandfather's direction, rebellion sticking out of her like porcupine quills. If she was his daughter, she'd be taught a thing or two.

To watch her response, he yelled out, "This coffee has grounds in it," followed by a brown, tobacco juice grin.

Hannah didn't skip a beat, pouring tea. Didn't look at him, either. "Shut up and eat them!"

A howl of delight from Emanuel Yoder. An intense look from her grandfather. A whispered, "Hannah!" from the pale-faced widow, Sarah.

Washing dishes with fury, spraying water and soapsuds across the linoleum, Hannah silently took her mother's admonishing, listening wearily as she quoted scripture about the virtues of a good woman.

"Hannah, you are choosing to be prickly. You are choosing to go through life irritated by the slightest thing, caused by your inability to give up. Such a flagrant display of disrespect, Hannah. It isn't funny."

"One of the men thought so."

"Your grandfather didn't. Your punishment will be to stay home from any of the *youngie ihr rumschpringas* this Sunday."

"That's not much of a punishment. I don't want to be with the *youngie*."

So that was the reason Jeremiah Riehl searched the barn floor most of the evening, the harmonicas' lilting tones setting the dancers' feet flying across the oak floor of the gigantic bay between two others filled with hay.

She wasn't there. All evening, he kept up his hope, until at midnight he finally gave in and went in search of Ben Stoltzfus, who was about to leave, in a sour mood himself, having lost his main ally when Hannah refused to accompany him to the hoedown.

"Going home already?" was his way of greeting Ben.

"Yeah. It's late."

"Need help?"

"With what?"

"That horse."

"I'm not driving him."

"Oh." Then, "where's your niece this evening?"

"You mean Hannah? I couldn't persuade her to come with me."

Without sounding disappointed or interested, Jerry let it go, changing the subject to the horse he had for sale, if any of his brothers needed a sound driving horse. They exchanged pleasantries the way two well-brought-up young men would, before Jerry asked how come Hannah had never joined the group of young men and women before this.

"Her dad is Mose Detweiler. Was Mose Detweiler. He was killed."

"Oh, that guy. Moved out West. Where was it? Montana?"

"No, North Dakota."

"Yeah, I heard about that. Sort of different, wasn't he?"

"Hannah's like him. She doesn't want to be here. Says she's going back. They're homesteaders, or were before he died. She's determined to keep those 320 acres. She'll break her mother, you watch, and her fifteen–year-old brother. She wants a windmill and a herd of cows. Dry as a desert out there. No other Amish. Got a mind of her own."

Jerry let it go at that, grateful for that bit of information. His interest only increased. He vowed to make her acquaintance, somehow, before she left. He could do no more than wait and hope she'd show up.

He could never drive up to the Samuel Stoltzfus farm and ask to speak to her; the culture in which they lived completely forbade it. All matters of the heart were conducted in secret and never mentioned until long after a couple had actually begun seeing each other. It would be considered brash beyond reason to approach a young woman in the light of day, let alone on the home farmstead.

He figured he'd been patient before, he could be again. He turned and went back to the lively sounds of the Saturday night hoedown that suddenly appeared drab and colorless.

Hannah stayed true to her word and began picking tomatoes on Monday morning. A fine mist settled across the tomato field as she picked up the first wooden crate of the day, bent her back, and began to find the ripened fruit under the prickly stalks.

All morning Hannah's back stayed bent as the late-summer sun burned off the mist and she continued to pick tomatoes. The backs of her legs ached, then her lower back. She stood up, stretched, rubbed her back, then bent over and threw more tomatoes in the crate. Teams of Belgian horses pulled flatbed wagons across the level fields and hauled the loaded crates to the cannery.

She became aware of a shadow crossing ahead of her, looking up to find the farm's owner, Daniel Lantz, standing in front of her with his arms crossed. Tall and wiry, his beard like a stiff, brown brush, his straw hat creased and worn, he drew his eyebrows down across his small brown eyes and said, "I've been watching you."

Hannah was hot and aching with fatigue, her mood at a genuine low, wishing she'd brought a jug of water. Her throat was so dry she could not have swallowed her saliva if there was any available.

She glared at him and thought, what a scarecrow.

"You're throwing the tomatoes. You'll bruise them. You need to place them in the crate, not throw them."

"Is that right?"

Taken aback, Daniel opened his mouth and closed it again. "I was just saying, if the skin of the tomato breaks, it makes a real mess on the bed of the wagon. You just need to be more careful in the future."

Hannah stood in the warmth of the sun and glared at him with so much dislike that he felt as if he was in the presence of danger. Turning on his heel, he left without a backward glance.

Hannah picked tomatoes for awhile longer, filled the last crate, and stalked out of the tomato patch with her head held high, her shoulders erect, and never returned.

She refused her mother's pleas, Manny's embarrassment and obedience, and said she'd do anything else to earn money, but she was not picking tomatoes for that picky stick man.

So Sarah had to go to her sister's quilting and answer their questions truthfully, saying no, Hannah hadn't yet found a job, leaving out any information where Daniel Lantz and his tomato picking was concerned. Often ashamed of Hannah's belligerence—where did it come from?—she found it only increased here in Lancaster County among so many friends and relatives.

Rachel drew her eyebrows as if made from elastic. "But, Sarah, you need to take that girl in hand. She is one *ungehorsam* girl. You can tell by the way she walks, so stiff and unfriendly."

Yes, yes, Sarah knew. She knew. But a mother's feathers are often ruffled by being admonished about her own children, and Sarah was no exception.

Who was Rachel to speak? That little Samuel of hers had been expelled from school in eighth grade. Annie told her that, and here sat Rachel, all high and mighty, telling her where she was going wrong with Hannah.

But being the cowed, humble person she was, Sarah agreed with Rachel outwardly, nodded her head, and said times were hard during this Depression, but they would keep trying. She told them about Hannah working in Harry Rocher's store in the town of Pine, thinking they would approve, but she was met with cold stars of disapproval for allowing Hannah to stay the night at an Englisher's house.

Sarah bent her head over the quilt, wondering how she could possibly have missed this quarrelsome bunch of women. Their disapproval was like a kick in the stomach, taking all the life's breath from her, leaving her bewildered and alone. How could any of them understand being poor to the point of desperation? Yes, times were hard, they knew, but not to the extent that Sarah did. They had no idea of the panic of scrabbling a tin scoop around in an almost empty sack of cornmeal, of children who went to bed hungry. Yes, hungry. To admit that even to herself brought back the cold fear of actually having to starve. Or crawl to the neighbors.

Perplexed, bewildered, Sarah stayed quiet, kept her peace. She could not keep thoughts of pity from crowding out the love she sought to keep. Yes, it was pity for herself, perhaps, but in the face of this cold-hearted onslaught of not understanding, the blatant unfairness was like a slap. Jesus said the poor would always be among us. Every fair-minded Christian, surely including her own sisters, recognized the poor and gave what was available.

"You don't have much to say, Sarah." This from Rachel and Emma, well fed, their crisp white coverings pulled over the oiled hair combed severely, so perfectly obeying the laws of the church, outwardly at least. Respected and well-liked, a beacon of shining examples by the way they dressed, they hid their refusal to accept Sarah's plight well beneath their wide black capes.

Sarah merely shook her head, her mouth unsteady with the tears so close to the surface. Lydia eyed her sharply.

"Did we hurt your feelings about Hannah? Well, I do feel sorry for you, but you know we're right. You do need to take her in hand."

"How?" Sarah burst out, so out of character, this meek and quiet sister defending herself with one harsh word. Down came the eyebrows, everyone's attention grabbed effectively. "Tell me how," Sarah said harshly.

"How did she get like that in the first place?" Emma wanted to know.

Sarah shook her head. She had always been like that. *Vonn glaynem uf.* Since she was small, she had been obstinate, her will unbreakable. Nothing fazed her; fear was not in her vocabulary. Had the move to the West only worsened the nature she had been given at birth?

"Nothing like hard work to break that stiff will," Rachel began. "Uncle Jake's Suvilla got in her head she wasn't going to be *gehorsam* and he sent her to his brother Sam's, as *maud.* They had the twelve children in fourteen years, milked twenty cows by hand, and grew strawberries. She was busy from four in the morning until nine at night. Really did the trick. She was glad to go home, glad to help her mother after a few years of Uncle Jake's wife, Lomie."

Rachel chuckled, comfortable from her viewpoint on the self-appointed tower on which she had hoisted herself by her own opinions.

"Isn't Suvilla the one with mental problems?" Sarah asked, quietly.

"I guess she does have some affliction of the mind, but only because she won't give up. The devil has plenty of room to stay as long as that will isn't broken."

Emma nodded, pulled a long thread through the quilt top, then dipped her head for another round of pushing her needle up and down to create tiny, even stitches on the nine patch Rachel had pieced from scraps.

"That's what Hannah needs to do," Lydia said, staring at Sarah.

Sarah laughed outright, a sound that came from her throat without intention. "She wouldn't go. You don't realize, you cannot make Hannah do anything."

"Oh, really?" Rachel's voice dripped with disbelief and something close to mockery. "That sounds more like an excuse than anything else. Mothers that do that—stand by their children when they know full well they are in the wrong—will only suffer sorrow and heartache down the road."

Sarah bent her head to the quilt, incredulous. Her own sisters. Her blood relatives. It seemed to her as if the dearest to her heart, the ones she had missed most, had turned into cold-hearted stone objects she no longer recognized.

Was it their mother's passing? Was it grief that caused them to become sisters with attitudes so alien to Sarah's remembrance? Compassion had been shelved, for one thing. They were perfect, in their own eyes. "Oh God," Sarah cried silently. "Have I experienced a time of awakening in North Dakota and returned to find myself changed? Or has the Depression done this to us, to them?" Well she remembered the openhearted giving, the jars of honey and preserves, and the pieced baby quilt when Hannah was born. They had done her peach canning, her applesauce, gaily coming and going in their dusty buggies pulled by spirited horses, fussing and clucking about their sister's first baby, Hannah.

Emma gave days of her time, getting her started on making little broadfall-type trousers for Manny and pinafore-style aprons for Hannah. She only remembered her sisters as kind and loving. She had spent days dreaming of her return, of being taken back into their generosity, of their open arms waiting to receive her, and of their listening as she spoke of the journey.

Oh, they had been sympathetic. They cried and wiped tears, discreet in their grief, reserved as was the Amish custom. But this coldhearted judgment of Hannah? The admonishing about being under her father's care?

This she could not grasp. Was it greed? A tight-fisted lust for money? Surely they had not fallen so far away from what God intended his Christian church to be.

Sarah searched her own soul as she sat quilting, smiling acknowledgment when necessary, joining softly into the conversation when it was expected of her. She filled her plate with unimaginable food, the serving dishes piled high with parsley potatoes, serving platters of fried chicken and stewed tomatoes and dumplings. Yes, times were hard, jobs hard to come by, scrimp and save and make do. With this food so plentiful?

Mentally, Sarah shook her head in wonder. She didn't care if she never saw another cup of cornmeal as long as she lived, but this thought she did not share with her sisters. They would blame Mose and bring up the whole shame of their past. Then start in about Hannah.

No, best to let it go. And she did, to the best of her ability. But that night, alone in the comfortable bed, where Mose's pillow lay untouched beside her, she cried. She talked to God. She asked Him for guidance. There was the monumental problem of Hannah. Should she take Rachel's advice? Make her go work for a stranger? How would she do that?

She knew there was no way to force Hannah to do anything. To return to North Dakota was like facing a giant beast and its open, slavering jaws ready to devour her. She quaked with a lack of courage. She knew her own cowardice. To again be subject to that kind of desperation was simply unbearable.

To stay, living with Hannah's powerful rebellion, was another beast, almost as fearsome. Give her time, some said. But Sarah knew. She knew Hannah would not bend. She would never forget the 320 acres of land, her strong love for the plains, the freedom of the wind and the swaying grass, the horses and yes, likely Clay Jenkins was at the back of all the rest of it.

So what if she made the sacrifice to return for Hannah's sake? Should mothers sacrifice for their children?

Sarah wasn't sure that going back to the prairie would only send her daughter back to Clay, an *Englisha mon*. She would leave the faith, leave everything she had ever been taught.

The next day, Sarah had a long talk with her father. She poured out her heart to her remaining parent, who listened attentively and recognized the problem for what it was, not what he wanted it to be.

Wise, aged, experienced, he pondered Sarah's plight, then went off to drive the corn binder in the late September sun.

CHAPTER 19

Hannah was lost. Low scudding clouds threatened a serious downpour. She was in Elam's open courting buggy, by herself, and had already taken a few wrong turns. Fred, the bay driving horse, was exhausted, his head lowered, his sides heaving, leaving Hannah in a mild state of panic. Justifying herself by blaming the stupid Lancaster County roads, she stopped the horse, which happily obeyed, and looked around her.

That was strange. There was a fairly high ridge, or at least a small mountain, to the left of her. All of Lancaster County spread out to the right, the woods, green fields and brown ones, dotted with white houses and barns, cement silos, and fences. Hannah snorted with impatience after acknowledging that she simply didn't know where she was.

Well, she couldn't drive Fred up that hill, he'd likely die. So she guessed she'd have to turn around and ask someone. The thought of actually driving into a strange place to ask for directions was irritating, but the only smart thing to do.

"Git up, Fred." Slowly, he complied, lifting his weary head and starting back the way he'd come.

Hannah had heard through a friend, Lydia, that there was a job available at a feed store, weighing corn, measuring and mixing feed, and waiting on customers. She was told it was about ten miles away, in Georgetown. She thought she'd already gone farther than that. Mam had wanted her to use the neighbor's telephone, but she despised that contraption. Dialing made her nervous, always afraid she'd put her finger in the wrong circle. Then, when she did hear a voice, it was crackly and unintelligible.

Against her mother's wishes, she left early, despite her grandfather's warnings that it would likely commence raining. She told him if it rained she had an umbrella, laughed off his warning of driving a horse and holding an umbrella at the same time.

So here she was, caught in a very sudden and serious downpour, digging around under the seat for the large black umbrella while holding on to both reins with one hand. Large drops of cold rain splattered on her back. She pulled on the reins and stopped Fred under the overhanging boughs of a large tree, thinking it would afford a bit of protection, which it did not, large drops falling off the swaying leaves.

This was a fine mess. She decided the best course of action was to turn into the drive leading to the closest farm, seeing the way the wind was getting up. The house was built of brick, the barn white, with the usual huddle of maple trees around the yard, the clean barnyard and well-kept grass surrounding everything.

No one was about when she stopped by the hitching rack. Feeling foolish, she quickly hopped off the buggy, her white organdy covering already clinging to her head by the force of the rain. She eyed the house, then the forebay of the barn.

Should she pull up to the watering trough, get her horse and buggy out of the rain? Would that be too bold?

"Hey!"

She turned to find a man standing just inside the wide door of the forebay, beckoning her with his right hand.

"Better get in out of the rain."

Sheepishly, she led her tired, dripping horse to the watering trough, looking to thank the man who had allowed her to get out of the cold rain.

"You're pretty wet," he observed.

No beard. Single. Hmm. Hannah observed this in one swift glance, her dark eyes fringed with wet lashes, her covering thoroughly drenched, her dress clinging to her with no coat for warmth.

"Who are you?" she said, quick and to the point, as always.

"You can call me Jerry."

"Jerry? That's different."

"Why don't you unhitch?" He almost added, "Hannah." It was her. It was. He felt as if a rainbow had descended out of the gray, wind-driven clouds and produced a miracle. A very wet and obviously irritated miracle!

"How did you get yourself into this predicament?" he asked, grinning at her across the horse's back, working loose the snap that held the britching to the shaft.

Her eyes flashed. "Looking for a feed mill, if you have to know."

"Whereabouts?"

"They said Georgetown, but there's an awful hill. Growing up here, I never realized that mountain was there."

"May I ask who you are?" As if he didn't know.

"I'm Hannah. Mose Detweiler was my father. He died in North Dakota."

"I heard about that."

"You did?"

"Yeah."

What else had he heard? All the stupidity associated with her family? She said nothing as they unhitched Fred. Jerry took the horse to a stall and gave him some feed and hay. Hannah wanted to follow, taking notice of the long middle aisle with stalls on either side. This was obviously one huge horse barn, housing more horses than the average.

She thought of the thin-necked, pot-bellied, long-haired nags of North Dakota, fed on grass and water, wherever they could find it, branded like cattle, half of them as wild as deer. She wondered what Clay would say about some of these horses' heads appearing above wooden half-doors.

Hannah was intrigued but too proud to move down the aisle and gawk like some poor beggar. Which she was.

"I am a horse dealer," he offered.

"Mm." Feigning disinterest, Hannah walked over to the barn door, her arms crossed about her waist. She was cold but determined he wouldn't see her shiver.

He thought about asking her into the house for lunch, which was where the rest of the family had gone, but he couldn't bring himself to do it. He wanted to keep her here, in the forebay, lit magically by her presence.

"Would you like to see the horses?"

"I could, I guess." She turned and led the way. He noticed she was almost as tall as he was and that her covering really was ruined by the rain. She could have worn a torn rag on her head and she still would have been the most beautiful girl he had ever seen or imagined.

"This is Duke."

"Hm. High and mighty name."

"He's a high and mighty horse."

She turned to look at him, her eyes wide. "Is he really?"

"Yes, he is. The best. His offspring are amazing. I can get hundreds of dollars for a foal."

Intimidated, Hannah didn't answer. From one stall door to another, she viewed black or brown horses, mostly for driving, sold to Amish men who knew a good horse with plenty of stamina when they saw one. She was quiet, unafraid to reach out and stroke foreheads, to cup a hand below a mouth. She was used to being around horses.

He was so full of questions, and so afraid to ask them.

They returned to the door of the forebay, watched it rain. Her hair was as glossy and black as her eyes, her profile like a princess. She was cold. She rubbed her hands across her bare arms, her voice shook.

"Are you cold?" he asked.

Immediately she snapped, "No!"

"We could go inside and get something warm to eat. Coffee."

"No."

Relieved, he asked how far she had to return.

"I don't know. Far."

"How will you get home? It doesn't appear to be letting up anytime soon."

"I'll wait."

And you'll be out here tomorrow morning, he thought. But he didn't say it. This girl was not the normal Amish type of girl. She was unfriendly, barbed. Quickly, before his uncle and nephews returned from the house, he said, "So, how was it, living in North Dakota?"

She shrugged, then turned to look at him and saw his friendliness, the dark light of genuine caring, and something else she couldn't name. She saw that he wanted to know, though, and not only for the wrong reasons.

"It was a lot different. Wild. Windy. Nobody around. We almost starved. My father was, well, not too capable. We lived like destitute people. It was scary. Dat tried planting corn, but it shriveled up in the hot sun. We didn't have a windmill like the other ranchers. We didn't have cattle. One of our horses died."

Hannah waved a hand, as if to dismiss the whole telling. "I'm going back. I hate it here. We have 320 acres of land from the government. All we have to do is live on it for ten years. Prove our claim. I'll make a go of it. We have two young cows and one old, mad cow, the one that killed my father."

Soberly, Jerry nodded his head. "Heard about that."

"Dat didn't fit to the West. He was a dreamer. He thought if he planted corn some God-given cloud would float above it and dump rain on it." She looked wide-eyed with surprise when he laughed, genuinely laughed, loud and long.

"You're not very reverent about your poor father."

"Well." Then, "It doesn't rain out there. Drought is common. The cattle roam around, branded, so the ranchers know which cows they own. I want to learn to ride and rope, have my own cattle. But my mother . . ."

She stopped. "I shouldn't be telling you this."

"Why?"

"I don't know. I just shouldn't. Who are you anyway?"

"My name is Jeremiah Riehl."

"And?"

"I live here with my uncle. My past is nothing to be proud of."

"What did you do? Kill someone, or what?" She was surprised again when he laughed like before.

"My dad and I had a fight. We didn't get along. My fault, a lot of it."

Instead of a suitable comment, she changed the subject back to North Dakota. "You should see the horses in the West. Some of them, well, most of them, are as ugly as goats. Tough, rangy, pot-bellied mustangs that can go twenty miles without breathing hard. Like the people. If it wouldn't have been for the Jenkins family, we'd probably all have starved to death."

Jerry glanced at her sharply. He felt his own bitterness in the word "starved." He didn't doubt for a minute that she would go back and continue to make choices driven by her unforgiveness, much the same way he had.

"How will you go back?"

"I don't know. I can't go back without money this time. I was on my way to Georgetown for a job at a feed mill. I have to save some money before I can go back. I'm thinking maybe my grandfather will allow me to take a loan. The Jenkinses are keeping the horses and three cows. We need a better well and some way of pumping water out of it, likely a windmill. The creek is probably dry by now."

Her speech was laced with passion, her planning shone in the intensity of her eyes, her hands moving in agitation. Jerry watched her face like a man hypnotized. He thought, *How could this girl survive in the West with all the uncouth characters, the claim jumpers, the cattle thieves, and the law sometimes helpless?* He saw the challenge and accepted the unreality of her plans. She would not stay in Lancaster County.

They went into the house and Becky served them bowls of steaming vegetable soup, slices of homemade bread, and apple butter. The fire in the cook stove felt so good that Hannah chose the chair closest to the heat, bent her head, and ate hungrily, the way a person who remembers an empty stomach does.

Becky knew enough to stay quiet, watching Jerry. Hmm. Shook up, he was.

When Hannah had finished her soup, she pushed the bowl away and began spreading apple butter on a slice of bread, her actions deliberate and concentrated. Jerry noticed the length of her fingers, the long, slim hands and arms. He pretended to eat, more than what he was actually hungry for.

"Well, if you don't want to drive your horse across the ridge to Georgetown, I could probably take you in the *doch-veggley*."

Hannah looked up from spreading the apple butter. "No."

Jerry raise his eyebrows and swallowed the retort that came naturally.

"I don't want the job. I'd have to drive a horse over that ridge every day from my grandfather's farm. I won't do that."

She pushed her chair back, surveyed the kitchen, the children around the table, and the window above the sink where the rain splattered and ran down in slices. "I'll let Fred rest awhile and eat something. Then I'll be on my way."

"Not in this rain," Jerry protested.

"I won't melt."

Becky didn't doubt for a minute she wouldn't melt. Like a stone, this one. "Would you like to borrow my bonnet?" she ventured kindly.

Hannah reached up to touch her ruined white covering. "Wouldn't help much now."

No smile, no appreciation for the offer. She rose, tall and slender, raised her hands to the heat of the cook stove and said firmly, "*Denke* for the soup. I'll be on my way."

Jerry opened his mouth, closed it again. He followed her out and helped her hitch up Fred, all the words he wanted to say crowding his chest. He watched helplessly as she sprang onto the buggy, pulled up the sodden gum blanket, lifted the reins, and looked at him.

"I'll be all right. A little rain never hurt anyone. My father would have given anything for a few drops of this to save his field of corn."

He had to say it. "Don't go back. Don't go without letting me know when you're leaving."

"Why would you have to know?"

"I would be worried, I guess." What an impotent answer! A limp, pathetic version of the desperate plea he felt in his heart, his whole being straining to keep her from making the same mistake her father had made.

"Yeah, well, that's nice of you, but I'm going. Somehow, I'll raise the money."

He didn't doubt she would do just that. The only comfort he could take with him after that was the length of time her eyes stayed on his, the amount of softening that took place in her hard, black gaze.

She drove out of the forebay into the driving rain without looking back or saying goodbye.

She came down with a terrible fever and sore throat. Her chest was filled with infection, her breathing came in short gasps, and her face was flushed and hot. The doctor was summoned from Lancaster, who pronounced her ill with double pneumonia in her lungs. He left medicines and pills and came back twice, begging Sarah and Hannah's grandfather to put her in the hospital.

Oh, never. The cost was much too high. Sarah tried every remedy she knew. She summoned her sisters, who came and stood over Hannah's bed like flapping crows, their voices hurting her head. She turned her face away, refused to open her eyes, willing them out of the house.

Onions. Raw, boiled, fried, slapped on her chest sizzling hot. Time after time, Hannah raked the stinking poultice off her chest and slammed it on the floor beside her bed, gasping for breath from the little effort it took to move her left arm.

Sarah steeped comfrey leaves in boiling water, added honey, and brought the cup to Hannah's papery lips, which was all she could do. Hannah refused to swallow the vile stuff.

Rachel said mustard and Echinacea poultices would be good. Emma suggested burdock root tea, which Sarah knew would not get past those clamped lips. They applied burdock leaves on her chest, hot and steaming, but odorless, which Hannah accepted. She fell asleep after that, resting deeply.

Back in the kitchen, Sarah shook her head at her worried sisters, taking their concern as a token of the love she had remembered, the love she held to her heart when she journeyed west with Mose.

"She'll likely get better," Emma commented.

"I would think so. Who is going to pay the doctor? He's been here how many times? Likely it will fall on Dat's shoulders." This from Rachel, shaking her head with long sighs of resignation.

Sarah assured Rachel she would do everything in her power to repay her father, who had already done more than enough. When Hannah recovered, she'd get a job, they'd see to it. Manny was already a big help to Elam and Ben. Hannah had been on her way to apply for a job at Rohrer's Mill when she had gotten caught in the rain.

"Rohrer's Mill?" Emma shrieked.

"What in the world, Sarah?" Rachel gasped. "A girl like Hannah working at a feed mill with all those men. That wouldn't be fitting. I would not let my daughter within a mile of that place. But then, you can't control Hannah the way I can handle Susie and Fannie."

Sarah nodded agreeably. This was true. She couldn't. But Hannah was not the type to like men. She was wooed reluctantly by Clay Jenkins. Wouldn't these sisters have a fit if they knew?

Suddenly, the need to stand up for herself was so strong it was like bile in her throat. Sarah coughed and cleared the passageway for the words that had lain dormant too long.

"Hannah could handle the job at the feed mill. She doesn't like men as a rule. She could hardly serve the table of silo fillers. I would trust her completely. She is a determined girl, but if it can be directed in the right way, she will be a talented young woman someday."

Her sisters stared at her, openmouthed. "Now you're taking up for her. I'm surprised at you, Sarah."

"Since I've said that, I'll say more. I will not stay here with Dat. Everyone in the family resents our living off his charity, which is understandable on your part. My decision is made. I will ask Dat for a loan to return, start our herd, and with God's help, we will prosper on the claim of 320 acres. Mose lies under the North Dakota soil, and I know now, that is where I want to be. He loved me in a way none of you could ever know.

"Your love is buried beneath your greed and avarice. All you know is to get ahead, pay off your farm, and snatch up another. You may believe my Mose was a failure, but he was the most successful man I have ever known, if you count the wealth of his love. Oh, he saw it. He saw and understood the downfall of many of his Plain brethren. It rode on his shoulders like a heavy burden. Yes, he was a failure where finances and management were concerned. But he laid up treasures in heaven far above anything any of us has ever experienced."

She paused for breath.

"You can't ask Dat for a loan!" Rachel exclaimed.

"You'll never pay it back!" Emma echoed.

So there it was. The only part of Sarah's speech they had heard was about the loan, which to them meant that Sarah was taking a portion of their inheritance, resulting in less money for themselves.

"I will. I will pay back every penny, with God's help. Hannah has the will, Manny has the strength and obedience, and I will be the rock of support they will need to survive. No, not just to survive, but to flourish."

Sarah's face was pale, her hands shook as she made the coffee, but there was a new firmness, a foundation beneath her words that the sisters had never known.

Quickly, sensibly, they tried to change their erring sister's course. Sarah remained steadfast.

They went to their father, husbands in tow, and begged him to refuse Sarah's request for a loan, citing many reasons why it was only common sense to withhold the loan. Circling around their aging father like a pack of wolves, they lunged at every angle, trying to secure the amount she had asked for.

Samuel Stoltzfus was well off, and he knew it, even with the depreciation on the farm he owned. The financial markets during the Great Depression were like a smothering blanket on any gain he might have expected in the future. God had a hand in this, he knew. Monetary value had replaced the fruits of the Spirit for too many brethren, himself included.

He listened to the undertone of greed in his daughters' arguments, shored up by the desperate pleas of obedient husbands to refuse Sarah. But he remained like a rock, firm and unmovable.

In his mind, he doubled the amount she had asked for, then tripled it, adding a windmill, a new well, and a decent house.

He'd ask Ben Miller's crew to install a windmill. He would. He sat at the kitchen table, his gray hair and beard surrounding his lined, aging face, weathered by hard work and a good temperament, his head and shoulders bowed by the wisdom of his years; like a head of wheat so filled with kernels, it bent him.

Once he had fully absorbed the insatiable grasping of his daughters and their collaborating spouses, there was no turning back. It was not rebellion, merely recognition of giving where giving was due. Sarah was the meek and quiet daughter, with the true love required of a married woman running in her veins. He did not doubt for a moment that she carried the same love within her heart as Ruth had for her mother-in-law and later for Boaz, as told in that beloved Old Testament story that was expounded at every Amish wedding.

"Wither thou goest, I will go. Thy God shall be my God." Hadn't Sarah proved her love, followed Mose to the ends of the earth, and believed that his God was her God?

Ah, yes, she had. Now, she was choosing to honor their love, with Mose lying beneath the plains, driven by the memory of the love that meant more to her than her own home, her own relatives, everything she had known. Sickened by the betrayal of her sisters' ravenous selfishness, she was returning to the land that had brought her to her knees, separated the worldly from the spiritual, what was true from what was a lie.

Samuel spoke with Elam and Ben and laid out his plans. At first, the sons responded with disbelief. But after hearing their father out, they slowly came to see his point. Their respect for him ran deep, so in the light of obedience, they "gave themselves up," in the often-used words of the Amish.

Hannah regained her strength, her lungs healed, and she was soon back to her forceful self. Manny told his mother that anyone as angry as Hannah probably got better by force of the strong will they lived with. But he smiled when he said it.

Sarah and the children had a long talk with her father. Hannah was wide-eyed and disbelieving. Manny grinned and all but bounced up and down.

He told them of his plans for a windmill, the crew who would install it, the cattle he would buy for them, and his plans to accompany them on the train to help give them a start. He wanted to meet the *Englische leid* around them and get a feel of the surrounding culture.

He spoke of his concern that Sarah and the children would stay true to their Amish culture and faith. He explained the need for *Ordnung*, the reason for modest dress, forgiveness, "*de lieve*," the love necessary for a successful *fottgung*. If they left Lancaster County in anger or self-righteousness, they would lose the blessing they needed to be successful.

Herr saya, God's blessing, is the ultimate goal, he said. If that is on your agenda, you will not fail.

Hannah listened, wide-eyed and silent. Her grandfather's words were priceless, but in her opinion came awfully close to her father's dreaming. Surely her grandfather didn't think along the same lines as Dat had. She knew full well it took hard work, foresight, and more hard work to get the homestead up and running. If he started in about the drought being a sign of *unsaya*, the unblessing so often spoken of—well, she didn't believe it. If it didn't rain, then it just didn't rain, and that was that. It made you tough and put every resource to use. You adapted, got a job in town to feed yourself, and you kept right on going, even if you only ate cornmeal and bread and prairie hens.

But she was grateful. She was more than grateful. Overjoyed, filled with a new and burning passion to excel. A windmill! A water tank like the Jenkinses had. Their grandfather to accompany them. It was much more than she could have ever hoped for.

Elam and Ben wanted to go. The harvest imminent, they knew they had to stay. It was hard, but they'd hear their father's account of things changing at the homestead.

Sarah was quiet, with a new resolve surrounding her like a set of fine, new clothes worn with a lift of her bowed shoulders.

CHAPTER 20

WORD GOT AROUND.

Samuel Stoltzfus was as bad as his son-in-law, that Mose Detweiler and his crazy venture, dead and gone now. Incredulous of his support of his widowed daughter, they tried to dissuade him, to make him see the light.

It took a month of planning, acquiring prices and agreements, and coordinating the schedules of freight trains for shipping the costly parts for the steel windmill. It was made in sections in Lancaster County by a reliable company to be shipped by train.

Most of the windmills in the West were made of wood, the lack of humidity preserving them for years of service. Windmills made of steel, used widely in the eastern United States, were better, and dozens of manufacturing companies produced them.

Ben Miller was a tall and swarthy man, red-faced and yellow-toothed from his love of a hefty wad of chewing tobacco lodged in his right cheek like a growth. Ambitious, his business of producing and installing windmills was known for many miles around. So when Samuel Stoltzfus came to see him about building one in North Dakota, his small green eyes squinted with delight. He immediately went to the door of his welding shop to spit out the long-chewed wad of tobacco before inserting a clean one.

"Ho! North Dakota! *Vass gebt?*" His voice carried well, too well in fact, leaving Samuel rubbing the ear closest to Ben.

"My daughter was married to Mose Detweiler."

Nothing further needed to be said. Ben nodded, understanding. He'd heard, knew Mose, watched the demise of a fine farm under his management. Long-suffering *schöene frau*. But nothing was said about her reason for returning. Unnecessary.

Samuel reasoned about this long before he approached Ben Miller. What the rest of Lancaster County did not know was fine with him, for he would carry a significant amount of shame from his remaining family and their overreaching concern about his charity to Sarah and her children. If Rachel and Emma wanted to air their grievances, word would spread, but so be it. Some would side with them; others would be aghast at their tightfisted selfishness.

They would need the windmill shipped as soon as possible. The prairie winters were nothing to take lightly.

Yes, yes, Ben had heard. In fact, he heard more than enough to wonder what was wrong with Samuel, thinking of supporting this venture.

"Surely you ain't leaving Sarah out there by herself?" he asked, adjusting his wide, black suspenders across the width of his barrel chest.

"She has Hannah and Emanuel. Manny they call him."

Ben reached under the rusty metal desk and produced a tin can, filled halfway with the dark liquid of his spitting. Pursing his lips, he sent a stream of tobacco juice expertly into the can, landing it with a fine, splashless plunk. He scratched his stomach after replacing the can, then put a foot up on a pile of metal and turned his full attention to his customer, figuring it wasn't his business. If the man wanted a windmill, he'd do his best to give him one and install it for him, no questions asked.

After the men finished the planning and negotiating the shipping costs and the price for the job, Samuel drove his horse away from Ben Miller's shop, satisfied that he had a trustworthy person to oversee the whole transaction from start to finish, in spite of the roaring in his ears and the questionably aimed stream of tobacco juice at frequent intervals.

At home, Sarah was canning vegetables and fruit in Mason jars. Tomatoes, peaches, corn, apples turned into sauce, zucchini relish, late cucumbers, anything she thought they might need. A new respect for food that was preserved and edible in the cold winter months drove her to work tirelessly all day, laboring in the heat of the wood-fired cook stove and the boiling water in the blue agate canner. As the jars cooled, she packed them in cardboard boxes with a thick layer of newspaper, labeling each and setting it aside.

She couldn't help thinking of the journey with Mose and how he had persuaded her that the jars of food would be too heavy for the horses. They had money and would buy food along the way. Plenty of small towns. Folks were generous. They'd be all right. They had been all right, had eaten well, in fact. The only downside was the disappearance of their money, leaving them destitute, scrabbling to survive.

Oh, she tried hard not to compare her departed husband with the planning and foresight of her father, but she could not help some comparisons. The journey on the train was so much wiser, but then . . . Sarah's thoughts drifted to the joy of pleasant days on the road, the crisp mornings when a light shawl that felt good on her shoulders, the clinking of the horses' harness, the swaying of the wagon, the crunch of steel-rimmed wheels on gravel roads. She fondly remembered Mose sitting beside her, his childish joy contagious, pointing out the different flocks of birds, the thrashers and dickcissels and indigo buntings, hearing their piercing songs long before they were in sight. His heavy arm about her shoulders, drawing her close for a kiss on her cheek. My Sarah, he had called her. And his Sarah she had been, in every sense of the word.

Sometimes, she wondered if he had been slightly demented toward the end. Perhaps he was only too determined. How hard it had been to let him go. But how hard might it have been to see him slowly losing his sense, his sound mind, had he lived?

This she must leave in God's hands. It was an enormous test of her faith, to let this wondering go. She would never know. His time had come, and God took him. So now it was up to her and the children to keep the homestead. A part of her mourned the loss of Lancaster County, her childhood, her heritage. Perhaps she could never go back home, like she once thought she could.

Did she only remember the perfection? Did she view her world through the pink haze of rose-colored glasses? The most difficult task that lay ahead of her was truly forgiving her grasping sisters, especially Rachel and Emma.

Unexpectedly, a smile came to her lips, her shoulders shook with mirth, and tears rose unbidden as she thought of Hannah's version of her two sisters: "cows." Flat and unadorned, labeling them along with her least favorite animal, a milk cow. Hannah should have been sharply reprimanded, for all the amount of good it would probably not do.

But still. She knew too that Hannah would board the train with a hefty chip on her shoulder, not caring whether she forgave Rachel and Emma or if she didn't.

And so Sarah planned her own journey, allowed her father to add burlap bags of potatoes and fifty-pound paper sacks of flour, cornmeal, oatmeal, and brown sugar. They packed coffee and tea, white sugar and baking soda, stacks of canned goods and round wooden boxes of cheese. It was a carload of luxuries, a God-send of security for Sarah. She felt as if she could face the harshest winds of winter, the worst drought in years—anything. There was a song in her heart, a new purpose supported by her aging father's love, his willingness to see this homesteading undertaking through to the end.

Of course, Ben urged Hannah to go to the singing that last Sunday evening. They were leaving the next day, Monday.

Hannah had just endured the final church service, shrugging off the nosy girls' questions, glad to return home and rid herself of all these people and their sharp glances and pitying looks.

As if she had a growth on her face, or two heads, or some strange disease like leprosy. That was all right if they didn't like her, she didn't necessarily care for them either.

People just weren't Hannah's favorite thing. They were just so false, most of them. Saying nice words, their eyes full of pity that they were so dumb, returning to the West like gypsies. Wanderers. Vagabonds. Taking all her grandfather's inheritance.

She'd show every one of these superior people. She'd be known for miles around, hundreds of miles around, for her pure bloodline of the best cattle. Her most important goal was to persuade her grandfather to buy the cattle from the Klassermans, not the Jenkinses.

The tough old longhorns they mixed with any old Angus or Hereford produced scrappy calves that survived blizzards and heat and drought. But in the auction ring, they weren't worth nearly what the Klassermans' Angus were worth. Calves took more care. Hard to birth, Hod said. Well, that might be true, but what about fast weight gain? What about good bloodlines?

Oh, the list of her dreaming could go on and on, but she needed to stop and take stock of what they had now. Debt to her grandfather, the drought, the two calves, and one mad cow. All the food was nothing but charity.

She told Ben, no, she wasn't going to the singing. Then it was the usual round of coaxing followed by the usual amount of excuses from Hannah.

"What will Rebecca Lapp say?"

Hannah sat up straight. "I don't care what she says. She doesn't give a fig about me, and I don't give one about her. She doesn't even know if I'm there or not. Besides, if you don't have

the nerve to ask her for a date, then I don't either. It's your problem, not mine."

Ben ground his teeth in frustration. She irked him so *hesslich*.
Speaking the truth like that. Why couldn't she be nice like other
girls? She honestly didn't care if she had any friends or if she
didn't. She was so odd, so different, wanting to return to the
West.

He left without her, disgruntled more at himself than at her,
berating himself for still not having the gumption to ask Rebecca
Lapp. He didn't notice Jerry Riehl watching his arrival, then
turning away, or that he wasn't at the singing at all that evening.

Hannah had not yet gone to bed, too keyed up about their
departure the following morning. In a way, she wished she
would have gone with Ben just to make the evening go faster.

She had washed her hair, put it back with the bobby pins
Doris Rocher had given her. The gold, shiny little clasps were
not allowed according to the *Ordnung*. Bobby pins enabled the
fast girls to adjust their hair in stylish waves, a fanciness not
possible without them.

Hannah loved to experiment with bobby pins. She could pull
her thick, dark hair up over her head and secure it with bobby
pins, or push it forward to let it droop over her forehead like
bangs. Mam would discourage this, asking her why she wasn't
content to wet her hair and roll it back along the side of her
head the way the other girls did, which Hannah didn't bother
answering.

An object hit the window. Hail? She waited, held her breath,
suddenly glad her grandfather and mother were asleep in the
same house.

Ping. Ping. Two more in quick succession. Whatever could
it be?

Going to the window, she pulled the retractable screen aside
and pushed the wooden framed window farther up, then stuck
her head out, her eyes searching the maple tree to the left and the

barnyard with dark objects milling around, the driveway like a ribbon of silver in the moonlight. No dogs were barking and the cows didn't seem disturbed. The night was warm and calm, a night like any other.

"Hannah!" A whisper from the base of the maple tree.

Vass in die velt? she thought wildly.

"Hannah! It's me, Jerry."

"What do you want?" she hissed, suddenly irritated by his daring.

"Come down. I need to talk to you. Please."

"No."

"Please."

"No. I'll wake my mother."

"Then I'm coming up."

"You can't do that. You can't come to my room. That would not be *shicklich*."

"I will, if you don't come down."

Hannah snorted, replaced the screen. Well, whatever he wanted, she wasn't going to put an apron on, or a covering. Her hair was still wet.

Oh, this was so aggravating. Why couldn't he tell her what he wanted from the base of the maple tree? She hardly knew him.

She didn't bother being quiet, simply went down the steps and through the kitchen, thinking that if she woke her mother, she'd tell her the truth. Jeremiah Riehl wanted to talk to her.

Jeremiah Riehl. What a name! Like a clown or a biblical prophet. She found him by the grape arbor, in the deep shadows behind the pump house. Her first thought was, coward. *Bupp*. Why not walk up to the porch and knock like normal people?

"What?" she asked, loudly.

"Shh. Someone will hear," he hissed sharply.

"So what?"

"Your grandfather would chase me off."

"Why would he? He doesn't know you. It's not like you were after me, or anything like that."

In the dark, Jerry rolled his eyes to the night sky, exasperated. Off on the wrong foot, a rocky start for sure.

"How do you know I'm not?"

"What?"

"After you?"

The usual derisive snort. "You have an awful long way to go. I'm going home tomorrow morning."

"I know."

"Is that why you came to talk?"

Why did she always make him feel like a boy in the first grade? Probably he should turn and leave, simply walk away from this bluntly spoken, intimidating girl and never give her another thought.

Almost, he did just that. In fact, he turned his body as if to leave, thinking what a belligerent person she was, how different from the realm of other girls, the circle in which they moved, polite, attracted to him, giggling, some of them coquettish, flirtatious. This one couldn't care one bit whether he left or didn't.

Was that the attraction? The age-old human condition of wanting what we can't have, and if we can have it, we don't want it. All this crowded into his head, followed by indecision and not a small dose of irritation.

"I came to ask if I can have your address. I want to write to you, if I may. I thought perhaps you'd write back to me. I'd like to get to know you better."

"Really? Why is that?"

"I don't know. Maybe because I find you interesting. Different."

"Well, I'll stop any chance of you courting me by saying that I don't know if I want to be Amish. There's this guy I know, Clay Jenkins, who wants me. Hod and Abby, his parents, saved us from starving more than once. He's really nice. Polite. I just don't know if I can do it to my mother. Leave, you know. Go English."

Jerry felt as if she'd put a fist in his stomach, leaving him scrabbling for his breath. Despair crowded out his usual sense of optimism. Boldly, without feeling, she had told him the worst. The unimaginable. He had always thought any girl who was so cold, so bereft of parental love that she could deliver the ultimate blow of *ungehorsamkeit* to undeserving parents, was not worth a passing glance.

Time stood still. The night became black, the oxygen sucked into a vacuum, leaving him without air.

"Why don't you say something?"

He had nothing to lose, so he spoke what was on his mind. "Hannah, I don't know why I have these feelings for you. I just do. I want to know you better, in spite of your leaving to go to North Dakota. I know you're not interested, but you could at least write to me every once in awhile and let me know how things are going."

"Why would you have to know? Why would you care? It's really none of your business how we're doing."

So it was that hopeless then. "I guess you're right."

"See, there are no other Amish out there. We're the only ones. And we're not worth very much. We won't own that homestead for another eight and a half years. We're getting a loan from my grandfather. We're getting all our food from him, to be shipped out with the windmill. We're just poorer than poor, taking an awful risk. And yet, it intrigues me to wonder if we're going to make it with the winter coming on and the start of our herd. Oh, you have no idea, Jerry, the things that I think."

Her voice was low, but filled with so much passion, every fiber of her being invested in the homestead in the West.

"See, if you'd see how we live, where the homestead is, how horribly poor and primitive, you would see me for what I am. You don't want to know me. Why not become interested in one of these Lancaster girls who live on a farm, in line perhaps to own the farm someday? A girl worth something. I have to look out for my mother and the rest of my family."

"You just said you might not stay Amish."

"I don't know what I'm going to do."

"Would it help if I persuaded you to stay?"

"Well, there's Clay." That statement held a bit of doubt. All was not lost.

"All right, Hannah. Then I'll have to let you go. And I will. I realize how young you are, and you need room to make your own choices. Someday, I hope to go to North Dakota to see where you live."

"No. No. Don't. Don't ever do that."

Puzzled, Jerry asked her why she said that.

"I don't know."

He stepped closer. The cloud that had obscured the silver of the full moon drifted away, bathing Hannah in the white light of moon glow, her dark hair with a sheen of diamonds, her eyes two pools of vulnerability.

He reached out to touch her hair. Instantly, she jerked away from his touch.

"I was just checking to see if it was moonlight on your hair, or diamonds."

"Smooth talker," Hannah said, but she was smiling, a small uplifting at the corners of her mouth.

Emboldened, he cupped her chin in his large, calloused hand.

"Hannah, if only you knew how beautiful you are, you would not set so much store in the state of your poverty. Don't you know that none of that means a thing to me? I don't care if you live in a cave, or a wigwam, if you have money or if you don't. That has nothing to do with . . ." Almost he said love, but caught himself just in time.

"With what?"

"With my interest in you."

She didn't answer.

Thinking he had said too much, he sighed, looked away across the darkened landscape, the black shadows behind buildings, the silver outline of the maple tree trunk.

"See, if I did say it was all right to exchange letters, you would lose interest. I am not a person that says entertaining things to young men the way the other girls do. I don't have anything to say."

"You talked to me that day in the rain."

"Oh, that." Suddenly she laughed, the deep laugh seldom heard.

"Do you have any idea how wet I was when I got home? I got sick, double pneumonia. The doctor wanted to put me in the hospital."

"You are surely not serious?" he asked.

"Oh, I was sick."

"See, I wanted to take you home that day."

"I know."

Then, the thought of her sickness, knowing the time of her leaving was in the morning, the permission to write to her unsecured, a great need to hold her and never let her go, keep her here with him, shook his frame.

He reached out to grasp her shoulders, surprised to find she did not immediately react and wriggle free with the usual sound of disdain.

Very softly, his hands slid down to her waist, imprisoning her arms. "Hannah, may I kiss you goodbye? Just as a token of remembrance?"

"No." She pulled away from him.

There was nothing to do but release her, let her go to stand by herself in the moonlight, her back turned to him.

"Are you afraid you'll remember me?" he asked gently.

"Of course not."

"What is it then?"

"I just want to go now. I want to forget Lancaster County and everybody in it. Why would I want to remember you? I certainly don't want to remember anyone else."

"Well, all right, Hannah. If that's what you want. May I ask you to write down your address, though? Could you please do that?"

"It takes weeks, sometimes longer, for a letter to arrive."

"That's all right."

She disappeared into the kettle house. The dim orange glow of a kerosene lamp in the window. Her bent head. A hand pushing back the curtain of dark hair.

She reappeared, handing him a slip of paper. He gave her his own on a white envelope. An exchange of promises. A slip of hope.

"Thank you, Hannah."

"Don't thank me. I didn't write to you yet."

He laughed. "Will you?"

"Maybe. If I can think of something to say."

They stood in the moonlight, each with their own thoughts, reluctant to leave, both of them now.

Hannah felt a flutter, a spark of interest, the moonlight carving his chiseled face, the dark hair that fell over his eyes, making him appear rakish, decidedly handsome. She'd go back to the homestead, sure, but what if this man actually meant what he said?

She wasn't sure how both of them stepped forward at the same time, but she found herself in his arms. One hand went up to stroke her hair, then dropped immediately when he felt her pull away.

"Hannah," he murmured. He could say that beautiful name a thousand times and never tire of it.

"May I kiss you now?" he whispered.

He smelled of sweet soap and shaving cream, toothpaste and night air, maple leaves and dew-wet grass. He was the only man that had not repelled her, even slightly. Before she could answer, she thought of Clay's slightly acrid and not too clean shirtfront, the stubble of his moustache when he had kissed her.

Without her answer, taking her slight yielding as an answer, he bent his head and found her mouth with his sweet-smelling lips. He kissed her lightly, almost like a breath.

It was Hannah who drew him closer, who would not break away. She had never imagined anything such as this. She was unprepared for the sweetness of him that rocked her and took away all of the irritation and natural rebellion that rose in her at the slightest provocation.

Her arms crept up around his shoulders, her fingers in his dark hair. It was Jerry who broke away and released her. She stayed where she was, her arms finally falling to her sides, her head lowered, ashamed now.

"Hannah," he said again. Nothing else fit into this night, this feeling.

Her hands found the edges of his black vest, clung to them. "I just . . ." She began to talk, but he stopped her with his fingers on her mouth.

"Don't talk, Hannah."

To his complete astonishment, she began to cry, softly at first, and then with childlike sobs and hiccups that threw him completely off guard. He gathered her straight back into his arms and kept her there, until the storm of weeping ceased. He produced a clean handkerchief that smelled like a different kind of soap.

"I am so sorry," she whispered.

"Sorry for what?" he asked.

"For . . . for that."

"That, if that's what you mean, was the most perfect, the most . . . There are no words to describe it. Why would you be sorry?"

"I shouldn't have allowed it. Now what am I going to do?" The old irritation welled up, her take-charge attitude firmly in place.

"You'll go to North Dakota on the train. We'll write."

She couldn't tell him that a letter from him was the last thing she wanted. She wanted to stay here with him. No, she didn't. She had no plans of living in Lancaster County. But surely they wouldn't always live apart. She had to be with him sometime in the future.

Confused, his leaving like nothing she could begin to explain, Hannah walked slowly back to the house, went upstairs and plunked herself into bed vowing to never, ever let Jerry Riehl back into her life. She couldn't.

CHAPTER 21

How could Sarah fully describe the return trip with her father? There was no way to stave off the fear of recurring starvation, the hopeless feeling of those days with Mose. Over and over she reassured herself with her father's presence, the freight car filled with food, the later arrival of the promised windmill.

She had forgotten the desolation of the plains, the sheer expanse of it. The flagrant emptiness was like an assault, a slam to the senses. Knowing her own unpreparedness, she prayed when they got off the train and on the journey to the homestead. She knew now, it would take much more strength than she had imagined.

It helped, though, watching the children's excitement. Even Manny, who was normally subdued, seemed willing to step into their past life with renewed hope and exhilaration. Eli and Mary simply loved the freedom of the prairie, the quirky gophers and wealth of flying insects.

The view of the buildings remained unchanged, though they had turned darker and with more gray undertones, perhaps. But they remained erect, braced against the never ending wind like a proud Amish fortress.

Here was the log house with the rusty tin roof, the door barred against the elements, windows closed and shuttered. The grass had reclaimed the yard, billowing up against the house. The barn looked half buried in it, only the tops of the barnyard fence showing.

Sarah shuddered, held her arms tight to her waist, thinking, thinking. She would never be able to clear her mind of the picture of Mose, her heart, lying battered and bleeding by the barnyard fence.

She got off the buggy as if in a dream, walked straight toward the barn and collapsed by the fence, where she stayed until her tears of sorrow were complete.

Her father helped the children unload, paid the driver, took care of the necessary steps as he let Sarah grieve. The door to the house unlatched easily. The floor was littered with the debris of the nosy rodents that had entered.

They resumed their life on the plains as before, seamlessly entering into a routine of cooking, washing, and cleaning.

Hannah remained a mystery to Sarah, during the entire journey on the train and for weeks afterward. If she didn't know better, she would have thought she had fallen in love, or was suffering from some other malady of the heart, like other girls did. But not Hannah.

Questions about her health revealed nothing. She was fine. Clipped words with her nose in the air, heavy eyelids covering any expression. Finally, Sarah decided it was the pneumonia, leaving her in a weakened condition, changing her fierce personality. Subdued, is what she was. Tamped down, the way you tamp down the good soil around a tomato plant when you put it in the earth.

Sarah stood by her garden, a withered brown patch of shriveled, dead plants. She shook her head as she scuffed a bare toe in the dust and dry grass.

Ah, but her father was here. The food would arrive in cardboard boxes. Safely. They would never go hungry, she assured herself over and over. The windmill would arrive and men to erect it and dig the well. She had to keep these thoughts, give herself over to the comfort of them, to keep the panic at bay, like a fire that keeps lurking wolves in the shadows of its heat and light. The time wasn't long, the distance between hopelessness and starvation, to this new beginning.

Her father smiled about the drought, said he'd never known there was an area in all of America where it simply didn't rain. "Our God is so much greater than we think," he said, smiling.

Sarah took solace in the fact that he did not despair in the face of the blowing grass and the emptiness. He rather liked it, he said, his hat all but leaving his head whenever it felt like it. Sarah laughed and pinned a strip of elastic from the inside of the crown to the other side, to be worn below his chin, the way they kept small boys' hats from blowing away. Rather than discard the troublesome hat, he stayed true to his teaching, the elastic cord keeping it firmly on his head.

Manny walked all the way to the Jenkinses to bring back the horses, asking Hod and the boys about the cows. Surprised to see their neighbors had already returned, they threw their hands in the air, delight creasing their weathered faces, standing there on the porch of the ranch house surrounded by their accumulation of earthly treasures, the stuff most people would label junk.

The dry brown grass, weeds, various thorny shrubs were all piled together with discarded wagon axels, wooden wheels, rusty spools of barbed wire, uneven sizes of fence posts, all things the Jenkinses viewed as useful and necessary.

Manny grinned, his shoulders already showing signs of manhood, his eyes alight with recognition.

"Yer back!" shouted Abigail.

"Howdy!" Hod yelled.

The kitchen door opened, revealing a sleepy Hank, who had been taking his noon break, followed by a jubilant Ken, who sprang out and off the porch in one leap, clapping Manny's shoulder with one hand and pumping his hand with the other.

"Glad to see you back, ol' buddy!"

"It's nice to be back," Manny said, smiling broadly.

He noticed the absence of Clay, but did not inquire, figuring he'd pop up somewhere, same as all the rest. He gladly accepted the offer of some leftover dinner, with a glass of chilled tea. He had forgotten the taste of Abby's beef steaks, rolled in flour, fried in lard in a cast-iron pan so hot the whole stove was splattered, including the wall behind it and the floor in front of it. His serving of beans would easily have fed his mother and the rest of the family, but he wasn't complaining.

Hunger was real. It was always imminent. He knew the gut-wrenching feeling of going to bed with a hollow, shriveled place inside of him, a place that was never comfortable and often kept sleep away. He knew the sacrifice of ladling small amounts of cornmeal mush in his own bowl so that Eli and Mary's stomachs could be filled, allowing them to sleep comfortably. So he dug his fork into the mound of beans, spread butter on an endless supply of leftover, cold biscuits, and was glad inside.

"So, ya gonna give it a shot without yer pa?" Hod asked, his chair pushed back, tilted on the two back legs, dangling a toothpick from his lower teeth.

Abby set to washing dishes, her mouth creased into a smile, so glad was she to have these neighbors returned, although it wouldn't surprise her a bit if they all turned tail and ran back to wherever they had come from. They didn't stand much chance without that oldest girl.

She watched Manny from the corner of her eye as she swabbed the countertop, thought he showed some promise maybe, but these people needed a plan put firmly in place.

She stopped wiping, listening as Manny spoke. *Huh. Good thing. Hmm. Buyin' cows from the Klassermans. Well, hoity toity. Somepin' wrong with ours?* But she stayed quiet and listened. *A purebred herd of Angus. Huh. Don't ask me to help out at birthin' time. They'd have their problems, so they would. Somebody was thinkin' some big ideas.*

She turned to Manny and said, "Where's yer sister?"

"You mean Hannah?" Manny asked politely, speaking after he'd swallowed.

"Yeah. The big one."

"She's helping my mother. They're unpacking and cleaning stuff. My grandfather will be finishing our house, putting up wall board, and finishing the floors. He wants to build an addition on to the kitchen."

"Well now, ain't that nice? If you got all that help. I'm speckting yer grandpappy's got food to tide you over. Winter's comin' on."

"The windmill comin' this fall yet?" Hod broke in.

"Oh yeah. It'll be here in a couple of weeks."

Hank said he'd want to see this new contraption. The Jenkins' ranch boasted the old wooden type, nothing wrong with it.

"Wooden, is it?"

"Oh, no. It's made of steel. Ben Miller has a welding shop in Lancaster."

Hod squinted his eyes, shifted his toothpick to a corner of his mouth, and said slowly, "Them Amish ain't all like yer pa, then?"

Manny's eyes grew wide, turned darker as he swallowed, then swallowed again. Ashamed of the quick tears that sprang up, he looked at his hands in his lap, then shook his head from side to side. "No, not all of them."

"Hey, sonny, didn't mean anything by it. Yer pa's gone now. Didn't mean to belittle him none."

Manny nodded.

Abby had her say after that, berating Hod up one side and down the other for making that boy feel bad, mentioning his pa that way, and didn't he have a brain in his head, talkin' like that?

Hank told his mother to quit talkin' to his pa that way, and was cuffed on the shoulder for it. Manny winced, trying to imagine his quiet mother hitting him or talking to his father in that manner.

Feeling uneasy, he rose to collect the horses, but was met instantly by a loud clamoring of everyone wanting him to stay. Hod asked Abby to refill his coffee cup, which she did, laying a hand across his back as she did so, a warm, tender touch as if she hadn't been talking gruffly only a few minutes ago. Hank rubbed his shoulder and told Abby she carried a mean punch. Ken guffawed about that, his mouth open wide, and Abby told him if they didn't all sit up and treat her respectable, she'd throw that mean punch around a whole lot more.

Manny was bewildered, then realized their anger and hard speech had no roots; it disappeared like tumbleweed on a wind. It wasn't fastened to old grudges and jealousies. These people were different. They said what they felt, took whatever came their way, and just rolled along with it.

Hod offered to help the old man at the house. Abby said she'd bring cornbread and a pot of beans. Hank asked how many pieces the windmill was in, and Ken said probably a thousand.

They all laughed. Manny said counting nuts and bolts maybe. So it was late when he returned to the homestead, the sun low in the sky. Sarah wore a tight-lipped expression that meant she'd been watching for him too long.

Old Pete was in good shape, the horse given to them by the Jenkinses looking as skinny and lop-eared as ever, his ribs like teeth of a comb, his stomach hanging low, his knees knobby and swollen, a mean look in his half-closed eyes.

Samuel Stoltzfus stood by the barnyard fence, pushed back his hat, and scratched the bald head beneath it. His eyes crinkled, then he laughed outright. "My oh, Manuel, is this what Western horses look like?"

Manny laughed, a joyous sound. "Ach, nay, Doddy. Not all of them. You have to remember that Dan died, so we had only

Pete and no way to plow this grass. We had no means of buying a decent horse, so the Jenkinses gave us this one. Gave him to us for free."

Doddy Stoltzfus, as the children called him, held Mary by her small brown hand, shook his head, and said he couldn't imagine what the family had been through.

Sarah stood beside him, holding Abby, the wind tossing tendrils of her dark hair away from the bun she had coiled on the back of her head, her faded green dress skirt with the gray, patched, and mended apron flapping, her large dark eyes pools of hurt and remembrance, biting her lower lip as she swallowed her tears.

She nodded, unable to speak.

"Now, I certainly don't want to make fun of God's creatures, but this horse resembles a large, brown goat. If he was sold at the New Holland Sales Stables, I doubt we could get a bid!"

"Out here you would. Lots of horses look like that, Doddy. You know why? They live on grass or hay. No grain, most times. Sometimes corn, if it's cheap at the granary in town," Manny said, grinning.

"He looks as if he could collapse," Doddy said.

"He's a lot tougher than he looks. These horses have the best record for stamina I've ever heard. They just go and go and go, their skinny necks stretched out, their legs just keep churning."

"Ei-ya-yi," Doddy said, good humored.

Hannah walked up to the group eyeing the horses. She smiled at Manny, a look in her eyes that reminded Manny they knew things, together. They were Westerners, and they knew what this horse could do.

She strode up to Pete, stroked his neck, lifted the heavy mane and smoothed the forelocks that fell down between his ears. "Good Pete. He has a lot of miles beneath those sturdy hooves. Were you talking about the brown one, Doddy?"

"I was. He's some horse."

Hannah laughed. "Tough as leather. He'd plow all day."

"Ah, I doubt it."

"Sure he would." This from Manny, standing beside Hannah, showing Doddy they were from the West now, knew the Western ways. They were seasoned in the art of old, ugly horses and knew their worth.

Supper was a lighthearted affair that evening. The end of summer was here, the worst of the drought over, the wind cooling in the evening, making their sleep deep and restful, refreshing their bodies to face another day.

The canned beef over new potatoes and canned lima beans and applesauce was so good, eaten in the slant of yellow evening light with the front door open, the sounds of grasshoppers and locusts like a symphony to usher out the day and welcome in the night.

It was sobering to think of the scant pot of cornmeal mush, the heat and drought, the fear and foreboding taking away any sense of survival. And now, here they were, making another attempt, without their husband and father, but with a new plan, with Doddy, a loan firmly in place, the agreement written by a lawyer, signed into a legitimate pact by both Sarah and her father.

With his faith in her and the children, anything was possible. Everything. Anything. A new fierceness took hold of Sarah, a new will to do it right this time.

She sat on the front steps with her father, long after the children had gone to bed, tired out by their endless roaming, the wind and the sun and the dust. The moon rose in the east, a great white orb so close to the prairie it seemed to rise from the restless brown grass like a brilliant round flower surrounded by the dark, whispering foliage.

"Ah, Sarah, I'm afraid I have to say this. I can see how a person like Hannah would want to return. There's a freedom out here. You can feel it in the wind, you can see it in the emptiness. It's a great land, and a restful one."

Sarah looked at her father's profile in the white-washed moonlight. Like a patriarch, an Old Testament prophet, with his white hair and full white beard surrounding his face like a curtain.

"You really think so, Dat?"

"Oh yes. Yes, I do. I can understand Mose liking it here. He had the pioneer spirit, the dislike of crowds. Too many people."

Sarah wrapped her hands around her knees, her fingers interlocked. "We just couldn't make a go of it. There was no money." She shuddered.

"I can only imagine, Sarah." Her father's voice was kind, full of caring, which brought an unexpected sob to Sarah's throat. She put a hand to her mouth, unsuccessfully suppressing the tearing sound of sorrow and remembered agony.

Quickly she coughed, trying to hide her emotion. Things like this were not easily spoken of. Far braver to hide it away.

"You will need chickens and a milk cow. A few pigs to fatten. We'll take care of that tomorrow, now that the horses are here. If you have eggs and milk, food goes a long way."

"Oh, eggs, Dat!" Sarah exclaimed, drawing in a pleased breath. "So often I was hungry for a nice soft-boiled egg with butter and salt."

Pleased at his daughter's grateful response, he spoke of perhaps not wanting to return. What if Elam and Ben wanted to come too? Here there was a simple appreciation of life's necessities, a deep thanks in everything, the way Sarah and the children bowed their heads over the most common bowl of food. They were not aware of this, he knew, but it came from the hardscrabble year they had only recently encountered.

Suddenly, thoughts of Emma, Rachel, and Lydia crowded out everything else. He could hardly contain his anger. What if he simply decided to stay? What if? He chuckled.

"What?" Sarah asked, facing her father.

"Oh, the girls. What would they say if I never returned?"

"You can't do that to them, Dat. They'd be furious. You must keep the home farm profitable."

"Until the day I die, *gel*? *Gel*, Sarah?" A brittle note of bitterness distorted the old man's normally friendly tone.

"You know they're all waiting to snatch up everything the minute I'm safely buried. They'll squabble like magpies over the kitchen cupboard that was your grandmother's. They'll fight for my collection of coins and knives. Then they'll sell all those family treasures and buy new linoleum and spanking new horses and shiny buggies, build another silo so the neighbors say, 'Must be Samuel was well off.'

"I can't stand it, Sarah. I can't believe I'm talking this way. I would never have, before. It must be the wild of the plains got into my speech. I'm sorry. You know I love all of you the same, but they have so much, and you went through so many trials. I can't see how they could possibly feel right with God. So greedy. Not wanting me to provide for my own destitute daughter."

He stopped, rubbed his hands together. Sarah could hear the rough, scraping sound of his calluses.

"What would they say of my loan to you? They'd have tried to stop the train. It breaks my heart in so many unexpected ways." He stopped, a deep sigh ending his speech.

"Ach, family. We all have our problems, some more than others. We always had a nice life together. Little squabbles, perhaps, but nothing like this. The Depression may have something to do with it. The desperation of the falling value of their land. I don't know."

Sarah nodded. She realized times were hard, in spite of the prosperous appearing farms and properties of her childhood home. She could not condemn her sisters, neither could she wallow in the mud of her own self-pity, a grudge against Rachel slowly drowning her sense of peace and goodwill. Of love and inner happiness.

If God was found in the love we have toward others, then how could Sarah continue her life with a grudge against anyone? Especially her sisters.

These thoughts chased themselves around in her head as she sat quietly with her father, the silver moon climbing steadily into the night sky. All around them, a shrill sound of insects, accompanied by the high yip of the coyotes and the bawling of the yearling calves brought a sense of being one with the earth.

The night smelled of dust, devoid of the moist dew, a dry scent of papery-thin grass, cracked, parched earth, and thirst.

"Where do the creatures find water after a summer of no rain?" her father asked quietly.

"Wherever they can, I suppose. Our well is almost dry. I don't think it would supply water through another drought."

"Ya, vell, we'll fix that." Then, "Did you want to return?"

For a long moment, Sarah searched for the right words. Finally she decided a forthright answer was best. "No."

"What made you do it?"

"Hannah. Mostly."

"And your sisters' jealousy?"

"That too."

"You do realize, Sarah, that Hannah will need company of her own kind. We cannot expect her to remain unmarried, as well as taking up with an *ausra*. With her temperament, I'd be afraid for her soul."

Better not mention Clay. "Hannah isn't like other girls her age. But without her, we would not have survived. She saw ahead the way Mose could not. She treated him with contempt many times."

Samuel shook his head, making noises of disapproval. "Children are expected to honor their parents. It doesn't say honor them if they live life according to the children's approval, or anything like that. Hannah lives her days with much confidence in her own opinion, and I imagine she often usurped his authority.

Mose was a gentle person, a *mensch* of soft-hearted views, his quest for spiritual perfection sometimes overriding his good judgment. No, Sarah, he would not have made it here, had he lived. In a way, it's a mercy he could be taken home to spend eternity with his Lord and Savior."

Sarah's voice caught. "But what is to become of me? I loved him so. He treated me kindly, always caring. Some days I feel as if I can't place one foot in front of the other, going through life without him."

"You have Hannah. And Manuel."

They drifted apart, sitting on the rough wooden steps, the old man lost in thought. It was well that his daughter had memories of her husband in that light of love. He knew, for him, it was more than he could honestly say.

His wife of fifty-two years. Dead now, and gone from him, never to return. His grieving was real, but he well knew it was a different kind of sorrow than Sarah's own. His sorrow was the deep, ingrained sadness of having spent all those years with a woman he still felt as if he hadn't known in the way many husbands share a closeness with their wives.

She had simply never given him her heart. That knowledge was a deep wound in his own heart, scarred and opened, scarred again. The house, the children, the garden, the social church-going, and the quiltings, had all meant more to her than he had. He had often longed for the sharing of innermost thoughts, times spent alone, on the porch swing in the evening, or the shared intimacy of pillow talk at night.

They farmed and raised ten children, prospered with the milking of the cows, the growing of abundant crops, traveled together side by side in the gray, canvas-covered buggy, without the ties that bind. Without the love they needed.

Oh, he had loved her, as much as he was able. But a warm flame is soon extinguished if met only with the icy blast of refusal. Eyes averted, mouth downturned. Always busy, her hands moving,

moving. Shelling peas, cutting corn, sewing, washing dishes. He longed for a pure light of recognition, a smile that meant *Denke*. The tiniest slice of approval, a warm and tender touch. Perhaps he had been the one who had failed. Failed to nurture the love that had withered before it could blossom.

Ah, but the children, each one more precious to his heart. Sarah, the woman of tribulation, marrying gentle Mose, and still they had so much more than himself. Thrown into poverty, perhaps, but wealthy in love.

In this way, Samuel Stoltzfus conducted himself and hid all the imperfections of the marriage away from his children, figuring they would not need all that unnecessary information, their mother dead and gone.

It was the way of it. He stretched and yawned.

"Bedtime for an old man."

"Ach, Dat, I hate to think of your leaving. Going back to Lancaster."

"Oh, but you know I have to, and soon, even before the windmill crew gets here."

"I know."

"I need to look after things at home. Elam and Ben still need teaching."

Sarah rose, tall and slender in the moonlight, her eyes large and dark. "We'll be all right."

"Yes, you will."

They stepped through the door of the house together, said their goodnights, each one to their own sleeping quarters, alone with their thoughts of the past as the moon made its way across the beauty of the clear night sky. The supplies would arrive tomorrow. The house would be covered with wall board and painted, like Abby's. The floors would be sanded smooth and varnished, making life so much cleaner, so much more normal.

Sarah knew she had nothing to fear, except the past rearing its ugly head like a horned beast, leaving her mouth dry, her heart racing. She knew the storms of the past winter. She still felt the cold in her half-frozen feet and heard the howling wind. This winter, she would not have Mose to lean on. No one to make decisions.

She gathered little Abby into her empty arms, knew there was no use wailing and pining like a weak kitten.

She must let go of her father. And somehow, bridge the gap between her and Hannah.

CHAPTER 22

O NE NIGHT AFTER DODDY STOLTZFUS HAD LEFT BUT BEFORE THE windmill crew arrived, Hannah woke up while it was still dark. She had no idea what time it was, but it felt like way past midnight. The flannel coverlet was drawn up well past her shoulders, half covering her ears, the nights having turned cooler as fall arrived.

Someone's voice had awoken her. It was not in the house but farther away. Instantly alert, she rolled onto her back, her arms at her sides, holding still and straining to hear.

Was it only the whisper of grass, when the wind didn't die completely away, even at night?

A banging. And most certainly voices. Low voices. Immediately, her heart set up a clamor of its own. Should she wake Mam? Manny? Wake anyone?

She lay still, listening. Yes, there it was. Someone was at the barn.

Every story she had ever heard about claim jumpers crowded into her mind. Hod Jenkins had spoken of them to her father, while she sat on the sidelines around the campfire in the yard. He had recounted tales of fist fights, even exchanges of gunfire, the law too far away and too unconcerned to help. The documents uncovered too late, many of the homesteaders, discouraged before the claim jumpers even showed up, willingly allowed them to take the land.

Knowing the subservient spirit of her mother, Hannah recognized it was up to her to save their homestead. Whether it was claim jumpers out there or cattle or horse thieves, they weren't getting away with this craziness. That was for sure.

She rolled out of bed, slipped a dark dress over her nightgown and made her way to the narrow stairs in bare feet like a ghost, her breath coming in ragged puffs.

The rifle. Beside the cupboard.

Her toe hit the former of a kitchen chair, sending sparks of pain along her foot. Her eyes scrunched as she bit her lip to keep from crying out. She found the rifle, her hands closing around the cold metal of the barrel, down to the smooth stock. Gripping it in both hands, she let herself out the front door, holding her breath as it sent out its usual creak of hinges.

She tiptoed across the porch, wishing the silver illumination of the moon away. A dark night would be so much better, but there was nothing to do about that now.

She hunkered down in the shadows of the house, where the dark night made her disappear.

"Hey, them's horses." A volley of evil language followed.

"They come back?"

"Nah."

A shuffling followed, as they removed saddles from horses whose heads hung low, tired out, glistening with sweat in the moonlight.

One tall, thin man, accompanied by a shorter, stockier one. At that moment, Hannah realized the need of a good watchdog. A huge German shepherd, like Uncle Levi's that he kept tied to a doghouse at the side of his barn. Her father disliked that dog, saying the only thing that kept him from taking off someone's leg was the chain attached to his collar. The way that dog carried on at the slightest disturbance, he didn't know how much faith you could put in a flimsy chain, as powerful as those lunges were, coupled with the harsh barking.

She needed a dog just like that. Well, the cracking of a good rifle was all she had. Hod said that most times it spoke louder than the law. Her father had nodded, a smile playing around his gentle lips. Hannah knew well, he would never shoot a gun in any man's direction. His faith forbade it.

If a man asked him to go with him a mile, he would go twain, as the Bible required of him. If someone took his shirt, he would offer his coat as well. He lived by the righteousness of turning the other cheek. He'd get slapped around and give up the homestead, rather than lose his faith.

Nonresistant. That meant putting up no resistance when someone came to take away what was rightfully yours. There was no gray area for her father. It was all black and white. Being Amish, you lived by the articles of faith written in the small, gray booklet, and by these rules you lived your life, secure in the knowledge that they were not too much sacrifice. They were the *Ordnung*, the giving of your life to Jesus Christ, living as He had lived on this earth.

Why did these thoughts of her father come now, like a barrage of right and wrong choices, igniting an uncomfortable fire in her conscience?

Well, that was all right. That was her gentle father. She was what was left behind, and she had no plans of giving up their 320 acres of profitable grassland. The windmill was coming, and they had a checking account in her grandfather's name to buy cattle.

"Wanna try the house?"

"Yeah."

They hobbled the horses.

Hannah felt the bullet pouch, drew back the clip, and inserted one. A soft click. She held her breath. They were coming. The grass rustled in the night wind, gently. A coyote yipped, far away. It was now or never. If she spoke, they'd know it was a woman. She'd have to let the gun speak for her.

She raised the heavy rifle to her shoulder, sighted down the black, cold barrel, aimed a few feet to the left of them, away from the barn. They should hear the bullet whistle past, but certainly not hit either one of them. Thou shalt not kill, this she knew, and had no intention of doing that.

She squeezed the trigger, her sturdy shoulder took the impact well.

Crack!

A loud yell—and another.

On they came. Hannah followed the first shot with two more. Her heart racing, a dry fear turning her mouth to cotton, she watched as they stopped, turned, and ran, silently scrambling to unhobble their horses. They threw the saddles on, jerking at the cinch, fumbling, muttering to one another about gittin' outta here.

To let them know she meant business, she fired once more, hoping her family would have the good sense not so show their faces.

She watched as they threw themselves on their mounts, turned, and galloped away into the dry, rustling moonlit night. Hannah stayed in the shadows of the house, her gun held across her raised knees, listening to the retreating hoof beats, until the quiet whispering of the grass was all that remained.

She rose from her cramped position, her knees like jelly, and stumbled up the porch steps, to find her mother and Manny, huddled by the door, Eli and Mary softly weeping.

"Hannah! Is it you? What is going on?" Manny whispered hoarsely.

"Who was shooting? Surely it wasn't you?" her mother croaked, her mouth and throat dry with the same fear.

"I was shooting. There were claim jumpers at the barn."

Sarah gasped audibly. "But, Dat, Mose, I mean . . . your father always said he didn't know what he would do if he found himself in those circumstances."

"Well, I knew. They're not getting these 320 acres." Such conviction.

Sarah shook her head, lit the kerosene lamp with shaking fingers, the glass chimney rattling between the metal prongs as she replaced it.

"Did you shoot?" Manny asked.

"Sure. I shot the rifle to scare them off. It worked."

Sarah gathered the terrified children to her side as she sat down weakly in a kitchen chair, stroking Eli's dark head as he sat on her lap. Mary stood beside her mother, arms around her shoulders, her eyes like dark pools in the light of the lamp's flame.

"But Hannah, is it right? Are we living by your father's rules?"

"Look, Mam. Dat is no longer here. We have our choices to make now, if we want to stay here in the West, all right? It isn't right to let those brazen, lawless men take what is ours. We worked hard for this, and will continue to work hard. I don't care what you say."

"But, Hannah. You know he wouldn't approve of what you just did."

Hannah took a deep breath. "Mam, listen to me. If this is how you're going to be, you may as well go back home now. We can't live by our father's dreaming if we're going to survive. I only scared them off. I didn't kill anyone. I never meant to. I know about nonresistance, but how far does that go?"

Sarah shook her head, suddenly miserable. Oh, this wild land. Amish had no business out here. How could they be expected to live by the rules of the church? Did those four gunshots mean they had crossed off one of the articles of their faith?

"Ah, but Hannah. Now we are not abiding by one rule, so now we are already started on the downward spiral, turning our backs to the teachings of our forefathers." Sarah shuddered to think of the lawlessness that had crept in so soon, like a thief in the night.

She turned to Manny, the obedient one. "What do you think?"

So much like his father, he took a few moments before he spoke. "I want to respect our father's wishes, Mam. But we can't just lay down and take the claim jumpers unlawful thievery, either. I don't know."

Hannah glowered from her stand by the door, one ear turned toward the night, alert for the sound of hoof beats.

"Here we are again. Everyone sifting through the *Ordnung*, trying to figure right from wrong, wondering, dreaming, looking back, when I am the only one who gets off my backside and does anything about anything." Her voice turned to a shout.

"You would have died without food if I hadn't gone to town. No one ever figured out if that was right or wrong, did you? Huh? No, you were too hungry." She paused for breath.

"So now, you'd better decide if you're with me or not. If this is how our future is planned, then I'll marry Clay Jenkins at the first opportunity. I want to live here. To be sensible, we might have to bend the rules sometimes."

"Oh Hannah, please. Please don't tell me you would marry an *ausra*. That is not even thinkable," Sarah said, wheedling now, begging her headstrong daughter to change her way of thinking.

As the night wore on, they remained seated around the kitchen table, hashing out the rocky path of survival and the Amish *Ordnung*, the meek and gentle spirit of Mose Detweiler the burning example, a flame to lead them in the coming years, almost extinguished by Hannah's pragmatism when compared to his righteous, biblical version of life. Sarah found herself often swayed by Hannah's power and the stark sensibility of her reasoning.

Nothing hidden, nothing sugar coated to make the swallowing of it easier. To live in the West required adaptation. Changes. Who was to care? No other Amish lived here. God saw them, of course, Hannah conceded to humor her mother.

But Sarah knew. And she could tell that Hannah knew: Hannah was wielding power over her mother and Manny by threatening to marry Clay. There was no doubt in Sarah's mind that it was possible. Hadn't she seen? Clay would marry her tomorrow. Well, Sarah had a wealth of power herself. The minute Hannah brought up the subject of Clay Jenkins becoming her husband, Sarah would mention the possibility of her grandfather's withholding his checkbook and the windmill. She knew only too well her aging father's disappointment, the deep and searing heartache he'd endure if Hannah chose to live outside the *Ordnung*, the way of righteousness by which he abided.

It was a great mystery, this heartache. Why was it so hard to see children leave the Amish? To see them openly disobey?

And Hannah on the brink of it herself. Sarah well remembered Uncle Levi's Abner, going off to war, disregarding his parents' warnings. He had lived many years untrue to the Amish faith, battling side by side with the *ausra,* the English soldiers in World War I. He was shot and killed. Uncle Levi and Aunt Barbara were never the same after that. How could they be, having no hope for his soul? To burn in hell, eternal damnation. Or did he have time to repent and ask forgiveness before his final moment? They would never know. They could hope, that was all. This life was no *kinnershpiel*, no child's play. There were consequences for wrong choices. God is not mocked.

The upbringing Sarah had lived by all her life was now viewed through the microscopic lens of her self-willed oldest daughter. Things she had never questioned, that she had taken as rules written in stone, the foundation of her character, were now shaken and rattled as never before. She had given her life to her husband, and now to Hannah, faithfully and without self-pity. She had done what was required of her, and here she was, her daughter holding the threat of marriage to Clay Jenkins over her head like a fierce, flapping bird of prey that threatened to peck her eyes out.

A shot of anger sparked in Sarah. It made her feel small and helpless, like a baby bird, dependent on Hannah's offering. Well, this was not right, according to the Bible. Her husband had been a different story. This was her daughter.

She pictured herself at the base of a pedestal, an intricately chiseled Roman pillar, prostrate, worshipping at the shrine called Hannah, bidding Manny to join her. The thought was so real and so revolting that it felt as if a hot wind blew from below the bed, enveloping her in an uncomfortable steam bath. Self-recognition brought wave after wave of anxiety washing over her and then receding, only to submerge her again.

So what was she to do? What was her next step? The coming days loomed before her, formidable as the tallest mountain. It sapped her strength, leaving her floundering for oxygen, as if her trek up the mountain had already begun.

She had felt courage on the night she had the talk with her father. She had recognized the need, felt the passion directed toward the success of the homestead. Now, a far greater trial loomed: taming Hannah and reversing authority in the family.

Sarah realized the thin line of helping Hannah find the balance she would need. To be harsh and unforgiving would germinate the seed of rebellion, drawing it from the earth like a warm summer rain. To allow Hannah to control her, passive and afraid, would only bring an unchastened, unhandy spirit, one that flared up the minute her authority was questioned. Like bread dough forgotten and left to rise, Hannah had risen out of proportion and down over the pan. Such dough is ruined unless brought into submission and kneaded into shape.

Sarah shook slightly, a rare moment of laughter overcoming her as she thought of Hannah's reaction to her comparison to bread dough. Oh, mercy.

She fell asleep, a prayer on her lips, her sweet face relaxed as she breathed lightly. The moon was low in the west, luminous and orange, before the first call of the sage thrasher woke the western blue birds, until the prairie hummed and warbled and trilled.

The birdsong woke Hannah when the first of the sun's rays poked a slanted yellow beam of light on the round rafters, the rough boards placed horizontally on top of them. She would be happy to wake up in a decent room, with wall board and paint, but that was beside the point this morning.

She rolled over, stretched, then raised herself from the hay tick and padded lightly downstairs to begin her day.

She had planned on accumulating all the firewood she possibly could before the windmill crew arrived. For one thing, if the family was expected to cook for them, it would take plenty of wood to keep the stove going. Plus winter was coming, and she had no plans of being cold ever again. Between her and Manny, they'd stack the northeast side full of wood, insulating the house as well as never getting lost in an unexpected blizzard.

So Mam could make a big breakfast, after which they'd set off for the creek bed to saw wood. As soon as the new windmill was up, they'd buy the cows from the Klassermans and buy a huge dog; it didn't matter what kind, just so it was big and had a fear-inducing bark.

She wished they had some kind of food storage facility, but that could wait if it had to, she supposed.

She didn't greet her mother, just watched her set about gathering the soiled laundry from the wooden hamper in the bedroom.

Finally she asked if Sarah would make breakfast soon; she had plans for herself and Manny to chop firewood.

"I thought I might be able to get the whites on to soak before I start the wash water."

Hannah snorted. "What do you mean? That doesn't make sense."

"I have enough hot water on the cook stove to pour into the small granite tub to soak the whites in lye soap. After that, I want to start the fire to heat the rest of the water in the kettle."

"Why didn't you say so?" Hannah asked as she bent to pull on a pair of warm stockings.

Sarah's patience was as dependable as the sun's rising, so Hannah was surprised when her mother stopped sorting clothes, faced her with her hands on her hips and said firmly, "I'm busy, Hannah. The rest of the food boxes still need to unpacked before the windmill arrives. I would appreciate your help today. You could make breakfast for all of us. It doesn't take long to make a pot of oatmeal and fry bread in a skillet."

"I can't see why that washing has to be done this minute," Hannah retorted, stretching her feet in front of her and wriggling the toes of her stockings.

"I told you," Sarah said shortly.

Hannah glared at her mother, then got up to go to the mirror above the washstand. She removed her hairpins, loosened her long dark hair, lowering her left shoulder to swing her hair behind her, raising her eyebrows to inspect a blemish on her usually flawless forehead. She claimed her head was itchy, saying she probably had lice, the way that train had been packed with people.

"Let me see. Come here." Sarah left her laundry to draw Hannah over to the doorway, where the light of the morning brought each strand of hair into keen sight. She raked the tips of her fingers through the top of Hannah's head, parting her dark hair to reveal the white scalp underneath, then lifted the heavy tresses to check thoroughly behind her ears.

The lice were harder to see than the white clusters of their eggs, and she told Hannah this, which caused her to pull away from Sarah with a sharp jerk and an exclamation of disgust.

"Well, you don't have lice, at any rate. I've seen them before, but they're most common in school-age children and smaller ones who play together. I don't believe you've been infested, Hannah."

They drew apart, each one going their own way. Hannah thought how much her mother's nearness reminded her of times when she rolled and plaited her hair to go to school, wetting it so miserably with cold water, drawing the steel-toothed comb through it without mercy, rolling it so tightly along the side of her head that it felt as if each hair was being pulled out by the root. After all that pain, she twisted the plaited hair into a bun on the back of her head, jabbing the hairpins through it without restraint. Every morning was a mild form of torture, like the one before.

But still. There was something about the smell of a mother, the soft, spicy scent that came from her clothes, the soft touch of her fingers, the way her chest rose and fell as she breathed. When her hands clamped down on her shoulders with a bit of pressure to turn her around, it was like a caress, a caring, a mother doing the duty that was like a bond between them. A part of Hannah missed this ritual, and she realized the absence of her mother's touch.

Unlike the last time she'd been held.

The thought of Jerry Riehl was so painfully embarrassing that she became rattled and forgot the bread frying in the cast-iron skillet. It burned as black as charcoal and she yelled at her mother when Sarah reminded her, her face flaming from the cookstove's heat, but mostly from her own bewildered thoughts.

She woke Manny, ate her oatmeal, and vowed to never catch sight of that man again. Why would she? Hundreds of miles away now, with no longing to return, there was no chance. So that was that.

She spread apple butter on her fried bread, drank her tea, and shivered.

"Chilly, huh?" Manny asked.

"Winter's coming," she answered soberly.

Manny lifted a spoonful of thick oatmeal and nodded. "We need firewood. And who is going to buy chickens and a cow? And pigs. Doddy told us to do that. I'll get the pens ready in the barn if you'll do the rest."

"I had planned on firewood making."

"Well, we can."

So that was what they did. Always the same. Hannah planned and Manny went along with it. Sawing and cutting all day long with only a short break at lunchtime. Manny was uneasy, watching the horizon, asking questions. He knew every minute where the rifle was, propped against a poplar tree.

"If we had a dog," he began.

Hannah put down the axe, wiped the sweat from her forehead. "I'm getting one, somehow. If we had Uncle Levi's German shepherd, they never would have made it to the barn. Bold. Honestly, Manny, they were settling in. If we wouldn't have been here, they'd have some sort of false documents. Something. They'd take our claim. The only resistance they understand is the sound of a gun."

Manny shook his head. His eyes went to the horizon, afraid.

They acquired ten laying hens, brown ones, young, and laying six eggs between them. Egg production cut back in the fall as the daylight hours shortened. Two baby pigs dug in the manure in the back stall of the barn, little ones with ribs showing, runts from the Klassermans' litter of twelve.

Good-natured Owen waved away the mention of a price, said they'd likely be laid on by the mother sow anyway, as dumb as she was. Owen went on to say he'd never met an animal with less brains than a pig. Didn't understand why the good Lord made them so ugly, but he sure enjoyed the bacon and shoulder meat with the fresh sauerkraut and dumplings Sylvia made.

The milk cow was small and brown eyed, a Guernsey, he said. Good rich milk, high in fat. Said they could all use some meat on their bones, to be sure and drink it down, make plenty of butter. Nothing better on fried bread. Or biscuits. Did Sarah make biscuits?

No? Ach, he'd bring Sylvia over to show her how. Nothing like biscuits made with lard. Flaky. So soft they would melt in your mouth.

Hannah stood, shifting her weight from one foot to the other, waiting until the flowery words of praise for all things edible came to an end. She could hardly get a word in to inquire about a dog.

"A dawk? You vont a dawk? Vell, I don't haf vun. Dey kill mine sheeps. Dey luf to kill calfs and lamps. I don't haf a dawk. No, no."

"Do you know of any place we can buy one?"

"No. No. Haf no business wiss a dawk. Ornery buggers. Bite mine lamp."

It took five hours to return to the homestead, trailing the fine-boned little cow with the swinging udder behind the wagon. It was a perfect day, the heat gone, the cooling winds that carried the scent of fall, the brown grass rustling by the side of the road.

"I'm hungry, listening about all that food. It will be hours before we can eat. It almost feels like, you know, last time," Manny said.

"I know what real hunger is, that's for sure," Hannah answered.

"Think we'll make it through the winter?"

"No. We'll have to get to town for oatmeal, flour, and sugar. We have plenty of everything else. Firewood. A dog. Need to get the cattle bought and branded."

"I hate to think of branding cows. It brings back too many memories of Dat. Poor man. I miss him every day. There's not a day goes by I don't remember his words. They're words to live by, Hannah. I will always love and remember my father."

Hannah stared intently to the right, and didn't answer at all. She didn't need to. Manny knew what she was thinking.

CHAPTER 23

WHEN SARAH BOUGHT THE CATTLE, OWEN KLASSERMAN WAS MORE than generous. Ten yearlings, coal black, muscular, lean, and healthy looking. One hundred dollars a head. No need to weigh them. One thousand dollars.

Sarah wrote the check with a trembling hand, struggling with her own thoughts of pessimism. Dark thoughts of disease and dying, winter blizzards, and loss. In spring, the birthing of calves. So much could go wrong, and would, she knew.

One thousand dollars in debt to her father. Another four hundred for supplies to finish the house. Then the milk cow and hens. To be in debt was a horrible thing. She would despise this loan until the day she died. She would never be free of it. But she didn't speak of this to Hannah or Manny.

The Jenkins boys rode over, with Clay this time. Hannah was waiting, trousers buttoned in place below her skirt, Pete saddled with the used saddle from Owen Klasserman. Manny was riding Goat, which was the new horse's name after Doddy Stoltzfus brought up the resemblance.

Hank and Ken were boisterous, open and friendly, their faces creased in good-natured grins. Clay hung back, his handsome, chiseled face taut, tanned to a reddish brown, the stubble on his face bleached white by the sun. He didn't greet Hannah directly.

She was given a fleeting smile, a hand waved in recognition, eliciting strange stares from his brothers. Well, no time to worry about Clay's behavior now. There were cattle to be branded, and they were about a year older than they should have been.

"You need a chute," Clay observed dryly.

"We don't have one, so how are we going to do this?" Hannah asked.

"Rope 'em, hold 'em down best we kin, I spect," Hank spoke up. They were eager, up to the challenge, their horses fresh.

"Why Angus?" Clay asked. "You know these purebreds aren't as tough as our skinny crossbreeds. They're Longhorn, Angus, Hereford, and Reds. They're anything all mixed together, which makes for easy calving and getting through the winter better. They're just all around an easier breed to raise."

"And when they're sent to auction, how much less do you get per pound?" Hannah asked quickly.

"I don't know. Never asked the German what he gets."

So now it was the German. Were they actually riled, these Jenkinses? Were herds of cattle held with as much pride as the farms in Lancaster County? For some reason, this upset Hannah, and when she was upset, she spoke what was on her mind. She faced Clay and asked him why he referred to Owen Klasserman as "the German?"

"I didn't mean anything by it. That name's a mouthful, is all." He held her gaze, his blue eyes as beautiful as she remembered, but devoid of the intense light he had always reserved for her. Bewildered, Hannah lowered her own, scuffed the toe of her worn black shoes in the dust and wondered what was going on.

As before, they cleared a large area, started a blazing fire, which Clay informed everyone was a bad idea. One spark would be all it took to get this prairie started burning. "It'll go up like tinder. Manny, you stay here and watch. Might not hurt to have a bucket of water settin' by. Get the kids to bring one."

The dust flew as the horses raced, wheeled, pulled the ropes taut, with Hannah hanging on to Pete and mostly incapable of helping at all.

Clay got mad and yelled at her to go make dinner. That stupid horse didn't know his head from his tail. He said the cows were dumb, but what could you expect from an Angus?

Hannah was seething. She had roped one, helped to hold it down. What was wrong with Clay? He acted as if there was nothing between them and never had been.

Well, she wasn't making dinner, either. She would stand right here and watch them fail to bring down these large heifers. Good, strong, quality calves, is what they were, and she didn't care what Clay said. He didn't know everything.

But it was heart-stopping to watch those boys in action. Always a step ahead of the elusive cows, always controlling their horses with the touch of a knee, a rein draped across the horse's neck, either from the left or the right. A quick called command, followed by instant obedience.

The fire died down to a bed of hot coals, the branding iron heated, sizzled through the heavy hair and thick skin of the year-old heifers. It was a grueling job, with repeated attempts at roping gone awry. The cows charged the dancing horses, dodged the ropes, and if they were fast enough to throw one, she was quickly on her feet charging anything that moved, including the terrified barn cat.

It was well into the afternoon when the branding iron sizzled through the last hide. They released the bawling, wild-eyed heifer, extinguished the fire, and rubbed down and fed the horses.

Sarah called from the house to invite the boys to dinner, so with Manny leading the way, they all washed up on the back lean-to and went into the house.

Clay stopped short, gave a low whistle, and looked around at the painted walls, the addition to the kitchen, and the gleaming floor. "Someone was real busy, I'd say," he told Sarah, smiling at her in his best manner, which made Hannah grind her teeth in frustration.

The nerve of him, treating Mam with his flowery manners. Fuming, she slammed bowls of mashed potatoes and canned beef in gravy on the table, moving from stove to table with her head held high, her nostrils flaring in her best belligerent manner, which, seemingly, did not even faze the elegant manners Clay bestowed on Sarah.

Hank and Ken dug their forks into mounds of mashed potatoes, grinned, made conversation with Manny, and never worried about the quiet drama taking place between Clay and Hannah.

Sarah figured the roping had not gone well and left it at that, filling water glasses, talking about the water level in the old well, the windmill crew's arrival, anything, it seemed to Hannah, that would exclude her.

Sarah served a warm dried-apple pie with milk and sopped up Clay's praise like a thirsty sponge, her face shining with appreciation.

Hannah glowered and refused the slice of pie Sarah served her. "You sure?" she asked, her eyes questioning.

"'Course I'm sure," she spat out.

Clay dipped his head to hide his amusement. Hannah ignored him when they all got up, retrieved their hats, and thanked Sarah again.

"Oh, it was nothing, really, boys. Your mother's cooking is far superior to mine. I'm just glad I have food to cook with. Glad to be able to feed you when you've done us such a big favor. Thank you."

"It was our pleasure, ma'am," Clay said, his teeth flashing white in his tanned face.

Hannah could not believe he walked out the front door and down the porch steps without looking at her. The nerve of him! What was going on? Had he forgotten the attraction, the long talks? He'd kissed her! She groaned inwardly, thinking of all the reasons he may have had to brush past her as if she were a piece of furniture.

She supposed she'd been clumsy and ill-prepared, riding poor, plodding old Pete, but could she help that? She had learned to rope and thought she'd made a good showing, helping to throw two of them, until Clay yelled at her.

Make dinner. Huh. Boy that had irked her. If she would have made him dinner just then, she would have fried him a few grass-hoppers and boiled some earthworms. Oh, he made her furious!

So much for Clay Jenkins. She'd write him off as thoroughly as she'd written off the other one. She cringed in humiliation even thinking of his name. Well, this just cemented the fact that she did not need a man to keep her happy. She was much better off without anyone. Getting married was so far off on the horizon, it wasn't worth talking about.

She asked Sarah why she thought Clay was acting strange. Shocked, Sarah turned wide eyes on her daughter. "I didn't notice anything different, Hannah. He was just being Clay."

"No, he wasn't. He openly ignored me and yelled at me."

"He had a hard day, being in charge of branding those heifers."

"Puh. We could have done it without him."

"Now, Hannah, I wonder."

"If only I would have had a decent horse. Someday, Mam, I will own a fire horse with a good bloodline. I'll have a stable full of them, like Jerry Riehl."

Sarah scraped a plate and lowered it into the dish water. "Who?"

"Someone in Lancaster. Remember when I went to the feed mill that day? When I got caught in the rain?"

"Yes, I do remember well. You became sick with pneumonia."

"I got lost. Drove into a farm. Where I found him and the horses."

"Interesting."

"Yeah. Well. Someday, I'll own horses like that. I'll ride a horse that will make Clay positively green with envy. Then he won't tell me to go make dinner."

Sarah lifted the agate roaster from the cook stove. Abby fell over, bumped her head on the chair leg, and set up a howl of protest. Drying her hands on her apron, Sarah hurried over, scooped her up, and held her close, rubbing a palm across the back of her head, crooning. She dropped into the armless rocker and began to rock back and forth.

Hannah finished the dishes, then came to sit with her mother. "See, if we breed these heifers as soon as our bull arrives, in less than a year, we'll have ten calves. If we keep them till they weigh six or seven hundred pounds, and we get seventy or eighty cents a pound, that's how much?"

She stared at the ceiling, her mouth whispering the sums. "That's five hundred and sixty dollars per calf. If we sell five and keep five, that's 2,800 dollars. We can pay Doddy Stoltzfus back, plus have seven or eight hundred in the bank. If we repeat that each year, Mam, we'll be wealthy ranchers with a herd of fine black Anguses, and horses the likes of which no one on these hick plains will have ever seen. I'll enter my horses in shows, and we'll collect one blue ribbon after another. I'll take them to state fairs and festivals in all the local towns."

"Ach, Hannah, I don't want to burst your bubble with my everlasting realism, but didn't Clay mention the fact that the Angus mothers have a harder time birthing their calves? I think we need to consider that. Perhaps divide the sum in half. We may have dead calves, or more unfortunate things. Maybe a hard winter."

"We have stacks and stacks of hay. If it gets too cold, they'll find their way to the barn. The Jenkinses' cows do. I'll ride every day, find the expectant mothers, bring them in, and sleep in the barn if I have to. I'll do anything, Mam. Anything to pull us out of poverty and depending on other people's charity."

There was a fierce light in Hannah's dark eyes, the set of her shoulders like granite. It frightened Sarah, this steely resolve. Unbreakable. Without bending to anyone's will. The reason she was so furious with Clay, Sarah thought, was she probably had meant to show him all she had learned, and with Pete. Well, it was sad.

How well she remembered instances during Hannah's school years. Bloodied knees, a black eye, torn clothing, notes from harried teachers needing help.

Once, she'd struck out in baseball and yelled and yelled about the unfairness of the pitch—too high or too low. Then she lost her temper completely, threw a stone, and hit the pitcher's shin, resulting in a serious injury.

Expelled from school, believing she was being treated unfairly, she never forgave the teacher fully, which always bothered Mose. He believed Hannah would not be forgiven if she didn't learn to forgive, even at the tender age of twelve. He'd repeatedly made her copy the Lord 's Prayer, over and over, until her head drooped and fell on the tabletop. Her breathing slowed and became shallow as she fell into a deep sleep.

Sarah remembered watching her lovely daughter in repose. A beautiful tyrant. And Hannah was still was just that. She could never be described as a sweet girl, not even a good-natured one. Half the days of her life were spent either irked at someone or feeling she had been unfairly treated. Perhaps it was well that she would never marry. Perhaps it was God's will that she live her life alone, growing old and presiding over her own ranch without the added nuisance of a husband, which was all the poor man would amount to. Sarah wondered about this Jerry Riehl—or was it King? What had she called him? Had he been the reason for her black, nightmarish mood? No, it wasn't possible.

She chuckled out loud, brought back to the present by Hannah's angry, "What are you laughing about?"

"Oh, nothing, Hannah. Nothing."

"What?"

"Just a passing thought."

"You have to tell me."

"All right. I was just wondering if your poor husband will ever amount to anything other than a nuisance. A bother, like an unwanted house cat."

"I hope you know I'm not planning on having a husband. Unless, of course, I'd go English and marry Clay." She watched for Sarah's response with narrowed eyes.

Quickly, Sarah caught herself. Her instant panic, her tendency to plead. She pretended she hadn't heard and gave her full attention to Abby, getting her to say, "*Gaul*. Can you say *gaul*?" It's the Dutch word for horse.

Louder, Hannah said, "I wouldn't want anyone for a husband, except Clay. He's the best-looking man I've ever seen."

Sarah feigned unconcern. "Is he?" and turned back to teaching Abby to talk.

Hannah flounced out of the house, down to the barn, where Manny was constructing a pen for the chickens, complete with a nesting box and plenty of hay.

"Aren't they allowed out during the day, Manny? I can see penning them up at night, but they should be allowed to eat bugs and stuff."

"What? With all the eagles and hawks and falcons that hover over this prairie? They'd all be dead in less than a week!"

"You aren't serious."

"Sure I am. Haven't you seen them swoop down all the time, eating the prairie hens and gophers?" Manny bent his back and began to hammer nails into a board.

"What will we feed them?"

"Laying mash from the feed store in Pine. They deliver with that rattling old truck for fifty cents."

Hannah had forgotten. They had money now. Money to buy necessities, to feed chickens, and have eggs for breakfast. They would live like normal people. Bake cakes and pies. A surge of exhilaration crept up her spine, giving her goose bumps.

Yes, they would not only survive, but prosper, with their aging grandfather's support. She could feel it, here in the dank air of the primitive barn, a testament to their father's lack of foresight.

A hovel made of logs. And yet, Mose had brought them here, secured the documents, laid the foundation for a successful ranch on these plains. She should think along those lines, instead of undermining his abilities.

Almost, but not quite, she remembered her father with kindness.

The silo crew arrived in Pine. A flatbed truck brought the hundreds of steel parts on a cold, dry day, when the atmosphere was heavy with dust and the smell of weary grass and dead insects.

Ben Miller stuck his finger up his nose, gave a good twirl, and said every hair in his nose holes was covered with dust and dirt, soot from the train, and if he couldn't breathe through his mouth, he'd have suffocated a long time ago. Back in Indiana, to be exact.

Whoever would think of moving out here in this flat land that probably even God only remembered from time to time? He forgot the rain, sure as shootin', and most of the trees too.

He talked the whole way to the homestead, then stood in silence, speechless, when he saw the dwellings that Mose Detweiler had built in the middle of a dry desert filled with dead grass and asphyxiated bugs, stinking groundhogs, and crazy little chickens that multiplied like rabbits. They were everywhere, dashing madly across the road, chirping and squawking, pecking and fluttering.

He told Ike Lapp that you couldn't begin to shoot a fourth of them. The rest of the crew consisted of two single men, Ben Beiler and David King, bachelors both of them, aged beyond their years of *rumschpringa*, unimpressed by the thought of marriage. They worked at manufacturing and installing windmills, traveling around the states whenever they felt like it. Both lived at home enjoying the coddling of their elderly parents, figuring they had nothing to lose staying single.

Ben Beiler was known as Bennie, David as Davey. They were chaps easy to get along with. Brown haired and brown eyed, both of average height, ordinary, clean shaven young men who had no astonishing features that separated them from everyone else, one way or another, both handsome or plain. They had never met a woman they could not live without.

When the dust rolled up toward the blue, cloudless sky, Manny came dashing in from the barn, shouting about the windmill crew's arrival. Breathless with anticipation, he stayed rooted to the porch, shading his eyes, calling to his mother and Hannah when the truck reached the yard. The driver was paid and sent back to Pine, and the four men turned to greet the occupants of the house.

Homesteaders. Ben Miller strode up and shook hands with Sarah and Manny, then clutched a reluctant, limp hand belonging to Hannah. Ike Lapp, Bennie, and Davey followed, meeting the favorite Amish greeting requirement of hand shaking.

"So," Ben Miller began, hooking thumbs like sausages through his suspenders. "This is where Mose Detweiler settled then, did he?"

Sarah nodded, a half smile on her lips.

"You're planning on keeping the acreage you got off the government then? Going on without him, are you?"

"Yes, we are," Sarah nodded.

Ike Lapp stuck his thin, white nose in the air and commented nasally about the lack of rain or trees.

Hannah thought he didn't need to make fun of them, so she asked him in a voice dripping with vinegar why he thought they were erecting a windmill. That got his attention.

It got Bennie's and Davey's too. They tried to deny it to themselves, and they did deny it to each other, but this tall, confident girl with the big, dark eyes fascinated both of them. Here was a girl with some spunk. When they walked through the powder-dry grass to the site they had agreed on, Bennie watched the arrogance of her shoulders. Davey thought her steps really covered some ground.

She spoke without thinking. She told Ben Miller if he didn't like prairie hens he should try living out here with nothing else to eat. They were quite tasty.

Bennie and Davey couldn't believe the family had lived here without money, without food, and barely decent shelter. Each one watched Hannah's face intently, stealing looks when the other wasn't watching. Obviously, this Hannah Detweiler was different, a force to respect.

They planned where the windmill would go. The well-drilling rig was arriving the following morning, so everything should be finished within a week's time.

The wind blew, lifting the men's hats, tugging at their trouser legs, and parting their beards. They retrieved their straw hats and clapped them back on their heads, only to have them torn off and whirled away. Ben Miller said they'd have to shut the windmill off or else their tank would overflow constantly in this kind of gale.

Sarah laughed. "It's not always this windy. I'm hoping we'll be getting some fall rains, now that the weather had cooled some." Manny squared his young shoulders and told them they'd get used to it.

Supper that evening was a lively affair. Sarah cooked generously, setting out canned sausages cooked with potatoes, lima beans, and onions, sauerkraut and fluffy white dumplings.

Ben Miller kept up a constant stream of Lancaster County news, interesting accounts of frolics, horse sales, and the high price of tomatoes. Some of his chatter bordered on gossip, blurring the line between truth and the questionable grapevine of which he was so fond.

"Elmer Beiler's Amos was scouted so bad the other night, he couldn't drive his horse and buggy home from Enos King's Emma, his girlfriend's house. They led his horse to the firehouse in Intercourse, tied it by the maple tree, there by the hitching rack. He got loose somehow and ran all the way to Bird-in-Hand without his harness.

"The buggy was taken apart so bad they still couldn't find one wheel. All the oil bled out of the hub and made a terrible mess on Enos King's barn floor. I don't know who put all that oil in the hub, but I bet the chaps who scouted them had more oil with them than what was on that wheel. Anyway, they carried his halter, whip, and neck rope all the way to the top of the windmill there at Enos Kings'. Henry Easch told me you could see it for miles around. They say Amos got *fer-late* with dating and told his girlfriend off. I heard the horse had a hoof condition and after galloping at that rate, he ruined a tendon in his front leg. Haven't heard if they put him down yet or not. Ach, such *dummheita*. Ain't never seen the likes. But I thought if Amos doesn't love his girlfriend better than that, she's better off without him. Amos has a quick temper. Wait till he finds out about this. The fuzz will fly."

And on and on. Ike Lapp stuck his white nose in the air from time to time, laughing uproariously, his beard sticking up like prairie grass, his Adam's apple bobbing up and down like a cork.

Hannah didn't laugh. She ate her sausage and sauerkraut and sat in her chair thinking how unattractive these windmill chaps were, greasy haired and pale as lard. She wouldn't cook for them if she was the boss. If they could sleep in the haymow, they could cook their own food. She slammed cups of coffee down and glared at all of them, including Benny and Davey, who, in her opinion, were about as helpful as two bumps on a log.

Until Manny told them about the cattle management here on the plains. They sat up, forgot making an impression on Hannah, their eyes alight, excitement in the way they sat on the edge of their chairs.

"Cowboying, you mean, son?" Bennie asked, extracting a toothpick and shoving it back between his lower teeth.

"Yeah. Oh, yeah. But there's a lot more to it than climbing on a horse and throwing a rope. It takes serious skill. I'll ask the Jenkinses to ride over and show you."

Hannah had never known Manny to be so talkative. His black eyes danced as he created pictures with his speech, his listeners rapt. Hannah broke in dryly to inform Bennie and Davey that it wasn't as exciting as Manny made it sound. There were no good horses around, so riding among those milling cattle was risking your life.

She didn't want a bunch of Lancaster County bachelors living out here on these peaceful plains. Next they'd all be raising cattle like a bunch of greenhorns, minding everyone's business but their own. Embarrassing to think about introducing Ike Lapp and Ben Miller to handsome Clay Jenkins, who, by the way, had nothing to do with her. So what should she care? She shared her thoughts to her mother after the men had gone.

"Hannah, stop it. You must not think along those lines. It's just wrong. God made these men, all individuals, loved by Him as well as all of us. Now you stop it. They may be thinking the same thoughts about you. Did you ever think of that?"

Hannah flounced one shoulder, than the other. "They both want me. They would both like to marry me. I can tell. I wish Manny would stop painting a spectacular picture for them. He makes it sound so enticing and romantic."

Sarah watched the expression on her daughter's face and thought, she surely isn't like other girls. But she said, "Maybe it is, Hannah. Maybe it is."

CHAPTER 24

The windmill arrived. The well-drilling rig ground its way along the level road, dust rolling in huge billows, prairie chickens running ahead of it, their necks stretched with terrified squawks.

The pounding of the well drilling equipment was a ceaseless clatter as they dug deep beneath the dry soil.

Ben Miller and his crew set to work pouring the cement foundation, with Manny's help, who was completely taken by Bennie and Davey. He told Hannah he hoped with all his might they would move out here to stay. They could start a small church service on Sunday; they had the beginnings of an Amish church already.

The Jenkinses arrived midweek, the men in awe of the steel windmill's construction. Hod proclaimed it the best windmill he'd ever laid eyes on. He had a bit notion to have the guy build him one. Until Abby got wind of his plans, squelching them properly with her rapid-fire tongue lashing, saying they had a perfectly good windmill, and he wasn't going to spend no money to build another one.

Clay took up for his father, followed by Hank and Ken, who chimed in, stating their case effectively. Another familial spat ensued, with Abby holding court like a small dog, getting everyone's attention with her wiry authority.

They stood as a group watching the windmill being set, a better construction, a better devised and assembled windmill, sturdier bolts, a gas engine in case of calm weather.

Hod laughed and told them to take that engine back to Pennsylvania. They ain't using it here, that's sure.

The well drillers hit a stream at 120 some feet, but it was a powerful one. The grizzled old man who ran the machine said it was one of the best, and he'd been digging wells for a long time.

"Lady, you ain't got nuthin' to worry about. Ye'll have good water for a thousand o' them black cows. Ain't no way this one's dryin' up. No way."

The promise of good water brought so much hope to Sarah, bolstering her spirits for days. With the dust and the wind, no rain all summer, she had repeatedly questioned their move back to the homestead when she lay alone at night with no one to talk to, no one to ask, except the fiery Hannah, who threw all Sarah's questions to the ground and stomped on them. To question, to think of quitting, was an unbearable weakness, according to Hannah. Sarah learned to keep her doubts to herself.

She wrote a check for the well driller and one for Ben Miller, cringing inwardly, wondering if this mountain of debt would ever be paid. She put her trust in God, having no one else. It came naturally, though, the submission, having practiced it all her life, although in the face of so much adversity, she needed to dig deep into the well of her soul to find the stream of trust and courage.

Sometimes, she imagined Hannah marching ahead, the flag of bravery hoisted in the air, leading her and Manny and the children. It was Hannah who had the pioneer spirit, the unflinching stoutheartedness that kept them going forward.

Had God made Hannah and given her this unusual personality for this purpose? Or was she a rebellious girl headed straight down the wrong trail? Sarah chose to believe the first as she watched Hannah sitting on the porch steps, her eyes scanning the prairie, taking in the endless possibilities of verdant, waving grass, her keen mind calculating, adding and multiplying, never dividing or subtracting.

And now, the glorious windmill and the deep, deep well, the tank of water that would never be empty. It seemed to Sarah that she could sense a new purpose in Manny, an eagerness in the glint of his dark eyes, a lifting of his young shoulders.

They were sad to see the windmill crew leave. Ben Miller's endless stories were a boon to their days. Bennie and Davey were brand new heroes for Manny. Hannah, however, could hardly wait to see them go and hoped those bachelors hadn't caught too much of the pioneer spirit. She didn't want them out here. At least Ike Lapp's nose got a bit of color. Actually, quite a lot. The sun and the wind had turned it into a deep shade of red that had started to peel like an old cherry. She just could hardly stand sitting at the supper table with that man. She told her mother to send their food down to the barn, but Sarah said no, you couldn't treat workers like ordinary barn cats.

Hannah cast her a look of disbelief. This comment, coming from her mother, surprised her. She realized that without her husband, she just might find a spark of new energy and get rid of the limp submission she had always portrayed.

The wind blew, the windmill spun effectively, the new steel water tank remained full and overflowing. The thirteen cows with the Bar S brand filed in regularly, milling around the tank, creating a quagmire of wet prairie soil, swatting their tails at the incessant flies, spreading mud and soggy grass into the clean, cold water.

Hannah didn't like that. The cows' water needed to stay clean, so every morning she strode out to the tank and skimmed the top and raked out the muck, keeping an eye out for the unpredictable black cow that had killed her father. Hod said she'd likely be all right; she'd just been riled that day from all the unusual activity with the calf branding. She had proved to be trustworthy when the new cattle from the Klassermans had arrived, so Hannah was not afraid, only vigilant.

She missed her grandfather's steady presence, his unfailing good humor. Sarah had been remarkably brave when she shook his hand, bidding him goodbye, their eyes saying the words that weren't necessary to speak.

Sarah had hoped he would stay but knew he couldn't. She knew her younger brothers would need him for the harvest. Another unspoken agreement was the telling of the loan he had given them. Her sisters would not need to know, the way they would raise a fuss. Her father knew it was probably the saving of Hannah, the keeping of her.

Ah, but it was a shaky deal, this loan, and her father knew it. It was risky, unwise perhaps. How much of it was done as a punishment to squelch Rachel's, Emma's, and Lydia's greed? Far into the night they had talked, her and her father, a golden memory so precious it was beyond description.

The bond between a father and a daughter was something she had never known existed. Always, it had been the women of the house who shared their feelings, her father always working, working, a man of few words. Now his words were priceless, each sentence laden with goodness, like mouthfuls of bread with fresh butter and honey.

The Klassermans arrived, the black Angus bull towed behind the spring wagon. Young and muscular, he was a real prize, Hannah could tell, as she stood by the barnyard fence watching their arrival.

She grinned up at their German neighbors, both rotund and sunburned at summer's end, dressed in freshly washed and ironed clothes, a broad brimmed hat setting low on Owen's head, squeezing his small blue eyes to an even smaller size. "Here comes the financial part of the Bar S," he called out. "A finer young bull ain't to be found."

Hannah nodded, still smiling. Manny came out of the barn carrying a pitchfork, his eyes alight with pleasure at the sight of their neighbors.

Sylvia heaved herself off the spring wagon, greeting them both effusively, then made her way to the house, carrying a heavy satchel.

Owen unhitched the sturdy brown horse and loosened the bull that had been tied to the spring wagon with a length of sturdy rope through the ring in his nose. "He's tired out, this vun," he chortled. "He had to run avays." True to his word, they led the black bull meekly to the tank, and released him, where he immediately stuck his chin over the side and began to drink.

Owen stood with his thumbs hooked in his fiery red suspenders and eyed the sturdy windmill, his florid face lifted to watch the spinning metal panels as they whirred against the blue sky. He checked the engine, the tank, and the large steel handle to shut off the turning wheel when the tank overflowed.

"*Ach, du lieva!* Dat is qvite da setup." He clucked and shook his head, walked around the sturdy concrete base to view the windmill from different angles, and asked who the company was that designed this thing.

Manny told him, gleeful, pleased to announce the fine craftsmanship of the Amish in Lancaster County.

Hannah wished she could elbow him in the ribs to get him to shut his mouth. Next thing, that whole crew would be out here again. Likely Mam would put them up and cook for them. Half the country would want a new windmill, and Ben Miller and Ike Lapp would bring their families and take up permanent residence. Bennie and Davey would both want to marry her, and that simply was not going to happen!

Owen Klasserman was taken by that windmill, like a fish with a hook embedded in its lower lip, reeled in to lay flopping on the creek bank. He looked up, muttered to himself and put four fingers into the cold water in the tank. He kept shaking his head, his blue eyes mere slashes of calculating light.

"Vot you say diss cost?" he asked shrewdly.

Manny shrugged his shoulders, his hands in his pockets. Hannah knew but she wasn't about to tell him. "You can't afford it," she said, cold as ice.

Owen's face whipped around to face her, his eyes opened to twice their normal size, his mouth turned into a perfect pink O. "Oh, ho, ho, Miss. You vatch me."

"Ben Miller is busy. He can hardly keep up with the demand."

Owen watched Hannah shrewdly. "I vait till spring. I vant to see hos dis operate in winter. How you gonna keep all dis ice avay."

"Break it," Hannah replied abruptly.

"Ah, ha. Outta da mouth of babes. You vait. Dis prairie put de Ben Miller to de test. Ah, hah."

They made an uneasy pact with Owen's announcement to delay till spring. Hannah's icy manner upped the cost of the bill by another fifty dollars, which she didn't need to know. That girl needed her wings clipped. Like a banty hen, she was.

Sarah wrote the check, thinking the amount was more than she'd bargained for, but didn't say anything. Hannah glared at Owen with large, black eyes as he pocketed the check, and he threw her a frosty look in response.

He mellowed somewhat, though, as Sarah set a wide slice of apple pie in front of him, accompanied by a cup of steaming black coffee. Sylvia asked if she had cream and sugar, Owen would appreciate it, and Hannah thought you could tell by his size that he wouldn't drink it black.

She thought of Clay, tall and lean, drinking coffee out of a thick, ironstone mug in Abby's kitchen, his blue eyes watching her without letting her know how he felt about her, now that she was back.

Sarah loved Sylvia's company. The sheer volume of her words and her heavy German accent were so *auhaemlich*, it reminded her of home and growing up among German descendants, with the flat, drawn-out vowels they uttered because the intricacies of the English language could be so hard to master. The only downside was that when speaking with Sylvia, Sarah could easily lapse into Pennsylvania Dutch, mixing it with English, sometimes in the same sentence, just like they did at home. But native-speaking Germans could not follow it.

Sylvia had brought *schnitz und knepp*, a dish Sarah had not eaten since the first move. Dried apples cooked with chunks of home-cured ham and spices, with a covering of thick, floury dumplings called *knepp*.

Sylvia also brought a pie made with thickened canned peaches that were baked into a pie crust sprinkled thickly with sugar, like sand. And *lebkucken*: butter cookies so heavy with shortening they fell apart.

The conversation flowed, Sarah's face became rich with color, laughter sparkling in her eyes, treating Sylvia like a sister.

Hannah didn't like *schnitz und knepp*. Whoever had come up with the idea of cooking ham with boiled dried apples, dark and curdled? That person surely had nothing else in the house to make for supper.

Hannah ate only a small slice of the peach pie, carefully scraping off some of the sugar and thinking it was small wonder this German couple resembled clean, pink pigs. But she didn't say it.

Sylvia had a fit about the house. She couldn't believe what a difference it made—the wall board and paint, the varnish on the newly sanded floors, curtains and colorful handmade rugs. A sink with a counter for Sarah to cook, roll out dough, and make pies and bread.

"Blessed. Blessed among vimmen. Eye-ya-yi. Viss da poor man dead and gone, so many udder blessings."

Hannah rolled her eyes and snickered. Sarah threw her a dark look. After the Klassermans took their leave, she turned to Hannah and delivered a firm lecture on good manners and resisted Hannah's pouting around after that.

When Hod and Abby came over a few days later, Hannah was in a better frame of mind—until she found out why they were visiting. They wanted a windmill!

Hod had won Abby over. She sat in the armless rocker and held Baby Abby on her lap, cooing and making the most ridiculous baby talk, which always came as a surprise to Hannah. This wiry, little woman, tough as nails, was reduced to the softness of flowery baby talk.

Abby loved this baby, who was growing up too fast. Her very own namesake was already crawling on the floor, prattling to herself, and stealing Abby Jenkins's heart so thoroughly that she never regained it.

Eli and Mary were fond of Abby Jenkins too. She always carried hard candies in her apron pocket for them. She asked about their schooling, her lined face softening like stiff dough turned out to rise. Her boys had grown up too fast, away from her, lured by the cows and horses, the vast land, and the excitement of every season. Crazy bulls and diseased animals, lost calves and thunderstorms, rodeos and bull riding.

A mother had to harden her heart after she realized she meant no more to her boys than a means of being fed and keeping clean, patched jeans and denim shirts in their dresser drawers. She'd thought she was through with the young 'uns till these people arrived needing help, and the poor, innocent children as hungry as calves without proper milk, and the poor father dead now. And now Hod's hankerin' after this windmill.

Hannah heard Hod asking for an address. She watched her mother, always ready to accommodate, produce a white envelope, pleased to help her neighbors acquire a new windmill like theirs. Hannah's eyes smoldered. She slouched in her chair and wished her mother would stop being so eager to serve everyone, so happy to help out their neighbors.

She'd been right about one thing. They'd have that whole bunch living out here right under their noses, just when Mam was loosening some of the restrictions of the *Ordnung*. Hannah had taken to wearing a dress without an apron and a small men's handkerchief on her head instead of a white covering. It was much more practical when riding a horse, cutting firewood, and forking hay, all of which turned a thin white covering positively gray.

You watch, she thought balefully, glaring at her mother's kind face. They'll arrive in droves, and I'll be back to keeping the *Ordnung* to the letter. Black apron pinned around my waist, white covering on my head. She knew her mother would live by her neighbors' consciences, her neighbors' scrutiny, crumpling beneath the gasps of *fadenkas*. "What would they think?" she would ask. According to Hannah, they could think what they wanted. If she felt better wearing a men's handkerchief on her head, then she would wear it.

Although she didn't know if she could ever turn her heart into the stone that would be necessary to turn her back and leave the faith, bringing a deep and penetrating grief to her mother. That was a leap across a yawning chasm, a division that had to be done by pushing love and obedience to the side, perhaps never to find it again.

If she chose that route, would the freedom to do what she wanted really be worth it in the end? Would it be worth casting aside the ways she had been taught?

Well, she sure couldn't tell now, with that Clay acting as if he'd never known her, let alone kissed her, and acting as if he couldn't bear the thought of her returning to Pennsylvania. Now here she was, back again, and him as hard to figure out as a thunderstorm. No matter how she tried, she couldn't understand why he even came around, sitting at the kitchen table with Hod as if nothing had ever passed between them.

He had about as many feelings for her as he did for Manny. Good neighbors, good buddies, and that was it. She watched

Hod's moustache droop into his coffee cup and thought that this is what Clay would look like down the road, lifting that row of hairs, beaded with moisture, out of the scalding liquid.

She swallowed and thought, "Ew." No, marriage was not for her. She had no plans of ever becoming dependent on another person. That was all marriage was. The joining of two hearts was just a nice way of putting it. What it really amounted to was just about the opposite. You lived with someone who had a big moustache or a large sunburned nose, or trousers that were too short, and let him direct your days, weeks, and months until he took over your whole life like a thief, and you weren't even aware of it.

It was yes dear, no dear, I don't know dear, until your whole self was numb and you didn't own a thought in your head. She'd never be happy like that. So, she resolved firmly, there would be no more quiet moments, no stolen times with Clay. If he loved her the way he tried to say before, he'd come around, and then he'd be in for a surprise. Sorry, sir.

Take Hod and Abby, for instance. She didn't want that windmill. Knew they couldn't afford it. The old wooden one still served its purpose. Besides, those longhorns could go days without water, like camels. But what always happens in the end? The woman give in, her words amounting to a soap bubble that rose out of the dish water and popped. And they weren't even Amish!

She thought Hod looked at her mother too much, so she got up and went outside, saddled Pete, and rode out to check on the cattle. She loved the word *cattle*. More than one cow. That's right. They had fourteen head of cattle. One big, mad cow, one unbranded bull, ten young heifers, and two bred heifers.

She wasn't sure how they would brand that bull. It seemed dangerous, no matter how mild his temperament. She'd ask the Jenkins boys. See how aloof Clay remained.

The day was perfect except for the sadness of the brittle, brown grass rasping together, the sound of no rain. Little puffs of dust rose from Pete's hooves. The wind was full of dust particles and the smell of it. She had meant to ask Hod if there would be snow in the middle of his predicted few years of no rain.

She could see the black bodies of their cattle, like lumps of coal on a great bed of hay. She rode on among them, turning to watch their ceaseless tearing at the dry grass, their long, rough tongues wrapping around it and ripping it away from the roots—chewing, chewing.

How many cattle would 320 acres support if it didn't rain? She'd ask Hod that question too. Wisps of dark hair loosened themselves from beneath her kerchief, the sleeves of her dress rippled in the stiff breeze. She should have brought a coat, a light shawl, or something, as chilly as it felt out here.

There was the new bull, easily found by its short, thick neck and rounded muscular shoulders that displayed his power. What a good bloodline they would have, Hannah thought. For miles around, their calves would be known. A goal, a dream. She'd make it a reality.

There was the large, black cow tearing peacefully at the grass, ignoring the horse and rider, intent on the business of filling her stomach. Or stomachs. Cows had two of them.

She thought Sylvia and Owen Klasserman might have two stomachs, as much as they ate.

Satisfied that all was well, she turned Pete back to the barn, her eyes searching the horizon for anything unusual. There was nothing, only the waving grass and the level horizon, the sky like a giant blue bowl above her. As far as the eye could see, there was nothing. To the east, the north, or the south. To the west were small brown lumps, the buildings of the homestead, their shelter for the coming winter. With chickens in their coop, cows roaming the acres, a milk cow in the barnyard, two horses, a wagon, a windmill, and a well, they were on their way.

Chills raised the fine hairs on her arms and ran along her spine. Anything was possible. Anything. Or impossible, if you chose to see it that way.

On the horizon now there was a shape, then a brown horse, the rider low in the saddle, the hat.

Clay Jenkins. If she would have been on any other horse, she may have been able to outrun him, but with Pete, there was no chance. So she sat, staring straight ahead, keeping her horse at a walk. She heard the dull clopping of hoof beats, the rustling of dry, brown grass, then heard her name, but she didn't acknowledge it.

"Hey!"

Slowly, she turned her head, the smile on her face forced and frozen. "Clay."

"What are you doin' out here by yourself?"

"What does it look like?"

He was close enough that she smelled the sweat off his lathered horse, heard the creaking of leather, the squeak of wood where the stirrups rubbed the leather bands that held them.

"I guess checkin' on the cows."

"Right."

There was an awkward silence, with only the sound of the wind in her ears, the snort from one of the horses as he cleared his nostrils.

"So how they doin'?"

"Good."

"Yeah, Hannah. A nice lookin' bunch. Decoratin' the plains with yer herd. All the same black color. Not an ugly one in the bunch. You wait though. Them Angus don't winter over so good. Come spring, you'll have a heap of trouble, come birthin' time. Angus is the hardest to birth."

Hannah was too busy swallowing her fury to give him the comfort of a reply. He thought he knew everything. Just everything.

When she didn't answer, he said, "Hey, I'm talkin' to you."

"Well, go ahead. I'm not talking to you."

"What was that?"

"Go away, Clay Jenkins. Just go home and leave me alone. If you rode over to make fun of my herd of Angus, then just leave."

"That's not what I come over for. My folks is at yer house."

"I know."

"Plus, I thought I might have time to catch you alone. Sort of take up where we left off, if you know what I mean."

"What do you mean?"

"You know. We were getting to be more than just friends. Getting to know each other better. Hopin' to know you even more, here shortly."

"It would be a waste of your time, Clay."

"Why?"

"I am never getting married. I have no intentions of being anyone's wife. Especially not yours, you being different from me. From our way of life."

Why was it that she so hated to use the words English and Amish? Like Angus and Longhorn, Hereford and Holstein. A labeling of a different breed, when they were all cows. So it was with humans, a label, a brand, the telling apart one from another. A necessity?

"You sound like you mean it," Clay said, quietly.

"I do."

"So if I come around tryin' to get sweet on you, it's a waste of my time? Is that what yer sayin'?"

When she nodded, she didn't look at him, knowing that if she did, it might well be her undoing. She knew the allure those blue eyes held, the look that came from beneath the brim of his brown Stetson. If she wanted to live life on her own terms, she had to watch her boundaries and know her limits.

In love, things were much the same as they were in finances and in the running of a successful homestead: You had to calculate and plan carefully. You couldn't afford any craziness. If you got caught unprepared, the way she'd been knocked off her feet by that Jerry Riehl, you wouldn't stay true to your goal.

She put that incident out of her mind, kicked her heels against an unsuspecting Pete's sides, and rode away from Clay, the triangle of the men's handkerchief on her head fluttering a farewell to the young man who leaned forward in the saddle, his forearms crossed in front of him, a light in his blue eyes, and a chuckle rumbling from his throat.

CHAPTER 25

THE COLD DID NOT COME GRADUALLY. ONE DAY, IT WAS CHILLY, AND you wished for a shawl when you rode out. The next week there was a band of frost like spiderwebs around the perimeter of the water tank.

Hannah got down to the serious business of preparing for winter. She would think the worst and prepare for blizzards. She worried about the amount of hay stacked to the west of the barn, whether it would amount to sufficient food for the cows. She fretted about this to her mother and Manny, saying if they had very many storms the size of the one they had had the previous winter, the cattle would not survive. They could not afford to lose one cow.

Sarah watched the shifting anxiety in her daughter's dark eyes and told her quietly to place her trust in God. He was the One who would see them through the winter, and if they were meant to prosper, they would.

Hannah ground her teeth to keep the onslaught of rebellious words inside, not wanting to hurt her mother's feelings. But there it was again—so much like her father.

Well, they'd go ahead and place their trust in God, but someone would have to think and plan ahead and then do the work. She asked Manny if he thought they could erect a shelter for the cows, a lean-to, sort of. Put heavy poles in the ground and cover them with sawed lumber and some tin for a roof.

They asked Owen Klasserman about a shelter. He said the cows could usually take care of themselves if they had the lee side of a barn and some haystacks. Here in the West, it was normal to lose a few cows over the winter, especially young ones. With wolves and coyotes prowling, you couldn't expect to keep them all.

Hannah told Manny that was all right for someone like them. They could afford it. The Jenkinses' rangy herd was too tough to die. They'd probably gain weight eating snow. She would not let go of the shed idea until Manny agreed to help her set poles and cut logs.

That was where Hod and his boys found them on a cold, dry October day, whacking away on some trees by the dry creek bed. Hod stopped his horse, his eyes quiet beneath his hat, watching Hannah as she laid down the axe and walked over to meet them. "Still puttin' up firewood, are you?" he asked.

Hannah shook her head and pulled the thin, patched coat tighter around her middle. Manny tipped back his battered straw hat and grinned up at the riders, his unfailing good humor intact. "We're cutting poles for a shelter for the cows," he informed them.

Clay spoke quickly, "Don't need no shelter."

Hannah chose to ignore him and turned her attention to Hod instead. "We can't afford to lose cows this winter. I thought if they have a shelter, they'd be able to survive. All of them."

Hod chuckled, a soft and low sound tinged with pity. "Clay's right. The Longhorns don't need no shelter. But you got the makings of a high-class herd, same's them other neighbors. They baby them cows. Same way with you. Yer gonna have to."

Hank, the quiet one, spoke up. "Don't know how you aimin' to set them poles. Ground's hard as a rock."

Hod nodded. "Ain't gonna be done. Not without a diggin' machine, which gets mighty expensive."

"We have money," Hannah said forcefully, hating the indication to their former shame, their hunger and desperation.

"Wal, if'n yer bent on havin' a shelter, then you best build yerselfs a lean-to on the southeast side o' the barn. That don't require no diggin' into the ground."

Hannah drew down her eyebrows, bit her lower lip. Why hadn't she thought of that before? Of course it would work. She wasn't about to tell them though. And she didn't, either.

Manny, of course, in his humble, guileless way, laughed and said, of course, of course, a great idea. That rankled Hannah, this being dependent on other people's ideas. She asked them why the southeast side. How did they know which direction the storms would approach? Take the blizzard of last year. There was no direction. The snow swirled and roared from everywhere.

Clay corrected her by saying there is always a direction. Hannah gave him a black look and said she didn't agree with him. His answer was swift and solid. "Who lived here on the plains the longest? You've only been here less than a coupla years, which, to my mind, pretty well labels all of you as greenhorns." This was said with a condescension that made Hannah so angry she wanted to rip him off his horse and . . . and, well, pound him with her fists.

Greenhorns! Who did he think he was? "We're not exactly new here. We survived, which is more than some folks do. Some don't last a year," she ground out.

Hod nodded, chuckled. "That's true, Hannah. True enough."

She cast Clay a look of triumph, but he was gazing steadily across the grass to the horizon, his mind elsewhere. As if she was a pesky fly buzzing around his head, she thought. They were all riding into Pine later that day for a beef barbeque at Rocher's Hardware. Did they want to come along?

Hannah wanted to go. Manny's eyes shone, thinking of going to town, meeting new people and tasting the local barbeque.

"S' gonna be bull riding and calf roping."

Sarah said no. Their father would not want them to go. His words spoke to her from his grave. He wanted to keep his children pure, unsullied by the world, to avoid all appearances of evil.

Her face serene and calm, Sarah spoke quietly of the Amish tradition of staying away from groups of worldly people who entertain themselves with unseemly activities. There would be music, which was a form of sin, and girls wearing jeans, uncouth men. No, it was no place for any of her children. If they obeyed her, they would stay at home.

"Just this once, Mam. Just out of curiosity. Please let us go," Hannah begged, her voice rising in a childish whine.

Eli and Mary watched, their eyes large and wondering. Manny took his mother's words as his law, his own conscience forbidding it if his deceased father had spoken of it. He could not go against his mother's wishes.

Sarah recognized this, knew the difference in her son and daughter. Hannah said she wanted to see the Rochers. They'd wonder what became of her. She was worried about Doris, knowing how easily she slipped into her melancholy state. "She probably misses me. Perhaps she needs me still, to work in the store or to clean her house."

Sarah would not budge. "No. You can visit Harry and Doris Rocher any other time. Stay away from the goings-on in town."

All afternoon Hannah struggled with her own will. She walked around by the southeast side of the barn and got nothing accomplished. How did the Jenkinses figure they'd get poles in the ground here, if they couldn't do it on the prairie? The ground was just as dry here as anywhere else. Sometimes those Jenkinses just irked her. Know it alls.

Well, if they thought an addition to the barn was in order, then they could dig the holes themselves. She wasn't going to do it.

Later that evening, she rode out on Pete, freshly bathed, wearing the triangle of dark blue on her head, a laundered and ironed blue dress with no apron, Manny's denim trousers beneath her skirt, telling her mother she was going to check on the cows.

Her hair was done to perfection, swept up along the sides and pinned in a bun low on the back of her head.

Sarah knew she was not checking on cows. Not after all that bathing and dressing. "Hannah, if you are going to town, please wear a head covering and a black apron, as our *Ordnung* requires." Hannah shrugged her shoulders and let herself out of the door without another word.

Sarah knew there would be no sleep that night. Hannah would be riding Pete for many hours. It would turn colder and she had only the light denim coat. Well, she would have to go out and sow her wild oats. She would have to learn the hard lessons all by herself. Her daughter's will of stone left her helpless, and her inability to guide and nurture Hannah was maddening.

Left alone with a thousand fears, a thousand thoughts of all the evil Hannah was subjecting herself to, was a new form of torture. Acceptance brought the realization that it was a necessary torture, this taming of Hannah.

Manny was furious, wanting to ride after her and bring her back. His frustration brightened his eyes with unshed, little-boy tears, but the set of his shoulders reminded Sarah of his impending manhood. Dear Emanuel. So much like Mose. So easy to love, to lay down his life for them. How could one child differ so much from another? She knew the tallest order was to love Hannah as she loved Manny. How could she, when the love she tried to give was flung back, discarded, unaccepted so much of the time?

Hannah rode hard, the cooling late afternoon air biting through her thin jacket. She followed the accustomed route along the dirt roads, now ground to a gray layer of dust, the dry, gray weeds hanging their heads by the side of the road as if taking the blame for the drought.

The road that led to the Klasserman ranch, the outer reaches of rusted barbed wire fence of the Jenkins ranch—she recognized it all and figured she'd have no problem returning, with the formation of the stars to guide her.

An exhilaration bloomed in her chest, like a white prairie flower touched by the morning sun. She was free and had won that freedom by asserting herself quietly, without anger or argument. She was old enough to be her own boss now, going on eighteen the way she was.

Enough of this thing of listening to her father's voice. He wasn't here. He was gone. Well, in Heaven, of course, but not here to tell her what was what.

They were just so old-fashioned, so anciently behind the times. There was nothing wrong with an evening of clean entertainment. So, well-fortified by her own cloud of justification, Hannah rode into the town of Pine, tied Pete to a clump of trees by the livery stable, and turned to enjoy the sights and sounds of a Western night in town.

The Rochers, of course, were delighted to see their Hannah back again. Harry grabbed her in a warm embrace, holding court over the large barbeque pit, his breath smelling strange and sour, which she suspected was due to an alcoholic beverage.

Immediately, the shame of her father's whiskey-making crowded out the cheers of the onlookers as Harry Rocher introduced Hannah to his loyal friends, Doris slipping a thin arm around her waist and kissing her cheek. The wonder of being loved and accepted by these friendly people erased the shame that had washed over her, so she turned a blushing, glowing face to the crowd, her large dark eyes with their lustrous light of excitement so beautiful that it took real effort for more than one man to turn their attention to their wives and keep it there.

She ate a plateful of the most delicious beef she had ever eaten. She ate a baked potato and applesauce, beans and home-made noodles. There were pies and cakes, cupcakes and cookies, breads and cinnamon rolls. Doris plied her with food, and more food. She begged her to come back and clean her house. Over and over, she did this, without taking no for an answer, her eyes too bright, her face pale and tired.

Hannah knew she should resist and tell this woman no. She had enough to do at home if she wanted to be a successful homesteader. But a part of her longed for the activities of town. Watching the ordinary people, labeled *worldly*, wearing dresses with pretty flowers and fashionable plaids, smoking cigarettes and cutting their hair, being allowed to do all these things without the threat of damnation hanging over their heads.

They were free and easy, conversation mixed with gossip and goodwill, enjoying the elbow room of their world. There were no restraints, no *Ordnung*. They could do as they pleased, every day. No wonder it seemed everyone was so happy.

There was an allure for Hannah. She felt the strong undertow of the world, beckoning her to come and taste this life of privilege. Being born Amish was not fair. She felt the harness of her birth, an uncomfortable slot where she was wedged tightly into a stall of expectation, the path of her life chosen by someone else, dictated and ordered by the authority that manipulated her parents' consciences as well as her own.

When the music began and the dancers swirled and stomped into an intricate pattern of color and movement, she could not hold her feet still. Sitting on the sidelines, erect, showing no emotion except for her eyes and the two bright spots of color on her cheeks, she carefully hid the movement of her feet. It was all so festive, so wonderfully lighthearted and carefree. The homestead and its cares, worries about the approaching winter, the safety of the cows, wolves and coyotes, all crumbled and fell away, as her heart swelled with the emotion of plucked guitars, drums, and harmonicas, a deep voice singing of a love gone wrong.

Had her love gone wrong? The love of her faith, her Amish heritage? Guilt stabbed her chest as she sat there on the metal folding chair, disobedient, leaving her mother and Manny at home to worry far into the night.

When she felt a presence beside her, she looked up to find Clay Jenkins, blond and handsome, clean-shaven, an invitation in his eyes.

"Dance with me, Hannah?"

Her eyes turned black with refusal, her tone clipped and severe. "No, I can't."

"You can't, or you don't know how?"

"What's the difference?"

"No, I mean yer religion. Or you never danced."

Down came her eyebrows and up came her chin. "I've danced."

"Well, come on then."

Her pride held her to the metal chair, resulting in a firm shake of her head, eyes lowered.

"You're just being stubborn."

A short girl with fiery red hair and a brilliant green flowered dress sashayed over to grab Clay's hand. "Clay, you haven't asked me to dance. What's wrong with you?"

"Hey, Jennie! Good to see you!" He grabbed her around her waist and whirled her away. Soon they were lost among the couples who whirled around the grassy town square, the smoke of the barbeque pit from Rocher's Hardware low above their heads, like a mist.

Hannah's eyes narrowed. There they were. Clay was holding her much too close. Jealousy and anger were hard to tell apart, but whatever it was, Hannah knew there was no way that Jennie was going to have the upper hand with Clay while she sat there like the dowdy Amish girl no one wanted. Jennie wasn't that pretty. Too short, for one thing.

Clay circled around, his eyes looking for her, and when he found her, they were a taunt, a mockery. *See, Hannah, I can have anyone I choose.*

It was too much. Like a boat tied to a dock, the winds blew and loosened the rope of restraint.

It was inevitable that he would ask her again. When he did, she rose, placed her hand in his and was brought up close by a firm hand on her waist, swept away among the crowd of dancers, a dreamlike quality enveloping her senses and erasing every negative thought.

How could anything like this be a sin? She was carried away with the looks of admiration cast their way. She knew what a startling couple they made, Clay so tall and blond and handsome, she almost as tall and dark as he was light. She reveled in the music, the joy of movement, the crisp barbeque scented evening air, being so close to Clay.

She had no trouble keeping up with the best of the dancers, whirled away from Clay on the arms of many other men who cut in, asking her to dance. She never tired, just wanted to keep dancing all night, waiting till daylight to ride home.

When it got late, the band played their farewell piece and amid thunderous applause, began to pack away their instruments.

Clay told her he would ride home with her and she accepted gladly. The night seemed very dark, the moon only a crescent that did nothing to light anything.

Without speaking, he walked her to the livery stable, saddled Pete for her as she stood watching, then went to get his own horse. She stopped to talk to Harry and Doris and promised to ride into town every Tuesday and spend the day cleaning or working in the store for a small wage. Harry promised to drive out and bring her back in the car, if her mother would allow it.

At the mention of her mother, and the word *allow*, the fairy tale of her evening of dancing in Clay's arms evaporated, leaving her heavy with dejection and an unnamed feeling of yearning.

She bid the Rochers a goodnight, and rode away with Clay, the lights of the town and its magnetism slowly fading in the distance.

The only sound was the dull clopping of the horse's hooves, the creak of leather, and the occasional yelp of a coyote. Hannah shivered beneath her thin jacket. She noticed that Clay had donned a heavy coat with a collar that looked like sheep skin. The cold night brought back the monumental worry of the fast approaching winter.

"I meant to ask your father—in the time of drought, are there winter storms, like usual? Or is the winter dry as well?"

"It depends. You can't tell. You gotta take it as it comes."

Hannah nodded, then realized he couldn't see that gesture, so she said, "Yes."

He remained quiet, after that, leaving her alone with her thoughts. Inwardly, she picked up the pieces of the responsibilities she had left behind when she rode into town. She came down to earth with a solid jolt, placed firmly back with her family, the homestead and, yes, her heritage.

She was a daughter of Mose Detweiler, the son of Mose Detweiler before him, born into a faith that would stand the test of time. Would she, herself, be able to stay true, to stand the same test? Tonight had been powerful and all-consuming; the desire for all things forbidden was too strong. She'd pulled away from her moorings, and now, with Clay beside her, she felt the loss of direction, the heaving and swelling of these turbulent waters. Waves crested around her, doubt pushing them over her creaking boat, almost sinking her.

What had her father always said? A doubter is *unfaschtendich* in all his ways. He is tossed about like the waves of the sea.

There it was, the thing she resisted the most wedging its way into her conscience—the voice of her father. Wryly, she shook her head, the darkness a comforting cloak. They stopped their horses at the corner where the barbed wire fence met the edge of the road.

"Should I ride on home with you?" Clay asked.

"No. There's no need."

"Well, Hannah, thanks for the dance." He guided his horse over until he could reach out and pull her close. She closed her eyes as he whispered, "I love you, you know."

Immediately she turned Pete and kicked the stirrups into his sides, startling the poor animal into an uneven gait that was mostly a headlong dash into the night. Tears poured down her face, the rushing night wind drying them as they fell.

Clay sat on his horse and listened to the disappearing hoof beats, shaking his head soberly before turning his horse and riding off.

Hannah rode blindly, allowing Pete to find his way in the dark, the battle within creating her helpless tears. Yes, she could love Clay, could probably be his wife, if she chose to do that. But she wasn't prepared for this evening, and now here she was, at loose ends and thoroughly rattled. She had to be careful, calculate every angle, same as with raising cattle.

Perhaps love came down on you like a winter storm, and if you weren't prepared, you'd perish, unprotected. She had to be very careful. She had to consider the truth. Her responsibility to her mother. The homestead.

Tonight had been a time away, a reprieve, a rest from the hard beating of the odds, surviving the prairie winter.

Foolish. She'd been foolish. Slipped off the path, in more ways than one. As this truth settled about her shoulders, cloaking her like a too-snug shawl, she shrugged, and then decided that all decisions were made wisely as the need arose. The time had not yet come to be forced into a decision.

Pete loped steadily along into the night. Hannah settled into his easy rocking gait as the cold wind spoke of the long prairie winter and whispered of snow and storm and fury.

The End

HOPE ON THE PLAINS

CHAPTER 1

THE BRISK WINDS OF AUTUMN FADED, LEAVING THE NORTH DAKOTA plains silent, dry, and dusty, the grasses that never ceased their brittle rustling hanging limp and brown. The sky took on a yellowish gray color, hanging above the Detweiler homestead as if it might crack and fall. The air crackled the atmosphere still and ominous.

Sarah shivered, rubbed her arms as she crossed them tightly to her waist, standing on the edge of the porch that looked across the level land to the barn, gray, weathered, its roof capping the logs with rusted tin, the fence around it brown and splintered. Every morning on that porch, the widow repeated her early morning ritual of gazing between the second and third posts of the barnyard fence, where her husband, Mose, had met his early death, gored by a displaced and angry cow with horns like sabers.

And she spoke to him. To his memory. She told him she loved him still, that today was another new day without him, but she was all right. She had the children. Hannah, strong, independent, a mind of her own; Manny, growing into another version of his devout father, conscientious, obedient; Eli and Mary, still so innocent, playing and playing on the endless prairie; Abby, the baby, growing, crawling, her little body a comfort to her mother when she held the child in her aching arms.

She turned, her eyes misty, her dark hair parted in the middle, the white head covering set on her sleekly combed tresses pulled into a bun on the back of her head. Still slim, her worn, faded dress a soft blue, a black apron tied at her waist, her feet encased in black stockings and sturdy leather shoes.

She stepped off the porch, her eyes drifting to their beacon of hope, the windmill, its rotating blades pumping the water necessary for a fledgling herd of thirteen cows and one magnificent bull. But the blades were still now, and the up and down movement of the pump silent.

There was no wind.

Sarah prayed, asking God to bless them with the wind. She never imagined praying for wind; in times past, its endless blowing could test the limits of her sanity.

She felt her daughter's presence before seeing her. Tall, disheveled hair as dark as midnight, her dress hanging loosely, surrounding her thin frame in ragged patches, worn thin beneath her arms and along the sides of her chest. And no apron—again.

Sarah didn't understand her daughter's aversion to the required black apron. It was part of the *Ordnung*, which was highly regarded in her own mind, the lack of it meant being partly undressed. No head covering this morning.

"No wind?" Hannah asked, her large dark eyes black with anxiety. Sarah shook her head, shivering.

"Well, we're going to have to go to town for gasoline. The tank was half empty last night. We have to get that engine started."

Sarah stifled a whimper. The engine terrified her. To think of pouring gasoline into a tank, the dreadful machine churning away out there surrounded by unpredictable cows and grass dry as bone, filled her with dread. But she hid this away, for Hannah's sake.

They ate their breakfast of fried eggs and homemade yeast bread, bowls of oatmeal spooned up and appreciated.

There was a time when breakfast consisted of barely enough watered-down cornmeal porridge to stave off the lurking hunger that made their stomachs, cramped and empty, growl with voices that drew down their courage and hope, leaving them to endure their days in wide-eyed incomprehension of what to do next. Until Hannah rode to town and worked for Harry and Doris Rocher, who paid her in enough flour and cornmeal to keep their stomachs filled and their courage up.

The 1930s were lean, the Great Depression causing hardship even in prospering areas of the United States. On the Dakota plains, stark reality was crying children, hurting with hunger and dark-brown questioning eyes asking silently for what no one could provide.

Sarah spread the fragrant butter on toasted bread, thanking God with every bite, her mind reaching out to her Heavenly Father as her spirit sang its praises.

"Hannah, when you go to town, will you wear an apron and your white head covering, please?"

Hannah's dark eyes met her mother's anxious ones, a quick rebellion thrusting its way between them, filtering out the love and obedience. "Why? There's no other Amish for miles, hundreds of miles. Who cares what I wear?"

"God sees. He cares. You are an Amish person, subject to an *Ordnung*. Hannah, your father's words should mean more to you than they do. You cannot still them by your disobedience."

"I am not Amish unless I choose to be, Mam." This with a proud toss of her head and a shrug of her wide, capable shoulders.

Fear clenched Sarah's stomach, a cold lump lodged in her chest as her oatmeal turned into a gray, inedible mass of anxiety. She longed for Mose's calming presence, his gently spoken words as wise as those of the biblical Solomon.

Nothing more was said, the dread in Sarah's mind obliterating further conversation.

Hannah rode off with Manny on the spring wagon, the triangle of a blue men's handkerchief fluttering from her head, and no apron in sight. Shameful, that patched dress worn thin.

Sarah knew that any further words of discipline would only fuel the fire of rebellion, so she let it go, turning to the dishes and her day's work, the crushing weight of her daughter's disobedience taking away the joy of the washing and ironing.

The mismatched team, one steady, thick muscled and plodding horse from Lancaster County named Pete, was hitched with a lean and rangy brown mustang, a gift from their neighbor, Hod Jenkins. He never acquired a decent name after Hannah said he looked like a goat. So Goat he was. Goat and Pete, a pathetic pairing, driven by a girl dressed in little better than rags, that ridiculous kerchief tied on to the back of her head, her shoulders wide and proud, her goal keeping her head high, her eyes alive and questioning.

She was a homesteader, the owner of the Bar S. A cattle owner. No one would have a finer herd. No one could get better prices at market time. They were well on their way, with the generous loan from her grandfather, the ten first-year heifers dropping calves next year.

They had a bank account, a checkbook, and cash in her pocket to buy gasoline. They needed coffee and baking powder and chicken feed. Laying mash for the flock of precious chickens was an unimagined luxury after the generous lending from their grandfather.

She drove the mismatched pair as if they were fine thoroughbreds, and the patched, jingling wagon with the loose wheel spokes a grand carriage, the picture in her head differing greatly from the actual lowly form of transportation, the endless gray dust that squelched out from the steel rims of the wheels launching into the still air before powdering the papery grass.

Hannah shivered in spite of herself. Her coat was too thin, too patched and worn.

On either side of the grass-lined dirt road, the prairie fell away, level, unmoving, and endless. As far as the eye could see, after the clump of cottonwoods and jack pines in the hollow where the winding creek was deepest and widest in normal weather, there was nothing but grass and sky.

The next road right led to the Klasserman ranch, a neat assembly of low buildings surrounded by heavy black Angus cattle, run by Owen and his wife Sylvia, a couple of German descent, hardworking, hard-eating and larger in size than most other folks who ran cattle and lived spare, lean lives that wore them down like polished wood, and creased and fissured their leathery faces. Not the Klassermans. They remained florid pink, smooth-faced and portly, their clothes pressed to perfection, washed until the whites shone blue.

After that road, a few miles farther, was the road that led to Hod Jenkins's spread. He had resorted to some barbed wire, the corner post leaning haphazardly, the wires rusted and sagging, like everything else around their place.

The sight of the corner post took away Hannah's proud thoughts and replaced them with a sort of humbling.

More of a put-down, she thought grimly, thinking of Hod's oldest son, Clay. Blonde and handsome, desperately in love with her, he was as bothersome as a determined green-headed horsefly. But he made her feel wanted and beautiful, everything she had planned to resist.

Would resist. For one thing, he was a person raised according to worldly standards. A non-Amish. An English. A chasm stood between them, a divide that Clay simply did not understand or try to. His comprehension of all things spiritual was distorted by his infrequent church attendance, Hannah thought. He claimed he went with his parents, Hod and Abby, but knowing them, they went on an irregular basis themselves.

Well, the neighbors' church-going particulars were none of her affair, so she wasn't going to ruin her morning thinking about Clay. If she was inclined to marry, which she was not, he wouldn't be included in the list of possible suitors. She'd have to travel back home to Lancaster County, join the Amish church, then take up the serious vows of church membership, which meant giving her life to God, accepting Jesus Christ as her master and the author of her faith, a prospect that seemed a bit daunting.

The Detweiler homestead was situated on 640 acres smack in the middle of nowhere, with not one other Amish family living closer than hundreds of miles, giving Hannah reason to question her future as far as staying Amish.

She put all of this out of her mind as they approached the dusty little town of Pine, situated among clumps of half-dead trees and rusted out cars, broken-down farming equipment, and peeling signs.

There was a livery stable, Rocher's Hardware, the feed store, two cafes, and a few bars, places of evil that Mose had warned his children were the devil's watering holes and to stay away from them.

There was a gas station on the edge of town by the railroad tracks where the redroot and tumbleweed sprawled among each other, both sifting dust and dirt and whatever blew past. Hannah stopped the team, gave the reins to Manny and pushed open the heavy door covered with cracked white paint, fly speckled, the long window splotched with grease and fingerprints. The loud bell that jangled above her head made her jumpy.

She didn't smile at the young man behind the counter, just looked him square in the eye and said she needed five gallons of gasoline and a can to put it in.

He looked back at her, then leaned on the counter, his elbows propping up his long bony shoulders, without smiling.

"You that Detweiler girl?"

"Yes."

"Hmm."

"I need the gas. Cows out of water."

"Oh, you got the engine, do ya?"

Hannah nodded, irritated, watching his slow movements, getting the metal gas can, dusting it off by blowing on it, wiping the top of the can with a greasy rag, then methodically thumping the numbers on the buttons of the high-backed cash register.

"That'll be two bucks and fifty-four cents."

Hannah counted out the money, ten quarters and four pennies, placing them on the counter before turning to pick up the empty gas can. She walked to the pump, waited and waited, then went to find the youth, who was bent over a red metal tub, his pant legs hitched above his ankles, fishing around in the cold water for a bottle of root beer.

"I need my gas can filled," Hannah said loudly. He came up with his drink, turned, adjusted his pants and said, "Git it yerself."

Ashamed to tell him she didn't know how, she stalked off, figured she could learn, unhooked the nozzle, and pressed a button.

Nothing happened. Red-faced, she tried again. Still nothing.

"Manny, get down offa there and help me with this thing," she shouted, holding the pump nozzle in one hand and the gas cap in the other.

Obediently he leaped off, hung the reins across the splintered dashboard, walked over, pressed not one lever, but two, and an aromatic stream of clear gasoline shot into the can. At the proper moment, Manny stopped the flow, capped the gasoline can, and hoisted it onto the back of the spring wagon.

At the hardware, they made their purchases, promised Harry she'd be back the following week, said hello to the wan Doris, who clasped her hand in both of hers and begged her to return.

The hardware store was more of a general store, stocking all kinds of groceries and housewares, fabrics, boots, and shoes.

The place had returned to its usual disregard for order of any kind, but Hannah knew there would only be time for an occasional day's work done there. The ranch required most of her time.

The ride home was even colder, the dry air slicing through their thin outerwear, cold and cruel. Manny said they could have brought a horse blanket. Hannah shook her head, chapped hands to warm them, and drew back a nose-full of mucus, her teeth chattering.

"This weather is odd," Manny remarked.

"Nothing's odd out here. If you expect the worst, it's normal. Terrible cold, high winds, drought, heat that scorches the grass, hailstorms—that's all normal. So why would we worry about a still day?"

Manny nodded, his eyes lifted to the yellow light that came from gray clouds, the air so cold and still. He didn't like it. The hairs on his forearms prickled with electricity.

The engine chugged away, propelling the pump into the well. Water gushed from the cast-iron hydrant, filling the galvanized tank to one half, three fourths, then to overflowing.

The cows smelled the fresh water, came from every direction, hopping, trotting and bobbing through the trampled brown grass. The sound of the engine stopped them in their tracks. Heads lowered, they stood grouped together, sniffing the air, ears forward like black flaps, their fear of the engine overpowering their thirst. The large cow, the one who had turned on their father, shook her head and pawed the ground, her breath whistling through distended nostrils.

"Watch her, Hannah," Manny said, tense and alert. Hannah nodded, shutting off the engine.

Snorting, blowing, the cows surged forward, dipped their noses and dry tongues into the tank brimming with cold water. Hannah stood watching the milling cattle jockeying for position, butting heads, tossing a smaller heifer like a half-empty sack of feed.

They started the engine again, leaning, yanking on the starter rope until it popped, backfired, sparks flying. The cows took off, panicked, bawling short, sharp sounds of craziness, their tails held aloft like baseball bats.

"Hey! Watch those sparks!" Manny yelled above the roar of the clattering engine.

"It'll be all right," Hannah yelled back.

When the tank was full, they shut off the rattling contraption, glad to regain the sense of solitude and sweet lonesomeness that clumped together out in this boundless land without end, bringing substance to an unstable world. It was always like that. A town, a loud engine, company coming, letters from Lancaster—everything was a tangle of noise and uncertainty. Alone on the prairie, everything came together and made sense. The sky, the earth, the cattle, hopes and dreams. Thoughts became reality, and reality became thoughts. A oneness with the land materialized over time, a fine, sweet message that flowed back and forth without effort. To feel the level dirt beneath her feet, knowing it held an uncountable amount of roots that would push new growth to meet the undying sunlight every spring without fail, was a promise of the future, a substance she could feel in her spirit.

If she listened to the neighboring ranchers, their past, their predictions of the future, she lost sight of this reassurance with the land. Folks just talked too much. They made her so tense and irritated. Take that Hod Jenkins and his boys. They'd as soon make fun of any new idea as try it out, stuck on that ranch that didn't know the meaning of the word maintenance. If a hinge on a door broke, they merely lifted the door to swing it open or shut on one hinge. Every empty tin can was plastered with buck shot, left to rust in the grass for someone to cut themselves on. Their herd of cattle was slatted with protruding ribs, pot-bellied, scrawny-necked and ugly, coarse hair hanging off them like dead grass. That didn't keep them from telling Hannah her fancy cows wouldn't winter over good and would need help birthing calves.

But she knew that without the Jenkinses, they would not have survived that first year. Generous and plain good-hearted, they took the Detweilers under their wings like a mother hen. Everything they had given, everything they had done, had been with the Detweiler's best interest in mind. Even as they begged them to return to Lancaster County because they weren't cut out to be homesteaders, the Jenkinses eyes were liquid with sympathy.

The cows watered sufficiently, they walked back together, the stillness of their companionship the only thing necessary.

They came up on the squat brown and weathered house, the dark smoke curling toward the ominous sky. Without speaking, their pace increased, anticipating the warmth of the cookstove, secure from the cold. They clattered up on the porch and yanked the door open to the smell of simmering chicken potpie, the children's chatter like birdsong, and the sound of Sarah's low singing at the table, where she sat darning a pair of stockings.

Sarah served them the chicken potpie in deep bowls of stone ware, and sides of applesauce and spicy red beets. She frowned when Hannah lifted her spoon and began to eat without the usual bowing of her head, eyes closed in silent prayer. Manny sat waiting.

Sarah reminded Hannah to pray before eating. After a whoosh of impatience and a shrug of her shoulder, she folded her hands and dipped her head, Manny following suit. They ate quickly, shoveling the hot food into their mouths, shaking their heads to cool their tongues when too much heat produced quick tears.

Hunger, or the sating of it, was not a matter taken lightly. "Why'd you kill a chicken?" Hannah asked after she wiped her bowl with a bread crust and jammed the whole piece into her mouth.

"I didn't. It's canned chicken from Doddy Stoltzfus's cellar."

Hannah raised her eyebrows and kept her comment to herself. Sarah lifted the cover on the cookstove, added two sticks of wood, and squinted at the billowing smoke before replacing the lid.

Eli played with blocks of wood and tiny bundles of grass tied with string, building a barnyard and feeding imaginary cattle. Mary pushed the wooden wagon, loaded the bundles of grass and took them across the floor, making galloping noises as she imagined a team of horses.

"Winter's coming," Eli piped up. "Better get more hay, Mary."

Abby crawled fast, wrecked the barn, and scattered the hay with baby squeals. Eli jumped to his feet, his hands grasping her soft, plump waist as he pulled and dragged her back from the cattle ranch. Abby set up howls of protest as she wriggled against the restraint. Hannah slid off her chair, bent to pick her up and held her on her lap, cooing and stroking her back.

"They should let you play. Mary, why can't she play with some of your blocks?"

"We need them."

"Our barn needs to be closed in," Eli chimed in.

Manny got down on the floor and helped them build a better barn, with blocks left over for a barnyard. He promised to build some cattle for them from blocks of wood with nails for legs.

"Grass for a tail! Grass for a tail!" Eli shouted, until Sarah held a finger to her lips, shushing him.

Night fell, darkening the windows with a smear of black. There were no stars, no wind, only the breathless silence. Inside, it was warm, their stomachs were full. Contentment lay in the folds of the white curtains, the simmering of the hot water on the back of the stove, in Sarah's drooping eyelids as she set cups of sugared tea in front of them. Night was closing in and she was ready to rest, weary with the work of the day.

Hannah said the engine worked well and the cattle had their fill of water. Now they would not need to worry about calm weather.

Sarah smiled sleepily, her mind only absorbing a portion of what Hannah was saying. She was thinking of long winter evenings with Mose, the times of happiness in Lancaster County when she was a new bride living in the small rental house at Uncle Levi's, her husband dark and handsome, their love so perfect and unspoiled, like a delicate rose. His kindness, his loving devotion, everything a man should be. She was blessed beyond measure in those days.

It was only her absolute devotion to the Bible and the art of submission that had taken her through the dark times that followed. She had not been blind to her husband's poor management of the family farm, but she felt it was not in her rightful place to assert herself.

Cows milked late, milk production dropped, and checks in the mail dwindled, leaving unpaid feed bills, horses dying of colic, mold in the grain, and wet alfalfa they should not have been fed. Sarah milked the cows until her arms were numb, her fingers stiff like newly stuffed sausages. And still she milked, trying to ward off the lurking mastitis, the dreaded clumping of the milk, and the blood mixed with the yellowish lumps as it came painfully through the teats.

When the Great Depression hit, the cows were sold to pay the feed bill. When the price of a good milk cow barely reached one hundred dollars and corn wasn't worth anything with no livestock to eat it, the slide into losing the farm became inevitable.

Yet he dreamed and refused to face reality, a cloud of goodwill and a rosy future would appear just around the next bend. They still had five good milk cows, a much smaller feed bill, plenty of hay, and corn to husk.

The bishop sent the deacon to talk to Mose about unpaid bills and the offer of allowing men into their house to "Go over the books," in his words. In his courteous manner he spoke of this being a help to Mose to relieve him of the burden of not being able to meet the monthly payments that were past due. Mose bowed his head, acknowledged that he needed help, and then went out and made his own arrangements. He set up the illegal whiskey still and turned all his grain into the *verboten* alcoholic beverage.

He felt despised, stomped on, hunted, and shamed. Excommunicated for this gross *ivva drettung*, the overstepping of set boundaries, he experienced public shaming to the fullest, his soft heart and easy-going manner wrecked, twisted, and wrung out to a fine pulp.

Still Sarah remained loyal and supportive. When the men went through their accounts, there was no alternative. The farm had to be sold for much less than it was worth. Mose made *frieda*, was taken back as a member of the church, his sins forgiven. Then, already, the decline of his good sense had begun.

Sarah sat, the darning needles clicking, her face serene in the glow of the kerosene lamp. But the dark circles that saddened her eyes into a shade of gray betrayed the pain of remembering, so intense at times that she felt as if she could not bear up beneath it.

Had she done wrong by being passive? How much could she have prevented?

Manny looked up from his building of a better farm, his eyes resting on his mother's, the sadness a common knowledge between them. Manny's was caused by his *zeit-lang*, and Sarah's by the pain of wishing that things had been different.

Still, she had carried his love and preserved it valiantly, in spite of his shortcomings, and for this, she felt rewarded and redeemed.

Sighing, she put away the darning needles, folded up the half-finished socks, and set the basket on the side cupboard. Her eyes felt heavy with sleep as she bent and lifted up Abby to wash her face and hands. Confused, she noticed an odd pink glow in her bedroom window. Was there a storm approaching so late in the evening?

CHAPTER 2

Sᴀʀᴀʜ's ꜱʜᴀᴋɪɴɢ ʜᴀɴᴅꜱ ᴘᴀʀᴛᴇᴅ ᴛʜᴇ ᴄᴜʀᴛᴀɪɴꜱ. Sʜᴇ ꜱᴛʀᴀɪɴᴇᴅ ᴛᴏ see. Her mouth opened, but no sound came from it. Then she called loudly, "Hannah! Manny!"

The pink glow turned into an orange line, low and wide, in the direction of the windmill.

The sound of their mother's voice froze both of them. They knew instantly there was something serious. They fell over each other, rushing to the bedroom. Both of them let out a hoarse, primal scream. Sarah directed as they moved swiftly through the house.

"Feed sacks. The sacks!" Hannah shouted. Manny burst through the front door, flung himself off the porch, and disappeared into the night, leaving Sarah and Hannah to run toward the dry burning grass surrounding the windmill.

Eli and Mary held Abby, their eyes large and frightened, Abby reaching toward the front door, wailing and crying for her mother.

They realized the situation was dire. The line of fire increased too fast to stop. Somehow, they had to reach the tank and immerse the sacks. They had to try.

Hannah stood at the edge of the fire, the heat sending a hard stab of fear through her sturdy leather shoes and into her stomach, feeding their desperation to stop the fire. The homestead was all they had.

"The tank. We'll flog a path through," Sarah shouted.

"There's no wind," Manny yelled.

"We can do this," Hannah ground out between clenched teeth.

The heat seared the soles of her feet as she dashed through the scattered flames. She saw the breaks in the line of fire, where the cattle hooves had trampled the grass.

Was there hope?

She threw the sacks into the tank, prodded them down as the greedy flames licked at the dry grass around them. As Hannah gripped a feed sack with clenched fingers, sucking air through clenched teeth, her nails bent backward, creating a searing pain. She brought it down on the low, crackling flames with a hard whoosh, the flames dying and leaving a black, charred area, stinking smoke and ashes showering them. One area blackened, and the flames leaped out of control in another.

Clearly, they had created a path to the water tank now. The dash to wet the sacks was possible without wading through a line of fire. The flames died down, only to leap up, hissing, brilliant. The sight of the fire devouring the dry grass banished any hope.

The night was still, the only sounds the crackling of the burning grass and the wet burlap sacks flogging the orange flames in bursts of smoke and ash. There were no stars or moon, only the canopy of black night sky and the eerie orange glow of the flames.

How long did they keep throwing those wet sacks around? Hannah didn't know, couldn't speculate, her world suddenly turned into a searing nightmare of heat, flame, and the stench of smoke and black ashes.

She noticed that the burnt grasses turned into bits of white, like tiny worms that appeared for only a second then disappeared. For a fleeting moment, she saw the homestead, its puny buildings tinder dry, gone up in smoke like a blade of grass.

They became hopeless when the surrounding line of flames grew in spite of the blackened path, the avenue of charred grass mixed with hot dust and dirt.

Hannah flogged on, beating the earth until her face burnt, her shoulders and arms numb with fatigue. The ever widening area of burned grass was only an unstable victory. She sensed the dancing, licking greediness of the blaze devouring dry grasses so easily, increasing the red and orange flames. Manny's face was as black as the night sky, with white lines zigzagging along his cheeks where the tears of desperation had fallen. He was like someone gone made, running and flogging with a maniacal speed of despair, a pace he could not hope to keep up.

Sarah worked grimly, a determination born of panic driving her on. They had to save the buildings. There was hope, in spite of the futility of these wet sacks beating on the flames. She cried out as she saw a new line of fire breaking out toward the direction of the house.

Dear God, is this your will? Are we simply not meant to be homesteaders? Are we meant to reside among others like us, secure together in body as well as spirit?

She knew the situation was dire long before Hannah and Manny did. But she figured that, as long as God gave her strength, she would fight on. The path to the tank grew longer and longer, the blaze spreading wider. How long until Hannah saw this?

She watched her daughter beating and beating, stomping on flames, her skirt charred and blackened, her face a caricature of herself, her hair, coming loose as the pins fell out, surrounding her face in tendrils, like a wild woman. Her eyes were swelling from the heat and smoke.

Sarah stood still, making raspy sounds as she breathed in and out, her chest heaving, her throat feeling charred and burnt.

Taking stock of the situation, the panic rose in her chest, filling her senses. They need to flee, to get away now. She calmed herself, not wanting the children to see absolute abandonment in her need for a headlong dash away from this heat and uncontrollable dry grass. She needed to think and speak rationally.

"Hannah!" she called loudly, her voice carrying above the sound of the crackling prairie fire.

Hannah was deaf to her mother's voice, lost in a world of agony and defiance, her determined nature now leading her to the brink of foolishness.

Sarah screamed in a high and desperate voice. "Hannah!"

Manny stopped beating the flames and ran over to his mother, his eyes dark with rings of white in the eerie glow.

"It's no use. We can't do it," Sarah choked.

Manny nodded, ran over to Hannah, and yelled in her ear. She elbowed him away and kept up her demented flogging and beating with a gunny sack half eaten away by the flames. She stomped and danced, her head down, her arms outstretched as if the power of her own determination would yet deliver them from this horrible evil.

Manny grabbed her arm, yelled and pulled her away. She fought him off, the gunny sack flung in his face. She beat his shoulders with her fist, kicked his shins, his legs and feet, screaming hysterically.

"No! No! Come on, Manny! No! No!"

Sarah ran and grabbed Hannah by the waist, pulling her away with supernatural strength. Hannah twisted and yelled, shrieking threats and beating the air with her fists. Manny grabbed her kicking feet and held on.

Without speaking, they gave up the fight. They had all they could do to get Hannah away from the flames. Sarah could not think of what this would do to her daughter, knowing what can happen to a person so unusually determined to be pushed over the brink.

The thought of her Aunt Suvilla sent shudders of fear through her. They hadn't known what was wrong. No one did. Put away, they called it. Put away in an insane asylum. Please, please, please. Her pleading came with her gasping breath as she begged for deliverance from so harsh a punishment.

In the end, their strength gave out. They had to rest. Crying and screaming, Hannah tore out of their grip and took off into the night and the disastrous orange flames. There was nothing they could do but lay spent and gasping, their muscles burning with fatigue. It was only the thought of the terrified children and the need to get away, that roused Sarah and set her on the path of action.

"Manny!" she panted. "Get the horses hitched. Take the lantern. Bundle the children into their coats. Go. We have to get away."

"Will it take everything?" Manny gasped.

She could not soften the blow. "Yes! Go!"

She thanked God for Manny's obedience and began walking in the direction of the fire. "Preserve Hannah's mind, Lord. Preserve her spirit," she prayed. Soon enough she saw her, stomping on the flames, as useless as she had ever seen anything. The windmill behind her, the arc of blackened earth, the ever-widening wreath of burning grass and white smoke against the cold, black sky—the hellish scene etched in her mind forever.

"Hannah!" she screamed. "Hannah!" Sarah went to her, wincing at the heat coming through her skirts and on the soles of her shoes, the fire's searing brilliance ever powerful, ever increasing. Sarah drew on Hannah's sleeve, tugged at her skirt, begging, crying, her breath coming in painful puffs of air. "Hannah!"

The sound of panic in her mother's voice broke through Hannah's maudlin stomping. She stood stock still, her dark eyes staring without seeing. Dear God, have I lost my eldest daughter? Suddenly a fierce and undeniable hatred of Mose's ill-timed journey to North Dakota speared its way into Sarah's mind.

She had submitted, had obeyed the whole way, the whole senseless, ridiculous way. She cried and screamed, lifted her face to the dark sky and allowed herself the luxury of regret and remorse. The power to save her daughter from this awful fate fueled the confrontation of who she was.

To this end, then, she had blindly obeyed. Her screaming broke through Hannah's sense of shock. With a broken cry, she threw herself down, groveling and clutching Sarah's blackened skirts, whimpering, a lost sound devoid of courage.

Sarah bent down and lifted her up. Supporting her with an arm around her waist, she drew her away. Pliant now, her head fallen forward, Sarah guided Hannah with an arm about her shoulders and then around her waist.

Murmuring half-prayers and half-endearments incoherently, Sarah stopped and turned to kiss Hannah's cheek. She tasted soot and ashes, and the salt of Hannah's tears. Broken, they stood together weeping hoarse sobs of pain and defeat, acceptance and helplessness.

"Come, Hannah," Sarah murmured gently. Hannah nodded. And then, in a gesture Sarah would never forget, laid her head lightly on her mother's shoulder. Dry, hacking sobs and coughs tore from her raw throat.

"It'll take the buildings," she croaked.

"Yes."

Mother and daughter, united now, turned back toward the house, tears mingling with ashes from their a baptism of fire, introducing the uncharted territory of homesteading in the West. So far, determination and the help of family and neighbors had kept them afloat. But from here on, on this terrible night, there was no direction.

They looked back and saw the ever-widening circle of flames. Spurred on by fear, they ran to the house, stumbling painfully on leather soles half burned away. Up on the porch, they grabbed the little ones, hushing, cajoling.

What to take? What to leave? No matter. The windows reflected the orange glow. Hurry. Oh, hurry. Will the horses outrun it?

A high yell from Manny in the direction of the barn. The wind. The wind was getting up. Sarah snatched quilts, blankets, towels, the checkbook, the coins in the crock.

For what? For what? Blindly they ran out into the night. She felt the wind. Plainly, she heard the distant crackling, the yellowish glow lighting the dark.

"The chickens! The cow!" Hannah shouted.

"I let them loose! Manny shouted back, hanging onto Pete's bridle. Goat snorted, his hooves digging into the earth. Fire terrified horses.

They threw themselves into the wagon, stuffing quilts under the seats. As Manny let loose, the horses reared and leaped, knocking him onto the seat. He grabbed the reins. The wild dash into the night began.

Hannah looked back at a wall of crackling orange. The buildings etched in black harbored their belongings—the cookstove, the plank table made by Mose's own hands, the beds and the washtubs, the dishes and pans. All of it would be devoured by one spark from the new gasoline engine.

She turned away, the picture of all her hopes and dreams an unbearable vision. She clung to the seat and hung on to Eli, wide-eyed and crying.

"You have to slow them down, Manny," Sarah called hoarsely.

He nodded. "Klassermans?" he croaked.

"They're closest."

Owen and Sylvia were deep in their first slumber of the night when Owen dreamed there was a woodpecker talking to him, his mouth in a smile, telling Owen he'd better check the front door soon. He woke with an unnamed dread and a cold chill, aware of his wife's soft hand shoving at his shoulder and saying, "Owen. Owen. Owen."

He swung his legs down from the high bedstead, his feet scrabbling for the stool he used to get in and out of bed. He missed it and fell hard on his hands and knees, a whoosh of air and a grunt pushing from his mouth.

"Ach, Owen. Get up." Sylvia, talking to him from the folds of warm blankets. Fumbling for his trousers, he placed one pink foot into an opening and jammed his toes into a pocket before untangling himself and trying again. The knocking was louder and faster now.

Muttering, he let himself out the bedroom door, wondering if he should grab the rifle or what. Such a pounding on his front door!

His eyes stretched enormously to see the blackened huddle in front of him. The story came tumbling out in swift sentences, sending Owen to the telephone to call the fire department and all the surrounding neighbors. He held the mouthpiece and yelled into it, the dim electric bulb from the ceiling making the desperate group appear more burned and terrified.

Sylvia appeared in her fluffy pink housecoat, her eyes popping then streaming with tears of pity. She couldn't help but think of the time spent on her hands and knees wiping the linoleum on the floor, and now here it was, covered with black soot. They smelled terrible, just terrible. But *ach*.

The wind confused them after days of silence. It moaned and sighed in the cold night and tore at the corner of the roof where the downspout wasn't fastened properly. It whistled around the corner of the porch, lifted the door mat and folded it in half, sent a half-dozen barn cats scurrying for cover.

Back at the homestead, it whipped the burning grass into a fury of heat and light. The flames danced across the plains, eating away at the dry, unpainted logs of the buildings. It licked greedily now, gulping wood and mortar, growing hotter and hotter as the wind rose in strength, riding before the storm that had been lurking in the gray bank of clouds for days, waiting to unleash its pent-up power.

The work of Mose Detweiler's hands was ravaged, gobbled up in less than an hour by the raging inferno, whipped by the oncoming storm. There was no one to observe, no one to record the actual time.

The fire engines arrived clanging, but by now the fire had spread wider and was completely out of control. Telephone wires crackled with the news until the poles went down, annihilated along with everything else in the fire's path.

The laying hens cackled and squawked as they ran before the wall of fire with the gophers and rabbits and prairie hens. The milk cow ran clumsily, her poor udder swinging and her eyes wide with terror until she succumbed to the power of the smoke and heat, like every other living thing in its wake.

When the ice and freezing rain started, appearing as wet splotches the size of dimes, driven sideways and slanting against the night sky, pelting the house's sturdy German siding, they all thought it was only the wind increasing. But soon they realized what the sound against the glass window panes was.

Manny's face lit up, the hope burning in eyes so like his father's, believing, with faith like a rock, that his prayers were answered. The homestead would be saved, there was no doubt.

Sarah turned her head and saw the ice and cold rain sluicing down the window panes. She silently calculated the distance between the windmill and the buildings and was afraid to hope.

Hannah stood still and listened. Bitter. Too late, likely. So much for God helping you out. And yet, for a fleeting instant, she hoped.

The freezing rain and the wind turned into a maelstrom of sight and sound, pounding against the north side of the house, then the south. The wind shrieked and roared. The cold deluge clattered against the windows, flung on the house as if giant arms were throwing it.

Eli held both hands to his ears, palms sweaty with panic and little boy agitation. "Mam, Mam," he whimpered, his black eyes like wet coals.

Mary went to him and held him in her thin arms. She stroked his shoulder and said, "It's only rain, Eli. And wind. *Yusht da vint.*"

Owen sat at the kitchen table, his round face sober, his eyes glinting in the electric light. Sylvia was in the closet, rummaging for clothes for Sarah and the two oldest children. They smelled bad. She could hardly breathe.

She filled the claw-foot tub with hot water from the spigot, the stopper to the drain attached with a small chain. She gathered clean towels, a bar of soap, washcloths, and two flannel nightgowns she had outgrown. Holding one up to her shoulders, she shook her head in disbelief. Had she really been that small once?

Back at the homestead, the wind whipped the fire into a hellish frenzy, its power growing until it could gobble up anything in its path. The greedy blaze devoured acres of dry grass, reducing it to flat, black ash that left little puffs of gray smoke and white dust whirling away into the night.

When the thunderous black clouds finally unleashed their pent-up rain and hailstones, the sky poured unlike anything the huddled ranchers had ever seen, and they thought they'd seen everything.

In only a few hours, the out-of-control burning turned the land into a black, stinking, mushy slime dented with ice pockets, hailstones sizzling and steaming in seconds. The clattering ice and rain made hissing and spitting sounds as it fell on the raging flames, firing shoots of white steam toward the roiling black sky.

Ranchers and firefighters stood by their various forms of transportation until the power of the deluge sent them inside.

Hail bounced off metal rooftops and windowpanes, and the torrents of icy rain made driving impossible.

The flattened brown grass bent to the onslaught. The cracked earth took on piles of ice and water sluiced into the broken, parched soil. The rain was too late for the crops, but it restored the water table beneath the grass.

Years later, the ranchers would speak of the fire, the sizzling and steaming clouds of it that people spotted as far away as Pine. The storm had saved them all. Hard telling where the fire would have stopped had the rain not come. They would have needed to dig trenches to save ranch buildings. Stretched to the limit by the local gossip, the night of the storm was told and retold, around dinner tables, in church yards, and in cafés and bars. Hashed and rehashed, until it was chewed to a pulp.

At the Klassermans, Sarah lay in the clean guest bed that Sylvia had made, little Abby held snugly in her arms. She was exhausted. Weary beyond anything she had ever experienced. The muscles in her arms burned with the extended force and movement of the wet feed sacks that had pushed her to her limits and beyond. Her legs ached and felt like stumps. Her lips were numb, scorched by the heat and smoke. Her face was chapped and dry. She reached up to feel the lashes on her eyes and eyebrows and was met with smooth, hairless skin.

She cried, then, hot scalding tears of hopeless despair, the loss of her eyebrows the final shove that sent her headlong into a chasm of anguish. She drew up her knees as she whimpered and sobbed, stuffing a fist against her mouth to keep from waking Abby.

The rod of God's chastening had fallen hard, more than she could bear. What had she done to deserve this? Must one person reap what another had sowed? When she became Mose's wife, they had become one. Was punishment meted out bit by bit to her as an accomplice in Mose's follies?

She squeezed her eyes together, moaning softly with the pain and humiliation. She had followed him, this wild land an anchor for his dreaming. Footloose, unstable he was. Oh, he was.

The future loomed, a bitter cup. Sarah's family could not be expected to come forward yet again. All Sarah and the children had were two worn-out horses, a rusted wagon that jiggled, clothes that reeked of fire and smoke, a few quilts, and she hoped, a handful of bewildered cattle that had been bought with her father's money. She prayed to keep from blaming Mose. She prayed that God would purge her heart and show her the known and unknown sins she coveted. *Vissa adda unvissa.* To be beaten back time after time, surely God was showing her something about her life—a wrong, a sin, a rebellion.

In the adjacent guest room, Hannah lay with Mary and Eli beside her on smooth and spotless sheets smelling of lavender and mothballs. The quilts pressed her ravaged body into the mattress.

She was bone tired. She could be dead the way her body felt, but she guessed that as long as her heart was beating and her lungs were breathing, she was still alive, so that was something.

Stupid old gas engine. That Ben Miller didn't install it right. Probably Ike Lapp did it. One spark, two or three, whatever. If the storm had arrived even a few hours earlier, the buildings would have been saved. She railed against God about how the Higher Power handled what she couldn't control. But her sensitivity to sin and wrongdoing steered her away from blaming the family's misfortune on God.

Well, all right then; here is what it was. The homestead was a soupy black mess that smelled worse than Sodom and Gomorrah. One windmill. Some frightened cattle. Two horses and a wagon. Everyone safe. They'd need to make a phone call to Lancaster. Her grandfather's neighbor could find him and bring him to the house.

News would spread. The biggest hurdle, as Hannah saw it, was going to be her own mother's need to return to the safety of Lancaster County. To persuade her to start over was the closest thing to an impossibility Hannah had ever encountered. Who could do it?

An iron fist closed around Hannah, the will to stay and start overflowing in her veins, revitalizing her fatigue. She envisioned a new house, long and low, a real ranch house, a barn, the grass lush and green and waving; the cattle fat and black, multiplying like rabbits, being driven to Dorchester where the auctioneer's gavel crashed down on the highest prices.

Everyone would know the superiority of the Bar S brand. Somehow, she needed to procure another loan. First thing in the morning she'd make that telephone call without Sarah knowing about it.

CHAPTER 3

THE COLD CAME WITH DETERMINATION, RIDING IN ON THE WAKE OF the storm a month earlier than usual. It came at night, freezing a lid of ice on the cow's water tank and coating the crumbling dry grass with hoarfrost resembling sugar crystals. The dry creek beds welled with turgid brown water that seeped into the cracked, parched earth and left slabs of thin brown ice along its banks that looked like torn slabs of moldy bread.

The cows grew winter coats and stood hunched against the cold, their eyes slashes in their faces, warding off the frost. Acres and acres of burnt prairie grass froze to a blackened permafrost, a sort of nighttime Arctic, someone's overwrought imagination come to life.

Owen and Sylvia kept them all safely tucked in the warm ranch house, the fire burning and crackling cheerily in the two wood stoves. As news of the fire spread, farmers and townspeople bearing bags of clothes and boxes of pans and plates, glasses, knives and forks, blankets and towels stopped at the Klassermans in their chugging cars and trucks.

Hannah made the phone call home, relating the events, her voice strong and without emotion. The word spread quickly, ears bent toward the shocking news. That poor Sarah. They shook their heads, clucked their tongues. Hadn't the poor woman had enough?

Ei-ya-yi. And they stepped forth. They couldn't blame hard times. In the time of tragedy, you gave freely, never questioning. Give and it shall be given unto you, packed down and flowing over.

And they did. The relatives gathered clothing and furniture. Some gave money. Samuel Stoltzfus, Sarah's father, sat at his kitchen table with tears flowing silently down his face, glistening in his white beard, the humble gratitude overflowing.

Jeremiah Riehl was shoeing a horse for a customer, Henry Esh, the horse leaning all his weight on the hoof tucked between his knees. Henry kept up an endless volley of local news peppered with gossip. Jerry's shoulders burned with the strength needed to keep the hoof intact. He was tired of listening to Henry's blather, and this horse was about the most contrary creature he'd shod all week.

He heard North Dakota. Immediately, he let go of the hoof, straightened his back and stared at Henry, his dark eyes intense.

"Yeah, burned up. They say there's nothing left. Burned up the house and barn. They say it wasn't much to begin with. That Mose Detweiler was an *aylend*. They say his wife will come back now, but the oldest daughter won't. Ray Miller said the only reason they're out there is because of her. She's something else. Must be like her old man. You know they say it rained so hard the fire was out in five minutes. Five minutes! I guess the way it sounds the weather out there is hardly to be trusted.

"So I don't know what's gonna happen. Old Samuel Stoltzfus is getting ready to go out again. Folks are giving things, and he'll probably end up with a railroad car load of stuff."

He stopped and went over to the open barn door to send a stream of tobacco juice into the crisp November air.

"Weddings going full sing, right now. Don't you think you better start courting someone? You're not getting any younger."

Jerry didn't hear that part of Henry's string of words. He was still thinking about North Dakota. About Hannah. "So how'd this fire start?" he asked.

Henry roared and slapped his knee. "Boy, you're a slick one! Avoid talking about what I just said."

Henry took his leave, driving the newly shod horse and leaving Jerry in a fuzzy state, his mind hundreds of miles away, out on the plains of North Dakota. He didn't understand his need to go and see for himself what had actually occurred, to see for himself what they had come through. Mostly, though, he wanted to see Hannah.

Was she suffering? Broken down? Where was the family staying? How could he go without raising suspicion?

When he heard of a group of men and boys going to help rebuild, he put his name in. He met the raised eyebrows of his sister and her husband with a bland questioning look, one of innocence, so that she told her husband perhaps there was nothing to her wondering if Jerry had been attracted to Hannah that day she had been caught in the rain. After all, it wasn't unusual for a young man to get the fever to go West. Not unusual at all.

Emma wanted to go. She felt she could persuade her sister to come back and live a decent life among God-fearing Amish instead of yoking herself to the world. Those western heathen were no good for the family, especially that Hannah.

Samuel said point blank there was no work for the women until the house was up. Emma blew up, enraged at her father for even thinking of helping them rebuild. What in the world was wrong with him? If Sarah planned on staying out there for Hannah's sake well, then, she was going to wash her hands of the whole affair, and she certainly hoped he wasn't too generous in his giving.

Samuel told his daughter in a patient, even tone that no, he wasn't too generous; other folks had given so much that he believed he'd need most of one railroad car to take it all.

Sylvia Klasserman had a minor breakdown that resulted in the neighbors erecting a sort of shack to house the family while they worked on rebuilding.

Sylvia was from an old aristocratic German family and was given to extreme cleanliness, a way of life that decreed that certain jobs be done on certain days. Washing on Monday, ironing on Tuesday, and so forth. Her washing was done in her Maytag wringer washer, rinsed twice, once in vinegar water and once in water containing blueing, her whites so white they shone blue. She ironed everything, even her bed sheets and Owen's underwear. Every six weeks she took down her white curtains and washed them, rinsed them in blueing, and ironed them. She washed walls and floors and furniture. She scoured the claw foot bathtub and the small sink beside it.

Her bread baking was done on Wednesday, her pie baking on Thursday. All her belongings had a place and were always in it or on it. Cast iron frying pans were hung by size, her turners and spatulas in certain compartments in certain drawers. When the tin of lard was brought out of the pantry, it was never returned before a good washing with soapy water.

When her immaculate house received two children and a baby, it scrambled all her ingrained priorities. The laundry was washed haphazardly, the ironing not even close to her specifications, not to mention the cleaning and dish washing.

And oh, that baby!

Sylvia didn't want to be this way. She wanted to relax and give over for the dear homeless family. But in the end, she just couldn't do it.

Abby Jenkins snorted and shook her head. She invited the family to stay at the Jenkins ranch. But Sarah declined; it would not be proper with Hannah's attraction to Clay.

When Owen and Hod got a group of locals to help construct a temporary dwelling where the family could live there while the building was going on, Sylvia did her best to hide her pent-up frustration until the glad day when they all moved out of her house.

The temporary dwelling was a shack, nothing more. Sarah shook her head at the irony of it. Here she was, back to where they began and probably with even less. All around them lay the blackened land. A dark desolation, the stark windmill creaking and spinning endlessly, the gray sky above it like pewter.

They had a good cookstove, and for this she was grateful. They made their beds on the floor each evening, but she was thankful for the heavy blankets and quilts. They made due with a rickety old table and chairs and clothes packed in cardboard boxes.

They carried their water from the tank, heated it in the agate canner, and used it to wash dishes and clothes. The rough planks that served as flooring were soon covered with black ashes and soot. It was everywhere. There was no way to avoid it. The land surrounding the dwelling was scorched and blackened, the gray skies and the cold prohibiting any new growth.

The cattle stayed on the prairie where the fire had been stopped by the storm. They found sustenance in the dry brown grass and for water made their way to the tank, where Hannah or Manny faithfully broke away the rim of ice.

The cattle had all survived, easily able to fend for themselves, standing far away from the fire on that awful night. Resilient, bred to fend for themselves, they went about the business of eating grass as if nothing had happened.

The locals had given without restraint. The family had no other clothes, so they wore whatever had been given.

Sarah looked funny in a too-short red shirtwaist dress with a collar. Even if she buttoned it all the way up, it still seemed as if her neck was exposed. She wore her covering and always pinned up her hair, laughing with Hannah about her ridiculous get-up. But she was clothed, and for that she was grateful.

Hannah reveled in the newfound luxury of rooting through boxes and choosing her own clothes. She tried on blouses and skirts, shoes and thin stockings. Sarah frowned as Hannah tried rearranging her hair and told her to stop it. That was enough of that.

Manny wore denim jeans. There were no buttons to attach suspenders, so he went without them, finding a leather belt and wearing it. He looked apologetic and knew he was not obeying the *Ordnung*.

One day, a black dot appeared on the horizon. It turned out to be a rattling truck, then another, and another. A freight train carload of material, a miracle in real life, had recently arrived from Lancaster.

Sarah stood in the doorway of the shack and listened to the chugging of the engines. As she watched them approach, she wept.

Across the edge, where the blackened earth lay frozen and dormant, the windmill rose cold and harsh, the paddles whispering of the desolation and loss, the gears creaking, the foundation charred and blackened.

There was her father, Samuel Stoltzfus. With him were Ben Miller, who had installed the windmill, Elam Stoltzfus, and a few men she did not recognize. Single men, without beards, none of whom she knew.

She grasped her father's hand, bit her lips to keep from crying, and blinked back the tears that threatened her composure. She had to remain strong in the face of these men. It was bad enough they were here to see the loneliness and devastation.

Sarah squared her shoulders, her mouth trembling, giving away the agony of what she'd been through, the vulnerability and weakness in the face of what God had wrought. Not a few of the men marveled at this woman who had an ability to carry on. For the life of them, they couldn't see it.

They heard hoofbeats. Hannah and Manny, riding in, the cold air flushing their faces, their horses sweating, lathered where the saddles rubbed against them, threw themselves off, the blackened earth puffing up like smoke. Hannah wore jeans, a short dress over them—Sarah made her do it—and a heavy denim coat.

Her blackened face was edged in soot, her eyes dark in her flushed and exhilarated face. Manny smiled, his teeth white in his dark face.

Hannah watched the group of men warily, without smiling. She took in the three trucks, the impatient drivers hanging out of the windows saying, "Let's go. Let's go. We don't have all day!" She saw her grandfather and recognized Ben Miller. She dropped the reins of her horse and strode over to greet them with long strides, tall shoulders flung back, a tower of pride and strength. Her eyes mirrored the black devastation around her, shrouded well, or so she thought, by the pretense of her self-confident swagger.

She greeted only her grandfather and nodded curtly to the rest. She recognized Jerry Riehl. What was he doing here?

A blast of irritation shot through her. He had no right to come out here and see this burnt land and a pile of twisted metal, the hellish scene of failure and disappointment. She wished she could reach out and erase that day when she told him her foolish hopes and dreams.

She would not meet his eyes.

The men spoke with Sarah. Where would the house be built? Hannah stepped forward and began to speak, overriding her mother's voice. She had planned the house. She went through the door of the shack and came back with a folded white paper and gave it to her grandfather.

The men turned and began to unload, heeding the drivers' impatient shouts. Unload close to the charred metal, Hannah said. Under a cold, gray sky bloated with snow, the men worked feverishly, knowing that when the snow began to pummel the charred earth, their job would become twice as hard.

Samuel Stoltzfus wished they could dig a cellar. What was a good sturdy house without a cellar, especially on a level land prone to storms of every description? Ben Miller eyed the clouds and said they had best get on with it.

They erected a lean-to of sorts for the men's quarters. Sarah cooked soups and stews from morning to night. She baked bread, fed the group of men from the donated store of food, the men consuming vast quantities at each meal.

The house was framed before the snow began. Fine pellets of snow blew through the air, pinging against the lumber and their bare hands and faces.

Hannah looked up; her eyes watched the lowering clouds and the resulting bits of snow and ice. If this turned into a full blown blizzard, they'd all be packed into that shack like a bunch of rats. Well, she wasn't going to be stuck in that tar-paper shanty with those men, that was for sure. She'd ride over to the Jenkins.

That Sylvia Klasserman was crazy as a bat. She'd never step foot in that house, ever again. You didn't have to go through life eating off your floors and sanitizing everything you wore. Them and the Jenkins were exactly the opposite.

With all of Hannah's forthright thoughts swirling around in her head, the wind picked up, scouring the prairie. She knew within an hour that she would not be riding to the Jenkins. The snow intensified and fell like white curtains across the burnt earth.

Ben Miller and his crew worked on. Samuel Stoltzfus lifted his face to the sky, his white beard separating in the wind, the black felt brim of his hat flapping. He said they'd best make sure there was firewood, the way Sarah described these storms.

With the power of the driving snow, they abandoned the work. The only safe haven was the tar-paper shanty, a small drafty hovel much too small to house the nine men plus Sarah and the children.

Hannah sat in her allotted space beside the cookstove. She glowered at everyone and kept quiet, not listening to the men's ceaseless talk. Worse than women at a quilting, they talked constantly, no doubt thinking this was all a grand adventure that they could go home and joke about for the rest of their lives.

Sarah moved between the stove and the table, cooking beef stew and chili, cornbread, and fried potatoes. She was glad for the men and the endearing company of her father. Let Hannah smolder in her corner. Let her pout and hiss like a bad-mannered cat. She would happily feed these men for the gratitude and the aura of protection they afforded her.

Manny was a part of these men. He sat with them, listened to their talk, the way they expressed themselves, soaked up the latest news on politics. The times in which they lived were a clear sign of God's displeasure, taking away their money and chastening them with unsavory, undisciplined leaders in Washington, D.C.

In spite of herself, Hannah found herself listening. When the subject turned to cows, the way everyone in these parts made a living, Elam expressed his incredulity by saying he couldn't see how, if this storm was an example, these cows survived the winter.

"Yeah, and it's only November," Ben Miller chimed in.

"They won't make it. There's no way," another concurred.

That was too much for Hannah, harboring all that uncomfortable ruined pride and resentment, stuck in this disgusting little shack with these odorous, unwashed men who flashed yellow teeth like slabs of cheese every time they laughed, which was much too often.

"They will too!" she burst out.

All eyes turned to the prickly daughter, beautiful but covered in quills like a porcupine. They'd soon learned to stay away. Her grandfather smiled his slow smile. He knew her well. "How do they do it?"

"It's bred into them. They're tough, same as the people here. In a storm like this they hunker together facing away from the wind and wait to eat until it passes. They paw the snow and eat what's underneath if they have to. Ranchers have hay and some of them have shelters. Our hay's all gone, though, so we'll have to keep any eye on them."

"What happens when the storms become too frequent and the snow too deep?"

Hannah shrugged her shoulders. In the lamplight, from his corner, Jerry watched her eyes lose their flash of enthusiasm, becoming dark and brooding. He could feel her covered-up vulnerability, her fear of the coming winter.

He wondered how they would survive, much less prosper, in a land where even the elements seemed to crouch on the horizon, waiting to wipe out even the most resilient.

"Well," Elam said finally. "One way or another, we're going to give it a go; huh, Hannah?"

Her lightning smile and grateful eyes vanished, replaced by condescension and the cold, lofty lift of her chin. "Yeah." Her voice was low, a certainty laced with doubt.

The storm blew itself out during the night. Everyone was roused by the quiet, the stillness that pervaded their thin walls, the sound of the wind and scouring snow gone.

Sarah dished up bowls of oatmeal, slabs of fried bread, blackberry jam, and honey. The men pulled on rubber boots, brown work gloves, shoveled snow, and continued building the house.

The locals rode over on horseback. Abby Jenkins dismounted stiffly, the mule she had ridden tired out from his trek through the drifting snow. She brought a cardboard box of cookies, bread, and broken pies that she had lashed to her saddle.

She was yelling about the indecency of staying in this little outhouse, as she put it, wanting to know whose hare-brained idea this was? She thumped the baked items on the makeshift table, pulled up a chair to the cookstove, and held out her hands to its heat.

"Almost froze," she said, searching Sarah's face for signs of suffering. She gathered Abby into her lap and wrapped another blanket around her, rocking her gently with her thin arms. "Poor baby. Poor, poor baby," she crooned.

"So you found out about Sylvia, did you? She's crazy. She ain't right in the head. Sumpin's wrong if'n a woman irons her husband's underwear and rinses her washing twice. Ain't never heard the likes. Ya shoulda come on over, stayed with me. I'da took keer of all of ye. Don't know why ya didn't. This shack ain't fit to live in. Reckon them men can't all fit inside, fer sure not to sleep. It ain't right. You leave these men to theirselves an' you an' the children come on over an' stay with me."

Hannah shook her head. Sarah told Abby it was a generous offer, but, no, the house would soon be finished. It was better this way. The men needed warm food.

Abby sighed. "Wal, I'll tell ya one thing. If'n this was my men, the house wouldn't be finished any time soon. Come spring, it still wouldn't be. You know Hod an' the boys." She took off layers of clothing, rolled up her sleeves, helped Sarah dice carrots and potatoes, and told her what the locals were saying regarding the fire. She chuckled.

"I thought I should tell you this, Sarah. That town in the Bible that burned so bad, the lady looked back and was turned into salt? That coulda been you, you know."

Sarah laughed, the sound genuine, always to glad to be in Abby's company. "Well, Abby, hopefully God wasn't punishing us for the sins of that town. My goodness!"

Abby laughed her own happy cackle. "No, yer a good woman, Sarah. Yer too good fer the rest of us. Yer like a angel come to live among ordinary folks."

Sarah blushed and shook her head vigorously. Hannah put clean plates on a stack as she watched her mother and Abby and felt the easy flow of their talk, the binding of their love. She was sure her mother would take offense if she dared mention that they were more like sisters than her blood relatives, so she said nothing.

"Now, yer daughter here. She's pretty normal. Full of spit and vinegar, ain't cha?" She jostled Hannah's shoulder companionably.

Hannah grinned. She thought Abby would make an admirable mother-in-law. She hated being in close proximity to Jerry Riehl. If she could wipe away every sensation of that thing he had called a goodbye kiss, she'd be fine. She couldn't look at him without thinking of it, which, truth be told, threw her into an inward struggle she couldn't stand, feeling as if she was out to sea, or something like that.

So she didn't look at him. In fact, she avoided him as if he had some disease he could easily transmit. She planned on showing him somehow that Clay was the one, not that she ever planned on getting married, but it would certainly throw him off. If he came out here thinking of any romantic involvement—well, it was just too bad. It wasn't going to happen.

The men came to eat dinner and could barely all fit. Hannah stepped back to allow Elam Stoltzfus to pass, stumbled backward, and fell into Jerry's lap. His hands went out instinctively to keep her from falling, catching her slim waist as soft as a dove's back. He laughed, enjoying her discomfiture, his hands falling to his sides as she shot up, outraged, crossing her arms tightly about her waist, then going to stand behind the cookstove, her face flaming.

Clay saw the disturbance. His eyes narrowed, drawing his mouth into a straight line of disapproval. That Jerry was far too good-looking. Brash, handsome, a threat—and Clay didn't like it. He still fully intended on claiming Hannah someday. He was willing to wait for the duration. Yes, he was. He could never forget about her. She inhabited his thoughts constantly. And here she was, dressed in English clothes, although her mother made her wear that ridiculous kerchief on the back of her head.

Sarah watched the incident with a mother's intuition. Jerry was far too handsome, far too suave for any normal girl to resist.

She knew that, like Clay, he was used to plenty of girls trying to get his attention.

Well, all too soon, Mr. Riehl would need to know that Hannah was different. She was not like other girls. She had her mind made up. Was this God's answer for Hannah's life? Because here was another roadblock, like Clay not being Amish: Jeremiah Riehl would never leave the prosperity of Lancaster County to come out here to these lonesome, unsettled plains, with their unpredictable elements and disasters, which, bit by bit, ate away at the pioneer spirit.

CHAPTER 4

THE SUN SHONE AS SOFT AND WARM AS A FINE SPRING MORNING, melting the snow and ice and creating a gray, blackened slush-like tundra. Another load of people arrived from Lancaster County, gawkers, curious onlookers who came simply to satisfy their nosiness, their snooping, their wanting to find out for themselves how dire these leftover Mose Detweiler folks actually were.

Sarah's sisters were among them. Emma and Lydia. Sarah pushed back the irritation, projected the sisterly bond, shook hands, and smiled saying, "So good to see you." But inside, she felt much differently.

"We have lodging in Pine. We're not staying overnight," Emma informed her. They wrinkled their noses, drew sharp breaths, asked how she could live like this. It was disgusting.

Sarah felt her courage rise up within. She drew herself up to her full height, which was taller than Emma, looked her full in the eyes, without a trace of her usual bowing, and told her she was doing what had to be done under the circumstances, and if she couldn't accept it, well then, she'd have to go back to her lodging in Pine.

A volley of accusation followed, raining down on Sarah like bilious hail. She was only doing this for Hannah, and where would it get her? they wanted to know. And if she thought her father was going to give her one penny to rebuild, she was badly mistaken.

Sarah did not give out any information, nor did she give them the pleasure of her usual apology. It was, quite simply, none of their business where the funds came from, or why she chose to live in North Dakota, or what she was planning for the future.

Her father had given her the funds from Lancaster County, his soft, dark eyes welling with tears. She would not need a loan for the house or the barn. There was more than enough right here.

Sarah had been seated, but now she rose in agitation, wringing her hands, shaking her head and saying, "No, no. I can't take this. How can *Herr saya* be received if there is always charity? We are always taking, taking, taking, Dat!" Her voice rose on an edge of hysteria, saying it wasn't right, yet again, to be recipients of other people's money.

Her father spoke quietly, calmed her by saying that God's blessing lay before her in the form of this money. All she needed to do was reach out and take it, thanking God with a pure heart.

And she had, until now. She was shaken by the deep dislike of her sisters, condemned by it, yet rose above it, receiving the courage she found deep within herself to stand up and be heard. To stay here was her decision, even if it was Hannah that helped her to make it. That was all right too. Her sisters needed to see that she was capable of making decisions and keeping them regardless of whether they were aligned to their way of thinking or not.

That was one drawback of living a cloistered lifestyle. It was normal, minding each others' business, opinions given freely, and this *right* to assert authority to an adult sister. To move away with this alarming amount of miles between them was new and rather frightening. So perhaps that was the reason Emma and Lydia had come in the first place. Perhaps they too felt the separation and wanted to come to see the devastation, and then, having seen it, were alarmed by it.

Sarah vowed to try to push away the comment that she would not get a penny to rebuild. If she acknowledged those words, she would have to accept their greediness. Instead, she chose to banish it, turn it away, and she felt much better.

Hannah sloshed around in the black mud, handing lumber and nails to the men. She cleaned up, ran errands, and did anything to help the building process along.

They used shingles this time. Hannah was thrilled to see the gray asbestos shingles nailed into place, hammers rising and falling with a speed she hadn't thought possible. In less than a day, the roof was on.

The following day, the men placed long slabs of German siding horizontally outside and covered the inside with sturdy wallboard. Then they installed the windows—six in all. The house was an icon of luxury. Seven windows! Two in the front room—the living room, it was called—two in the kitchen, and two long, low windows that allowed them to see the prairie on every side.

After two days, Emma and Lydia left on the train after two days, and, as usual, their willing husbands left with them. "Obedient puppies," Hannah said.

Sarah reprimanded her sharply and said the West was making her uncouth. "Whatever that means," Hannah muttered to herself, then went to find Manny.

The barn began to take shape, another long, low building. Hay would be stored in an adjacent lean-to, allowing easier access, all Manny's planning. He said here on the level grasslands, with no hillsides to build into, there were no bank barns. So why stack hay upstairs?

Jerry found Hannah, standing tall with her arms wrapped around her waist, viewing the barn's beginning. He walked over without hesitation. "So, what do you think?"

She nodded.

"Look okay?"

She nodded again.

"Do you like the house?"

Another nod.

Jerry laughed, a true, uninhibited sound. "You know, if you keep nodding like that, your head might fall off!"

His sense of humor caught her off guard and she laughed outright, that short, sharp blast of sound that very few people ever heard. He laughed with her.

"You do like the house, don't you? Does it look the way you imagined on paper? You know, you did pretty good, for a girl, making a drawing that precise. We could easily build with what you had drawn up."

Hannah looked at him, her mistrust rising to the surface like foam. "You're just saying that."

"What do you mean, 'I'm just saying that'? I meant it. I was impressed. You did a good job."

Only for a moment he saw her lower lip tremble, a second of transparent vulnerability. Jerry tore his eyes away from the perfection of her mouth, steadied himself, and asked about the fire, his quiet voice drawing the story from her.

Yes, the gas engine was the culprit. Unbelievable, still. He stood and listened, tried to stay calm and composed, but took in every flash of her dark eyes, every movement of her mouth. He could read her fear, sensing her determination, and could only guess at the cost of giving up the fight. For Hannah, the price must have been an awfully high.

Suddenly her story was finished. She glared at him with all the old animosity back in place. "Why did you come out here?"

"Same reason everyone else did. To help where there was a need. If I ever saw a need, it was right here. I honestly don't know how you did it. I admire your courage. A lot."

"So you're going back?"

"Yeah."

Unexpected, unexplained, the intense longing for him to stay shook her. It left her feeling unsure of anything that had ever happened in her life and anything that would occur in the future. Why did he do this to her? The first thing she had to do was get her priorities straight, which was to walk away and stop listening to his compliments. As if he was lifting her up to set her on a pedestal that she was bound to fall from. There could be no yielding here, no caving to those compliments.

His ridiculously handsome face. She wished she'd never met him. Wished he'd go home, now, this instant.

The sisters had brought a trunk load of Amish clothing, having decided between themselves that it would be the saving of Sarah's family, keeping them true to the *Ordnung*. Who else would see to it? Sarah waved and bowed down like an obedient white flag of defeat where that Hannah was concerned. So they took the matter upon themselves.

Sarah was grateful. She knelt by the trunk and lifted out one freshly sewn garment after another, examined the sturdy broadfall trousers and cotton button down shirts, the dresses and aprons without hems in a brilliant array of blue, purple, and green. She almost wept to see the amount of stiff white organdy coverings, a necessity for living out the faith.

Without the head covering, she felt undressed, exposed, as if the covering completed the obedience to her Mose, now deceased, taken away, leaving only his gentle words and strict adherence to the way of life described as Amish. The least she could do was carry on the traditions and stay true to his teaching.

Gladly, then, Manny wore the new Amish clothing, complete with the straw hat pressed down on his dark hair. With Hannah, however, and her prickliness, her hidden rebellion, there came a myriad of questions. Why? What was the difference? Dat was dead and gone. Who was there to see what she wore?

Patiently, Sarah explained. "You were born to this, Hannah. It is your duty to remain obedient."

In the too-small drafty tar-paper shanty, Sarah sat on a chair, trying to keep the new clothing off the ever-present smears of black soot that the men perpetually tracked through the door, covering the floor like a remembered curse. She plied her needle in and out of a hem so fast it made Hannah dizzy to watch.

"You may not understand now, Hannah, but later in life you will realize the value of it more than you do now. To separate ourselves from the world does not mean that we feel superior, or that we flaunt our righteousness. We are only trying to live simple lives in order to please God, to abstain from worldly pleasures that often lead to sins of the flesh."

Hannah interrupted. "There's no difference, Mam. These folks that you label worldly are not nearly as worldly in their attitudes as Emma and Lydia. You call them good, God-fearing women, with all their greed and jealousy?"

To this, Sarah had nothing to say. She bit her lip, but knew that Hannah spoke the truth. The danger of dressing plain to hide a cauldron of hidden sins rose before her, and she trembled in its presence. Her sisters meant well, she knew, but to tell Hannah this would only infuriate her.

"Hannah, listen. We cannot look on the mistakes of other people to justify our own lives. What Emma and Lydia say or do does not give you license to desert the teachings of our forefathers. That is like pushing them down to lift yourself up, which only results in a hard fall. They are only trying to preserve their own homestead and their own way of life. Think, Hannah, how you strive to manage these three hundred and twenty acres of land. Think of your hopes and dreams. So too they are trying to keep their farms, pay their mortgages, to hand them down to their children, and their children's children.

"Look at us. Off on a wild goose chase, in their opinion, robbing them of what is rightfully theirs. You can't blame them.

Now, the worldly thing to do would be to become angry, to separate ourselves and not speak to them; to think ourselves mistreated, the victims, if you will. When, in truth, you know your father had his shortcomings, his wandering ways. Godly wisdom is easy to be entreated; it tries to see both sides, and this we have to follow if we don't want to create a family rift."

Hannah snorted with her customary derision. "I can't believe you're acknowledging any wrongdoing on Dat's part."

"I didn't say it was wrong. I only said he was . . ." Her voice fell away, the needle held between her thumb and forefinger stilled. Her hands lay in her lap, loose, the strength leeched from them by the vast, open, uncharted void between the two of them.

How was one parent to uphold the virtues of the other, when his whole walk in life had reflected his unwise choices, which bordered on insanity? Hannah was no longer a child. That time of budding acceptance and worship, looking to a father as the one who does no wrong, was past. She well knew of Mose's failures, and even made up a few of her own, feeling him inferior to her own choices.

"Well, Hannah, let's just say we're taking on the challenge of your father's journey. That was your choice. So are you different from him? Better? Your dream of the Bar S and the better herd of cattle? Is this not so much like your father and his dreaming?"

The second she finished talking, Sarah knew she had wandered into a territory where she should not have gone. Blind anger clouded Hannah's dark brown eyes and her face contorted with rage.

"You think I'm as dumb as Dat, then, huh? That's all you think of me? I can't believe what you just said!" Hannah rose to her feet, grabbed her coat and scarf and let herself out of the thin, tar-paper door, closing it with a quick flick of her wrist. The whole shanty shook with its impact.

Sarah took up her needle and jabbed it through the blue fabric straight into the tip of her finger underneath, drawing a drop of crimson blood, staining the new dress. She did not weep at her daughter's outburst but merely looked at the bloodstain on the fabric, taking it as an omen.

Our blood runs thick, she thought, with the ways of our fore-fathers who looked on their path of life through eyes of humility, eyes filled with the wisdom of the simple lifestyle, the denying of the flesh. All of this is the secret to a lasting inner peace, a happiness that cannot be explained, like Jesus said.

The job of raising Hannah rose before her like an insur-mountable cliff yet again. She could not become idle, noncha-lant. She must stay alert, seek guidance, and warn Hannah of the follies of the world. She would no longer allow Hannah's perception of life to shut her out, the willing, passive mother who had no backbone, no strength to meet the strong words of rebellion. She needed to take Hannah in hand, firmly, but with love, and likely with a thousand gifts of patience.

Hannah stormed out of the house, blinded by her own outburst and the unbelief that curdled her blood. Her own mother! She was not one bit like her father. He would never have acquired the windmill, these cattle, and now, this house. This wonderful house that sustained her battered spirits. He would not have pressed on in the face of so much adversity. Then she remem-bered the hunger, the impossibility of their situation, and how he had pressed on until he bordered on losing his mind.

Hannah stood in the cold air, the sky the color of a bat-tered tin pail. She knew another storm was brewing somewhere above the plains. She felt sick with the realization of her moth-er's words, which pounded into her.

She threw a saddle on Pete, jerking the cinch until his ears lay flat and he shifted uncomfortably from side to side. She hit his teeth hard with the bit and flattened his ears as she yanked the bridle over them. "Hold still, you old nag!" she shouted.

She rode past the house, kicking the stirrups against Pete's side, leaning forward as if she was on a fast racer coming into the finish line. She galloped past the house and the workers who lifted their straw hats and stared after her in bewilderment.

Hannah rode hard past the windmill, through the burned area, throwing up little puffs of black ash, until Pete had worked up a good lather. She was breathing hard, her face numb from the cold, her hands like frozen claws. Should have worn gloves, she thought.

She held a hand to her forehead, palm down, searching for the familiar huddle of black cattle. Turning from right to left, she surveyed the level prairie. There were swells, hidden hollows, gentle bowls of earth that weren't visible to the human eye, so sometimes they weren't easy to spot.

She urged Pete on, then pulled abruptly on the reins. There they were. Breathless, she counted each black cow. Thirteen. One big mean one with bowed horns and the audacity to use them. Two cows that would be dropping calves in the spring, and ten young heifers. The bull. There he was, wide-shouldered and magnificent. They were all there. Every last one.

A few of them lifted their heads, observed her, then bent to tear mouthfuls of grass, wrapping their powerful, rough tongues around the tufts of dry grass, never stopping to chew or swallow, as far as Hannah could tell.

They didn't appear to be losing weight, in spite of the cold and the surprise snowstorm. She figured they would, though, till winter was over. All she asked was that they survive. They needed every cow, every calf, to repay her grandfather's loan.

A fleeting thought ran through her mind. How long till the wolves became hungrier? She knew they were always hungry, always on the move, dark denizens of death to anything weakened or alone. It was only when the snows of winter drove them to a bold desperation that the cows' lives were in actual danger.

She planned on borrowing more than one rifle from Clay. She'd teach herself to become a sharpshooter, able to hit a running target from yards away. She'd teach Manny, too, and together they'd keep an eye on their cows.

She glanced up at the mottled clouds that hung like moldy cottage cheese, dark clumps among lumpy gray and white ones. She wondered what that meant. She'd become fairly skilled at predicting the weather on these plains but she'd never seen anything quite like this. Her eyes roamed the level land, the endless swell of cold, rasping grass like hay that met the gray horizon, the sky cold and mysterious above it.

The sense that there was something much greater than herself washed over her, giving her a cold chill. When things ran amok, and everything seemed out of control, propelled by wheels of fear and doubt, it all came together out here, alone, without anyone's interference.

It was the vast earth and the sky with nothing in between that caused bewilderment. Was that another trait of her father? He'd spoken of the babble of voices, the constant debates that gave him so much grief. Had he been unhinged then, as he was before he died? Was she so like her father that she needed vast amounts of empty space, muddled dreams, and unrealistic ventures to stay sane? Her mother's words lay like lead in her chest.

Quickly she justified her motive for keeping the homestead, knowing her father would never have stooped to asking for a loan to better himself. Never. That was the difference. She wasn't afraid to forge ahead, to look to the future, to plan.

That was where he went wrong, muddling along without a plan, dreaming about miracles that didn't happen. And yet, here she was with the small herd, winter storms, wolves, lack of feed, which added up to nothing short of a miracle if they all survived.

She lifted her shoulders and shook her head, a small grin playing across her mouth. One day at a time. She had Manny. They'd try their best. Heartened, she rode home, unsaddled

Pete, and went to see how many days before the men would leave. They had been laying the floor, and working on the doors and trim. The chimney was finished.

Ben Miller acknowledged her with a smile. "One more day!" he shouted.

Hannah gasped. "Really?"

He nodded proudly.

The house had all come together in the last few days. A new cookstove stood against one kitchen wall, the stovepipe entering the stone chimney between the two windows. A row of store-bought cupboards housed a real porcelain sink with running water and a drain like they had back home. A large living room with plenty of space for a table and chairs. A hallway with bedrooms on either side. An indoor bathroom with a bathtub.

Ben Miller said there were only a few families who had dared install a bathtub back in Lancaster County. The bishops discouraged every new form of luxury, but this was only good hygiene and common sense. The bathroom contained a commode and a sink to wash hands and brush teeth—things Hannah thought the homestead would never have.

It was all charity, though. People had given away their hard-earned money so the family could gain a new foothold out here in this no-man's land. Well, so be it. That was another of her father's weaknesses. He had been too proud to accept charity.

Hannah and Sarah followed on the heels of the builders, polishing windows, washing walls and scrubbing floors.

The day came when they carried in and placed all donated furniture. The end result brought tears to Sarah's eyes and a deep sigh of happiness. Oh, this house. She could never have imagined a house half as big or as cozy or as handy or as filled with lovely furniture, even if it was other peoples' cast-offs. No matter. Every piece was a pure luxury. It may as well have been plated in gold, so precious it was.

What did anything matter? The arm of the brown sofa was worn smooth and faded in spots, but it was a sofa. A couch. A soft spot to enjoy, to sit down and relax with her knitting or mending.

What if the kitchen rugs were mismatched? They were rugs much better than anything they had ever owned. They unpacked dishes and marveled at the smooth pots and pans. Like a loving caress they wiped the plates and cupped their hands around tea cups and tumblers like a warm embrace. They lined drawers with leftover wallpaper and glued down the edges.

The pantry was stocked with food, staples that would sustain them long after winter was gone. Dried peas, flour, cornmeal, brown sugar, dried navy beans, oatmeal, lard and white sugar, baking powder and salt. Jars of canned tomatoes and cucumbers, mixed pickle and applesauce.

Sarah wiped the dust from her forehead yet again, her eyes red with fatigue, a smile on her face as she told Ben and Elam where to set the corner cupboard. They would have dishes to put in there too.

Ben surveyed his handiwork, narrowed his eyes, and told Sarah that he'd love to build his wife a house like this.

"Maybe we'll just have to sell out and move out here. There'd be plenty of work for the windmill installing, that's for sure. I can't tell you how many of these ranchers asked about your windmill. But I don't know what the wife would say. She'd be out of fix, for sure. Davey here, he's thinking along the same lines. Why not? Grab on to that pioneer spirit and run with it. Break the mold. Get away and try something new. See what the wife says."

Hannah thought, Oh boy, Davey. He'll want to get a wife out here, which means me. Set her mind like cement.

They slept in the house that night. Mary snuggled beside Hannah on thick flannel sheets and covered with heavy quilts, breathed heavily and was asleep. Hannah lay thinking at the miracle of this house. All because people shared their money, their possessions. She hoped every person who donated even one item, no matter how small, would be rewarded ten times over. She remembered that passage from the Bible. She hoped it was true.

She thought of all the electric lamps and irons and appliances the local townsfolk had contributed. She felt sorry for them, not realizing they'd never be used, and she hoped her mother would have the good sense not to return them to the kindhearted people.

So what was so terrible about electricity? It would certainly be nice to pull a string and be illuminated with bright light on demand, instead of straining to see by the light of a smelly old kerosene lamp. Or, the way it used to be before coal oil—candles. She heard the wind moan around the eaves and wondered when the storm would arrive.

Across the hallway, Sarah lay holding Abby until she slept, then slid out of bed and down onto her knees. She folded her hands, bent her head, and prayed. Over and over she thanked God for the generous giving and asked Him to bless each individual for their kindness.

She wished Doris Rocher abundant happiness and many customers for Harry. She prayed that Betsy from the café would have a thriving business and Leonard Heel from the feed store a healed back. She mentioned all her acquaintances by name, and when she finished, she simply laid her head on her folded hands and softly wept with pure gratitude until the flannel sheets were wet.

Outside, from the curdled black clouds, the first winds of December brought snowflakes the size of a quarter, flung them against the sturdy ranch house and whirled them down along the good German siding, where they began to accumulate in a hour's time, just when Sarah lay her head on a pillow made of blessings.

CHAPTER 5

HANNAH WAS DOWN AT THE BARN CHECKING TO SEE WHAT REMAINED to be done, the snow coming down steadily, a world of white around them, when Jerry found her.

"Hannah."

She turned, wide eyed.

"We're leaving."

"Are you?"

"Yes."

She stepped back, afraid he would hear the impossibly loud banging of her heart.

"I want to wish you the best." His voice quivered. He shook his head. "You're a brave girl. I admire you, honestly. A part of me wants to stay here, protect you, watch over you."

Her eyes became hooded, the old bitterness a curtain of anger. "You sound like God."

"You know I'm not."

"Yeah, well, I can take care of myself."

"Can you?"

"Of course. Manny's here. My mother. Clay."

Jerry couldn't help himself. "What does he mean to you? Clay."

"Nothing. You should understand that I'm never getting married. He wants me to marry him, but that . . . well, you know."

The silence stretched out. The interior of the barn was lit by a dim gray light, the new yellow lumber permeating the air with the acrid smell of pine. Through the door, a rectangle of white swirled in restless little arcs of wind tumbling the snow around.

"What?" Hannah couldn't take the silence, so static with unspoken words it was like the air during a prairie thunderstorm.

"Hannah." Jerry moved toward her, holding out both arms. "Just let me hold you. Something to remember me by."

"No!" Hannah stepped away, her back against the sweet-smelling lumber.

"What would you say if I decided to move here if Ben Miller and Davey do? I don't mean to be rude, but you could use a few good horses here in cow country. Not to mention a farrier."

"I don't want you out here." Blunt, the sharp edges like a serrated knife. From a distance they heard Davey's high-pitched yell announcing the driver's arrival.

Another moment of her heart hammering against her ribs and then he stepped closer, gripped her shoulders in his large, calloused hands, gently drawing her toward himself, speaking her name as his eyes searched hers.

"I know, Hannah. I know you don't." His lips closed over hers in a gentle kiss of goodbye, and then he released her.

"I don't know why you think you have the right to do that, Jerry Riehl. Go home to Lancaster County and find some Susie or Becky and marry her. Stay away from me!" She ran the back of her hand roughly across her mouth, her eyes bright with frustration and unshed tears.

"Jerry! Get out of here!"

But he held her again, with a hold like a vice. Crushing her to him, he bent his head and kissed her again. This time, he meant it. "Remember me, Hannah." And then he was gone.

Hannah had never been so angry, or so thoroughly shook up. She fell back against the wall, her chest heaving with agitation. In case he didn't know it, he had just lost his last chance. That was a serious breach of good manners, or Amish *Ordnung*, or whatever you wanted to call it. If he moved out here, she would move to Utah, or California. She'd get a job picking tomatoes in some fertile valley. Oh, he had just now ruined his chances forever! But she moved stealthily to the side of the doorway, watched the two cars, her mother and Manny waving, dark figures standing alone on the prairie, the cars moving steadily away, through the gray white world of burnt earth and falling snow.

Hannah breathed out, a long sigh of spent emotion. So now the men were gone. They were alone, her and Mam and Manny. She expected a rush of euphoria, an intense feeling of joy, but all she could manage was a weak smile that wouldn't stay in place before sobs caught her unprepared. She stifled them with a balled up fist and swiped viciously at her streaming eyes with the corner of her scarf. But nothing could stop her feeling of desolation as she watched those two cars lumbering through the snow.

She stamped her foot in frustration, blew her nose into a wadded handkerchief, and then took a fist and slammed it against the door frame, resulting in bruised knuckles that throbbed painfully through the remainder of the day.

Sarah was in high spirits, humming a song as she cooked their dinner, rushing to the window to exclaim about the falling snow. A gift from God, this snow. Imagine the dried-out earth receiving this moisture that would give new life to the grass around them. She reveled in the wonders of the new cookstove.

Abby discovered the water in the commode, threw wooden blocks into it, delighting in the splash, her high shrieks a signal that ended all her fun. "No, no," Sarah scolded. Abby wailed in protest, hiding her face in Sarah's skirts.

There were so many new and useful things. The pantry contained many shelves, a corner that Sarah declared was the best idea any man had ever thought of.

"You're *grosfeelich*, Mam," Eli chirped.

Sarah laughed, a trilling, happy sound of the heady joy she felt. "Then I guess I will just have to be boastful for awhile, won't I?" she said lightly, whirling from stove to table with the grace of a much younger woman.

Mary watched her mother, put a hand over her mouth and giggled. This was a new Mam, one she had seldom known. Hannah gave away her bad mood by frowning, her eyebrows heavy above dull eyes. "Hope the food lasts, is all I can say."

Sarah chose to ignore this, knowing it would only bring out the worst in her if she chose to answer the endless, senseless argument that was Hannah's style, caught in the net of her own dark mood.

"Think Ben will move out?" Manny asked, sitting at the table, lifting lids and sniffing the delicious aromas.

"I hope so. Davey Stoltzfus too. Jerry Riehl even spoke of it."

"Yeah, and he's a horseman. Imagine the Jenkinses and the Klassermans when they see his horses!"

"When," Hannah spat out. "You don't even know if he's going to move out."

Manny eyed her levelly and thought, so that's what's wrong. Must have gotten tangled in some upsetting conversation with him.

"I hope he does," Sarah said, easily.

"Why?" Hannah wanted to know.

"For the same reason Manny says. The horses."

Hannah snorted.

They ate the good hot vegetable stew and bread with apple butter, silently chewing their food in the bright new kitchen with the patterned linoleum like a rug in the middle of the room. The tablecloth was checkered in red and white squares, the snow casting a white, winter light over everything.

A sturdy house, food in the pantry, the windmill churning away not far from the buildings, the cows out on the prairie finding grass, the unfinished barn housing their two old horses and aging wagon, the neighbors living close enough to help in an emergency. God was above all, and they were blessed beyond measure.

All day the snow fell steadily. It was a beautiful snow, not a storm. The wind whirled it playfully, as if God was smiling down on them, presenting them with the clean white beauty of a winter barely begun. It piled on the good shingled roof and slid off with a sound like falling water, a dull whump as it hit the snow below.

Down at the barn, Hannah and Manny were hunched over a rough drawing of the interior of the unfinished barn. "If we have two stables on each side with a wide enough walkway, we can push a manure spreader back there and clean out slick as a whistle," Hannah said.

"As if we'll ever own a manure spreader," Manny muttered.

"Sure we will. Maybe not next year or the year after, but sometime." Hannah straightened her back and viewed the dim interior of the barn. She began to whistle, then hum, and then went back to whistling.

Manny set up two sawhorses, flopped a wide piece of lumber on top and began to measure. Hannah grabbed a handsaw, ready to cut the board after it was marked correctly, still whistling, nodding her head to the internal beat only she could hear.

Manny stood up, watched her with narrowed eyes. "You're happy," he said dryly, thinking it didn't happen too often.

"Oh, skip, skip, skip to my Lou,
Skip, skip, skip to my Lou,
Skip, skip, skip to my Lou,
Skip to my Lou, my darlin'."

Manny frowned. "That song is senseless."

"Not if you're dancing."

Alarmed, Manny stared at his sister. "You never did."

"I certainly did. That's where I was the other week—well, months, weeks, how long ago was it? I danced with Clay. It was the best thing I ever did. I could dance all day, every day. I'm good at it. You wouldn't believe it." Hannah grinned, lifted her arms, and did a quick two-step, leaving poor Manny blushing, shaking his head in embarrassment.

"Stop it, Hannah. What would Dat say?"

Hannah shrugged and did another two-step, then another. "I'm never getting married, Manny. I hope you know there is no one who I will love enough to be his slave and be tied to a house like a common goat and have a bunch of kids. Nope. Not for me. It's easier to flirt and be happy and see how many men want you to be their wife, and you know you're never going to be."

Manny lifted another board, carried it back to the far end, and bent to position it before pulling out a handful of nails. Lifting his hammer, he began to pound in the nails.

"Nothing to say to that, huh, Manny? That's because you don't know what to say. I'm right. I control my destiny. If I choose not to marry, that means I can be the rightful owner of the Bar S, make my own money, make all my own choices, do what I want with no whining man to cook for or wash his dirty socks. *Nein. Nein.*"

Hannah laughed out loud, that short, raucous sound that came from deep within. Manny kept hammering away without giving her the satisfaction of a reply.

"Aren't you going to say anything?"

Manny finished nailing the board, looked Hannah straight in the eye, and said, "Then you'd better not let Jerry Riehl do what he just did."

Hannah dropped her hammer. It landed on the toe of her boot and bounced off, unnoticed. She coughed, choked, and cleared her throat as her eyes widened and a deep flush spread across her cheeks. "What are you talking about?"

"Next time he wants to say goodbye, you'd better make sure there is no one else in the barn."

"You weren't! You were standing right out there with Mam. I saw you!"

"I was in here. What do you think the back stall door's for? A fast escape when . . ." He couldn't bring himself to say *kiss*, so he stopped.

"When what?"

"Nothing." Angrily, Manny pushed past her and began sawing another board, the movement of his arm jerky and his face hidden.

"That wasn't my fault, you know. He thinks he likes me and has the right to do that. He's bold and despicable, and I can't stand him!"

"Didn't appear like that to me."

That remark was a battering ram to Hannah's wall of protective pride. She flew into a volley of angry words, telling him that he knew nothing about anything, and he couldn't tell how she felt, no matter what he saw. "Snooping, nosy little brother. You ought to be ashamed of yourself!"

"Oh, I'm not ashamed. You're the one that should be. Stringing two of them along the way you are."

"I'm not stringing anyone along!" Hannah shouted, her dark eyes snapping with denial.

"What did you just say? You were dancing with Clay, and Jerry just kissed you this morning."

"It wasn't my fault!"

"Wasn't entirely his, either."

Hannah balled her fists, her head thrust forward as she stalked out of the barn, sizzling with wounded pride. Her feet stamped down hard in the ever-deepening snow as she walked blindly, without thinking, heading toward the tar-paper shanty that had been their home for the past weeks.

How could her own beloved Manny turn against her like that? What did he mean by that last sentence? The one about it not appearing to him as if . . . As if what? As if she wasn't willing? Well, she wasn't.

Like tangled yarn her thoughts knotted and folded in over themselves until she yanked on the door handle of the makeshift dwelling and heard a man's cough.

Her attention was brought up sharply when the cough was repeated. Peering through the gray gloom of the near windowless dwelling, she thought someone had left a pile of clothes or quilts in the corner. Then she heard another cough, raspy, like gravel tumbled in a creek bed.

"Hey!" she called out, bold and unafraid.

Immediately the pile of rags shifted, shoulders appeared, a head covered with an old cap, a gray blue scarf tied over the top. Two eyes like raisins in a flushed face etched like a map with blue and dark red veins crisscrossing the cheeks.

"S'cuse me, ma'am. Beg pardon." The breathing came in irregular puffs, labored. "Musta got sick. Come down with the flu." More harsh, short breaths.

"Well, tell me who you are," Hannah demanded, short on patience and still holding onto the residue of her outrage.

"Lemuel. Lemuel Short from over by Crock's Landing." A series of short, harsh barks followed.

"Well, that doesn't help. Never heard of a Lemuel. You sure it isn't Benuel? Lots of Benuels where I come from."

"No, ma'am."

"What am I supposed to do with you?"

"Just let me rest a minute, ma'am."

"You'll freeze."

"No, no, I'm out of the snow. Thank you kindly, ma'am."

"I can't just let you lay there."

He coughed so violently that Hannah became alarmed, closed the door, and waded through the deepening snow to the house.

She clattered up on the porch, stomped her boots to rid them of the clinging snow, opened the door, and yelled loudly for her mother, who looked up with frightened eyes as she opened the oven door. "Hannah! What is wrong?"

"There's a man in the shack."

Sarah straightened up, her eyes wide in the white, snowy atmosphere. "What man?"

"Come and see for yourself."

Sarah grabbed her heavy black coat, a hand-me-down from her sister, Emma, and shrugged into it. A scarf on her head, boots on her feet, she followed Hannah across the yard to the shanty and let herself inside, more timid than Hannah had been.

"His name is Lemuel Short," Hannah hissed.

"Mr. Short?" Sarah called softly.

Immediately a head wrapped in the old blue gray scarf with small black eyes appeared.

"Beg pardon, ma'am. Just resting awhile then I'll be gone. Just let me rest and I'll be on my way."

Sarah heard the harsh cough and instantly recognized Lemuel Short as a test from God, who had given, shaken, pressed down, and running over. Now it was her turn to give back by ministering to this angel in disguise. Not a trace of doubt. Clear-eyed, strong, the banner of her faith rippled in the soft wind of her voice. "Good afternoon, Mr. Short."

"Ma'am. Thank you."

"You will come to the house. We'll get you better. I have a pot of *ponhaus* cooking, and we'll make you a hot toddy. My name is Sarah and this is my daughter, Hannah."

Sarah reached down to help him up. He reached out a hand and tried, but fell back, then tried again. Hannah met Sarah's eyes, a question answered by the lifting of Sarah's chin to the left.

Together each inserted a hand under his armpits and lifted gently until he stood on his feet. He was of average height, clothed in ordinary country outerwear, smelling of wood smoke, kerosene, and tar. His denim trousers were soaked from walking in the snow, his knees trembling.

"Ready?"

He nodded.

Awkwardly, they maneuvered him through the small doorway, across the snowy yard, and up onto the porch, where he stood gasping and coughing, retching horribly while managing to mutter weak apologies.

Manny came wading through the snow, plowing through at a half run, billows of loose snow like a wake behind him, his eyes dark questions in his face.

"Help," Hannah mouthed.

They got him to the sofa where he collapsed and lay gasping amid his apologies. Sarah worked quickly. First she unlaced and removed his boots and then the gray wet socks. His toes were as white as if there was no blood circulating at all.

Softly Sarah said, "The large agate tub with warm water." Hannah obeyed promptly for once. Eli and Mary stood wide-eyed, Abby sitting with her fat little legs thrust straight out, her thumb in her mouth, watching every move.

Tenderly Sarah rolled up the sodden denim of his trousers and unbuttoned his coat. Lemuel sat up and helped Sarah remove all his outer garments, his hands shaking like spring leaves, his jaw wobbling until his teeth clacked together.

When she removed his scarf, Sarah could feel the heat. His face was flushed, his small brown eyes red-rimmed, shimmering with fever. Sarah realized the strength of his sickness. He may already have pneumonia or worse. Well, there were onions. She made a tincture paregoric. She would see what she could do, with God's help.

She brought a clean sheet, made up the sofa while he sat on the chair with his feet in warm water. Hannah came over and told Sarah in a hiss that he smelled awful. Why couldn't he bathe and wear some of Manny's clothes?

"He's too sick," Sarah whispered back.

"He stinks! He smells like a billy goat!"

"Shh."

Hannah moved off in a huff. What a predicament. Now they weren't more than settled in their nice new house and here comes this sick, smelly old man to mess everything up. He was probably a thief. Or worse. They'd probably all be dead by morning. She was going to sleep with Dat's rifle under her pillow. All that coughing and carrying on could well be a bluff, and as soon as they went to bed, he'd sneak around stealing stuff and . . . Oh, it gave her the creeps.

The house smelled of cooking onions and paregoric, chamomile tea, and *ponhaus*. It was enough to make her lose her supper, especially with the rank odor that steamed off his soaked clothes. Like a wet dog. Fleas and lice, she guaranteed.

He coughed all night. Spat and honked and wheezed like a goose caught in a trap. Hannah knew because she heard every sound as she sat on the side of her bed with Dat's rifle across her lap, figuring he might get the others, but he was not getting her. She had a ranch to operate. The Bar S.

Mam had the fuzziest soul. She was all love and compassion and tenderness, treating Lemuel Short as if he was royalty. She could just see the Bible verses Mam had before her. "Inasmuch as ye have done it to the least of these my brethren, ye have done it unto me." She probably thought she was entertaining angels unawares. Well, that was all right as far as it went, but Hannah was not taking any chances.

In the morning, Hannah was in bed, the gun clutched in her hands. Lemuel Short had fallen into a deep sleep, his mouth open, all manner of wheezes, whistles, and sawing sounds coming from his dark, toothless cavity.

Sarah drew her dress tightly around her shivering form, lifted the lid on the cookstove and threw a match onto the prepared paper and kindling. The sun had not yet risen, but the sky was a vast dome of reflected white light from the level snow-filled land that nestled right up to the horizon. She stood at the window, shivered again, the comforting sound of the popping, crackling fire filling her with peace.

They were so well *fa-sarked*. Taken care of. Every need had been supplied. If she praised God for the remainder of her life, she would never have thanked Him enough. She folded her hands, bowed her head, and, thanked her Heavenly Father for sending Lemuel Short and allowing her to be His servant. She prayed for Lemuel's well-being and for guidance.

Hannah was summoned to the breakfast table, flopped in her chair with a sour expression, and stuck a thumb out in the general direction of Lemuel Short, raising an eyebrow at Sarah.

"Sick," Sarah mouthed.

They ate fried *ponhaus* and buttered toast, then relaxed around the table with mugs of tea sweetened with a dollop of honey. The sun burst above the plains, filling the house with strong yellow light till the red horizon gave way to winter's icy blue sky.

Sarah remarked about not being able to get used to the light. So many windows. It spoiled her, being able to see out across the prairie. Manny smiled at Sarah, told her she deserved every window, and hoped she'd enjoy them for a long time.

Hannah choked on her tea. So much sugary talk. It was enough to gag her. Plus, that man on the couch was going to have to move along. She didn't want to spend one more night in this house with him and his life-threatening noises. She'd even caught herself holding her breath, waiting until he exhaled safely, his rattling intake of air enough to make her imagine he was dying.

The whole thing was unsettling, to put it mildly. She wished she'd never gone into that tar-paper shack. He would have moved on by now. He would have made it as far as the Klassermans. Sylvia could keep him.

That brought the first smile of the day, thinking of meticulous Sylvia ministering to poor, smelly Mr. Short. She'd probably get Owen to take him to the livery stable in town. Well, he was here now, and by the looks of her angelic mother, he'd be here awhile longer.

CHAPTER 6

Hannah was right.

Lemuel Short stayed on the couch, smelling the same as the day he arrived, Sarah ministering to him like a most devoted nurse. With the snow piled up to two feet and no telephone nearby, there was no use summoning the doctor. Stranded on the prairie, miles from the nearest neighbor, there had been no sense of isolation until the sick wanderer had arrived.

Sarah realized his situation was grave. She used up half her store of onions, vinegar, paregoric, tea and mustard poultices, and still his fever would not break.

The morning after, the snow was still coming down but thinner and slower. A weak sun showed its face in the gray clouds and the wind slammed into the north side of the house with such force that Sarah straightened from her job tending to Lemuel, her eyes wide with alarm.

It was indeed fortunate that everyone was in the house when the wind sprang up. Manny said he didn't know how they would have made it back to the house, the wind whipping the loose snow to a blinding, stinging frenzy, obliterating anything and everything in its path. A wall of moving snow driven by the hissing, humming wind scoured the top layer of it, then the snow beneath, leaving jagged patches of bare, brown grass, a jigsaw of

high, impenetrable drifts like jagged little mountain ranges as far
as the eye could see, which wasn't any great distance.

Hannah paced and muttered to herself, a caged lion sick with
anxiety. She worried about the cows, wondering if they could
survive. She wanted to ride out and see for herself, but that was
impossible.

Lemuel Short sat up for a short time, his small raisin eyes
watching the oldest daughter's agitation. He could tell she was
of a different nature than her mother but kept his observations
to himself.

It didn't help Hannah's short temper that she sat up every
night with the rifle on her lab, robbing herself of restful sleep,
priding herself that she was the only one who remained vigilant.

Mr. Short was not to be trusted no matter how sick he was. Her
lack of sleep, coupled with the anxiety and frustration of listening
to the howling wind and blowing snow, almost drove her mad. She
took to chewing her fingernails down to the quick and drinking
black coffee that made her so jittery she spilled everything, slopping
soup on the tablecloth and dumping tea on the floor. She yelled at
Eli when he crawled underfoot with Abby astride his back, yanked
her off and smacked her bottom, till she set up a red-faced howl of
protest. Eli pinched her leg, a firm pinch between his thumb and
forefinger, resulting in a cat-like yowl from Hannah. Poor Eli was
promptly cuffed on the ear by his tightly wound sister, whereupon
he slunk away and folded himself up in the corner of the couch
opposite Lemuel, his knees drawn up to his face, the forbidden
thumb finding its way to his mouth.

Sarah sighed, her eyes snapping with impatience. Eli heard a
"Psst." He sat very still, rolled his eyes in Lemuel's direction and
quickly removed the disobedient thumb.

"Little boy," Lemuel whispered.

Out came the thumb again, only to be quickly hidden from
sight in his trouser pocket. A smile, quick and furtive, appeared
as quickly as it disappeared.

"Your sister bigger than you?" Lemuel whispered.

Eli nodded, his dark eyes slanted toward the sick man.

"Not to worry, Son. You'll outgrow her one day." Lemuel winked, one raisin eye disappearing beneath a blue veined eyelid. Eli laughed outright. Hannah glared in his direction.

The following day, Lemuel's fever broke. He spent a long time soaking in the new claw foot tub, dressed in Mose's clothes— clean, wrinkled, taken from the small bundle Sarah had thrown on the wagon the night of the fire.

He was so thin that the shirt and trousers hung on his gaunt frame. He was bald across most of his head but had a wealth of gray hair hanging to his shoulders in the back. After he had shaved, he appeared to have shrunken in size, his weathered face revealing a life of hardship.

Hannah guessed he was close to seventy years old, but he said he was only fifty-nine. In his quiet, breathy voice, there was an underlying rasp, an unsettling timbre that rattled Hannah.

He began to sit up at the table to eat, didn't even know enough to bow his head when Sarah told him there was always silent grace before a meal. He didn't put his hands below the table, either. Just sat there with a foolish expression in his small eyes nearly hidden in flaps of loose skin.

Hannah knew because she watched him when he thought her head was bowed. So, right there, that told you a lot, she thought. No teaching about God, which meant he would think nothing of holding them all hostage after he had his strength back. Rob them probably, take everything and perhaps leave them all dead.

Manny strongly disagreed and said he had none of those mannerisms. Sarah plied him with more food, more soup, but he ate very little. Finally, he turned his attention to Hannah.

"Miss," he said softly.

Hannah didn't reply, the soft-spoken word left her floundering, unsure.

"Miss, I can see you're anxious about something. Do you care to tell me?"

Hannah left his sentence hanging in the air. He gave her the willies, those dark, unblinking eyes watching her like a squirrel's.

Manny answered for her, his face flushing at her outward lack of good manners. "We're all worried about the cows."

"You have cows?"

"Yes."

"Ah, so did I, so did I. At one time. Do you care to hear my story?"

Sarah nodded eagerly, Manny a mirror of his trusting mother. Hannah sat back, folded her arms and glowered. Likely the yarn he would spin would be filled with lies, a colorful pack of fabrications he told to everyone he met, spreading words of untruth thick as flies across the table, lies only she could decipher.

"I had a spread in Montana," he began. "A wife and two children. I was young."

"Where in Montana?" Hannah asked.

"Just across the border. The North Dakota border. It was called the Sun River Range. Good grasslands. I was building up my herd. It was a lonely life—but a good one. I loved my days, my herd of cattle, and the isolation. I guess that's what Mae couldn't take. She left me and took the children, in the fall before the winter came. Went back to her parents in the East, where we both come from."

Here his voice slowed, faltered. In spite of herself, Hannah found herself listening, her eyes downcast, the palm of each hand wrapped around an elbow.

"I followed, left my heard of cows. I found her, but all my pleading didn't do any good. Her parents wouldn't allow her to return even if she wanted to. The children, Jack and Rory, cried and wanted their daddy. But they were like stone—the parents and Mae.

"So I came back, had plans to sell out, give it up. Could hardly do it, but knew it had to be done. All my hopes was wrapped up in my homestead."

Hannah blinked and swallowed.

"In the end, the whiskey got me. I started to drink to dull the edge of the pain. Guess it was a rebellion, an inner anger that burned slow and mean, pitying myself. Never stopped drinking.

"It was my homestead, my ranch, my wife, and my children. It consumed my life, glass by glass. I lived for the dull numbing it brought, the bottom of the emptied glass the fulfillment I needed. It erased most of my sense of failure, but never all of it. As long as I live, I'll hear my boys crying as I turned and walked away. A sound I'll never get rid of. Or the sight of Mae and her parents. Like hawks, they were."

He shook his head, the veined lids falling over the small black eyes. "I wandered, held different jobs, always got into fights, was fired more times than I can say. Rode the rails."

Manny broke in, "What's that?"

"Hitched a ride in a boxcar. On the train. Hundreds do it."

"Like real hobos? Tramps?" Manny asked, his eyes alight.

Sarah smiled, "We used to have them come by our place back in Pennsylvania. *Vaek-laufa.* Road walkers, in English."

Lemuel nodded. "You speak two languages?"

"Yes. We are raised speaking Pennsylvania Dutch first, then we learn English as we grow older."

Lemuel nodded again. He seemed satisfied to drop the subject of who they were, or why they spoke Pennsylvania Dutch.

"I got away from God. Don't hold to no religion. Figured if there was a God, He was right cruel taking away everything I had."

There it was! Hannah sat up sharply, an intake of breath hissing between her teeth. "If you don't believe in God, what would keep you from . . . from, you know, getting rid of all of us and keeping our homestead? Claim jumpers will do that. How do we know all this sickness was only to fool us?"

"Hannah!" Sarah said sharply, her disapproval obvious in her tone.

Lemuel held up a hand. "It's all right. The girl's only being careful. I didn't say I don't believe in God. I said I got away from Him. I done wrong. Now I don't know how God will have me back. I done a heap of sinning. Not sure I didn't leave a man to die once. Among other things."

Well, here they were. Sitting ducks. Hannah was disgusted and began chewing the corner of her thumbnail, her eyes dark and hot with an inner light.

Eli and Manny slid off the bench, began to play with their wooden spools and fences. Silence shrouded the table, a prickly quiet.

Sarah sighed, toyed with her coffee cup, obviously at a loss for words.

"You think the cows will survive this?" Manny asked finally.

"They'll survive the storm better than the wolves that will soon be starving, hungry, and powerful mean. Got a bull out there?"

"Oh, yes. And a cow that's meaner than him." Without thinking, Hannah spoke ahead of Manny. Manny looked at her, blinked, but kept quiet.

"If I were you, I'd soon be riding out. I saw you have a right good windmill. They'll be in, if they're thirsty. Best thing would be a lean-to, stored hay. Don't know if you have either one."

Quickly, Hannah shook her head. That was the hard part. The part that kept her up at night.

Lemuel spoke again. "They should be all right. They might need a little help here and there. Riding out, starting a good strong fire at night, all these things will help repel them wolves. Have you heard them?"

"More coyotes than wolves."

Lemuel nodded. "They'll be the enemy once calving begins."

Fear shot through Hannah. "They tell us purebred Angus have trouble calving." She spoke quickly, the words tumbling out of her mouth, her mistrust pushed to the background.

"No. Someone had it all wrong. Them little Angus calves are small in the head. Delicate. Most ranchers have part Angus for that reason. They drop calves better than some breeds."

Hannah's eyes shone. She leaned forward. "How do you know?"

Lemuel shrugged. "Common knowledge."

Hannah clasped her hands together beneath the table, like a child, she was so delighted.

They rode out. Manny took the lead on Goat. The sun shone with a weak light through the gray veil of the sky, obscuring the brilliant winter blue. The wind had calmed but was still fickle, little spirals of snow puffing up unexpectedly to fling the flakes in stinging whirls against their faces. The horses walked in a few inches of snow, brown grass sticking up like strubbly hair, then plunged into drifts that came up to their chests. All around them the prairie looked level, the snow an even blanket of white, gray shadows swirling a pattern like cold marble. It was all a fine deception. The drifts arose, then faded away, the horses stumbling on clumps of frozen grass.

The air was frigid. Hannah's teeth chattered uncontrollably. Her fingers were like ice picks. She had no idea the cold was so intense. The fabric of her coat was like a window screen, letting in the icy drafts that swirled around her. She watched Manny, hunched in his saddle ahead of her, Goat's sturdy legs breaking a path through yet another drift.

She was shivering violently now, her teeth chattering like pebbles. "Manny!" she shouted.

He stopped Goat and turned to listen, his face wind whipped and raw.

"I can hardly keep going. I'm so cold!" For Hannah to admit anything quite like this must mean it was serious.

"We haven't found the cows yet!" he yelled.

"I know, but I can't go on."

Undecided, Manny gazed across the unforgiving white prairie. To find the cows was necessary for their peace of mind and worth the cold that penetrated like thousands of needles. Hannah was always the one who knew everything, who goaded him and tried him to his limit. So now it was his turn.

"You have to," he shouted back.

"No, Manny. I'm too cold." Hannah bit back her plea for mercy.

Manny goaded Goat without looking back. Hannah had no choice but to follow. She bit her lower lip to keep her teeth from chattering and tasted blood. She couldn't feel her fingers or her toes. Like dead chunks of ice, they were encased in her hard leather boots, stuck in the creaking, frozen stirrups.

Riding above the snow, the cold like sharp needles against her skin, they continued without sighting even one black cow. Impossibly cold, fraught with anxiety and lack of a good night's sleep, Hannah stopped Pete, dismounted, and began to scream at Manny, flailing her arms in circles and stomping her feet against the frozen earth. She felt as small and insignificant as a pinhead in the center of a tilting white orbit that was eventually going to swallow her alive.

Stupid cows. Dumb bovine creatures that couldn't even think for themselves. Let Manny ride on and get lost. She had to help herself or turn into a frozen lump of ice and snow.

Manny stopped Goat, turned in his saddle to watch his sister dismount. Without emotion, he watched her wild motions, stuck his gloved hands beneath his armpits, and waited, squinting his eyes against the stark white light and stinging snow.

When a section of the snowdrift on his right broke away, he blinked. Shading his eyes with his gloved hand, he squinted and blinked again.

Vass in die velt?

The cows!

They had not seen them because they were looking for black objects. Here they were, backed into a snowdrift and, by all appearances, alive and well.

As Hannah continued to flail and scream, chunks of snowdrift continued to break away, black legs carrying the snow until it broke into pieces and slid down the animals' sides, revealing the thick, black hair on their backs covered with powdered snow—like salt on burnt toast.

Manny yelled, twisted in his saddle and pointed. Hannah continued her wild pounding and arm swinging, until her feet stung with returning circulation.

She stopped and heard Manny's voice, saw his outstretched arm.

"What?" He didn't hear her question, and Hannah saw nothing. Quickly she mounted her horse, looked in the direction he was pointing.

"There they are! Manny! Manny!"

Cold and almost hysterical at the sight of the emerging cows, Hannah came undone, crying and laughing intermittently. There was no one to see, no one to hear, except Manny and the crazy old snow-covered cows that ran mooing and bawling over the frozen ground, frightened by the sound of Hannah's screams.

She rode up to Manny. "How many?" she yelled.

"They're all here," he yelled back.

"The bull?"

"Yep, every one of them. That old one, the mean cow, she looks to be calving soon. In a month or two—maybe before that."

"Should we keep her in the barn?"

"What would we feed her? We have barely enough hay for the horses."

Hannah nodded.

Supper that evening was a cozy affair. Sarah was in good spirits and some of Hannah's anxiety had lessened, now that they knew the cows had survived the storm and would likely continue to survive in the coming months. Manny was tall and manly, pleased with his ability to lead Hannah, finding the cows while she mostly cried and floundered around.

He wouldn't always be the follower, which was new knowledge that caused him to hold his head high and his shoulders wide. Hannah wasn't as mighty as she wanted him to believe.

Sarah had put the agate roaster filled with navy beans and tomatoes, cane syrup and salt pork, in the oven hours ago, filling the house with a mouth-watering aroma. She roasted potatoes, and fried slabs of beef, sliced thin and salted and peppered to perfection. She had made warm cracker pudding with canned milk and she had thickened canned peaches, a treat in the middle of winter.

Lemuel Short stayed all that week. Not that Hannah was interested in having him stay that long. He simply had nowhere else to go and no means of transportation.

"What's the harm in it?" Sarah questioned in a whisper, washing dishes with Hannah in the afterglow of their warm and wondrous meal.

"He's bold and old and his eyes look like raisins," Hannah hissed back to her mother, wiping a plate with a corner of the tea towel she was holding.

"It's all right," Sarah said softly.

Lemuel must have heard, opening the subject of his leaving less than an hour later. "I must be on my way," he stated simply.

"But how will you go?" Sarah asked.

"On foot. The way I always go," he answered.

"You can't. It's too cold. The closest neighbor is miles away. I'm not sure that Sylvia Klasserman would appreciate visitors at all. She's pretty meticulous."

Lemuel Short chuckled. "Nothing wrong with that. My Mae, she was no housekeeper. The house was crawling with flies over unwashed dishes. Never swept the floor. Baby rabbits, ducklings, chickens ate the crumbs from our table. Wandered in and out of the house like children. They were her children. She took better care of them chickens than her own babies."

His soft voice rolled to a stop, turning into a sigh of regret tinged with remembrance colored in shame. "It was not good. Seems now I could have done more. Mae wasn't happy. She didn't care."

Hannah thought of Doris Rocher and felt an intense longing to see her. She wondered how she was surviving the winter. She hadn't realized the winter storms would isolate them quite like this.

Were there any happy women in the West? Surely not, now that hard times had come in what history would call the Great Depression. Things weren't so good in the big cities back East, either. Her grandfather had spoken of businessmen committing suicide in New York City, wealthy men who lost their fortunes overnight, and folks migrating to California to the fertile valleys for work picking fruits and vegetables. It was hard luck for countless people.

Perhaps here on the prairie, what was considered hardship back East was only normal, resulting in an easy slide through lean years. But then, not everyone had a grandfather with money laid by and no mortgage on his farm. Already, young men from Pennsylvania were moving to Ohio and Indiana. Would they move even farther west?

Nope. Didn't have to, as far as Hannah was concerned. Certainly not the dashing Jeremiah Riehl. Didn't he think he was quite the fellow, though? Going around kissing girls like it meant nothing. He ought to be ashamed of himself, considering everything. He probably told a dozen girls in Lancaster County the exact same thing. She conjured a picture of Jerry marching along blowing a brass horn and a gaggle of silly girls following him like goslings.

How could Manny accuse her of wanting Jerry? Hadn't he heard her biting words of refusal? She had meant it too. Just a trick of one's mind, thinking about the Great Depression, followed by young men moving west, followed by thoughts of Jerry. Just the way a person's thoughts flowed along, as uncontrollable as a river. It wasn't that she'd tried to think of him.

Actually, if she ever did decide to get married, she'd pick someone who wasn't handsome. Someone who was much too humble and kind to go around thinking he could win her over. Look at Clay. He was every bit as conceited as Jerry. Nothing humble about him either.

Take Lemuel Short, this rail-thin, wizened little man who drowned his sorrows in whiskey. He likely kissed Mae, wooed her, lured her to the West, without a humble thought in his head. Look where it had gotten him. He should have stayed humble and asked a girl who was common-looking, with eyes like raisins, just like him. With a large nose maybe, or stick-thin figure.

He hadn't said, though, what Mae looked like. Later that evening, she asked him and then regretted it instantly.

Poor Lemuel's voice shook, his small eyes seeming to take on a life of their own, lids fluttering like a trapped butterfly, working furiously to keep back the tears.

"She was like a fairy princess. Hair like spun gold and eyes so blue the sky was only a reflection. Lips like a rose."

His deep sighs were like the roaring of a bull to Hannah. She wanted to clap her hands over her ears and leave the room. Simple, doddering old man. Quite his own fault.

There, she had love figured out again. Best to stay away from it if you weren't humble. If you thought too much of yourself, you were bound to be attracted to the same kind of man. Handsome. Good looking. Swaggering and thinking himself a real winner.

That's where most girls went wrong. For the thousandth time, she knew she wasn't like most girls. She wondered how Jerry figured, saying that he wanted to bring horses to the West. Didn't he know horses wouldn't always be in demand?

Look at all the automobiles and tractors popping up like thistles. Not to mention electricity, railroads, and about every modern new thing you could think of. The only thing was, there would always have to be cows, rodeos, show horses, and the need for a good farrier. He could probably make a go of it. Word got around surprisingly fast out here on the plains, especially if you had a telephone.

Jerry had some outstanding horses in that barn in Lancaster. Her hands went to her cheeks, hiding the flush that gave away her thoughts. That day still rattled her as helplessly as it ever had.

Enough now!

She was not going to make the same mistake Lemuel Short had made. What kind of a name was Lemuel Short anyway? Honestly. She shrugged her shoulders, worried the hangnail on the side of her thumb with her teeth, and watched from beneath hooded eyes the little man seated there on the couch with Eli on one side, Mary on the other leaning against him. Baby Abby sat on his lap. He held the Little Golden Book of Hansel and Gretel high so that everyone could see, reading in a good, steady voice punctuated with sighs and squeaks and harrumphs until they were so involved in the story they were oblivious to everything around them.

The children with no father, the father with no children, both supplying what the other longed for. Sarah stood by the kitchen table, the balding, stoop-shouldered man dressed in her dead husband's clothes, a bewildering, mysterious sight that she could not begin to unravel.

CHAPTER 7

THE HIGH, UNDULATING CRY OF WOLVES REMOVED HANNAH FROM her curtain of sleep. Her bedroom was cold, but the sound sent a frigid chill up her spine. Her open mouth was dry and her tongue stuck to the roof of her mouth, her breath coming in short, quick gasps. Her heartbeat accelerated at the sound of their howls.

They had come, then. She pictured them, high-backed, long-legged, bony, the ragged hair along their backs like the teeth of a saw, bad-tempered, their driving hunger propelling them toward the rich smell of cows.

It was more than she could bear lying there helplessly, a mere dot on the endless white expanse that was their home, their acquired portion of prairie, their homestead. For a fleeting instant, she grasped a vision of herself sleeping soundly in the winter wonderland that was Lancaster County, a job secured in some little dry-goods store, unaware of the appalling dangers of the West. She regretted the move—almost.

She jumped out of bed and made her way along the hall, startled at the soft voice from the couch asking, "You heard?"

Too frightened to speak properly, she nodded. Lemuel Short sat up, quilts wrapped securely around his legs, her father's nightshirt sliding to the side, exposing the veins on his thin neck. The candle in her hand flickered.

"If I was younger, I'd ride out with a lantern," he stated.

"Should we?" Hannah asked, like a child.

"If you have good horses. Be foolish to try it on middling ones." Pete and Goat were definitely middling.

"Will they be able to defend themselves?" she asked in a quivering voice.

"If you have a bull and one ornery cow with horns, they'll give it a good shot. What worries me is how hungry the wolves are."

Hannah nodded. She sat in the chair facing him and set the candle on the oak table, twisting her hands in her lap, her eyes large and dark.

"Should I wake Manny?" she asked.

"I'd let him sleep. You can't ride out if your horses are middling."

"I can't go back to bed, either."

"You don't have to." Sarah appeared, a heavy flannel wrapper secured about her waist, her hair loosened, worry lines creasing her delicate mouth like parentheses. "Surely it is the worst sound a rancher could hear at night." Her words were soft, gravelly with sleep, but devoid of Hannah's panicky tones. "You won't ride out?" she asked.

"Lemuel thinks I shouldn't with the horses we have."

"A wise choice, Hannah. I couldn't bear to see you and Manny ride out." Sarah shuddered, a small involuntary movement, then seemed to shrink in on herself.

Lemuel threw aside the quilts, drew his trousers up over his flannel long johns, hitched up the nightshirt and scratched his stomach. Hannah hurried out to the kitchen, where her mother was putting the kettle on, lighting the kerosene lamp—automatic movements she made many times without thinking.

Lemuel followed, sat down at the table, coughing into his red handkerchief, apologizing, begging their pardon.

The long drawn-out wail sounded again, mournful, primal calls of hunger and loneliness. Hannah's eyes showed the terror she felt, the despair following on its heels. "Could they attack a year-old heifer, bring her down successfully, do you think?"

Lemuel watched the flame in the lamp, his wrinkled face like unironed linen, etched and crisscrossed with blue and red veins, his raisin eyes glittering like wet river pebbles.

"I'll just tell you that if the cows are smart, they'll stick tight, and the bull and the mean cow should be able to protect them. If they spread out, face the pack separately, you'll lose some."

"We can't afford to lose any!" Hannah burst out.

"Sometimes life on the range teaches you what you can afford and what you can't," Lemuel stated. "It's not always up to us. Nature throws us some punches, you know. You gotta go with it."

Real appreciation shone in Sarah's eyes while Hannah resisted his easy speech. No wonder he didn't make it and took to the bottle. You had to fight for everything you got. You had to be smart and cunning, no matter what Lemuel said.

They rode out in the crisp, biting morning, the sun on the snow blinding them as they set off. Hannah's teeth chattered from fear, the dreaded unknown, the pit of her stomach like a stone. She didn't feel the cold, only the specter of possible death before her.

Manny was grim but composed, riding Goat like a true knight, his face toward the sun, courageous. They rode into deep snow, the force of the horses' churning legs sending it spraying, instantly slowing them down. Out to windswept high places, and they could increase their speed.

Their eyes searched the snowing plains, longing to see the familiar salt-and-pepper cows sprinkled with frosty snow. There was nothing. They rode to the east for miles, turned north in a sweeping arc, the horses' breath coming in short, white puffs. A thin dark line appeared below Pete's bridle, the sweat staining the light brown hairs of his face.

Manny shouted and pointed a gloved hand. A tight bundle of cows. Hannah rose up in her saddle and strained to see, her eyes squinting against the early morning sun.

At the horses' approach, the herd scattered and ran off in their awkward hump-backed gallop, snorting and wild-eyed. There was no evidence of a struggle, the snow around them smooth and windblown.

There was the bull, and the mean, horned cow. Quickly Hannah counted. Only counted eleven; there should be twelve yearling cows.

They came upon the grisly scene before they could brace themselves. Snow trampled into the consistency of cottage cheese, deep hoof marks, huge paw prints, then the awful pink color of blood mixed with snow.

The bones protruded, a rib cage with bits of hair, meat, and gristle, the empty eyes staring and wild-eyed, horribly panicked from the ripping, clawing feet and slavering mouths that brought her down.

Half eaten, the cloven hooves barely attached to the devoured leg portion, snow and old dried grass mingled with the remains of the yearling heifer. The struggle to save herself must have been fearsome, the cow and smaller bull trying to stave off the wolves.

Hannah dismounted after Manny. They stood together, heads bent, unable to grasp what the wolves had accomplished.

"I hate those big brutes. They'll kill anything just to kill," she yelled, angry and needing to avenge herself. She wanted to ride home, get the rifle and hunt down the bloodthirsty pack and kill them all.

She would.

She turned with swift, jerky movements, placed her foot in the stirrup, and flung herself astride her horse.

"Where are you going?"

"For the rifle. I'm going to hunt down this pack of wolves until I've killed every last one!"

"You can't do that!" Manny yelled after her, then mounted his horse and tore off after her.

They shouted at each other the whole way home. Manny tried to talk sense, tell her the wolf pack roamed for miles on end, much farther than old Pete could manage even if she rode hard for most of the day.

"Shut up! I don't believe you!" Hannah shouted over her shoulder.

In the end, it took hours of reasoning by Lemuel with Sarah's tearful pleas and Manny's words injected at opportune moments, until Hannah relented.

The cows had to come in. They had to be brought into the corral, today. No matter that they had nothing to feed them. They'd starve out there anyway. In their weakened state, the wolves would finish off the whole herd.

Lemuel told her the horses were spent. She could go nowhere now, likely not all week, unless they had a warm spell. The wolves would be back to finish their kill, but they would not necessarily be able to kill another one. The cows would not starve on the prairie. Better to leave them. They'd be in for water from the tank.

Break up the ice, make sure they had access to water. In spite of giving in to Lemuel's advice, Hannah took matters into her own hands after dinner. She saddled Pete and rode off to the Klassermans against Lemuel and Manny's advice.

They'd drive the herd to the Klasserman ranch. Hannah was crazy with fear, obsessed with the possibility of dead yearling carcasses dotting the prairie, a ruined mess of blood and mangled flesh, protruding bones that were an open invitation to the golden eagles and buzzards from the sky.

She couldn't bear to think of their ability to pay back the loan taken away by the ruthless hunger of scavengers in winter. Nature wasn't that cruel, and God surely wasn't, either. So that left only the devil and his unclean mischief.

Half-frozen, she barely clung to the saddle as Pete stumbled into the Klassermans' barnyard, exhausted from wading through deep drifts of snow.

Red-faced Owen Klasserman lumbered through the snow wearing so many clothes he resembled a human snowman, lifting a fat, gloved finger and wagging it as he spoke.

"You dumb voman. Vott iss wrong mitt you? Ei-ya-yi-yi-yi. You easy freeze. You kill dat horse."

Hannah threw herself off the saddle, her feet like blocks of ice, her knees crumpled so that she sat down hard in the snow, Pete heaving, his head hanging straight out, the way horses do when they are beyond reasonably tired.

"Get up, Hannah. Get up!" Owen shouted, disgusted that she had had the gall to ride that old horse through the drifts. She could have become lost or disoriented, lost on the prairie, frozen to death. The plains in winter were not to be taken lightly. Owen knew this well.

Nearly crying, Hannah stumbled into the barn after Owen. He removed Pete's saddle with excessive grunts, scolding and lamenting in between.

"Dis horse too oldt for your dumbheit," he scolded.

"We don't have a better one."

"Den you must stay home."

"I can't." Almost losing control and giving way to little-girl tears of rage and frustration, Hannah told Owen between shivers and chattering teeth that the wolves had killed a yearling heifer.

Owen's blue eyes popped open. "I told Sylvia. I told her I hear them volves."

Hannah followed Owen to the house, past the swept porch and the broom hanging from a nail by a short length of rawhide.

Sylvia threw up her hands, a glad light in her blue eyes, her apron stretched tight across her doughy hips, waggling a red, plumpish finger and scolding just the way Owen had.

Hannah removed her boots, carefully staying on the colorful rag rug, setting them neatly side by side. They led her to the table, where a steaming cup of Dutch cocoa waited along with a variety of cookies, sweet rolls, and breads.

The kitchen gleamed in the winter sunlight. The gas range shone like a mirror, the curtains above the sink so white they shone blue. African violets were blooming in an array of colors, lined up in coffee cans like a harbinger of spring. The patterned linoleum floor was waxed to a high sheen, not a crumb or scuff mark anywhere.

Hannah resolved to be a housekeeper just like Sylvia if she ever had her own house. It would not include a husband to clump through the kitchen with bits of manure clinging to the soles of his shoes.

"The wolves got one of our heifers," Hannah explained. "We have no lean-to, no shelter of any kind, and no hay stored because of the fire." She took a deep breath. "So, the reason I'm here is to ask if there's a possibility of driving our cows to your ranch where they could be taken care of."

Owen drummed his fingertips on the oilcloth table top. "You can't drive them over. Likely dese cows is already hungry and not so strong. To keep volves away iss not easy unless you camp out on the prairie." He shook his head. "Too hard. Too hard. How you gonna keep firewood? How you gonna take it dere?"

Hannah's eyes widened. "You mean there's nothing to be done?"

"Without stored hay, no. Especially not without goot horses. Do you vant me to call Jenkins on the telephone? See vhat Hod says?"

Hannah nodded, grateful.

So a yelling into the telephone mouthpiece ensued, punctuated by many "Vot's? Vot you say? Huh?" Finally he handed the phone to Hannah, who took it with trembling fingers. Hope was slipping away too fast, the awful prospect of letting those cows out to fend for themselves beyond her comprehension.

"Hello?"

"Hannah?"

"Yes."

"Hod here."

"Yes."

"You crazy?"

"Owen says I am."

His deep, relaxed chuckle came through the line. "Believe me, you are." That deep, automatic chuckle again that seemed to iron out every hopeless obstacle in her way. "So you lost a heifer, Owen tells me."

"Yes." She hated the tears she felt were forming.

"Well, there ain't a whole lot you can do if this snow keeps up. Them cows might do good on their own. Learn to stay tight. You got that mean one and the bull. But, tell you what. Pickin's are gonna get pretty slim so what we'll do is watch the weather. If'n we git a warm spell, we'll take the tractor and try to haul some hay over there to yer windmill. Yer biggest problem is no hay. Them cows won't starve, but they might not do too good, either. You might lose a few more heifers to them wolves. Boys and I might ride out, see what we can find. Wouldn't suggest it now, the way the snow's piled around. You get yerself home now, Hannah. Sit tight and see what the weather does."

"But I can't wait to see if it will warm up," Hannah said. "It will seem like every day and night is a week long, sitting there while the wolves chew up our whole herd."

Hod laughed outright. Abby pestered Hod to give her the telephone and he handed it over to her.

"Hannah!"

"How are you, Abby?"

"Doin' all right. How's them little ones? And your ma?"

"We're cozy and warm. We have plenty to eat. We're blessed."
Now she sounded just like her father.

"You shore are."

"We have a man staying at our house, Lemuel Short. He's
homeless and wandered into the shack. He almost died."

"Mercy sakes, Child. You can't trust them people." Abby let
loose a hailstorm of warnings about folks helping those vagabonds and how badly it turned out. "Best send him on his way,"
she admonished.

The very next morning, late, a posse of men arrived on horseback. Hod and all his boys and two men neither Sarah nor Hannah had ever seen before. They rode in, their horses well lathered,
nostrils expanded, breathing rapidly, their necks stretched out
after the men dismounted.

The boys hung back and led the horses into the barn as Clay
led the way to the porch. Sarah became alarmed, watching Lemuel, whose small, kind eyes turned hard as glittering pieces of
coal. He sat on a kitchen chair like a bound animal, straining
against unseen forces, twisting his hands and leaning forward,
his elbows on his knees. Then he sat up straight, breathing
rapidly.

There was an insistent rapping. Hannah opened the door
and stepped back to allow the men to enter. Sarah stood off to
the side observing. Manny came out of the wash house door,
clearly surprised, then alarmed.

The teakettle's low humming was the only sound after the
men had all filed through the door, standing at attention as they
watched the tallest of the two strangers. He was dressed just
like Hod, heavy denim overcoat, jeans, a woolen scarf, his black
Stetson jammed down halfway over his ears, face brick red from

the cold, a mustache like a dark brush, stiff, as if each hair had been frozen.

"Mornin', ma'am," he said to Sarah, who smiled politely and nodded. He looked at Mr. Short, who sat upright, one palm on the table, his face white and without expression.

"Lemuel? Lemuel Short?"

Features etched in stone. No reply.

The man reached into a pocket of his overcoat, produced a badge, the gold star of his profession. The sheriff. Lemuel's expression remained unchanged.

"We've been lookin' for you, Mr. Short. You need to accompany us back to Pine."

Lemuel remained mute, as still as a carved statue. The accompanying sheriff told him he was under arrest, quietly, as solemn as a minister. It was only when he produced the silver handcuffs that Lemuel reacted, leaping sideways, rocketing from his chair with the speed and agility of a much younger man. There was no evidence of his cough, his weakness eclipsed by his desperation.

Chairs overturned as a scuffle broke out. Sarah, standing by the stove, lifted both hands to cover her face. It was only a matter of seconds until Lemuel was subdued, the cold metal of the handcuffs clicked into place. His head was bent, the skin on top shining from beneath his thin, gray hair, as vulnerable as a child. For a fleeting instant Hannah wanted to believe he was innocent of whatever wrong he had done in the past. Or *was* it the past?

"Sorry, ma'am, for the inconvenience," the tall, burly sheriff said. "But I don't believe you want Mr. Short in your care any longer. He's wanted for killing a man in a bar fight in Lacoma, about a hundred miles west of here."

Sarah nodded, wide-eyed, a hand to her mouth.

"You need some heavy clothing," the sheriff ordered brusquely. Lemuel could not raise his head. It was as if there was a rock on his shoulders weighing him down. He did not resist as they loosened the handcuffs, standing patiently as he put on his overcoat, one of Mose's homemade denim ones, and wound the old scarf around his head.

Hannah carried the look of his eyes with her for days. When he lifted his head, his eyes reminded her of a wounded animal caught in a trap. The desperation gave way to a sad acceptance of his fate, his words soft and filled with sincerity.

"Ma'am," he said to Sarah, "if I die in prison, your face will get me through until the end. You're one of those rare people that shine with an inner light. Your prayers alone is all I need. Pray for me every morning and evening so that God can accept my repentance. I deserve to burn in hell forever, but with your prayers opening the way for my own feeble begging, I just might make it."

Hannah straightened her shoulders and bit her lips to keep the weakness at bay.

"I'm ready," he told the sheriff, then walked through the door into the blinding world of sun on snow, his head held high.

Sarah sank into a chair, a shuddering breath releasing the tension in the room. She shook her head. "At a time when I should have spoken to him about salvation, words wouldn't come. Now he'll go to prison without hearing about Jesus Christ, and all I have is my German Bible. And Mose's . . ."

Manny broke in. "He wants to be forgiven, Mam. He'll find the way. I believe his story about his past. I do. He was just a bitter man. I'll help you pray for him."

"Thank you, Manny."

"He could have killed us all," Hannah said with conviction.

"But he didn't," Sarah said softly.

"We have to stop trusting people, Mam. We're such ignorant, greenhorns from the East. We lived in a cloistered society. Being raised Amish to live in peace and forbearance might be all right as long as you stay in Lancaster County. But we're here in the West now, where tramps are murderers and wolves destroy cattle, snowstorms can threaten your life, and drought shrivels anything you plant. We need to become smarter, wiser, or we're not going to make it."

"God will take care of us," Sarah said quietly.

"And what if He doesn't?" Hannah burst out. "We have no guarantee on this earth that He'll magically turn everything in our favor. That's how Dat thought. He lived by those principles and dreamed his way into poverty and starvation."

Sarah watched the heated passion in her daughter's face. She sighed, a weary sound of resignation. "Perhaps if we were as smart as we should be, we'd realize homesteading is folly and return to our native land. Perhaps God is allowing all these frightening things to show us we are not living according to His will."

Hannah didn't consider her mother's words, just tossed them aside like apple peels, keeping what she wanted to believe.

"So you're saying it wasn't God's will that Dat traveled out here?"

Miserably, Sarah shook her head. "I don't know, Hannah. I don't know."

Manny sat up. "Well, Mam, we're here now. We're in debt. We're blessed to have a sturdy house and our health. We have sound minds to think this through. I think we'll get through the winter and, to my way of thinking, the cows will learn to fend for themselves. To try and put everyone else in danger by bringing the cows in, providing hay, is foolish. I don't care what you say, Hannah.

"It will be a setback to lose more heifers, but it would be worse to lose our lives or cause our neighbors to lose theirs. I don't believe the weather will warm up, according to Hod and the boys. Clay says it'll likely keep snowing. He knows more about the prairie weather than we do, so I think we need to take his advice."

Instant rebellion rose in Hannah. "It's just dumb, Manny!"

"What?"

"Letting those cows out there to weaken."

"What is better? Bring them in and let them starve around the water tank?"

"Hod and the boys will bring over hay."

"How?"

"The tractor. They said they would."

"Well, if it's possible, they will. It might not be possible and you know it. For once in your life, Hannah, consider someone else's opinion and let go of your own."

Hannah met Manny's gaze, direct, calm, filled with conviction. She hated for him to tell her what to do, but she knew there was no choice. Even as she watched his face, the brilliance of the blinding sun on snow faded, casting shadows beneath his dark eyes.

Sarah looked up, then turned her head to watch the sun's disappearance, the mountain of gray clouds swelling and inflating even as they sat there together.

"Is there plenty of firewood in?" she asked softly.

CHAPTER 8

THE LIGHT GREW DIM AND FALTERED. THE KITCHEN TURNED OMI-
nous, dark shadows appearing in corners that had been filled
with sunshine.

Hannah's dark eyes flickered with fear. Manny's face paled
as the light was erased, turning the house even darker.

Sarah rose, lifted the glass chimney on the coal-oil lamp,
struck a match with her thumbnail, lighted the wick, and
watched the steady yellow flame before replacing the chimney.

Hannah stood and went to the west-facing windows, meeting her adversary head-on, arms crossed around her waist like
steel armor. As far as she could see, the level snow-covered land
stretched before her, pure white, indented by blue gray shadows.
The horizon was smeared into the land, as if the boiling gray
clouds were gobbling up the earth, destroying it as the winter
storm approached.

There was no wind, only a threatening calm, a quiet portent. The hairs on her forearms rose with the quick chills
along them. The urge to fling herself on a horse and round up
the cold, hungry cattle was overpowering, followed by a helplessness and loss of ability she could not name.

No one could prepare a person for this all-encompassing
force of nature. It sent you whimpering into yourself. As she

stood there, the clouds shifted, steely gray and flat, as dark as a moonlit night, the snow on the prairie brighter than the sky itself.

Had all the rain that did not fall during the summer packed itself into a vast cloud that stayed above them in the gentle, drought stricken days of autumn? How did one go about understanding the weather patterns in this God-forsaken land?

There! She had finally thought the unthinkable. Had not God forsaken them in their hour of need? Hannah felt alone, isolated, punished by forces beyond anything she could control, like a tiny vessel pummeled by the seas, hundreds of miles out away from the security of the land.

So then, ultimately, God did what He wanted to do, leaving His mortals to flounder around for themselves. There was no mercy in the face of this fast approaching storm.

What about the sheriffs and Lemuel Short? If they were caught in what appeared to be a maelstrom of wind and snow, they'd lose their way and freeze to death. It might be just as well for poor Mr. Short.

Sarah busied herself building up the fire. She jumped back as the cookstove lids rattled, followed by a puff of white smoke that belched from the fire pit. Alarmed, she raised questioning eyes to Manny. "You think the chimney is clogged with soot?"

Quickly, Manny threw on his coat and boots, pulled himself up the porch posts and onto the roof, as agile as a cat, Hannah watching from below. He waded through the snow on the roof of the porch, but the wind had blown most of it off the house roof, allowing him to reach the stone chimney. He lowered a long pole, wiggled it around to test for a buildup of soot, then shook his head, perplexed.

"There's nothing there!" he yelled.

There was a cry from the kitchen as the cookstove puffed out more billows of gray wood smoke. Manny slid off the roof, landing in deep snow, then shook himself, his face and hands already red with the cold.

"Must be the air," he said. "A downdraft. Before the storm."

Hannah watched the pewter gray sky worriedly. "Think we'd better find a rope to attach from the house to the barn?" she asked.

"Might be a good idea."

They found pieces of rope and knotted them together until a long line could be attached to the barn, propped up here and there by pieces of wood as high as a clothesline. Sarah continued to deal with the cranky stove, waving her apron to dispel the onslaught of wood smoke that coughed out of every crack at regular intervals.

The children coughed and wiped their streaming eyes. Abby began to cry, rubbing her eyes as she tried to rid herself of the bothersome fumes.

When the storm hit, it sucked up the smoke and spewed it out of the chimney, raising the red-hot coals underneath into leaping flames and heating the stove top to a cherry red glow. It was as if the stove had no controls, no levers to open and shut the draft, leaving the fire to burn hotter and hotter.

Sarah realized she could only throw on a few sticks of wood at a time. It would be better to be cold than let the fire rage out of control and threaten them with the loss of their house and perhaps their lives.

The wind shook the well-built house in its teeth. Snow scoured the windows like gravel flung by a giant hand, rattled against the window panes, and bounced off to form a drift against the walls. There was nothing to see except a dizzying whirl of snow and ice, the sky and the prairie blending into one.

Hannah wrapped herself into an old quilt, the edges frayed by many washings, and pouted. She picked at loose threads, loosening thin patches of worn fabric, and pitied herself with a deep and abiding sympathy. She refused to answer her mother's worried inquiries, turned her face away, closed her eyes, and shut out the whole business of life that included storms and wolves and cattle and deceased fathers who had made insane choices to move their family to a land that was simply unlivable. She railed against her mother's subservient demeanor and was angered by Manny's disobedience.

Why hadn't someone stood up for them when her father had made poor choices and lost the farm? Why had they all followed him like docile sheep out to this—there it was again—this God-forsaken, impossible land?

The drought and the fire had been one thing, but these awful blizzards were a new and terrible thing.

A metallic sensation welled up in her mouth; a stone settled in her stomach. Real fear had a physical taste, like moldy bread served on a rusted plate.

Sarah cooked a fine vegetable stew seasoned with scraps of canned beef. Above the roar of the wind, the metal spoon clanking against the glass jar brought an intense homesickness, as she remembered her mother opening a jar of beef chunks, dumping them into the heated browned butter in the pan, the fragrant meat simmering in its own juice before she thickened it with a heavy white mixture of flour and water.

Beef gravy over mounds of mashed potatoes eaten with fresh hull peas from the garden, homemade white bread with freshly churned butter and raspberry jam.

Had they taken it all for granted? *Undankbar*. Unthankfulness, one of the deadliest sins. Was that why God had sent the Great Depression, forcing them into the unreasonable slide of unmet payments, unpaid bills, and collectors like wolves slavering on the porch? Surely Mose had not seen where they were headed. Or had he?

Chunks of canned beef had not been available for many Amish families. Some smart housewives learned to cook bacon or bologna rinds, frying them into a deep, dark gel, adding milk and thickening it with flour like gravy.

Blooney dunkas. Bologna gravy. And it was good. Turnips had taken the place of potatoes after they were gone toward the end of winter. A stronger flavor, one many children disliked, but what Elam King's Salome had said was true: "A child who is hungry enough will eat almost anything."

Who could have foreseen it, this Great Depression? Money, as the stalwart Amish had come to know it, suddenly became worthless. Uncountable debt. Land without value. Unthinkable. The old, white-bearded men shook their heads and blamed the president. The crooked politicians who would bring down the greatest country on earth.

They argued, their words circling among themselves, but no one really understood the root of the problem or how to fix it. So they always circled back to the president. They tightened their suspenders, pulled their straw hats low and went to work. They did without, made do with what they had, and were more thankful for leaner rations than they'd been in fatter times.

Wasn't it something how you could make dresses from feed sacks? Housewives repeatedly devised ways of dyeing the letters and objects printed on the rough cotton material. The children owned three shirts or dresses, one for Sunday, one for school, and one for *voddogs*, usually the everyday one patched and patched again, then handed down to a younger child and held together by still more patches.

Well, they'd certainly been prepared for the lean times here in the West. Real poverty was something the housewives of Lancaster County could not have understood, even in the grip of the Great Depression. Turnips and bologna gravy was one thing; but to go to bed with a yawning pit that hurt from being empty, a stomach shriveled and aching for lack of food, was quite another.

The aroma of the fragrant vegetable stew filled the cold, dark house. Sarah dished it up, bowls of thickly cut potatoes and carrots seasoned with beef and onion and parsley. She cut wedges of sourdough bread and spread it with dark molasses from the barrel.

Hannah refused to leave her self-inflicted cocoon of quilts, turning her face away and keeping her eyes closed, her mouth a hard line of determination. Manny glanced her way, shrugged his shoulders, and began to eat hungrily. Sarah lifted her eyebrows and was met with a shrug of Manny's wide, young shoulders. Let her pout.

"Hannah, come on. Aren't you hungry?" Mary called before she lifted her spoon to begin eating the stew.

"She probably doesn't feel good," was Eli's verdict.

Abby waved her spoon and gurgled happily, as Sarah tied the cloth bib around her neck.

The wind roared like a freight train. The snow hissed against the window. A death song for the cattle, Hannah thought, allowing bitter thoughts to hold her in their grip. They would never survive this. The ones that didn't starve would be eaten by ravenous wolves, specters of death descending on them through the ever deepening snow.

Manny could not rouse her to help feed the horses. Little Eli accompanied him along the rope to the barn, red-faced and gasping, his chest expanding by his sense of being one with his brother. Sarah fussed over him, saying he was a right young man, and made him strong hot tea flavored with molasses.

Mary sang a little German school song in her sweet, low voice as she played on the floor, building a tower with wooden spools for Abby.

Kommt liebe Kindlein,
Kommt zu dem Vater.

Abby squealed when the tower fell over, wooden spools rolling in every direction. Eli dove after them, reaching beneath the oak cupboard, the couch, and pushing aside the roll of quilts that encased Hannah's legs.

"Move. I need those spools," he directed.

Angrily, Hannah kicked out, hitting the side of his head, sending him from a good-natured crawl to a sprawling, indignant roll on his back. He gave a loud, insulted yell, which brought Sarah from the bedroom where she had been putting more covers on the beds.

"She kicked me!" Eli howled.

Sarah stood there, quietly taking in the situation. The storm shook the house, rattled the windowpanes, moaned and whistled around the edges of the roof, setting her teeth on edge and allowing no great amount of patience where her eldest daughter was concerned.

With brisk steps she strode over to the couch. Without a word, she gripped the corners of the quilt in both hands, threw her weight backward and heaved, rolling Hannah out of the quilts onto her stomach, leaving her sprawled in an ungainly position across the couch.

"Get up! Get out of these quilts and go to your room. If you're going to act like a six-year-old, then I'll treat you like one." With each word her temper increased, until she reached out and gave Hannah a hard cuff on the shoulder.

Hannah was shocked into obedience. She sent a desultory glance in her mother's direction, got herself onto her feet, and slunk into her room, closing the door with a firm slam.

Sarah reached down, grabbed the quilts, opened Hannah's bedroom door, and tossed them inside before closing the door with a decided click.

Sarah didn't speak for a long time after that. She washed dishes, dried them, and put them away. She cleaned the stove top with an emery board, piled on more wood than she should have, swept the floor, and got the children ready for bed.

Night came early, and with the darkness, the sound of the storm seemed to grow louder. Tension already ran high and taut, a tight rope that none of them had the skill to navigate, so they may as well go to bed. Things would be better in the morning light.

Hannah finally undressed, put on her long flannel nightgown and crawled beneath the heavy covers. Her teeth chattered and she was ravenously hungry. She wasn't about to set foot out her room to eat cold, congealed vegetable stew. Or face her mother's wrath. What in the world had come over her? She should have displayed some of that gumption to her husband! Likely he wouldn't have dared to even think about moving out West.

That certainly was a put down, your own mother treating you to a solid smack on the shoulder. At her age. She cringed in embarrassment.

What in the world? Her meek and quiet mother. Well, she'd seen that side of her before, and it was a scary spectacle. Her large dark eyes, that solid, tall body made of muscle. She could be tough if she wanted to be. Most times, though, meekness and goodness covered the tough side, like fluffy frosting on a layer cake.

The cold burned her nose. She should get up and open the door to allow some of the heat from the wood stove to circulate, but there was no way she was going to let her mother know she was cold.

She dreamed a long, unsettling dream that night, one that set her eyelids to fluttering, small squeaks coming from her throat until her eyes flew open and she was fully awake, staring wide-eyed into the roaring, snow-scoured night that was as cold as an icicle.

She thought about the dream, reliving her feelings of desperation. The wolves were devouring the cattle, one by one, the great horned cow the only one remaining alive. She had devised a plan—she couldn't say what it was—to save the cattle's lives, but she was hampered by her mother constantly slapping her shoulder.

Manny was nowhere around in her dream. Well, that was certainly frightening! Perhaps her dream meant something. Maybe it was God's way of speaking to her. Who knew? Very likely it meant that she could have ridden out and saved the cattle if her mother had only allowed it.

That might not be the case, though. She knew she could very well have been caught in this deadly blizzard if she had disobeyed.

She didn't go back to sleep for a long time, partly because she was so cold and partly because she thought she would surely lose her mind listening to the wind and the snow. Anxious about being in debt, and about the cows, she wondered what they would do when the snow melted and uncovered fourteen carcasses half-eaten by wolves or starved to death.

That blizzard was only the second in a series of winter storms unlike anything the local folks had ever seen. Some of the older men and women remembered worse winters, when the bitter winds drove the snow into ten-foot drifts that dotted the prairie like mountain ranges.

It was in late March that the snow began to become soft and heavy. The edge of the roof was lined with shimmering, glassy icicles. It became a dangerous route to pass beneath them when they dripped icy water or let loose entirely, crashing to the snow with a grand display of shattered ice.

The sun shone with varying degrees of warmth, but eventually the day came when the snow was shallow enough to attempt navigating. Still, Sarah would not allow it, saying the storms could raise their heads and arrive in less than an hour, which wouldn't allow a sufficient amount of time to ride home safely.

Only after the Jenkins boys rode over did she allow it. Hannah found herself feeling awkward and tongue-tied, her feet clumsy when confronted by the young men—Clay, Hank and

Ken. All of them were attractive, curious, eager to know how the family had fared during three months of winter.

How was Hannah expected to tell them the truth? The endless dark hours of anxiety, the dread of another approaching storm, the certainty of finding only cattle remains, her night sweats and attacks of panic?

To her own sense of pride, she had never cried. She refused to do that. She had battled her own inner demons, to be sure, the determination to survive unaided while she bitterly railed against the storms and doubted God's mercy.

Sarah remained the firm foundation for all of them after that evening when she sent Hannah to her room. It was Sarah who rallied valiantly when Hannah fell into another swamp of despair, wallowing in her lethal self-pity, covering herself in the muddy slime of blaming her father for all of her woes, unwilling and unable to see that it was she who had orchestrated the move back, who had goaded the remainder of the family into the pioneer spirit.

Clearly, it had been Hannah's choice. But the price was unforeseen, and the toll it took on her emotional health uncalculated. So now, standing before the Jenkins boys, she found herself ill at east, unsure, incapable of hiding her terror at having lived so isolated and alone.

Clay was pale, blond, clean cut, as lean and handsome as she'd ever seen him. Clean shaven, his gray Stetson pulled to his eyebrows, his eyes shone like blue ice. Hank was a mirror of his brother; Ken was even taller than his siblings.

Their eyes bore into Hannah's face, curious, alive with interest. Hannah was thinner, dark circles under her huge, brown eyes. There was an intensity about her that seemed unsettling somehow. Manny was good natured, saying they'd come through okay. Really. A large affable grin sealed his sincerity, and the Jenkinses believed him.

Tight-lipped, Hannah suggested they all ride out together to check on the cows. A nervous tic at the corner of her eye, her lips twitching, her voice hoarse, her fingers restlessly easing out of her gloves and stretching back into them.

Clay watched her silently. She hadn't taken the winter well. He noticed the too-wide eyes, the blue veins that showed at her temples, the cold blisters that lined her upper lip, appearing painful.

"Horses need to rest awhile before we ride farther," Clay suggested to his brothers.

Manny invited them in for coffee, gladly brought them through the door to his welcoming mother, who met the three boys with hands extended, her dark eyes alight.

"Oh, it's just a pleasure to see your faces!" she beamed. Gladly she served them mugs of hot coffee and brought out the sourdough bread and the jam she kept for special occasions.

She asked so many questions that Clay finally laughed and said he couldn't find all the answers for her soon enough. Yes, Hod and Abby were both in good health. Abby had had a bit of pleurisy, a cough, but got herself over it without seeing a doctor. "Not as if'n the doctor could have done a whole lot, stuck in town the way he was."

Amid all the talk and slurping of hot coffee, Hannah remained stone-faced, one thumb and forefinger picking constantly at her cold sores until they bled.

Clay cringed as he watched her apply a clean handkerchief, watched as she tried to conceal the spots of red blood. No, he decided, she had not come through the winter well. An ordeal is what it had been.

It was only when he stretched and suggested they ride out that she came to life, springing up with cat-like energy and grace, yanking at the sleeves of her coat to tear it off the wooden peg on the wall. Her fingers shook as she tightened the cinch on her saddle. The bit rattled against Pete's teeth as she tried to insert it into his mouth.

They rode out in single file, Hannah falling behind, old Pete working to lift his wide hooves through the wet snow. The sodden earth, a quagmire of mud, rotting roots, decaying grass and, where the fire had burned it off, a black, slimy mush of soot, ashes, and snow, sucked at the horses' hooves.

"You go west, Clay!" Hank shouted, jerking a thumb in the spoken direction. Clay turned in his saddle, looking for Hannah. "Go with me?" he called to her.

"She can ride with me," Hank offered.

"Naw. You go east. Take Manny and Ken with you." Hank gave his brother an exasperated look, but was too proud to object. He knew well enough that Clay was sweet on Hannah. Good luck with that one!

Clay sat astride his horse, relaxed and waiting for her to catch up. Hannah's pale face was pinched, wan, and much too thin.

"You musta forgot to eat most of the winter," he said, watching her dark eyes focus anywhere but on his.

"Yeah, well. It was a long winter," Hannah snapped.

"That's when most people enjoy their food. You know, hibernate like bears and get fat!"

"I got sick of sourdough bread."

Clay laughed. Hannah's eyes scanned the prairie with a furtive look, almost like a person obsessed. She bit her lower lip, her gloved hand went to her mouth repeatedly until she remembered the gloves, lowering her hands to fiddle with the buttons on her coat.

"You're more nervous than a cat on a hot tin roof," Clay observed.

"You would be too if your whole life depended on these cows."

"Now, Hannah. There's more to life than makin' a livin'. You won't starve."

Soberly, Hannah nodded. "We almost did one time. Probably will again if these cows didn't survive. You know that."

"I told Hank to shoot if they see 'em, so listen for a gunshot." They rode on. Clay produced a pair of black binoculars that he put to his eyes to scan the white prairie. Once, Hannah thought she saw a dark lump but it passed from her vision.

The sky was blue, studded with small gray clouds like sheep's wool, dirty and thick. The air was cold but the sun shone on their faces, not warm but with a softness of promised spring. A dark line appeared on the horizon. Hannah shouted, pointing a shaking gloved finger.

Clay shook his head. "It's them cottonwoods north of the Klassermans. Doubt if yer cattle stuck that close."

"Think not?"

"They had a wide area to travel if they wanted to find food."

Hannah could not have answered if she had wanted to, with the hard knot of fear forming in her chest. Clay probably knew they would never find their cattle and was only humoring her.

"Let's ride to those cottonwoods anyway. Maybe they went there for some kind of shelter."

"Sure. We can check." Clay goaded his horse, leaving a weary, mud-splattered Pete behind.

CHAPTER 9

THE COTTONWOOD TREES WERE MUCH FARTHER AWAY THAN THEY appeared. Clay had to halt his horse repeatedly, waiting until Hannah caught up. They rode together, Pete's sides heaving, a good lather of sweat appearing beneath the cinch and around the saddle blanket. He walked faithfully on, his head bobbing, his ears flicking, listening for commands.

There. Wasn't that line of trees too dark? Hannah lifted a hand to her forehead, shading her eyes from the sunlight. There was a band of black, irregular shapes too thick to be trunks of trees.

Was it a ravine, or a bank behind the trees? Did the prairie have a drop-off point? She tried to call out to Clay, her eyes riveted to the dark objects beneath the cottonwood trees.

The cows!

Clay yelled. He whooped and hollered, raised a fist and pumped the air.

Cows exploded from beneath the bare branches of the trees. Thin, long-haired, spindly looking things, every last one.

Hannah wasn't aware of Pete or Clay or the fact that he was shouting hoarsely. She was counting, babbling numbers to herself through eyes that blurred with tears running down her cheeks of their own accord, down her cheeks and dripping off the end of her nose, running into her cold blisters, the salty tears stinging and hurting.

Twelve. Thirteen. A dog? Two dogs. What were dogs doing among the herd?

Hannah screamed at the same time Clay shot his rifle into the air. The small ones were not dogs. They were calves! Healthy little black calves. Two of them!

Hannah screamed again, then slumped in her saddle, crying with great, uncontrollable sobs that wrenched hoarse sounds from her throat and mucus from her nose running down into her cold sores. She didn't care about anything. Nothing.

There was the bull, still wide in the chest, but definitely gaunt, his ribs showing beneath his ragged coat. There was the mean cow, looking more belligerent and wild-eyed than ever.

The herd scattered and came together to watch warily, the new young mothers bawling for their spindly calves.

Clay shook his head as he dismounted. "Look at this!"

Hannah was afraid to dismount, afraid her legs would not support her, so she followed Clay from her perch on the saddle.

"I'd say that old cow gets the credit for saving your herd. Look at this." He held up a bleached ribcage, the frozen tattered paw of a wolf.

Hannah nodded. She swiped at her streaming eyes, her chest heaving.

"Once them wolves know whose boss, they don't hang around. Once these cows could back up to these cottonwoods, that ornery old cow let 'em have it. The bull, too. Look at this. Here's another one. That pack of wolves took a lickin'."

Hannah nodded, swallowed. She tried to laugh, pointed at the crazy antics of the wobbly, long-legged calves, then began crying hysterically again.

Clay looked up at her and then dug in his coat pocket for a handkerchief, producing a well-used and rumpled red one.

Hannah honked and snorted, wiped her eyes and took a deep breath to steady herself.

"Wal, Hannah, I'd say the Bar S is off and running," Clay said, accepting the red handkerchief as she handed it back to him. "It won't be long until those cows is sleek and fat, munching grass like you ain't ever seen," he laughed.

Hannah laughed too, a hoarse sound bordering on a sob. "It was a long winter, Clay. I was so worried. I had bad dreams. One day just blurred into the next until I thought the storms would never stop and we'd die, all of us together out on this homestead in the middle of the prairie."

He caught her hands, hauled her off the saddle, pulled her against him and cradled her head against his chest, swaying lightly, the way he might comfort a child.

"It's been rough for you, Hannah. Too rough. I could see it in your eyes. I wanted to come to you, to see how you were doing. But it would have been foolish. I still have feelings for you, Hannah. I'm still waiting."

Hannah nodded. "I know. Let's just be friends for now. You know I'm different than most girls. I don't want a husband or a boyfriend right now. And there's this Amish-English thing to consider."

"I'll wait. It's all right." He pulled back to look into her dark eyes. "I'd love to kiss you, Hannah, but that mouth . . ."

Hannah laughed and slapped him with her gloves. "I need to keep these cold sores. Scares you away."

She thought of the other person she needed to scare away. Now there was a brazen one! That Jerry Riehl. The dark horse. The one who was impossible to forget.

Hadn't she tried on so many sleepless nights when yet another storm ravaged the prairie, the house on the homestead a black dot in a vast land, scoured and pummeled by forces they could not predict or control? Hadn't she tried to push thoughts of him from her mind?

Why now, here in Clay's arms, thankful and filled with an emotion she herself could not fully understand, did Jerry's face, no, his . . . It was too humiliating how much she wanted him. She needed to stop all thoughts of love and romance or any entanglement with Jerry or Clay. Either one distracted her from the business at hand, which was to keep the cows alive and healthy, gather hay for the winter, keep the windmill working, help her mother plant and harvest a garden, and hope for the best.

Sighing, she stepped away from Clay. They stood apart, watching the cattle. It almost scared her how thin a few of them were. She noticed the swelling of udders, a few more calves would soon be born.

"Them mothers are gonna need grass to nurse them young 'uns," Clay observed. Hannah nodded.

When Manny, Hank, and Ken found them, another celebration broke out with Indian whoops and raised fists pumping the air above their heads.

The herd was here, they had survived the worst winter. Manny's face was a mixture of awe and deep reverence—so much like his father—and little-boy tears, all strengthened by his own will to appear grownup and nonchalant in the presence of the Jenkins boys.

They rode home, threw themselves off their horses, and ran toward the porch to announce the good news to Sarah.

As soon as the weather, permitted, Sarah cooked a celebratory meal and invited the Jenkinses and the Klassermans. The arrival of sighing breezes, running water that formed joyful little puddles that eddied and swirled from banks of melting snow, was enough to call for a gathering of friends and good food.

The wind was still harsh, as if it was reluctant to announce its defeat, but that was all right. What was a bit of dashing cold if you could feel the sunlight on your face and listen to the sound of melting snowbanks?

Sarah baked an entire ham, basting it with molasses and brown sugar mixed with hard cider. The whole house smelled of sweet, baking ham, an aroma that always took Hannah back to her grandparents' kitchen at Christmas time.

They peeled potatoes, breaking off the long white sprouts before they could apply their paring knives, the potatoes wrinkled and dusty from having lain in the cold cellar, which was attached to the wash house.

Sarah laughed at the long white sprouts. She laughed at the wrinkled carrots and smiled as she peeled onions. The winter's dark anxiety was being erased now as the warm sun melted the snow banks, a sign of hope, of survival. The grasses would spring up and cover the prairie in verdant waves of thick, hardy growth that would sustain every cow and calf.

The kitchen was filled with brilliant sunlight that cut rectangles of yellow light on the scrubbed and polished floor. The aroma of baking ham mixed with the earth smells of cooking potatoes and carrots.

Sarah wore a gray dress with a black apron, her hair, like the wings of a raven, parted neatly in the center. Her crisp, white covering had been washed in soapy water with a few shavings of paraffin thrown in to starch and stiffen the fabric. Her cheeks glowed, her large eyes turned gray with that certain hint of sadness that had darkened them the day Mose had died. It seemed they had never regained their original luster.

Hannah never wore a white head covering anymore, choosing to pin a diagonal half of a man's handkerchief as far back on her head as possible, her own black hair arranged loosely with decided tendrils framing her face. She was especially attractive in a dress of deep purple, a black apron tied around her slim waist. Her face glowed with a wellspring of renewed hope and energy, her step quick and light, every shadow of anxiety gone.

Manny's dark hair was neatly trimmed in the traditional Amish bowl cut, his face pale from the months of winter, his jaw square and clean shaven. The children were dressed in their best clothes, Baby Abby as cute as a button in a pink dress with a row of tucks sewed into the hem, to be lengthened as she grew. She crawled, pulled herself up, took tottering steps, her fat little hands clinging to furniture as she babbled excitedly to herself.

Sarah, however, could only dream of the desserts she would have liked to make, choosing instead to ration the scant amounts of flour and sugar that remained after the long winter. She knew another year would go by without income, the calves needing time to grow before being sent to auction. Her father was more than generous, but in spite of this, she remained frugal, guiltily aware of using anything to excess.

The Jenkinses were the first to arrive, clattering into the barn-yard in the rusted old pickup truck that had once been blue but now was striped with gray, speckled with brown rust, and splattered with snow and dark mud.

Abby alighted with the eagerness of a young girl, beat Hod to the porch, and stepped inside without bothering to knock or announce her arrival. She scooped up Baby Abigail and plunked her bony little frame in the armless rocker.

The baby set up a desperate howl, lunged, and wriggled away from her until she gave up and set her down. She raced on all fours to her mother who picked her up, nestling her head on Sarah's shoulder before lifting it to peek at Abby.

"Oh now, come on. It's me, little one. It's only me. You know who I am. Come on." She reached out both arms, her fingers wiggling, beckoning, but Abby merely bent her head and hid her face in Sarah's neck.

Sarah laughed. "She'll warm up to you, Abby. It's just been so long."

"Hasn't it though? Oh, it's been a long one. Terrible. Thought I'd go crazy with them winds a' howlin'. Pure miracle yer herd made it, ain't it? Beginnin' to think God's favorin' you."

Sarah shook her head. "Oh, please don't think that. God just knew we couldn't get along without the herd. We wouldn't be here if it wasn't for my father back in Pennsylvania, you know that. Or you and Hod. We would have starved that first year without your kindness."

"Oh now, don't go makin' up stuff. We never did nothin' 'cept loan you some food. Anyone else woulda done the same."

Sarah smiled and looked into Abby's eyes. The two women had been thrown together on this bleak prairie, and they were grateful for the friendship, the companionship, that grew and flourished in spite of their differences.

Sarah frowned, concern drawing a line between her eyes, when Abby began to cough, a deep-seated, rasping sound from low in her too-thin chest. To hide her alarm, she bent to open the oven door, lifting the lid on the roaster, inserting a fork, and then replacing the lid.

"Ah."

Abby thumped her chest with a fist, tears forming in her brilliant blue eyes. "Got myself a real cough a coupla weeks ago. Don't nothin' seem to help. Cooked enougha onions to steam the men clear outa the house. Tried mustard till I blistered my chest. Guess with the warm weather it'll go away."

"I would hope so. Get Hod to take you to the doctor in Pine."

"I wouldn't take a half-starved cat to that joker. He don't know a thing 'bout nothin'. Mind you, Sarah, you know that Rocher woman? Her husband owns the hardware? I forget her name. She's sort of spindly, looks like a washrag someone left floatin' in the dish water too long. She doesn't like it out here in the West. Somepin' wrong in her head. Doc Brinter tol' her she got TB. Tuberculosis. Now you know that ain't true. Them TB people turn lemon yellow, so they do. Ain't nothin' wrong with her, otherin' she needs to quit pityin' herself. That Roger knew what was good for her, he'd take her back home. Land sakes, she's a pain in everybody's life, not jes' her own. Isn't Hannah goin' back?" She fixed her blue eyes on Hannah.

"I don't know," Hannah announced.

"Wal, you should. Everybody said you was doin' her some good, keepin' that house in order, keepin' her spirits up."

Hod and the boys stomped up on the porch, ridding their boots of slush and snow, tracking mud up the steps and onto the rug, unaware of having done anything out of the ordinary.

The boys had ridden their horses, racing along the way they always did, smelling of horse sweat and that vague rancher's scent of cows and mud and manure, their coats and hats slick with saddle grease and leather. Their faces were ruddy from the cold, their hair smashed to their foreheads by their tight hat bands, then billowing loosely down the back of their necks and around their ears.

Clay was growing a mustache, Hank the beginnings of a full beard. The youngest, Ken, looked stubbly and pimple faced, as if he needed a good face washing and a shave.

Why had Hannah never noticed this before? She never realized these boys lived their days in happy oblivion to how they appeared, with yellowed teeth and unwashed faces, hair that was much too long and separated into clumps, never being washed often enough.

Perhaps they had never been in this new sun-filled house in the middle of the day, either. Without meaning to, Hannah's dark eyes measured the Jenkins boys with the fastidious yardstick she used to appraise all men.

Those white, white foreheads! They'd grow old like that. The lower part of their faces would become lined and wrinkled, actually deeply crevassed, the way Hod's was from exposure to sun and rain, sweltering summer temperatures and blasting winter winds. Their hair would always be glued to their heads by those greasy Stetsons. They'd hardly ever take a decent all-over bath, or brush their teeth with baking soda. They'd always

clump through the house with whatever clung to the thick soles
of their boots, and never know the difference. This is how they
were raised by Hod and Abby. Hannah tried hard to measure
them in a new and better light, but she knew there was no use.

She was who she was. For a moment, the thought took the
light from her eyes. This was not the first, nor the only time,
she had felt this aversion to men. Today, though, it was sobering, this knowledge of why she was never seriously attracted to
anyone.

Look at Lemuel Short. She'd been right about him for sure.
But the Jenkinses were here now, and she needed to do her best
to make the dinner a success.

The Klassermans arrival caused quite a stir, with Owen yelling across the room, followed by his pink, exclaiming spouse.
If anything, they had increased in size, the long winter whiled
away with many culinary forays, no doubt.

Sylvia seemed almost shy, a tad apologetic, but soon realized all was forgiven. Her meticulous housekeeping and lack of
endurance when the Detweiler's house went up in flames had
been forgotten. Oh, she had tried to be the good Samaritan and
house them all, but in the end, her nerves wouldn't take it. Owen
supported her to this day, thank God.

Sarah served up the meal with Hannah's help, Abby and Sylvia shooed out of the way. Talk rose in lively spurts as Owen,
Hod, and the boys discussed the winter, the cattle market and
the local news, everything swirling and tumbling about like a
creek in springtime. Hannah strained to hear, but it was useless.
She was unable to decipher much at all with two or three of
them talking at once.

The table was stretched out to accommodate them all, spread
with a freshly washed and ironed white cotton tablecloth. The
plates were flowered china, a design of pink roses and blue
forget-me-nots entwined with green ivy, the gift of an anony-
mous donor back in Pennsylvania.

There were small cut-glass dishes of sweet pickles and red beets, saved for an occasion such as this. The applesauce was a bit dark in color but tasted just wonderful all the same.

They enjoyed the thick sourdough bread without butter, but with plenty of jam, red and shimmering in tiny glass dishes. The potatoes were mashed with salt and one precious tin of canned milk, covered liberally with thick, salty ham gravy, rich and dark. Stewed carrots and onions, *knepp*, those tiny little white flour dumplings simmered on top of sauerkraut, an old Amish favorite that Hod and the boys ate until every bit was scraped from the serving bowl.

There were noodles too. Rachel's homemade noodles, cut thick and wide, simmered in chicken and parsley broth, flavored with small amounts of hard cheese. Browned butter would have been perfect, but without milk, this was simply impossible. So they did without.

Hannah filled water glasses and coffee cups, refilled serving bowls, laughed and talked and smiled, aware of Clay's hungry eyes and Hank's near worshipping looks, never responding fully, always aloof, always on the outer edge of any warm conversations.

She glowed when talk turned to the near miraculous survival of the herd, but spoke very little, still loathing the amount of tears she had allowed Clay to witness, and him pulling her into his arms at every opportunity.

It irked her, these men doing things like that. Why couldn't he have walked away and allowed her to have her moment of bawling when her eyes were red and her nose ran like a child's? But no, he had to pull her into his arms again. She reached a hand up to tentatively feel the healing cold sores, suddenly grateful for their awful appearance. She should try to sprout them on a regular basis!

Sylvia ended the meal by disappearing into the washhouse and reappearing with a stack of homemade pies, carrying them triumphantly, like a torch, to the table where she set them down with a flourish, her face as red as a cherry, amid yells and thumps of boots and claps that fell on her shoulders.

"Apple pie!" she trilled, her cheeks bunched up around her eyes like fresh, pink bread dough.

"Cherry pie!" she shouted, unveiling a huge pie baked in a monstrous blue agate pie plate as big as a frying pan.

Wedges of pie disappeared like snow in summer. Forkfuls of flaky crust bursting with sweet, thickened fruit disappeared into hungry mouths, Sarah and Hannah no different from the rest of them.

"Deprived too long," Hod said, chuckling, his face creased in smiles of pleasure.

"Now don't you go making as if'n I never bake you a pie," Abby said, shaking her fork at him.

"You don't!" Hank yelled, good naturedly teasing his mother.

"Wal young feller, if that's how you 'preciate my hard work slavin' over that there stove, wal, you kin bake yer own pie next time!"

Hod laughed outright, reached over and patted Abby's thin shoulder. "Now, Ma. We're only funnin' you, is all."

They shared the same look Hannah had often seen between Mose and Sarah, her parents who were closer than anyone she knew. So here was another couple who had been married even longer, living together with that mysterious harmony, that bewildering sharing of thoughts and emotions that Hannah could never understand.

She had no longing to be patted on the shoulder as if she was a dog who had obeyed. She would never see that kind of appreciation by a man for having baked him a pie. For one thing, she hated the thought of pie baking. For another, a man could survive real good without pie. He could eat cake or, if she didn't feel like baking him a cake, he could eat bread with molasses on it!

That's what married women turned into the minute they sealed their fate with that innocent "Ya" in answer to the minister's questions about promising to love, honor, and obey. All that stuff. Dutifully being turned into a slave of sorts. No, not really a slave, but . . .

Hannah sat drinking black coffee, the taste of pie like a sweet afterthought, contemplating this thing called marriage, her eyes dark and brooding, her mouth compressed, listening to Sylvia's high, breathless voice as she gave out instructions for successful pie baking.

Hannah snorted inwardly. Sylvia had probably eaten half a pie and had no room for air, so she had to take helpless little breaths. She was huge! Hannah watched the rise and fall of her bosom, the lifting of her fork, a skinny, tiny utensil held by the thick, fleshy fingers. She marveled at the ability of an insignificant fork entering a normal sized mouth with enough food to build up this pyramid of a woman.

Owen was no different, discretely loosening the top button of his too-tight trousers beneath the table, but she'd seen him and looked away quickly when his bright eyes met hers.

Hannah decided she didn't like people who ate too much, and all men who went through life without washing or brushing their teeth. In fact, she didn't care a whole lot for hardly anyone. She wished they'd all stop talking now and go home. They'd said everything that was important and a whole pile of things that weren't important, so now it was time to go home.

Abby coughed and coughed. She left the table to go out to the washhouse to hack and gag, bringing up phlegm and mucous, sounding like she wasn't able to get her breath.

Hannah spoke without thinking. "Hod, why don't you take your wife to see a doctor?"

"She won't go."

"Well, she needs to."

"I know."

She met Hod's blue gaze and what passed between them was definitely not even close to the glances of understanding that Hannah had witnessed between him and Abby. He doesn't care enough about her, she thought.

She's about as tactful as a wire brush, that one, Hod thought, with a look so vinegary it could sour mile. She needs to be taken down a notch, sittin' there like the queen of Sheba and all his boys moonin' around, and she knows it. Don't care. Clay was the worst. He needed to talk to him right soon. No use wasting is time and breath on that bad-tempered filly.

CHAPTER 10

ONE DAY IN LATE APRIL, THE COLD WINDS SUBSIDED, SHUDDERED, and gave up, allowing the warm sunshine to turn the playful breezes into mellow, friendly little puffs of air that tugged at skirts and sent hats, untied kerchiefs, and bonnets flying.

They hitched Pete to the plow, tilled the garden, planted left-over wrinkled potatoes and seeds of beans, squash, and toma-toes they had saved. Seeds were dropped in the furrows with painstaking precision, careful to let not one seed go to waste.

Calves were born and frolicked with the herd of cows as the grass shot up from the blackened earth.

Cold rain seeped into the soil and replenished the already snow-soaked earth. Prairie dogs sat on their skinny haunches, their front feet dangling as if waiting to pray, then shot into their burrows with the speed of lightning. Prairie hens ran with-out direction, squawking like alarmed old women, necks out-stretched, running simply for the sake of leaving one spot for another. Butterflies hovered, took off in their dizzying flight, leaving a trail that was impossible for birds to follow. So they survived, flitting from clumps of columbines to low-lying bunches of purple violets, their wings lifted then lowered, as they guzzled the nectar.

Hannah worked from sunup to sundown. Her bare feet walked across stubbles of new growth, slimy black ashes, and new grass shooting up from beneath winter's brown growth.

She learned the ways of birthing calves. She knew when to spot trouble and when the time of birth was near. She was not one to be overly religious but her heart lifted to God of its own accord every time she came upon a mother licking her newborn calf, a healthy, black calf with a wide chest and sturdy, knobby knees, the cleft hooves splayed as delicately as toenails on a newborn baby.

The milk cow gave birth to a brown calf and what the calf did not drink found its way into the house. They all enjoyed glasses of creamy, sweet milk, the top cream turned into butter and cheese.

Haymaking time came, sending all of them into the fields. Manny raked the hay with Pete and Goat hitched up to the mower. Everyone helped fork it onto the wooden wagon. The haymaking never stopped. It was the one single thing that would keep the anxious nightmares at bay on those awful dark nights of winter.

No matter that Mam said prayers were more trustworthy. Prayer was what triumphed over anxiety. Hannah listened half-heartedly, refusing to allow what she knew was her own version of security to be ridiculed by her devout mother. Hay in the haymow. Stacks of hay in the barnyard, by the windmill, hay in every corner they could find. It was certain to keep the cows fed, ensuring survival and, ultimately, the success of the ranch.

Hannah's face turned dark, browned by the sun. Her arms became muscular, her hands calloused, the soles of her feet as tough as the cows' hooves.

A new concern raised its head in spite of things going so well. Pete was wearing out, and Goat was running on his last legs. Something had to be done about dependable horsepower, and Hannah had no idea how to procure another decent horse.

The calves they would sell before winter would barely tide them over this first year. She refused to ask her grandfather yet again for a loan. But something would have to be done.

She talked it over with Manny, who had no real solution except to ask the Jenkinses, which, Hannah felt sure, would result in the generous gift of another pitiful creature like Goat.

"I mean, Goat's all right. We couldn't have managed without him. He helped us through lots of haying. I'm sure the Jenkinses have half a dozen horses like Goat that they'd be glad to get rid of."

"I'm not going to the Jenkinses."

"We could get a tractor."

Hannah laughed. "Mam would never allow it. She's so Amish it isn't even funny."

"We all are."

"Not me."

"Oh, come on, Hannah. You're always bluffing and blustering. You'd never hurt Mam by disobeying her."

Hannah shrugged and changed the subject back to the problem of a horse. "For now, we're going to have to let it go and hope Goat holds up for another year or so."

The letter arrived with the Klassermans driving in and waving a handful of letters as their impeccably clean station wagon came to a halt. "Ve're back from a visit to the dentist. Picked these up at the post office for you."

Sarah wiped her hands on her apron, leaving streaks of brown dirt from weeding the onions. She used the back of her hand to push back the windblown strands of hair that had blown loose around her face.

"Oh, good! Thank you so much. I was starting to wonder if everyone in Lancaster County forgot about us. Not that I could blame them."

"Ya. Ya. But they didn't. Relatives don't forget," Owen smiled.

"Yer garden looks beautiful," Sylvia observed, hitching her bulk to a more comfortable position.

"Lots of horse manure. We spread it on throughout the fall when we cleaned out the stable and plowed it in before we planted. Nothing better."

"Ya, ya. Vell, ve must be on our vay. Haf you heard? Abby Jenkins finally vent to a doctor. She has the double pneumonia. Stubborn voman."

"Oh, dear." Sarah's dark eyes filled with quick tears. "I must go visit her. Take her some food or offer to do the washing or cleaning. Maybe I'll send Hannah."

The Klassermans took their leave, leaving Sarah to stand in the driveway by the porch as she riffled through four letters before sitting on the edge of the porch to rip open one long white envelope, gripping the white paper with both hands and moving slightly back and forth as she read.

"Oh my. Oh my," she repeated, her lips moving silently. Elam and Ben had agreed to give up the farm. "Lord willing, we are making plans to begin our move west," her father wrote. "The pioneering bug has bitten us hard."

Sarah lifted her face to the sun, her eyes closed, absorbing every word, the vast open sky and the waves of grass etched into her heart and soul. This was her home, this unfettered land. And now her father and two brothers were planning to come and begin a new life on the prairie with them.

She lowered her head and red on. "Ben Miller's and Ike Lapp's see great opportunity in building windmills, so they are in the planning stages, same as we are. I believe the two young bachelors will be accompanying them. Word is getting around that a young horse dealer by the name of Jeremiah Riehl has shown interest in moving his horse trade to North Dakota. He is also a farrier.

"Your sisters remain of the same mind. I pray to God they will yet repent of their overbearing ways, but for now, we are on good terms. I have not dared mention our future plans to them. Rachel's health is not the best. I'm afraid if she's confronted by these sudden goings on, she may fall victim to a stroke."

Here, Sarah lifted her face to the sky, propped herself up with two palms facing outward. Kicking both feet in the air, she howled with abandon, a most unladylike move and not like her at all.

It brought a concerned Eli and Mary from around the back of the house where they were playing horse, a rope tied around Eli's waist. "Mam! What is wrong with you?" Mary asked worriedly.

"Oh, nothing, Mary. I'm just reading a letter from Daudy. And just think, Daudy and Ben and Elam and Ben Miller—a whole bunch of Amish people—are moving here. Here! Here to North Dakota with us! We won't be alone anymore! We can have church services and we can have people like us to share our Sundays."

Eli looked at his mother and frowned. "We don't need those people."

"We don't," Mary echoed.

Sarah laughed aloud, reached out to grab the rope around Eli's waist and hauled him in for a tight hug and a resounding kiss. "Your hair smells like a cow," she said, nuzzling his cheek.

"Ah. Ah," he grunted, trying to squirm out of his mother's arms.

"You need a head washing," Sarah said.

"Not now. He's a horse," Mary reminded her before pulling on the rope to lead him away. Eli whinnied and kicked one leg out to show his mother that he was a horse to be reckoned with.

Sarah watched them, smiled, and went back to her letter reading. Emma had a boil on her back. My goodness! That should be treated by a doctor for sure. Amos King's Naomi was published to be married to the widower, Jacob King.

My, my. Naomi was going on forty years of age. Jacob King *sei* Becky passed away only a year before. He had nine or ten children. Just wait until Hannah hears this!

She read and reread each precious letter. She laughed and cried, then took a deep, cleansing breath of pure unadulterated joy, allowing the wonderful news to sink in, to spread through her limbs and give them new life.

Oh, wonder, blessed, benevolent Father, the Giver of all good things. Her heart sang praises, her soul was lifted to the heights of the unending sky and rode the prairie breezes like the notes of a song.

Every bit of hardship had been worth this moment. Every dark night of suffering and indecision. She had eaten the food of despair and tasted the bitter cup of sorrow. Many times she had drunk thirstily from the cup of grace and was able to go on.

She wished her mother was alive, and then realized as quickly that her father would not be moving here to the prairie if she were. Her mother would never have allowed it.

She got up, went into the house, put the precious letters in a cupboard drawer, and then came back out to finish weeding the onions. She worked as if in a dream; she caught herself talking, murmuring things out loud, making plans, the future full of possibilities, full of security from shared responsibilities.

Sarah adjusted her covering and listened to the sighing of the wind in the prairie grass. The rustling was now so dear and familiar; it was like her own heartbeat. Without it, her life would be devoid of a certain endless rhythm, a breathing of earth and sky, a oneness with nature, with God. This experience she could never have found in Lancaster County amid the hustle and bustle of life.

The realization dawned like the parting of storm clouds to reveal the sun. Here was her destiny. Here the land would shape and form her into a being created for God. Humbled, Sarah wept.

Hannah grasped the letters with white-knuckled fingers, her lips moving as she read, her eyebrows drawing down in irritation.

Sarah cast silent glances in her direction, busying herself with warming a pan full of ham noodle soup for their evening meal.

Was it only her imagination or did Hannah's face lose its ruddy brown color? She watched Hannah lay the letter aside and stare stone faced out of the window without comment.

"What do you think, Hannah?" she asked, quietly.

"I don't know." Her words were flat, lifeless, as if all the air had been taken from her. Without another word she got up and let herself out through the door. Sarah went to the window, watching her daughter's long strides as she went to the barn, disappearing behind a stack of hay.

She'd never understand Hannah if she lived to be ninety years old. Didn't she want her grandfather and her two uncles to come? Surely she would be happy to have them come out and start their own homestead.

She shook her head, lifted a scalding spoonful of soup to her mouth, tasted it, grimaced. Too salty. She peeled a wrinkled potato, threw it in, added more water, toasted bread in the oven and went to the door to call the children.

Supper was a silent affair, after Manny's joyful whooping, which was struck down immediately by Hannah's scathing words, sharp like daggers.

"If we'd want all of Lancaster County to live with us, we'd move back to Pennsylvania where it's jammed full of all sorts and shapes of Amish and Mennonites, Dunkards, and whatever else in the world exists there. What does that long-nosed Ike Lapp want out here? I can't stand him. He'll probably bring a whining, long-nosed wife and a brood of sniveling kids!"

Here Sarah broke in, shaking her spoon in Hannah's direction. "The world does not turn only for you, Hannah. God loves us all. He made us all, and He must be saddened by your blasphemy."

"I'm not blaspheming. I'm just saying it the way I see it. I don't want people crawling all over the prairie like lice. Those two bachelors will be like that, as unwelcome in my opinion. You know they're going to want a wife. Guess who'll be available?"

"Do you realize how much you are like your father?"

Hannah snorted, the trademark of her derision. "Not much. I'm not wailing and fasting."

Sarah realized the futility of the endless sparring of words, a contest she was certain to lose. Unwise, this volley of regrettable words. So she resigned herself to allowing Hannah the upper hand—sometimes she had to—and said no, she did not do that, and let it go, thinking bitterly that Hannah had nothing to worry about with her attitude, as prickly as a cactus. No man would dare get close to her.

Manny said the homesteads would be miles apart and no one would likely be closer than the Klassermans, which did nothing to change Hannah's foul mood. She washed dishes, banging them against the granite dish pan till Sarah thought they would fly into dozens of pieces, like falling icicles. But she said nothing.

Sometimes she almost despised her own daughter. When those eyebrows came down and spread across those brown eyes, she wanted to physically slap her. Why, when a mother and daughter's heartstrings were so interwoven? Often she wondered if she was a bad mother, if, somewhere along the way, she had missed some element of child-rearing, or some giving of love.

Hannah stalked out of the door, stiff-legged, her large feet slapping against the porch boards, and disappeared, a tall figure becoming smaller and smaller until she appeared as only a dot on the prairie. Sarah turned away and whispered a prayer for her safety.

Hannah was furious! How dare they invade her privacy? This land was their homestead. Theirs. Hers and Mam's and Manny's. She didn't want the prairie dotted with Amish homes, Amish folks sticking their noses into her business, giving advice, superior voices clanging against her own particular way of doing things.

She knew how to start the ranch. Was well on her way. Hadn't Clay said so? This is exactly what would happen. They'd all move out here, figure out a way to grow corn, feed their cattle better, moving ahead and leaving her and the Bar S scrounging in the dust. They'd end up with inferior cattle poorly fed, insufficient horse power, and no modern equipment to cut and rake hay.

She sat down in the fast-growing grass, yanked out a flat stem, aligned it between two thumbs and blew vehemently. A sharp, high whistle split the air. She did it again and again. It satisfied a deep longing to assert herself.

Let the clouds in the west and the sky know that I am Hannah. I can be a homesteader. I can run a successful ranch without dozens of other folks telling me what to do. Perhaps the trains that would bring them would all run off the tracks, a regular train wreck. The scared Amish would take it as a bad omen, a sign from God that they should all go back to Pennsylvania and stay there!

Grandfather Stoltzfus hadn't written that Jerry Riehl was coming with the rest of the herd, just that there was a rumor that he was interested. Well, he could send a few good horses out, but he may as well stay in Lancaster County if he thought he had a remote chance with all his kissy romance. He was about the last one she wanted to see, that was for sure.

Hannah sighed and threw the blade of grass aside. A whole shower of troubles had rained down on her head in the form of a bunch of letters, leaving a sour taste on her tongue.

She had a notion to whack off her hair and go English! She could tell Clay she'd marry him just to get away, but that would open another can of worms, no different from her original troubles. She groaned, threw herself on her back, and watched the puffy cloud formations to the west. The sun's light was already casting a pink glow, the rustling grasses changing color as it sank lower, turning the undersides of the puffy clouds to a lavender hue.

Birds wheeled silently without so much as the flap of a wing, gliding along effortlessly, little black etches against the evening sky. A lark called its plaintive cry, another answered. Hannah pictured the bird clinging to a tall grass stalk, tiny feet clenched perfectly as it opened its beak to begin its song. She knew which insects they preferred, and which jays lived in the rotten branches of the old cottonwood trees.

She often sighted herds of antelope, the leader with his black, two-pronged horns, running like music, the strains of perfect symmetry, beauty in motion. She always hoped fervently that they would not encounter barbed wire, knowing they sometimes became entangled, dying a long, slow, torturous death. It was almost more than she could bear.

Hannah knew that many of the local ranchers considered them pests, but to her way of thinking, they were the most beautiful creatures of the plains, even if their meat was often unfit to eat, tasting of a bitter goat flavor. They would have been more than happy with the strong-smelling meat before the loan from Daudy, when starvation lurked in every corner of the old log house.

She watched the shadows play along the every-moving surface of grass, clouds playing with the wind, teasing the sun. If those ambitious Amish men came out here to live, would they notice or appreciate the endless wonders of this land? Would they use common sense, or would they look on the fertile earth beneath the grass and, ambitious and eager to turn the prairie into a profitable landscape, go crazy with dollar signs?

Well, there was nothing she could do about it. Let them come, let them face a drought, winter storms, and whatever else God chose to send them. They'd learn.

Back at the house, Sarah's thoughts ran along an opposite line. She could hardly grasp the fact that her life would resume in the ways of her childhood, the beloved closeness of a group of like-minded people, who understood the importance of *Ordnung*, were obedient to church doctrine, forming an invisible protective fence around the family, making choices and decisions for her, and abiding by a discipline they believed came from God.

It was a way of life that allowed one to walk in the footsteps of Jesus. It was what she had been born into, raised as a child to accept the manner of dressing, the church services held in homes every two weeks, the strict adherence to using the horse and buggy, and the shunning of electricity and the automobile.

Oh, it wasn't that it set them apart as elite members of God's family. She never wavered in her attitude that all like-minded Christians who believed in God's Son, Jesus Christ, and who lived as they had been taught, would enter into the same rest with other good and faithful servants.

The Amish way of life was her lot, and a beloved one. Even a few families, those of her own father and brothers, living within a distance she could travel with a horse and wagon, were a gift. A rare and precious gift she would never take for granted.

They would hold an Amish church service, even without an ordained minister. Tears sprang to her eyes as she hummed the slow melody of the "*Lob Sang*." Page 770 in the thick black *Ausbund*, the book containing the verses written by men of faith while incarcerated in the damp, stone-walled prisons in Passau, Germany. *Unser fore eldern*. Our forefathers, who chose persecution over the doctrines they found questionable and forged a way of life they preferred.

She giggled, a maudlin, hysterical little sound, as tears ran unchecked down her face. She had no pickles or red beets. She had served the last jars to her neighbors. What were church services without the pickles and red beets served with traditional bread and cheese and pies?

How gladly she would spread the white tablecloth! With a song in her heart she would clean and polish, sweep and mop, rearrange the furniture to make room for benches forming a line of people seated facing the minister.

Evening shadows lurked in the corners of the house after the sun disappeared below the horizon. Sarah lifted the glass chimney, struck a match, and lit the oil lamp. She called the children in from their play, set a basin of warm water and soap on the porch, and washed their hands and faces by turns. They washed their feet until the water turned black from the dust and dirt they had accumulated.

"Now, into your nightclothes," she announced.

"I'm hungry."

"I don't want to go bed. It's not dark yet."

Sarah smiled at Eli and Mary as she spread slices of sourdough bread with new butter and molasses. They drank cold well water, then became droopy with sleepiness, their eyes taking on that certain dull, half-alert look, until she shooed them off to bed.

Together they knelt by the side of their small, single beds, clasped their hands, bowed their heads, and recited the same German prayer Sarah had prayed as a child. Then she tucked them in, kissed them goodnight, and softly left the room, the door slightly ajar.

She found Manny on the front porch removing his shoes, his wide shoulders slumped with weariness.

"Where's Hannah?"

Sarah shrugged her shoulders, picked up the dish pan of dirty water, and threw it out over the yard before wiping it with the washcloth.

"She went for a walk," she said quietly.

"She's upset, isn't she?"

"Yes. She read Father's letter."

"She'll get over it."

"I'm not so sure. Oh, Manny. Life would be so perfect if only Hannah would . . ." she almost said, "Be like you," but she caught herself. How, she wondered, could two children, raised the best she and Mose knew how, be so different from each other?

Sarah sat on the rough-hewn bench, her hands in her lap and sighed. "She's so hard to figure out."

"She's a loner, Mam. She simply doesn't like people. She loves this land and has no desire to see if filling up, especially not with our people. Plus, she has a real problem with Jerry Riehl, the horseman."

Sarah looked at Manny sharply. "What do you mean?"

Manny shook his head. "I can't tell on her, Mam. But he is certainly interested in her. Seriously interested."

"How do you know?"

"I just do. They all want her. Everyone who lives around here would like to have her for a girlfriend, a wife, and she knows it. Look at the Jenkins boys. They fall over their feet to please her. She couldn't care less. She's downright mean to Clay sometimes.

"It's why they all want her: they know they can't have her. She presents a challenge to them. I guarantee you, Mam, Hannah will never marry. Pity her husband if she ever does."

They sat together in the gathering darkness, mother and son, a companionable silence between them, the night easing itself softly around them, folding the dark, low-lying house in its whispering embrace.

A quarter moon sliced its way up through the blanket of night clouds on the horizon, the stars arranging themselves in their age-old positions, twinkling and blinking.

From out of the night, a lone, dark figure appeared, silently stepping into the yard, wordlessly, as if part of the night, a being devised from the earth and sky and vast stillness around her. Without speaking, she stepped up on the porch, opened the screen door, and let herself inside.

"Good-night, Hannah." There was no answer, but then, Sarah didn't expect one.

CHAPTER 11

Hᴀɴɴᴀʜ ᴅᴇᴄɪᴅᴇᴅ ᴇᴀʀʟʏ ᴏɴ ᴛʜᴀᴛ Gᴏᴅ ᴍᴜsᴛ ɴᴏᴛ ʜᴀᴠᴇ ʜᴇᴀʀᴅ ʜᴇʀ begging for a train wreck.

The spring rains ran their course, then stopped as if all the rain clouds had been cut from the sky with a giant scissors, leaving the yellowish, copper tone that spoke of drought and dust, the sky cloudless and sizzling with white heat. Everywhere Hannah looked, from one horizon to the other, there were ripples of heat above the waving grass, the sun a fiery ball that saturated the earth and sky with heat. The wind dried out the heavy new growth. Dust rolled from wagons and horses, trucks and tractors, anything that moved across a road, leaving an imprint in the inches of loose dust that clung to everything.

By the middle of July, Ben Miller and his brood arrived, settling into a tent, of sorts, while the building began on his 1200 acres. Ike Lapp and his wife and children chugged in on the back of a flatbed truck, the wooden sides flapping and creaking dangerously, threatening to spill all of them out over the side.

Hannah stood by the door frame, her arms crossed, watching the clattering apparatus rumble up to the porch. She stayed right where she was, letting her eyes convey her disapproval.

Of course, they all climbed down, the six offspring of various sizes, the lean and hungry wife who couldn't have weighed more than a hundred pounds.

Sarah received them warmly, her eyes wet with unshed tears of welcome. Manny stood by her side, pumped Ike's hand with enthusiasm that seemed genuine, inquired about the children, always mannerly, always proper and polite, pleasing his mother.

Hannah turned away, went inside, out through the back door and across the prairie to the windmill. Likely Mam would cook them a good dinner while she listened to news from home. Well, she'd do it alone. They didn't need to feel like this was a celebration with everybody fussing and fawning over them, as if they were important moving out here where they probably wouldn't make it anyway. Hannah vowed to have nothing to do with them. Ben Miller either. Talk about shunning! They hadn't seen anything!

When Sarah told her that Ike Lapp's family were moving on a claim only six miles east of them, Hannah was furious. Sarah listened to her displeasure until it ran itself out, then told her she didn't have to be neighborly, if that's how she felt, but she herself would do as she pleased. "They're poor, Hannah. They have only 320 acres. You know how hard it was for us."

"Yeah, well, the summer's turning out dry, so we may not have enough for ourselves, let alone peddling everything to that Ike Lapp family."

Sarah set her mouth in a firm line and turned away.

The calves arrived one by one, little, wet and black, their long, spindly legs knobby kneed and wobbly, their tails whacking at flies only hours after they were born. Their eyes were large and liquid, with slanted lids and heavy lashes, the prettiest animals Hannah had ever seen.

One after another, the mothers dropped their calves that nursed successfully without any serious complications, which was a miracle of sorts, Hannah knew. Thirteen cows and now there were eleven calves. The herd was swelling in size, the calves capering among their mothers, exact little replicas of the Black Angus breed.

Hannah was never happier than when she was sitting astride Pete, out by the cows, milling around with them, checking on the health of the babies and the mothers who had not yet calved. She knew them all apart by small differences, a whorl of hair on a forehead, a longer neck, a heavy tail, or a peculiar set of nostrils. Some small difference was always there, and she named each calf to match their oddity.

She hoped they could have at least seven or eight of the calves weighing close to eight hundred pounds till late fall or early winter, make a successful drive to Pine, and meet the cattle truck that would take them to the large auction in Dorchester.

She believed that with Manny's help, they could accomplish this, if certain new and nosy neighbors would stay out of it.

Oh, it irked her! Here was Mam, cooking and baking, riding off with Manny in the wagon like two saints, leaving her alone, uninvited and never letting her know what they were doing. They could at least tell her which family they were visiting.

Fueled by a strong dose of anger, she yanked the old, brittle saddle with the cracked wooden stirrup off Pete's back and hurled it into a dark corner of the barn.

She hadn't bargained for this. She had battled, even anticipated drought and winter storms. They'd survived the awful fire, the long winter, met Lemuel Short, acted like greenhorns and took in the poor man.

This, now, this wave of Amish people migrating out here, thinking it was all one big lark, wealth hidden everywhere they looked, was going to be a tough load to shoulder. Nosy, judgmental, deciding right from wrong for themselves as well as everyone around them, it was enough to make her yank off the *dichly* and go cut her hair. That would give them something to talk about!

You just watch. Mam would give half of her garden produce away. That wife of Ike Lapp, whatever her name was, looked as mean and hungry as a wolf in winter. The children picked their noses and examined whatever they had dug out.

Hannah shuddered. She picked up the saddle, hoisted it on to the wooden rack, hung up the bridle, then leaned on the fence, one foot hooked on the bottom board, her arms crossed on the top rail, watching Pete walk out to meet his only companion, Goat.

They possessed two of the oldest, most battered and worn horses she had ever seen. Ribs like washboards, skinny and distended necks, scrapes and cuts and swollen knees.

Hannah shook her head and wondered if they'd last another year. That Goat was as worthless a horse as she'd ever seen. He had no eye for cutting cattle from the herd, just ran pell-mell among them like a happy calf. You could yank on the reins, yell directions, and still he simply did not get it. He was stupid. Stupid and loathsome, and constantly dropping loose green bowels that made a mess wherever he went.

It never stopped. But, it was all they had and Hannah would never mistreat poor Goat. Manny had more patience, so he rode him among the cattle more than Hannah did, mostly to save the poor horse from Hannah's frustration.

They practiced their roping skills on the calves, making them wild-eyed and skittish. Clay told them it was not a good idea, but Hannah told him that a bit of chasing wouldn't hurt them. He narrowed his eyes and set his jaw and thought—wait until you try and drive them to Pine—but didn't say it aloud.

Two half-dead horses and saddles that were falling apart, bridles held together by rivets and pieces of twine. Comfortable, serviceable buildings, a windmill, the start of a good herd of cattle. Hannah guessed they weren't doing too badly. With a satisfied nod, she turned away.

What was that? Dust rolling out toward Pine? Someone was approaching. Hannah fought the urge to hide, stayed where she was, squinting, the wind tugging her black hair out from under the flapping men's handkerchief that served as her head covering. A loose brown dress, one sleeve torn, pinned haphazardly down the front, the skirt, well below her knees, blowing in the ceaseless wind that caressed the plains all day long.

A pickup truck hauling a cattle trailer. Nothing new or different, it resembled the Klassermans' rig.

Her bare feet were planted apart, brown and strong, and she stood there unwavering as she watched the truck draw the trailer up to the barn, followed by a cloud of brown dust and grit that rolled over everything as it came to a halt.

Hannah didn't recognize the driver or the two passengers. She crossed her arms and glared, hoping to convey the message she felt inside: Move on. Don't bother me.

Her squinting eyes tightened, the lids drooped and closed momentarily as a long sigh escaped through her lips, a whoosh of air expelled by the jumping craziness in her chest.

It was him!

He walked up to her, at ease and unselfconscious, lifted his straw hat, the wind picking up the dark hair underneath, the light in his eyes meant for her.

"How are you, Hannah?"

She nodded.

"I need a place to keep three horses until I get a lean-to built. I bought the old Perthing place out past the slough. What is it called? Swamp . . . or something?"

Another young man joined them, tall and thin, straw hat pulled low, thumbs hooked in his suspenders. Hannah met his dark, curious gaze with her usual coldness and her flat, unwelcoming stare that usually froze the friendliest person.

"This is Jake. Jake Fisher."

Hannah nodded, lifted her chin a few inches and kept it there. Jerry Riehl and Jake Fisher. Sounded like horse thieves or something.

"I don't want your horses."

Jake looked at her, startled.

Jerry said, "Well, you're going to get them. I don't know where else to put them.

"There's the Klassermans. The Jenkinses too."

"I don't know them."

"So?"

Jerry stepped closer, stared at her, his eyes bright with anger. He was here now, and he had a plan firmly in place. This obstinate girl was not going to stop him.

"I'm leaving them here, Hannah. I want to keep them in your barn. I have salt blocks and grain, so feed them until I can come and get them."

"No."

Jake looked at his friend, a small smile playing around his mouth.

"Manny will do it. So will your mother. If you want to be so bull-headed, go right ahead. It's not going to make any difference."

Hannah's eyes blazed. "Yeah, well, I'm not my mother. Or Manny. So don't come here expecting a bunch of favors because you're not getting them. I don't want a gaggle of bossy Amish folks as neighbors. We were doing just fine on our own, so don't expect me to be of any help."

"If I remember correctly, your whole family was not doing so great after the fire. You would not have been able to stay on your homestead without your grandfather's help, and you know it." Jerry's face had gone white, his nostrils flared.

For once in her life, Hannah did not know what to say. Any smart retort that came to her mind fizzled and died before the blaze in his eyes, a reflection of her own.

With that, he stalked off, yanked the bar on the trailer door, let down the wooden ramp, and walked up, calling to his horses.

Hannah stayed where she was, her tanned face suffused with anger.

She had never seen horses like the ones he led down that ramp. Sleek, well-fed, their necks arched and thick, rippling manes and tails like poetry. Their eyes were calm, without the whites showing, well-trained by the way Jerry led them down easily, without any coaxing or commanding.

A black one and a dark brown one with a beautiful mane and tail as black as a crow.

The third horse he led down made her draw in a sharp breath. Golden! A golden horse with a mane the color of molasses in milk. Or oatmeal. The tail was arched and flowing almost to the ground. A groan of longing rose in her throat, and she brought her fist up to her mouth to silence it.

She would never let either of them see what she was feeling. Never.

Her eyes followed the golden horse, taking in the waving mane, the deep, wide chest, the long symmetrical legs, the perfect withers. A white blaze on the forehead. Hooves perfectly trimmed and shod. Likely he had done it.

They led the horses over, Jerry holding the black one and golden one. "Meet my horses, Hannah."

She lifted her chin and stared coldly.

"The black one is Duke. The brown one is King. Haven't named the palomino. You can name her. They're all riding horses, not drivers, so don't go trying anything crazy. Keep them penned. They won't do well turned loose. This is strange country for them. One scoop of grain and plenty of water. Make sure they have hay.

"You ever hear of the Perthing place?"

She shook her head.

"Some old guy hung on to the place at the turn of the century. Wasn't mentally capable and they found him dead in the house. After that, the winds and whatever else got at the buildings and basically destroyed them. But it is actually a ranch of over a thousand acres. I bought it for a song. Figured if I bought it then decided to go back home, I'd probably make a nice profit."

Hannah snorted.

Jerry looked at her. "Think not?"

"Nobody wants swamp land."

Jake Fisher watched Hannah's face. When she spoke in that low, husky voice, he could see the irresistible charm of this girl who sizzled with anger.

"But that swamp land might be all right in dry weather. Does it ever rain here in summer?"

Hannah shook her head. "Hasn't so far."

"Then I should be making heavy hay when the rest of you are traveling pretty far to cut and load some decent hay. So I might not be as dumb as you think I am."

They stabled the horses, Hannah keeping her distance, showing no interest, scuffing her feet in the dust, her hands gripped together behind her back.

Jerry gave her a few more clipped instructions, saying they would need some exercise, so they should be ridden.

Hannah's heart fluttered against her chest, but she gave no sign. Goat stuck his head over the top of the fence, whinnying. Hannah cringed as the men turned to look.

"S' wrong with your horse?"

Before she could catch herself, she laughed. "Nothing. That's a product of the North Dakota plains. They all look like that. They're tough and rangy and full of worms."

Both men laughed genuine laughs that came from finding her blunt, truthful words hilarious. They both eyed her with new appreciation.

She didn't laugh.

"I'm guessing he needs his teeth filed." Jerry climbed over the fence, grabbed Goat's unsuspecting chin, and pried his mouth open with two fingers. He ran his hands along Goat's teeth, whistled and said it's a wonder this horse wasn't dead! Never saw a worse set of molars.

Hannah's defensiveness was back in place. She didn't say anything. This was where it would start. She'd be bossed around and told what to do. They were here ten minutes and already they found fault. Well, she'd have to tell them now so they'd get the hint.

"You can just leave if this is what you're going to do. Come out here to start ranching and thinking you're better than anyone else, telling us what to do. You can just forget it. It's none of your business if that horse's teeth come down all the way to his knees. It's my business and I'd appreciate if you'd go home and stop bothering us."

Jerry nodded once, turned and left, a bewildered Jake in tow. Hannah nodded her head in their direction, then turned and made her way back to the house. Let him think what he wanted. Just wait until he caught sight of the herd. That would give him something to think about.

He had the nerve, not taking no for an answer. She'd distinctly said no. He had brushed her aside like a housefly.

Why had he gone and bought that old ranch? He could easily have gotten all the acres he wanted for free. All he had to do was live on them for ten years.

Out here throwing his authority around! Didn't he know there was a depression and times were hard? Perhaps he thought he was better than them. He lived above most people's standards.

Well, she wasn't touching those horses. That was Manny's job, since they thought Manny and his mother were so sweet and welcoming. Which they were, but that didn't mean *she* needed to be.

The horses stayed in the barn. Manny took responsibility for their care, slavishly feeding them the grain Jerry had provided, leading them out to drink, brushing them, exclaiming about this wonderful horse flesh to anyone who would listen, and always, without fail, at the breakfast table, the dinner table, and the supper table.

Manny knew his own sister well enough to keep her out of the conversation. He knew her refusal to help had nothing to do with the horses themselves but everything to do with their owner.

Sarah stood on the porch, watching Manny lead Duke first, then King, and last the palomino, riding each of them in turn. She felt Hannah's presence beside her. Silence hung between them like a heavy curtain, separating the thoughts and the words that should have flowed so easily.

A waste, Sarah thought. A waste of precious hours lent to us by our Lord. A total, unfruitful waste, to be so miserable with one's own will that it directed foolishness of endless pouting and a bold refusal to comply. It was enough to send a tremor of frustration through her.

Quietly, Sarah asked, "If the brown one is King, and Duke is the black one, what is the name of the light-colored one?"

Hannah stood like a statue, staring straight ahead. Her lips parted but no sound came out until she cleared her throat and said roughly, "Doesn't have one."

Sarah looked at her. "Why not?"

She was rewarded with an offhand shrug.

"Let's think of one."

"I already did. Mistral."

Sarah's eyebrows went up. She gave a short laugh, shook her head. "Never heard of it."

"It's a wind."

Sarah gestured with her hand. "You mean like this wind?"

"No. A master wind. In France."

"Really? You think it fits her?"

"Didn't you see her run? If we raced those three, she'd win."

Ah, here was her chance, Sarah thought. "So, go ahead and race them."

Hannah shook her head.

"Why not?" But a seed had been sown, sprouting in Hannah's mind, although Sarah knew her daughter would do her best to stomp all over it.

When Jerry and Jake showed up with the necessary tools to file Goat's teeth, they greeted Sarah, who sat on the front porch cleaning green and yellow beans, thankful for the fine vegetables, in spite of the drought. Thankful for Manny's expertise in rigging up a long pipe underground to a hydrant close to the garden. The windmill's clanking and whirring powered by the constant wind supplied them with the necessary water for the garden.

Every evening and every morning, Eli and Mary filled blue and white speckled granite buckets, lugged them to the long rows of vegetables, and poured water on the plants, cup by cup. The children never complained. They were too glad to have something to eat when the snow and the cold slammed the house like a battering ram.

Old enough to remember the pinched pain of their empty stomachs, they worked with energy, making a game out of arriving at the hydrant together.

When Jerry and Jake arrived, they stopped watering and stood upright like two curious rabbits, watching quietly as the two men dismounted. They didn't stop at the house or look for Hannah and Manny. They just went ahead, climbed the fence, caught Goat by the halter, yanked open his mouth, and set to work.

To the children, it looked like the work of a serious murderer, sawing away inside a horse's mouth. They looked at each other, nodded, and raced for the house, clattered up on the porch, their eyes wide with alarm.

Eli pointed a shaking finger and said, "Why is he doing that?"

"He's killing him dead!" Mary shouted, agitation making her voice shrill and loud, which brought Hannah from her job at the wash tubs, scrubbing Manny's trousers with lye soap.

She glared at the two men, tucked a few stray hairs under her *dichly* and stalked off, stiff legged, pumping her arms.

"What are you doing?" she demanded.

Jake Fisher stopped, but Jerry kept on going, told Jake to keep his hold on Goat's mouth and not to worry about her.

"Release that poor horse this instant!" Hannah screeched.

Jerry kept working with the file, took his time, and didn't give her so much as a sidelong glance.

"Stop it! You'll kill that horse!"

Jerry finished, told Jake to let Goat go, bent to gather his tools, and turned to face the dark fury in Hannah's eyes.

"He'd die sooner if we didn't do that. Now his grass and hay can be chewed properly and he'll digest his food better. He'll fill out now."

"You don't know a thing, Jerry Riehl."

Jerry didn't bother answering, merely lifted one eyebrow and laughed, a sound that only served to increase Hannah's bad temper. "How's the exercising going?"

"How would I know? I don't touch your horses. I didn't give you permission to bring them here, so it's Manny's chore, not mine."

Jerry busied himself opening the gate and threw back over his shoulder, "Too bad. I was thinking of giving the palomino to you, but I guess you're not interested."

Hannah was so taken aback she had absolutely nothing to say. She forgot herself enough to let her eyes widen and her mouth hang open, clearly showing her shock, followed by disbelief. She caught herself just as Jerry led the palomino out, stopped and lowered his face a mere foot away from hers.

"You know you want her, Hannah," he stated in a husky whisper as he lowered an eyelid over one dark eye and gave just a hint of a smile.

What a self-righteous . . . Hannah ground her teeth, curled her hands into fists, stamped her foot and yelled. She yelled and shouted words that she had no idea she could be capable of using to disparage someone.

She told him to get his horses out of there in a week or she was going to turn them loose with the cattle, and if he never found them again, well, that was just too bad, now wasn't it!

Jerry tightened the cinch on the palomino's saddle, his shoulders shaking, his face well hidden, hiding his laughter from her. "Guess if you did that, it would be more of an invitation to cattle thieves than they already have, with that fine-looking herd of Angus cows you have. Or maybe you haven't heard?"

Hannah's big dark eyes came up and met his immediately.

"They made off with twelve of that Owen's cows. I forget his last name—German guy. Heavy. At night. Hauled them out in a big truck and trailer, they think. Better watch your herd, I'd think. Better be careful, Hannah."

CHAPTER 12

THE DROUGHT WORSENED.

The sun beat down mercilessly. Tin roofs creaked and snapped, grasses swayed and shriveled to a melancholy brown color that spoke of the prairie's desperate need for rain. The creek bed whispered itself to nothing, dry, jagged cracks appearing like dark scabs on the parched earth.

The wind blew hot and dry, laden with brown dust particles and the smell of dying vegetation. Cows moiled around the water tank and wandered far to crop the grass that had turned to hay on the stalk. Wild flowers gave up their glad colors of yellow, pink, and blue, hung their heads and became hot and dry and dusty like everything else.

The newly arrived Amish thought surely the end of the world was nigh. They had never experienced anything like it, these blue skies that refused to send even a spattering of raindrops. Sarah smiled and shook her head, saying, oh no, this was a normal North Dakota summer. The rains would come. That's why we have so many acres, the cows travel far to get their fill of grass.

For awhile, Hannah and Manny rode out to sleep on the prairie, keeping watch like shepherds over their herd after Jerry had told them of cattle thieves. When nothing happened, they figured it was over. The Klassermans were the ones known to be wealthy and were therefore an easy target.

Ike Lapp built a horrible little stick house out of thrown away shingles and corrugated metal, the roof flat and wide and rusted to a deep brown. They moved their belongings and their seven skinny children into it, hung green blinds in the windows and called it home.

Ben Miller, of course, designed a long, low ranch house with dormers in the roof and bought logs from some fancy company in the Northwest. He built a barn the size of two or three ordinary barns put together, maybe four.

His windmill was up and running with orders pouring in from folks for miles around. The Midas touch, he had. Just about everything went well for that man. He even invented a homemade sprinkler for the garden, and chuckled and laughed his way through the dust-filled days. He said the women were blessed, now weren't they, all that laundry that dried in a few minutes flat. No mud to worry about either.

Nothing much was heard from the vicinity of the old Perthing place. After Jerry took his three horses back, Hannah figured he must have built a barn, and didn't care about anything other than that.

They all got together to have church services in the summer before the arrival of Grandfather Stoltzfus, Elam, and Ben. Hannah refused to go. Her excuse was that she didn't know if she was ever going to be Amish, and why should she try to figure it out at her age?

Sarah and the children rode home from services at Ben Millers, renewed and refreshed, their faces alive with smiles and conversation, an invitation to dinner at Ike Lapps the following Sunday.

All of this was like a reviving drink of water to Sarah, a long awaited renewal of her faith, her roots. She was surprised to find herself missing Mose so keenly. It was like an ache that settled into her chest and didn't leave all day. She believed it was the atmosphere of knowing friends he had known, the chattering of the women punctuated by the men's voices rising and falling, peppered with guffaws of laughter that made her curious. Sometimes, when he was alive, she had gone to sit quietly with him, listening to the men's talk, which was often more interesting than the endless pursuit of the best apple pie or child-rearing practices.

But she was blessed. She was thankful to have Manny and the little ones. Baby Abby was asleep on her lap and of course, the blistered Hannah, burned with what God had handed her, preferring to pick out the sour grapes, digest them like vinegar, then blame everyone else for her self-chosen path of prickliness. She guessed this is where you loved without condition; loved, kept your mouth shut, and allowed God to do the work of teaching your daughter.

Sometimes, she found herself watching Mary, looking for signs of determination, unkindness, or a strong, selfish will. She remembered Hannah at Mary's age. She'd had trouble in school, slandering the teachers, repeating uncouth rhymes the boys taught her, and yes, it had always been someone else's fault. The teachers were too strict, they picked on her, girls were stupid, jumping all that rope. And on and on.

It wasn't that she went unpunished. More than once, Mose had taken her to school to apologize. Could a person really determine their fate, born with a nature that rebelled from a young age? Like a mule, Hannah was. Set and determined. Though her caring parents disciplined her, spouted Bible verses to her, and tumbled holy prayers around her head like a waterfall, all of it passed her by, untouched, unimpressed.

Lord, have mercy. Sarah's lips trembled with whispered prayer.

Toward the end of summer, Hannah broke out with a fierce, red rash, followed by a sore throat and a high fever. It was when she was cranky, hot and bed-ridden, her eyes closed against the misery of her days, the heat oppressive like a punishment, that she found out about Clay.

Abby Jenkins came to visit, thinner than ever, still coughing, her eyes rheumy, but shrugging it off as if it was nothing. Her skin was stretched across her cheekbones, her wrinkles like crumpled waxed paper that had been smoothed out again.

She took one long look at Hannah and said she had a bumper crop of German measles, that she'd better stay in bed because she didn't want no lasting effects.

They left the door open, so their voices were heard clearly, sentences spoken between sips of spearmint tea. Abby spoke barely two sentences without coughing, which served to irritate Hannah to the point of clawing at the thin sheet covering her itching legs.

"You heard about Clay, did you?" she asked Sarah.

"No, we haven't heard anything."

"He's takin' the car every Saturday night and goin' to dances with that Judy Harris. She's that redhead from Pine. Says he'll likely ask her to marry him come fall."

Hannah stopped breathing in order to hear every word.

"Always hoped him and Hannah would git hitched but then, I guess yer traditions wouldn't allow it, an' I doubt as Clay would hold too much to some of yours. Afraid Hannah might be better off on her own anyhow, leastways as long as she don't like folks much. But now me? I coulda get along bein' her mother-in-law. I'da let her set. Jus' stayed away. Best thing. She'da been awright."

Sarah smiled as she listened to Abby. She saw the open bedroom door and figured Hannah could hear this. Her own feeling about the whole Clay thing had always been to pray that Clay would stay with his own kind, or recognize early on that Hannah was a peck of trouble.

Now, seated with Abby at her kitchen table, Sarah's smile was bright and genuine and her congratulations heartfelt. To her way of thinking, there had never been a Clay and Hannah. The drama was certainly not over. Hannah did what she wanted, so who was to know the outcome? Marriage might be a small thing, or perhaps there would be no marriage at all.

Oh, Hannah, Hannah. Suffering with measles in this heat, her skin as prickly as her nature, she was only beginning to see all that life would offer.

Sarah smiled at Abby, but felt her mouth tremble as she held back tears. "Yes, Abby, I have no doubt you would have done right by Hannah. You're a genuinely good-hearted soul. I owe you so much. You'll be rewarded some day for all your giving. You were more concerned about us than we were about ourselves."

Abby laughed, then coughed and coughed. "Ah." She cleared her throat, wiped her eyes with a corner of her flowered apron.

Hannah lay in bed absorbing every word between Abby and her mother. So he'd gone and done it, then, what he'd threatened out by the windmill a month ago.

Always after her, a lone wolf circling her, trying to bring her down. He was nice enough and attractive enough by far. But just so everlasting wanting to touch her, hold her, be with her, so that the minute she saw him arrive on horseback, her main intention had been to stay away from him, or at least make it clear she wasn't interested.

Well, so that was that. There he went. Good.

Her throat felt as if she'd swallowed a mousetrap, and her breath tasted like it too. Her skin felt hot and clammy, worse than a dose of poison ivy. Likely the whole family would come down with this contagious thing, and since she had it first, guess who'd be the nurse? She turned her head to the wall and tried to block out the sound of Abby's cough, rasping like sandpaper on a rough board. She sniffed, reached for her used and rumpled white handkerchief, grimaced at the stains, and called for Sarah to bring her a clean one.

When Sarah returned to the kitchen, Abby shook her head. "S' partly what's wrong with that girl."

"What?" Sarah lifted innocent eyes to her neighbor.

"She coulda got her own handkerchief."

"But she's sick."

"I don't care. She's grown up. Let her get her own or use her soiled one."

"Well." Sarah didn't know what to say to this.

"That tone of voice comin' from that bedroom door? Makes me feel like takin' holt of them sheets and rollin' her outta bed!" Abby's eyes glittered, her mouth in a firm line. "She needs to be stood up to, Sarah. Yer ways with Mose was okay, but this girl ain't yer husband. She needs to know you ain't puttin' up with none of her mouth."

After Abby took her leave, Sarah foundered, unsure about anything as far as Hannah was concerned. She'd thought it best to love her and leave the rest to God, but now she wasn't so sure. She respected Abby, loved her, and took her advice seriously. Well, one thing for sure, she had a very irate patient to look after, so perhaps true wisdom would be given her.

As it was, the whole family came down with the German measles, except Sarah, who'd had them when she was thirteen.

Hannah was left with red, flaky skin, the rash driving her wild with its cruel itching, like bugs crawling lightly over her skin. Her fever left, her throat healed, and her appetite returned. She cooked oatmeal and ate huge portions, fried bread in the cast iron pan and ate it with raspberry jam. She ate prairie hen gravy on new potatoes, green beans, and applesauce.

Color bloomed in her cheeks, her dresses became tight across her chest, her teeth shone white when she smiled, which was quite frequent, for Hannah.

Goat grew into a sleeker, fatter version of himself. His thin neck filled out and his ribs became rounded with flesh. The long, miserable hair hanging on his stomach disappeared. His strength rebounded and his stamina returned.

Manny couldn't stop talking about it. He said if teeth made so much difference in horses, why did every ranch for miles around not know this? He'd get Jerry to teach him and they'd supplement their income, at least enough to stock up on supplies before winter.

Hannah turned a deaf ear, pretended she hadn't heard. She'd never once acknowledged any difference in Goat. She ignored it all, including Manny's talk.

She strode around the house caring for Eli and Mary, rocked Abby when she cried with the fever and painful red rash.

They received another letter from their grandfather. They would not arrive until next spring. Complications had risen between Emma, Rachel, and Lydia, although he did not go into detail. Sarah fretted and worried and longed to speak with her father. What had happened? Why hadn't he gone into more detail?

Manny came in for the evening meal, his face blazing with fever, his eyes unnaturally bright. He staggered to the couch and flopped onto his back, one hand thrown across his forehead. "I am so sick," he whispered.

Alarmed, Sarah and Hannah rushed over to him. His face was dry and radiating with heat. His lips were cracked and peeling. His nostrils were distended as he breathed shallow breaths.

They bathed him in vinegar water to bring down his fever. He seemed to be fairly comfortable after that and fell into a deep sleep, allowing them time to care for the little ones.

With the heat during the day and interrupted sleep at night, Sarah and Hannah were exhausted, moving around the house half-awake, perspiring and quick to take offense.

Eli's rash appeared quickly, which seemed to alleviate his fever and sore throat. He was cheerful, propped up on pillows, writing and drawing on his small slate with a piece of broken chalk.

Mary lay in a deep sleep, her fever alarmingly high. But after the red rash appeared, she too felt much better.

Manny, however, seemed to languish in the grip of a fever they could not break. When the red rash did not appear after the fifth day, his tossing and moaning increased. Sarah sent Hannah to the Klassermans to use the telephone to summon Doc Brinter from his office in Pine.

Hannah saddled Pete, obedient for once and seriously alarmed. It was unthinkable that something might happen to Manny. God wouldn't allow it. He was not that cruel.

She knew Pete was slower than Goat would be, but there was no reason for her to accept the new version of him, which would prove Jerry right. She rode Pete hard, lashing him with the ends of the reins, her breath coming in shallow jerks, her mouth dry with fear. They'd been so worried about cattle thieves, which proved to be nothing, and now here they were, stricken with this illness in the middle of another champion drought.

Now, though, she thought along the same lines as everyone else. They were homesteaders, facing things head on. Gladiators of the plains. Fearless. Hadn't they already proved themselves? Already they sounded like Hod and Abby, talking to the new families who'd come to live on their claims.

Hot puffs of wind smacked her face as she rode. All around her the brittle grass rustled, a brown gray mass of dried out vegetation that rolled away to meet the hot sky at the horizon. Hannah loved the dry season now that she knew the cattle would always have something to eat, and the windmill would always pump cold well water for them. She could never get enough of watching the calves turn into sturdy little replicas of their mothers, and she couldn't help but count the pounds they were adding into dollar bills.

She rode up to the Klassermans, summoned the doctor, and after a drink of yeasty, sour-smelling homemade root beer, she was on her way home. She allowed Pete his head and his pace as well. The day was warm, so she'd have to take it easy, after the mad dash to the neighboring ranch.

Doc Brinter's car chugged up to the low ranch house only minutes after she'd unsaddled Pete. This was frightening in a way she herself didn't fully understand. How could he have driven all that way in so short a time?

She let herself in through the wash house door. The smell of soap and vinegar was strong in the stifling heat of the low house. She placed her bare feet carefully, her heart in her throat, listening to low voices from Manny's room. She walked to the door, stopped to listen to the doctor's voice, and then her mother's soft, rasping whisper. She could hear Manny's shallow breathing.

"You do understand, German measles are a virus," the doctor inquired. There was no answer from her mother.

Hannah watched Sarah's face, fearful of her mother's features set like stone, as if her submission had been stretched too far, turning into anger that God would allow this, her oldest son, her sweet Emmanuel, to be taken so sick with this horrible, fiery, skin-altering disease.

The doctor stayed for a long time, working to bring down Manny's fever, talking in quiet tones to Sarah, who remained in that odd realm, as if she could not fully comprehend anything that was happening.

Finally the doctor, kindly though he was, spoke to Sarah sharply. "You are his mother, Mrs. Detweiler. You need to pull yourself together and listen to what I'm trying to tell you. You are responsible for him."

He showed her a small white envelope filled with aspirin, white tablets to be crushed on a spoon and given in pudding or applesauce for the fever. A liquid medicine for pain, in a dark glass bottle with a stopper. To be given every three hours, as long as he can swallow.

Sarah's head jerked up and her eyes widened. "What do you mean, as long as he can swallow? You mean the time will come when he won't be able to? You're trying to tell me my son will die?"

Hannah was frightened to hear her mother's voice rising to a hysterical pitch, her face contorted with something Hannah had never seen.

Doctor Brinter was no longer young. He had seen plenty cases of German measles, and he knew all too well the lingering high fever, the red rash so long awaited that never appeared, followed by a slow, painful end.

"We'll have to wait and see. The rash should have appeared by now. If you want, we can transport him to the hospital in Dorchester."

"Can they help him there?" Sarah asked, her words like ice picks. Hannah looked at her sharply.

"They can keep him comfortable. As I told you, this is a virus."

"Answer my question!" Sarah shrilled in a high, unnatural voice that drove fear into Hannah.

Dr. Brinter turned and beckoned Hannah to follow him, then spoke in quiet tones, left a packed of pills for Sarah, who was showing signs of shock and instability. He told her, kindly, his eyes never leaving her face, that there was a real possibility that Manny would not live if the rash did not appear. Hannah swallowed, blinked, and struggled to remain composed.

"Just keep a constant vigil. There is a possibility of seizures if his temperature goes too high. If the measles, the lesions from the virus itself, do not appear within the next few days, he will probably not survive this. By all appearances, your mother is unfit to accept what I must tell her. So you are the one to keep watch."

He reached out to lay a heavy hand on her shoulder, patted a few times. "You appear to be a strong young woman. Bear up for your mother and the little ones."

"What . . . what about the hospital? Wouldn't it be best to take him there?" Hannah asked, laying a hand on his arm.

The doctor hesitated, then shook his head. "I'm sorry, Miss, but no. With the cost, I doubt it would be best. The hospital in Dorchester is famously understaffed, so it would be better to keep him here."

The overwhelming responsibility lit on Hannah's shoulders with a crushing weight, turning her breathing into shallow gasps. How could she sit by Manny's bedside, waiting for a rash to appear? What if seizures overtook him? What about Mam?

She stood at the window, looking out, watching the doctor leave as he carried his black bag and stowed it in the trunk of his car, opened the door, and slid behind the wheel. He started the car and slowly drove away, a cloud of gray dust swirling up behind him.

Oh, God.

Hannah wasn't aware that she had called on a Higher Power as she groaned under the weight of this heavy calamity that had fallen upon them, just when things were going surprisingly well. If something happened to Manny, she wouldn't be able to go on.

Alone, standing in the heat and dust of the drought-stricken day, Hannah clamped her jaws shut like a vice. Manny would live. He had to. She hadn't come out here only to be flogged and beaten back by circumstances she couldn't control. She would get him better. She had no choice.

The heat shimmered in a rippling haze that spread across the land. Manny's fever would never come down unless they could cool him off. She made her way to the door of his bedroom, where he lay moaning and turning his head from side to side, his tanned face flaming with the elevation of his body temperature.

His hands plucked at the thin sheet covering him, then threw it off as if the light touch burned his skin.

"Manny, don't!" Sarah screamed, her voice high and unnatural. A shot of pure anger coursed through Hannah's veins. There was her mother, the one who should be shepherding them through this, slowly losing control, acting like a child.

Hannah drew back a well-muscled arm and delivered a ringing smack to her mother's face, sending her head to one side, almost knocking her off the low chair on which she was seated.

"Stop it, Mam! Get ahold of yourself!" she shouted. Sarah slid off the chair, a crushed, crumpled heap lying inert, staring at Hannah in disbelief before she curled up in a pitiful fetal position and began to sob.

Hannah had often seen her mother cry, but she had never heard anything like the deep primal wail that tore out of Sarah's throat.

She had survived so much. Now, when she could touch and taste joy again, now to be dealt this blow of Manny's sickness and questionable survival. It was her undoing. It left her battered, exposed, and vulnerable, pushing her to the brink of insanity.

Hannah left the room.

Manny's anguished moans melded with her mother's hoarse sobs, and there wasn't much she could do about either one. A bucket of cold water. Some rags. Vinegar for a fever.

First, she went to speak to Eli and Mary, telling them how sick Manny was. Mam was tired but she would soon feel better. She promised them molasses cookies and milk if they would take care of Abigail and stay quiet.

"Is Manny going to die?" Eli asked, his eyes liquid with fear.

"No. He'll get better."

Mary sighed, "Good."

Hannah pressed a cold cloth to Manny's forehead, but he immediately clawed it away, writhing and calling out, mumbling words that made no sense. Hannah put the cloths back in the bucket, then pulled up a chair by his bed. She reached out to stroke the long, dark hair away from his face, alarmed at the absence of perspiration or tears, his lips hot, chapped, and dry.

He needed water.

After repeated attempts, the white pills and all the water except the small amount that dribbled down his chin, remained in Hannah's hand.

"Manny. Please listen. You have to take these pills." Hannah spoke in soft tones, begging him to drink the water, but his teeth remained clenched.

Hannah sighed, reached out to set everything on the night table and watched her mother's form silently heaving in her agony. She thought this weakness of her mother was unnecessary, walked over and touched her shoulder, said, "Stop it now, Mam."

Sarah pushed herself up with both palms, her white covering sliding sideways, her dark hair pulled away from the severe bun on the back of her head, her eyes swollen from the force of her weeping. She sagged against the wall, ashamed, a creature of despair and lost hope.

"Forgive me, Hannah. Did the doctor leave pills here for me?" Hannah nodded and handed them over, watching as her mother swallowed the pills with the glass of water that should have gone to Manny.

CHAPTER 13

Long into the night, Hannah sat alone. Her mother had taken not one pill, but two, and lay now in a deep sleep, a small figure beneath the thin cotton sheet covering her.

From time to time, Hannah ran her hands lightly across Manny's arms and chest, searching desperately for a sign of the red rash that should be appearing, the one single thing that would ease his pain and misery. His skin remained smooth and dry, the heat so frightening toward morning that she could no longer bear to touch him.

The doctor arrived early, dressed in his immaculate black suit, his tie slipped behind his buttoned vest. Already the sun was hot, the house retaining yesterday's heat. He soon produced his white handkerchief and wiped at the beads of perspiration that formed on his upper lip.

Hannah's dark eyes searched the doctor's. Seeing the hopelessness, her spirit shrank within her, as a promise his regained health folded.

Sarah moved softly, like a ghost, into the room, wringing her hands in anguish, her face without color or expression.

Hannah felt the calm and saw it in her eyes, knowing she had reached out and found the all-seeing, benevolent Father who directed her life and kept her in the palm of His Hand. If this was God's will, she would bear up beneath it.

"Mrs. Detweiler, how are you this morning?" the doctor inquired.

Sarah nodded, "I'm all right."

"Good. Good. I understand you lost your husband in the not too distant past. I extend my condolences."

Sarah nodded again and asked, "Is my son still doing all right?"

"Yes."

"Can we possibly get him to a hospital?" Sarah asked.

"We can do that if you wish. But to move him might be an effort. The ambulance from the hospital would have to transport him. You have no telephone, I gather?"

"No."

"Then I will use one, if you will give me directions to the nearest ranch."

"I can accompany you to the Klassermans," Sarah offered.

Hannah gazed steadily on Manny's face, serene now, in a deep sleep. She agreed to let her mother go, knowing the anguished vigil would be too much for Sarah.

After they left, Hannah cared for Abby, changed her diaper, dressed her, combed Mary's hair and made breakfast for the children. She set the kitchen right, swept the floor, washed dishes, and wiped the countertop and table. She gave Eli and Mary instructions on feeding the milk cow and checking the level at the water tank.

When she returned to Manny's room, he lay as before, his face without color. Panic seized her. She bit down on her lower lip to keep from crying out.

Surely not.

But his face was warm.

Warm? Not as hot as before?

Hannah tore off the sheet and bent to peer at his chest, his stomach, and his legs, with the dark hair growing over them. She rushed to the window, grasped the heavy window blind and yanked with too much force, sending it crashing to the floor. A blaze of hot, morning sunlight illuminated the room. Without attempting to replace the fallen window blind, Hannah retraced her steps to the bed and bent over Manny.

Was that a red welt appearing on his shoulder? Yes! It was!

Without thinking of his pain, she grasped his shoulders in her strong hands and pulled him forward like a limp doll. His head fell sideways. She reached behind him to prop him up, bent her head and saw that his back was covered with red pustules, the scaly, disfiguring rash on his skin like a beautiful, long awaited sign.

Manny's eyes flew open. Irritation crossed his face. "Put me down," he said hoarsely.

But Hannah was crying, her eyes squeezed shut as tears ran down her cheeks. Her lips quivered and a glad cry escaped her lips. "Manny!"

It was all she could manage, before she lowered him, turned away and, with heaving shoulders, fixed the window blind.

Manny lay back, opened his eyes, and croaked like a frog as he told Hannah he would die of thirst if she didn't bring him some water. By the time she brought the glass, his chest was already breaking out in angry spots, the awful virus leaving his body through his skin.

"Look at you, Manny," Hannah quavered.

Manny bent his head, felt the lesions on his skin, asked if he'd been very sick.

"Manny, you were so ill. So terribly sick!" Hannah burst out.

"Measles, huh?" Then he lay back, exhausted, and fell into a deep, restful sleep as the rash continued to grow and spread.

When Dr. Brinter and Sarah returned, Hannah met them at the door with a glad cry. She threw herself into her mother's arms and began to weep hysterically.

They rushed to the room and quietly observed, Sarah weeping now, the tears a flow of healing water.

Dr. Brinter bowed his head and thanked the God of healing. He placed a hand on Sarah's back, and she went weeping into his arms. At once she stepped back, ashamed. To be in a man's arms, to lay her head on a strong chest, no matter how briefly, awakened in her a longing she had forgotten existed. Mose. Mose. If only you could be here to share this moment.

Dr. Brinter told them the Lord had chosen to save Manny's life. He would live. He left an ointment for the itchiness and then left instructions for the ambulance driver when he arrived. Then he let himself out the door before Hannah or Sarah could gather their wits to thank him properly or ask how much they owed him.

They were quarantined now. No visitors until the measles were gone. They thoroughly disinfected house, scouring the walls and floors, washing the bedding and curtains in bleach, wiping down the doors, cupboards, and furniture.

The dust blew in and around them, the sun shone on the dry grass, but a happiness soaked every wall and doorway. The dust could settle in on the freshly washed floors, but what did that matter? Manny would live, would regain his health, ride the plains with Hannah, shoot coyotes, and chase antelope.

Thankfulness had always been a way of life for Sarah, but now it was magnified tenfold. She spent her days hugging her children impulsively, squeezing poor Abby until she struggled to free herself. Eli squealed and wriggled out of her grasp but sat there blinking afterward, a small, silly grin playing around his mouth.

She celebrated Manny's health in song, humming and whistling softly under her breath. She cooked great quantities of stew, thick with chunks of canned beef, carrots, and celery from the late garden. She baked potatoes, fried prairie hen rolled in egg and flour and seasoned with fresh herbs.

Manny gained weight, his cheeks filled out again, his skin healed and tanned under the hot summer sun.

Hannah bloomed, her cheeks reddened, her teeth shone white as her lips parted in smiles about everything, and sometimes, about nothing. To be truly delivered from the awful death of a loved one left a lasting impression on her.

Then one Sunday, without warning, uninvited and unannounced, Ike and Barbara Lapp and their seven children came to visit, driving two surprisingly nice horses hitched to a spring wagon painted black.

Sarah met them on the porch. Manny hurried out to help Ike put away the horses.

"Why, what a surprise!" Sarah exclaimed, throwing up her hands. "Come right in, Barbara."

Hannah sniffed, went to her room, and closed the door firmly. If Mam needed her, she could come get her. No need to visit with Ike Lapp. They had the nerve, uninvited, at that.

The children circled each other shyly, Eli and Mary uncertain how to start a friendship, so they sat with the grownups while Sarah busied herself in the kitchen making coffee.

Manny kept a conversation going with Ike. He rather liked the man. Not too much ambition, but he had a great love of life and a dry sense of humor that sent Manny into peals of mirth.

They had brought along Barbara's sister's daughter, Marybelle. She was a quiet, skinny girl with large feet, hair the color of ripe wheat, slanted eyes so blue they were shocking, and a splattering of freckles like dark sand over her tiny nose.

"She just arrived last week with the Henry Esches."

Sarah called from the kitchen, "Who?"

"Didn't you know? You know, Amos Escha Henrys, from the Gap."

Sarah brought a tray bearing four cups of steaming coffee and placed it on the low table by the couch. She thought, a hand going to her mouth, "Amos Escha? You mean Amos, the one who has the threshing rig?"

"Yep, that's the one. He moved his family out here last week. He's going to try his hand at raising wheat. There's a new seed wheat, an early variety, and he thinks if he gets it in in the fall, he'll be able to grow a good crop before the drought hits. He's sitting on close to a thousand acres right now. In a tent."

Ike Lapp lifted his coffee cup, sipped, grimaced. "His wife is so fat, I don't know how she'll take to prairie life. She takes a lot of feed."

Manny sputtered, choking on his coffee.

Ike laughed heartily, a sound without guile, just pure, light-hearted merriment, the joy of a humorous situation shared with others.

Barbara, pinched and thin, chortled with him. "Marybelle, why don't you take the children to see the windmill? Your Uncle Ike helped erect it, one of the first ones out here."

She looked at Ike, who rewarded her with his smile. "Where is the windmill?" she asked, her voice low.

Manny jumped to his feet. "I'll take you. Come on, Eli. Bring your friends. Sorry, I don't know your children's names."

"Oh, they'll let you know soon enough," Barbara said, waving a hand in dismissal.

They all filed out the door into the heat of the afternoon. Barbara began to talk the minute they were gone. "Yes, well, about the girl. You notice her name is not plain, not truly Amish. Well, her mother, my sister Anna, ran off with the local grocer, and she is the product of that marriage. Anna was only sixteen. Left the Amish, left all her teachings, ended up in Georgia or some such state down South. Just a year or so ago, we got this letter from a mental institution asking us to come and get Mary-belle. A horrible place." She said the word "horrible" with a slight shudder.

"Guess Anna took up with a snake hunter who lived in a swamp and raised rats and mice to feed the snakes he captured. It got the best of her and they took her away. I don't know if she'll ever be right again."

Listening to Barbara, Sarah's face went slack as she thought how she'd been to the brink herself, and so recently. A great welling of sympathy for Anna washed over her. Poor girl, making such wrong choices. Whose fault? Sarah felt a deep sadness for the woman, incarcerated now in a place where no human being should ever have to live.

"Anyway, this Marybelle stayed with the snake hunter and lived in his house with him. She kept it clean enough and kept some food on the table. It's hot there. You think it's hot here. This was like liquid heat. Like swimming in humidity. He's a drinker; passed out drunk most of the time. So we took her. She didn't want to go. I believe she had a nice enough life. He was good to her, when he was sober. She seems sensible, no ill effects from her life in the swamp.

"She told me she wasn't afraid of the snakes. They milked them for the venom and sold it, I guess. Alligators and mosquitoes, bugs—the whole place simply buzzed with hundreds of insects. Thousands.

"We're trying to teach her about God, but she doesn't really seem to understand." Barbara stopped for breath.

"How old is she?" Sarah asked.

"Older than she looks. Guess how old."

"Fourteen?"

"Almost fifteen. But immature. Needs discipline. Wants her mother and misses being near the water."

"I bet."

Hannah lay on her stomach, her room like an oven with the door closed and no breeze. The buzz of voices rose and fell. She dozed and woke up sweating, seized by an irritation. You watch, she thought. Mam will invite them to supper. She'll waste all our food on those starving little brats.

Sure enough, she heard the clatter of pots and pans, the sound of water running, footsteps. A knock on her door. She had a notion to crawl out the window. Here, this situation, was precisely why she resisted the Amish migration to North Dakota.

Instead of roaming the prairie on Pete and being left alone on a hot Sunday, she was expected to keep up appearances, help make supper, talk, smile, and go to church, when she'd rather go lose herself on the plains, completely unknown, forgotten by anyone who came from Lancaster County.

Stupid old Ike Lapp with his oversized, hooked nose and yellowed teeth. He looked like a horse!

Her happiness about Manny's regained health was overshadowed by her own dark nature, leaving her annoyed, in no mood to shake hands or make small talk. Meddling old man! Hoping to creep out of her room and sidle down the hallway to the bathroom, Hannah opened her door and slid through noiselessly.

"Hannah!" She sagged against the wall, clapped a hand to her forehead, and rolled her eyes.

"Hannah! Get over here! Didn't know you were home," Ike called. Hannah arranged her features into some semblance of normalcy, her lips in a tight smile that only served to provide an aura of frost around her. If she were a horse, she could buck and kick, break through the door and take off running, but as it was, she was stuck. Strangled by company.

"Well now, Hannah," Ike Lapp chortled, saying her name as if she was the title of a story he was about to write. "Still the same. You don't want anyone around, but they all want you!" He slapped his knee at his own hilarious observation, sending Hannah to the kitchen in a huff, where she greeted Barbara in a voice strung with icicles, resulting in a firm jab in her ribs from her mother's elbow and followed by a dark look of warning.

She mashed potatoes in the torrid kitchen, the steam rising up over her face, listening half-heartedly to Barbara's high-pitched voice, which irritated her worse than a whining mosquito.

Sarah told her to open the table and add at least eight leaves, as there would be fifteen of them. She stood at one end of the table and yanked. Nothing happened. She knew someone would have to pull it apart from the other end, but there was no way she'd ask Ike for help. Of course, watching her like a hawk, he rose to the occasion, helped her pull the table apart, added leaves, chatting all the while like a woman.

"You heard about the new barn? Down on the old Perthing place?"

Hannah shook her head.

"Quite a barn. That Jerry has some excellent horses. Never saw better."

Hannah didn't answer so he continued to ramble on about nothing. She didn't care how many horses Jerry had, or if his barn was covered in gold. She only half listened, wishing he'd go sit down and be quiet.

With a clattering on the porch, Manny and the children came in, windswept and red-faced, the constantly blowing dust powdering their hair and shoulders. Hannah caught sight of Marybelle. Now what? She wasn't one of the Lapp bunch, sure as shooting. Boy, was she a looker. That hair like a palomino.

Hannah blinked. Blinked again. Tucked a strand of hair behind her ear. She couldn't stop looking at her. What was it about that girl? She looked to be about fourteen, but carried herself with a practiced grace, her shoulders back, her head held high. Her eyes were astonishing—slanted, huge, and blue.

No one acted as if there was anything going on that was out of the ordinary. She was too proud to ask, so she remained in a fog of curiosity that only became thicker as the meal went on.

Ike Lapp ate with his usual bad table manners, but Barbara was surprising, holding her fork in a proper manner, speaking quietly to the children, spreading elderberry jelly on their bread and cutting it in half for the little ones, who ate quietly, without speaking.

She watched Marybelle, sitting across from her, cutting the chunks of beef, spearing her carrots. What was it about her eyes. Like a knowing, a telling of something. Was it sadness? Experience? Hannah decided that her eyes were older than her face. And those freckles!

Ike Lapp was rambling on about the need to add onto his house and insulate it a bit. "I could cover the whole thing with mud and call it an adobe house. Isn't that what they do farther south?"

Marybelle looked up from her plate at the same time Hannah did. Their eyes met but neither one acknowledged the other.

After the Lapp family left, Sarah threw herself on the couch, thrust her feet in front of her, and sighed, her eyes half closed. "Wonderful! Just *wunderbar*." She grabbed Abigail and nuzzled her little face, then turned her toward her chest and kissed her all over.

"What a blessing! What an opportunity for good old fellowship. Making Sunday supper for company. Just the way I was raised. And now we can keep up this old tradition of visiting, just showing up at someone's door and being welcomed in. What about that Marybelle?"

Hannah jerked to attention. "Is that her name? Fancy," she said sourly.

Sarah related Marybelle's life story. She was surprised to be met with a snort, a shrug of disinterested shoulders, as Hannah evidently found her story uninteresting. She brought her little story to a close, closed her eyes to relax, and let it go. Typical Hannah. Pessimistic. Always looking on the dark underside of everything.

Suddenly Hannah said, "Well, if she's not lying and *was* raised in a swamp, she should be dried out by now."

No one laughed. They all fastened cold eyes on her face until she felt a prick of humiliation, one eyelid twitching uncomfortably. She got up and walked out of the door into the evening shadows.

Out to the water tank where the grass was trampled until it disappeared, the roots dried out and mashed into the dust by the wide, cloven hooves of the cows that milled around their only source of water in the blazing sun.

They were all there, every one, fat and black and sleek, chewing their cud contentedly, others cropping the short, brown grass. The calves were growing into well-built heifers or steers at an alarming rate. Hannah couldn't believe how well the tough prairie grass fed these cattle, all the feed they needed without a cent paid out.

Haymaking had gone well, but they'd need to resume, starting tomorrow morning. She could never let her guard down, never relax about the amount of hay they'd need.

The calves were growing, but not all of them would be sold. Only enough to make a nice payment on the loan.

She watched them cropping grass, well-built, firm in the front shoulders, wide chests, straight spines and muscular legs. They'd sell well at auction. Compared to the Jenkinses' slat-sided, pot-bellied creatures, these heifers would bring a good price.

She loved to smell the dry, trampled earth, the wet smell of mud where the clear cold water ran out over the sides of the tank and mixed with the dust. She could stand for hours, listening to the whine and clanking of the great wheel as it turned, the huge metal paddles taking full advantage of the slightest breeze. The long steel rod that pumped up and down glistened in the late evening twilight, the life of the wind and the water pump.

Manny often climbed to the top, hung by one arm crooked over a metal rung, his eyes shaded with his hand, dark hair blowing in the wind, his trouser legs flapping like a struggling bird. That he had been restored to health still seemed like a miracle. So easily he could have slipped away from them, leaving her to work the homestead by herself.

Well, Mam too, but she couldn't ride and shoot and rope and make hay. She'd have to get a dog. After they sold the cattle, she'd buy a decent dog, teach him to watch the herd; maybe two dogs. Then, if one of them couldn't be there, the dogs could take over. Plus, they'd be good in winter at keeping the wolves away.

A deep satisfaction spread through her, a sense of well-being, like the wearing of a new garment.

Proud. She was proud of her accomplishments. If she hadn't worked in town at Rocher's Hardware, they would have starved or have gone crawling to the Jenkinses, the same thing they always did. Yes, they'd had help after the fire, but so had plenty of other folks. If anyone else had a fire, they would help in return. It was the way they did it.

Hannah knew that pride was squelched down among their people, stepped on, destroyed by acts of humility, half-disguised tut-tuts of, Oh, it isn't so. Go on. A wave of dismissal, turning a scarlet cheek.

But still, it was pride. Perhaps people like Ike Lapp had none. He had no reason to have any, never amounting to a hill of beans. Happy as a pig in mud, though.

Take Ben Miller. In the middle of the Great Depression, when times were unbelievably hard for most ordinary folks, here he comes, raking in opportunities by the handful. 'Cause he was smart, that's what it was. He saw things, took life by the horns, and ran with it.

She had one big obstacle coming up, and soon. They had to do something about better horses. That teeth filing, or floating, as Jerry called it—why did she always imagine large yellow molars floating out of a horse's mouth? It did make Goat appear to be a better horse, but he was still the same lazy, winded old bag with the jounciest gallop God ever gave a horse.

Pete was also on his last legs. The long journey from the East, coupled with her father's insane plowing of the prairie grass. It still made her sick to think about Pete standing with his neck outstretched, sweat running from his belly, his withers.

They had no money until they sold the calves, and then, all of what they made at auction should go to pay back her grandfather's loan.

Pete and Goat would never manage the round up or the long drive into Pine, perhaps Dorchester, or farther. The summer's drought would produce fewer cattle than usual, which meant the small town of Pine might not have an auction this year.

They could have them trucked, but Hannah didn't want that. Ever since she had set foot on this prairie, she'd wanted to join in a real cattle drive, and she was going to do it.

A thrill shot through her. All she needed was a good horse for herself and one for Manny. So if that meant being nice to Jerry Riehl and Jake Fisher, then she'd do it. Yessir. She would.

CHAPTER 14

WHEN THE HOT WINDS FADED TO A LUKEWARM JOSTLING OF GRASSES, and the house cooled off at night, Hannah knew the worst of the summer was behind them.

They redoubled their haymaking efforts, teaching Mary to drive the horses hitched double to the creaking old wagon, so that both she and Manny could fork hay, one on either side, expertly trampling it so that they could stack it high before returning to the barn.

Manny would mow one day, they'd load it the next. There was an urgency to their work now, knowing how soon the mellow winds could turn sharp as a knife blade.

They loved their work. Alone on the high plains with nothing but the sky and the land, flocks of wheeling birds bursting from the waving grasses like hurled stones, exploding into the sky until they formed a perfectly synchronized turn and settling again in a whir of sturdy little wings.

The hay smelled sweet, dusty, and earthy. The sun was sizzling on their faces. Dust settled in the cracks of their arms, between their fingers and toes, and behind their ears where the sweat trickled down. The wagon groaned and creaked; the horses' harnesses squeaked and flapped against their backsides. The wind blew and blew, raking across their faces, flapping dress skirts and handkerchiefs tied in a double triangle around their heads.

Rabbits were unafraid, hopping in front of the horses like lead dogs, escorting them along the flat rows of mown hay. Prairie dogs eyed them with undisguised curiosity before popping into their holes, allowing the wagon to rumble across, only to reappear moments after, sitting upright, their eyes like marbles bulging from their heads.

Occasionally, a small herd of rust-colored, white, and black antelope appeared on the horizon, the sight of the haymakers spurring them into a headlong flight, seeming to float above the prairie on wings. So smooth was their running they could have been on wheels. Shy deer emerged from hollows, bounding away on stick legs.

Hannah felt good about the hay storage. There would be no anxiety this winter, no appetite-seizing panic that left her wild-eyed with fear. No Lemuel Short, either.

Hannah burst out laughing, thinking of poor misguided Lemuel. He had been quite an actor, though. Very good at his craft.

"What's so funny?" Manny grinned.

"Oh, nothing. Thinking of last winter. Poor Mr. Short."

"We were fooled. Thoroughly taken across."

"We sure were!" Hannah shook her head.

"We learn." Manny laughed, a happy sound Hannah often heard these days. He was alive, ripe with youth and good health, his arms muscled from the constant hard work, his long dark hair swinging almost to his shoulders. He never wore a hat. Devout in his faith, Amish to the core, there were no homemade straw hats available. Sarah never bothered ordering one from Lancaster County, so, his old one in shreds, he went without.

It became a family joke, Manny without a hat. In winter, he wore the serviceable black felt hat with the wide brim, but never took to wearing one in the summer.

Forking hay furiously to get the load done, by dinnertime they were ravenous. Sitting atop a load of hay, the sun directly overhead, her stomach hollow, saliva collecting in her mouth as she thought of fried bread and *schmear kase*, Hannah chewed on a strand of hay and, without telling Manny, plotted her trip to the old Perthing place.

He'd try and persuade her to stay.

On the day she was prepared to go, a car, a red convertible with the white top down and a white stripe of along the side, came chugging up the road.

Hannah stood to the side of the living room window so as not to be seen and watched the slow approach, trailed by a cloud of the usual brown dust. It was Harry Rocher, and his wife, Doris, her hair piled on top of her head and covered by a white, gauzy headscarf. She was dressed in a pale yellow dress.

She remained in the car, watching with her normal pinched expression as Harry approached the house. Sarah was in the garden, hoeing up the dry soil around the gnarly celery. She laid down the hoe, dusted her hands, wiping them on her patched gray apron as she walked toward Harry Rocher.

"Hello."

Harry Rocher stopped just as he was about to step onto the porch when he spied Sarah and smiled. "Mrs. Detweiler."

"Yes, Mr. Rocher. It's good to see you again. If Doris would like, we can have a cold glass of tea together."

"No, no. I doubt if she would. I came to ask if Hannah would be willing to lend assistance at the store. My wife, Doris, is unwell. She went back East for a time but has returned. Why, I can only guess. Perhaps to make my life miserable. This time, I'd be willing to pay Hannah a small wage, beings as you're fairly well established here."

"Let's go in and ask Hannah, shall we?" Sarah asked. The poor man. Thin as a rail, like a stick man, with that stricken look about him, like a whipped puppy.

Hannah met them at the door. It was all arranged. She would work two whole days, spend the night, for five dollars. She was expected to resume her duties as before, cleaning, organizing at the store, and do some cooking. Mr. Rocher would transport her, if it was allowed.

The cogs on Hannah's brain wheel caught and set her thoughts in motion. Perfect. This would be her biggest need, the most pressing reason for a horse. Her ride to work. Jerry didn't need to know her boss had a perfectly good car. She needed a horse to ride to Pine.

"No, there's no need for you to drive your car. I always enjoy riding my horse to town. Thank you." Harry agreed, grateful for her promise to help out.

Hannah spun in a circle on her tiptoes, arms outspread. "Just perfect, Mam. Five dollars a week till the snow flies will stock our pantry with everything we need—flour, cornmeal, oatmeal, coffee, tea—all of that stuff. We can make our own way this winter. Nobody has to look out for us, not the Klassermans or the Jenkinses, and none of the greenhorn Amish either."

She gave one last exaggerated twirl on one foot. "We are westerners. Real ranchers, planning our cattle drive. Homesteaders who made it pretty good, without our father."

Manny smiled and Sarah laughed outright. She wanted to hug her again, with abandon, the way she'd thrown herself in her mother's arms after Manny's measles rash appeared. Since then, a certain self-consciousness had come between them, as if they were much more aware of each other. That move had been so uncharacteristic of Hannah, exposing a new vulnerability she had never been aware of. And now Sarah knew that beneath Hannah's veneer of disloyalty and unkindness was a profound love of family that she had never displayed with such abandon.

This created a shyness in Hannah, a wariness of her mother's trying to force that vulnerability again and corner her into a sort of submission, into changing and being a better, more unselfish person, when she planned on clapping that veneer firmly back in place, and keep it there.

"Yes, Hannah, we are survivors, aren't we?" Sarah said.

Hannah spread her fingers. "Remember when Eli got lost that time? Dat's death, winter storms, fire, diseases, starving hungry, cold, drought, heat."

"Lemuel Short!" Mary shouted.

Eli giggled and blinked his eyes owlishly. He remembered Mr. Short and had loved every story he told while sitting on his knee.

"He was a good man underneath all of his troubles," Sarah said.

"He was not. He was an actor," Hannah said, forcefully.

"Whatever. I still do feel sorry for him in prison. If we could, we'd go visit him and take him some food."

Then there was nothing left to do but dress in her most brilliantly colored dress, comb her hair becomingly, brush Pete and saddle him, tell Mam and Manny she was going to visit Ben Miller's, and then ride off in that direction.

Summer's end was all around her. The grass looked as it always did after a drought, but the assortment of weeds by the dusty road were bent double, heavy with seed pods and dust. The butterflies had left, except for the dizzy white moths that fluttered over everything. The crickets and katydids set up a racket, undeterred by the long, dry summer.

Hannah wasn't sure exactly where the Perthing place was, so she kept a steady eye on the horizon. The prairie could be tricky when you were searching for something, like the roof of a building or a creek bank or a lone tree. Everything appeared level, but there were deceiving swells, the land rising slightly, and then falling away to a large hollow, like a shallow bowl. The road was straight, disappearing to a point in the distance.

Hmm. Not much as far as she could see.

Pete was acting strangely. His head was lower than usual, and he kept stumbling, as if his feet were too heavy to clear the ground. She tugged on the reins, chirped, making the sound most horses understood as a sign to quicken their pace. His sweat-soaked ears flicked back, then forward, but he did nothing to increase his speed.

She wondered idly whether he had had a drink of water before she left home. He certainly was not in top form but, oh well, he had a lot of miles on him and the day was as hot as the middle of summer. Would this heat never end?

She noticed the swaying, then. The unnatural rhythm, as if Pete couldn't carry his back legs properly. She had just cleared the saddle, her feet hitting the ground, when Pete went down in the back, his legs folding up like a massive accordion.

His front legs stayed stiff, his neck outstretched, the whites of his eyes showing his alarm, as if he did not understand what was happening. Then his front legs buckled, and he went down on his knees, grunting with an expulsion of air. He rolled sideways, his legs bent and the saddle half buried beneath him.

Hannah stood helplessly by. This was a fine pickle. Out in the middle of nowhere with a horse down. Great!

She tugged on one rein and called, "Pete! Come on here! Get up! Pete!" But he never really made an effort. He just lay there as if he planned on taking a long nap.

Why was a horse so large when they were laying there helplessly? He was like a mountain of flesh, and as immovable as one.

The sun beat down on both of them, as if purposely making things worse. Hannah's mouth was dry and perspiration beaded her brow. All around her, the wind kept up its steady, even rustling of the grass, tossing it, and tearing at her perfectly combed hair, flapping the triangle of her *dichly*.

Hannah tried to get Pete back on his feet, lifting, sliding her hands beneath the impossibly large mound of his body. Her face reddened with exertion, her temper steadily becoming shorter, like a length of rope being eaten by fire.

She straightened and took a long breath, folded her hands into fists, and stamped her foot. Now what? Keep walking?

Keep looking for this old place even if she couldn't see a roof or the tip of a windmill for miles in every direction?

She could leave Pete, turn around, and go back home. But who would ever get this horse back on his feet? If she walked the long dusty road home, it would be a few hours, at least, before she could return with Manny and Goat and the spring wagon. Even then, what could they do?

Hannah plunked herself down. She studied the rise and fall of Pete's heaving sides and thought he didn't appear to be in pain or particularly stressed. He had never done anything like this before.

She was thirsty. She wondered if this was how people who were lost in the desert felt. She couldn't sit in the heat and the wind and dry out; she'd have to walk in one direction or the other.

On her feet again, took stock of the situation. Pete lay in the middle of the narrow dirt road. If an automobile or a truck came barreling along, it would plow right into him. She renewed her efforts imploring Pete to stand, tugging on the reins, calling his name, but he only opened his eyes wider and grunted that strange whooshing sound.

Hannah was just about to start walking back toward home when she heard, or rather, felt, the dull clop of hoof beats. Someone was riding toward her. Help was on the way. Billowing dust clouds preceded a galloping dark horse, his legs pounding the parched earth. The hatless rider, judging by the width of him, looked much like Ben Miller.

Self-conscious now, Hannah raked at her disheveled hair and the wildly flapping *dichly*, which had slid back on her head, tugged by the mischievous wind.

The gladness in her eyes darkened, replaced by a dull sheen of pride.

Jerry Riehl.

Oh, of course, she thought bitterly. Damsel in distress, plunked right down in his path. The chivalrous rescuer—big, bold, and brave!

The magnificent horse slid to a stop with an easy touch on the reins. Hannah could tell it was easy, not the usual western way of the Jenkinses, sawing and pulling on the reins attached to the bit in the iron-mouthed mustangs they rode, half-broke and cranky.

"Whoa! What have we here?" Jerry sat astride his horse with the easy grace of being one with the animal, smiling down at her with his white, even teeth in his dark face.

Why did she think of the scent of toothpaste and aftershave? She glared up at him, figuring that if she could convey all that ill-will, he'd have no idea she remembered ever kissing that grinning mouth, and, even more important, that she was certainly *not* glad to see him.

She just had this bit of a problem with a downed horse.

"You don't have anything here. I do," she stated, flat and hard as a sheet of granite.

His chuckle increased her irritation. Sit there and laugh, she thought bitterly.

"Yeah, you definitely do."

There was no way to answer that so she didn't.

Jerry leaned forward and crossed his arms on the horn of the saddle as his horse snorted, side-stepped, and pranced as if there were springs in his hooves.

She wished he'd fall off. Flat on his righteous backside.

He dismounted, all fluid grace and expertise, swinging the reins to the ground and leaving his horse standing there, still as still, as if he was made of stone. Trained like that, Hannah knew.

Jerry ignored her as he ran his hands across Pete's back, felt his ears and checked his legs, which were now stretched out full length.

"How'd he go down?" he asked, straightening up and running one hand through his dark hair.

"He just went down."

"No, I mean, did he collapse suddenly, or did he act strange? Did his gait change? Did he maybe go down in the back?"

"His walk wasn't right. He swayed. And then his back legs kind of lowered."

"And then they went down?"

Hannah nodded.

Jerry walked around Pete and considered the problem. The wind blew, lashing the grass to a rustling frenzy. It grabbed Hannah's kerchief off her head and sent it spinning away, across the now almost horizontal grass.

Jerry lifted his head and searched the horizon at the same time they heard a pronounced rumble, deep in a bank of roiling clouds to the north.

"Does a storm crop up at midday out here?" Jerry asked.

Hannah shrugged.

"At any rate, there's one on the way," he concluded.

"It won't hit us, coming from the north."

"How do you know?"

"I've lived here a lot longer than you have. I should know."

"You mean to say, in the few years you've been here, it hasn't happened? Doesn't say it couldn't now." His eyes watched the clouds.

In spite of the hot sunlight, there was a decided change in the atmosphere. A prickly kind of feeling, as if each blade of grass now crackled instead of rustling. A boom in the distance rattled the ground beneath their feet.

Jerry said sternly that they'd have to try and get Pete to stand up, then perhaps get him to the ranch, if he could walk. He guessed Pete had kidney problems, going down at the back like he had.

"Are you feeding him corn?" he asked.

Hannah snorted. "Yeah, we raise a lot of corn out here where it never rains."

A quick flicker of irritation rose in his dark eyes. He turned. "Come on, put your hands beneath his withers. When I pull on his head, push. Heave toward the front."

"What does that have to do with it?"

Another boom of thunder sounded in the distance. A split second of jagged white lightning appeared in the steadily darkening north. Jerry stood far too close to her, lowered his face, his dark eyes boring into hers and ground out, "Do as I say for once."

She refused. What were two hands going to amount to? Nothing. That mound of horseflesh could not be moved by any mere human, she was sure. He thought he could come out here from soft little Lancaster County and tell her what was what, the weather and everything. Well, he couldn't.

Jerry urged Pete, lifting his head by his neck and drawing him up and forward, straining, calling his name in a level voice. Hannah stood and watched him, her arms crossed, her skirt blowing wildly in the wind. She hadn't tried to retrieve that *dichly*, he noticed.

Another boom of thunder. The wind increased. Jerry shouted something Hannah didn't understand. Suddenly he loosened his grip on Pete's neck, stalked over to his horse and lifted the reins. He looked at Hannah, his eyes snapping, his dark hair blowing up off his forehead, accentuating the stark wings of his black eyebrows.

"I'm leaving. I don't trust that storm," he shouted against the ever-increasing wind.

"It won't hit us. It'll go to the east. Round by Pine." Her words deterred him, but only momentarily.

"You better leave the horse. Come on, I'll take you home."

Hannah shook her head, crossed her arms tighter, her shoulders hunched forward.

Jerry mounted his horse. "Come on!"

"I'm not going with you."

"You can't stay here."

"I sure can."

Jerry's eyes scanned the north. The prairie appeared yellow, drenched in a strange glow against the backdrop of storm clouds as black as night. As they watched, the sun's heat became weak, losing its power, like the wick on a kerosene lamp when it's turned down.

Another rolling, menacing boom rattled the ground beneath their feet. The air around them crackled.

Hannah watched the light fade and felt a prickle of doubt. She weighed her options: stay here, in the middle of nowhere, unprotected, a sitting duck for the wind and the probable hail, or get up on that saddle with Jerry.

The choice was easy. She'd stay right here. Storms always— usually—followed a pattern. The wind was roaring in her ears. She turned to watch the storm and braced herself against it. She had never seen cloud formations quite like these. The dark-as-night wall, which was the storm, she figured, preceded by a writhing gray mass of either rain or wind, she couldn't be sure which. Hod had warned them of cyclones, the twisting, turning whirlpools of monstrous wind and destruction.

Hannah screamed as she felt a grip around her waist; she screamed again when she felt herself being lifted and hauled like a sack of feed across Jerry's lap. She yelled and kicked, but his arm was like a vice and held her fast, pressing the breath out of her until she was fortunate to be able to take small, desperate intakes of air.

She could only grasp at air, her hands flying down the side of the now galloping horse. She was completely at Jerry's mercy. The ground was so close she could have touched the tall weeds on the side of the road, whizzing by in waves of dark grass, streaks of brown dust, and parched, cracked earth.

Hanging by her waist like that, blood rushed to her face, and her head began to pound. The horse increased his speed into a headlong, mad gallop, his hooves flailing and pounding, the neck by her left side moving in rhythmic lunges. She felt as if her life was in danger.

Her anger dissipated, replaced by a sick fear she had never known. He didn't care about her. The truth was worse than the hard, cutting slice of pain that tore into the side of her face, her outstretched arms, and her bare feet. The pain was indescribable, like thousands of knife points stabbing her skin. She cried out in a choked, pleading voice, but all that emerged from her throat was a guttural sound like a choking animal.

Determined to endure this and stay alive, she hung on, resigned to whatever happened next.

What did happen was that hail assaulted every exposed inch of her body, and the vice-like grip around her waist tightened. She could not breathe. She tasted blood in her mouth and realized the hail was cutting through her skin.

Booms like falling timbers. Weird flashes of blue light. She couldn't breathe. She couldn't breathe. Then, the hail ceased and gave way to a cold, drenching deluge that soaked them. It was like being under a waterfall.

She struggled to stay conscious. The world turned into movement, a pinwheel of sound and color, of wet and cold and pain, always choked by the grasp around her middle.

The horse's hooves no longer pounded; they splashed, plopping through rivers of water and flying brown grass that blew loose from the weakened dry roots and hurled itself against them by the storm's force.

She heard a shout, struggled to stay conscious. Waves of pain and cold set her teeth to chattering, jouncing around as if they were no longer a part of her.

Another shout. Then they crashed headlong into the smell of dirt and hay and manure and blessed stillness.

She felt his hands around her waist, pulling her off the horse and lifting her to the ground, helping her to stand against the rough lumber of a stall, where she slid down, the barn floor solid and unyielding beneath her.

She was as soaked as if they'd dragged her through the watering trough. She pulled at her skirt, too weak to make much difference.

Rain pummeled the metal roof like bullets. Lightning flashed, followed by rolling crashes of thunder that spoke of the bottled-up fury contained in the summer clouds that had refused to give their rain.

Hannah had read of sailors who were weeks at sea, kissing the earth beneath their feet after arriving safely on shore. She now knew exactly how they felt. Never had she blessed a metal roof like she did this one.

CHAPTER 15

Conversation was useless, as the storm hung over the old Perthing place and pounded the metal roof with a wind-lashed deluge that sounded as if buckets of water were being thrown against the metal.

There wasn't much light. Only a grayish dark world and the smell of leather, horse sweat, manure, and dry hay. The black horse's nostrils quivered as they moved in rhythm to the heaving of his flanks, sweat dripping on the floor of the barn.

Hannah's chest rose and fell as she breathed, each intake of breath a sucking of air driven by desperation. She shivered, wrapped her arms around her waist, puddles of dirty water mixed with hay and straw pooling beneath and around her.

She was aware of Jake Fisher and Jerry dragging off the soaked saddle then rubbing down the magnificent horse. There was no other word to describe him, this massive black animal made of powerful muscle and tendon. Hannah marveled at his incredible ability to almost outrun a fast-moving storm, keeping his hooves pounding through mud and water at a pace that never slowed, staying on his feet in the slimy muck made of dust and dry, parched earth pasted to the falling rain.

"She all right?" Hannah heard the words, not meant for her ears.

There was no answer, only the sound of the lashing rain and wind.

The care of the horse went on for too long, in Hannah's opinion. Evidently the horse's comfort was far more important than her own well-being, as they busied themselves without so much as a glance in her direction, which, she finally decided, she wouldn't have seen anyway because of the dark interior of the barn.

She was cold. Her middle hurt, right across the top of her stomach, where she'd been flung over the horse like a dead calf. Exactly the way Clay slung a dead calf across his saddle.

Hannah was unaccustomed to humiliation. Now she couldn't bear to think of herself sprawled across Jerry's saddle. She couldn't think of it. Let him mention it once and he'd be sorry.

She was wet. Wet? She was soaked! She was as wet as if she'd stayed right there with Pete. Likely the poor old horse had died, alone on the prairie in a pounding storm that hurled hailstones on his faithful, fallen body. She had meant to stay, meant to stay right there with him.

When the rectangular shapes of the barn windows appeared to be turning from dark gray to a lighter color, the rasping, hissing sound of driven rain turned to a softer, whispering sound. Jerry walked over and stood above her. He said nothing, just stared down at her.

Then, "Cold?" he asked.

She didn't raise her head. All she could think of was being slung across that saddle and the headlong dash through the hail and wind and rain.

"Your face is bleeding."

She didn't lift her face or bother answering. Just sat there like a log.

"Can you hear me, Hannah?" Not a trace of tenderness. Nothing.

"I can hear you," she said, low and harsh.

He loved her voice. It was so low, almost like a man's, and husky. Well, she was angry now, so he'd better be careful.

"You can come inside with Jake and me."

"For what?"

"To take care of the bleeding and get you into some dry clothes."

"You should have left me alone. I'm as wet now as if I'd have stayed with Pete."

"You think?"

When there was no answer and the silence dragged out, Jake walked over and said he was making a run for the house.

Jerry nodded, "Go ahead."

When Hannah refused to look at him or answer his questions, he plunked down beside her, raised one knee and laid an arm across it. With the other hand he touched the dirty, sodden fabric of her dress. She slid away from him, leaving a wet trail through the dirt.

"What if a cyclone would have touched down? You'd have had no protection whatsoever. None. I couldn't leave you out there."

"Pete's probably dead."

"He's an old horse. He has kidney problems."

"You don't know how old he is. Or if he has kidney problems."

Touchy. Testy. He could never say the right thing. "Come on, Hannah. Let's go inside."

"No."

Jerry sighed. "Don't you ever do as you're told?"

"Hardly ever."

"Why?"

"People are dumb."

He bit off the words that came to his mouth and asked instead, "What were you doing out riding so far away from home?"

"Nothing."

"Just riding?"

"Yes."

"Well, if you won't come inside, can I take you home after the rain quits?"

"I can walk."

"No, you can't. I'll ride King, and you can take the palomino."

Hannah turned suspicious eyes in his direction. Still trying to see that she got that horse, although he knew perfectly well she wasn't going to take him. Sly, slick, and deceiving, that's what he was.

"I'm not taking the palomino."

"Why not?"

She shrugged. Jerry got to his feet, stood looking down at her. In the half-light of the storm she was so hauntingly beautiful. Dark lashes on a firm, beautifully contoured cheek. That petulant mouth, just enough of a pout to intrigue him, wondering what had ever happened in her life to make her so obstinate, so hard-hearted.

He had never met a girl—no, any person—quite like Hannah. Nothing suited her, nothing pleased her. Everybody annoyed or irritated her. If he had a lick of common sense, he'd stay far away from the Detweiler ranch. But a challenge like Hannah was intriguing and captured his interest the way the plains of North Dakota had.

"Well, if you won't come inside to dry out, and you won't ride the palomino, then I suggest we ride King double."

"Don't you have a buggy?" she asked, picking at the bits of hay clinging to her skirt.

"It's tore apart right now." Partly true. He was replacing one dry wheel, oiling it.

The rain was still whispering across the roof, the day was turning steadily lighter, as Jerry remained standing, hands on his hips, looking down at Hannah, marveling at her sodden, rain-washed beauty. Not one other girl could sit in the middle of a barn littered with dirt and hay and straw, soaking wet, her hair plastered to her head like a shining dark cap, its tendrils drying out, framing her face, and be the most attractive thing he'd ever seen.

What he wanted to do and what he did were very different things. He walked away, opened a gate, led King and the brown gelding out to the watering trough, and then began to brush King's sleek sides with long strokes of the grooming tool. He could learn as he went along, what worked and what didn't with Hannah.

Obviously, holding her close, certainly as close as he had before he really knew her, was off limits. He wasn't the kind of person that would cringe about past mistakes, but he acknowledged that there was definitely a learning curve.

Like an untamed horse, she had never been taught to listen, due either to an absent father or a weak mother, or perhaps through no one's fault. Perhaps she had been born with this irritation. Who knew?

King saddled and bridled, he brought out the palomino and began to brush him in the same easy manner, ignoring Hannah. When he was finished, he turned to her.

"Ready?"

"I told you, I'm not taking the palomino."

Jerry counted to ten, then said it was still raining anyway, they may as well go into the house, dry out a bit, and get something to eat.

"No."

So, he left her there, sitting on the dirt floor of the barn and went into the house. He opened drawers and slammed them shut like the bang of a rifle. He made a sandwich with quick, jerky movements of frustration, wolfed it down with bitter swallows of hot coffee, grabbed his old felt hat, and swung out the door.

Jake Fisher went on with his carving of a wolf and didn't say a word. Jerry better be careful, he thought, or he'd be in over his head with that one.

Jerry noticed the storm clouds passing on, leaving the northwest washed blue through rents in the residue of black storm clouds. He'd risk it then. He opened the barn door wide, allowing afternoon light to stream in along with the smell of parched earth reawakened by the rain.

Hannah blinked, turned back to threading a piece of straw through her fingers.

"Look, I'm busy. We're working on the house. Get up on the palomino and follow me. I won't ride the whole way. We've got work to do." He raised his eyebrows, waiting.

She got to her feet—she was so tall—and pulled at her damp skirt, smoothed her hands across the front of her dress to rid herself of any clinging straw and hay.

He watched as she walked over to the palomino and without a word, swung up into the saddle and walked him through the barn door, ducking her head slightly to clear the overhead beam. There was nothing for Jerry to do but follow.

The earth had changed to a washed brown. Everything shimmered with raindrops, like jewels, clinging precariously to brittle brown grass that had been softened by the deluge. It was a joy to breathe in and absorb the scents of the settled dust, the wet grass, and the rivulets that still trickled beside the road, vanishing shyly into the moistened roots.

The horses felt the change and tugged on the reins, wanting to run. Hannah felt the tugging, the step sideways, the dancing, as if the palomino was walking on air. She felt the tightening of his muscles, the gathering of unleashed power beneath her, the golden horse waiting for her command to run.

Ahead of her, Jerry was up on King, looking as if he was having difficulty holding him back. Excitement welled up in Hannah, but she knew she could not let it show and allow Jerry to see any willingness to accept his horse. If she did, she'd be indebted to him, the last thing on earth she wanted.

Jerry brought King to a stop. Hannah caught up. "He wants to run. I'm going to give him his head for a few miles to settle him down. We'll go slow and look for your horse afterward."

Nothing could have prepared Hannah for the surge of speed, the clean, flowing gait of a well-bred horse. The comparison to their old horses was like night and day.

She had never known such speed existed on horseback. She became frightened, realizing that she was hurtling along on the back of a lunging animal that reveled in this breakneck speed and had no intention of slowing down. Quite simply, this horse loved to run, loved to race with the brown horse well ahead of her.

The distance was closing in. She could see King's flailing hooves as Jerry bent low, his hat pulled down over his forehead, the gathering of the horse's withers, loosened when hooves dug into the earth, sending mud and water and bits of grass flying up to hit the palomino's chest. His nose was close to the bobbing flanks. Hannah ceased to think. There was nothing in her mind, just getting past Jerry to show off her riding skills.

She leaned forward, loosened the reins, shook them the slightest bit, and was rewarded by another, stronger gathering of hoof, tendon, and muscle.

Now to Jerry's side, to his horse's neck. A shout from Jerry. On they went, thundering across the wet, muddy road with the remnants of the storm hanging like banners to cheer them on.

Nose to nose, and Jerry reined in, laughing and throwing his hat on the ground, his dark eyes shining into hers. In the exulting of the moment, Hannah forgot her pride, all her foolish refusal to cooperate, everything. She stood up in the stirrups, pumped an arm upward and yelled across the wide, rain-washed prairie that she had won! If they had been neck and neck in the beginning, the palomino would have won effortlessly.

"I held King back," Jerry stated, slanting his eyes at her. Hannah laughed and shook her head, then laughed deeper and more genuinely. Jerry had heard that sound only once before.

They both turned to look at the same moment, taking in the sight of an old bay horse, his neck outstretched, his ears lifted in welcome, alive and, by all appearances, quite recovered.

"Pete!" Hannah flung herself off the palomino's back, reached Pete with a few quick steps, gathered up the reins that dragged on the ground, and held on to them. She rubbed the scruffy head, sliding a hand beneath his mane where his coat was as smooth as silk.

She forgot Jerry, who sat in his saddle taking it all in and wondering at this girl, this Hannah Detweiler, with a hard, impenetrable crust covering her like a burr on a chestnut. But what, really, was on the inside?

The palomino followed Jerry home, and no decision was made. Hannah rode Pete home and arrived to loud acclaim from the porch, Sarah and Manny having been quite beside themselves with worry.

Jerry went home to the place they called a house, although it wasn't a house by anyone's imagination. It was merely a leaking old board shack they'd cleaned out and planned to insulate against winter's arrival. The barn had taken up more time than they'd planned, and here was summer on the way out with nothing much else done.

He had to put the thought of Hannah behind him. She addled his wits, making a mess out of his common sense. He needed to focus on the work at hand.

Jake fried steaks rolled in flour in the cast iron skillet. He thickened the pan juices and poured the hot gravy over biscuits that were so hard, you couldn't eat them unless they were softened with it. He was the worst cook ever, but Jerry never said anything, knowing full well he could do no better and would probably do worse.

"Supper," Jake announced.

Jerry pulled up a chair, ate the salty gravy marbled with streaks of fat and dotted with white lumps of flour. The biscuits had to be cut with a serrated bread knife; a table knife couldn't dent them. But after the gravy soaked through, they were edible.

Jake was younger than Jerry by a few years. They'd gone to school together and attended the same church service. They liked the same girls and drove the same kind of horses. They were more than impressed with North Dakota. The wide open spaces got into their blood, and they lived for the day when they could move out here and stay.

Unlike Jerry, Jake came from a family that was as tight as a ball of yarn. Jerry teased his friend, saying that if he accompanied him out West, the whole family was sure to follow.

At night, Jerry detected homesickness when Jake became quiet, a faraway look in his eyes, not answering when Jerry spoke to him. Jerry knew he was back with his family, the sisters and brothers he loves, the kindly father who spoiled him just a bit, and the mother who doted on his every whim.

Poor as church mice they were. Especially now, with the value of land falling, the cash flow cut off by plummeting sales and the stagnant exchange of everything.

But he loved horses, Jake did, taking an avid interest in all the work of shoeing, filing teeth, and, especially, breaking a young colt. So the partnership worked well, for now. But Jerry knew the time would come when Jake would return to his family, the ties that bind as tight as glue for him.

Jerry had brought these three horses, but he had eight more being sent as soon as he wanted. His problem now was to complete the fence-making before winter. He couldn't imagine letting the horses run wild with no boundaries, slapping a brand on their backsides, and hoping for the best.

He wanted fences with boundaries for his horses, grain from the local feed mill in town, salt blocks, and minerals. His goal was to start up a horse auction. To get the locals involved, he thought maybe he'd have a barbeque to introduce himself. Observing how these old ranchers kept their horses, he knew he'd have to settle for some inferior ones in the beginning. Not all of them. The Klassermans had a few horses that equaled some of his.

Jerry loved the solitude, the days on end without encountering another human being, the wide open spaces, the unexpected, uncontrolled scenery of waving grass, and a sky so immense it was all right to feel insignificant.

The way he had felt most of his life. His father was a harsh, exacting man, ensuring none of his boys would turn out *grosfeelich*. His way of raising children was to work them hard, give them no money to spend, and then they'd stay out of trouble, especially if they were put in their place frequently enough.

Jerry had been his mother's favorite, for some reason, which only increased his father's dislike and jealousy. After he turned eighteen, he left home, but his sister and her husband took him in. There he learned what a normal family was like.

To love without judging, to be able to please someone, anyone. It was a different life. After his introduction to horse training, he had found his vocation, his meaning in life. But as he grew older, the horses were not enough. He wanted to have a companion by his side, someone to love and build a future with.

He'd dated plenty of girls, but all of them left him empty and bewildered. He thought something might be wrong with him; maybe he was not able to love a woman because of his upbringing, his anger toward his sniveling, spoiled mother as solid as his rebellion toward his father.

So he let go of girls, as the years came and went. Until Hannah showed up, soaking wet and angry. She had grasped his interest in those two strong brown hands of hers and taken over his thoughts, his waking hours, his whole life, the way God was supposed to.

Of late, things had gotten worse. He felt as if he was running out of time. Would he actually have to go through life without her? She had no interest in him, absolutely none. All that girl thought about was her herd of black cows.

What was she doing riding out in his direction anyway? She'd never made herself clear. Visiting the Ben Millers? Highly unlikely. At any rate, old Pete was on his last legs, whether she admitted it or not. He couldn't see how her and her brother did all that haymaking with those two worn-out horses. They had enough hay to feed twice as many cattle as they had. Someone had worked hard, all summer long.

So, there she was again, soaking wet in his barn, years later. A very different set of circumstances this time—a different barn, a different place. Who would have thought they'd end up in North Dakota?

Life was strange. He wondered if she'd ever forgive him for the mad dash to the barn. He had never been quite so irritated with anyone in his whole life, except his father, of course. You simply couldn't tell that girl anything. She knew everything and wasn't afraid to let you know it. Why did he even think of her?

By all outward appearances, she was unfit to be anyone's wife, hard-headed, often rude, and ignorant. Likely the best path for her would be the life of a single cattle queen. A baroness of the West. Or that was what she imagined herself to be. There was no doubt about it, she was a dreamer. He could see the resemblance between her and her father.

And yet, here she was, by all appearances her Bar S well on the way. It was only a stroke of luck that the fire ruined the house. That, and God's Almighty wisdom, His ways. All that help they'd received was all to their good.

But Jerry also knew that they had a well-to-do parent somewhere. Someone had to give them their start with those cattle. Someday, he hoped to be close enough to her to hear her story, which, he supposed, contained a lot more fear and trials than she would ever let on. That was exactly the reason she intrigued him and kept him always wondering about her. What made her say and do the things she did?

He looked at Jake, who stood over him with another biscuit and question marks in his eyes. He nodded and the biscuit clattered onto his plate. Jerry raised his chin in the bread knife's direction. Jake handed him the salt shaker instead. Jerry shook his head and said, "Knife."

Jake handed it over with one hand and cut off a bite of steak with the other. Feeling the shanty shake in the teeth of the wind that sprang up after the storm, they both looked up from their gravy-soaked biscuits and shook their heads.

"I have a feeling we're in for quite a few surprises living out here on these plains," Jake observed. "It seems like the wind and the heat and the rain all have a mind of their own."

Jerry nodded and tried to sop up gravy with his biscuit. Giving up, he stuck it in his mouth, chewing it like a pretzel. "We'd better worry about this little pile of sticks we live in." They both winced as a piece of metal flapped wildly, making a steady buzzing sound like a giant angry wasp. There was a decided breeze coming from between the rotting logs, flapping the towel that hung beside the wash basin setting on a bench.

"We need to come up with a plan. We don't know how to go about procuring lumber here in the booming town of Pine. Or roofing, or windows, not to mention door handles and plumbing supplies. We may have to keep our deluxe plumbing system we have now," Jerry said, smiling broadly.

"Won't hurt us," Jake said dryly.

"What if we get company?"

"No one will bother us. That . . ." Jake jerked a thumb in the general direction in which Hannah had arrived.

"Hannah?"

"Yeah, her. She could come calling."

Jerry shook his head. "She won't be back anytime soon, I have a hunch."

Jake chose to keep his curiosity to himself.

After they washed the dishes, wiped out the frying pan and hung it back on its nail on the wall, they went outside to see how cheaply they could get by the winter-proofing the old, falling-down remainder of a half-log, half-sod house that had stood for a century or more, attacked by all kinds of rain, hail, snowstorms, and extreme temperatures.

The wind scoured the rusting metal, bent the tired, brown weeds and grass up against the old logs, swung the door back against the wall on its hinges with a loud clap.

Somewhere in the distance, coyotes set up their high, yipping bark, answered by another set of yelps close by. Jake said they needed a dog if they were planning on raising horses successfully.

"They wouldn't touch a colt with the mother nearby."

"Think not?"

Jerry nodded. "Think about Hannah Detweiler's cattle. They were out all winter, with no hay for them at all. That was nothing short of a miracle."

Jake thought it would take another miracle to get Jerry back to normal.

CHAPTER 16

The whole thing was bad timing.

Stuck behind the counter at Harry Rocher's hardware store, to look up and find that Jerry Riehl was the one that had set that annoying little bell to tinkling. If he hadn't already spied her, she'd have ducked behind the cash register and crawled away, which, for one panicked moment, she almost did.

Her practiced glare firmly in place, she looked at him standing tall, slim, and wide in the shoulders, her faded purple dress too tight in the sleeves.

When his dark face broke into a welcoming smile, his white teeth gleaming and looking ridiculously handsome, her glare intensified.

"What are you doing here, Hannah?"

"What does it look like?"

"Well, since you're standing behind the counter, I'm guessing you're employed here."

"Smart of you."

A flicker of irritation passed through him. Why did she always make him feel like a bumbling second grader? "I need doorknobs and hinges," he said, brusque now, turning away to inspect a bin of bolts.

She came out from behind the counter and led him to the section where all sorts of hinges were displayed, along with a variety of door handles. Standing back, she turned on her heel and left him to decide. No use trying to help him out.

When he had chosen the hinges and doorknobs he wanted, she was involved with another customer, a small boy who silently handed her a slip of white paper.

Jerry stood patiently, watching as she bent over the counter, propped her elbows, her too tight sleeves revealing her muscular arms. For an instant, something like fear of her wafted across his vision. Definitely someone to be reckoned with.

But when she spoke to the thin, wide-eyed little boy, her smile brought one to his face as well.

"Your mama had no time to come get her own thread and buttons? So you had to come the whole way here by yourself?" she asked.

The boy nodded, whispered, and bent his head.

Hannah came out from behind the counter, got down on her knees and placed her hands on his shoulders, squeezing gently. "Can't hear you."

"My bike. I rode my bike."

Feigning astonishment, Hannah said, "My, you are little to be riding a bike. You deserve a piece of candy for that."

The boy's face lit up as if an internal light switch had been flipped on, watching every move she made until the bit of wrapped chocolate was in his hand.

Jerry stood, without realizing his own soft expression, his eyebrows slightly raised and his mouth open. So she had a tender heart for children, a well-buried kindness that rose to the surface on occasion. Somehow, to witness this scene balanced the muscular arms and her glare. He knew he'd continue his pursuit, but this was certainly a boost.

Hannah helped the boy first and left Jerry standing there holding his armload of doorknobs and hinges. No apology for keeping him waiting when he unloaded them on the counter, she merely pecked the keys on the cash register, a hidden face, presenting only her profile, the perfect contours of cheekbone and jaw, the small, flat nose. Oh, she was beautiful!

His heart set up a sweet pounding, like an ache. To begin a conversation, he mentioned the little boy. When there was no response, he tried the weather; no response then either. As she bagged his purchase, he became desperate and asked when she'd be ready to race horses again.

A flicker of interest, the lifting of her eyes, and looking straight into his. "We'll be driving part of our herd and part of the Klassermans' to Dorchester the last week in October before the snows come. We need horses. Pete is . . ." The slightest tremble of the firm lips. "Not strong enough," she finished, her voice husky.

"It's his kidneys."

She nodded and held his gaze.

Suddenly, it was as if they were conversing with their eyes. The interior of the store with its yellow light bulbs overhead illuminating the shelves and dark walls, the shadowed objects, disappeared, leaving them both in a world where only the depths of their eyes existed.

Help me.

You know I would give my life for you.

Ride with me. I'm scared.

I'll be there for you.

And then it was over, the moment broken by the jarring sound of the bell above the door. Jerry cleared his throat, ran a hand across his eyes, and left. There were no words, and if there had been, they would have ruined what he had just experienced.

He rode home, bouncing high on the saddle, flinging himself into the wind, a song like the high notes of a wailing bugle in his chest, an exhilaration of his spirit that rode high in the heights of the prairie sky.

Hannah rode home with Harry Rocher in the red car, a scarf tied over her head, black and warm.

The day was too cool to have the top down, but that was what he liked, so she crossed her arms, pulled the light denim jacket tighter, and didn't say anything.

Harry talked nonstop, his considerate face thinner, pulled down, as if the years had not been kind. His hair had thinned and turned white at the temples. His hands were long and lined with heavy blue veins across the backs.

Old hands. An old face, long before it was time. Curious, Hannah asked about Doris. It was strange that she had worked in the store all day without being asked to do one chore for Doris in the house.

Harry talked then, his voice rising well above the rushing air and the sound of the motor. "She's going downhill, fast. I don't know what to do. She says if I don't accompany her home to Baltimore, where her folks are, she's going to file for a divorce. I don't want that. It would be a public scandal. But I don't want to live in Baltimore, in the city, with the heat and gut-wrenching smell of saltwater, the humidity that is so stifling you can't breathe in the summer.

"Her parents are aging. They need our help. I don't want to go, and I don't want a divorce. She's beyond miserable. I'm afraid if I don't consent, she'll lose her mind, and I'll have to put her away. I can't do that, either."

Hannah considered his words that were peppered with self-pity. Hadn't he promised to care for her in sickness and in health, or any other circumstances presented by God? Perhaps English vows were unlike the Amish vows.

"I hate Baltimore," he said, his grip tightening on the steering wheel. "She hates it here. I love it. I love the people, the open sky, the land, snow, drought, dust—all of it. This is where my heart is."

Hannah thought of her mother. Lancaster County was where her heart was. But she had followed Hannah's father withersoever—as the Bible said. His God had been her God, or rather,

her father's version of God, his own translation of dreams and miracles and high-mindedness.

Call it what you wanted. Straight into near starvation they had gone. Hannah realized again that the reason for having survived that winter were both sitting here in this car. It wasn't a miracle. You simply went out and did what you had to do, whatever came your way.

"Well, seems your choice is pretty clear. You need to go home to Baltimore if you want to do the right thing. You're supposed to give your life for your wife."

"And she's supposed to submit to my will," Harry said, the kindness in his face vanishing, leaving him looking old and thin, his face papery with wrinkles, his eyes hard.

Hmm. Here was a side of Mr. Rocher she hadn't seen. When they pulled up to the door, the dust following them, blowing across the open car, the porch, seeping into the house and away across the prairie, Harry turned to her.

"Next week, same day?"

"Till the end of October. Then we drive the cattle."

Harry nodded. He hesitated, ran the tip of one finger around the smooth rim of the steering wheel. He straightened his back, reached into his pocket for a rumpled, red handkerchief and busily dusted the glass of the gas and speedometer gauges.

"What do you think I should do, Hannah?" he asked.

"I told you."

"But you have no idea. The smell of fish hangs over that city like a plague. The noise, the stench, the ships in the harbor, smelling of rust and oil and old saltwater. I can't tell you how much I loathe that place."

"Then get a divorce."

"I can't."

"You mean, you can't give up to take Doris home."

Harry gazed off in the opposite direction. Finally, he thumped the steering wheel with his clenched fist and said he never should have married her. Hannah shrugged, got out of the car, and went into the house without watching him drive away.

Big baby. She had no sympathy. Grow up. Do what it takes to face life. You're married to a squeamish little woman who is afraid of her own shadow, so get over it. She didn't blame Doris.

Her face clouded over with her disgust of Harry's indecision. She stormed into the house to find her mother bent over the open oven door, poking a fork into the aluminum roaster filled with a steaming mound of *roasht*.

The house smelled like Christmas dinners and weddings. Sarah straightened and smiled at Hannah but her smile faded as she saw her dark countenance.

"You're upset, Hannah."

Hannah gave a quick snort of derision, then gave her mother an account of Harry's life. Sarah nodded, feelings chasing over her features like light and shadow. She could not judge Mr. Rocher harshly. No. Buoyed as she was by the foundation of her upbringing, it still had not been easy. After she had ridden away from her home on the hard seat of that covered wagon, resentment had crept up and rode on her shoulders like a heavy burden, more times than she could tell. The private and bitter struggle, so much more than her daughter would ever know.

English hardware-store owner, Amish wife of a dreamer. Was there a difference, when the hardest task for all members of the human race was to relinquish the hold on your own will and allow someone else to present you with their will, expecting the nearly impossible?

No! It was called life. Living here on earth, giving your life, if not to your spouse, then for the sake of Christ alone.

Christ, who had bled and died, tortured by Roman soldiers, for her, for all of mankind. Without this belief, the bedrock of her faith, she would not have done it, and now, prospering here on this bleak and unforgiving land.

Or was it? She had come to love it. She had come to love her home, her neighbors, the vast realm of prairie, the magnificence of an ever-changing sky, a kaleidoscope of times and seasons, the hard work of producing vegetables from a garden that, except for their efforts, would remain unwatered.

The dust and the heat, the storms of winter, were all a part of her life, her love. This is where the children were, where Mose lay beneath the soil of the homestead.

All of this went through her mind in a second, as she listened to her daughter. The judgment of the young, the inexperienced. Sarah knew well the time would come for Hannah's own test, the times when God would send her an unannounced quiz, when she was least prepared.

But she smiled, nodded, listened to Hannah's words swirling through the kitchen like hard, pecking birds. Birds that needed to be avoided and chased out the back door.

She lifted the lid on the boiling potatoes, inserted a fork, poured off the water, called to Mary to set the table, turning her head to avoid the cloud of steam that rose above the pan.

The gravy was made, the green beans from the garden boiling in their buttered water. She applied the potato masher, pounding the potatoes with a strong arm, inhaling the rich, earthy smell of them.

She could never cook a good meal without gratitude, ever. The lean times were forever stamped on her memory.

Sarah dished up the steaming *roasht*—bread cubes, celery and onion, bits of cooked chicken, butter, salt and pepper, mixed well and baked in a roaster. Every edible part of the chicken had been used—the liver, gizzard and heart, neck meat and bits of skin, the rich broth simmered for yellow gravy.

"I am so hungry." Hannah elaborated each word before bowing her head, or slightly inclining it, actually. More often than not she'd be gazing off somewhere above everyone's head, her thoughts anywhere but giving thanks, while the rest of the family bent their heads, closed their eyes and actually gave thanks.

Everyone ate the evening meal with a healthy appetite. Sarah had to refill the serving bowls more than once, especially the *roasht*.

"You keep butchering these chickens and we're going to be without eggs," Hannah said, laying down her fork.

"This one was caught in the fence by her foot. She was unable to free herself without breaking it. I figured she'd never be able to escape the night varmints."

"Varmints?"

"Sorry. A word borrowed from Hod and Abby."

"I guess if we start to say varmints, we're genuine western folks, huh?"

Summer waned, like a brilliant full moon that steadily lost its light, until only a delicate sliver of light hung in the night sky.

The sun was warm, but only at midday, the mornings as crisp and dry as crumpled toast, the evenings laid bare with encroaching cold.

The moisture from the infrequent thunderstorms had long evaporated or soaked into the bone-dry soil like an inadequate whisper. The prairie grass looked thin and beaten, as if it had given up hope, knowing winter would whip the remaining life from it.

Hannah watched the sky, tested the direction of the wind, her eyes clouded over with worry. The cattle drive would not be possible without rain. The cows needed water to make the long trek to Dorchester.

Manny spoke of trucking them. Why not hire a local truck with a cattle trailer? It was by far the most logical thing to do.

Hannah would hear nothing of it. She knew well the times she had dreamed of doing a real cattle drive. The thrill of roping, chasing, and branding, doubled by the excitement of sleeping out on the prairie under the stars, the cattle watched by vigilant riders. Besides, it would take a big chunk out of her profit to hire a truck and trailer. They'd do it the old way.

Hod Jenkins didn't think it was a good idea. He hung out of the door of his rusted old pickup, squinted at Hannah and her mother as they stood on the porch steps. The motor idled, a low, rumbling sound, so they both moved off the steps and went to talk to him, standing in the dry, chilly air.

"You and that brother of yours better brush up on them ropin' skills. Them cattle's wilder 'n deer."

Hannah shook her head, her mouth set in a stubborn line. "Our cattle aren't like yours." She had a notion to add, "skinny-ribbed, horned old horrors." He should be ashamed to drive those long-haired skeletons to market.

Hod wagged his head. "You'll find out."

Hannah gave him a black look. "Yours would never make it, as skinny as they are."

Sarah winced, looked at the bed of the pickup where an old gate was stacked to one side, a roll of rusted barbed wire and a digging iron leaning crazily against it.

"Longhorns is supposed to be skinny, Miss High and Mighty." His blue eyes shone with an unusual glint of anger.

"Yeah, well, all right then. If Clay doesn't want to join the drive, will Hank and Ken do it?"

"I couldn't tell you." Hod opened the door of his pickup, climbed out and stepped away a few paces before sending a stream of tobacco juice like pressurized water from a hose. The ill-smelling brown liquid landed with a dull splat in the dust, raising a small cloud that settled quickly over it.

Hannah swallowed and felt the bile rise in her throat. She watched as he settled the wad of liquid-sounding tobacco strands further in his cheek, wiped his mouth with his forefinger, then dragged it along the side of his jeans, which appeared to have been the recipient of many tobacco juice encounters.

Dust covered his greasy hat, settled in black granules around the band surrounding the crown, and lay in the creases and pocket flaps of his vest. His shirt had been blue at one time, but resembled the color of stagnant water now. His boots were cracked, the heels both worn down until he walked on the outside, the too-long legs of his jeans frayed and brown from dragging along in the dust.

Hannah swallowed again and imagined the odor of his unwashed socks, if he wore any at all.

Sarah, however, was blind to all of Hannah's magnified scrutiny. She seemed to think Mr. Hod was the most important visitor of the month. She fired questions about Abby's cough, listened to Hod's words that became increasingly garbled with emotion, his head bent as he said that all the pills from the doctor hadn't eased her cough. He was afraid she'd have to accept the inevitable hospital stay.

Immediately, Sarah offered to go to Abby. She'd ride back with him and take Baby Abby along, knowing how much Abby loved her. She hurried back into the house to change, leaving Hannah standing with Hod, who was leaning against the rusted sides of the pickup, the motor still rumbling in small, muffled chugs.

Hod turned to look at Hannah. "So yer pretty set on doin' this cattle drive?" he asked.

"Yes."

"How come?"

"I don't want to pay a fee to have them hauled."

"You know it'll cost you, the way them cows will lose weight on their long walk. If I was you, I wouldn't do it. How come old man Klasserman don't know any better? You sure he's sendin' 'em?"

Hannah nodded. "He said he was."

"His cattle's ornery."

Hannah frowned. "You have no idea what his cattle are like."

Hod squinted, his blue eyes slits of light, gazing off across the plains. He hooked two thumbs into his belt loops, wagged his elbows and gave a sound between a snort and a laugh.

"You are one determined young lady. You have no idea how hard it can be, keepin' them cattle on the move, all in the right direction. You'll have cars, mebbe a coupla trucks. They'll scare 'em straight across the prairie. So then when one of you tries to turn 'em back, the rest will be hightailin' it somewhere else. You better pick good men."

"Manny's going."

"He can't rope worth a toot."

Hannah bristled. "Sure he can."

Hod shook his head, then faced her, lowered his frame closer to her and said forcefully, "You think you know everything. You ain't seen nothin'. I'm only warnin' you once. It'll be tougher than you think. And when you get there, they'll all have lost weight. So don't come cryin' to me iffen you don't get nothin' for them black cows."

Hannah looked away from him, off across the garden.

"You got any spare horses?"

"No. You going to let the boys go?"

"That's up to them."

"I need a horse."

"Wal, git your own. Them Amish have some fancy lookin' horse flesh paradin' around."

Hannah wanted to stamp her foot in frustration. Instead, she watched her mother emerge from the house wearing a purple dress with a black apron pinned around her waist, the stiff black bonnet on her head. She always dressed according to the *Ordnung*, the laws branded into her, giving her life.

"All right. We're ready." She smiled at Hod, who pulled himself away from the side of the truck, opened the door for Sarah, then went around to the opposite side and closed his door before leaning out the window and wagging a finger. Probably the one he'd used to wipe his mouth, thought Hannah.

"Mind what I said. You need to think about it."

Hannah didn't give him the benefit of an answer. Filthy, arrogant old coot. Seriously, who did he think he was?

Well, she'd show him. She would brush up on her roping skills, her riding, everything. She'd have Manny, Jerry, and probably Jake. So those Jenkinses could just stay home, then.

As she stalked off to find Manny, she yelled to Mary and Eli to stay close to the house because they were going to work cattle.

Pete was stiff and slow, loose and wobbly in the hind legs. Goat was more interested in the occasional mouthful of grass than anything else. Manny wasn't being very enthused, Hannah interrupting his harness mending, but he did what she asked, his nature far too dutiful to resist.

The cows had multiplied in number, of course, with twelve healthy new calves grown into young cattle and probably weighing six or seven hundred pounds. Manny guessed a few of them would tip the scales at closer to eight hundred. In spite of the drought, they'd had plenty of thick, dry prairie grass and fresh water from the tank, all sufficient to produce twelve half-grown cows.

The young cattle were well-rounded, filled out nicely in the chest and shoulder area, their heads well shaped at the top, with square, black mouths that moved constantly, ripping at the grass or laying contentedly, chewing their cud.

Hannah's eyes shone as she sat in the saddle surveying her herd. "What do you think, Manny?"

He nodded and smiled.

They practiced riding and roping, chased cattle, missed many more times than they actually roped one. The horses were soon winded, Pete sagging in the back, Goat snacking on yet another mouthful of grass.

Hannah dismounted, sat in the grass, and told Manny that unless they had better horses, they couldn't make the drive, that was all there was to it.

Manny nodded, agreed. "We'll ask the Jenkinses."

"I already did." Manny looked at her, his eyebrows raised. Hannah shook her head.

Manny straightened his shoulders and sighed. "Guess I'll have to make a trip over to Jerry Riehl. He'll let us use a few of his, likely."

Hannah tried to hide the exhilaration she felt at his suggestion.

CHAPTER 17

THE RAIN DID NOT COME.

The days grew shorter, the air around them containing only a dry, bone-chilling cold, especially at night.

Manny split and stacked wood from the fallen cottonwoods in the creek bottom, shoring up the supply leftover from the year before, the thought of the previous winter's blizzards goading him on.

Hannah continued to watch the skies, biting her lower lip in anxiety, knowing if the rains held off, there could be no cattle drive. With Manny's help, Jerry had given his consent to bring two extra horses, which only served to double Hannah's anxious watching of the empty sky.

They set the date for separating and branding the cattle. They would be sending eight of the heaviest ones, along with ten of the Klassermans, which brought the total to eighteen head of unruly young cattle, a fact Hannah could no longer dismiss.

The well-attended, most important cattle auction was to be held at the fairgrounds in Dorchester, about thirty-five miles away.

Hannah allowed a week for the branding and separating, the preparation of the food, depending on the fact that the rain would come. She forged ahead with her plans, in spite of Hod

Jenkins's warnings, Sarah having joined forces with him, advising Hannah to call it off, in spite of risking her anger which, inevitably, came thundering down around her ears.

Frustrated by the lack of rain and unwilling to give up her plans, Hannah railed against her mother, accusing her of siding with Hod just to go against her, that she didn't know a thing about cattle drives.

Whereupon Sarah informed her daughter that no, she didn't, but anytime you went against an experienced person's advice, you were setting yourself up for failure. It was too dry, too risky.

Undeterred, Hannah forged ahead with her plans, until one afternoon Sarah had a glimpse of her deceased husband in the glittering determination in Hannah's eyes and the set of her mouth. In the way her head jutted forward on her neck, as if her goal was closer as long as she kept her face forward. Well, Hannah hadn't taken to fasting and praying, but that was the only difference.

Sarah was drying strips of beef in the oven for jerky, to be taken on the drive, a labor of love, and one she enjoyed. It was just so unsettling, this dealing with her daughter's determination.

How can we go through life running parallel with the one we most disdain? It was uncanny, the likeness to her father, holding on to a dream with an iron grip, regardless of the circumstances that warned against it. But to face Hannah and throw this fact in her face would be unwise, like throwing gasoline on hot coals, an inevitable explosion.

She lifted the limp strips of beef from the herbal mixture, patted them in place on the thin aluminum sheet, and placed it in the oven. All she could do was place her trust in God and pray that He would keep the riders safe and the cattle healthy, somehow.

On the day of the branding, Jerry and Jake met the Jenkins boys for the first time. Loquacious as always, the Jenkinses were quick to make new friends and easy to talk to, giving easily understood instructions. They spent a good half-hour inspecting the horses, asking questions, circling them, whistling in admiration, then bargaining for a horse just like these.

Jerry didn't say much; he was watching Hannah. She had been a puzzle ever since she'd watched them ride in. She had not acknowledged his presence, or the palomino, and refused to touch the horse, acting as if he didn't exist.

So, that was the way of it. Jerry ignored her, took to the Jenkinses like a magnet, then sat back and watched Clay and Hank go to work. They rode as if there were no horse and rider, just one animal that thought and moved together.

In spite of the belligerent cows' savage advances, the bellowing, pawing, dust-throwing of the bull, they showed no hesitance, merely rode among the cows with authority, packing them into a moving, black mass, trundling them across the prairie to the water tank where the rest of the crew was expected to hold them.

Jerry watched, eyes alight. When he wasn't watching her, Hannah untied the palomino's reins, mounted quickly without looking at Jerry, and rode out to the tank. He went on talking to Manny, who was astride the roan, an older horse, but a large one, well-formed, clean in his limbs, and sweet tempered. She felt sadness for Pete and Goat standing by the barnyard fence watching the goings on, Pete offering a gentle nicker occasionally. Goat was too busy taking chomps out of the top board of the fence, eating splinters like hay.

The Jenkins boys rode back, leaving instructions on holding the cattle, then started a roaring fire which soon burned down to a bed of red hot coals.

Out at the tank, however, things took a decided turn for the worse. The ill-tempered, outsized cow suddenly displayed an unwillingness to be ordered about, charging with all the weight and fury of a great buffalo and scattering the two men, who had no experience with being sidelined by a horned monster the size of that one.

Jerry yelled, wheeled the black in the direction of the barn, the cow intent on chasing them all, followed by whinnying horses, and the bawling, excited cattle. A few of them ran across the bed of hot coals, scattering them and igniting the bone-dry grass, which only added to the melee of animals and riders. Panicked, half-grown cattle stuck their tails up like broomsticks and thundered off across the prairie.

Hannah was mad. She saw red. What a coward, she thought. She stayed by the water tank and watched all of it, holding the prancing palomino in check and snorting inwardly. So much for those two helping on the cattle drive. It couldn't be done with those creampuffs. And Manny was no better. She lost no time in loping off in their direction, after everything was controlled, including the fire.

From her perch on the palomino, she told them all how unbelievably unnecessary that whole pile of chaos had been, and if they couldn't do any better than that, they may as well all stay home.

Even Manny's face turned red with indignation after the tirade from his sister, thoroughly embarrassed by his unlikely display of cowardice, then feeling bad for Jerry who was being good enough to lend them the use of the two horses.

He had just opened his mouth to tell Hannah a thing or two, when there was a combination of shouts and hoarse yelling, followed by a spray of dust and the sound of hooves, as the fiercely determined cow streaked toward Hannah on the palomino, who twisted his body in a flash to avoid the red-eyed, crazed old cow, unseating Hannah in the process.

She felt the horse turn away from under her, felt herself sliding off the saddle, airborne for a split second before her shoulder hit the ground, her head snapping back, the rest of her body following with a bone jarring expulsion of breath, a folding in, as if she did a slow somersault, which she was never sure if she did or not.

The palomino was off in a wild flight, the stirrups slapping his sides, the reins flying of their own accord. The belligerent cow stopped, turned and eyed Hannah who was up on one elbow, faced with the enraged, pawing cow that had killed her father.

With no thought for anything other than getting away, she scrambled to her feet, running like the wind, yelling and shouting, horses wheeling, the cow lumbering off amid the galloping of horses' hooves, all one big chaotic explosion of movement and noise around her.

She slumped against the barnyard fence, gasping for breath, one half-breath after another, turning into a painful tearing in her chest. She slowed her breathing, tried to get out from under the terrifying weight on her chest and around her middle.

The first one to reach her side was Clay, his face ashen.

"Hannah!" His voice was terrible.

She remained calm, kept herself level-headed, fought for breath and nodded, watching Clay's face.

"You all right?"

She nodded again.

Surrounded now by the rest of the crew, Manny's face hardly recognizable as he worked hard to keep his emotions in check, Hannah was soon able to assure them that she was all right.

Clay felt her shoulder and asked her to turn her head both ways, then checked her arms and knees, asking her to bend and straighten them.

"I will be okay," Hannah said, soft and low.

The cattle were sorted and branded that day, but not without a sensible and serious discussion about the upcoming cattle drive.

When the air turned brittle with cold, they stood around the coals left over from the branding, Clay holding court.

"This thing of drivin' these cattle ain't gonna work. You saw what happened today. None of you is experienced. You gotta give it up."

He didn't spare any feelings or try to decorate the facts with flowery praise. He just kept talking, building his case, counting the reasons that stacked up to a considerable height.

The most important thing was water. "There ain't none," he stated, bluntly.

Hannah broke in, "It will rain, soon."

"What if it don't?"

"We'll go anyhow."

"How you gonna keep these cows alive? How?"

"It will rain, I said."

"You ain't God. You don't know whether it will rain!" Clay shouted, clearly upset with her stubborn refusal to accept his advice.

Jerry suggested they wait out the next three days, and if it rained a significant amount, they'd go. If not, they'd truck them.

"We're not trucking these cattle."

Sure enough, the following evening, a dark gray mountain of clouds blew in from the northwest. Hannah could smell the rain long before it arrived. The smell of wet dust, a raw, earthy smell that set her senses quivering. She stood on the porch, exulting, clapped Manny's shoulder and did a little dance of "What did I tell you?"

He grinned, always good-natured, always glad to give Hannah the top rung of the ladder, the best spot on the totem pole.

There was only one thing wrong with the cold rain that rode in on the wings of a genuine deluge, driving cold needles of wet, sluicing raindrops into every crack and crevice where it could possibly go.

Sarah shook her head and said no, they had better not attempt it. The dusty path that led to the house turned into a slippery bowl of pudding—like brown sugar cornstarch pudding. The creek filled, the yellowing willow leaves swayed, let loose, and were hurled across the prairie, leaving some bare, dark branches, whipping and glistening in the wind and rain.

The roof of the house was shining wet, like polished metal, the wooden sides of the house turned dark yellow, like maize, rivulets of water splashing down from the roof and across the windows.

Hannah thought the rain would surely quit after the downpour, but it only let up for an hour or so, with walls of soft, gray fog like sheep's wool hovering between the sky and the horizon, before it began again, a fresh shower of rain driven by a whining wind.

The Klassermans rode through the wet night, the headlights of their truck piercing the dark like glaring white eyes. They splashed up onto the porch, their pink faces like wet ceramic, chortling, laughing, pulling off their rubber boots with red-faced effort.

"Ach, de rain, de rain. When she finally arrive, she arrive full force," Owen said loudly, his pink gums showing above a row of even, white teeth.

Sylvia whooshed and blew through her nose, shaking her head like a dog, drops of water flying every which way.

Sarah laughed and ushered them in, happy as she always was to receive visitors. Long gone was the memory of Sylvia's meticulous behavior. She had *schenked und fagevva*.

"Come in, come in, out of the rain. How unfortunate for you to be out in this weather at night," she said, holding out a hand for their wet outerwear.

Owen rolled his eyes with importance. "Oh, but very necessary. I decided it is far too foolhardy to attempt to drive my cattle to market. We will truck them. I will drive it mineself. My wife will not hear of me allowing your children to drive them on foot."

Sylvia rose to the occasion, patting her massive bosom with one hand, flapping it like a large, startled bird. "Oh, *nein*, *nein*. I say to mine Owen, *ach du lieva. Vot iss diss?* Such dumbheit. Ve cannot ride dis horse, chase dis cattle, so vy allow some young ones to do it? No. No. We use the truck. The truck iss only sensible choice."

Hannah sat at the kitchen table, her ears heating to a deep, dull red, her eyes sparking with frustration. How many things had gone against this long-awaited cattle drive? Drought, too much rain, uncooperative neighbors, Jerry and his willy-nilly partner, Jake, who were afraid of cows. Honestly. Now what?

"Hannah?" A large, glistening pink face was thrust into her own personal territory, the kitchen table and a perimeter of ten feet around it. "Hannah, mine darlink girl. Haf you been well?"

Hannah wanted to say no, I had measles and was almost killed by a cow yesterday, but what she said was, "Yes."

"Yes? You are well? Oh, goot, goot." Again, the fluttering of that large pink hand. Sylvia was breathing hard as she lowered her flowery bulk into a groaning kitchen chair and proceeded to give Hannah an hour by hour account of her lost barn cat.

Why didn't you just shoot her? Hannah thought sourly. She couldn't stand cats. Mewly things, rubbing themselves up against your leg when both hands were occupied pegging wash to the line, until you became fuzzy all over, finally reaching out with a backward heave of your foot that sent the sniveling thing out of reach.

"So you vill also truck your cows, I presume?" Sylvia asked now, reaching gratefully for the soothing cup of peppermint tea Sarah brought to her.

"I don't know." Well, she didn't. See what the morning brought.

What it did bring was more rain. Slanting, steady sheets of rain that didn't give any indication of letting up. The creek rose, full and muddy, churning with dead grass and dead roots, the banks swallowed by the ever increasing water.

She heard nothing from Jerry Riehl, but the Jenkinses waded through the brown slop to let them know they'd haul their two trailer loads of cattle, then come back for hers tomorrow around noon. If they wanted, they could all ride along. Clay was hauling the cattle, and Hod was taking the car.

Sarah didn't ask Hannah's opinion, just nodded her assent happily and said she'd look forward to the auction. Manny nodded, smiled and said yes, that would be great. Eli and Mary bounced up and down, clapping their hands.

As soon as Hod left, Hannah informed her family that no one had asked her opinion. Sarah searched Hannah's face and said kindly, "But, surely, Hannah, you wouldn't attempt anything as dangerous . . ."

Hannah broke in. "We could have done it. In the rain. No one gave me a chance." And then she pouted. She walked around the house with her nose in the air and wouldn't speak to anyone, stalking from room to room, window to window, scowling bitterly at the bad timing of all this rain, this endless pouring that soaked into the earth, puddling around the house, and destroyed her long-awaited plans.

It wasn't so much about the profit. It was the novelty of the whole thing. Range riders. Cattle drivers. Western horsemen. Dust and rain and cold and hail. Eating beef jerky around a roaring campfire, the cows bedded down close by, strong coffee as the sun tipped the edge of the earth.

Perhaps they'd just have to move farther west, to Wyoming or Colorado, where there were even less people and cars and ranches. If you could truck your cattle to market, it was far too close, too civilized, too full of other people sticking their noses in your business.

That Clay and his high opinion of himself! At least Jerry had the right idea. Even if he didn't know anything about cattle drives, he kept his mouth shut.

She refused to load the eight head of cattle. The Jenkins boys and Manny did it by themselves, in the pouring rain. Hannah stood behind the curtain in the kitchen and watched, the mass of glistening wet cows being separated, moiling around as if they knew this was the first step to a serious departure from all they'd ever known.

When they clattered into the house for dry clothes and a cup of steaming coffee, Hannah went to her room and stayed there until Manny knocked and said that Hod was here with the car. If she wanted to see her cattle sold, she'd best get her clothes changed.

She rode in the back seat, her head turned to the window on her left, the dismal landscape jarring to her senses, the way there was no letup in the clouds, even now.

Her mother sat in the front seat with Abby on her lap, talking in quiet tones, difficult to hear above the sound of the steady chugging of the engine. The windshield wipers' hypnotic rhythm made Hannah feel slightly crazy, not wanting to watch the movement, but quite unable to tear her eyes away.

Eli and Mary fidgeted until Hannah delivered an ill-tempered pinch on Eli's trouser leg, resulting in a shocked silence, followed by peace and quiet.

Hannah's mood worsened to see a tear in the dark rain clouds, as if a hole had been cut with a giant knife, allowing a glimpse of blue, then a shaft of yellow sunlight pierced the parted clouds, and the rain was over.

The town of Dorchester was large, a rain-washed sprawling cluster of businesses and houses, trees, paved roads, slippery mud, people, and cars. The fairgrounds were a cluster of long, low buildings, trees, and acres of dead grass awash in more mud.

Trucks and cattle trailers were everywhere, engines grinding, steel cables squealing as gates were lowered, black cattle, longhorn steers, baldy-faced bulls, all bellowing or mooing or dodging men with cattle prods.

Children ran wild. Their clothes plastered with mud, their hair damp with the last of the raindrops. Automobile horns blew warnings as another trailer wedged itself like a giant digging iron between two trailers, men standing by the open gate in the back and giving the driver calculated stares.

There were a few horses tied by an ancient hitching post under the dripping foliage of a tree, but mostly there were old, bent Ford trucks, and all manner of trailers, some expensive looking, built of steel and painted white or blue, with the insignia of the owner's ranch inscribed on the side. Other trailers were merely wooden racks fastened to a metal flatbed with screws, baler twine, and good fortune.

Hod let them out at the entrance to the auction barn, a building made mostly of gray corrugated tin and rust, a few splintered doors with paint peeling like molting chickens. The smell of food was powerful, and Hannah swallowed.

The interior of the building was higher than it appeared from the outside, with an oblong center, the floor strewn with sawdust. On two sides, seats were built one behind the other, stacked toward the ceiling, so that folks were in layers and everyone could see over the heads of the people in front.

About half the seats were filled with what appeared to be farmers or ranchers, perhaps all ranchers. Various colors of Stetson hats bent in all sorts of shapes and silhouettes adorned most men's heads. Their women were like weathered flowers, brittle and creased, their faces pounded into crevices of flesh by the harsh winters and blazing heat of the summers, riding the herds with their men.

Keenly aware of their Amish dress, Hannah walked with her back straight, shoulders squared, a fierce scowl on her face, her brown eyes looking straight ahead, unwavering. Sarah carried Abby and held on to Eli and Mary, hurrying after Hannah's long strides until they were seated, somewhere above the third row.

Glad to find a spot to rest, her arms aching, Sarah smiled at the children, breathed deeply, then dared a peek at her oldest daughter, who sat like a stone, unmoving.

"Hannah?" she breathed.

Hannah glowered at her mother, held a finger to her lips. "Hush. Everyone is looking at us. I hate my clothes. So Amish."

Sarah looked around. She did not see anyone looking at them. All eyes were glued to the ring below them, where a heavy-set man in a red shirt was picking up a sheaf of papers, riffling through them, bending to speak to another even bigger fellow endowed with a face as red as his shirt, crowned with a white Stetson set back on his head like framework for the brilliance of his visage.

Hannah watched the two men, decided she'd never seen anyone as ugly as they were. What in the world caused their faces to be so red? They looked boiled, like a piece of liver.

She jumped with a squawking sound that came from the ceiling. Eli began to cry, and Mary grabbed Hannah's hand with both of hers. "Testing. Testing. One, two, three."

Hannah decided the men's faces were red from bellowing, if that was the way their voices were expected to carry. But Sarah pointed to a black box hanging from the ceiling, said it was something electrical to carry the man's voice. Mose had described them for her in New Holland at the sales stables.

The sale began with a roan-colored steer with horns like curved swords entering the ring, a huge growth protruding from his lower abdomen, his massive head shaking the horns from side to side, the large hooves stirring the sawdust.

Two men held evil-looking black whips, cracking them repeatedly over the bewildered animal's head. Confused, the

roan steer dashed first in one direction, than another, the grotesque growth swinging as he moved.

"Here's one for the killer!" shouted the auctioneer. "Nothin'
but ground beef for this one. Yup! Who'll give me ten? Twenty?
Five dollars, now five dollars, five, five, five. Yup!"

The bidding didn't last long enough to even make sense.
Hannah had no idea if the price was per pound or if that was
the amount for the whole steer. If they got that amount for eight
heifers, they'd be paying their grandfather's loan back for a long
time.

Hod came up the aisle, smiled at Sarah, and sat beside her,
taking Abby on his lap. He handed a candy bar to Eli and one to
Mary. A Mallo Cup. Chocolate covered marshmallow. Hannah's
mouth watered but she didn't let on, bent to help them unwrap
the candy, told them to remember to thank Hod, who was too
busy watching the cattle being sold to notice their thank you's.

He better be worried, Hannah thought. That sickly wife of
his was coughing her lungs into pieces. He was going to have
some hospital bill to pay if he didn't get the poor woman some
help soon.

Or perhaps it was Abby herself, refusing to be treated. She
turned in her seat, the smell of chocolate so powerful she asked
Eli for a bite, and looked straight into the eyes of Jerry Riehl!

CHAPTER 18

"How'd you get here?" It was the only thing she knew to say, her mind going blank the way it did.

"I rode King."

"In the rain?"

"Yeah. I brought the palomino for you."

Hannah blinked, had no comprehension.

"You mean . . . ?"

"I felt bad for you. I knew you had your heart set on that drive, so I thought I'd risk it, hope the weather cleared, and we'd get the cattle sold and ride back together. You know, camp out, take our time."

"You mean . . . ?"

"Yeah, if you want to."

Hannah licked chocolate from her fingertip, swallowed, and blinked.

"Only us two?"

"Us."

Well, now what? What was she supposed to say? She didn't trust him. Not at all. He'd get her out on that wild prairie and start getting all sweet on her again. Huh. Uh . . . but he'd brought that horse the whole way. What was wrong with him, thinking she'd go back with him? Alone. The two of them. She couldn't.

"Sorry. I don't want to."

Jerry looked comfortable with her answer, shrugged, said all right or okay, something like that, and began his descent.

Hannah opened her mouth and then closed it again. Well, he had more nerve than common-sense thinking, no, assuming, she'd go. His appearance and offer of riding home ruined the whole sale. She knew how badly she wanted to go. Knew, too, that her pride would never allow it. Or should it?

If that black box from the ceiling kept up that squawking all day, she would personally shoot the stupid thing down. She craned her neck, peered at it with half-closed eyes, then down at the crimson-faced auctioneer. She wanted to stand up and tell him to shut up, wave her arms and get his attention good and solid, but she'd end up buying some cows, and Lord knows, these cows were nothing to look at, long-haired, skinny-necked creatures with wild red eyes.

The afternoon dragged on, with bunches of cows in various sizes and colors being sold for different prices, some high, some low.

Hannah had not seen any cattle that looked as nice as hers, but she figured they'd keep the good ones till last. She didn't know.

She watched as they prodded four black Angus heifers into the ring. The auctioneer's tone took on an excitement, yelling about the Klasserman ranch. Immediately, the bidding began at a brisk pace, the price escalating beyond anything she'd heard all day.

Sure enough. The bidding rounded out at almost a dollar a pound. Unbelievable! Hannah's heart raced, her tongue felt like sandpaper in her dry mouth as she drew in her breath in short puffs. If they got that price, they'd be able to pay back more than half of the loan from her grandfather.

Another group of the Klassermans' cattle was sold at an even higher price. Immediately afterward, all eight of her own cattle were herded in, looking every bit as good as the Klassermans', calm, doe-eyed, beautiful young cattle with nicely rounded bodies, sleek hair, and short muscular legs, spaced well.

The auctioneer's face took on a purple hue. "Here we have a new group of cattle. Young, good-looking stuff that'll increase the likability of your own herd. Says here they're from the Bar S. I'd say them folks know a thing or two about cattle raising."

Hannah's hands went to her mouth to stop its trembling. She was ashamed of the quick tears that rose to her eyes. Knew a thing or two about cattle raising? She thought of all the mistakes, all they'd been through to get started, the harsh winter, the anxiety, the wolves. No, they didn't know much at all.

"Whaddaya gimme for these excellent, top o' the line cattle?"

Hannah held her breath as the bidding floundered, slow to start. Folks buying cattle knew the Klassermans but were unsure about the Bar S.

Down to twenty-five cents a pound.

Hannah couldn't breathe. She felt as if she was suffocating.

And then it started. Yup! Yup!

The man taking the bids yelled out, waved his arms and hopped like a banty rooster.

All the way up over a dollar a pound. A dollar ten. Fifteen. Hannah was crying now, she could do nothing about the emotions that came from good fortune, from relief after having suffered so much.

The cattle were sold for the unbelievable sum of a dollar thirty-nine, way over anything Hannah had expected.

She swiped fiercely at her eyes, looked at Sarah, who gave her a wide smile through misty eyes. "We're on our way, Hannah," she mouthed.

Hannah didn't know what love felt like, one way or another, but she figured this was about the closest thing to it.

She wouldn't have gone with Jerry if Clay wouldn't have made her so angry, parading around with the red-haired Jennifer in jeans. Imagine! Right in front of her, he tried to buy that palomino horse from Jerry for Jennifer, his girlfriend. He knew full well how that would rankle, bargaining with an arm draped across Jennifer's shoulders.

So, after that scene played out, she looked straight at Jerry and told him she'd changed her mind. She'd ride home with him, even smiled into his astonished eyes, for Clay's benefit.

The rest of her family rode home with Hod. Manny looked puzzled, but then shrugged his shoulders, having given up a long time ago trying to figure Hannah out.

When it was time to go, Jerry silently handed her a pair of his old trousers. She took them, turned her back, and pulled them on. She looked over the amount of items tied on the horses' backs. Bedrolls, knapsacks, everything looked in order.

Well, this was something, now wasn't it?

Jerry asked if she wanted to go someplace to eat before they started off. Hannah didn't know what he meant, so she said no, not wanting to enter some stranger's house and sit at their table.

"Well, there's a great place to eat just outside of town. Their steaks and potatoes are unlike anything I've ever eaten. You sure you won't come?"

"If it's a café or restaurant, then yes, I will."

So that was how she found herself in that intimate setting with Jerry, his dark eyes watching her beneath the canopy of dark hair, cut exactly right, not too long and not too short.

She had never eaten inside a restaurant before except for her humiliating encounter with the fiery-haired Betsy, an episode she'd just as soon forget.

She looked around, took in the boards with dark knotholes, the red Formica-topped tables, the scattering of ranchers and wives or girlfriends decked out in gaily printed dresses, some of them dressed like men, in shirts and jeans. The trousers for women that Sylvia Klasserman called dungarees.

Instinctively, she pulled her own legs under her chair, hoping no one would notice the men's trouser legs sticking out from beneath her skirt.

She hated being in public dressed in her Amish clothes. Half-Amish, the way she refused to wear the required white head covering. The thing about adhering to a belief, being born into a way of life, wearing clothes meant to convey modesty, a conservative lifestyle, was that people stared.

The ordinary, English people. They looked at you, a certain changing of the eyes, an expression of surprise, another look, the rearranging of their features, usually followed by a half-smile or a sliding away from any eye contact.

So often, Hannah only wanted to fit into the mainstream, be out in public looking like everyone else, unnoticed, unseen. The blending in she longed for.

If she was going to cross over, forget about obedience, now would be the time to do it, before her grandfather arrived, before more people flocked in like unwanted crows, and they ordained the inevitable minister.

As if Jerry was reading her mind, those intent brown eyes on her face, he asked, "Why don't you wear your covering?"

Hannah shrugged, lowered her eyes. When she looked up, he was still waiting for her answer.

"It's unhandy. Gets awfully dirty working at the hay and in the barn."

Evidently that answer didn't suit him, the way the corners of his mouth dipped down.

"You're still thinking of leaving the Amish? I know you were seriously considering it at one time. Why?"

Hannah's eyes flashed. "You know, if you're going to sit there asking me all these nosy questions, I'm not riding home with you."

Jerry realized his mistake the minute he saw the irritation flicker in those large, secretive pools of black. So much like a colt. So much like an unbroken horse. He could be patient, but if he was wasting his time and would only be hurt in the end, there was no sense in putting himself through this.

When the food arrived, Hannah ate very little, too preoccupied with the daunting reality of having someone seated across the table who possessed the backbone to bark out those personal questions like that.

She was in no position to take his questions into consideration, the truth being that she simply didn't know the answers. To admit this would be a serious failure on her part, like walking ahead of him on a narrow trail above a precipice, losing her footing and hurling down the side, complete with pebbles rattling and dust rolling. She had to be very careful, always alert, so he would never be able to decipher the code to her locked away fears and insecurities.

They rode along, side by side, Hannah astride the palomino, pensively mulling over the idea of a name for this beautiful creature.

Goldie?

Honey?

Creamy?

All of them feminine, childish. This was a gelding, after all, one that needed a strong name like "Buck" or "Freedom" or maybe "Roger."

The late evening air held the promise of frost, the sun sliding toward the horizon, painting the prairie with reddish hues. Hannah loved this time of year, the autumnal splendor, the invigorating wind that played among the grasses, so she was content riding along on the smooth-gaited palomino, sneaking furtive glances at her companion, who rode along as quiet and unobtrusive as if he was alone.

When dusk fell with the softness of the plains, Hannah glanced at the twin bedrolls, then felt a warm blush suffuse her face. She certainly hoped that one thin roll of blanket would be enough to keep the chill of night away.

Suddenly, she wanted to be at home, safe in her bedroom, with Mam banking the fire, getting the little ones off to bed.

What was she doing out here in the middle of nowhere with the arrogant Jerry Riehl?

She sniffed, blinked, and looked long and hard at the thin blanket. Then she said that she hoped that blanket was warmer than it looked.

Jerry reached back to adjust it, as if to reassure himself. "You'll be warm."

"Well, just so you know that if I get cold, I don't expect to sleep anywhere near you. You'll have to keep the fire going, because I won't do it." She figured that would put him in his place.

He acted as if he never heard what she said, just pointed across the waving grass and said that bunch of cottonwoods looked suitable and would she be willing to stop for the night?

"You heard what I said about that thin bedroll."

"I heard."

He expertly tethered the horses, the hobbles keeping them close, cropping grass with a satisfying sound of their teeth tearing at the wet growth, grinding it in their back molars.

Jerry started a fire, just as expertly as he did everything else, his movements calculated, sparse. When the dry grass and twigs were cheerfully burning, he added heavier dead growth from the trees, filled a small granite coffee pot with water from a metal flask, threw in a scoop of coffee, arranged it on an iron grate, then stretched out with his back to his bedroll, his hands crossed in front of his stomach.

All this time Hannah stood like an unnecessary fence post, feeling about as useful and attractive, wishing he'd ask her to help, to do something with her hands.

He looked up at her as if remembering her presence. "Sit down, Hannah."

"I will if I want to."

He grinned unexpectedly. "Or, you can stand there all night. Do whatever you want. Makes no difference to me."

Hannah's face flamed. "You know, if you wanted my company, you're not very appreciative."

"Sure I am. I appreciate the fact that you're standing there." He laughed, a short, hard sound.

"I won't sit with you until you promise not to ask me any questions that are none of your business."

He didn't reply, just took the toe of his boot and stirred up the fire, sending a spray of sparks up toward the gray, early night sky.

"Sit down," he said, finally. She sat.

"Look, I meant well in asking you to accompany me, thinking you'd be happy to go on this adventure since having to give up the cattle drive. But if you're going to be as soft and welcoming as a cactus, you may as well get on that horse and ride on home."

Hannah didn't say anything, merely drew up her knees, smoothed her skirt down over her feet, rested her chin on her knees, her arms around her legs, and stared darkly into the fire.

A night owl screeched its high trilling note, sending shivers up and down her spine. The grass around them waved, rattling the night song of the plains, a constant rustling, like waves of water.

"So stop asking me stuff I don't like to answer."

"All right. What do you want to talk about?"

"Nothing. Drink coffee. Listen to the owls."

He poured her a cup of bitter, boiling hot coffee, strong enough to make her splutter. "This stuff is horrible!"

"You think?"

"I can't drink it."

"Sure you can. Want me to add some water?"

When she nodded, he got to his feet, tipped the metal flask and dribbled a few splashes of cooling water into her cup. She watched his hands, brown and calloused, the nails rounded and clean, the fingers long and tapered. He had nice hands. They were very close to her own. She'd just have to lift a finger to touch his knuckle.

For a wild instant, she wanted to do just that.

He moved away. She felt his absence like an ever-widening chasm.

"Tell me about you, Hannah. Tell me about your life. What makes you the way you are?" He settled back against the cushioning of his bedroll, his eyes squinting in the firelight. "I was hoping if I'd be alone with you, I could uncover some of the barriers, the many layers of protection you seem to wear."

"What for?"

He grimaced, swallowed his anger. So blunt, so forthright, always jousting, her sword of defense held aloft. He decided to meet her with a sword of his own.

"You fascinate me."

"What is that supposed to mean?"

"What I said."

"How could I fascinate anyone?"

Jerry believed this statement was real. Had she no idea of her own beauty, her own allure, the captivating eyes and the mouth that smiled only on occasion, like a rare flower that only showed its face for a day, then wilted away? The fiery temperament, the joy she had shown at her success today?

He sighed and watched her face. "Well for one thing, not too many girls would have returned to North Dakota after all you experienced. You rose from the ashes, literally. You made it through the worst winter in a decade, your cows intact."

"We lost one."

"Right. But today you showed your dreams are now reality. Your cows are on the way to turning a profit. It's quite amazing."

"You think? Mam says it was the grace of God alone."

"You believe that?"

"Of course. I was raised a God-fearing young Amish child."

"You will remain?"

"Why are you so intent on my answering that question?"

"Your . . ." Here Jerry waved a hand along the back of his head, his eyes squinting, as if trying to gauge her response before he aired his opinion. "Your covering, or absence of it."

"You want to know why I never wear one? I'll tell you. It's because the strings get in the way. It gets dirty, it wasn't made for ranch work, and there is no bishop or minister to come tell me what I can do and what I can't. This little triangle of a handkerchief suits me just fine."

Jerry nodded. "Okay."

"I'm Amish."

"Then come to church."

"If I come to church, everyone will think I approve of them. It will be like telling them it's all right that they rode that train out here to our North Dakota, our prairie. They're going to keep coming until we have a regular old settlement like the one we left. We'll be right back into it—neighbors, gossip, scrambling to make money, all of it. I don't like people. They give me a headache."

Jerry listened, said, "Like your father."

Hannah nodded, then shook her head back and forth, correcting the nod. "I'm not like him. You should know that."

"You're a loner like he was."

"Well, maybe. But there it stops."

"Tell me about your childhood."

"Why would I? There's nothing to tell." But she did. She told him about the farm causing her father's worry, the money never quite reaching to cover the bills, her mother's absolute devotion, her backbone like jelly, always submitting.

"Dat could do no wrong," Hannah said. "That was nice, for us as children. Our home was secure, a warm place filled with the smell of baking bread, the odor of ironed linen and cotton, wooden spools to make towers, cracked linoleum, and the smell of Lava soap. Mam was an excellent housekeeper, taught us well, allowed us to have baby kittens and piglets, lambs and baby goats in cardboard boxes behind the stove when they were newborn.

Hannah hesitated. "The hard part began when we lost the farm. My father did a very foolish, untrustworthy thing, and we left. We left amid horrible rumors and shame on our heads like rain. It hurt a lot. I was about ready to start my *rumschpringa*, so naturally I felt the cruelty of our downfall. I resented my father a lot. Anger built up inside of me, I suppose."

She spread her hands, shrugged, her face pale in the glowing coals of the fire. "So now you know why I'm, well . . . the way I am."

"It was your father's downfall," Jerry said quietly.

"I don't know. I guess. I didn't like the men who came to our house to help. They made Mam cry. Dat was quiet, brooding. Everything, my whole world, changed after we lost the farm."

"You weren't the only ones. Many families lost everything. City people, English businessmen, thousands of ordinary wage workers. It was not unusual to not meet your mortgage payments."

"I know. But when it happens to your own family, it doesn't make it any easier."

Jerry nodded. "You know, I came out here with my horses to get away from Lancaster County, just like you. I loved the idea of starting a new settlement. The thrill of trying to make it. You should see what we did to that old wreck of a house. We're just getting started, and we're doing it as cheaply as possible, but you should absolutely come over and look at it."

Why was she disappointed that he didn't say he came out here for her? Hadn't he said that once?

She should not think these thoughts, ever. She was failing her own resolve to stay single, untroubled by thoughts of love, a genuine slippery slope into unhappiness and betrayal.

But his face had an arresting quality. She couldn't seem to stop herself from watching him, the way his chin jutted a bit, the cleft in it just made for a fingertip to touch. His dark eyes, so often half-closed with his heavy eyelids, or squinting in the firelight or sunlight. His nose was wide at the top, stubby at the bottom, with perfectly formed nostrils.

Well, she could think these thoughts, then hide them away. He'd never have to know.

Jerry admired her ability to remain quiet, to spend long minutes in restful silence. The first time he met her, this had caught his attention. He would pursue her further, unafraid, if it wouldn't be for the fact that she was not devoted to her faith, her birthright, her culture.

His peace lay in the love of the brotherhood, the rightness of it. How could he love God if he could not love the brethren? He was steadfast in his baptismal vows, living his life as defined by the will of God and the acceptance of the blood of the Lord Jesus.

He could not be certain that Hannah wanted to share his beliefs. But this, this evening by the fire, on the prairie, was something. She had spoken far more than he had allowed himself to hope.

Suddenly, she got to her feet, turned her back and rid herself of the cumbersome trousers, kicked them into the grass, returned to the fire, and began to unroll her blanket. She stood, hands on her hips, her head to one side, considering. "No pillow?" she asked.

"Your saddle."

"It's getting awful cold."

"That blanket is one hundred percent wool. You won't be cold." He got to his feet, brought her saddle over, and stood by her bedroll with a question in his eyes.

"Two people together are much warmer than one," he said, his eyes warm with humor.

All she said, with the coolness of an icicle was, "You think?" Then promptly wrapped her coat tighter around her slim form, slid into her blanket and, knocking her head up and down on the saddle a few times, grimaced, and complained, "I won't sleep a wink. To use a saddle for a pillow can only be comfortable for giraffes. My neck should be about three times longer. It stinks. It smells like horses. Why couldn't you bring at least a small pillow?

"I never slept with a girl in North Dakota," he said dryly.

CHAPTER 19

THE NIGHT TURNED EVEN COLDER. THE FIRE DIED DOWN TO A SMALL circle of red coals, an ominous red eye that kept Hannah awake. To relax and fall asleep meant the coals would die to gray ashes and she would certainly freeze.

At first, the woolen blanket was sufficient, its heavy weight like a comforting arm the entire length of her body. But when the frost settled in, the temperature dropped even further. Shivers began to ripple along her shoulders and the backs of her legs. Her face was so cold she curled up even tighter, pulled the odorous blanket up over her head and tried to concentrate on the pockets of warmth she could find.

She wondered vaguely if your nose could crack right off your face, if it was frozen solid, or if the tissue and blood vessels kept it warm enough to stay fastened to the rest of your face.

Repeatedly, she opened one eye to peer at the glowing coals. When the call of the wolves sounded through the woolen blanket she clutched around her head and became rigid with fear. The long drawn-out wails rose to a hair-raising crescendo, floating above the prairie like ghosts of the wolves who howled before them, a long drawn-out cry that jangled Hannah's resolve, ruined her pride, and goaded her into action.

Flinging aside the useless thing he called a blanket, she scrambled to her feet, scavenged around in the pitch black night, her back bent, her hands scouring the campsite for more wood. Sticks, logs, anything. She was slowly turning into a human icicle, about to be eaten by wolves, and if her judgment was right, he was the same as dead, sleeping so soundly the only thing that would wake him would be a shotgun or a herd of buffalo, not necessarily in that order.

What if there was no wood? She wasn't about to wade through the frosty grass to the group of ash and cottonwood trees. Not with the wolves running in packs, howling their heads off.

She could see them. Huge, long-legged brutes, black or gray, some brownish gray, silver-tipped hair on the darker ones, their long powerful legs efficient machines that propelled them easily over the roughest terrain, their wide foreheads and large, pointed ears, and red eyes that saw everything, like the devil.

No wood anywhere. The fire out. Her teeth rattling together like strung beads in the wind.

Then, instead of feeling despaired, or helpless, Hannah got mad! She stomped over to the sleeping mound called Jerry, drew back her foot and gave him a solid kick, then another.

Immediately, his dark head appeared, followed by his hands clawing at the blanket, muttered words of confusion cutting through the night air, all unintelligible, which did nothing to assuage Hannah's temper.

"Get up! Where's the wood? I'm freezing!" she yelled.

"Wood? What wood?" he asked stupidly, running a hand through his hair.

"Wood for the fire."

"Oh, here. Right here."

Jerry picked up a few small sections of a dead branch, scattered the dead ashes into a few glowing red coals, and soon had a crackling flame that ate away at the dead wood, sending light and warmth into the dark like a promise.

"You're shivering," he observed.

"Yeah. What do you think? It's zero degrees and there's a pack of wolves howling. Very restful."

"Why didn't you wake me before now?"

Hannah didn't answer, mostly because of the clacking activity of her teeth.

A high, ripping howl began, rising higher and higher, until it turned into a cacophony of intermittent yelps and mournful cadences that could only be described as ghostly.

Hannah hated the wolves ever since the previous winter when that sound was like a dagger, attempting to slice away her hope for the future, slavering jowls of primal beasts devouring her cattle.

"They aren't close," Jerry observed.

"So what? Get this fire going." But she was glad he'd said they were at a distance.

He did get the fire roaring, loading the small flames with carefully placed wood, until the heat toasted her face and hands. He brought her blanket and wrapped it around her shoulders, then set her saddle at her back to lean on.

"It's much colder than I thought possible," he said gruffly.

"You have a lot to learn yet," she answered.

He chose to ignore that comment, poured water into the pot, and set it on the grate, than stood over her, his hands balled into fists and propped on his hips.

"Will you share your blanket?" She could hear the mockery in his voice.

"Get your own."

"You sure? I could warm you up just sitting beside you."

"No."

"All right," he said cheerfully, retrieving his blanket, wearing it like a shawl, lowering himself so close to her, their shoulders touched.

Hannah moved away but put only inches between them. The truth was, she was still shivering all along her back, even if her face was roasted.

"Still cold?"

"No," she lied.

"Good. You'll warm up. Sorry I slept so soundly. I sure didn't want you to be miserable, but I guess girls sleep colder than men do. I don't know much about girls, never had sisters, you know."

Nice of him to be all chatty in the middle of the night. She stared into the fire and thought if he was all nice and apologizing for every little thing it was likely because he wanted to kiss her again. She'd thwart that before it started.

She tugged at the blanket and said sourly, "You don't have to apologize. And you better not think of kissing me, either, if that's why you're being so nice."

Hannah was startled when a loud guffaw came from his mouth, followed by rolling peals of laughter rising into the night sky.

She ended all this by saying, "That's not funny."

"Sure it's funny. You must be thinking of when I kissed you before. You never forgot that, did you?"

"I forgot. Of course I don't remember." But her face felt on fire.

"Then why did you say that?"

"I don't want you to try it again."

"You sure?" He laughed again, all good humor and benevolence in the middle of the night on the freezing prairie with one small fire and wolves loping off somewhere in the distance.

After that was out in the open, there was an awkward silence, as if each one knew what the other was thinking, but trying to be calm and nonchalant, as if nothing had ever happened between them. Yet the memory of it lay there like a rock, an unmovable object that grew as the minutes ticked away.

Hannah stirred, crossed her arms, crossed her ankles and uncrossed them. She cleared her throat.

"I'm never getting married. I have no plans of falling in love or allowing a man into my life. I can run the Bar S by myself, with Manny's help. And, if too many Amish arrive, we'll move on, to Wyoming or Colorado. So you know that now."

Jerry shifted his weight so his shoulder hit hers. He turned his face to look at her, just watched her brooding, dark eyes for a long minute, before saying, "You know, Hannah, that is the saddest thing I have ever heard. Why would you want to be like that? Wouldn't it be better to share your life with someone? Someone who would cherish you, treat you with love and respect? Don't you want the companionship of a good husband?"

"Never met one that I liked well enough to want to marry him. Husbands are nothing but trouble. Like dogs. They get crazy ideas in their heads and away they go, leaving their wives to stumble along behind them happily ever after."

"Your father did that. Not all men are like that. You can't measure every man by the past mistakes your father made."

Hannah considered this. She looked over at Jerry, who was watching the orange flames dancing in the mirror of her dark eyes. He wondered how many other fears and secrets were well-hidden in the depths of those dark pools.

Many girls had dark eyes, but hers were so dark you could hardly tell where the pupils began or ended. Hers were the darkest eyes he'd ever seen. His eyes moved to her mouth, the swelling of her perfect lips that made him turn away and wrap his blanket tightly around himself, like a woolen armor against what he knew would be an act of poor judgment.

To have kissed her before was one thing, done in an offhand, "see if I can get Hannah to like me" sort of thing. He'd kissed lots of girls; they all fell for him. Sometimes he'd had to be rude just to get them to lose interest.

Hannah was a thing apart. The more time he spent with her, the more the truth wrapped itself around his heart, like a giant elastic band that pulled so tight it hurt, only to be released again, but always there.

He often asked himself the question—was it the thrill of the chase? Longing for something he could not have, like the foolish fox jumping for the out-of-reach grapes in his reading book in school?

Was it the fascination of her cold heart? Or was it a love that was alive in the spirit of God? The thing so many folks sense, notice, and follow? Feeling the obedience of God's will.

All he knew for sure was that he wanted Hannah. He wanted to stand by her side for the rest of his life. How lightly the phrase was tossed about—"If it's meant to be, it will be." He could not take it as lightly as that, like a dandelion seed blown by a puff of air.

She surprised him by speaking in a husky voice. "He was just so, I don't know, unstable. Carried away with thinking himself to be a prophet, a person set aside to receive special favors from God, while the reality of it was, we were starving. Jerry, do you have any idea what it's like to be so ravenously hungry your stomach hurts and you give your bowl of cornmeal mush to your little brother because you see the hunger in his eyes? And your father, the husband and leader of the weaker vessels, is flailing around, and praying in the bedroom, thinking that God will send manna or something?"

He could hear the resentment in her grating voice. What had she gone through? He grasped the idea of a husband that had been planted in her brain like a virus. She was afraid to trust. Afraid to live the life her mother had lived.

"See, that's why I haven't made the decision to be Amish. If I stay with our people, I'll be expected to marry, and marriage is forever. No separation, no divorce. I am not my mother with her sweet temperament. I couldn't handle being tied to a no-good dreamer leading me with a rope tied around my neck like a nanny goat. Most men just irritate me."

"Most men? Does that 'most' mean there is still a chance that I'm not among the ones that irritate you? Or, wait a minute. You gave me a few good solid kicks awhile ago, caused, no doubt, by irritation."

Jerry laughed, the easy sound that rolled from the depths of his chest. Far away, the wolves' lament turned into shivers, raising the hair on Hannah's forearms. The fire leapt into the night sky, sending sparks to share the darkness with the stars.

Hannah's head drooped onto her chest, her eyelids fell as the heat suffused her body. Jerry shrugged out of his blanket, draped an arm around her shoulders and drew her close as he would comfort a child.

"Thanks for sharing, Hannah. It gives me a lot to think about. And I promise not to kiss you, okay?"

They rode home together in the gathering cold, the clouds bunched together like heaps of dirty wool, puffing away across the prairie sky, changing the light as they thinned out and stretched, allowing a few shy rays of sun to slant through, then disappear.

The powerful gait of the palomino made her heart sing. Sometimes, for no reason, chills chased themselves up and down her spine, quick tears springing to her eyes. The sizable check would be put in the bank, the full amount paid on the debt to their grandfather, leaving no money to buy golden horses. But she was here, now, up on this horse that was like something she could only dream about on this breezy autumn day with the air crisp and invigorating, breathing new life into the parched, arid earth.

And she had to admit, the person riding with her was like a magnet to her sight, her eyes constantly turning to the denim jacket across the wide shoulders, the way he rode so easily, as if he was one with his horse. Both knew what was required of the other, a thoughtless unity that was as graceful as the dance of wildflowers hidden among the lush grass in spring.

She was sorry to see the homestead, knowing this was the end of the ride on the palomino, and yes, the end of his company as well as Jerry's.

They both dismounted and stood by the horses, unsure now, a silence stretching between them.

"You want to feed and water the horses?" Hannah asked quietly.

"I should, I suppose," he answered.

In the barn, she stayed a safe distance away, watching as the horses lowered their heads and drank thirstily, the gulps of water passing up through their long bent necks with a quiet glugging sound.

"You can stable them, if you want. We can see if my mother has something to eat."

She didn't tell him that the dried, over-peppered meat he'd supplied for breakfast was barely enough to tide her over. She was starving, positively light-headed with hunger. That awful coffee he made was so strong it was almost like syrup, with a bunch of bitter grounds huddled on the bottom and clinging to the sides of the cup like fleas.

Together, they walked to the low ranch house, welcomed warmly by Sarah. Manny was out checking the herd; he'd noticed a limp on the old cow last night.

Sarah served them leftover vegetable stew with a layer of fluffy white dumplings covering the fragrant chunks of potato, carrot and onion, a broth made of tomatoes and beef. She apologized about the lack of butter, but there was plenty of plum jam.

They had discovered a gnarled old plum tree hidden behind two big oak trees down along the creek, about a mile away. The fruit had already begun to ripen and fall, staining the brown, trampled grass purple, flies and hornets zig-zagging drunkenly, sated with too much sugar and the flesh of the rotting, fermented plums.

It was like a windfall, a blessing to be able to preserve this fruit for the winter months. They'd gorged themselves on the sweet fruit for days, until stomachs rumbled and trips to the new commode became hasty affairs. But now they had this jam, the promise of the old plum tree once again laden with fruit.

Jerry seemed hesitant to leave, sitting back in his chair, his eyes half-hidden by his lowered lids, his hands crossed on his stomach.

Sarah's cheeks were flushed, her eyes large and sparkling with good humor. Why not? Here was an attractive young man in the company of her daughter, so could any mother be free of thinking thoughts of love and romance? She saw no signs of either one in the bristly Hannah, who lowered her head and slurped the stew, stuffed her mouth with dumpling and bread and jam until she could hardly swallow fast enough, without her cheeks bulging.

Had she simply no social skills, even? Most girls would react to Jerry in a normal fashion, eating daintily, smiling, trying to be attractive, perhaps batting eyelashes on occasion.

Sarah turned to the stove with sinking heart. She wanted to shake Hannah! Hair disheveled, *dichly* discarded the minute she walked into the house, her apron knotted around her waist instead of being pinned neatly, in the Amish fashion. Men's trousers—whose?—protruding from her skirt, worn boots, castoffs from the Jenkinses.

Didn't she care, ever, about the impact she made, going through life so unhandily, so unconcerned about her appearance?

"You're still wearing my trousers. I'd let you have them, but with two bachelors, laundry is something we don't look forward to."

"Oh, that's right. I forgot I was wearing them."

Sarah was horrified to see her turn her back, hike up her skirt in front, shimmy out of the denims, and kick them across the room.

Jerry didn't seem to be embarrassed, so Sarah bit back the dismayed "Hannah!" and busied herself at the sink.

"Well," Jerry said, stretching his arms above his head. "I'd better get going. This isn't working on the house. I figure Jake is about tired of working alone. Thank you for the good dinner. I usually don't drop in at lunchtime unannounced."

He smiled at Sarah with his white teeth, so evenly spaced in his tanned face and, to her shame, she felt herself blush.

She answered quickly that it was nothing, there had been plenty left over, glanced at Hannah, hoping she had missed the obviousness of her girlish response.

Nothing to worry about there. She'd picked up one of her boots and was picking loose pieces off the heel with a table knife. "I need a new pair of boots," she stated flatly.

"Well, perhaps it will be possible with the money from the sale of the cattle," Sarah said, kindly.

"Huh-uh, Mam. Not one cent of that money will be spent. We can repay Doddy Stoltzfus up to half the loan. No new boots."

"What about stocking up on winter supplies? There's the doctor bill to pay."

"I'll go to work. I am working."

Jerry thought, Ah-ha. So there was a reason for her being at Mr. Rocher's hardware store. She was being paid wages to survive the long winter. In a flash, he realized the futility of offering the palomino to Hannah. If this was the tight ship she ran, she would never accept the horse without being in debt, the thought of more debt hounding her like a pack of dogs.

He was relaxed now, ready to leave, without the daunting task of trying to get her to accept the palomino. He would be surprised if old Pete made it through the winter, so maybe her pride would be flattened out of necessity.

He thanked Sarah again, looked at Hannah, who was still worrying the heel of her boot with the knife.

"Hannah."

She looked up.

"Thanks for riding home with me. If you need anything, let me know."

Hannah nodded, her gaze dropping to her boot.

He smiled at Sarah, then let himself out the door, walking to the barn where he saddled King, took up the palomino's reins, and rode home, acknowledging wearily that he had gained absolutely nothing where Hannah Detweiler was concerned.

She was like a mist, or a vapor, a puff of smoke, someone you could see but could never really hold. The closer you came, the more unsure you were.

Back in the kitchen of the ranch house, Sarah frowned, her brows lowered in concentration as she scraped the dishes, and asked Mary to take the scraps to the chickens.

She spoke sharply when she addressed her daughter. "Hannah, should you be using that table knife to scrape manure and what-not off that boot? You weren't very polite to Jerry Riehl, working on that heel and ignoring him when he left."

Hannah gave her mother a weary look. "What was I supposed to do? Stand up and gush over him the way you did?"

Her anger slow to rise, Sarah had time to release a breath, take another one in, before turning away to finish the dishes.

Hannah's behavior was forgotten when a cloud of dust heralded the arrival of two sheriffs from the town of Pine, who wasted no time getting out of their gray, dust-covered vehicle and striding up on the porch.

They were tall, formidable looking men, their faces weathered like old saddles left in the sun, the rain, and the scouring wind. Their serious expressions brought instant fear. Manny appeared in the doorway of the barn before making his way to the house, coming in through the wash house and standing quietly by his mother's side, as if his presence would support her.

Sarah's hand went to her mouth, her dark eyes widened as alarming thoughts crashed through her head. Were they conveyors of bad news this time? Wasn't that the way you were contacted if there was a death or an accident?

But when the older of the two began to speak, there was a moment when she realized this was not about news of home.

"We're asking you to be alert, perhaps keep a rifle or shotgun handy. That Luke Short. . ."

"Lemuel," the other sheriff corrected him.

"That Mr. Short that stayed here. He broke out of prison with another inmate. They're believed to be between this area and west of Dorchester. He knows you're good people, having helped him before, but don't let him close. Don't allow him into your house. They are both armed and dangerous. It might be a good idea to get a dog. All ranchers have them. Be very careful going out to your cattle, on the road, at night. Just be reasonable and don't take risks."

Sarah nodded, took a deep breath to steady herself. "All right. We'll do our best."

Hannah heard her light words, as if all hope and conviction had been abandoned, only a shell of herself remaining.

After they left, Sarah sat down on a kitchen chair, put her elbows on the table, and placed her head in her hands.

Hannah looked out of the window to avoid seeing her mother's distress, thinking that perhaps the sheriff was wrong. Manny went over to his mother and put a hand on her shoulder.

"We'll be all right, Mam. I'll keep the rifle handy."

Sarah lifted her head. "It's not that," she said to the opposite wall. "Do we really have to live like barbarians? Plain old shooting a rifle to protect ourselves? This wild land will be my undoing, at times like this. Mr. Lemuel Short was a nice man, and I believed every word he said. If he comes around, we can't just up and shoot him like savages."

Hannah tried not to snort, but she did anyway. "What did I tell you?"

"Oh, hush. Just hush. For once in your life stay quiet, Hannah. You don't know everything."

Hannah stalked out of the door and out to the barn, took up the pitch fork and threw hay around blindly, not caring where it landed or who ate it. Why couldn't her mother be strong? Why this caving in at the slightest adversity? So what if old Lemuel came around with his chronic cough and his craziness? She wasn't a bit afraid of him, and she couldn't imagine his consort would be too awesome, either. Get a dog, the sheriff had said. As if it was so easy to find a grown dog to haul home and get to barking obediently. She wasn't about to get a dog.

Here they were, well on their way, a sizable amount of money to put on her grandfather's loan, Amish neighbors to keep her content, and now this little man to upset her. Sometimes she just wearied of her mother's collapsing at the slightest provocation.

Hannah jabbed the pitchfork into the haystack, turned and left the barn, then stalked back to the house and went to her room without speaking.

When her mother knocked on her door, asking what was the matter, that she shouldn't worry about Lemuel Short, they'd be all right—Hannah didn't give her the satisfaction of an answer.

And when Manny took things into his own hands and brought home a skinny, mean-looking German shepherd dog, half-grown and rambunctious, an ugly dog that barked incessantly at nothing, or anything, she told him that dog would end up chasing young calves, and then what?

Manny smiled in his good-natured way and told her that's what dogs were for, to train and teach them how to work for you.

CHAPTER 20

On a dry, bitter cold afternoon, Abby Jenkins passed away, leaving Hod and the boys bereft, like floating debris on a flooded river, carried along by the churning wake of their grief, unraveling to an extent that they forgot everything else—their ranch, the cows, or how to go about living their lives without her.

Sarah divided her time between the Jenkins' place and her own, driving Goat in the spring wagon, with Eli and Mary beside her, Baby Abby on her lap, alone and unprotected. She did their washing, cooked meals, and cleaned the house until she became gaunt and weary, the work load being too much for her.

Hannah offered to help and took her turn, allowing her mother to rest. She hated going to that sad, empty house, but she bit her lip and went anyway. The boys stayed out of her way, slinking out to the barn like feral cats, as if it was an embarrassment that Abby had left them alone.

Hod talked to Hannah, though, showing her the wooden cross he'd made to put on her grave. Together, they walked out on the brittle prairie, where a sad pile of soil had been dug, her casket lowered, the soil replaced, an oblong mound of testimony to the truth of her death.

Hannah stood in the blowing wind, her skirts whipping about, her gloved hands clutching the lapel of her denim overcoat, watching as Hod slowly tapped the cross into the ground at the head of the grave.

He straightened and looked off across the land, his old, greasy Stetson smashed down on his head, his blue eyes holding the most desolate light Hannah had ever seen.

There were no tears, only the captured grief that lay in his eyes, a sadness so deep it seemed to change the color of blue to a deeper shade, like early twilight, after the sun is gone.

He spoke gruffly, as if the pain was like gravel in his throat. "It's been a good run, Hannah girl. Every year I spent with this woman was like a minute. I loved her with the kind of love I could only wish for all my boys. I know she had her times. She didn't always love the land the way me and the boys did. But that was beside the point. She gave her life for us, for me and them boys. Nothin' can measure the worth of a good woman. She appeared rough around the edges, but didn't have a mean bone in her body."

He shuddered slightly, the imprisoned emotion shaking his empty hands. "I can see her, crossin' over to that there other side, findin' her baby girl. They say there's thousands an' thousands a' angels up there, but she'll find her. She'll scoop her right up and be happier'n she's ever been."

Hannah felt the sting of tears and blinked furiously.

"Wal, we'll be goin' back now, Hannah." He placed a hand on her shoulder, and they both turned to go back to the house. Hannah wanted to say something, anything, words of comfort, words of remembering Abby, but they wouldn't come. There was no way to force words out if they stick in your head and stay there. Or her heart, she wasn't sure where.

At the house, the boys watched their return, seated around the old oak kitchen table with the blue checked tablecloth, drinking coffee that was strong like a fortress, cup after cup.

Hod went to the stove, poured himself a cup, sat with the boys, motioned Hannah to sit.

"Coffee?"

Hannah shook her head. Ever since she'd downed that slop Jerry called campfire coffee, she hadn't touched it. Those coffee grounds still reminded her of dead, black fleas.

"Now, I want you and yer' mother to go through Abby's things. Take what you kin use. No use lettin' it all go to waste. She ain't got no relatives hereabouts, an' the few she does have back where she come from wouldn't want it. I got her Bible, her weddin' ring and her dress. The rest you kin go through. The boys'll git the furniture after I'm gone. I'm thinkin' that'll be enough."

Hannah surveyed the somber faces, the downcast eyes, wondering where the red-haired Jennifer was. She couldn't remember seeing her at the funeral, when the church in Pine was filled with sober-colored dresses and ill-fitting dark suits that were worn without comfort, bared white foreheads hidden beneath slouched Stetsons, the faces below the white foreheads sunburned and weather-beaten.

The mourning and support of the mourners was much like every funeral Hannah had ever attended. These hardy ranchers were linked by deep bonds forged from survival on the plains, an ingrained love of this high, vast, empty land, and the unpredictable weather the subject of so many neighborhood get-togethers.

"I'm gittin' hitched."

At first, Hannah had a mental picture of Clay being hitched to a spring wagon, till it dawned on her what he meant.

Hod looked at his eldest son, his face blank, his eyes fogged, until he shook himself, and the beginning of a smile played around the corners of his mouth.

"Wal, I'll be."

"That all you got to say?"

"No. I ain't done yet."

There were smiles on every face, even Hannah's.

"First off, it comes a bit sudden, this announcement. I'm guessin' it comes at a good time, without yer Ma to do fer you. I wish you the best, son. Give you my blessin'. Hope yer little Jenny will be everything fer you that yer mother was to me."

Was that a light of revenge in Clay's eyes as they met Hannah's? She looked away immediately, left soon after, bringing down the reins on Goat's flapping haunches, chilled to the bone, one thought chasing another through her head until she felt as numb from the cold as she was from those words that became weary sentences.

He had loved me.

He wanted me to be his wife.

I should have left and gone with Clay.

He's still the best-looking man. Well, almost.

I hope he's happy. But she knew that wasn't true.

Before the snow came, Lemuel Short pounded on the door, a stringy-looking individual in tow.

Sarah was alone with the little ones, Hannah and Manny had ridden off with the German shepherd, now named Shep by Manny. Hannah ignored the dog like a virus, wouldn't touch him or talk to him, so he had learned to keep his distance, and he wouldn't wag his tail at the sight of her.

Sarah stood by her bread making, slowly wiping bits of dough and flour from each finger before putting her hands in the dishwater to finish cleaning them. She licked her lips as the dryness of her mouth alternated with the pounding of her heart. Yes, she was afraid.

God, help me. Stay with me now.

The pounding erupted again, the latch rattling like chains. Eli and Mary stopped their schoolwork, their eyes wide, as they looked to their mother for assurance.

Wiping her hands on her apron, she scooped up Abby, told them to continue their work before going to the window, peering sideways, then drawing back, her eyes darkening with fear.

It was him. Both of them.

It was useless to try and hide; they'd heard the children.

She opened the door, blinked in the strong sunlight. "Mr. Short?"

"Don't Mr. Short me. I need food."

He drew his revolver, a small, evil-looking handgun that gleamed with a dull, gray sheen, matching the gray pallor of the little man's face.

His companion, or the man who accompanied him—companion seemed too nice a word—glared over his shoulder, his white face twisted into a leering snarl, a face Sarah could have never imagined.

It was a face absent of any human warmth, decency, or kindness. It took her breath away, leaving her mouth open with shallow rushes of air expelled and inhaled, her nostrils dilated, her limbs weak with terror.

Sarah did not speak. She didn't have the strength. Turning, she went to the pantry.

Eli and Mary recognized their friend, Lemuel, their eyes warm as they opened their mouths to speak, saw the handgun, blinked, then lowered their faces to their lessons, their hands holding the yellow lead pencils, without moving.

Abby toddled after Sarah, beginning to whimper. When Sarah didn't respond, she began to cry.

"Get the baby!" Lemuel yelled, a maniacal note creeping into the end of his sentence.

Sarah obeyed.

The pantry was not well stocked. There was very little she could give them, except cornmeal or oatmeal, flour, other dry staples meant to be used in cooking and baking.

There were canned vegetables and the plums. A few jars of applesauce, but all the canned meat and most of the potatoes had been used up.

Sarah harbored a secret concern, one she had not confided to the children, about the amount of food left for the coming winter months. And now this.

She found a paper sack on a high shelf. Carefully, she placed a jar of plums, one of green beans, and one of small potatoes.

"You better hurry!" Lemuel shouted.

"I don't have a lot to give you," she said hoarsely, returning with the three mason jars of canned goods.

"Where's the bread?"

Sarah turned, pointed with shaking fingers. "It's all gone. I was making bread when you arrived."

"You're holding back. You had more than enough when I was here before. Sit down."

Lemuel Short pushed her roughly into a chair, where she sprawled, struggling to regain her balance, clutching Abby to her chest.

The revolver was within inches of her face now, a cold, gleaming weapon that made her throat constrict with horror. She tasted bile in her mouth, and fought rising nausea.

It was then that she found the leering face of the second man pushed into hers, his cruel, white hands on her shoulders pushing her back into the chair. Abby screamed and struggled to get away. Sarah held on to her.

"I can see you won't do as we say, which means we'll have to use other measures," the man said, his voice as slick and oily as bacon grease.

He drew back a hand and swung, hitting the side of Sarah's face, sending her head sideways, the slap like an explosion through her head. There was only blackness before a blinding burst of light. The kitchen floor came up to meet her, then tilted at an awful angle, steep and slippery.

She heard the cupboard doors slamming, Lemuel muttering. Abby screamed and went on crying until he shouted at her to cut that out. Eli and Mary put their heads on their folded arms, crying quietly at their desk in the living room.

"There ain't nothin' 'cept these canned vegetables," Lemuel mocked. The second man whipped out a length of rope, ordered Sarah to get up and get back on the chair.

"What you doin' that for?" Lemuel asked, then shrugged his shoulders as he tied Sarah's hands to the ladder-back chair.

She knew struggling would only cause her situation to be more difficult, so she sat quietly as the rope cut deep into her wrists, shutting off the circulation to her hands.

"You get smart with us, you'll get worse," the second man snarled.

Sarah had never been in the presence of anything this cold and calculating. She had often heard the word evil. She read it in her Bible and knew it meant something bad. But it came down to this cold-hearted invasion of her own self-worth, this treatment of her that smashed all her rights to the fringes of human dignity.

She now saw that evil was the absence of basic human emotion—kindness, caring, empathy, the will to do good. These men were shells. Empty, crumbling wasted men without a residue of common humanity.

She had always believed in the good of every human heart. She couldn't think of any person as evil. Now she could.

The second man eyed Mary, holding her with a malicious glint in his eyes. When he walked toward her, Sarah let out a piercing scream.

"No! No! Mary, run! Run! Oh go! Eli, run!"

Immediately he whirled and turned his face to Sarah, allowing the children time to get to the door, slip through like ghosts, clatter across the porch, and down the steps.

To the barn. To the barn. Sarah's mind screamed direction. Burrow in the hay. It's cold, Eli. Mary, hide in the hay.

"Shut up, lady! Just shut that mouth!"

Lemuel Short had opened a jar of the beans, spilled them into a bowl, eating greedily, smacking his sips as he stuffed them into his mouth with his hands.

The second man found a scarf hanging from a nail on the wall. He grabbed it, approached Sarah with a mocking smile, and tied

606 Hope on the Plains

it like a vice around her mouth, knotting it in the back, jerking her head like a doll, until it rolled and wobbled on her shoulders.

He smacked his hands together, dusting them off, and said they could eat in peace now. Shut her up good.

They were well into the third jar of beans, the revolver lying on the table between them, Sarah bound to the chair, her eyes watching every move. Abigail came to stand by her mother's knee, crying quietly, gazing up into Sarah's face, before she laid her head on her lap, inserted her thumb in her mouth, and bravely quieted.

That was so much. God was with her here in the presence of evil. A Psalm of David entered her mind as a softness, a mere powder puff of comfort, but it was enough. "Yea, though I walk through the valley of the shadow of death, I will fear no evil." She sat without terror now.

The two men became relaxed and got up to search for more food, leaving the revolver on the table surrounded by empty bean jars.

"Make her bake the bread dough. Man, I could use a loaf of bread. Some bacon. Butter. She always had that stuff before."

Suddenly, the door was flung open!

Sarah screamed, but the sound was muffled by the scarf around her mouth. Only the bulging of her eyes and the veins in her neck gave away the fact that she had made any sound at all.

Shep! Dear God, the dog! Then there was Manny, shouting commands, his face white and terrible, followed by Hannah entering with a pitch fork.

The dog barked, growled, and latched onto Lemuel Short's leg and would not let go. Glass mason jars went flying across the room, shattering in the corners, the sound of breaking glass mixed with hoarse curses and shouts as Hannah knocked the revolver off the table with the pitch fork.

The second man lunged after it, but Hannah was too quick, dropping the pitch fork and grabbing it up, holding it in two hands, as steady as a rock.

"You want a bullet or the pitch fork?" she asked, her voice calm.

"Leggo! Leggo!" Lemuel Short writhed in the dog's grip. Manny loosened his mother's hands and used the rope to tie Lemuel's hands before ordering Shep to let go. The scarf was used to tie the second man's hands.

"Sit," Manny ordered, pushing them both into chairs.

Sarah grabbed Abby, held her sobbing in her arms.

The second man lunged for the back door. A short command from Manny and the dog was all over him, jaws locking on an arm, a shoulder, a leg, amid piercing screams.

Manny bound them together with many lengths of rope, tied them to chairs. They were bound and restrained far too well to think of getting loose.

It was Hannah who rode to the Klassermans, whipping Goat into an uneven trot that drained every ounce of strength from his already weary body.

She found no one at home, the doors locked firmly, the only sound the milling around of a few cattle around the haystacks, the wind whistling along the ornate eaves of the house.

There was nothing else to be done. Hannah grabbed the straw broom, turned the handle toward the closest window, and shoved, cracking the pane into splinters. Risking cuts on the palms of her hands, she reached through until she found the metal clasp on top of the wooden sash, turned it to the left, and pushed up with both hands.

"Thank you," she whispered, as she extended one leg through the opening, bent her back, and slid through. She found the black telephone, the sheriff's number, and dialed carefully, holding her breath with concentration.

It was soon over after the telephone call to the sheriff's office, although Hannah had to leave a winded Goat in the Klassermans' barn and ride home on one of their mean-tempered broncos, which almost unseated her before the ride home started.

The house was filled with men, the yard jammed with automobiles. Hannah opened the barn door to lead the horse through, was calmly sliding the saddle off his wet back, when she heard her name whispered. Chills slid up her back. Her eyes opened wide.

"Hannah! Hannah!"

She turned, tried to locate the whispers. One dark head appeared from the loft, followed by another.

"Eli! Mary!"

"Can we come down?"

"Of course. It's over. The sheriff is here."

"We watched you leave on Goat, and we thought we'd better stay here. Do they . . . are they still here? Those men?"

"Get down. Come on. I'll tell you about it."

Two pairs of legs appeared, one after another they scrambled down, threw themselves at Hannah, who hunkered down and held them as if she would never let them go.

She found Sarah seated on the rocking chair inside the living room door, rubbing the bruises on her wrists, a red, ugly welt appearing on her right cheekbone, dark bruises on each side of her mouth where the scarf had dug into her tender flesh.

Hannah stood, unsure. The words that should have been spoken were all jammed up inside of her, so she said nothing.

Sarah nodded, held her gaze. "I'll be all right."

Manny stood in the kitchen, a hand on Shep's head, the only restraint the dog required. Jealousy flickered through Hannah, the one thing Manny had done that out-maneuvered his sister, and it didn't sit well with her.

Shep was the undoubted hero. She eyed him. Looked into those yellowish brown dog eyes. He stared back at her intently, and his tail did not move an inch.

I know you don't like me, you dumb dog. I don't like you either. But maybe I should.

Hannah never watched them untie the two men, or escort them to the car. She could hardly stand to look at their wrinkled, sullen faces. Baggy old trousers with holes in them from the dog's teeth. Blood all over everything. Green bean juice on their coat fronts. Greasy long hair and yellow teeth like a mule's. She had no mercy on them. She didn't pity either one, not even a thin slice of sympathy.

Sarah and Manny talked with the sheriff and the investigators who asked questions and wrote reports.

Hannah didn't talk, mostly for the fact that she didn't like these men, either. Why did they have to ask all these nosy questions? They could stick them into the jailhouse without knowing every tiny piece of information. It was a wonder they didn't ask what kind of bean seeds they'd planted, and what type of jars they used to preserve them.

They should all leave now, go home or to the sheriff's office in Pine, or wherever it was that they all belonged.

The man asking all the questions had a congested nose, speaking with a nasal twang, the way your voice came out if you put a clothespin on top of it. He kept sniffing, drawing air through his thin nostrils, until Hannah wanted to give him a handkerchief and tell him to use it! Blow as hard as he could. She bet it would be wondrous!

His sideburns were so long she couldn't tell if he has thought about growing a beard along the side of his face, then changed his mind but didn't finish shaving it off. Maybe he couldn't grow anything on his chin.

Sarah was unfailing in her kindness, speaking clearly, trying to remember to the best of her ability, Manny helping her over the difficult places.

Hannah glared at the dog, then at the sheriff, sniffed back at the investigator until she'd had enough. She told them all that her mother needed to rest and would they please finish up.

Of course, they were the law, so they only raised their eyebrows in her direction and stayed on course.

It was only after everyone had finally driven out the gravelly road and the last bit of dust had settled that they realized the fire had gone out. The house was cold, the floor littered with broken glass and splotches of blood, and Abby was hungry and needed her diaper changed.

They all worked together, setting things to rights. They spoke very little until the kitchen floor was swept, Hannah had scrubbed it on her hands and knees, Sarah set the bread to baking, and Manny and Shep fed the livestock.

No one except Abby was hungry, a sense of shock permeating the house like a sour odor. They tried to talk about the incident, but the horror was too real, so their voices stilled and became quiet.

Sarah wondered if it wasn't the same for all of them. The disbelief cut through their comfort level like the ragged edge of a saw. How could a nice man like Lemuel Short, a sweet, fatherly type, turn from his humanity into this animal? Which one was the real Lemuel Short?

For Sarah, the hardest part had not been the physical abuse. It was when the children recognized him, the gladness in their eyes as they looked up, only to have their trust so horribly shattered.

As was her own. Would she ever be able to look on strangers with the same kind of trust as before?

After she finally laid her head on her pillow, sighing deeply, she held her throbbing wrists, then switched to the opposite side, the side of her face that had not been smacked.

He just plowed his fist into the side of my face, she thought wryly. Well, just add this one to the long list of new experiences on the plains, this hateful, unforgiving land of drought and cold and sweltering heat and now thieving men turned into monsters.

She shivered involuntarily. She tried, bravely, to fight these thoughts. How many days had she put on a fresh, new face to begin another day, the rest of her life projected on a screen by the move to North Dakota?

How many battles had she won with goodness, faith, and trust in God and mankind? But now, it was time to face the dark visage of reality. She was afraid. So horribly afraid.

What would keep this incident from being repeated? Couldn't you blame this endless expanse of dried-out land for producing people like Lemuel? He had told her his story and she had believed him. Not every woman could survive, no matter how deep her faith.

Allowing these thoughts to inhabit her mind made her feel like a traitor, like someone who betrays their country.

Somehow, in her heart, admitted to no one and seen by no one, she raised the white flag of surrender. Just go home, return to civilization as we have always known it. But then, there was the Ben Millers and Ike Lapps, the new Stoltzfuses, and the bachelors. Her father and brothers would be coming in spring. Safety in numbers. Or was there?

She saw only the expression of trust on her children's faces when she closed her eyes, so she kept them open, watched the stars winking through the gap in the bedroom curtain, rubbed her wrists, and fought the negative thoughts with prayer, until God seemed to be in the room with her, comforting her in her time of greatest need.

And yet, she wept far into the night, the heaving of her quiet sobs the sound of so many high-plains women before her.

CHAPTER 21

THE BITING WINDS OF WINTER SEEMED TO INTENSIFY EVERY WEEK, A dry cold, as harsh as a saw's teeth. Into November, December, past Christmas, and there was no snow, only the endless gale winds that swept from the north, scouring the land with their harsh moaning sounds, bending the dry, brittle vegetation, boiling up clouds of cold gray dust that covered every available surface with a fine and cumbersome grit.

Hands and faces were chapped, dried out with the strength of the arid cold. The cows tore at the haystacks and drank water from the holes Manny chopped in the frozen water tank. The windmill spun and creaked in the cold, forming a swollen river of ice where the tank overflowed.

Many days were bleak, sunless, without cheer. Mary and Eli hunched over their school work, their heads in their hands propped up by one elbow. The provisions in the pantry ran low, supplemented only by Hannah's wages from Rocher's Hardware.

Wolves howled at night, and the terrifying ripples of sound kept Hannah from restful sleep. She trusted the cows to defend themselves, but the high, primal pitch of the wolves baying sent shivers of unease up her spine.

They dressed in coats, scarves, worn gloves and boots, rode out past the tank, across the windswept plains, their guns held across their saddle horns. When they came upon the wandering herd, Hannah knew before they counted that they weren't all present.

Surely they had defended themselves this winter, if they were capable of defending themselves in the deep snows of the preceding winter.

They came upon the grisly scene of mutilated calves and cows, not a few, but six carcasses in various stages of mutilation. Hannah's face showed no emotion, pale as the gray sky, her eyes black daggers of hardened resolve.

Manny picked up his gun, dismounted, and stood looking down at the remains of a calf, not believing the amount of destruction.

"Why? Why?" he asked finally.

Hannah shrugged coldly.

"Why didn't they stay around the buildings? Shep would have alerted us to any wolves."

He turned away and poked the flopping leg of a dead yearling, his face a mask of pain and anxiety.

"Wolves couldn't run in the snow," Hannah said, her words hard and clipped.

"You mean last winter?"

Hannah nodded.

They counted the cattle. The large, oversized cow, the bull, and three remaining young cows. Five head of cattle.

"Not much left," Manny remarked, shaking his head.

"Enough. I have my job. You'll have to get one. We have enough. As long as we're able to keep food on the table, we'll keep the homestead. We have others, now, Amish brethren to help us through."

Manny looked at Hannah. "You said that?" he asked, a small smile on his face.

"It's true. They won't let us starve."

They rode back slowly and talked of penning the remaining cows. Wild as deer, especially that old, oversized one. They'd

need better horsepower to round them up, then there was no
promise they'd stay within the confines of the posts and few
strands of barbed wire that enclosed most of the barnyard.

"It will snow soon," Manny said, trying to bolster his spirits
as well as Hannah's.

"Yeah, I think so."

"Will you tell Mam, or shall I?" Manny asked, always thinking of his mother's well-being.

"You can."

Manny told Sarah. Her face registered no surprise, no alarm,
nothing. Manny wasn't sure his mother had heard him correctly,
and repeated his words.

When she looked at him, it was like looking into someone's
eyes where there was no emotion, no feeling, a barren place calloused by too much suffering.

"Mam!" he said sharply.

Sarah started, blinked, said yes, the wolves had done them a
nasty turn, but perhaps they'd move on, God willing. Words spoken without caring or conviction, only spoken out of necessity.

The winter months came and went, days marching in slow
succession. Firewood was becoming scarce, vegetables rolling
around in the bottom of the bin, an ominous sound portending
tight, empty stomachs that struck fear in Sarah's heart.

She wrote letters questioning her father's and brothers' reluc-
tance to commit themselves to a date—sometime in April or
May.

The letter Hannah brought back from town deepened a gnawing unease, almost like an excitement at the idea of surrender.

Dear Daughter,

I hope you are all well.

*This letter is written in Jesus' Name, hoping you can take
this news as it is written, in love, to all of you.*

I regret to inform you that our move to North Dakota has been cancelled for the present time. I have other daughters who think it unwise, and since Ben and Elam have taken up a farrier business from Jeremiah Riehl, we have chosen to stay.

Snow is abundant this year, but milk prices are holding steady, so it is a joy to load the milk cans on the bobsled and take them to town.

Sarah's hands shook. She gripped the paper until her knuckles whitened, her dark eyes boring into the words from her thin, white face, her mind refusing to accept this monumental disappointment. She read on.

I thank you for the check you wrote and sent to me. It is a generous repayment, and I'm glad you are doing well, the cattle thriving.

Sarah blinked, tried to collect her scattered thoughts, as they raced in paranoid circles. Dat, we aren't thriving. The cows are dead, torn apart by long, lean wolves of the prairie. Thin, hungry animals that live from day to day on what they can kill, running across a lean and hungry land that shows no mercy to homesteaders.

She put down the letter, grasped the thin remnants of her old coat around her body, leaned forward, and rocked from side to side, her eyes closed, dry, the absence of tears a testament to the hardened spirit within.

Snow. Milk. So much rich, creamy milk they hauled it away on a bobsled with Belgians, huge, healthy animals that ate oats and corn and were stabled in a barn made of stone and heavy lumber, painted white, a row of cupolas marching across the peak in perfect symmetry. It was all she had ever known.

She could smell the heavy cream, feel the smooth sides of the glass butter churn, the slow creak of the iron handle that turned the wooden paddles, the schlomp, schlomp of the agitated cream that solidified into butter.

A physical longing stabbed through her stomach, but she only clutched her arms more tightly. It was little Abby coming to rest her head on her mother's knee, that shook her from her reverie. She lifted her head, smiled wanly, gathered Abby in her arms and bent her head over the cold little form.

The house was so cold. She was trying to stretch the firewood, hoping to make it last till spring, but without snow, the foundation and the cracks around windows and doors would seep cold and dust particles that moved about the house like a physical discomfort. Woolen socks and cracked leather shoes were not enough to keep toes from numbing and chills from racing across thin shoulders.

She added a stick of wood to the stove, closing the damper to make it last longer. She longed to open the draft, hear the roaring of the fire, the crackling, leaping flames that devoured the wood and turned the stove top cherry red.

Hannah spent her days stalking from the house to the barn, a tall, thin cold-wracked pack of anxiety, her dark eyes lifted to the sky, searching for snow, the elusive white moisture that would warm the foundation of the house and replenish the grasses that fed her few remaining cattle.

Manny rode the old horse, Goat, trying to keep the cows as close to the haystacks as possible, the mean-natured cow, always a threat without a better horse to dodge her belligerent advances. The bull was more stoic, enduring a bit of prodding with aplomb, until the old cow became too agitated, and he'd begin bellowing low and mean, throwing dust up over his shoulder with the strength of a mighty cloven hoof.

The cold intensified, a strange, dry sub-zero temperature that blackened fingers and toes without warning. Hank Jenkins landed in the hospital in Dorchester, two of his toes partially amputated, they were so badly frozen. Hod said in all his days on the plains, he'd never seen anything like this, as if the clouds withheld every snowflake, every bit of ice that needed to fall.

There were the church services to look forward to, the fellow-ship with the Ben Millers and the Ike Lapps, but all that cold, dry winter Sarah could not put her heart into the fledgling community.

The sermons were preached by the new Elam Stoltzfus, who was not an ordained minister, but since they needed a speaker, he had plenty to say concerning the Bible and the Plain way of life.

Somehow, the weak singing led by Ben Miller seemed a spinoff of the real thing, that two-toned swell of song that rolled to the ceiling of an Amish house and rolled out the window on the beauty of the notes. It seemed unholy, somehow, the person's words, thinking himself a gifted speaker when, in reality, he was not.

Ike Lapp's children were thin and riddled with cold sores, hacking coughs, and mucus that ran in an endless yellow stream from their poor, red, chapped noses.

Houses were cold, even Ben Miller's, the one with the best stove among the Amish.

There just weren't very many trees for firewood. The feed mill sold coal, but there was no extra money for Ike Lapps or the Detweilers. Ike said he was experimenting with twisted hay. It didn't last long, but made a hot fire. His wife shot him a look of reproach, and Sarah could not blame her.

But twisting hay is what it came to toward the end of February when the cold became unbearable. They shivered through their scant breakfast, the hot cornmeal mush steaming in the cold air, burning their tongues in their haste to fill their stomachs.

When had it come to this? How like a thief in the night this cold crept in and left them with scarce provisions. Hannah still traveled to the Rochers' store two days a week, one for items they needed to keep real hunger at bay and one to help buy seeds and raise some money for other necessities or to repay their grandfather.

Doris Rocher was wasting away, thin as a stick, refusing food, whispering words to Hannah, words of homesickness and irritation, saying she was going home on the train by herself for the second time, and seemingly proud of this fact.

Hannah had no patience for this self-absorbed woman. Her husband ran a hardware store, perhaps only minimally successful, but then, weren't many places of business just that in these years of hardship? Doris had a nice warm house, heated with coal, snug and cozy, plenty to eat, a telephone, and electricity.

Hannah worked all day, rearranging shelves, dusting, making signs, and then she was sent to the kitchen to clean for Doris. Harry gave her a pleading look, one she knew well, the same hangdog look he displayed every time he looked at his wife.

Don't go looking for pity from her, Hannah thought. There is none. It's gone.

"All right," she said brusquely, brushing him off like a whining fly.

"Try and lift her spirits, would you, Hannah?" he asked, his eyes like a basset hound.

Hannah turned away, sickened, kept a straight face, and set to work, ignoring Doris who sat propped on a chair with a pile of pillows holding her up like a sagging rag doll.

The kitchen was pleasant, or as pleasant as any room could be on a gray wintry day with the wind buffeting the wooden siding, rasping around the cracks in the window like teeth on a comb. The bulbs on the ceiling cast a yellow haze over everything, the corners illuminated with reading lamps.

White lace doilies hung over the backs of the chairs, over the stuffed arms of davenports and the Queen Anne chairs, which were upholstered in flowered prints. China cabinets displayed ceramic dogs, cats, ladies with parasols, teapots, rabbits, horses, men in top hats, and row upon row of glass objects.

Doris lifted a hand, crooked one finger to beckon Hannah closer.

"What?" Hannah asked loudly. Talk to me, she thought. You can speak.

"I want the ceramics washed," Doris whispered.

"All of them?" Hannah asked loudly, raising one eyebrow.

Doris nodded.

"Shall I put them back after they're clean?"

"No. No. In a trunk. Upstairs in the blue guest room there's a small wooden trunk. Newspapers are in the washroom. Wash and dry them and pack them in the trunk."

Hannah did as she was told. She enjoyed washing the odd little glass and ceramic creatures, rinsing and drying them, rolling them in newspaper and packing them away.

Halfway through, Harry walked into the room, stood and watched Hannah with an odd expression before asking Doris what was going on.

"I'm packing." The curt words were loaded with malice and ill will. Like a concealed weapon, she showed him the gleaming barrel of her mental and emotional revolver.

She received the response she was hoping for. Harry fell on his knees, took his wife's hands in his visibly trembling ones, and begged her over and over to reconsider.

The longer the theatrics continued, the faster Hannah worked, slamming the newspaper wrapped objects into the yawning trunk.

"Careful there!"

If Hannah would not have to depend on the wages from this man, she'd break every one of those piddling ceramics and make him drive her home. What was wrong with these people? He obviously would have a nicer life without her, so why not let her go? And if she wanted to go home so badly, then go! Leave already. What a bunch of malarkey! Like two children that needed disciplining.

She thought of her own mother, the adaptation she had made, the grace in which she had accepted the ranch, never complaining, always cheerful. Well, Manny's illness had been rough. Even the experience with old Lemuel Short had been hard for her. But still she was stoic and accepting. She was here in North Dakota for the long haul, supporting Hannah's dream of the Bar S.

Superiority flapped its wings and settled on Hannah's shoulder, making her oblivious to the intense struggles her patient mother suffered still.

"Oh, Harry! Sell the store. Sell out, I implore you. Return to Baltimore with me. If you don't, I must go alone. I will die in my hometown without the support of my betrothed."

"Oh, my darling woman, we are more than betrothed. We are united in marriage. We are as one flesh. We cannot separate!" Harry's voice rose to a strident crescendo.

Hannah fled to the back room. Her hands over her ears, she hunkered down, determined to shut out the sound of those falsely sticky-sweet voices.

What an absolute farce! It sickened her. If one cared for the other even half of what their mouths uttered, they would reside in peace, either in Baltimore, Maryland, or in Pine, North Dakota.

She was going to march in there and let them have it. She carried a few more newspapers to the table, plunked them down, took a deep breath, and asked them to stop.

Harry looked at her. Doris narrowed her eyes. "If either one of you loved the other as much as you say, then you'd be happy together, it doesn't matter where."

And that was only the beginning. In the end, she was fired by an irate Harry Rocher and his indignant, resurrected wife. Hannah collected her pay and Harry drove her home in stone cold silence. He ushered her out car door with a curt, "Goodbye," leaving Hannah standing in front of the ranch house in the raw wind, watching the car disappear into a cloud of dust that rolled across the brown plains.

Sarah reacted to Hannah's news with consternation. "Hannah, how will we survive? It's our only hope, now that the herd is depleted."

"We still have some. It's not depleted."

"But we need to have a way to get provisions until the herd is built back up, which could be two years. Jobs are scarce. If it doesn't snow, when spring comes the drought will continue. And how will we live?"

"I'll get a job. Didn't Manny find anything yet?"

"Not yet."

Hannah went to feed the horses, stomped angrily around the barn, yelled at Manny for dumping saddles and bridles in the corner instead of hanging them on the nails provided for that purpose.

She found Pete lying down, was not surprised to touch his neck and find it stiff and cold, his eyes glazed over with the dull look of death.

So, that was that, she thought. Dead. Finally, the poor old thing. Well, they were down to one scrawny horse, five head of cattle, a long year of drought, clouds that refused to send rain, and, very likely, God Himself had forgot about them. Bitter thoughts, but better than no thoughts at all.

They dragged Pete out using a bewildered Goat, left him lying on the prairie, figured the coyotes, vultures, eagles, crows, and whatever other hungry scavengers would find him and have a square meal.

Manny didn't think the wolves would come so close to the buildings, and, if they did, well, the dead horse would be easier than bringing down a cow.

They came in from completing the task, twisted a wagonload of hay to supplement the firewood supply, then pulled it to the stoop of the wash house, covered it with a piece of canvas, and let themselves in the back door, stomping their boots to keep their feet from becoming numb.

The house was not warm, but it was more comfortable than outside. Sarah had used one turnip and two potatoes, cut them in chunks and stewed them with prairie hens, simmering the pot on the stove until the rich broth permeated the whole house with its savory aroma.

The news of Pete's death was taken without surprise, the poor horse unable to rid his body of any liquid matter. They knew it would only be a matter of time.

Hannah was strangely quiet while they ate. The good stew was sopped up with crusty bread, turning the children's cheeks red, giving them renewed vigor to talk and laugh, punch each other, lift their faces, and giggle at their own silliness.

Baby Abby looked at the ceiling, squeezed her eyes, and opened her mouth, howling like a coyote, trying to be silly and get her share of attention from everyone else.

They laughed. Outside, the wind scoured the house with dust that it picked up and flung against the walls, crackling against the windows, then roaring away into the night.

Hannah brooded beside the cookstove, her legs thrust out in front of her like two slim saplings, her eyes black with too much thinking.

"The hay really helps with the cooking," Sarah said, out of a need to raise Hannah's spirits.

"Yeah, that's good. We don't have many cows to eat our store of hay."

"Is it serious again?" Sarah asked.

"What do you think? Pete's gone, I was fired. If this drought continues, there's only one thing to do. Get another job, both Manny and I. I don't know what we'll do if it doesn't rain in the spring."

"God will provide," Sarah said softly.

Manny nodded, a reverence showing in his soft brown eyes.

"Yeah. Well, it's good you can say that. What if He doesn't? What if this is the beginning of a three- or four-year drought?

Would you stay?" The question was like barbed wire hurled at Sarah by Hannah's hands.

Sarah winced, hoped it didn't show. Firmly, she sat on a kitchen chair and turned to face Hannah with a steady gaze.

"No one would. Not even the town of Pine would stay."

"You don't know. You're just saying."

"Hannah." That lilt at the end of her name, a sweet, soft warning. So, the divide was beginning again. She was thinking of giving up. Panic mounted in Hannah's chest as she watched her mother's face.

"We can make it. I can get another horse. From Jerry."

Manny raised his eyebrows, looking at his mother over the uncovered head of his sister.

They both rode to Pine on Goat. An embarrassment to be seen on the back of the poor, scrawny creature, so Hannah walked after the buildings came into view.

Faces red with the sweep of raw air, hands and feet numb with the cold, they walked through the feed-mill door, accosted by the stares of a group of grimy men peering out from under their stained, battered hats. The owner behind the counter was lean and wrinkled, his eyes bulging out of his head like egg yolks.

"What kin' I do fer ye young 'uns?"

Manny straightened his shoulders, spoke in a clear tone, asking for work.

"You them Detweilers?"

"Yessir."

He stroked his beardless chin, chewed on the eraser of his yellow pencil, picked a piece of it off his tongue, examined it, wiped the tips of his fingers on his trousers, squinted, coughed, wiped his mouth with a filthy brown handkerchief and shook his head.

"Wish I could. Times is hard. You got your cattle yet?"

"Yessir." This from Hannah.

"Wolves ain't got any? Yer lucky. Most folks lost quite a few. Easy for them with no snow."

"We lost five, sir," Manny said, providing the truth.

Hannah glared at the mill owner, swept the onlookers with her proud stare, pulled Manny away by the shoulder and clomped across the creaking wooden floor and out the door, banging it shut behind her.

"Hoity-toity," remarked Abram Jacobs.

The sewing and alterations place was stuffy, a small room blue with cigarette smoke, acrid with the smell of human perspiration.

The owner shook her head, the ashes tumbling from the cigarette she held between thin lips. "Have a waiting list," was all she said.

Manny did no better at the garage, the mechanic telling him he had enough to do without training a young 'un.

They stood together on the lee side of the driving wind. Hannah said there was one more place, but she'd rather go hungry than work for her.

"Who?" Manny asked.

"That Betsy at the café."

"What's wrong with her?"

"She reminds me of the old cow. The one that killed our father."

Manny smiled, shrugged his shoulders.

That was where Hannah found employment. Three days a week. Had to find her own way there and back. Goat. The only available form of transportation.

But she lifted her chin, squared her thin shoulders, and told Betsy she'd take it. She had no other choice. It was that or allow the long, bony fingers of starvation to clench all of them in the grip they had known before.

She could do it. She could go ask Jerry Riehl for the palomino, still uncertain which job would be most difficult.

CHAPTER 22

Hannah thought God must have remembered them when Jerry Riehl arrived in his light buggy, driving a horse she had never seen. Now she would not need to ride over on Goat, that poor thing had enough to do pulling the work load around the ranch without Pete.

Jerry was not the same, open, friendly person he had been. His face seemed pale, set.

When Hannah followed Manny out to greet him, he smiled at both of them, but it was a pinched smile. Tension played around his mouth, his eyes turned often to the leaden sky.

"Is this usual, the normal way, to have no snow?" he asked.

"First winter we've seen like this," Manny replied.

"There will be no planting in the spring if we get no snow or rain. Jake wants to go back. Ben Miller says it's foolish to stay if we don't get any moisture. Wolves got a bunch of Ike Lapp's heifers. His kids are going hungry."

His words raked themselves across Hannah's mind, inflicting a deep and awful hurt.

"It'll soon snow!" she burst out, to hide the pain. "One of these days the blizzards of March and April will arrive and the grass will spring up like never before."

Jerry found her eyes with his. Their gazes held. He saw the feverish determination in hers, she saw the doubt in his. Each one knew the clash of wills with the other.

"Come on in, Jerry. We'll find us a cup of coffee," Manny said, cheerfully.

Hannah followed them to the barn, watched them unhitch. Here was a real buggy horse. Sturdy, long and lean, built for stamina, the miles eaten away by the tireless hooves placed on the road. This horse could easily run ten or twelve miles without exertion, the light buggy pulled along like an afterthought.

"Nice horse," she said amiably.

Jerry nodded. "No relation to King or Duke."

"Doesn't surprise me."

"Where's Pete?"

"Well, between the coyotes, vultures, and whatever other hungry creature roaming these plains, he's pretty much eaten up," Manny said, shaking his head at the thought.

"So, he didn't make it then?"

"No."

"Poor old coot. He was a good one."

"Yes, he was. My father drove a double team of those Haflingers' all the way out here. Hundreds of miles," Manny said, proudly.

Jerry shook his head.

Hannah fought down her rising sense of irritation. How could he be proud? The thought of that journey was a memory she would like to erase, a humiliation.

"You have to admire the pioneer spirit of the man," Jerry said, giving Manny a wry smile.

Manny grinned back. "Yeah, he had that. His faith too. He was a big believer in God's generosity, always looking for miracles and blessings along the way."

Hannah glared and said, "He was a dreamer. He lived in a world of unreality where things were made of fluff. Like a dandelion seed on the wind. That was our father."

"Hannah!" Manny stopped, suddenly knowing that to press his point would only bring the eruption of the volcano of bad memories Hannah harbored within herself.

"It's true."

Sarah was glad to see them come in out of the cold. She set steaming cups of coffee before them, apologized for the lack of food, pie, or small cakes to set out.

"I can't imagine the pantry has come to be so low so quickly," she said softly.

"You have enough, though?" Jerry asked, his voice tinged with so much kindness that Hannah felt a lump rising in her throat.

They spoke of the weather, the drought, the cold, and the dust. Hannah did not join in.

Did they ever speak of anything else? It would snow and rain. Spring always brought moisture.

Tension mounted as Jerry spoke reluctantly of Jake Fisher's thoughts about returning to Lancaster County, and Ike Lapp's inability to keep his family fed comfortably.

Sarah's eyes turned involuntarily to the pantry.

Hannah spoke then, her words hard, falling like metallic objects. They were hard to listen to, rife with disgust at anyone who even thought of returning. Pioneers lived through drought, worse than this. Amish in Lancaster County were the wrong people to settle the West, living in ease and comfort all their lives, cloistered, their sense of community stronger than the slightest sense of adventure.

Jerry's eyes snapped, his suppressed anger rising like steam. "Hannah, you do realize if this drought does continue, we will be forced to leave. It has nothing to do with what we want. Think of our horses, our cattle. Your cattle. No rain, no grass."

"You are only settling on a future, surmising it will not rain. Of course it will. Spring always brings moisture," she said tartly.

Jerry left that day with no idea that Hannah was in need of a horse. Hannah was so angry she decided to walk to the café in Pine if she had to. She'd never ask that arrogant man for so much as a stick.

Manny took it on himself to ride over to the Jenkinses to ask for a horse, telling them of Hannah's need. Of course, Hod provided.

A brown horse with a black mane and tail, an evil glint in his bulging eyes, large yellow teeth he bared repeatedly, as if the sight of them would buy him instant control over any human being.

He took a strong dislike to Hannah, who promptly named him Buck, knowing half of North Dakota's wild-eyed, half-broke mustangs were called Buck.

Hannah was as determined to ride him as Buck was determined she wouldn't. Dust flew from the area surrounding the barn as he shied, crow hopped, and kicked his way across the dead grass and dirt.

After one especially bad hopping, he arched his back and leaped like a grasshopper, unseating Hannah, who slid sideways off the saddle, landing on one shoulder, her legs folding like a piece of fabric beneath her.

She got to her feet, grasped her stomach and gasped in pain, every gulping breath a shooting pain in her ribs.

Manny caught Buck, then came to stand by her, watching quietly, knowing his sister well. Any word of condolence would be batted to the ground like a whining insect, her pride so thoroughly battered that no could help.

She was bent over, taking small painful breaths, her eyes wide as if she was astonished. After a while, she straightened slowly, ran a hand across her left side, grimaced, flopped a hand on her shoulder, and squeezed. She gave a small laugh, almost a sob.

"Give me the reins."

"You can't, Hannah. You can't."

"I can, and I will."

Manny stood helplessly, as Hannah, white-faced, her mouth contorted with pain, grabbed the reins, swung herself into the

saddle with obvious effort, and kept her seat as the horse immediately began his maneuvers to unseat her.

Sarah came from the house, shouting, waving her arms. This
was too much for her, so she tried to put a stop to the horrible
spectacle of Hannah's life being in danger.

"Manny, you must stop this!" she pleaded.

"You know she won't stop, Mam."

They watched as she kept her seat, a firm hand on the reins.
She goaded the unruly horse with the stirrups, kicking her legs
to the side to bring them crashing against his sides, which only
served the purpose of antagonizing him further.

The horse hunched his back, hopped, kicked, and shied
sideways, but Hannah remained seated, grim with pain and
single-mindedness. She was staying on this cranky horse, there
were no two ways to look at it.

Unseated again, she landed hard on her backside. Her chin
flopped onto her chest, and her teeth gouged a formidable hole
in her tongue, blood pouring from the wound and forming a
grotesque appearance of serious injury, when in truth, the worse
abuse was to her pride.

Sarah cried out, grabbed Hannah's arm, her face terrible
with fear and outrage. "Hannah! You must stop! You have to
stop this nonsense and come to the house. That horse will do
you serious harm."

Hannah took up her skirt hem to staunch the flow of blood,
refused her mother's pleading, grabbed the reins from Manny,
and got back on the horse, who eyed her with belligerence, and
began his antics all over again.

When she flew through the air a third time, coming down
hard on one knee, her head flopping forward like a rag doll,
Sarah cried out and ran to her, crying in earnest as she tried to
pick her daughter up.

This time, Hannah followed her mother to the house, hob-
bling on one good leg, dragging the other, blood running from

her mouth, splattered with dust and dirt, sniffing back the blood and mucus that poured from her nose.

She was spitting and gagging on the porch, so Sarah stayed with her, watching to make sure she wouldn't be sick, or faint from the pain.

They went inside as Eli and Mary watched wide-eyed, their pencils poised above the tablets they were writing on.

"What happened?" Mary quavered.

"Oh my, children. Weren't you watching from the window?" Sarah asked, applying a cold washcloth to Hannah's mouth.

"Ouch!" Hannah yelled, flinging the washcloth across the room.

"She was trying to ride a new horse," Sarah called back over her shoulder as she bent to retrieve the washcloth.

So be it, then, she thought. Let her suffer. She rinsed the cloth, put in the washtub with the other soiled laundry, and set to punching down her bread dough.

Hannah hobbled to the bathroom, bent to peer into the mirror. The painful throbbing in her mouth had to be more than a cut in her tongue. It was. She'd knocked a tooth out, a bleeding black spot where the tooth should have been. At least it was on the bottom. No one would notice. Must have gone clear through her tongue.

No cold washcloth was going to do a bit of good. She'd have pain for days, so she may as well get used to it. She opened a drawer, got out a clean rag, and applied it, then sat on the wooden rocking chair and closed her eyes.

The sound of Sarah punching bread dough, working it, kneading with her hands, was strangely comforting. It told Hannah that her mother would let her alone to handle her wounds in her own way, that she was capable of doing just that, and life would go on the way it had before.

The scratch of the children's pencils on paper, Abby's soft guttural baby talk, the crackle of the fire in the firebox of the kitchen range, were all comforting, normal sounds of everyday life. She'd heal. No use telling anyone she had a missing tooth. It was no one's business.

But her knee was on fire, shooting pains that went from her ankle to her thigh. Tentatively, she moved her foot from left to right. Then she lifted her heel off the floor, resulting in more stinging pain. She could bend it all right, so nothing was broken. Her ribs, she couldn't say. There was a tender spot so sore she could barely place the tip of one finger on it. Likely she had cracked or broken ribs, but that wasn't anyone's business either. She could hide that, as well.

But that night when she went to lie down, she cried out with the sharp sensation in her back, bringing Sarah to the door of her bedroom. Hannah told her she believed there was a mouse under her dresser; it had scared her, running over her foot.

"We'll have to set a trap," Sarah said, and left the room.

There was only one way Hannah could rest, and that was gently rolling on her left side, drawing her knees up to help balance the weight on what she now believed to be a broken rib. Probably more than one.

Luckily, her job at the café started the following Tuesday, which allowed her almost a week to heal. There was no question of getting back on that unruly horse's back until she had healed.

As it was, she rode painfully into Pine on Goat, white-faced, perspiring beneath her layer of heavy coats, the pain almost more than she could bear. Her family needed to eat, so she had to do this. There was no turning back, no self-pity. It was an obstacle that she needed to face, and she did.

Betsy greeted her at the back door with words that were less than kind or caring. "You look washed out, girl. Like you seen a ghost. Well, come on. Git going here. We're on behind. Got a special going. Seems like folks are dirt poor, but these men can come up with a dollar for a cup of coffee and eggs and home fries.

She yelled at Bernice, the sallow, pimply-faced young woman who was shoving a mound of fried potatoes into a huge, black, cast iron skillet.

"Show this one around. Name's Hannah. And watch yer mouth. She ain't used to the kind of language comes from your mouth."

Bernice didn't say hello, offer a hand, not even a nod. "Call me Bernie. This here's the egg pan. Lard up here on the shelf. Them's the eggs. We got sausage, bacon, or steak, but don't use a lot. Folks ain't got the money. Sometimes, the judge from the courthouse comes by and he gits steak. Eats the bloody thing half raw.

"This here's the deep fryer, potato cutter. Hamburgers made in the same pan as the potatoes. Fry 'em hot and crispy. Bread here on the shelf. We hafta make the soups yet. Bean soup, vegetable soup, and rivvel soup with milk. Saltines on a plate. I'm the cook. You're the helper. You do whatever I say, and we'll git along great."

Hannah nodded and thought Bernice was like Buck, all eyes and yellow teeth. Hannah disliked Betsy, Bernice, and every customer she was forced to serve. She hated the way the men ogled her way of dressing, waiting quietly without saying a friendly word while she set down platters of potatoes and eggs, filled coffee cups, her mouth throbbing, her ribs stinging with pain.

If Betsy or Bernice brought their food, there was instant banter, loud laughter, jokes thrown across the room, but the minute Hannah appeared, the silence was stifling.

Well, nothing to do for it. Her mouth hurt too much to talk anyway, so let them gawk at her Amish dress and the *dichly* pinned to her head.

Bernice said her appearance at least shut them up. "Can't stand that Roger Atkins," she said. "He thinks he can come in here and eat like a . . ." She caught herself, then continued, "Like a hog, then leave me or Betsy no tip. Not a penny. Complains about the price of a dollar for his coffee and eggs. I told him the other day if he don't wanna pay it, he can go home to his old lady and eat hers. That made him mad!"

Hannah moved fast, learned what needed to be done, and went ahead and did it without asking. Weak with pain and hunger, she almost cried when Bernice told her they were allowed a half-hour break after the lunch rush.

They were only allowed to eat breakfast leftovers, soup, or bread. Meat was too expensive, and it cost too much to drink the sodas, but they were allowed one cup of coffee or a glass of tea.

Hannah sank gratefully into a rickety old chair in the corner, balanced a bowl of bean soup with one hand and two thick slices of buttered toast on the other. She ate carefully, out of anyone's sight, soaking the toast in the hot broth, eating and savoring every mouthful in spite of the pain.

Surely she had never been so grateful for a hot bowl of soup. Her outlook and energy revived, her cheeks blooming with an attractive blush, she carried out the legendary steak to the judge from the courthouse, the one Bernice had mentioned.

Gray hair lined his temples, but he was younger and far more attractive than Bernice had let on. The judge looked up from the paper he was reading, his brown eyes kindly taking in the strange appearance of this tall girl who brought him breakfast.

The courthouse was in Dorchester, but there was a small, squalid room behind the garage in Pine that served as a sheriff's office. When he came to the dusty little town of Pine with paperwork, or he needed to pick up reports, he liked to stop at Betsy's café for a steak with his eggs.

No one could fire up a grill as hot as Betsy, producing legendary steaks, perfect eggs every time, and biscuits as big as saucers with the consistency of a pillow. Spread with homemade plum jam, it kept him coming back at least once a week.

He had no interest in any of the women who worked at Betsy's, but he enjoyed the easy banter with which he could joust verbally, always giving Betsy a good argument. She knew he was smart—all judges were brilliant—so it was a challenge to voice her strong opinions on any subject. All these farmers and ranchers knew in these parts was the weather, hay, and cows, always in that order.

His name was Dale Jones, in his forties, more or less, never married, never met a girl he couldn't live without. He enjoyed his work, kept a neat house on Ridge Street in Dorchester with the help of the Widow Mary Billing, who was at least sixty and as thin and wrinkled as a strip of beef jerky.

Dale Jones's life was predictable and well-ordered. He presided over the small country courthouse, sending mischief-makers and miscreants to jail, sentencing thieves and drunks and murderers, which were rare but frequent enough to keep him riffling through the occasional law book.

Hannah walked out as if she owned the place, tall, thin, and disdainful, carrying the tray as if she was queen for the day. She placed it in front of him with the long, tapered fingers on her well-shaped hands, stepped back, and glared at him, then turned on her heel and left.

Dale Jones blinked twice. He felt an ill-timed flush suffuse his face, the need to follow her to apologize for being here at the café, in fact, to make amends for his existence, and for the fact that it didn't snow this winter. He watched the swinging door until it was still, then shivered with the sensation of a cold winter wind swirling over his table.

He picked up his fork, broke the yolk of an egg, lifted his head to look at the swinging door to the kitchen again. He was afraid she would return; afraid she would not.

The judge picked up his serrated steak knife, proceeded with his usual sawing motion, severing a nice mouthful, the crispy outer edge falling away as he worked. He used his fork to spike a piece and thrust it into his mouth.

Back in the kitchen, Betsy ordered Hannah back out to his table. "The first rule is, serve the food, let him eat, then go see if he needs a refill of his drink, or if he wants anything else."

Hannah eyed her boss, cold-eyed, her arms crossed, fingers gripping her elbows. "He can ask."

Betsy stepped closer, shoved her face into Hannah's startled one. "You wanna work for me, you do as you're told. I run the show here. You don't. Go!"

Hannah went. She had never felt so silly, so unnecessary. How do you ask someone if their meal is to their liking? What if it wasn't? What if he didn't want a refill? What if he wished she didn't exist?

She reached his table. He looked up.

Hannah arched a perfect eyebrow, decided to tell it like it is. "Look, I'm not comfortable asking you if your food is good, or if you need more water. I'm new at this, so if you want something, you'll have to ask."

Dale Jones sat back in his chair, arched an eyebrow back at her, and asked what she meant by that?

"I don't like to serve someone."

"Then you had better look for another job."

"There is none."

"Hard times?"

Hannah nodded and left.

Betsy returned, immediately began her garrulous queries, whereupon Dale immediately changed the subject, asking who the new girl was, with just the right amount of nonchalance.

"Oh, they're homesteaders. Buncha Amish came out here thinkin' to git rich with horses and windmills and whatever else they got goin'. This Detweiler family's been here awhile. The old man was killed by a crazy cow, wife and kids hangin' on. This is the oldest daughter. Tough as nails. The only reason they stay here. Don't look fer any of 'em to outlast the drought, if it keeps on."

"How do they make a living?" he asked.

"Cows. A herd they started. Gardening. The mother's old man back wherever they come from helps 'em out. S' what folks is sayin', although I can't rightly tell."

Dale Jones nodded, chewed, contemplated the word "Amish." He slanted a look at Betsy.

"What's Amish mean?"

"Beats me. They dress weird. Sloppy-lookin' homemade stuff. Supposed ta be better'n normal folks, but I kin tell you right off, this Hannah ain't. I know lotsa people behave better'n her."

"That's her name? Hannah?"

"Yep."

Betsy changed the subject to the drought, the awful, bone-chilling cold, and if it didn't rain until spring it would fix the ranchers.

"This area's gonna be like the Dead Sea. No life, if'n it don't rain. You think it wouldn't affect you, huh? Sittin' in that court-house, rakin' in the money. Who's gonna go to court if there ain't nobody around to thieve and carry on?"

Dale Jones ate his steak and shrugged his shoulders. He wished Betsy would go back to the kitchen and allow him to finish in peace. He was not in the mood to listen to more of her gloomy prophesies.

But, of course, she drew back a chair and settled herself into it, leaned back and searched his face.

"You hear about the hardware?"

Dale Jones shook his head.

"They say he's sellin' out. To who, I couldn't say. Wife's crazy in the head. Fred Bird says they're moving east. Back to Balti-more. Harry come in here the other day, looked sick, fish out of water, eyes buggin' outta his head. Shoulda seen him. You know Harry? He's a good man. Good man. You watch, she'll take him back to wherever they come from, he'll leave his heart and soul out here on the plains. He won't last long, you mark my words."

"Who's Fred Bird?"

"You know Fred. Tall and skinny. Ranches out your way. Runs a few cattle, some sheep. He owns part of the feed mill."

Dale Jones nodded, pushed his chair back and reached for a toothpick. His eyes slid to the kitchen door. Betsy noticed. A hot jealousy swelled in her chest.

When the door swung open and Hannah appeared with a tray of clean glass tumblers, Betsy saw Hannah through Dale's eyes.

Creamy, tanned skin, huge dark eyes surrounded by long black lashes. How could anyone have lashes like that if they had no cosmetics available? That tall, easy grace. The small straight nose. Her shoulders held high, her head on the slim neck.

Ah, Betsy knew the confidence of youth. She knew too that hers had dissipated over the years. A once-firm waistline had developed soft rolls, like the black rubber tube of a tire. Jowls, a heavy neck.

Betsy sighed, was suddenly grateful for the ebb and flow of her regular customers, the life she lived in her café, serving ordinary folks in ordinary ways. She didn't need Dale Jones.

CHAPTER 23

APRIL CAME AND WENT. THE COLD BLEW ITSELF OUT AND A WARM, DRY wind took its place. The grass bent and rustled, broken and battered by the winds of winter. Some yellow-green color appeared at the base of the buffalo grass, the sedges, and switch grass, all native grasses that made up the tough, hardy winter pastures.

Some of the ranchers, like the Klassermans, had introduced bromegrass, also crested wheat grass that was better for hay. No new growth showed on any of it, only the rattling of hollow stems, bent by the endless gale, covered by the gray brown dust and sand-like grit.

Hod came over, folded himself down on the porch step, and said he needed help going through Abby's things. They could have most of it.

So on a day when Hannah wasn't working at the café, they drove Goat the seven miles to the Jenkinses, the children riding on the back of the spring wagon, glad to be out of the house and away from the homestead for a day.

They found a dusty box of journals, old black-and-white speckled composition books with crumbling, yellowed pages, scribbled with lead pencil marks like the scratches of chickens.

"Go ahead n' read," Hod urged them. "You won't hurt nobody. She didn't have anything to hide."

Hannah sat and read, spellbound, surrounded by heaps of old dresses, shoes, tablecloths and white china, dresser scarves and faded magazines.

The first entry was July 21, 1913. Hannah strained to read the barely legible scrawls. *Hot. No rain yet. Garden dry. Two calves born. One of 'em got scours.*

July 24, 1913. *Been so hot all day. No rain. Trying to water whenever I got extra water. Clay took his first step. Miss my momma, but don't do no good thinking on it.*

Hannah got up, went to a rocking chair by the window where the light poured in, revealing much more writing than she had thought was there.

Some days the wind makes me crazy, like I'm about to lose my mind. I have to be stronger or I won't make it one more day. Can't let Hod know, he got his heart set on this here place.

August 3, 1914. *Things isn't good. The baby is scrawny and sickly. I don't want to lose another one. God is watching over us. I hate this prairie, the wind, the separation from other folks. Can't tell Hod.*

Hannah caught her breath. She chewed on the inside of her lower lip. Surely Abby wasn't writing the truth. Surely this was not the way she truly felt. And Hod had no idea.

September 10, 1914. *Getting ready to winter in. Got squash and potatoes in. The onions. Beef cows doing good. Baby taking on some weight. The wind makes me wonder how on earth I will survive the winter. God will watch out for me I guess. I get these awful pains in my heart, standing and looking out across the prairie. There is nothing, as far as I can see, except grass and sky. How is a woman supposed to survive without the pleasure of company. My homesickness is like a growth in my stomach, crowding out my breath, barely allowing me enough air to breathe on my own. I feel only half alive.*

Abby! Hannah sucked in a breath. She held her finger at the page she was reading and turned the composition book from left to right, searching for truth, as if there would be an inscription on the cover that labeled it fiction. She read on, incredulous.

November 11, 1914. *Cooked cornmeal mush. Hod brought home a hundred pound sack. Snow came last night. Good thing we got the meal done. Now I can fry mush. Hens all but quit laying. They'll start again in spring. I dread the night coming on. That's when the loneliness is worst. I wake up with my heart pounding, feel like I'm going crazy. I have to get out of bed so Hod don't know. Don't need to worry him.*

November 23, 1914. *I think I need help. Nights getting worse. Fear something terrible. Need to get help. Maybe I can be strong. Hope so.*

"Mam, come and read this," Hannah called, holding out the black and white notebook. Sarah was folding a stained linen dresser scarf, its border crocheted with a colorful variety of threads. She placed it carefully in a cardboard box, smoothing it with her palm, as if it was a caress for Abby herself.

"Let me see," she said, reaching out for the proffered book.

She read quietly, then lifted startled eyes to Hannah. "What?" she whispered. "Not Abby."

"That's what I thought."

"But she was everything a pioneer woman should be. Tough, resilient. Nothing fazed her. Nothing."

"The death of her little girl baby," Hannah corrected her mother.

"But this? This suffering? You can feel it in the composition book." Sarah shook her head.

Together, they read more entries over the course of time. The cold, the heat, the length of time Abby lived without seeing anyone but Hod and the babies, which must have been Clay, Hank, and Ken.

"Listen," Hannah said. *I am like a bottle filled with tears during the day. The stopper comes out at night with Hod sleeping beside me. Tears run out of my eyes and I can't stop them. But I don't wake up fearful no more, so must be these tears are a good thing. Maybe they'll stop soon, then I'll be all right. God is watching over me, I can tell. Especially when Hod is out riding the prairie.*

February 13, 1916. *Days are terrible long. Hod confessed his sin to me. Don't want to write in this book what it was but I made a trip to town and had a talk with her. Marcella Brownleaf, he said. Part Indian. It's going to take me awhile but I'll get over it. He went to the tavern. Otherwise, it wouldn't have happened. Bible says to forgive, so guess I'll follow God's Word.*

Hannah lifted her face and shrieked to the ceiling. "Mam!"

"Shh. Hod will hear."

"She's an awfully good Christian woman, Mam. I bet you anything this is the reason she seemed to rule Hod and the boys. I bet he lived the rest of her days trying to make it up to her. You know, it gave her the upper hand over him."

Sarah looked at Hannah. It was moments like these when she loved her daughter. When Hannah forgot herself long enough to be happy, animated, absorbed in something of interest.

"Could be," Sarah nodded, smiling.

"Listen."

December 3, 1916. *No Christmas presents, Hod says. Wolves got too many cows. No money. We have food, no empty stomachs. Killed all the old laying hens. Stuck the meat in Mason jars and cold packed it.*

"Sounds like it," Hannah said grimly.

When Hod came in, they packed the journals with the things they would take back home with them. Hod waved them away, saying it was just woman stuff written in there.

"I don't need no books to mind the past. Them days was heaven on earth, every day. Me and Abby and the boys, God's green earth, some good horses, and a buncha ornery cows that bucked the tar outta each other.

"We built this here home with hard work and lotsa good luck. Coundn'ta found a better woman, always happy, kept herself busy, never pined for her ma and pa the way some of 'em done. She was a good woman. None better."

A slow anger burned in Hannah. She couldn't look at him sitting there with his blackened hands spread across his denim-clad knees. Unwashed denim, she'd wager. As satisfied with his own past as she'd ever seen anyone. The man had no idea of the sadness poor Abby had dealt with.

"Where are the boys?" Sarah asked. "We'll soon be through here, so Hannah and I can cook supper for you, leave it on the back of the stove."

Hod looked at Sarah, then nodded, shook his head repeatedly, saying now that would be just awful nice of her.

Reluctantly, Hannah placed the books in the boxes, carried them out to the spring wagon, returned to find her mother peeling potatoes, with Hod hovering at her elbow.

Potatoes! Why did the Jenkinses always have food? It seemed as if their pantry and cellar was always well-stocked, even during the days of drought that stretched on and on.

Hannah decided to ask and was given a good enough answer. They had over one hundred fifty cows. Wolves got a few calves, coyotes maybe, but those longhorns were hard to bring down with their horns. "Take a few away, we won't know the difference," Hod said.

Did he know the Detweilers had only five cows remaining? Her pride firmly in place, Hannah decided to keep that bit of information to herself.

"So, how's the winter treating your herd?" he asked, at the moment Hannah decided not to tell.

"We lost five." This from Sarah, who wouldn't think of keeping anything from Hod.

He whistled low. "So you have what, five more? Six?"

They left the Jenkins ranch that day with Hannah refusing to speak to her mother, a dark cloud of outrage riding above her head. It was none of Hod's business how they were faring.

Besides, he didn't have to stand there and give that low whistle, then search Sarah's eyes before looking at the bright blue overhead light, the dry sky that stayed the same throughout the winter months.

Did Hod see something in Sarah's eyes? They acted like, well, almost if there was a secret attraction, the way they could tell what the other was thinking.

Sarah lifted her face to the sky. "You know, Hannah, if the heat arrives, the grass already parched, what will keep the cows alive? How long will the wells continue to give water, if it hasn't rained for a year?"

"It isn't a year."

"Yes, it is. Our last rainfall was in May of last year."

"You're keeping a journal?"

"No."

"Well, then you don't know."

Sarah rode in silence, Abigail like a sleeping rag doll in her arms, jostled by the movement of the wagon, the steady sound of Goat's hooves on the hard packed dirt. Everywhere, as far as they could see, was a kind of defeated springtime. As if the earth gave its best, valiantly trying to produce one green shoot, then gave itself over to the drought.

There was still hay in the barn. The grass cured on the stalk all around them. As long as the windmill turned and the well gave its water, replenishing the tank, they'd be all right. She had to keep her job at the café, no matter what.

Manny still had not found work, but kept busy cutting trees for firewood. Hannah estimated they had enough old windfalls in the creek bottom to last another four years, maybe five. So, according to her way of thinking, their situation was not dire, yet.

Sarah rode beside Hannah, harboring a secret wish that God would shut the clouds from giving rain for awhile longer. She didn't know where these thoughts came from. She just knew that Abby's journals were past echoes of her own nights, and too many days.

With a glad fierceness, she had returned to the homestead, to the plains, to stay with Mose's grave, her beloved, who lay buried beneath the sod, his soul departed to his God. But her fierce desire to survive, to prosper, had begun to sputter, and now she found it hard to find the remnant of a spark.

To go home. To find peace and fellowship with her sisters. Estrangement was real. It was the amputation of a family tree's limb, injuring the entire tree. She could not speak of her waning need to fellowship with those who had moved here—the Ben Millers and the Ike Lapps, the new Stoltzfuses. Hadn't her heart leapt when Jerry Riehl spoke of their wish to return home? And then, her father, waiting to arrive. Had that been God's will as well?

Her last letter home had been filled with the situation surrounding them, an act of God, circumstances beyond their control. Would they still have failed, in the face of this drought? She glanced sideways at Hannah. Her face was unknowable, set in stone.

What was she thinking? What would she do when confronted with the fact of their failed homesteading? She wouldn't mind at all if the rest of them returned home. She'd be only too glad to watch them leave.

Sarah sighed deeply. Perhaps it would begin to rain, and they would continue on as before. They would build the herd, build their lives, the church would grow. Clearly, she was confronted with two choices. Which one did she truly desire?

And still the rains did not come. There was no point in planting the garden; the seeds would lay in a row of dust.

When the sun took on the shine of summer's heat, the shimmering waves that spoke of midday fierceness, Sarah stood on the porch, a hand turned palm down to her forehead, shading her eyes from the unrelenting glare, watching the brown grass rustling in the wind. She could see no way to survive. She would wait, say nothing. Someone would surely come to speak of these dire conditions.

Manny walked up on the porch, sweat staining the back of his shirt, his hair lined with moisture. Beads of perspiration formed on his upper lip, and for a moment, Sarah thought she could detect a certain desperation in his dark eyes.

"Getting hot, isn't it, Mam?" he asked, always pleasant, always hopeful.

"Yes, it is."

A comfortable silence stretched between them. Both looked out over the arid land and made no comment, as if they knew their words would be like a cloud of small flies, bothersome and useless.

Sarah had just turned to go in to check on her bread dough, when she thought she saw the beginning of a gray cloud in the west. She hesitated, took her stance by the porch post, one hand held to her forehead, squinting out over the expanse of prairie to the horizon.

"Is that what I think it is?" she asked.

"Where?"

Sarah pointed with a shaking finger. "Does that look like a storm cloud to you?"

Manny looked, then squinted, straining his eyes to see what appeared to be a narrow brown mountain ridge.

"I would say it looks like a storm cloud, except it's the wrong color. It's a yellowish gray brown."

They stood, watching. The cloud increased in size. As it approached, the wind picked up, sending tumbleweeds and loose vegetation hurling ahead of it.

Sarah ducked her head, closed her eyes and spit the dust and grit out of her mouth. Dry grass smacked into them.

There were no prairie hens, no rabbits, gophers, or birds run-ning ahead of the storm, the way it sometimes happened when a thunderstorm moved across the prairie.

On it came. The wind whipped the corners of Sarah's apron, slapped her skirt to her legs, and tore at her covering until the pins pulled her hair.

It roared across the prairie, surrounding them with a thick wall of dust and whipped-up dirt, flung along by the force of the ever-increasing wind.

Sarah cried out, remembering the windows. Inside, Eli and Mary stood wide-eyed, pulling down the wooden, paned windows.

"Will it rain now?" Eli asked, his brown eyes hopeful.

The faith of a child, Sarah thought. Abby ran to her, flung herself into her arms, and held tight, her face hidden in Sarah's neck.

Manny came through the door, struggled to close it behind him, his face pale in the disappearing light. The house took on a yellow sheen, a dark aura of weird light, as the wind shrieked and moaned around them. It was as if the whole house was being scoured by buckets of sand, a hissing, rasping sound above the roar of the wind.

Sarah sat down weakly, gazing at Manny in disbelief. He shook his head. It was literally a storm of dust and dry wind, hurling anything loose ahead of it, grass and weeds, loose boards and scattered hay.

They both thought of the windmill at the same time. Manny grasped the arms of the chair, pulled himself, a question in his eyes.

"No. No. You can't go out in this. The windmill will . . ." her voice faded away.

"Mam, this wind will propel the gears to a frantic pace. It will break the mechanism that operates the pump."

"We have Ben Miller."

And still the wind blew, the dirt scoured the house. Dust seeped in between the sash of the windows, beneath the door frame, even drifting down from the ceiling, as if an invisible hand was scraping it down.

The wind increased, the sound like a scream, setting their teeth on edge. They both thought of Hannah, in town, hoping she would be all right, wondering how long the wind would stay.

Eli huddled on the couch, drew his knees up to his chin, his hands to his ears, blocking out the sound. Mary began to cry softly, cradling herself with her thin arms.

"Come, Mary," Sarah said, above the roar of the wind. She crept into her mother's arms, with Abby, her arms stealing around both of them, reaching out for all the security she could find. Manny sat with his mother, pulled Eli into his own arms, huddled together at the mercy of wind and dust.

In town, men raced for their automobiles, tried to beat the storm to their distant homes dotting the outskirts of the small group of homes and businesses. Many became stranded along the roads, careening haphazardly into ditches or mounds of scattered weeds and dirt, unable to leave the small amount of safety their vehicles afforded.

The town hunkered down, prepared to wait out the worst of it. Betsy seemed to take it in stride, shut doors and windows, talking above the roar of the wind and saying this would bring a change now. "It'll blow the drought out. The rains'll come now."

Hannah stood, stiff with fear and disbelief. The battle that raged within her was worse than the storm of wind and dust outside the café. Her mother and Manny were barely managing to have enough will and determination to stay, no matter how hard they tried to convince Hannah otherwise.

Would this send them straight back to Lancaster County, their land of milk and honey?

Manny had attended the meager church service on Sunday, came home to his supper of bread and stiff, salty cornmeal mush, and talked of Ike Lapp's plight. Talked of that Marybelle, mostly, how she was withering away, much too thin, without proper food.

Hannah knew he cared for her; she could tell by the dreaminess in his eyes. She knew too that for a young man harboring thoughts of a rosy future with the doe-eyed Marybelle, there would be only hardship and disappointment on the prairie.

Only rain would save them. Perhaps it would appear after this, in the form of thunderstorms, the way Betsy said it would.

How had it come to this? This grinding down of wills, flattening hope, leveling even the staunchest spirit? Even Sarah turning into a white-faced, grim-lipped ghost of her former self?

Doddy Stoltzfus would come. His brothers, Ben and Elam, would bring renewed hope. Wasn't hope the necessary ingredient for pioneers?

Hannah sat in the darkened café, the electric lights blinking above them at first, then not blinking back on, leaving them in the gray storm-riddled light of midday.

In the afternoon, when the sun would have been slanting in through the tall front windows, a thin light appeared through the blowing dust and grime. The roaring ceased, trickled down to a more manageable gale, the kind of wind that flapped at skirts and sent light objects flying off porches, twirled leaves and bent tall grasses. Betsy said she may as well go home, if she wasn't afraid the wind would start up again.

Hannah shook her head, waded dust to the barn, hopped on Goat's back, and entered a world of brown dust and dirt that clung to every available surface, flattening the already skeletal grasses and whipping the dry earth into drifts like snow. Where the wind had scoured the loose dirt, only a bare, swept area remained, wide, deep cracks like broken glass separating the soil.

Hannah tied her handkerchief across her mouth and nose, to help breathe better. She could not stop turning her head, her eyes searching every surface, hardly able to absorb this world without life.

It was like the end of the world, when there would be nothing left. A sense of foreboding made her shiver. Was there ever a time when it simply did not rain for more than a year? That in itself seemed an impossibility. It always rained, even here in the West, didn't it?

She had no one to ask, no one who could assure her that the rain would come. Well, God, but He wasn't very reliable, so far.

Yes, she did believe in God. Of course she did. It was unthinkable to go through life without acknowledging a Higher Power. It was just difficult to think of asking for rain, then believing it might happen. When, in truth, it might not.

Look at her father. He called it faith. Was it? Or was he merely determined, assuring himself over and over that God would hear him and do what he wanted if he fasted and prayed hard enough.

What was faith? Assuring oneself that God would do what you wanted? Or was it never asking for anything except God's will, not your own, be done? Faith was a mystery to Hannah, elusive as the wind. You were supposed to be able to move mountains with it, if you owned even a tiny bit, like the size of a mustard seed.

No one could ever move mountains, so did that mean no one had any faith? Maybe faith was not ours to have, but it was supplied by God at the exact moment He wanted us to have it.

Well, enough of these thoughts. Hannah shook herself, freeing her mind from the numbness of unreality that lulled her into a stupor. Nothing seemed real. The prairie seemed like an alien land, a barren place without humanity.

Some places on the road were drifted so high with dirt that Goat had to wade through. His head nodded faithfully as he put one foot in front of the other, staying on course, his horse sense taking him home.

Hannah dreaded her arrival. She knew the question of staying or returning to Pennsylvania would have to come up, and soon. What would she do?

Five battered, wind-driven cattle that lived on worthless, dry grass and water in the tank, likely coming from a well that sank steadily deeper and deeper each month.

She would wait to come to a decision until she spoke to the remaining Amish friends. What about the Klassermans? The Jenkinses? Would these sturdy local folks let the drought get the best of them? She wouldn't believe it until she actually saw them leaving.

As she neared the buildings, she saw the weird angle of the wind mill. The blades of the giant wheel, the metal paddles that caught the breeze so efficiently, spinning the great circle that propelled the water pump up and down, bringing gallons of cold water from the underground stream to the surface hung lifeless, at odd angles, completely still.

She heard the high bawling of the thirsty cattle before she saw them.

CHAPTER 24

THE RIDE TO THE HOMESTEAD IN THE FACE OF THE ONSLAUGHT caught Hannah's breath, held it, left her lightheaded, dizzy, her limbs weakened with the force of the windmill's ruin. Always quick to size things up, calculate the cost, deciphering the best plan, Hannah's mind went blank. There were no thoughts, only the black, painful realization that they were ruined, finished.

There were no funds to pay Ben Miller to restore the windmill. Every available source of water had dried up months ago. Underground streams ran quick and full, but with no means of bringing the water to the tank, it was useless. Hannah envisioned a deep, dark flow of life-giving water beneath bedrock, layered with ancient stone and packed, dry soil, dead roots of any growing thing, destroyed from beneath, and pounded to powder by the merciless scourge of hot wind and fiery sun.

She was brought to the present by Buck's nickering, Goat stretching his neck to rid himself of the reins, his nose reaching for water. He pressed his face deep into the brackish hay-strewn moisture in the bottom of the trough, lipped the sides as if it would give him a few more drops.

Hannah peered to the bottom of the galvanized water trough to find only a layer of soggy hay and silt, dust turned to mud, leaving a foul, swampy odor. She straightened, led Goat to his stall, hung up the saddle and bridle, stood in the middle of the barn and gazed blankly at the water trough, her mind refusing to accept the inevitable, unable to focus on a solution.

Her breath came in quick gasps, as panic overtook her, seized her in a cloying grip like tentacles from some alien creature.

She walked to the side of Buck's stall and leaned against the rough boards as she struggled to gain control. She thumped a fist against her chest, licked her lips, swallowed, tried to regain some sense of calm, knowing there was only one solution.

Kneel before Ben Miller's mercy. Cast themselves on someone else's benevolence, the thought nauseating, repulsive. Strutting bantam rooster that he was, he knew everything. Never let her get a word in edgewise.

She found Manny and her mother white-faced with fear. There was no water.

Hannah would not meet their eyes. To protect herself, she did not want to acknowledge the questioning, the defeat, so she sat on a chair and put her head in her hands, unapproachable.

Abby's chatter, the hum of the children's low voices, the sighing of the wind in the eaves, were the only sounds in the room. The house stood, squat and low, the ruined prairie spreading out on every side, falling away to the edge of the horizon, the windmill rising like a battered sentry, fallen by the very power that had brought them life-sustaining water: the wind.

The roiling, eternal wind, that movement of air around them that never ceased, harnessed by the clever windmill, only to be stripped of its power by too much of it.

This homestead. Built by hands of generosity, caring hands that helped them back on their feet after the brutal fire, standing here, a testimony to her father's hopes and dreams, a harbinger of prosperity and peace, the lush grasses feeding the herd as it grew into a vast number of fine, black Angus cattle.

The herd was Hannah's dream. She invested so much of her time in the fledgling herd, nurtured and cared for by hard work and planning.

She saw the vacant buildings, the interior destroyed by wild creatures of the plains, the dust and desperate sadness of failure. The evacuation of men and women who had met the end of their ability, leaving these echoing dwellings containing nothing but the ghosts of what might have been.

Cars would rumble by, the occupants turning their heads idly, viewing the abandoned buildings with disinterest, a vague knowing of another person's collapse. Another victim of drought and the Depression.

The knowing raked across Hannah's body like a physical pain. She clutched her stomach, leaned forward over her crossed arms, spoke to the floor in ragged edged words of defiance.

"We're not giving up, so you and Manny can stop looking at me with all that stupid pity. I'll ride Buck. I'll find Ben Miller and bring him back. He can fix it."

She lifted her head, her eyes black with a dangerous light. Sarah lifted a hand, shook her head. "No, Hannah. No. We are done. Manny and I . . ." her low voice was sliced off by the dagger of Hannah's outcry, a volley of harsh and rebellious words that pressed against Sarah, smashed her down into a chair, and held her there, robbed of an answer.

Manny stepped up, pleaded, spread his hands in supplication. "Come on, Hannah. Can't you see?"

"All I see is your refusal to try," she spat.

Fueled by the force of her anger, she saddled and bridled Buck, who sidestepped every time she tried to place a foot in the stirrups.

There was no help from Manny, so Hannah's determination swelled with every misstep. It was her's or the horse's will, and he was not winning.

She arrived at the Ben Miller homestead, stiff and sore, so thirsty her mouth felt as if it was stuffed with cotton. Buck was lathered with white foam, breathing hard, wild-eyed and cranky. He tried to bite her shoulder when she led him into the barn, so she swatted him with the ends of the leather reins, which only angered him further, resulting in a good strong kick with his left foot.

"Whoa, there!" Ben Miller stood in the barn, short, wide, the same generous grin he always wore creasing his round face. "Some horse you have there."

"Yeah, well, he serves the purpose." She told him of her mission.

Ben raised both eyebrows, then bent his head, wagging it back and forth like a big dog. "Hannah, I don't know how to tell you this."

She froze.

"We're quitting. Going back home. No one can outlast this drought. Senseless. Unwise. We know better. We know where there is a much better land of opportunity. I made a mistake, falling in love with the whole pioneer-spirit idea. Lost a lot of money. But so be it."

Hannah's eyes hardened, her chin raised. "Quitters."

Ben Miller spat with force. Hannah swallowed and looked at the wet spot on the dusty barn floor. Anger sizzled across Ben's friendly blue eyes, reddened his face.

"You best listen to reason, girl. I'd rather be alive and a quitter, then dead and still hanging on."

"I'll stay with my cattle."

"Hannah, listen. It's very serious. If it doesn't rain this summer, there is no possibility of survival."

She knew this to be true, but bucked against it anyway. "Sure there is."

"Well, I ain't standing here arguing with you. Come on into the house. You look like you could use a meal. How about a drink of water? Tin cup there on the wall."

Hannah lunged, filled the cup and drank greedily. So they were leaving, Hannah thought, as she entered the house to find cardboard boxes and satchels piled everywhere.

Ben's wife, Susan, met her with glad eyes, a wide, welcoming smile. "Oh Hannah, we're going back. I'm so happy, I'm counting the days till the train departs for eastern civilization."

"Good for you." Spoken abruptly, devoid of warmth.

Ben glanced at her sharply. "Do you have time to make a cup of tea for Hannah?"

"Of course. Oh, of course. You do look hungry. Susan bustled around her kitchen, talking, putting yellow cheese on a blue platter, some cured meat, saltine crackers, and small, brown cinnamon-speckled cakes.

Cheese. Saltine crackers. How long since she'd eaten either one? For a moment, Hannah thought of comforts, things she'd always taken for granted, the butter on her bread, the eggs from the hen house, flour and sugar and coffee. It would certainly be easy to settle into the old way of life, but that was precisely why she resisted.

It was too easy. Life as dull and tasteless as vanilla pudding without sugar. Going back to Lancaster, marrying someone, having many children, she knew no cheese or butter or saltine crackers would ever spice her life to anything interesting.

"Let's go," she said to Ben.

"You should give me an idea how badly the windmill is damaged," he said.

"It's wrecked some."

"Is the main structure still standing?"

"Yes."

Ben drove the spring wagon loaded with tools. At the homestead, he eyed the battered windmill and said he'd need help, he couldn't begin to do the work by himself. He paced the area around the windmill, repeatedly lifting his gaze to the battered paddles, talked to himself, and finally drove off in the spring wagon pulled by two tired horses, saying he'd be back with more men, a welding machine and, he hoped, lots of luck.

This was all said without the usual rolling good humor, leaving Ben Miller as dry and brittle as the surrounding plains, which struck fear in Hannah as she stood in the wind, watching him drive off.

He returned the following morning with Ike Lapp, Jake Fisher, and Jerry Riehl, the spring wagons piled with tools. They brought a galvanized milk can of water, warm and tasting of metal, but it was blessed water, slaking their thirst as they drank cupful after cupful.

Ben Miller took Sarah aside, stood in the yard, in the heat of the late morning sun, the wind tugging at Sarah's skirts, flapping the edges of Ben's straw hat.

Hannah paced the kitchen, the sight of the two people talking in the yard drawing her to the window repeatedly. What were they saying?

The conversation went on too long. At one point, Sarah reached into the pocket of her skirt, produced a handkerchief to wipe her eyes. Ben was going back. Would he persuade her mother?

The men swarmed the windmill like black insects, crawling up the rungs as loosened paddles occasionally fell to the ground in chilling spirals. What if the wind caught one and flung it haphazardly to slice into the body of an unsuspecting victim?

They repaired, hoisted, welded, all day. By nightfall, the windmill was spinning, the giant arm pumping fresh water from the underground stream. It poured from the pipe, sloshed into the tank, bringing the thirsty cattle in a headlong dash, jostling and shoving into position, drinking for a long time.

Hannah stood, her arms crossed, noticed the beginning of the falling off of the cattle's flesh. They were thin. Thin and thirsty, unable to escape this heat and brittle grass. She asked Ben Miller for a bill, proudly, her eyes boring into his with a fervor he could not understand.

"Hannah," he said quietly. "I know you don't have the funds to pay me. I'll strike a bargain. You agree to give up and return to Lancaster County with us on the train, and your debts are paid. There is no way on earth anyone will be able to make a living, let alone survive in these conditions."

Almost, Hannah let go. Let go of hope and determination, let her dreams evaporate like steam on a cold winter morning, allowing the sight of the ribs with the cowhide stretched over them to determine her choice.

But, what if? What if it rained? What if this arid, dusty prairie turned into the lush paradise her father had envisioned? Each new day there was a chance the rains would come. There was water now.

She shook her head, met Ben's pleading gaze, shook it again. "No."

Ben sighed, looked off toward the house. He felt a deep widespread pity for the widow Sarah, and her son, faced with an awful decision. But so be it. He had his own family's welfare to consider.

Jerry stayed behind, sent Jake with Ike Lapp and Ben Miller. He asked Hannah to walk with him, he wanted to talk to her. Her first impulse was to refuse, but the thought of the broken windmill and the cow's ribs had softened her somewhat, so she told her mother and Manny that she was walking with Jerry.

The night was dry, wisps of heat rising from the dust on the road. The stars above them were blinking on and off like tiny white lanterns in a sea of night, the wind rustling what remained of the waving prairie grass. There was no moon, but the road was discernable by the bright light of the stars.

They did not speak. The silence stretched between them, taut as a bowstring, uncomfortable. Hannah cleared her throat, pushed a strand of dark hair behind an ear. She bit her lip, her hands hung loosely at her sides. What did he want?

Jerry stopped, turned. "Hannah," he began softly.

She made no reply.

She heard his sigh, or was it merely a sound of the wind?

"I'm so afraid I'll mess this up."

Still she did not answer.

"I want you to know that I'm not forcing a decision on you. I just hope that somehow I can find the right words."

Her heart fell. Was he asking her to marry him? Her breathing stopped for a long moment, then resumed, leaving her light-headed, her heart clattering in her chest.

"You know and I know . . ." He stopped. "We both know there are dire conditions here. It will be tough for anyone or anything to survive. I'm not sure it's possible."

She cut him off. "It's possible."

He chose not to challenge her response. She felt him reach for her hand. She withdrew it, fast. His hand came in contact with her skirt, then fell back.

They walked on in silence.

There was no yipping of coyotes, no howling of wolves, no prairie hens skittering through the grass by the side of the road. Only a barren silence that stretched for many miles on either side of them, a wide circumference of a pitiless stretch of forgotten land, blessed neither with rain or snow. It was a land that threatened to creep into a heart or soul, rendering it barren as well, creating human beings who stopped feeling and experiencing life fully, turning them into dull, lifeless versions of the prairie itself.

Jerry felt a rising alarm as they walked. Hannah seemed as firm and as obstinate as ever. Would she clench the bit in her teeth, headstrong and self-willed until she met her own doom? The thought of a future without the presence of Hannah in it was simply not possible.

"Wisdom easy to be entreated." These words were put into his mind. He took a deep breath and tried again.

"I know what your ranch means to you."

"No, you don't."

"Maybe I don't."

"You don't. Not if you're planning on returning to Lancaster. You have no idea."

"Did I say I was going back?"

"Yes."

"I'll stay, if you'll stay."

She stopped walking, startled. "Everyone else is going back. My mother wants to return as well."

"And you?"

"I'm staying."

"Jake is going back."

"So?"

He turned and grasped her shoulders, his grip firm, drawing her toward him until she could smell the steel and oil of the windmill, the perspiration of the day's heat.

"Marry me, Hannah. Marry me while Ben Miller is here to perform the marriage. We can get a license from the courthouse. We can live together, but don't necessarily have to, well, you know, live as man and wife. We'd be married in name only, and you would have a man to help you with the cattle, protect you from the riff-raff that ride around and prey on out-of-luck homesteaders. I know you don't love me, Hannah. You love only the land. You don't have to love me. We'll just live together, try and make a go of it, if that's what you want."

Hannah could always draw on the strength of anger, swat any choice or confrontation aside like an annoying insect. Anger and rebellion were her strength, especially with people. They served her purpose well, to hide the weakness beneath, erase the softening, the opening of her heart, and the trust that went hand in hand with love.

But now, they fell from her grasp. It was, by all means, a solution. Could she do it? What if she fell in love with him and he could never love her, stick thin and mean as the old cow that had killed her father?

He drew her closer. She wriggled out of his grasp, stepped away, breathing hard.

"Don't do that."

"What?"

"Touch me."

"All right. I won't."

"I will do it if you promise not to touch me or try to kiss me the way you did before. Married in name only. The only reason I am allowing this is to save the homestead. Do you have money? Means of surviving the drought?"

"Yes, I have some money put by."

"Then yes, I will marry you."

Jerry's heart sang, lifted the song to the heavens and danced with the stars, leaped from star to star, flinging the notes with abandon. He wanted to hold her, and yes, of course, kiss her, pledge his undying love for all eternity, now and forever, with God's richest blessings bestowed on both of them.

He put his hands in his pockets and said, "It's settled then."

"You understand, of course, that this is a marriage out of necessity. It will save the homestead. So don't go around thinking I'll fall in love and be a real wife, because it is not going to happen."

"I know. I agree to keep my part of the contract." It would be enough to sit across the table from her, three times a day. It would be enough to talk to her, every day. Learn her ways, learn the reason she was as hard to please as a wild horse, and as untamed. He looked forward to the challenge.

Suddenly shy, she fell silent. The wind whispered the words of promise neither one could say.

The following morning, Sarah sat down weakly, Hannah's words like an approaching cyclone. She threw both hands in the air, wagged her head back and forth, disbelief clouding her eyes.

Manny reacted with a stare, and silence.

"Are you sure?" Sarah finally uttered.

"You're going back, aren't you?"

"We are."

"Well, then. I'm staying. We are staying. We're going to try and make it through the drought."

The ceremony was held the following week. Heat shimmered across the prairie, but the summer breeze flapped the curtains in the living room as Ben Miller preached the Amish wedding sermon of creation, Ruth and Boaz, Samson and Delilah, and the story of Tobias from the Apocrypha.

Hannah sat, dressed in a blue Sunday dress and a black cape and apron, which replaced the white Swiss organdy normally worn by the bride, simply because it was not available.

She was breathtaking in a neat, white covering. Her hair was done loosely, combed in waves and darkly shining. Slim, sitting with natural grace, Jerry stole glances of admiration all through the service.

Hannah looked at him once, then kept her eyes averted. She was going to have to watch out. Dark haired, dark eyed, with that long, tanned face and wide mouth, he was startlingly handsome in a white shirt and black vest and trousers.

They were pronounced man and wife, given the blessing of old, the same vows that had been repeated for hundreds of years, a tradition that would stand the test, and be carried on until the end of time, a precious heritage, the birthright of the Amish.

Now, of course, Hannah was blind to this, her eyes covered by her own will and determination to save the homestead at all costs. Her vows were spoken without love or spirituality. This was the only way of obtaining what she most desired.

If the drought continued, they'd get by. He had money. She would tell Betsy she was quitting at the café, which was a joy of enormous size, not having to make that long, hot ride into town.

The wedding meal was simple, mostly supplied by the remains of Susan Miller's pantry, and most of Jerry's. Potatoes mashed with milk and salt, the usual *roasht* made with only bread cubes and onion. Thin gravy made with a whisper of chicken broth.

There was wedding cake, however, made with lard and white sugar, eggs and white flour, a rare and special treat.

Hod Jenkins sat with Ken and Hank, uncomfortable in stiff collars, Clay with a red-faced, sweltering Jennifer. The Klassermans sat side by side, perspiring great splotches on their Sunday finery, madly fanning themselves with white handkerchiefs, wondering if this service would ever end.

There was a general upheaval afterward, packing, hauling things to the rail car in Pine, an endless, wearing task as the summer heat mounted. But the day came when it was time to go, time to part, time to leave Hannah in the care of her new husband.

Sarah swallowed her tears, put on a brave face, knowing any display of emotion would only draw out Hannah's indignation.

Manny shook their hands, taller than Hannah now, wished them both *Gottes saya*, then turned to search the small crowd for the petite Marybelle, already awaiting the promise of a rosy future in Lancaster County.

Mary sniffled a bit as she clung to Hannah, produced many facial contortions as she desperately tried to keep her tears to herself.

Eli said he was going to raise pigs in Lancaster County and have bacon at every meal, then shook hands gravely, like a well-mannered little preacher.

Hannah held Abigail's small form, soft and pliable, molding her into her own body, kissing her soft cheeks over and over, before handing her to Sarah, tears dangerously close to the surface.

The train whistle blew, a short, sharp blast, followed by another. Ben Miller's family boarded the passenger car. Jake Fisher shook hands, clapped a hand on Jerry's shoulder, thought for the hundredth time that Jerry must have become mentally ill out here in this forsaken, dry land. No one could pay him enough to marry Hannah Detweiler.

As the train pulled slowly out of the small, dusty station, the whistle sounded again, high and piercing. Steam poured from the underbelly of the locomotive as black smoke poured into the hot sky.

Hannah did cry, a great gasping sob as she saw her mother's face pressed to the dusty window, a handkerchief to her nose. Crying. Her mother cried to leave her with Jerry. This knowledge brought her own unstoppable sobbing.

Jerry heard and turned away quickly, jamming his hands into his pockets to keep from reaching for her.

Hannah snorted once, lifted her defiant eyes to his and said, "Let's go."

Jerry followed her to the spring wagon, and they rode off across the desolate prairie, sitting side by side on the hard, wooden seat in the bright morning sun, with the dust and tumbleweeds blowing ahead of them.

The End

HOME IS WHERE THE HEART IS

CHAPTER 1

Spring arrived on the North Dakota plains like a flirtatious young girl that whispered promises of warmth and sunshine, melting icicles and turning snowdrifts into untrustworthy mounts of sodden slush.

The long drought had come to an end thanks to the melting snow and ice that replenished the arid soil, turning the prairie into a quagmire of slick brown mud and crumpled yellow grass.

Hannah stepped off the porch, a woven basket full of wet clothes balanced on one hip and an apron containing wooden clothes pegs tied around her narrow waist. A married woman now, she still resembled the same Hannah Detweiler she'd always been.

Dark-haired, with dark eyes like wet coal, defiant, missing nothing, she strode to the wash line like a soldier, threw down the basket, and proceeded to hang clothes on the line in quick, furtive movements.

Hurrying back to the house, she looked neither right nor left, her mind churning on the best way to accomplish all that needed to be done when spring actually arrived.

The two-year drought had depleted her herd of cows to five head. Jerry said he'd had money put by when they were married in the fall of the year, but lately he'd given no indication of a stash of money or a checkbook. Her mother and siblings had returned to the home of their birth, with all the rest of the Amish folks who'd been bitten by the pioneer spirit but chickened out when it stopped raining. Soft Lancaster County stock that had everything handed to them by their fathers, and their fathers before them.

What did they expect in North Dakota?

Her mother wrote lengthy accounts of their lives back in Pennsylvania. Manasses (Manny) had begun courting Ike Lapp's adopted daughter, Marybelle, who was working as a hired hand for Sammy Stoltzfus, Rufus's Sammy. She lived with her aging father and two brothers on the homestead. Mary and Eli went to school in Leacock Township. Hannah read every letter with interest, but always threw them down as soon as she was done, as if she couldn't bear to think too much about the contents.

Deserters. That's what they were. It still stung about Manny. She never thought he'd leave the ranch. After all they'd been through, he followed his mother back East like the obedient puppy he was.

Well, she had Jerry, who'd married her, which was something. She had told him there would be no love involved. She wanted to stay on the ranch and his money was the only way they could. It was an arrangement that worked well, so far. Jerry was kind, talkative, but kept his distance. Like brother and sister, they lived together in the sprawling ranch house made of lumber that had been shipped from the East, already weathered gray, with a porch along the front, and a barn with a low-pitched roof and a barnyard. The windmill churned about three hundred yards behind the barn. There were five head of Black Angus cattle, four of Jerry's horses, and a few good mousers, wild as cougars, that slunk around the perimeter of the barn.

Beyond, there was only the vast immensity of the North Dakota plains, stretching in all four directions to a level horizon, limp brown grass, dead from the long drought, huddled in clumps of leftover dirty snow.

Hannah loved the land with an unexplainable passion. The emptiness and solitude suited her reclusive nature. She could breathe, expand, fill her lungs with the air no one else breathed, a luxury that was priceless.

People were like clinging vines, parasitic growths that wound their way around your well-being until the life was choked out of you. Most people annoyed Hannah. Especially men. Loud, sure of their own decisions, acting so superior to women, she couldn't stand any of them. Well, maybe Hod Jenkins. He knew more about this prairie, the weather, cattle, everything, than anyone she'd known.

If her mother had not been so devoted to her Amish heritage, she could have married Hod after Abigail died.

Hod loved the land, same as Hannah. She looked out across the wet prairie as she hung up the second basket of clothes, watching for Jerry. He'd ridden to the Jenkinses' without saying why, so she supposed he'd be back before dinner.

That was another thing she hadn't bargained for—marrying Jerry. She cooked three meals a day, but she hated it. Told him so, too. He'd grin good-naturedly, get down the cast-iron skillet, fry a few pieces of beef, and eat it with bread she had baked.

The bread was coarse and hard as a rock. She sawed at it with the bread knife, served it, and never said a word, so Jerry didn't either. The poor man tried to sop up the lumpy ground beef gravy to soften it, but it acted like a metal spoon and shoved all the gravy around on his plate. His mouth twitched, Hannah had seen it, his desperation to keep from laughing. She'd yanked her plate off the table, ran the dishwater, and hid her flaming face. She couldn't help if she couldn't bake a decent loaf of bread. Besides, he'd better count his lucky stars that she baked anything at all, with provisions so meager and times so hard.

Jerry didn't say much, ever. There were a thousand questions she wanted to ask him, but would never risk throwing them out into the air heavy with tension. Especially her insatiable wondering about this new winter wheat everyone was talking about.

What if they could raise a profitable crop along with the cows? Acres and acres of soft winter wheat that was sown in the fall, sprouted sturdily in spring, soaking up the cold rains and flourishing in the summer sun.

Other than Hod Jenkins, Jerry was the only person Hannah felt the slightest twinge of respect for. He was tall, wide in the shoulders, his long, dark hair often hiding his expression. A solid jaw, a wide mouth, and eyes as black as her own.

Jerry had loved her, pursued her, even kissed her at every opportune moment a few years ago when he thought he had a chance with her. Which he didn't. Still didn't, in spite of being married to her. She'd made that very clear. Only for his money, the last chance to get this homestead up and running. If they failed now, she saw no reason to keep trying.

She swept the wide, varnished boards of the living room floor, shook a few rag rugs out the door, then took up a soft cloth and began to dust the tops of the furniture.

The playful breezes set a loose board to whirring at the corner of the house, so she made a mental note to tell Jerry. Or, better yet, she'd fix it herself. She finished her cleaning, went to the barn to find the wooden stepladder and a hammer, rooted around on the tool bench until she found a few nails, and carried it all back to the house in quick strides.

She was settling the stepladder, trying to find a level spot so she could climb up to the eaves and fasten the loose board, when she felt hoofbeats vibrating the ground beneath her feet.

A rider appeared, bent low over his plunging horse, galloping in a headlong dash and throwing mud and dead grass, the white lather coating the wet coat of the winded animal.

Hannah stood rooted to the ground, not a muscle moving, as she watched the horse and its rider approach.

Closer he came. She gripped the handle of her hammer. Her breath quickened. A small man, he was wearing a flat-crowned, greasy hat, the brim flapping drunkenly. Soiled clothing, a coat that flapped open, revealing a torn shirt. When the horse slid to a stop, she knew who it was before she actually saw the sizzle of desperation in his eyes.

Lemuel Short! Old, wizened, hardened by another stint in prison, coming back to haunt her. The horse hung his head, his sides heaving, drops of sweat and flecks of foam dropping to the mud below.

"Hide me," Lemuel rasped. "They're after me!"

Hannah gripped her hammer and tossed her head. "I'm not hiding you. You want me to get in trouble with the law, same as you?"

Lemuel Short, small, tough, and wiry. He had terrorized the whole family after they'd shown him all that dumb kindness, nursing him back to health with the Scripture about loving your enemy seared into their consciences.

She looked up into the cold metal barrel of a pistol held by a thin claw that shook violently. Hannah didn't think. Propelled by a fierce disdain for this desperate little liar, she stepped up as fast as midsummer lightning, swung her hammer, and knocked the revolver out of his hand.

It clattered to the ground. Hannah swung the hammer again, hitting the haunches of the sweating horse, frightening him into a swift gallop, Lemuel hanging on to the saddle horn as he fought to insert his feet into the stirrups.

Hannah heard the receding hoofbeats, the unintelligible screams of the escaped prisoner, shrugged, and bent to retrieve the revolver, turning it over and over, noticing its silver gleam, the deadly shape of it. Stolen, too, no doubt, same as the horse. Well, it might come in handy, so she'd hang on to it. She turned to finish the job of nailing down the loose board, unshaken, her hands steady.

She wasn't afraid of him. Never had been. The sheriff would find him again and stick him back in jail, same as he always had.

She whistled low under her breath as she watched Jerry's arrival, forgetting about the silver revolver lying in the grass until he rode up to the house and stopped his horse, a question in his eyes.

"What?" Hannah asked.

"What yourself. What are you doing up on that stepladder?"

"What does it look like? Fixing a loose board."

"And what is this?" Jerry dismounted in one graceful, fluid movement, bending to lift the pistol in one hand and giving a low whistle. He looked up at Hannah. "I guess this fell from the sky?"

"Not exactly. Remember Lemuel Short?"

Jerry nodded, his heavy eyebrows drawn down.

"He rode in on a lathered horse and asked me to hide him. I told him I wasn't going to do it. He aimed that thing at me, and I knocked it out of his hand with my hammer." She jutted her jaw in the direction of the gun, shrugged her shoulders, and climbed down the stepladder, cool and unruffled.

Jerry watched her fold the hinges of the ladder, his mouth dropping open in amazement. Finally he said, "I hope you're aware of how easily you could have been killed."

Hannah gave her legendary snort. "He's like a harmless little rat. He's afraid of his own shadow. He thinks he can go around scaring people. Puh!"

Jerry looked at Hannah with an undetermined expression, then turned to go into the house. Over his shoulder he said he was hungry. Which meant she was expected to follow him and come up with a tasty dish in less than half an hour.

Instant rebellion! What was it about men, looking at a clock three times a day and thinking about their empty stomachs and a handy wife to cook them a delicious meal? She'd never get used to it. Never. What she felt like doing was telling him to get his own dinner. He knew how to fry mush, or a few strips of beef.

She walked stiffly into the house and began slamming cast-iron pans about on the cook stove top, harder than necessary so Jerry would know she was not pleased with him.

Jerry threw himself on a wooden chair on the porch, removed his straw hat, and raked his hands through his long, dark hair. He listened to the banging in the kitchen, smiled ruefully, and then looked out across the prairie.

What he wanted to do was go to the kitchen, tell her to go ahead and finish whatever she'd been doing outside, and he'd prepare dinner. But after living with her for a winter, he knew this was no ordinary girl who could be won with love and kindness.

He had married a hornet's nest of self-will, single-minded ambition bordering on obsession, the success of the ranch occupying most of her thoughts. Without fear, she was bold, having no respect for men, needing no lady friends as far as he could tell. She was the biggest challenge he had ever undertaken.

He had loved her for years. Ever since the day she drove that open buggy into the forebay of his barn in Lancaster County, soaking wet and irritable as the proverbial wet hen. Did he love her still?

His gaze was soft, filled with a nameless emotion, as he pondered their six months of cohabitation. They lived together but certainly not in peace and harmony. He had never held her hand or slipped an arm about her waist. He'd promised to keep his distance. Their marriage was only one of convenience. She needed his money to keep the ranch going.

What would the Amish in Lancaster County think if they knew? This was certainly not what he had been taught. Or she. Defeat rose its hideous visage and swept through him in a cold chill. It was just much harder than he had imagined. She did everything she could possibly think of to irritate him, to drive him to the edge of patience and understanding. And he had never figured out why.

He was ready to admit that God alone could change her temperament, change the way she looked at the world through her dark, angry eyes. He had always thought that love never failed, love opened doors, broke down barriers, acquired the seemingly impossible.

He wasn't so sure anymore.

Each day was a genuine battle. She needed good old-fashioned discipline but woe to the person who would deliver it. He grinned, listened to the pans banging and the dishes clattering. He'd continue praying, believing there was a reason he had always loved her, and see what God had in store for them both.

Jerry sat down at the table, waiting until she joined him, then bowed his head in silent prayer before lifting his fork to shove the fried meat to the side, helping himself to some green mush that vaguely resembled beans. Applesauce on the side, or was it some kind of preserve?

Grease and blood pooled around the meat. Underdone again. Grimly he cut it with his knife, lifted a forkful to his mouth, and chewed, ignoring the taste of raw meat and blood. Hannah ate very little, choosing the unnamed vegetable and bread and molasses. So Jerry helped himself to another piece of meat, which seemed to be a bit better than the first.

She wanted to ask him what he'd learned at the Jenkinses' but figured if he wanted her to know, he'd tell her.

He finished his food, leaned back in his chair, and told her about Hod and his two boys riding out on the prairie for a cattle check. Mild winter, less snow, but the wolves got too many of the calves. They figured at least ten or twelve of them.

Hannah nodded, her eyes averted as she toyed with her fork. "It's always been that way," she said dryly.

"Why wouldn't we try to raise something else, like sheep or goats or simply forget cattle and raise horses?" Jerry asked.

Hannah considered his question and for once came up empty. She shrugged. Jerry pushed back his plate, tilted his chair on two legs, his shoulders wide, hands in his pockets, his too-long hair falling into his eyes. Hannah looked away.

"I mean, surely there is something we could do to make a living, to keep the ranch going until it's ours, that isn't quite as dependent on the weather, which seems to be the biggest problem so far."

"Smart man," Hannah answered, a touch of mockery in her voice. Jerry chose to ignore the bait for an argument.

"There's this new strain of wheat. Winter wheat. Sow it in the fall, reap it in early summer before the drought hits. Hod talked about it. But you need to till acres and acres and with this soil . . . I don't know. I can only see reasonable profits with gas-powered tractors. Unless we find a tough breed of horses. Belgians? Mules? What do you think?"

A shadow crossed Hannah's face, a slice of dark remembering . . . the dying horse, the heat, the fanatic belief of her father. She clenched her jaw, her eyes hard and glistening. "What makes you think we couldn't use a tractor?" she asked.

"Hannah, we're of the Amish faith, and our bishops don't approve of modern machinery. So, if we're going to consider this winter wheat, I would suggest mules. They're tough and they're easy to keep. So, why not?"

"I won't allow any animal, horse or mule, to plow this prairie," she said, with so much force that she left her chair in one quick motion. Jerry raised his eyebrows and leaned forward until the front legs of the wooden chair banged against the oak floor.

"I didn't say that was a definite plan."

"Well, it's not."

"Why?"

Hannah turned to face him, her hands on her hips. "You weren't here to see my father kill Dan in the plow. He ran that horse until he fell over. Dan's breathing, the foam and sweat, the way the sun beat down . . ." Her voice trailed off. She turned to grip the edge of the sink and gazed across the brown landscape.

Jerry could tell how agitated she was by the rise and fall of her shoulders. He wanted to go to her, place his hands on her shoulders, and comfort her as best he could. But he didn't have the courage, so he stayed put.

She whirled around. "Of course, what would you know about that? You were safely at home in Lancaster County, shoeing horses and counting money, pitying those half-crazy Mose Detweilers that lit out for North Dakota after they lost everything!"

"That's harsh, Hannah."

"No, it isn't. You can't tell me you didn't hear about my destitute, misguided family. Everybody did. Our reputation was mud. Mud!" she shouted.

Jerry watched her, wondering where all this was coming from.

"You know you remember."

"I'm not going to defend myself about what your family did or didn't do. Of course, I remember hearing about you, but I certainly didn't know you, or worry about it."

"You probably laughed with all your buddies about those pathetic people who had no clue what they were doing."

There was no right or wrong answer to her senseless accusation, so Jerry got up, reached to the wall hook for his straw hat, and strode out the door to the barn. He forked loose hay into a neater pile, swept the forebay, and pondered Hannah's outburst.

Was her past so painful, the shame like a hidden disease? Who could tell what a headstrong daughter had suffered with the public shaming and all? Hadn't he heard something about a homemade distillery and whiskey?

Perhaps Hannah wasn't so hard to figure out after all. People were not all cut from the same pattern, that was sure. Some could live through a traumatic childhood and come out unscathed, turning into loving, normal adults, while others wallowed in thorny nostalgia that served to hurt only themselves. Was her bitterness a product of her past?

He decided to buy mules and asked Hannah to accompany him to a ranch ten miles southeast of Dorchester, close to a small town called Bison.

Hannah was cleaning, her apron front black with the cleaner she was using on the stove top. She kept rubbing vigorously without looking at him.

"Are you riding?"

"No, it's too far. Hod Jenkins is taking us in the truck."

"Us?"

"Oh, come on Hannah. You want to see the mule farm. This guy has other horses, too."

"I told you, I won't stand for farming with horses."

"Well, just a couple of mules for making hay."

She squinted her eyes and looked at him like a stray dog that hadn't decided whether he'd be friendly or take off running.

"I'm not dumb."

"I know."

"Well, then."

"Come on. Change your clothes. Wear a covering. You look extra pretty with a white covering on your dark hair. Better than that men's handkerchief you insist on wearing."

"What do you care?"

"You're my wife."

She almost told him she wasn't his wife, but she was, so there was nothing to say. Plus, she had to admit to herself that she wanted to see the mule farm. She ducked into her bedroom and closed the door firmly behind her.

He looked at the closed door, a small smile playing around his mouth. When she emerged, the snowy white covering was pinned to her sleek, black hair. The deep purple of her dress brought out the heightened color of her cheeks, her large, dark eyes snapping with anticipation.

She took his breath away, so he turned, kicked off his boots, and went to the sink to wash his hands and face. He was drying his face on the roller towel when he caught a glimpse of her watching him with an inscrutable expression, one that baffled him and tormented him for days. What was she thinking? Could he ever win her love?

She'd made it clear from the beginning that this was not a union based on love, and he had agreed, with a young man's audacity that he was invincible. Everything was possible, wasn't it?

In the spring, a young man's fancy turns to thoughts of love. Perhaps that was the ache in his chest, the concealed sadness and lack of hope. He'd thought he could do this, but after the long winter was over, the soft breezes everywhere, she was not responding to his kindness and seemed farther away than ever, an iceberg drifting away in dark, frigid waters, abandoning him.

Well, she was wearing her covering, so that was something.

The pickup truck rattled up to the ranch house, its blue color faded to gray, the fenders laced with rust, dust clinging to everything, mud splatters and bits of yellow grass on top of all the rust. Wooden racks sagged at various angles, flopping and waving precariously, while empty gasoline cans and pieces of rope and barbed wire, paper bags, and feed sacks puddled into corners or slid around to each side, depending on the direction the truck was headed.

Hod's window was down, a greasy coat sleeve slung across the door, his once-white Stetson aged into varying shades of brown, gray, and yellow, his weathered face like fissures in old canyon rock.

His eyes lit up at the sight of them, his tobacco-stained teeth appearing as his face crinkled into a smile like a discarded paper bag. "Ain't you a sight for old eyes there, Hannah? Better looking 'n that husband o' yourn."

Jerry grinned and bumped Hod's arm with his fist. This impressed Hannah more than anything. Jerry's easy relationship with Hod and his boys, Hank and Ken. Clay, the oldest, had married Jennifer, a girl from town who, in Hannah's opinion, wasn't worthy of him. Hannah had almost been persuaded to be his girl and leave her family and the Amish way of life. She wasn't exactly sure what had held her back, other than her mother's prayers, she supposed.

Jerry held the door for her, and she scrambled inside, scooting over beside Hod to allow room for him. She hadn't realized a truck was so narrow. She had to sit sideways to allow Hod to shift gears with that odd-looking stick with a porcelain knob at the end, which meant she was jammed up against Jerry with no room for her feet.

"May as well hold 'er on yer lap, Jerry. This Ford ain't new. Think they're makin' the 1947 models wider, I heard."

"We're fine," Jerry said, smiling at Hannah, who was looking straight ahead with the high clear color in her cheeks that meant she wasn't fine at all.

Hod looked over at her. "Loosen up, honey. My word, we ain't goin' to yer ma's funeral."

Hannah gave him a tight smile, and he shrugged his bony shoulders and talked nonstop to Jerry. Never could tell about Hannah, pickin' her moods. Worse than an ornery old cow.

Hannah rode along, alternately jostling against Jerry, or trying to slide away from him, which meant she'd interfere with Hod's driving. She was acutely aware of Jerry's nearness, the length of him, the hard strength beneath the sleeve of his denim coat. He smelled of hay and horses and wood shavings and toothpaste.

He'd smelled of mint toothpaste once, long ago, when he kissed her. If he dared to put his arm around her, she'd bite him!

CHAPTER 2

THE TRUCK SLIPPED AND SLID THROUGH RUTS FULL OF MUDDY SLUSH. All around them the prairie lay flat, waiting to be awakened at the first kiss of the sun. Gray skies were woven with patches of white and blue, scudding along as if threatening the land with another blast of winter's fury.

Hannah half-listened to Hod and Jerry's conversation, her eyes roving over every corner of the Ford's windows, taking in the barbed wire and rotting old posts of a derelict ranch, the well-kept buildings of another. But mostly she searched the horizon for cattle, observing the size of herds, their well-being, and which ranchers raised wheat or corn, or simply cut the prairie grass and used it to feed their livestock.

It was good hay, nutritious, that native shortgrass called buffalo grass. Sedges and switch grass, the never-ending, God-given supply that kept all the overhead costs of these ranches to a minimum.

She jabbed her elbow into Jerry's arm, pointing to the right, where a distant herd of antelope streamed over a rise like brown and white liquid, as smooth as the wind. Those antelope sightings filled Hannah's soul the way she imagined Bible reading and prayer filled her mother's.

The untamed freedom of wild creatures—their lack of restrictions and rules and authority—thrilled her innermost being. It was spiritual for her, raising a belief in the God of nature, of a creation that was so huge and vast and awesome, it could only produce a deep humility.

The way the antelope coexisted with wolves and coyotes, prairie dogs and foxes—it was all an endless circle of life. One Hannah understood and wanted to belong to as she raised cattle and cut grass for a winter's supply of hay. She would be strong enough to withstand anything nature threw at her.

Living on the plains was an endless challenge. The future was unpredictable. Seasons came and went, with their surprises and dangers, leaving all the ranchers and farmers scrambling to make ends meet, to face the drought and snow storms and wind and fire, the wolves and lawless men, and to rise above the despair.

Hannah glanced quickly at Jerry's profile and wondered if he felt what she experienced when she sighted the antelope. Nothing in his eyes or the set of his jaw gave away his feelings, so she looked steadily ahead as the truck ground its way through water-filled ruts and potholes.

It would be exciting to see what actually occurred after a drought, as far as the return of vegetation went. Would the wildflowers reseed themselves? Hannah thought of her mother squeezing tomato seeds onto a rag, leaving them to dry for planting in the spring. Leaving pole beans and chili beans to dry, the seeds rattling in the leathery pods like dead bones. But how long could soil be dried out before roots and seeds died? She wanted to ask Hod, but decided to listen instead.

"Yeah, this dry spell's been a doozy. Guess you heard how many people from town's moving to Illinois?"

Hannah shook her head. Jerry said no, he hadn't heard.

"Guess a buncha folks is raisin' turkeys. Cheap land. Rains there, mostly. Sounds as if some folks is thinkin' turkeys is good profit. Ralph went, you know, Ralph at the feed mill. His wife's been bellyachin' as long as I've knowed her to git him to move off these plains. Good ol' Ralph. He'll hate them turkeys. Dumb-er'n a box o' rocks. A turkey chick will drown in its own water bowl. Abby tried raisin' them dumb chicks every year. Mighta kept one outta a batch o' twelve."

Hod turned the steering wheel sharply to the left, reached down to shift gears, rolled down the window to send a stream of brown tobacco juice out of the opening, then rolled the window back up.

Hannah swallowed and looked straight ahead.

"Owen's been thinkin' on movin', didja hear it?"

"The Klassermans?" Hannah whipped her head around, shock and surprise widening her eyes.

"Sure."

"Why? Why would they consider moving?"

"Wal now, honey, that I couldn't tell you. Guess you'll have to ask 'em the next time you see 'em. I heard he's tired o' the battle. Think he lost a good bit o' cattle. That's the trouble with them fat Angus. They're fine till the goin' gits tough. Now, look at my steers. Them longhorns is uglier than a mud-splattered cat, skinny and mean. But they'll git through jest about any-thing. They'll travel for miles, exist on scrub and old dead grass if they have to. The Klassermans' is too soft."

Hannah sat up, clutched the dashboard, her mouth com-pressed to a grim line. Doubt stabbed her chest. She flinched from Hod's words. The Klassermans' ranch, the well-rounded, beautiful Black Angus herd had always been her goal. And here was Hod, the true survivor of the plains, who took every disas-ter as it came, met it head on with real grit and good humor. As tough as the land itself. Would Jerry be up to the challenge? Or would she always be holding him here without his heart really being in the land?

For one panicked moment, she regretted the desperation that had driven her to marry him. Her heart pounded in her ears. She chewed her lips as she listened to Jerry's gravelly voice.

"Are you serious? I've been thinking a lot about cattle raising since the rest of our group moved back to Pennsylvania. Whether it's a good idea to attempt it at all in these parts."

A shot of anger coursed through Hannah. These parts. Huh.

Jerry continued, "I finally came up with the conclusion that you have to have something for the land, for the life, living on this wide-open land. It has to be in your blood, the way milking cows or horseshoeing, or anything else gets in your system and stays there. I'm about to agree with you about the Angus, too."

Hannah drew in a sharp intake of breath. "I'm not raising longhorns." Hod looked at her. Jerry didn't. They bumped along in silence.

"Seems to me you don't have much say so in the matter, missy," Hod said. "Yer married to this feller, Hannah. He seems to have a good head on his shoulders."

"You know I don't like longhorns."

"Wal then, you jest might have to move to Illinois and raise turkeys."

Hannah searched Hod's profile for signs of laughter and was shocked to find there was none. He meant it.

The subject was dropped, the cab of the truck filled with uneasy silence. Hannah was relieved when the truck nosed its way to the left, following a path of brown mud and bits of gravel to a set of gray buildings clustered around a stand of cottonwoods. Leafless and wind-blown, they appeared dead from the drought and hot, pulsing winds.

The buildings were well-kept though, fences mended, roofs in good repair, barn doors hung straight. And yes, there was one of Ben Miller's windmills, tall and straight, whirring away, the long steel arm driven by the paddles of the wheel pumping water from underground streams, the only source of water in the years of drought.

The house was long and low, like theirs, Hannah observed. The yard was bare and windswept, without clutter. Two medium-sized dogs came tearing around a corner of the house, barking uproariously, their short, pointed ears alert, their short legs muscular and pumping like pistons.

A curtain was pulled aside from the low windows that faced the driveway. There was no sign of an automobile or truck. The dogs took up their position at the door of Hod's truck, alternately bouncing on their short legs and barking.

"Which one of us wants to get chewed up first?" Jerry asked Hod, laughing amicably.

Hannah stared out the window, thinking that if this was a horse farm, she'd eat someone's hat. There was not a single horse to be seen anywhere.

Hod opened his door, swung to the ground, and was instantly surrounded by the yelping, jumping canines. "All right, all right, that's enough. Calm down. I ain't gonna hurtcha."

The door of the house burst open and a small, thin man appeared, poking his arms into a denim overcoat, a black felt hat with a narrow brim pulled low on his forehead.

"Hey, hey. Knock it off. Here. Shut up! Toby! Tip! Cut it out." The dogs quieted immediately, sat on their haunches, their mouths wide, tongues lolling, pleased to have announced their master's visitors.

"Hod Jenkins! How's it going, old man?"

Hod grinned, stuck out a weathered hand, and gripped the man's hand. "Good. Good. Couldn't be better." He turned to the truck, lifted a hand, and beckoned with his fingers. "Brought you someone interested in mules."

Jerry got out, held the door for Hannah. Introductions were made, with Jerry's easy friendliness and Hod's teasing making short work of feeling accepted and liked, in spite of their Amish clothing.

The man's name was Obadiah Yoder. He looked at Hannah's white covering and said his mother used to wear one of them. He came from a plain background, he said. River Brethren. Used to baptize in rivers. An old, old religion that went way back. They still didn't accept automobiles.

Now he and his wife weren't practicing members anymore. Being the only ones for hundreds of miles, they'd fallen away from some of the old practices. Never had any children, but hard telling what would have happened if they had, being the only River Brethren for miles around.

When Jerry nodded in agreement, Hannah held back a snort. What was he agreeing about? There would be no children for them, so he didn't have to hang on to his Amish ways for them.

"So, you want mules?" Obadiah asked.

"I'd like to look at what you have, see if I can get a team of four."

"Four?"

Jerry nodded yes. "You could kill a horse on this land."

Hannah swallowed, felt the heat creeping into her face. Now, why did Jerry have to say that? She felt as if this Obadiah Yoder could see the fact that her father had done just that, the memory of it like an exposed wound that festered with contempt.

"So, you're planning on tilling the prairie?"

"Well, there's all this talk of winter wheat, so I figured it might balance out the loss of calves and help keep a steady profit going," Jerry said evenly.

"It's gonna hafta rain, sonny," Hod said dryly.

Hannah ground her teeth. What was all this honey and missy and sonny? As if they were mere children. What did Hod Jenkins know about getting ahead, with his ranch in disrepair and the prairie crawling with ugly cattle that were nothing but a set of horns, long hair, and ribs?

Jerry said something about yeah, they'd have to depend on rain. *Oh, just shut up*, Hannah thought, crossing her arms and biting down hard on her back molars.

Obadiah chuckled, a sound like a prairie hen trying to attract a mate. Hannah glared at him through half-closed eyes. "Well, if you want to look at mules, then I guess I'd better send Tip and Toby to get them for me, huh?" he asked, his lean face wrinkling into a full smile.

He looked at the dogs, who watched his face intently. They stood on all fours, shifting positions, whining and begging. When Obadiah said, "Hep, hep," they were off like a shot straight across the prairie, disappearing into vague shapes in less than a few minutes.

Hod whistled. Jerry shook his head. Hannah wanted to stay quiet and aloof, but she couldn't help being intrigued by the dogs' instant knowledge of their master's orders, the eagerness with which they flew to obey.

"What kind of dogs are they?" she blurted before she could catch herself.

"They're Blue Heelers," Obadiah said. "Bred in Australia, also called Australian sheep dogs. They're easily trained. Herding animals is bred into them. I've had them most of my life, although these two are exceptional. Never had better dogs."

Hannah nodded and thought of the many ways they would be valuable on the ranch. Manny had left his dog but it had disappeared like fog in a hot sun the minute he left on the train. She looked at Jerry, who was paying no attention to her, watching the direction the dogs had gone instead. She wouldn't have to answer to him for every little thing she wanted, since their marriage wasn't the way most people's marriages were.

She had no money of her own, that was the thing. She had to ask him for everything, which included these dogs. Did he even like dogs?

Hannah heard the hoofbeats long before the brown mules trotted into their line of sight, the dogs dodging in and out of the moving hooves, never making a sound, simply pushing the mules in the direction of the barn, steadily working together as a team, guiding them through the wide gate into the wooden corral.

After Obadiah closed the gate, he reached into a pocket of his coat and handed each dog a treat that looked like beef jerky as he praised them for doing so well.

There were eight mules. Hannah climbed onto the second rail of the board fence and looked them over, her hands clutching the top rail, wondering why this fence was so much higher than most corrals she'd seen.

The mules stood facing her, their long, narrow faces like corncobs, their ears the size of a good sail on a boat. One was as ugly as the next. Mud brown. Big hooves, ratty tails that had long hair only on the ends. Her father said man created mules, breeding a donkey and a horse, so God really did not create them, which had rendered them useless to him. He would never own a mule, or use one to plow his fields. A camel was almost better looking than a mule! Hannah had seen pictures of camels in a Bible story book, so she knew their eyes were huge and soft, with sweeping black lashes like little brushes. There was simply not one nice feature about a mule!

Jerry stood apart with Obadiah and Hod, conferring, a man's conversation that excluded her. The wife. She had absolutely no say in the matter. Hannah couldn't believe she was caught in a situation very similar to what her mother's had been. Quiet, taking the back seat, obedient. Every ounce of her rebelled against it. She didn't want these mules. She was not about to make hay to keep these knock-kneed, flop-eared creatures alive. She stiffened when she felt Jerry beside her.

"Hannah."

"What?"

"What do you think?"

"Does it matter what I think?"

"Of course."

"They're mud ugly!"

Jerry laughed long and loud. He reached up to grasp her waist to pull her off the fence, which frightened Hannah so badly that she jumped off backward and almost lost her balance. She stepped back, away from him, refusing to look at him.

"Hannah."

"What?"

"I know they're ugly, but they're God's creatures too."

"No, they're not."

Jerry cleared his throat. "I know what you mean, but these mules are good mules. Top of the line. I mean, look at the power in those long, deep chests."

"They'll be tired after the first hour carrying those ears around!"

Jerry whooped and laughed. Hannah tried not to smile, her face taking on all sorts of strange contortions.

"Hannah, listen. It's our only hope of putting in a crop of wheat."

"We could get a tractor."

"You know what I want."

"Then why do you want my opinion?"

Jerry sighed and looked off across the prairie. "I know you don't want the mules, but you do want to try to raise the wheat. We already discussed this, didn't we?"

Hannah shrugged.

"So, it's mules and wheat or no wheat," Jerry said evenly.

If only she didn't feel as if she was giving in to Jerry, it wouldn't be so bad. Her whole being wanted to refuse him, watch him flounder and wheedle and beg, then refuse him anyway. Guilt welled up in her, like a blot of black ink that she could not ignore. For a fleeting instant, she wondered at the need to control the men in her life, the disdain for her father, her superiority over her brother, Manny. And yet, she was helpless to stop it. She didn't want the mules, it was as simple as that.

"How much money do you have?" she asked, short and blunt.

"Enough."

"To buy two dogs, too?"

"He doesn't have more than these two."

"You get the mules. I get the dogs."

"You can't buy these dogs."

"I know. I want two just like his."

Jerry caught her gaze with his own, hers black and defiant, but with the beginning of a golden light behind the darkness. What passed between them was mysterious, not decipherable to either one, but its evidence was known. Like two opposites that melded for a split second, producing a miniscule spark of recognition, they both knew the first inch of a long journey had begun, here on Obadiah Yoder's farm, west of Dorchester on the North Dakota plains.

The shining, two-bottom plow was drawn through the crumbling soil, still dry after the snows of winter, the brown mules plodding along under the warm spring sun with seemingly no effort at all.

Hitched four abreast, the new leather harnesses gleaming, Hannah was taken straight back to her childhood in Lancaster County, watching her father plow the soil with his Belgians. She loved to hear the mules' hooves hitting the earth, the clanking of the chains hooked to the plow, the creaking of the leather as it moved with the mules' muscles.

Jerry stood on the steel-wheeled cart, balanced seamlessly, driving the mules with one hand, and turned halfway to watch the soil roll away behind him, pulling the lever whenever he came to the end of the space that would be wheat.

The summer had flown by, with haymaking, a new and bigger corral built around the barn, the beginning of the new herd of longhorns grazing around the windmill.

They had sold the Black Angus cattle to Owen Klasserman, who had dispersed of his cattle, his farm equipment, and then sold his ranch to a wealthy cattle baron from Texas.

Sylvia cried great wet tears for Hannah, as well as every neighbor woman for miles around, saying she would never have better neighbors, no matter if they traveled from one end of the world to another.

Hannah swallowed her snort, endured Sylvia's soft, perspiration-soaked hug and felt not the least regret to see the shiny, pink couple ride away, probably never to be seen again. She did write the news to her mother, who responded in a month's time saying she was so happy indeed to hear that Sylvia was able to move out of North Dakota.

So, nothing had changed. Her mother, Manny, and Mary and Eli were settled in, happy to live on the homestead in Lancaster County among a growing population of the Amish faith in an area of Pennsylvania called the Garden Spot by many. Which is certainly what it was. Fertile soil, plenty of moisture, a hub of industry between the capitol city of Harrisburg and the seaports of the East Coast.

Hannah never failed to compare Jerry with her father, Moses. All his steps counted. He never seemed to hurry, yet things were accomplished in record time. Everything was well thought out, reasoned, and bargained for, with Hannah being the sole person he sought out when he needed help.

Rains came in the form of thunderstorms, although sparsely. The prairie rebounded after the drought, sprang to life as moisture revived every tiny seed that had dried out and lay in the dust, creating a kaleidoscope of unimaginable wildflowers. The south slant of unexpected swells of land were dressed as delicately as a new bride, with the lacy, lavender pasqueflower. The low places harbored chokecherry, buffalo-berry, and gooseberry bushes, which Hannah discovered when she was out training their two dogs.

She had had them for over three months now, and by the way they responded to her commands, she knew they were on to something. They were like hired hands, the way they knew instinctively where to look for cows or horses. They routed out prairie dogs, badgers, foxes, even terrorized deer that outran them, their legs carrying them like wings.

They had named the dogs Nip and Tuck, which suited them perfectly, the way they tucked into a group of cows and nipped at their heels.

Hannah named them, and Jerry thought she was awfully clever. He told her so, and watched the color spread on her cheeks like an unfolding rosebud. He told himself the long wait for her love would someday come to an end. More and more, he realized the difference in her, when she felt she performed a task to his approval, versus when she failed to meet the stringent requirements she set for herself.

Jerry could never tell her his discovery. She would viciously deny it and then stop communicating altogether, pouting for days, punishing him with her silences. It wasn't only the silence that got to him, but the resentment and bald-faced disapproval that was like a slap in the face the minute she was aware of his presence.

He knew now, though, that the harsh judgment she ladled out on those around her, she also ladled out for herself. She didn't like herself, so how could she stand anyone else?

A work in progress, he constantly reminded himself.

Jerry plowed the land with ease, the prairie soil falling away behind his plow, the mules plodding like a cadence, a symphony of sound and wonder. Skylarks wheeled across the hot, azure sky, and dickeybirds called their vibrant chirps. Grasses bent and swayed, rustled and shivered in the constantly teasing wind.

There was a stack of winter wheat seeds bagged in pretty muslin prints sitting against the wall of the forebay. It was their first crop on the prairie, and hopes ran high thinking of next summer's profit, God willing. Almost forty acres of wheat. Jerry calculated, counted low. Even with that amount, they would be able to buy many more longhorns, which was still a sore subject with Hannah.

Jerry figured that Hod Jenkins was the real authority on long-term survival. Not Hannah, nor those German Klassermans, nor any fancy government brochure that touted the merits of life on the high plains.

You had to live it, experience it, and not for only a few years. Jerry didn't know if he had a love for this Western land or not. He knew if he was meant to be here for Hannah's sake, God would provide for them, for sure.

So he insisted on longhorns, or they would not raise cattle at all. Hannah yelled and slammed doors, threatened and shouted, said she wasn't going to lift a finger to help him with those arrow-tipped monstrosities, and when he'd laughed, she got so mad she threw a plate against the wall, then stayed silent for weeks, talking only to the dogs.

That time she outdid herself, refusing to cook, so he made his own salt pork and eggs, ate a can of beans, made toast by holding a long-handled fork inserted into a thick slice of bread over hot coals. Then he applied a slick coat of butter, ate it in two bites, and made another.

The house turned blue with smoke, but neither one acted as if they noticed. Hannah threw her apron over her nose and coughed until she choked the minute he went out the door. She slammed the lid on the cook stove, when it lay crookedly until she nipped it with her finger and heard the skin sizzle before she felt it, then lived in pain for hours afterward. A huge, watery blister formed on the tip of her finger, burst, and an angry red infection set in. She treated it with wood ashes and kerosene, lay wide-eyed in bed at night thinking of blood poisoning and lockjaw, remembering in vivid detail the story her grandmother told of Uncle Harry who died, skin and bones, his jaw locked so tight no one could pry it open, even in death.

She wondered if she would go to hell for being stubborn, then got so scared she tiptoed across the hall and asked Jerry if he thought she might have blood poisoning or might get lockjaw. He said it looked as if it was healing already, that he didn't think she'd need to see a doctor. She looked so genuinely terrified that he reached for her, only to comfort her as he would a child, but she stepped back, slipped into her room, and shut the door with a resounding click.

CHAPTER 3

THE WINDMILL CREAKED AND GROANED AS THE GREAT PADDLES ON the wheel spun in the wind. Cold water gushed into the huge galvanized tank from the cast-iron pike that ran into it.

Brown, speckled, gray, black, or brindled cows with various sizes of horns roamed the plains around it. There were exactly nineteen head. They resembled Hod Jenkins's herd somewhat yet there was a certain sleek roundness to their bodies, the absence of long, coarse hair.

Jerry set out mineral blocks, salt blocks, and wormed his cattle. Hod said once a year was plenty. Jerry nodded his head in agreement and then went ahead and did it more often, which resulted in healthier cows. They'd done it in the spring, when they acquired the herd, and with the forty acres plowed, it was time to herd the cows for their de-wormer, as Jerry called it.

"Why don't we de-horn them, too?" Hannah asked, testy at the thought of all those contrary cows swinging those horns at her.

"I don't think so. Those horns will keep the wolves away this winter."

"Hmph. Hod lost ten calves."

"Out of a herd of a hundred and twenty."

"It's still ten calves." Hannah turned and flounced off, her men's handkerchief bouncing on her head. At times like these, Jerry wished he could shake some sense into her.

They saddled their horses without speaking. Jerry's horse, King, was a brown gelding, magnificent, huge, with a heavy black mane and tail as luxurious as a silk curtain. Hannah's horse was a palomino, the horse Jerry had made many attempts to gift to her, which she accepted now, as his wife, although she never spoke of those past offenses.

Nip and Tuck whined and yelped and tugged at their chains, but Jerry felt they were two young to help with this serious work. What if one of them got hooked by those massive horns? They had better wait until they were older and more experienced, he claimed.

Hannah argued her point. How would they ever gain experience but by being allowed to help? Obstinate now, more than ever, she refused to get on her horse. She stood like a tin soldier, her limbs stiff with resolve.

It was already past the time that Jerry had planned on starting. The black flies were thicker than water, which meant there was a storm brewing somewhere and he was not about to stand there and try to persuade Hannah in a patient manner.

He lost his temper. Stalking over to Hannah, he shoved his perspiring face into hers and said, "Fine. Stand there all day. I'll herd these cows into the corral by myself. You're not going to take those puppies out on the range."

He swatted the pesky little flies out of his eyes, leaped into the saddle, kicked his heels into King's side, and was off across the prairie in a cloud of dust.

Hannah's mouth dropped open, disbelief taking her breath away. She felt the beginning of a sob forming in her throat. The tip of her nose burned as quick tears sprang to her eyes.

Well! He didn't have to get all mad. Goodness. She had the distinct feeling she'd been wadded up like a piece of paper and thrown in the trash.

She blinked. She sniffled. She wiped a hand across her nose, hard.

This was an interesting turn of events. For one thing, she had to save her pride and let him bring in the cows by himself. If he wanted her to stand here all day, that is what she would do. She would stand here by the fence and watch him try to herd those despicable longhorns by himself. He'd never accomplish it.

Jerry disappeared over a rise. That was disappointing. She had hoped to be able to watch him wear himself out on King.

She unsaddled the palomino and put him in the barn, gave him a small forkful of hay to keep him happy, then hooked her elbows on the barn fence, her boot heel on another rung, and looked in the direction Jerry had gone. She swatted at the bothersome flies, then got tired and slid down by the fence into the dusty grass.

Hannah wondered if there was any trace of her father's blood left in the soil after all these years. She was sitting at the spot where the angry old cow had brought him to an untimely death.

Even now, the awful incident brought a feeling of overwhelming despair. She knew her father was in a better place, heaven being his only goal, the many prayers and devout reading of his Bible preceding him in death.

It was the story he lived before his demise, the shame Hannah still carried with her, the sensitivity to the loss of their homestead, the humiliation of the ride to North Dakota. Like tramps. No, like Amish gypsies. Different, weird people that traveled roads and highways with two tired horses, asking ordinary folks to stay a night here, feed their horses there.

"Would you spare a pound of butter for travelers?"

"Would you allow us water for our horses?"

"Thank you. God bless you. You'll be blessed." As if they were some ragged apparition sent from heaven to test people's ability to be kind.

There was a disgrace, an indignity attached like a loathsome parasite to all those painful memories, a part of her past she would never shake.

Ordinary folks, English people of class and citizenry, would peer through the opening of the covered wagon to find them seated among their belongings, unwashed, raggedy-haired, poor, stupid misfits. The people would stand there and stare, make clucking noises of banal sympathy.

Hannah felt like an orangutan at the zoo, a strange monkey, an amazing sight. If she allowed herself to think, it was like drowning in wave after wave of embarrassment, impossible to rise above it. She could control the self-loathing as long as no one took advantage of her, or used their authority in a demeaning manner, making her feel as if she was in the back of the wagon again.

Evidently, neither one of her siblings suffered from the same malady. They were all sweet and simple and obedient to this day, same as her mother. Bland as bean soup!

She'd been lost in her own thoughts, wrapped up in the past, which effectively sealed her off from Nip and Tuck's constant yapping, whining, jerking on their leashes, then starting all over again. "Hey! Quiet down there. It's not that bad." She walked over to play with them, scratching the coarse hair between their ears, rolling them over to rub their bellies, but keeping them tied the way Jerry wanted.

She heard the distant chuffing sound of an automobile, lifted a hand to shade her eyes to see if she could catch sight of who was coming to the ranch. A dark car with gold lettering.

She straightened and saw the gold star on the side of the car. The sheriff. Her heart fluttered, then began to pound. Please don't let it be a death message.

The car rolled to a stop, the cloud of dust thinned and was blown away. The passenger door opened first, the dark shirt and trousers, the white Stetson. The door on the driver's side opened with an identically clad sheriff, tall and sober, unfolding out of it.

"Hello."

Hannah nodded, her mouth gone dry. The dogs set up a racket, bouncing on two hind legs as they strained on their leashes.

"We're making the rounds of Elliot County. Have you seen anyone here on the ranch that answers to the name Isaac Short? Older fellow, small and skinny."

"Isaac? Only Short I know is Lemuel. He was here in early spring—April or May. Riding a horse. Wanted me to hide him."

"Lemuel, you say."

"Yes. When my mother still lived here, he stayed with us for months. Gave us a story that was all a lie."

"Mind if we search your house and outbuildings?"

"No."

So Lemuel was still loose. Nothing she was going to worry about, that was for sure. She watched for signs of Jerry, waited until the men completed their search, acknowledging their warnings politely, her hands behind her back, tipping forward then backward from toe to heel.

"You have a man here with you?"

"Yes."

"Well, you make sure you're not alone, unless you have a sizable dog to protect you. I understand you don't use firearms in self-defense. Your faith."

It was only then that she thought of the revolver. Her eyes widened as she put her hand over her mouth.

"What?" Instantly alert, the trained sheriff picked up on her astonished expression.

"I forgot. When Lemuel Short was here, he threatened me with a pistol. I knocked it out of his hand. I swung a hammer quick before he saw I had one. I have the revolver."

That was, of course, a tremendous help in tracking him down, so Hannah received words of praise for her quick-wittedness, her bravery. They thanked her and left.

Well, that was something now, wasn't it? She felt good from the inside out. She watched for Jerry, anxious to tell him, then decided against it. If she told him now, he'd never leave the ranch. He'd stick close like an unwanted burr, and she had absolutely no intention of putting up with that.

Her stomach growled. Time for lunch. She'd skipped breakfast, for some reason she couldn't remember. Oh, Jerry wanted oatmeal, she remembered. She had eaten so many bowls of rolled oats as a child, and again here on the prairie when starvation was very real. So now, when she could choose other foods, she did.

She heated a saucepan, added leftover ham and bean soup she'd made a few days ago. With rivvels. She loved rivvels. Like small lumps of noodles, they were pure energy. All that good flour and egg mixture dropped in tiny chunks into a bubbling pot of soup. She put rivvels in chicken corn soup and vegetable soup, or any other stew she threw together.

She got out the sourdough bread which, as usual, was hard as a rock, but toasted in a pan and spread with lard or butter, it was edible.

Her meal completed, she wiped the tabletop, put her dishes in the sink, then looked around the house with a sense of satisfaction. The afternoon sun slanted through the west-facing windows, bathing the front living room and kitchen in the golden glow of late summer. The deep gleam of the polished oak flooring added a warm luster to the white walls. The brown davenport and wooden rocking chairs both had a scattering of bright pillows and throws. Jerry's rolltop desk stood against the east wall, where the wide door led to the kitchen.

Hannah had been fortunate to be able to keep all the furnishings when her family returned to their home in the East. With

Jerry's belongings, the house was filled up nicely, except for one spare bedroom.

Mam had had no desire to take the furnishings, even if she could have. It was not what she'd brought when her and her beloved Mose had made the trek out West. That had all burned in the fire. The furniture that graced the rooms now had all been generously donated by concerned members of the Amish congregation in Lancaster, and by well-meaning neighbors here on the plains.

The day the gasoline engine threw sparks and ignited the tinder dry grass had been one of the worst days of Hannah's life. But now, so many good things had come out of that fire. The generosity of friends and family had gotten them back on their feet.

Charity or not, Hannah had never looked back.

She walked back to the barn, still searching for Jerry as her eyes scanned the position of the sun, then moved back to the direction he'd gone when he left. He would likely ride in alone, knowing how hard it was to round up cows that had no intention of leaving their buffet of thick broom grass.

A small brown dot appeared on the horizon, turning into a bobbing, weaving mass as it neared the ranch. Hannah shaded her eyes, thrilled at the sight of Jerry on King, driving a tight knot of lowing cattle that seemed to be walking along without being agitated or cranky, as they often were.

Quickly, she moved to the gate, swung it wide, then fastened it with a piece of rawhide before disappearing into the barn. She knew how frustrating it was to drive a herd of cattle successfully for miles, only to have them veer in the wrong direction at the last minute because someone was lounging on the corral fence. She could watch Jerry work now, without being seen.

On they came, led by the largest, oldest cow, the brindle bull behind her, his massive horns swinging, his eyes rolling. As they neared the buildings, Jerry pushed them harder, yelling and swinging his rope, maneuvering expertly from right to left, tightening loose ends and keeping them in a rectangle of movement, never allowing any stragglers.

King took her breath away. It was as if he'd been bred to chase cattle, which Hannah knew he had not been. If he was still back East, he'd likely be pulling a gray-and-black market wagon, in the rain, with a driving harness and blinders on his bridle. He'd only be half the horse he was here.

Jerry wore no hat, saying they were useless in the prairie wind. His thick, dark hair flopped up and down, blowing every which way depending on the direction of the wind. His skin was darkened, fissured by the elements. It suited him. If he lived out here another forty years, he'd look much like Hod. Hannah swallowed, thinking of Hod's tobacco juice.

The cows were coming faster now, bunched together, the lead cow becoming agitated as the ones behind her pushed her forward. She bawled, her eyes rolling, but on she came.

Jerry yelled, "Hey! Hey! Get up there! Hup!"

Hannah gripped the barn windowsill until her knuckles were white. Would the lead cow go through the open gate? So close now, only a hundred yards.

On they came. Hannah held her breath, feeling weak and dizzy. She could smell that bovine odor, the tart, sweet scent of cows. She heard the nineteen noses breathing hard, the hooves milling up the dusty ground around the barn. A cloud of dust and black flies followed the herd, sometimes almost obscuring them for a moment.

And then they were in, smoothly, without one straggler. Hannah was relieved, ecstatic. She ran out of the barn, unfastened the rawhide in one quick movement, swung the gate wide and lifted the wooden bar to place it in the proper notch.

She dusted her hands and looked up at Jerry, ready to receive his praise for her quick work. To her chagrin, he wheeled King around and dismounted, working the girth and throwing the reins before dragging off the saddle and throwing it on the floor of the barn.

Without looking at her, he walked off in the direction of the house. Her first instinct was to catch up to him and tell him about the soup on the stove. But she stayed, watching him go. What was wrong with him now? He'd done an excellent job of bringing the cows in. Why was he acting like this now, when everything had gone well?

She climbed the fence, sat on the top rail, and surveyed her herd of cattle. Still nineteen. Why did it seem as if this herd, these strange-looking cattle, were truly hers, her way to becoming successful now, with Jerry by her side?

Or, rather, she was by his side. Without doubt, Jerry was far superior in everything to any man she had ever known. She couldn't begin to compare him to her poor father, may he rest in peace. Even the Jenkins did not have the skills, the work ethic that Jerry had.

She knew he intrigued her, the way he planned ahead, asked for advice and took it, both priceless attributes when it came to managing the ranch. Those forty acres of plowed ground, done so effortlessly, the four plodding mules doing what they were meant to do, without fuss or fury.

Well, she couldn't tell him these things or he'd think she was starting to like him. Likely he'd try to put his arm around her shoulder or her waist like he was always wanting to do. Those arms were a trap, one she had no intention of being caught in.

When Jerry returned from the house, she stayed on the top rail, but did dare to look down as he approached. He was looking up at her, then climbed up, threw a leg across a post and perched on it.

"How did it go?" she asked, in a small voice.

"How did what go?"

She glanced at him. His face was pale and sick-looking.

"What's wrong with you?"

"I got sick. Hannah, I don't want to hurt your feelings, okay? But I absolutely hate rivvels. We, uh . . . you know, eat lots of rivvels. I know you love them, so you go ahead and make them for yourself, but I'll need potatoes or something else instead. Sorry."

Hannah wished she could disappear like a cloud of dust. Her embarrassment turned into anger, and to save herself she retorted, "You can make your own meals from now on, then."

"Hannah, I told you, I'm sorry. I knew this would hurt your feelings. I didn't mean to."

"Yeah, well, you did. So get over it. What do you want me to do as far as worming these ugly brutes?"

"We need them in the chute, one by one."

"I know that much."

"Can you give an injection?"

"I think so. Manny or my . . . my father always did it."

They worked together the remainder of the day sorting cattle and getting them into the narrow chute, lowering the gate behind them like a trap door and shooting the needle into their tough hides, putting pressure on the plunger and forcing the worm medicine into the cows' bodies.

Jerry was quick and vigilant, avoiding the horns as he drove the cattle with a sturdy black whip, one he mostly cracked above their heads, or used the handle to prod them along. He told Hannah that he didn't believe any of them were truly dangerous, or a threat to their lives. You just had to be careful around them, that was all.

Hannah looked at him, trying hard to cover her admiration.

The work was dirty, with dust coating everything. The cows milled about in the soil, throwing up everything under their feet with their ungainly cloven hooves. Hannah's eyelashes, the top of her head, everything seemed painted with the cloying dust. She choked, blinked, swiped at her eyes, then yanked the man's handkerchief from her head and tied it over her nose and mouth the way the Jenkins boys had taught her.

After the last cow had gone through the chute, Jerry walked over and told her she had done a great job. "Another man couldn't have done better.

Hannah looked at her feet and refused to meet his eyes. She didn't say thanks. She didn't smile. She just walked off and told him she was going to make rivvel soup for their evening meal.

That evening, though, things seemed to be changing, if only enough to allow Jerry a miniature ray of hope for the future. Hannah did make a small pot of rivvel soup for herself. But she cooked a pot of potatoes with ham and red beans for him, which was actually an overcooked mush with lumps of gristly ham and beans so hard they would have bounced off the wall if someone had thrown them.

But he was ravenous after losing his lunch so he enjoyed the dubious-looking mess and was grateful. He figured she'd learn as time went on, although he wished she would try and befriend some neighbor women who could teach her a few of the basics.

They sat together on the porch, Jerry on the steps, leaning back against a post, one knee drawn up with an arm slung across it. Hannah sat on a wooden chair, her legs crossed, swinging one foot, her elbows resting on her top knee.

Crickets chirped beneath the wooden floor of the porch, seeking out the only dark moist corners they could find. Grasshoppers leaped and chewed their noisy way through the grass by the fence, and evening larks called their plaintive call to one another as the sun slid behind the horizon.

A cow lowed from the corral. Another one answered. "How come they're still in the barnyard?" Hannah asked.

"I want to make sure none of them get sick."

"Good idea."

"I'm not looking forward to winter. Out here, everything is just so unpredictable. The blizzards, or no snow at all, or freezing, bitter cold and a wind that never stops."

"I love the prairie winters."

Jerry looked at her sharply. "You're serious?"

"Of course. Every day is a challenge. I love getting up in the morning without knowing what will present itself. It's never dull. Getting enough firewood, for one thing. You know the cottonwoods and oak trees in the creek bottom won't last forever. Will we have to buy coal from town? Or will we travel farther to find enough firewood?"

Jerry looked at Hannah with an unnamed expression. "So this challenge, this day-to-day onslaught of obstacles, the surprises, is what keeps you here?"

Hannah's gaze was riveted on the disappearance of the orange orb of the sun setting in its usual display of grandiosity. She jutted her chin in the general direction of the sunset. "Yes. And that."

Jerry watched the sun disappear, felt the twilight creeping over the plains, shadows of night encroaching, the air turning cooler and carrying a hint of frost, a harbinger of the howling winds of winter. He felt a foreboding, a portent, shivered, then shook his head from side to side. "You are different, Hannah."

"Don't you feel the same way?" she asked.

"I do, at times, yes. But I can't say I look forward to winter. And I miss the social life of Lancaster County, the hymn sings, church, the frolics and hoedowns in the barn. I miss the friends of my youth." The minute the words were out of his mouth, he knew he'd spoken too plainly.

Her foot bobbed faster. She removed her elbows from her knee and sat up straight, glaring at him with baleful eyes. "So you regret out marriage? You wish you could return, exactly like my mother and all the rest of them did?"

"I didn't say that. I just mentioned the fact that I miss the goings-on back East."

"There are churches in Pine. We could go to any church we choose."

"Hannah, we are of the Amish faith. I have no intention of leaving and changing my beliefs, or the way of life we were taught from our youth. I'm very comfortable living under a bishop and ministers who look out for our souls."

Hannah had nothing to say to this. They sat in silence that was fraught with unspoken longings, doubts about the future, about the marriage they both knew was as empty as the prairie itself. Jerry could not have known how difficult the path would be, seeing how Hannah drew into herself with no visible sign of harboring even the beginnings of a natural love for her husband.

His patience was God-given, this he knew. But when he thought of the years stretching before him, one after another, filled with only a swirling mist, a substance devoid of anything real, he felt only doubts and a nameless dread.

"You're always better than I am," Hannah remarked, as shadows deepened around them."

"No. No, I'm not. You know that."

"You don't have to stay."

"I want to stay here with you."

Her foot bobbed faster than ever. "You'll get tired of me. I'm not a very nice person."

"Hannah, I married you for one reason. I love you. It's up to you when you're ready to return my love."

Jerry could only watch as she lowered her face to her knee, and whispered very soft and low, "Thank you."

Chapter 4

THE NEXT MORNING, JERRY WHISTLED AS HE BRUSHED HIS MULES, working from the top of their broad backs, down their sides, their haunches, to the tops of their oversized hooves. He threw the black leather harness across their backs, tightened cinches and buckles.

He needed only two of the mules today. The drill used for sowing wheat was not heavy. It was easily pulled by the best two of the four—Max, the largest one, and Mike, the slightly smaller but energetic one. He knew if Mike didn't get worked enough, he'd be frisky.

Four mules—Max, Mike, Mollie, and Mud Mule. It was the naming of the mules that brought their first real laughter together. They could not come up with a fourth reasonable name that started with "M." So, Jerry suggested Muddy and they shortened it to Mud. Hannah forgot herself and snorted in laughter, which encouraged Jerry to carry on about their precious Mud Mule until they both were laughing so hard they had tears in their eyes. The poor mule was no beauty, as mules go, his nose even longer than his teammates', his eyes slanted and bulging like a frog's eyes. His tail was much shorter and had less hair on the end of it.

After that whispered, "Thank you," last evening, Jerry could take anything. It was like a sip of water to a parched throat. She was human after all. She said she appreciated his love. The sky was blue, the sun was golden, the birds singing songs of joy as the wind whispered a rhythm of longing and love.

What could go wrong now? Nothing. He felt as if he knew the right way, the times when she would need a firm refusal, the times when he could win her with kindness.

Jerry poured the sleek kernels of seed wheat into the hopper, the fifty-pound bags weighing almost nothing, the muscles in his arms rippling with strength, a song on his lips and his heart filled with hope. Back and forth the mules plodded steadily, the creaking wheels on the drill releasing the millions of wheat seeds into the well-harrowed soil, waiting for the autumn rains and sunshine.

He was thrilled to see Hannah walking toward the field, Nip and Tuck bouncing and jostling around at her feet, the wind blowing her skirts in all directions, her gray apron flapping unhandily. He loved to watch her walk. Her long-legged stride covered a good distance in a short time, effortless, as graceful as any of God's creation.

Impatience was in her way of moving, her long, slender neck leaning forward just a bit, her jaw elevated, jutting forward slightly, as if her mind was running ahead of her feet.

Now what had she thought up? What was important enough to come all this way with her fast gait? He caught her eye, pulled on the reins, called to the mules. When the squeaking of the drill stopped, the silence around him held nothing but the soft sighing of the wind, a sound like the breath of God or the whisper of angels' wings, as he often imagined the wind to be.

"Hey, Hannah!" he called.

As usual, no greeting. Only the exact reason for her arrival. "I'm going to the new neighbors."

"Why don't you wait until I can go with you?"

"No."

"All right. Are you sure they moved in already?"

"No, but I plan on finding out."

"Be careful."

She had already turned, but flapped a hand over her head to show she'd heard, and then she was gone, out of earshot.

Jerry shrugged, called to the mules. He was almost certain no one had moved in at the Klassermans' place, the way Hod said these Texans were planning on enlarging everything, both the house and the barn. But hey, let her find out for herself.

Jerry watched Hannah lead the palomino out of the barn, run the grooming brush all over, thoroughly, then throw the saddle across his back. He wondered if she'd take Nip and Tuck.

Hannah rode off in a cloud of dust, the sun shining down on her squared shoulders, her men's kerchief blowing in the wind. And then, nothing, as far as he could see. Emptiness all around him, the sky gigantic in its unknowable immensity, the grasses waving like dancers, pirouetting in every direction until he imagined the prairie to be made of water, with waves and eddies and whirlpools hidden in its depths.

Hannah rode hard down the dusty road that led north, away from the ranch, into the prairie where she could feel the freedom of being on a horse's back, feel the power and strength beneath her, thrill to the rush of wind in her face.

She missed the Klassermans already, if she admitted it. It was always nice to know the next ranch over was inhabited by someone she was acquainted with. So now, it seemed strange to be riding along the same road without knowing who, if anyone, she would meet.

Why would someone from Texas move to the plains? Surely they weren't thinking straight. Well, if they thought they were going to move out here and buy up every acre they could, they wouldn't get very far. Folks in these parts didn't take kindly to someone throwing their weight around. They liked things the way they were, and the way they had been for decades, and no upstart from Texas was going to change the way they raised cattle or grew wheat or built long, low houses—or anything.

Hannah smiled, slowed the palomino, gazed around at the swells and dips of the land as she caught sight of a badger slinking away beneath a thick stand of swamp grass. He was fat and clumsy, his bright eyes popping out of his striped face.

She noticed dust rolling on the horizon and kept to her side of the road as a truck approached, the sound of the motor an invasion of her senses. Wheezing and gasping, the truck careened out of a low place, covered in mud, the front fender missing, wooden racks clapping and swaying, as if the whole haphazard mess would let loose and splinter into a thousand pieces on the road.

Wasn't Hod Jenkins. This truck was even worse than his. Inside was a small man, barely visible above the steering wheel. No passenger. Hannah reined in the palomino as the truck wheezed to a stop, acutely aware of being alone with no ranch in sight.

Well, she was on a horse, so she'd be fine.

The window on the driver's side was being cranked down with a painful squeaking noise. She saw an elbow, followed by a small, wizened face with a bill cap pulled low over the eyes. Those ferret eyes. She'd know them anywhere. Hannah drew up her shoulders, straightened her jaw, and said, "What?"

"Sittin' high and mighty, there, aintcha?" Lemuel Short rasped, his words like fingernails on a chalkboard, followed by a series of coughs and throat-clearing, and a splat of phlegm that landed at her horse's feet. The palomino sidestepped, snorted. Hannah reined him in, spoke to him soothingly so he'd settle.

"Can't handle a horse like him, huh?" Red blotches of color suffused the small man's face, pock marks like fissured rock, bristly stubble over everything, the desperate brown eyes glinting like a cornered badger. From his shirt collar, blue veins protruded on his brick-red neck, as scrawny as a pecked chicken.

"I can handle him. Stop spitting on him." She glowered down at the man she had protected, sheltered, even cared about, even after all his lies and half-truths he'd used to gain the Detweiler family's sympathy. Almost, she had come to like him.

"Where's my gun?"

"I have no idea."

"What'd you do with it?"

Hannah shrugged.

"You better tell me. I mean it!"

"I wouldn't give you the gun even if I knew where it was."

Lemuel did not answer. To meet his eyes was like gazing into a volcanic pit, seething and churning with a nameless emotion that jarred her from the disdain she felt for him. A quick wave of shock rippled over her body. Whatever humanity Lemuel had once had in him had disappeared, leaving behind this icy creature who could be capable of anything.

He coughed and spat. Hannah loosened the reins and dug her heels into the palomino's flanks, leaned forward and prepared herself for the surge of power that would come when her horse took off. She didn't look back.

She flew down the dusty road, the wind in her face, the steady *thock-thock* of galloping hooves, the horse's great muscles propelling them forward. She focused only on the amazing sensation of the horse's pure power.

Then she heard it. Low at first, like a whine. The sound of a bumblebee in wood. The whine turned into a roar, then a high, crazed screech.

Hannah turned to look back over her shoulder. The sight that met her eyes was almost comical, if she would not have sensed the danger. Bent low over his steering wheel, both hands gripping it, Lemuel Short had every intention of running her down. The truck careened through dust and low places where the mud flew up in showers.

If the ancient, wheezing piece of junk he was driving went any faster, he'd catch up. Better to veer off to the right, onto the open prairie, even if she had to slow down on unknown territory.

The prairie could be deceiving, appearing as level as a kitchen table, but filled with surprises. Badger or prairie dog holes, rises in the most unexpected places, or hollows that were not visible to the eye.

She slowed her horse, then laid the reins flat against the left side of his neck, steering him to the right. It was called being neck reined and was gentle on a horse's mouth. Obediently, the palomino slowed, then cantered at an easy, rocking pace, his ears flicking forward, then back, alert to his rider's commands.

Hannah turned in the saddle, saw the truck slow, but didn't wait to see if he would pursue her. There was no way he could navigate the prairie in that old truck—certainly not fast enough to overtake her.

She still was not seriously frightened, but it was hard to forget that look in his eyes. He was old, small, and desperate, like a dark wisp of smoke that could be nothing or could be deadly, depending on the size of the fire at its source.

He probably stole that wheezing old bucket he drove. If he came after her on the prairie, he'd break an axle or run out of gas. At least she'd never have to worry about car problems for herself. Not that she wouldn't have loved to drive one of those late models, long and sleek, the kind you occasionally glimpsed in Dorchester. No one in Pine had enough money to purchase a decent car. They all drove around in rusted-out pickup trucks that dated back to the twenties.

Jerry was as Amish as *schnitz und knepp*, that century-old dish of home-cured ham and apples with dumplings. It didn't make a difference that they lived out here on the plains by themselves. He considered himself of the Old Order and fully expected to remain there, honoring the dress code and corresponding with the Lancaster County ministers via mail. No automobiles for them.

She shrugged involuntarily. She'd been desperate enough to keep her homestead that she'd married him, and now she had to follow his rules—or at least try. But it had worked and that's what mattered. She still had her beloved homestead on the plains.

Things were becoming steadily more complicated, though. Take last night. Oh my. What had possessed her to thank him? A burning shame washed over like rain. Now what? She didn't give two hoots if he loved her or not. She certainly did not love him, didn't even really need him except so she could stay on the plains. She would be happier on her own if she could be.

And so, her thoughts kept time to the horse's hoofbeats, until she realized she'd have to turn directly north, to the left, or she'd miss the Klasserman ranch.

No sight of Lemuel Short and his decrepit old junker. Good. She leaned forward in the saddle, eagerly scanned the surrounding land for the neighboring buildings, and wondered who these Texans would turn out to be. Friendly? Wealthy? Hostile? What would they think of her peculiar Amish lifestyle?

She really didn't care. Folks in Pine had been less than welcoming to the Detweiler family at first, but they'd warmed up to them eventually. So would the Texans.

Her calculations had been right. She caught sight of the dull gray galvanized roofing of the large barn their former neighbors had built. They'd raised a large herd of Black Angus cattle with German determination and a work ethic that far surpassed her own father's lackadaisical ways.

She still found it hard to believe they had actually retired and went back to the old country, especially now, the way Germany was still healing from the war. They received no newspapers and had no radio so the images of World War II were strictly hearsay. Sometimes Hod would rant on about the whole mess, in his words, and Hannah had no interest in any of it. They were self-sufficient, or almost, so what went on in the world was of no concern to her.

"Whoa!" She pulled back too hard and too fast on the reins, startling the palomino to a haunch lowering stop that almost unseated her. She grabbed the saddle horn and settled back down in her seat. What was that?

It looked like railroad cars lined up in a circle. Or wagons. The way a wagon train parked in a tight circle for protection from the Indians years ago. She counted eleven white horse trailers and as many trucks. There were men wearing white hats everywhere.

They were building, digging post holds. Horses everywhere. And not one single cow. It was like watching an anthill, or a beehive, only everything seemed to be white. Even the horses!

Hannah gasped. Those horses were white and they were enormous! Or was it only the fact that she was observing all this from a distance? From her slightly elevated standpoint, a rise in the deceptively level prairie, it seemed otherworldly, as if she was in a dream where the scene was devoid of color.

She wasn't aware that she was shaking her head back and forth and murmuring, "No, no, no. I can't go there." She remained rooted to the exact same spot, the only movement the wind flapping at her skirt, the legs of her trousers, the horse's mane, riffling through the autumn grass, and the constant flicking of the sensitive, waiting ears of her mount.

Were there no women? Only men, wearing those wide-brimmed white hats. No, she wasn't going there without Jerry. She clicked her tongue, laid the reins to the left, and was on her way back, fleeing now, half-afraid one of those white-hatted men would see her and follow, chasing her off his property. That would be embarrassing. Like she was a common spy, or worse yet, an intruder, a tramp.

She retraced her route, keeping an eye out for Lemuel Short, but there was no sign of him. The sun was still high overhead, although she could tell by the angle of her shadow that it was well past noon. And Jerry would be hungry.

Would all her days from now until her death be punctuated into three separate pieces? Breakfast. Dinner. Supper. Every day. If she lived to be seventy years old, that was a lot of ruptured days.

She'd wake up in a good mood and then realize she had to make him breakfast. A few hours of work and then there was another meal to be reckoned with. Figuring out what to cook was the hardest part. There wasn't much of a variety after two years of drought, and Jerry was as stingy and tight as her Uncle Jonas who'd had a reputation for being the most frugal person anyone had ever heard of.

Well, they hadn't met Jerry Riehl. Every bit of bone and gristle from a piece of meat was given to the dogs. Vegetable peelings went to the hens in the henhouse. All leftover grease that remained in the frying pan was left until the last meal of the day, to reuse again and again. Leftover bachelor philosophy is what it was. One of these days, she'd get tired of his tightfisted ways and tell him so.

Marriage vows didn't necessarily include cooking. You promised to care for them, in sickness and in health, although there was no mention of exactly how. As long as Jerry wasn't losing weight, it meant he had kept his health okay, right? There was nothing saying she had to cook *well*.

As she approached the ranch, Hannah searched the wheat field for the nodding mules and Jerry's straw hat, but found the field empty. The team was standing by the corral fence, so she figured her calculations were right on the dot. Jerry was hungry.

She stabled the horse, carried herself to the house with her long strides.

She smelled the dinner before she saw him standing by the kitchen range, spatula in hand, batter down the front of his white shirt. He turned when he heard the screen door slap closed.

"Hannah!"

No reply, as usual.

"You're back so soon." A smile spread his mouth wide, creased the dark eyes with a glad light. Almost Hannah dropped her guard, but she caught herself in time. Almost, she forgot herself and blurted out the whole story of the strange goings-on at the Klassermans'. She almost mirrored the enthusiasm in his eyes with her own. But she held back.

"It's not too soon," she said gruffly, as she turned and disappeared into the bathroom to wash her hands.

"I'm making pancakes."

No answer, only the running water and hand wringing, the drop of the lava soap into the dish. When she reappeared, her face was dark with an unnamed emotion.

Jerry stood eyeing her, his hands on both hips, the pancake turner sticking out of his curled palm like a growth. "What's wrong with you?"

"Who said there was anything wrong?"

"You look troubled."

"You can't tell."

"Sure I can. Something isn't right at the neighbors'."

Hannah didn't reply. How did he know? She walked over to the stove and peered in the cast-iron frying pan. "You're burning your pancakes."

Quickly he inserted the turner under a bubbling orb of batter, lifted it, and bent his head to examine the color. Straightening, he announced, "Wrong!"

His face, his shoulders, everything was too close. His nearness was too much like a magnet, starting with those crinkling brown eyes that enveloped her with that disturbingly happy light, a glow that was so genuine, so real, a light she had begun to accept, which was a weakness, a letting go of . . . something. He continued to smile at her, the light in his eyes changing to a darker one, with even more magnetic power.

Hannah stepped back, called over her shoulder, "I see you trailed mud into the washroom, like you always do." Harsh, grating words. The tone accusatory.

Jerry flipped the pancakes, felt the rebuttal, was used to it. One step forward, two back.

"No syrup?" he called.

"Molasses."

"Boy, what I would give for a glass jar of maple syrup."

"I hate that stuff."

One eyebrow arched as he stared at her. "Maple syrup? Hannah, come on."

She didn't answer, slammed two plates on the table, added glasses, knives, forks, and spoons. They ate in silence. The clock ticked on the wall, the pendulum clicked, catching the afternoon rays of the sun when it swung left.

Hannah was ravenous and devoured three pancakes with a thick coating of molasses, washed down with milk. Jerry watched her eat, loved the way food disappeared in small, neat bites, efficiently consuming as many pancakes as he did.

"You want coffee?" she asked, when she was finished.

"Is it hot?"

"Did you heat it?"

"No."

"Won't take long."

And so they chipped away at the solid wall between them, like digging mortar from between bricks with a toothpick, leaving all Hannah had seen, all she had experienced, uncovered and untouched.

He didn't need to know about Lemuel Short. As far as those white people at the Klasserman ranch, he could find that out for himself. She didn't know who they were or what they were doing, so there was no use talking about it.

CHAPTER 5

To stand beside Jerry on a mild autumn afternoon, to allow him to show her the small green shoots of wheat appearing above the tilled prairie soil, to feel the same sense of hope and accomplishment, was something she had not prepared herself for.

Anything that had to do with the prosperity of the homestead struck a deep emotion in Hannah, one that eclipsed every other aspect of her life. It was beyond comprehension, glorious.

The success was coming with almost no anxiety on her part, no staying awake worrying how the poor, worn-out horses would ever pull a plow through this awful soil. It seemed like a luxury no one deserved, least of all, herself.

For the first time in his life, Jerry experienced Hannah's face alight with approval and happiness. She was so beautiful. So unreal. Like an untouchable photograph.

"I can't believe it!" she said.

"You can. It's real! If this warm weather holds, we'll be the proud, new wheat growers of the county. The best winter wheat."

"How high does the new growth need to be to survive the winter, do you think?"

"Oh, a couple more inches. It's well-established. If you look across this whole field, you can already see the drill rows."

Hannah nodded. "The whole field has a green haze, like a veil."

"It's a promise. If all goes well, we'll have a strong stand of rippling, golden wheat by next summer. With rain, of course. And the Lord's blessing."

Hannah chewed her lower lip. "And, no hail, fire, or any other natural disaster."

"You're worrying, Hannah."

"No, just thinking out loud." The wind tugged at the black scarf on her head, tossed her apron away from her dress skirt. "It just makes me sad for my father."

"Why?"

"Oh, he had the same dream we do. The same goal. He just didn't have the resources, the horsepower, nothing. It seemed like all he had was a firm determination, a rock-solid faith that God would help him out. I used to get so mad at him and he knew it."

Jerry grinned. "You know, if you don't stop getting angry with me, I'll have an accident, and you'll regret it."

"Stop saying things like that!"

"You don't need me, only my money."

Hannah felt the furious blush of color rise in her face. She tried to speak, opened her mouth to deny his words, but it would be hollow, false, if she tried to answer him otherwise. The truth was what he had just said. It was exactly the way it really was.

"You married me for better or for worse. So, I'm worse."

Jerry laughed outright, a burst of pure glee, bent over and slapped his knee. "One thing about you, Hannah, you are the most honest person I know."

"Not always."

"When aren't you?"

Hannah shrugged and turned to go. "Time to check the creek bottom for more firewood." Jerry turned to follow, wondering what exactly she had meant.

They had a good supply of firewood and more than enough hay. The longhorns roamed the homestead, growing fat and lazy, contentedly chewing their cuds, luxuriating in the never-ending supply of cold, fresh water pumped into the tank by the whirring windmill. When the wind took on a decided bite and temperatures lowered each week, Hannah's eyes turned to the young blades of green wheat, wondering what, if anything, would keep them from being destroyed by the frequent heavy snowfall, the plummeting temperatures, the wind shrieking and moaning as it blew walls of ice particles around like miniature darts.

How could a whole field of tender new wheat withstand those natural calamities?

There was a mild day, when the wind stilled, strangely, leaving a deep quiet that Hannah felt in her bones, a solitude that took away her calm and shoved her through the house with manic energy.

She cleaned the pantry, a bucket of soapy water by her side, yanking out barrels and bags of flour, salt pork, cornmeal, tins of lard, scrubbing and wiping until her hands burned from the strong soap. She rearranged the containers on the shelves, scrubbed the floor to a deep shine, then stood back to survey what she had accomplished.

Deciding she could not take the strange stillness, she began cleaning the kitchen, yanking everything out of the cupboards, wiping down shelves and doors and the bottom of drawers, washing utensils and dusty pans and bowls her mother had frequently used to make pies and cakes, a duty Hannah refused to do. If her bread was like slices of lumber, how could she hope to bake a decent cake? Pies were completely out of her range, so she may as well not even attempt it.

In the hours before dinnertime, the house took on a strange yellow glow, as if the sun was shining through a veil of smoke. Putting down the cleaning rag she was wielding with so much energy, she straightened, pushed back a lock of dark hair, then stepped out on the porch to cast an anxious eye from one horizon to the other. She tried to recall when she had seen a sky like this. Wasn't it before the blizzard that had kept them all housebound for almost a week, when they used a rope to ensure their safe return when they went to feed the horses in the barn?

She licked her forefinger and held it up to the open air to determine the direction of the wind. As calm as it appeared to be, the right side of her finger felt cooler, so she decided the air was from the north, perhaps a bit to the east. Her brows drew down. October, though. The last week in October was too early for a snowstorm. So, she imagined there was no real danger. She calculated the amount of firewood stacked on the back stoop, the plentiful hay, the leathery resistance of the new breed of cattle, those skinny creatures with long horns that ran a close contest with the mules in a race for ugliness!

She snorted her derisive, dismissing sound from her nostrils. She couldn't believe she'd been such a pushover, allowing Jerry to get rid of those beautiful Black Angus cattle. Here they were, no better than the Jenkinses, with a herd of weird-looking cattle that would bring a poor price at the cattle market in Dorchester. They may be sleek now, but till spring, when they dropped their calves, they'd be nothing but leathery, long-haired hides stretched across bony skeletons. They wouldn't make any profit on them.

She heard the dull sound of hoofbeats, swung her eyes in that direction to find Jerry riding in on King, Nip and Tuck bouncing along by his side.

She turned and went into the house to resume her work, not wanting him to see her standing in the yard as if she was eagerly watching for his return.

When he came into the house, whistling, a spring in his step, his dark eyes alight, she went back to her cleaning, vigorously applying the rag to the cupboard doors, ignoring him.

"Hannah!"

She didn't answer, so he went on.

"It's a great day to ride over to the neighbors'. There's no wind and it's mild. Do you want to ride with me? Just to see if anyone moved in?"

She hadn't told him what she had seen, and he didn't ask, so he wouldn't know that the place was swarming with strange, white-hatted men. She stopped wiping cupboard doors, straightened her back, and looked at him. "I don't like the looks of this weather."

"What's wrong with it, Hannah? It's a gorgeous fall day. Like the Indian summer in Pennsylvania."

"The atmosphere is yellow. It's too still."

"Oh, come on. It's October."

"The last week in October."

"Have you ever seen snow this early?"

Hannah wanted to say yes, but she couldn't say it truthfully, so she went back to her cleaning, shrugging her shoulders.

"Let's eat lunch real quick and then ride over. We can take the dogs."

Hannah said nothing, just picked up her pail of soapy water and disappeared through the washhouse door, flinging the water across the backyard. She set a pot of salted water to boiling, threw in a few handfuls of cornmeal, and went to the bathroom to come her hair and wash her face. She'd go. The lure of the horseback ride and the open plains was too strong to refuse.

To wear a white covering or not? That was the question. She knew Jerry loved to see her dressed in the traditional white head covering. But what if there was a nip in the air later in the day? She'd need her black headscarf, tied securely beneath her chin.

No, she'd wear her head covering. With the green dress, she would look more attractive. Not that she cared what Jerry thought, though. But there were new people to meet, and they may as well know from her first appearance that they were different, saving themselves the explanation that would eventually have to be given.

She tied her good black apron over the green dress, pinned her covering to her head, and made her appearance, going straight to the stove to stir the boiling cornmeal mush.

"You always look so nice in your white covering."

Hannah didn't give him the satisfaction of an answer, simply got down two bowls, the sugar and milk, a few slices of leftover salt pork, and a loaf of bread.

They sat down together, their chairs scraping loudly on the wooden floor. Without looking at her, Jerry bowed his head, and Hannah followed suit, as they prayed silently, or Jerry did anyway. Hannah was thinking about the neighbors being so white and forgot to pray.

She often did that, a habit formed in childhood. She told Manny once that God knew she was thankful for her food, and if she remembered to tell Him once a week or so, that was probably all right with Him.

If she watched Jerry, though, his bowed head, his closed eyes, his lips moving in the most devout manner, she felt guilty, and quickly offered her own thanks. Formal prayer was not always her way, but living with Jerry, for whom she had to carry at least a bit of respect, was different somehow, than her own father, who was given to long and pious prayers, silent or otherwise. He often read the old German prayers from the small black *Gebet* (prayer) book, his words rising and falling in a tearful, emotional cadence that only brought a hardness, a rebellion in Hannah.

He had been so absolute in his devotion to God, and so hopelessly muddled in his way of providing for his family, unable to accept defeat, without a clear vision for the future, expecting a miracle from the God he felt would accept him as superior, special.

And He may have, Hannah thought. Who was she to judge? She just knew there was a difference in her own father and Jerry. (She never thought of him as her husband; it was too personal.)

Their marriage was a partnership for the saving of the homestead. Nothing more.

They rode out, deciding at the last minute to leave the dogs at home. They'd had plenty of exercise, running with Jerry when he was checking the cattle. They set up an awful, pitiful whining and yelping, clawing at the wire fence that enclosed them, their brown eyes begging, pleading with all the power of children not wanting to be left alone.

Hannah looked at Jerry. Their eyes met. Hannah watched the crinkles appear on his face, watched the slow smile spread his lips, and she knew he felt the same empathy for their dogs, and opened the gate.

They tumbled out, falling over each other, wriggling and giving short, ecstatic yelps of happiness, then ran circles around Jerry, Hannah, and the horses. Hannah laughed outright, that short, deep burst of sound that came from deep within, a sound heard so seldom that it never failed to shock Jerry.

They mounted their horses, still smiling as the dogs catapulted themselves ahead of them, streaks of brown, black, and speckled gray, their legs almost invisible, they pumped them so fast.

Hannah laughed again. "Those stupid little dogs. They'll wear themselves out," she said.

Jerry was busy holding King back from running with the dogs. His head was up, his neck arched, his haunches lowered as he danced, stepped sideways, fought the bit. He shook his head and snorted, then came up, his front legs leaving the ground. Jerry leaned forward, kept his seat, and told him to settle down.

Hannah kept her own horse in check, scanning the sky with anxious eyes. She did not like the feel of the atmosphere, the yellow light, the sun a hazy blob of illumination, like a bobbing lantern in the distance, or the headlight of a car. It wasn't normal, the stillness, the complete lack of even the faintest breeze.

She kept her worries to herself, knowing Jerry would think she was being too cautious, which she supposed she was.

Where had this come from, now? This lack of speaking her mind. Surely, she wasn't changing that much. She used to tell Jerry anything she wanted, she didn't care what he thought. Why didn't she do that now?

She watched his back, the way he rode his horse, that certain skill that always amazed her when she saw it in the Jenkins boys. When had Jerry acquired that same skill? It was unsettling, this grudging admiration she felt. She had to do something about it, but how?

She trained her eyes on her surroundings, choosing to watch the emptiness, that vast expanse of nothingness where you could not see anyone or anything, yet you often had the uncanny feeling of being watched.

God's eyes, she reckoned. God was everywhere, a fact she'd accepted from her birth, one of her earliest memories. Hearing her mother speak of *da Goot Mon* (the Good Man) was as natural as breathing, so whenever Hannah had the impression of being watched, it was all right with her.

The dogs had chased up a prairie hen, the poor fowl running in zigzags like a rabbit before finally having enough sense to take wing. Of all the creatures of the plains, those prairie hens had to be the dumbest.

She watched the chicken's awkward flight, flapping its wings furiously, squawking in wild-eyed alarm. The dogs' faces lifted, tongues lolling from wide mouths, before giving up the chase and finding another scent to follow.

A flurry of dickcissels rose from the swell of grass to the right like a burst of thrown wheat seeds, their shrill cries telling of their alarm. A larkspur sang its plaintive song from a hiding place, probably somewhere on an extra-large tuft of grass, the bird blending into its native background in much the same color.

They arrived at the corner where the dirt road led off to the right, a row of aging fence posts held up by their hidden length in the dry prairie soil, rows of sagging, rusted barbed wire strung between them.

No one seemed to know anything about this short length of useless fence, or cared about it, so Hannah always used it as a road sign, the right turn to the Klassermans'. It seemed strange to think of them being gone, having put all the hard work into the homestead and then deserting it.

They were no longer young, and certainly not the tough, sinewy type like the Jenkinses, the Moores, and dozens of other natives that dotted this land. Descendants of the pioneers, proud, unflappable, despising change, suspicious of strangers, harboring entire textbooks of knowledge in their brains, their hearts filled with a deep and abiding love of the land, a fierce loyalty to the plains and the elements.

Hannah was proud to be one of them. She believed she carried the same spirit of optimism within, the way the Jenkinses rode with the ebb and flow of the seasons, the extreme weather, the loneliness of being on the prairie for days on end.

The wind, though. She knew well that sometimes the wind was hardest to take. It blew hard for days and nights, on and on without ceasing, moaning around the corners of buildings like unhappy ghosts, ruffling grasses, blowing dust only days after a miniscule amount of rain, drying out any small amount of moisture that fell from the skimpy clouds.

And so she rode behind Jerry, never beside him, to avoid conversation. She liked it this way, her thoughts her own, the solitude a gift, not having to answer to anyone, only the horse beneath her and nature around her.

The road went to the left, then curved right and the sight of the ranch was immediate. No horse trailers. A few cars parked by the house. No activity. Everything strangely quiet. What had happened to them all?

Jerry rode on, never imagining that Hannah had ever been here before or knew anything about these people. She kept her distance, observed without saying a word.

They rode up to the familiar barn, stopped at the corral, dismounted, and looked around. Nip and Tuck were told to stay while they tied the horses to the hitching rack beside the closed barn doors.

Hannah thought that seemed odd, on a balmy, quiet day, to have all those doors closed. There were no white horses to be seen anywhere. No cattle or dogs.

Jerry looked at the parked vehicles, long, low, gleaming in the dull, yellowish light of the semi-dreary day. He gave a low whistle, admiring the teal green color of the Oldsmobile, the brilliant, earth-shaking opulence of the red Ford.

"Obviously, there are no people of poverty here!"

Hannah nodded. "Should we go to the house?"

"I guess. No one seems to be out here."

Together they walked to the house, the dear ranch structure that had housed Sylvia Klasserman and all her eccentric German ways, her florid pink face and enormous girth, the baklava and croissants, cinnamon rolls and raisin bread. Hannah swallowed an unexpected lump in her throat, realized she was blinking furiously to keep back unwanted tears.

No one came to the door, so Jerry knocked again. Hannah felt terribly ill at ease, when the door was pulled open from inside by a man who seemed to be about their own age and size.

From behind the screen door, his face broke into a grin of friendliness as he shoved open the door and spoke in a quiet, well-modulated voice. "Come in. Come in. I'm assuming you're neighbors?" The sentence rose at the end, making it a question. His way of speaking was completely foreign to their own, although the words were spoken in English.

Jerry stepped back to allow Hannah entry before him, a hand laid lightly on the small of her back. She went ahead quickly, so he'd drop his hand.

It was still the Klassermans' house, only it smelled different, the furniture was different, the rugs and pictures changing the living room into something more structured, neater. Gone were the crocheted doilies, the figurines and artificial pink roses, replaced by wooden chests, serviceable trays, green ferns in ceramic pots, throw pillows and blankets in neutral colors, all done tastefully and expensively.

The young man introduced himself. "My name is Timothy Weber. I'm from Salt Lake City, Utah."

Jerry proffered a hand. They shook firmly, met each other's gaze directly. "I'm Jeremiah Riehl and this is my wife Hannah." Hannah nodded, shook hands, and asked, "How do you do?"

"I'm doing well, thank you, Hannah. And you?"

"Good."

Timothy Weber stood back to survey them with curious eyes, taking in Jerry's straw hat with the strip of rawhide circling the crown, his denim coat without pockets, his broadfall trousers, as well as Hannah's skirts and head covering. "So you're . . .?"

"Amish. From Pennsylvania."

Timothy whistled softly. "Never heard of them. A religious sect?"

"Yes."

"Well, this is interesting. Very interesting. We'll have to talk. But first, let me seat you. Here, Jeremiah, is it?"

"Call me Jerry. Everybody does."

Timothy grinned an infectious grin. "Tim. Call me Tim."

He really was a nice-looking young man. Brown hair, cut short in the manner of the English, a thin brown moustache above a wide mouth, a prominent nose and expressive blue eyes, hooded by a wealth of brown eyebrows.

Tim seated them on the sofa, a large, deep davenport upholstered in gray. Expensive, Hannah thought, as she reached back to arrange pillows behind her back. Tim seated himself in an oak rocking chair and stretched his denim-clad legs out before him. Hannah looked around, wondering if he had a wife, children, or parents? Who were all those men, with the white trailers and white horses?

"So," Tim began. "The reason it is interesting to me that you are of a religious sect is because we are too. Oh, I meant to tell you. My wife is taking a much-needed nap. I told you we're from Salt Lake City. You probably have heard of the Mormons? The Church of the Latter-day Saints?"

"Yes." Jerry nodded.

"We are of that religious order." His voice turned quiet, and his eyes became averted. He lifted both hands to examine his fingernails, as if mentioning his church made him nervous, self-conscious.

There was an awkward silence. Then Tim sighed. "We moved here to begin a new life after leaving our way of life among the . . . the brethren of the Mormon Church."

Jerry raised his eyebrows, watched Tim's face, but said nothing. Tim took a deep breath, a smile appeared on his face, one that showed his white teeth but did not spread to his eyes. "So, here we are. Pioneers on the prairie. North Dakota. Bought this ranch. I raise horses."

White horses, Hannah thought. She wanted to know what the breed was called but of course, she couldn't say that in Jerry's presence.

"Tell me about your . . . way of life."

So Jerry outlined the Amish faith briefly, the *ordnung*, the way of obedience, the journey from Lancaster County, Hannah's family homesteading the 320 acres, and that now they were the only Amish remaining.

"Why did your brethren return home?" Tim asked.

Hannah spoke up. "The two-year drought."

"You mean . . ." Tim looked from Jerry to Hannah and back again.

"It didn't rain for two years."

"Oh, come on! I have a hard time believing that." Tim laughed, slapping his knee at the joke he'd just heard.

"No, I'm serious." Hannah felt a stab of anger. Boy, did he have a lot to learn.

"You can't sit there and tell me you had not one drop of rain in two years!" Incredulous, Tim leaned forward, an intensity stabbing the room's muted yellowish glow.

"Close to it." Hannah glanced at Jerry, saw his pinched look.

Tim chuckled, a derisive sound that bordered on mockery. The moment was saved by a fluttering sound, a door closing quietly, light footsteps crossing the hallway, followed by the appearance of a vision dressed in white. Almost, Hannah recoiled, thinking a heavenly being was in their midst.

Her hair was blond, an unnatural white blond, unlike anything Hannah had ever seen, surrounding her head like a halo, purely angelic. Her eyes were large, almond-shaped, and blue, her face small and pointed, like porcelain. Doll-like, she appeared to be made of wax.

"I heard visitors," she trilled, in an unnatural child's voice.

Hannah drew back, aghast. How old was this wife of Tim's?

She walked over to Hannah and sat next to her, extending a small, white hand, exclaiming in short sentences how happy she was to see them, and how they would be close friends, how charming her head covering was, and . . . how had they arrived?

Hannah looked out the window toward the corral and noticed the fading light, the restless horses. She spoke a few words of acknowledgment to the girl's overtures, listened to Tim's introduction of his wife, Lila, then rose and said they must be on their way, she believed there would be a change in the weather, but not before Lila mentioned the fact that she was sixteen years old.

CHAPTER 6

THEY WERE SORRY TO SEE THEM LEAVE SO SOON AND URGED THEM TO stay for tea and cakes. But Hannah remained adamant. Jerry told Tim they'd be back as soon as they could, but he'd better follow his wife because she was well-versed in the ways of the weather on the plains.

As soon as they were able to get away from their pleading hosts, Hannah hissed a warning to Jerry. "We have to ride hard." That was all she said, but Jerry heard the warning in her voice. They weren't at the first bend in the road before the yellowish cast turned much darker, changed to a leaden, grayish sheen that held no promise of anything gentle or good.

The dogs were flat out, running to the best of their ability, but could not keep up with the horses' galloping pace. When they fell behind, Hannah slowed the palomino and yelled to Jerry, who turned, and slowed King as well.

Hannah dismounted, pointing a shaking finger to the north-east. "See that?"

Jerry shaded his eyes, his palm turned down, squinting, then shook his head. "What? I don't see anything."

"That gray line. It looks like a wall."

Jerry still didn't see it.

"We're in for it. That's snow. If we ride hard enough, we'll make it. If not, there's a real chance we could get lost."

"Come on, Hannah. Not in October!"

"The dogs can't keep up. You carry one. I'll take the other."

"We can't, Hannah."

"We have to."

"They'll find their way home."

Hannah shrugged and got back in the saddle—there wasn't time to waste arguing. Kicking the stirrups in the palomino's sides, she rode leaning low across the saddle, listening for King's hoofbeats behind her.

The wind picked up immediately, followed by the first gritty snowflake. Hannah became wild-eyed, watching as King flashed by, Jerry low on his neck.

She put the end of the leather reins on her horse's sides, screaming and goading him on. They had not yet reached the crossroads where the barbed wire fence sagged on the right, which meant they had a long way to go after they turned. At least four or five miles.

The dogs were no longer behind them. Hannah twisted her body in the saddle and called their names, but she knew it was futile. They'd find their way home, he'd said. Did he even know how bad snowstorms could be on the plains?

A few hard flakes of snow, and then there were thousands, biting into her face like fierce, sharp teeth. She lowered her head even farther. The horses slowed of their own accord, turned left and increased their speed until Hannah thought she must be rocketing through the air. She gasped for breath and gritted her teeth against the stinging, icy bits of snow that were assaulting her face.

King was still visible, the flying hooves and charging body with Jerry's dark head so low it appeared to be part of the flowing black mane. Hannah was gasping for breath, wiping her nose on the shoulder of her coat, nose and eyes streaming. Her ears felt as if they were being torched.

Oh for a black, woolen kerchief to tie around her head. The flying bits of snow thickened. Ahead of her, King was turning from a brown horse with a flying black mane and tail to a blob of gray, an undulating blob of non-color with invisible hooves.

Panic rose in her chest. She screamed, trying to get Jerry to slow down. The possibility of being lost in a blizzard on the plains loomed before her, the stark reality a slap in the face, a painful blow that took her breath away. She didn't realize she was muttering and sobbing, "No no, no. Please God, no."

Not this way. She didn't want to die, frozen, on the prairie, blatant evidence of her own dumb choice, unlearned greenhorns without a lick of common sense.

It's only October. It's only a squall. Over and over, she told herself this, to keep the terror at bay.

Then, she couldn't see King at all. The wind blasted through her thin coat, the snow like knifepoints. The world turned into a gray void with no top or bottom, no left or right, and she had no idea where she was headed.

Give a horse its head, it'll always find its way home. The thought was a comfort, for a short time at least. When the palomino slowed to a trot, Hannah knew there was no use pushing him faster; he'd set his own pace.

Her teeth chattering, eyes streaming, black hair plastered to her head like a rubber swimming cap, Hannah held on with her knees, shivering so hard her arms raised and lowered of their own accord like a chicken after its head is severed on the chopping block. Grimly, she reminded herself to stay calm, stay reasonable.

Her world was a whiteout now. Everything was obliterated except for the orb of whirling snow and the icy, driving wind.

"He'll get me home," Hannah whispered. Over and over. "Home. Home. He'll get me home."

A hard bump. A lurch. Hannah grabbed for the saddle horn. Too late! The palomino went down, falling with a grunt, the air expelled from his nostrils as Hannah flew off the saddle, down over the horse's bent neck, hitting the ground with a crunch on her left shoulder.

A knife edge of pain shot all the way from her fingertips to her neck. A ripping, tearing monster of agony that took away every sensation, the whirling whiteness of the storm, the downed horse, and the cold. Everything.

She slid blissfully into unconsciousness.

Jerry let King have his head, knowing Hannah was on his heels. He didn't become too concerned until the snow became so thick he had trouble keeping the side of the road in his sight. After that, it was up to King. Trusting his horse was the only way. He had never been so cold in all his life. He turned in the saddle, repeatedly calling Hannah's name, but the wind tore his words out of his mouth and flung them away. He imagined the wind laughing at him, a hysterical, evil cackle that robbed him of the small amount of confidence he had.

He prayed for God's deliverance from the grip of this awful storm. He prayed for deliverance if it was God's will, though, always putting his life in God's hands.

Whether we live or whether we die, we are the Lord's. Over and over, this verse coursed through his mind. The pain of his cold hands was almost unbearable. He envisioned black, useless fingers. Hanging the reins across King's neck, he sat up to tuck his numbed hands under his armpits, but felt only more cold and ice.

He sucked in a lungful of air, blew it out, then shivered uncontrollably. Calm. Calm. Stay with it. He talked to himself repeatedly. King slowed, picked up his head to trot, then slowed again. Each time he slowed, Jerry turned, his eyes boring through the whirling whiteness, hoping for a glimpse of Hannah on the palomino.

He was becoming sleepy, while shivering like a wind-blown leaf on a tree branch. He released his hands from beneath his armpits, slapped them against his chest, kicked his feet out of the stirrups and pumped them up and down, whacking his knees against the sides of the saddle.

King plodded on, his faithful ears still turning back, then forward, pricking through the whirling, spitting, hissing gray world being flung in Jerry's face, a cruel reminder that he was a mere mortal who had made a stupid decision, a miscalculation. Why hadn't he taken Hannah's warnings more seriously?

Not that she'd ever take his warnings. He winced when something hit his left knee, then shouted weakly, the sound like a mewling kitten.

The corral. Thank God! He stopped, waiting for Hannah.

The realization that she was not directly behind him arrived slowly. Finally, to stave off his rising panic, he dismounted on legs that seemed to be made of liquid. He fell, his bare hands scrabbling in the deepening snow as he righted himself, wobbled to the barn, his stiffened fingers fumbling with the latch like a young child.

Surely Hannah would be here soon. He unsaddled King, rubbed him down, fed him, gave him a small amount of water, his ears tuned for the sound of Hannah's arrival. *Please, please.* Over and over he begged. *Keep her safe, Lord. Keep her safe.*

He made his way to the house by unspooling a long length of hemp rope, missing the house several times by a good one hundred feet each time. First to the right, then to the left, before bumping solidly into the side of the house, cracking his nose until tears ran down his cheeks.

Somehow, he kept enough of his senses to start a fire in the cook stove, open the draught until a roaring fire turned the stove top cherry red. Repeatedly, he went to the window, fighting down the dragon's fiery panic, the imagined monster that took away his sense of hope, his ability to pray and believe that God would look down with mercy.

Please. Please.

Hannah struggled as if she was under water, bravely fighting to open her mouth and fill her lungs with life-saving air.

She was so cold. So terribly cold. *She was a child, playing in the snow, her crocheted mittens soaked, her hands red and wet and freezing. There was Manny. She'd get his mittens. She ran after him, calling, calling, but he seemed never to hear her at all.*

She was crying when she regained consciousness. The palomino was down and, by the looks of it, had either broken or otherwise injured his foot. He made no attempt to regain his footing, merely huddled in a heap of golden hide and cream-colored mane and tail, his eyes closed against the whipping wind and snow.

Hannah's first logical reasoning was to stay where she was. She knew that to wallow about on level land in zero visibility was courting death, and she had no intention of dying this way. She took stock of her situation.

One downed horse. No one to rescue her this time. A saddle and yes, a saddle blanket. Both impossible to remove. If she could somehow loosen the girth strap, she'd be able to use both to try and keep from freezing. Then she'd have to wait out the storm and hope for the best.

She moved, which sent an electric shock through her shoulder. She felt like she might lose consciousness again, which really made her mad.

She took her right hand and grasped her left shoulder, pushing and prodding, squeezing her eyes shut against the pain. Nothing broken, just bumped and bruised.

Hannah got to her feet, crying now, the pain almost unbearable. She slipped a hand beneath the wide girth strap, and pulled. She pushed, working the girth up over the belly of the horse, shaking her numb, red hands over and over, alternately muttering and crying.

When the girth strap would not let loose, she fell on her backside, hard, then went back to tugging the saddle and blanket loose from the horse's body. She realized the importance of these two items, the difference between life and death. Gritting her teeth, she squeezed her eyes shut and kept pulling, over and over, yanking, urging the palomino to roll just a bit. Just a bit.

Only when the tears froze on her numb cheeks did she realize she was begging, crying, pushing on the horse's stomach with one hand, yanking on the wide girth strap with the other.

She lifted numb hands to cup her flaming ears and the side of her head. How long could a person.expect to survive in these harsh conditions?

She freed the saddle with a mighty heave, then the blanket. Quickly she found the lee side of the horse, away from the driving snow.

She tucked herself in, pulled the fibrous, itching saddle blanket over her body, rolling up in a tight fetal position, then reaching out with one hand to draw the saddle over her head and shoulders. A blessed reprieve, if only for a short time. She felt the absence of the wind's fury, the stinging of the icy snow. Exhausted, she reveled in the still, dark cocoon of the horse's body, the blanket, and the saddle.

Thank God for the trousers and boots, the woolen socks on her feet. She was still shaking with the cold, miserable with goose bumps going up and down her spine and across her shoulders, her ears and hands burning with the extreme cold and moisture of the melting snow.

Her teeth clacked together. She put her hands between her knees, rolling and grimacing with the pain. Well, she was here, now. In the biggest mess she'd ever been in. She guessed it was up to her to figure something out, with Jerry on his own and the dogs having gone their way. She hoped he wouldn't be dumb enough to start out on his own in this storm. Many more people than she cared to admit had died on the plains in a blizzard.

Had they discussed this together? She couldn't remember. She had no choice, no other option but to stay where she was and hope the storm would soon blow itself out and she could attempt to find her way back home. She would freeze to death if she tried to get to their homestead, if the storm continued through the night.

The horse afforded some heat. Why did he lay here? If his leg was broken, Jerry would have to shoot him. There was no repairing a horse's leg bone. She regretted not having taken him as a gift. The horse with no name, as she recognized him. If she would have accepted the gift of the beautiful palomino, she would have felt beholden to him, like she owed him the favor of being his friend, which she resisted.

And now she'd gone and married him, to save the homestead, and was in the same unsteady boat in the same swamp of her own will.

Perhaps it would just be easier to die out here on the prairie that she loved. Frozen stiff.

A fierce resistance to her own demise roared through her, leaving her shaken and unable to understand her intense, overwhelming fervor for life.

She would not die. She had this makeshift cave of sorts, the heat from the horse's body, if he lived through the night.

The sound of the blowing snow scouring the blanket told her the storm was still roaring across the prairie. Like a freight train, this wind. There was no stopping it, no directing it where you wanted it to go, or when you wanted it to cease.

She felt as if God was above the storm, mad at her, teaching her a lesson, like a child being punished. He certainly was not showing any mercy, no matter how much she cried and begged.

Well then, if this was what He thought she needed, then she'd take her punishment, and take it right, without complaint.

Her father had spanked her many times as a child so she figured this was the grown-up version of a "paddling" in the woodshed, where her gentle father would get down on one knee, grasp her shoulders tenderly, and explain to her in great and lengthy detail how she had disobeyed and, in order to correct her for doing wrong, she needed to feel the pain of the thin, flat piece of wood. To disobey made the Lord sad. Children who were left to their own devices, who never learned to submit to their parents, would find it hard to submit to God in later years.

Hannah stoically endured the few whacks of the board, which hurt, but not much. She never cried. Her father cried, which she thought was awfully strange. Why would you spank someone if it was that heartbreaking? What was so bad about chasing the cows into the pond? They liked the cool water. They just looked funny when they ran! Hannah never really felt bad about chasing cows. She never understood all this sorry and repent and all that. He could have tried to see it her way.

As she lay shivering beneath her makeshift tent, many incidences from her childhood roamed through her mind, like a herd of memories that found no comfortable way to disappear, so they just wandered around, bits and pieces, snatches of mischief, episodes of anger and disobedience.

Repeatedly, she had been chastised, talked to about sin and repentance and the eyes of God. About Jesus, who died on the cross. Countless times, she'd heard different ministers speak of these things, in many different sermons, and had always been completely and thoroughly bored.

Nothing ever stuck to her heart or mind it seemed. She could listen to the most fervent sermon, and remember only the bristles on the speaker's cheeks, or his too-long, greasy hair, or the way he unfolded his severely ironed handkerchief. Three hours of sitting on a hard, wooden bench was much too long, so she found ways to amuse herself, usually whispering, playing with straight pins, or watching flies or, if she was fortunate, looking out a nearby window.

Her father had patiently explained the new birth, but that never made much sense, either. She understood the basics of the Christian life—to do good, stay away from evil, and accept Jesus Christ as your personal Savior. Actually, she wasn't sure if she had ever done exactly that, in a deep, meaningful, spiritual way. She wasn't normal, maybe. Formal worship, like prayers and Bible reading, simply didn't interest her.

But so many times, beneath the enormous sky on the emptiness of the prairie, she felt as if she was a small dot, a worm, the pinhead of every human being, so small, so unimportant. And yet, God being as big as the sky and as tremendous as the wind, He *knew* her, every ounce of her. He knew her thoughts and her actions and how rebellious she was and how ignorant to other people.

But He had given her that nature, hadn't He? Well then, He would be able to change her heart when it was time.

Lying in the increasing discomfort of dripping snow, where the heat from the horse's body caused a melting stream to constantly trickle along her back, sent wave after wave of cold through her spine. She inched away, only to allow a fresh wave of cold to enter beneath the elevated blanket.

Oh, misery! She writhed with pain, allowing herself only inches to relieve stiff joints and aching fingers and toes.

How long? How long would the storm blow? She tried to will away nighttime, the encompassing blackness with no stars and no moon. Once night came, it might not leave before the horse, the saddle, and the blanket with her beneath were completely obscured in snow. Drifts on the plains were often two, three feet high, which would shroud their dead bodies until the spring thaw.

Who would find her? Jerry? The Jenkinses? A whole pile of rescue workers from the town?

She wasn't ready to die. She wanted to stay right here in North Dakota and keep the homestead. She loved her life on the prairie, the cows, the wildflowers, the animals and birds, the ranch house and barn, the mules and Jerry's horses.

Him? Jerry? Did she want to stay here in the world for Jerry? If only she could understand God and love and all the good things other people understood then perhaps she'd have a chance at loving her husband. But what exactly was love? Who could explain it to you? Help you find it?

And now she was getting sleepy. So terribly tired. The thought of closing her eyes and succumbing to a blissful cloud of sleep was the single most enticing emotion she had ever felt.

She'd heard somewhere, though, about the danger of falling asleep when a person is freezing cold. But she had to sleep. Had to. She couldn't stay awake. It was not possible.

Her eyelids fell. She drifted off into a place where the wet smell of the snow on the horse's body, the shivering goose bumps and pain, the knives of ice and frozen snow, disappeared to be replaced by an unimaginable place of softness and comfort, warmth and light.

Jerry paced. His hands knotted behind his back, he walked from room to room, his neck thrust forward, his dark hair falling in his eyes, a black stubble of whiskers growing across his ashen cheeks. That it should come to this.

He loved her. That was the pain of his existence, his single reason for staying with her in this ranch house, so far away from family, from his friend, Jake, from any human being who could make this vigil bearable.

When he heard the dogs barking, he ran to the door and flung it open, ushering them in to the warmth. Icicles hung from their thick fur and clumps of snow stuck in their paws. He hurried to get towels to wrap them in and brought them fresh bowls of water, thanking God that they had found their way.

Grateful for the dogs' company, he kneeled on the floor between them and prayed to the One he knew intimately. He begged his Lord and Savior to spare Hannah's life, but always had to add, "If it is Thy will." God's blessed will, which was to be honored above all else, even the treasure of his love for Hannah.

There were times of peace, when he felt his soul yielding to God, pliable, soft, accepting of his fate. Then came a desperate need to see her face, hear her voice, to apologize for letting her drop behind on their mad dash through the storm that grabbed him in a grip like a vise, until he thought he would surely lose his mind.

The storm battered the house, the wind and snow like flung pellets of stone against the windows. When darkness came, he began to shiver. His limbs turned to water, his breath came in short, hard gasps of agony.

Oh, Hannah. Hannah. Your suffering is more than I can bear. He would have gladly laid in the snow himself if it meant he could save her.

Please stop. Stop. Stop the snow and the wind.

His thoughts were becoming maudlin. If only he had gone back, if only he hadn't assumed she was behind him all the time.

He flung himself down on the davenport and cried hard, painful sobs of anguish and despair.

Had he been too selfish in his single-minded pursuit of her? He had to have Hannah at all cost. He'd given up the security of his Amish community, the horse-shoeing business, a bright and enterprising future, to live her with her—and for what? Oh dear God, for what?

His breathing slowed and became even as he fell to his knees, his face buried in his hands, groaning softly, begging God without words.

He sat up, drained and exhausted, cold and shivering. He lit a kerosene lamp with shaking fingers, had to blow at the match flame three times before it would die.

The fire in the cook stove had gone out, not an ember remained. Dully, he threw in a handful of kindling, held another match to it, opened the draft to watch it burn.

He added larger pieces of wood from the wood box behind the stove, noticed the few pieces remaining, but could not bring himself to go to the back stoop to collect more wood. He'd have to know, then, how deep the accumulation of snow had become.

He felt guilty as he spread his hands to the warmth, knowing that Hannah would have nothing to warm her freezing body.

And still the storm raged on.

Jerry resumed his pacing. He went to the windows, touched the glass with his fingers, as if he had power to stop the onslaught of deadly snow and ice. He put more wood on the fire.

I love you, Hannah, with all of my heart and soul. If it's not God's will that we live together in love, then I pray you will know perfect peace in Heaven.

He felt calm now, accepting his destiny, abandoning his own will to God's. What was his selfish, paltry, little love compared to God, who had sent His only Son so that we may live?

He stood still. Was the storm lessening? Was there only a slight change in the wind? Or was it all his own hope that made it seem so?

He sat down, weakly. He listened, holding his breath, hardly daring to exhale, for fear it was like a mirage, a cruel hallucination.

Decidedly now, there was a weakening of the storm. He whipped his body around to look at the clock. Almost eleven o'clock at night.

He couldn't wait until morning. He simply could not. He'd take a lantern and the dogs. His only hope was a lack of wind. All he needed were starlit skies, a moon, and a bit of calm.

He was on his feet, running to his bedroom for warm clothing, an extra pair of socks, tears running unchecked down his face.

CHAPTER 7

IT WAS COMMON KNOWLEDGE ON THE PLAINS THAT A BLIZZARD brought to a halt all outside activity. It was dangerous, foolhardy, to attempt a rescue or to search for lost cattle or horses if a storm of this velocity swept through the area.

If only they had never ventured out. Jerry stepped off the porch, alarmed to discover the depth of the snow. It was a good two feet in some places; other places were windswept, and fell to less than a foot.

The barn loomed dark through the snow that was now falling more slowly and thinly, as the storm gave its last gasp, giving Jerry a burst of elation. If he could only get to her before the inevitable wind unleashed its power on the unprotected prairie.

With fumbling, frantic movements, he saddled King, mounted, and held the lantern out from the eager, bouncing horse. With a whispered prayer, he gave King his head, bowing his own head to the spitting snow, the tail end of the storm.

How far would she have come? He tried to concentrate and stay on the road, though the road and the prairie were all one solid blanket of white now. If only there were trees, embankments, fences, neighbors, the way the countryside appeared in Lancaster County. He'd need a keen sense of direction, and the skill to search beyond the small circle of yellow lamplight.

The cold had not worsened, thank God. King was tiring already, so he slowed him to a walk. The snow was up to his chest in some of the lower areas. Jerry could only lean forward, his eyes straining above the glow of the lantern, piercing the darkness with a desperate gaze. The thought of this being foolish, being out at night alone directly after a storm, crossed his mind and left him with a rising sense of despair.

Should he have waited until daybreak? King charged on, plowing through the deep places, increasing his speed where the power of the wind had swept the ground almost bare. If only Hannah could be on a rise of ground and visible. He guessed the palomino would have wandered home, found his way, if he had remained upright. He knew the power of these storms, the mind-sucking confusion that robbed even seasoned Westerners of all sense of direction and level-headedness.

All the gopher holes, the prairie dog and badger homes that dotted the grasslands like set traps, meant that the palomino could have gone down. He likely did. All Jerry could hope for was Hannah's safety, that she had remained by her horse and stayed conscious. The saddle and blanket were her only hope of even a bit of shelter.

He pulled on the reins and stopped King. He had to get his bearings. Lowering the lantern, his intense gaze swept the level land as far as he could see. He calculated he'd come more than a mile, which meant he had about three more to go until the turn to the Texan's ranch. If the barbed wire and sagging posts were visible, he'd know he was on the right track.

But who knew how far off the road the palomino might have drifted? The sense of futility settled in and left him slumped in the saddle, his arms draped across the saddle horn, the lantern too close to his horse.

Should he return to the ranch, keeping his own safety in mind? He knew well the astounding fury of the wind after a winter storm, sending walls of thick snow scudding across the prairie without mercy on man or beast. A shiver went up his spine. He prayed, asking the Lord to guide him.

He sat motionless, the vast darkness around him, the great white void of the treeless plain suddenly becoming a menacing pit that had swallowed Hannah, never to surrender her frozen corpse.

He shook his head to clear it. After praying, why did such thoughts wedge their way in to his mind? He needed a stronger, better faith.

A sense of his own weak humanity encompassed him. *Miserable creature that I am*, he thought, *chasing my own will and desire*. Chasing Hannah and living out here in this tough, unforgiving land, his only reason being to obtain her love, something that seemed to be as elusive as a thin wisp of fog, a mirage in the desert.

He groaned within himself, could not accept her demise. *How can I sit here crying Lord, Lord, when perhaps all this is a lesson, a hard-earned lesson in self-denial?* He knew there were countless young women dotting the hills and valleys of Pennsylvania, young women of worth. Respectful, well-brought-up girls who never asked for more than a reasonable husband, a roof over their heads, food, and children to raise, filling their husband's quiver with offspring who adorned his table. Young women who were taught submission and the blessing of a meek and quiet spirit, who understood God's will for a woman, and strived obediently to be a helpmeet, a friend, lover, nurturer, using all of the gifts God bestowed on women.

But they weren't Hannah. This knowledge unfolded in his chest and bloomed to fill his heart with its essence. He bowed before it.

As if on cue, the moon slid silently from behind silver-white clouds, throwing the snow-covered landscape into waves of blue-white and shadows of dark gray. Every rise and hollow was visible, the impotent yellow light of the lantern a pitiful mockery. He threw it into a snow drift, where it hissed and died. He'd find it in the spring.

A wild elation rose up, a sense of clear direction now. He goaded King, his head swiveled from side to side, his eyes burning from the cold and his intense, piercing gaze. He knew if he found the fence, he'd have gone too far. She had been riding behind him at least halfway from the Texan's ranch.

This merciful calm. Surely God was on his side. But how long until the wind began to howl, burying them both in its strength?

The moon's white light on the snow proved to be even better than the limited yellow glow of the coal oil lantern. One by one, stars appeared, lending their merry dots of illumination, shoring up Jerry's flagging confidence, allowing him a few minutes of courage. He rode on, scanning the snow for any mound that could be Hannah buried in the snow.

And there it was.

A bump, a protrusion that was much bigger than a clump of grass, too small to be a rise, a swell or an unexpected hillock on the otherwise level, snow-encrusted land.

He turned King in the proper direction and slowed him to a walk. His heart leaped as the mound of snow gave way, the light color of a horse's head and neck appearing, followed by a resounding whinny, the low, urgent sound of a horse in pain.

Ah, so that was it. Her horse had fallen. He threw himself off King and waded to the palomino's head, reassuring him, then dug frantically, scraping snow off the upended saddle, the frozen blanket, heaving it off the inert form curled beside the horse.

"Hannah?" he called, unable to comprehend her stillness. He fell on his knees and touched her cold, white face. "Hannah."

Louder now, he grasped her shoulder and shook with all his strength. A low moan escaped her lips but her eyes stayed closed. Thank God, she was alive!

He called her name again and again but was unable to revive her. He straightened and took stock of their dilemma.

A downed horse. His unconscious wife. Likely hypothermia had set in. Gtting her to the house was his first concern. He'd have to get her up on King, somehow, before he would be able to get himself into the saddle.

If only she'd wake up. "Hannah! Hannah!"

Another low moan, but no reason for him to think she would regain consciousness. Well, there was only one way, and that was to heave her up onto the horse's back.

With herculean strength, he picked her up and tried repeatedly to drape her across the saddle, afraid of hurting her already frozen body, knowing he could not leave her here while he went to summon help.

Finally, he was able to position her across the front of the saddle before placing a foot in the stirrup and leaping up himself.

He had to call to King repeatedly and grab the reins to stop him from leaping into action. He carefully cradled Hannah in his arms like a child before allowing King to walk away from the pitiful form of the palomino. The injured horse's eyes were wild, his neck outstretched as he tried repeatedly to gather his legs beneath him and stand, only to topple over in the deep, light snow, sending up a cloud of white powder as he sank onto his side.

Jerry well knew the palomino would never walk again, but Hannah had to be his first priority. He'd have to be put down, but he'd left his gun at home. He couldn't bring himself to think about it now.

The cold stabbed through his coat. The breeze raked a cold, ominous hand across his face, sent a shiver of alarm through him. He figured he had four miles to go, maybe more. He adjusted Hannah's weight, cradling her shoulders firmly before leaning forward and calling to King to go.

He released the reins and felt the surge of power beneath him, but knew it would be short-lived the minute King's legs hit a deep drift. Snow was flung into his face, the wind picking up by the minute. *All right, God. The rest is up to You. I'm done. I've done all I can do. If it is Thy will that we survive this, then guide my horse. Give me strength to hold on.*

The reins flopped loosely in Jerry's hands. It was up to King. The horse was powerful, a magnificent specimen of his breed, but to arrive safely to the ranch in the face of these obstacles would take every ounce of his strength. It would be the ultimate marathon of his life.

The moon faded and disappeared as a prevailing blackness surrounded them. One by one, the stars were erased from the cold, menacing sky. The breeze became stronger, playing with King's mane, slapping against Jerry's face like a punishment, grabbing his courage and flinging it away.

King was smart, Jerry knew, but would he find his way? Hope rose in his chest as King leaped to increase his speed when the snow lay thinly on the high spots. He raced across these areas, then plowed through the drifts with unbelievable strength.

The snow, the prairie, the sky, everything became one, then, as the wind began to wail and howl, the song of the elements. It battered Jerry's face with stinging ice, flung his woolen stocking cap into the vast, blowing vortex of the onslaught that followed every blizzard, sending tremendous clouds of snow racing across the miles and miles of prairie. There were no mountains, no tree lines, nothing to slow the great blitz of the North Dakota wind.

And still King lunged, gathering his muscular, rippling haunches beneath him, his breath coming in powerful exhalations, his nostrils distended as he sucked in the oxygen he needed for the pumping of his great heart, the expansion of his vigorous lungs. His head was lowered, his thick neck distended, as he used every muscle in his resplendent body, sensing the danger, knowing he was pleasing his beloved master.

He never stumbled and he slowed only when it was absolutely impossible to keep up his pace, his ears flicking back, waiting for a voice, a command. Jerry urged King, spoke softly to him, but the power of the wind tore his words away from his mouth and sent them uselessly away.

But King knew. He knew Jerry was urging him. He sensed the danger, and so he stayed on course, faithful to his training, obedient to the one master he adored.

Pain crept up under Jerry's eyelids and his ears were on fire with the cold. His right arm was cramped, sending dull throbs of pain into his shoulder. King slowed to a walk, snow up to his wide chest. When it thinned and lessened, he lunged forward.

On and on. Jerry placed complete trust in his horse. He had no idea where the buildings were situated, had no idea how far they had come or how much distance they were required to travel before there was any shelter. All he knew was that as long as King stayed on his feet and kept moving forward, if he could keep Hannah and himself in the saddle, they still had hope of survival.

Over and over he repeated, *It's up to You. It's up to You.* And it was. It was simply whether God chose to save them both. *Whether we live or whether we die, we are the Lord's.* The verse brought calm and a renewed spirit.

And then King stopped. Jerry lifted his head and saw the looming gray wall of the barn and yelled a harsh, maudlin sound he wasn't aware of making. He lifted Hannah's form and held her against his chest with superhuman effort as he swung a stiff leg across the front of the saddle and let himself fall, still holding Hannah as best he could. As he sprawled awkwardly in the deep drift by the barn wall, he let her limp body roll into the snow.

He yanked the barn door open, led the heaving King inside, then returned for Hannah. Staggering under her weight, he laid her in the loose hay by the horse stalls. Without a lantern, he worked quickly and efficiently. He rubbed the horse all over with a feed sack as he talked, crooning and praising King, alarmed at the amount of sweat and lather. He stroked his wet neck, cupped a hand to the still muzzle and laid his forehead against King's.

Then, he led him to the watering trough, but took him away after a few sips. He fed him well, without sparing the hay or grain, then lowered the bar on the gate to his stall.

Jerry checked the length of rope to the house. Still there.

He bent to pick up the inert form of his wife, grasped the rope firmly in one gloved hand, and struggled to open the door and close it again before embarking on the long, arduous trek to the safety of the ranch house.

He told himself to stay calm, to take one step, one moment at a time. Visibility was almost nothing, except for an occasional glimpse of the rope he grasped with a desperate grip. He had come this far, but what if he lost the rope, missed the house by inches, and they both froze on the prairie, the fate of many hardy pioneers who lived on this harsh land before them?

His shoulders ached. His arms burned with the strain of his cold muscles called to perform this heroic effort.

The porch loomed in the whirling darkness, sending a surge of adrenaline through his bursting veins. He staggered up the steps, let go of the rope, lurched across the floor of the porch and fell against the door.

Then there was a blessed calm. A dark stillness. He realized the roaring in his ears was merely a remnant of his time in the wind.

Gently now, he laid Hannah on the sofa, alarmed at the stiffness of her limbs. Quickly, he lit a kerosene lamp, stoked the fire, opened the draft, and was rewarded by an instant crackling as the wood began to burn. He held his hands to the warmth, felt the tingle of pain in his frozen fingertips.

He shed his coat, vest, and one flannel shirt, then turned to Hannah, carrying the lamp to place it on the oak table beside the sofa. A doctor was needed, that was one thing he knew for sure. He crossed off that possibility immediately.

Hypothermia. Did people die from this condition? Why was she still unconscious? Helpless in the face of her still form, Jerry

stood gazing down at her as she lay still, barely breathing, her
face a waxen, ivory pearl . . . unreal.

"Hannah?"

No response. Gently, he touched her face, her ears. He
opened the buttons on her coat and lifted her limp arms to pull
the garment off. He didn't know what to do about the frozen
skirt of her dress, the trousers that were caked with ice. The
smell coming from her clothing was offensive, like an unwashed
horse. Perspiration from the horse's body, he guessed.

He should rid her of those frozen clothes but, if he did, and
she woke up? Well, he. . . . It was unthinkable.

He got two towels, dried off her skirt and trousers and pulled
the boots from her feet, thankful to see the layers of woolen socks.

The stove turned red hot, roared, the draft beneath the burning wood causing it to go wild. Quickly, Jerry shut off the draft,
then resumed his duties.

He rolled Hannah into a sheep's wool comforter, then
another. He pulled the couch across the oak floor, kicking rugs
from his path, until he was satisfied that the heat was close
enough to begin the warming process.

He touched her face. "Hannah?" Nothing.

Soon enough, when the heat penetrated her frozen limbs, her
ears, she would have to be brought back to consciousness. The
pain would wake her, he knew. He applied cold washcloths to
her ears, until he saw a bit of color returning. He would likely
need to put her hands in cold water, too, to thaw them. Hot
water would be unbearable.

The wind howled and whined, threw grains of snow and ice
against the window panes. An overwhelming gratitude rose in
Jerry, for the heat from the stove, the good solid walls and roof,
and their deliverance from this awful storm.

He stopped applying the washcloths. He felt her fingers on
both hands. So cold, almost as if there was no life.

He laid his head on her chest, heard the quiet flicker, the weak beat of her heart. He caressed her cold face. "I love you Hannah. Please wake up."

He kissed her cheek and smoothed her hair. He knew without a smidgen of doubt that he could wait as long as the Lord saw fit for her love. God had brought them through this for a reason. He traced the contours of her cheekbones, memorized the way her lashes fell like delicate feathers on her perfect face.

She drew in a sharp breath. Jerry stepped back. She coughed, softly, drew in a ragged breath, then choked. She kept choking, gasping for breath.

Jerry laid her on her left side, propped up her shoulders and supported her head. Her eyes flew open, dark pools of terror and pain. She whimpered, drew up a hand to drag it across her right ear. Her fingers flopped like helpless strips of cloth.

She blinked, squinted, struggled to swallow. She tried to form words, straining to use her tongue, but no sound emerged. He thought she said dirty, dirty, and began to apologize for her wet, frozen clothes. But she was thirsty. So thirsty, there was a desperation. He brought a tumbler of cold water, raised her shoulders, and held it to her lips.

"Just a few sips, Hannah, or you'll get sick." He knew she was conscious when she glared at him, grasped the glass in both hands and drained it, then leaned over the side of the couch and threw it all up. He held her head, wiped her mouth with a washcloth, then cleaned up the floor with rags and soapy water.

She drew in a sharp breath. A resounding "Ow!" came from her mouth, followed by howls of protest. She yelled and hollered and whimpered. She grasped her fingers with the near helpless fingers of her other hand, squinted her eyes, and rocked from side to side, loosening the comforters in her struggle.

"Do something!" she wailed.

Jerry lowered his face to hers. "You need to drink only a little at a time. Cold water for your fingers and toes. No heat. It will only make it worse. I'll make you hot tea."

She turned her face away and told him to shut up. He hid his grin. Definitely awake! So, he put the teakettle on the stove and shook a few tea leaves into a sturdy, white mug, adding sugar. He filled an agate basin with water from the faucet.

"Put both hands in this water."

"I can't," she yelled, louder than ever.

"You have to, Hannah. Listen to me. It will only get worse if you don't."

It was a long night. She refused the basin of cold water, cried and begged for mercy. She wouldn't allow him to remove her socks, said she could do it herself, which she obviously could not, so he didn't make any further attempts to ease her pain.

She did sip the hot tea, though, which was something, he supposed. The odor coming from those comforters was a nauseating smell that filled the room. How she could be unaware of this was beyond him, but he said nothing.

He must have dozed off shortly before daybreak. He awoke to morning's white light across his face. He sat up from his blanket on the floor and quickly realized that Hannah was missing; there was only the heap of smelly comforters on the sofa. He sat up, rubbed his eyes and saw the bathroom door was closed.

Oh. She must have found her way to the bathroom then, which meant she had been able to walk. He listened. Complete quiet.

He rapped softly on the bathroom door, placing an ear on the wooden panel. "Hannah?"

"Go away."

"I'm just checking if you're okay."

"I'm not okay. I'm frozen stiff!" she screeched.

Jerry turned away and felt a deep release of laughter. She was going to be okay.

When Hannah emerged, her dark hair wet, her face pale and thin but, mercifully, clean, a woolen blanket around her body like a giant shawl, she walked painfully to the sofa and sat down carefully. She pushed aside the comforters and asked him to take them out on the porch.

She was shivering uncontrollably. Her hands shook as if she had a palsy. Tears slid from beneath her lowered lashes, until Jerry asked her gently if there was anything he could do for her. He tried to take her hands, but she yanked them away and glared at him.

"Hannah, it's hard for me to see you suffer."

"It hurts so bad," she whispered.

"Do you want to try cold water?"

"I already had a bath. I could hardly do it."

"I believe it. You're strong, Hannah." He thought, strong-willed and determined, but didn't say it.

"I smelled horrible."

"Just horse, is all."

She didn't want to talk after that. She simply sat on the couch and suffered in silence, her stinging fingers repeatedly going to her ears, the tip of her nose. She watched in baleful silence as he fried steak in the big cast-iron pan, sliced bread, and soft-boiled four eggs for himself and two for her.

Hannah almost fainted from the delicious aroma of the frying steak. She was so terribly hungry, but there was no way she could hold a spoon.

He quietly filled two plates and brought them both to the couch and sat down beside her. He set her plate between them, then bowed his head in silent prayer before lifting his fork to his mouth with a bite of piping hot steak.

Hannah swallowed. She glanced sideways at the soft, gelatinous egg, the buttered toast. She swallowed again. As if it was the most natural thing in the world, Jerry cut a bite-size piece of toast, loaded a spoon with the soft-boiled egg and held it out to Hannah's mouth, a question in his soft, brown eyes.

Her hunger overrode her pride, and she opened her mouth like a fledgling. And so they ate breakfast together quietly, without speaking. She met his eyes once, and they held their gazes exchanging questions and answers.

He wiped away a bit of egg from the corner of her mouth. She looked at her helpless fingers. "They hurt so bad."

In answer, Jerry lifted them both to his mouth and kissed the tips of each finger. Drawing her hands away, she put them back in her lap, hurriedly, with averted eyes.

"You could have died, Hannah," Jerry said tenderly, his voice raspy with emotion.

"So I owe you a big thank you," she said, with only a trace of sarcasm.

They both listened to the wailing of the wind, turning their faces to watch clouds of roiling snow being hurled across the prairie, and they knew. They recognized the stark reality of what might have been, and what God had wrought. The perfect lull in the storm's aftermath, the timing that had been so critical, and the fact that they were here, together, warm and safe.

CHAPTER 8

ALL THAT DAY, HANNAH DID NOTHING. SHE SAT ON THE WOODEN rocking chair, wrapped in the woolen blanket, her dark hair tied into a ponytail, her eyes swollen and red, alternately clutching her fingers as she grimaced in pain, or holding a warmed washcloth to her ears.

Jerry kept busy feeding the livestock, tending the two stoves, stacking up wood in neat rows from the pile by the back stoop, repairing broken gates inside the barn, coming in every few hours to see how she was faring.

She could not sleep. The pain kept her awake, so she sat, bearing it stoically, refusing any remedy Jerry suggested. He cooked bean soup in the afternoon and offered to share it with her but she shook her head. "Tea would be nice," she said, flatly.

Jerry could barely make the tea fast enough. What a sweet request. Oh my.

He sat with her, eating his bean soup as she sipped her tea. He decided to say nothing but to allow her time to ask questions, if there was anything she wanted to know.

She whispered so soft and low that he could barely decipher her words. "It was awful."

He nodded.

"He fell. The horse."

"I know."

"Where is he now?"

"He's down. About four, maybe five miles from here."

"Is that where you found us?"

"Yes."

She said nothing more. He waited for her to ask more questions, but she didn't. In fact, she never asked any questions after that, not once.

The wind died down, as all prairie winds eventually do. The sun shone and melted the snow, but only partially, where the wind had swept it clean. Patches of winter wheat showed green—limp and bedraggled, but green.

Hannah's frostbitten fingers and ears healed, but she seemed changed somehow. Her eyes were large and dark in her pale, thin face, and they seemed to have dimmed. The fire that used to flicker in them so often seemed to have been snuffed out. Jerry wished he could read her better, understand her thoughts, what was causing the lethargy, the deflation of the static energy that normally propelled her from morning till evening.

One day, when another dark bank of clouds rode in from the northwest, another blizzard in the seething black mass, Hannah stood at the window with her arms crossed like a vice around her waist, her shoulders jutting with tension. "I don't know if I can stand another blizzard again," she said through tight lips.

Jerry was repairing a saddle with an awl and strips of rawhide. He looked up from his work, a question in his eyes. "The cows will be all right," he said slowly.

"I'm not thinking about the cows," she snapped. "I think once you've nearly lost your life, the weather takes on a different kind of menace. I can't really explain it the way I would like to, but it's almost as if you're not sure you have it in you to sit here and just . . . well . . . you know, take it. Take the wind and the

lashing of the snow and the cold and the loneliness . . . and the
. . ." Her sentence dangled between them, unfinished, mysterious.

Now was not the time to point out that she was the one who
had chosen to stay here, to fight through the miserable winters
and dry summers.

"This one might not be so bad," Jerry said, bending his head
to his work.

She said sharply, "You need a haircut."

"Why don't you cut it?"

"I never cut my own hair," he replied matter of factly.

"Who's going to cut it?"

"I guess you'll have to."

"No. I don't know how. I can't. Go to town or something."

Jerry laughed.

Hannah scowled.

"You could do it," he said, almost teasingly.

"I never cut anyone's hair and I'm not planning to start,
either."

"Good. I'll just let it grow, then. Eventually, I'll put it in a
braid, the way a lot of the pioneers did."

Hannah almost smiled. "I miss my mother."

This was so unexpected that it took Jerry a few seconds to
absorb her words. He busied himself shoving the awl through a
soft piece of stirrup, his hair falling over his eyes.

"I miss my mother, and Manny. Eli and Mary are probably
going to the same school in Leacock Township that I went to." A
wistful note crept into her voice so Jerry looked up from his work.

"Would you like to go to Lancaster for a visit?"

Much too quickly, there was a sharp refusal, a vehement shaking of her head. Then, "You never talked about the palomino."

"What is there to say?" Jerry asked gruffly.

"Was he still alive?"

"Yes."

"And then?"

"Hannah, listen. There is nothing harder in the world than putting a bullet into a horse you love. The only reason I could do it at all was to relieve the pitiful creature of its suffering.

"So you had to put him down?"

"Of course." He hadn't meant for his words to come out quite so sharply.

"I guess now you think it was my fault."

"Of course not. It was a blizzard. There was nothing you could have done differently."

Hannah was silent for a while, standing at the window and watching the storm approach. Then suddenly, without turning she said, "You probably wish the palomino was still alive and I was dead."

"Stop it, Hannah." This was spoken sternly.

"Would it have mattered to you if I'd have died?" she asked, almost coyly, but not quite.

"Yes, Hannah, a great deal."

"You would have headed back East so fast it wouldn't be funny. You'd marry again. Have a nice life. One without all this sacrifice."

Jerry stuck the awl back into the stirrup, got to his feet, and went to the window. He grasped Hannah's elbows from behind, and turned her to face him.

"What are you saying? What is wrong with you?"

"Well, you would have. You know you'd go back East if you didn't have to stay here on the homestead to keep up your end of the deal."

He could not deny it. Yes, he would. But he didn't say it.

Hannah twisted from his touch and flounced to the kitchen, banging pans on the countertop.

She baked a cake while he continued his work fixing the stirrup. Jerry couldn't tell what was going on in her head, but a comfortable silence settled throughout the house like the pleasant aroma coming from the cook stove—a companionable calm that brought a hum of contentment to Jerry's lips.

She had never before confided any of her feelings to him. And here, in one afternoon, she'd said all that—her mother, her fear, and the palomino. Suddenly, without thinking, he asked, "Why did you never name the palomino?"

"I did."

"You never called him by any name."

She lowered her face and blushed furiously. "That would mean I accepted your gift, and I never did. If I accepted the horse, I'd have to accept you."

"I see." Then, "You have accepted me."

Clearly rattled, Hannah lifted a flaming face, her eyes dark, miserable pools of embarrassment.

"Well," she said.

"Can't you do better than that?" When he looked at Hannah's face, his eyes traveled to her eyes, which now held a mysterious, warm light that threw his world off its steady axis.

"Someday." She let her eyes hold his, with only a hint of sparkle in their translucent depths, followed by the merest hint of a soft smile.

It was only a hint of acceptance, but it was as much as he'd ever hoped to receive. He sank to the low stool where he had been working, his breathing ragged and uneven. Whoa. Steady there.

He left the house, carrying the repaired saddle, then simply sat on a pile of hay with any empty expression in his eyes. If he lived to be a hundred years old, he'd never figure her out.

Someday, she had said.

He wavered between sobs of frustration and wild shrieks of glee. Did that soft light in her eyes mean her fierce resolve was crumbling? Was there the slightest crack in her rigid armor of bitterness and self-will? Too soon to tell. Perhaps that was most of his fascination with Hannah. She was so complex, so hard to comprehend. You never knew which way her mood would take her. He wondered, though, if that night on the prairie had not dispersed some of the worst of her rebellion.

He shook his head to clear it, jumped up, and began to clean stalls as if he had only one afternoon to do it.

The mules' gigantic ears pricked forward. Mollie yawned, stretched her mouth wide, bared her immense yellow teeth and then closed them with a clack. Then she bent her head and went back to nosing around for a forgotten wisp of hay.

True to Hannah's words, each storm that drove in from the northwest seemed to be a test of endurance. She found herself pensive, brittle, pacing the kitchen when Jerry was not around, wishing he'd go outside and leave her alone when he was in the house. He always tried to ease her unhappiness with cheerful words which, she decided, was like running your fingernails down the blackboard at school.

She didn't sew, wouldn't read, and hated to write letters. She refused to get on horseback if there was an inch of snow on the ground. She argued endlessly about Black Angus versus longhorns, and was simply a burden both to herself and to Jerry.

She wanted to go to town. She wanted to visit the Texas folks but, no, she would not go. For one thing, she didn't trust Bobby, the quarter horse. He was sorrel and chunky and cranky. She'd never seen a sorrel horse she liked. Even Nip and Tuck failed to pull her out of her slump.

Jerry told her the first thing they'd do in the spring would be make a trip to Pennsylvania to see her mother. Hannah averted her eyes and closed them off with lids like little feather-lined window curtains and didn't say anything.

Jerry's hair grew down to his shoulders, so Hannah told him one evening that if he didn't cut his hair, she would.

"Go right ahead," he answered, unconcerned. He didn't think she would do it.

Armed with a towel, a scissors, and a brush and comb, Hannah approached Jerry. "Sit up straight," she commanded.

He obeyed.

Instantly, the comb was dragged through his long dark hair, tearing at the snags until his nose burned and tears sprang to his eyes.

"Let me do that." He reached for the brush and comb, but she pulled them away. He sat down and bent his head, resigned.

"Take it easy."

Hannah said nothing, just proceeded to rake the comb through his long, tangled hair until he thought half the hair on his head had been pulled out by the roots. He gritted his teeth, bearing the pain.

She leveled her face with his, sighting along his floppy bangs, estimating, and then slowly drawing the blades of the scissors precisely where she wanted them.

Her confidence increased as the curtains of hair fell away from the scissors and she formed the traditional bowl cut of the Amish, leaving his hair longer over his ears than the bangs on his forehead.

Jerry thought he'd been shot when her scissors crunched into his ear, snapping a deep cut along the top where his skin was thickest. Making some sort of involuntary grimace and a whoosh of disgust, he leapt to his feet, a hand going to his ear that was already spurting blood.

Hannah moved back, a hand to her mouth, her eyes wide with fright, too embarrassed to utter a word of justification for her actions. He went to the bathroom and held a cold washcloth to his throbbing ear, trying to staunch the spurting blood.

When he returned, the scissors, comb, and brush lay on the table, the towel in a heap on the floor, with no sign of Hannah.

Her bedroom door was closed, and remained that way until the following morning.

At breakfast, she burned the toast. Not just burned it, but completely blackened it until it was as black as soot, smoking and shrunk to about half its size. She burned her fingers as she retrieved it from the oven and had to hold them beneath the gush of cold water from the faucet at the sink.

"I'll make more toast," Jerry offered.

Hannah didn't look up from her cold water therapy. She didn't let him know she'd heard him. She looked at his hair from the back and it looked all right. He must have finished cutting it by himself. There was a large, angry cut in his ear, about three-quarters of the way up. She decided he'd get over it, but wouldn't talk to him all day, so he gave up trying and kept to himself.

When Jerry came in from the barn late that evening, Hannah was sitting in the oak rocking chair, perfectly still, her hands folded in her lap. As he hung up his coat, she turned to look at him. "I think I'll go crazy if I don't have anything to do," she said.

Her words were spoken in short, hard jerks, as if she didn't have enough breath to complete the sentence. Her face was thin, her eyes huge, a frightened look on her features, as if she had seen a ghost lurking in the house while he was at the barn.

"Well, Hannah. I don't know what to tell you. We're pretty much snowed in. We have no telephone, no mail, no neighbors. You've lived here longer than I have, so surely you knew what the winters were like, didn't you?"

"I did, but it was different when my family was here. And the Jenkinses would come."

"We can ride over there."

"No." Her answer was decidedly emphatic and forceful. She would no longer venture out on horseback in the snow, saying it was foolish. If you were caught on the prairie once, you'd have no one to blame but yourself if it happened again. She had no desire to check on the cattle or watch for the herds of flowing antelope. Nothing.

"Hannah, you've changed."

"I don't want to die. It was close enough, that time."

"I mean, your sense of adventure is gone."

"It has nothing to do with adventure. It's foolish, is all. I'll ride again when spring comes, and not one day before that."

That night, after Jerry had gone to bed, she sat alone on her rocking chair and thought of Abigail Jenkins's diaries, those recordings of times like these, when the long, tedious days of winter drove her to questioning her own sanity, her fear of being pushed over the edge by the power of isolation. To be alone, day after day, in an endless expanse of white, while knowing one storm would eventually be followed by another, the time crawling by like snails.

Suddenly, without warning, Hannah began to cry. Her nose burned, her mouth wobbled, and quiet heaves of her chest ended in silent hiccoughs of distress. She let the tears and the overwhelming need to be sad rock her in its grip. She didn't try to hold back or prevent it.

She wanted her mother. She was so homesick for the sight of her kindly face, the soft etchings that would eventually turn into wrinkles. She wanted to eat her mother's food and listen to her words, knowing that she was there for her, no matter what. She wanted to put her fist into Manny's arm, to see him grab the spot where she'd clubbed him good and proper, grimace and sway, bent double, and then come after her, yelling his revenge.

Sweet Mary, so innocent and loving. A child. And Eli. She groaned within herself and let the tears come, welling from her eyes in soft trickles down her cheeks.

They were her family. She'd spent every day, every week, every month and year of her life with them. How could she be expected to live without them?

Jerry had said she was changing. What did he know?

She just knew that, suddenly, in the dead of this North Dakota winter, the homestead was no longer quite as important. It had lost some of its shining luster like a tarnished silver teapot. The Klassermans were gone, with the sleek black cattle she had envied, planning to fashion the homestead after their example. Now here she was, her land containing these rawboned, hairy old longhorns that she could as soon shoot as look at.

The homestead was not the real homestead without her family. There! She'd admitted to herself what she'd tried to stuff away without her head knowing what her heart had tried to reveal.

Perhaps if she loved Jerry the way other women loved their husbands, she would feel as if he was her family.

She didn't know. All she did for Jerry was cut his ear, burn his toast, and kill, yes, kill his best palomino. That poor horse! So faithful, left on the prairie for the eagles, ravens, and wolves. She felt as if it should have been her left out there. For the first time in her life, she wasn't absolutely sure of what she wanted, what she knew, or if she had ever known anything.

If only that incident had never happened. Lying out there on the prairie without knowing if she'd live or die had taken away all her confidence. It was like she'd been bucked off a horse and wasn't quite able to summon the courage to get back on.

Well, she'd have to do better. She couldn't sit in this house and weep around like a starving barn cat, that was one thing sure. Sniveling, whining, complaining. That simply was not her.

She dried her tears, blew her nose, and went to the window to look out at the stars, feeling the same sense of despair she had felt when she began to weep. She sat back in the rocking chair and began all over again.

Which is where Jerry found her. Unable to sleep and knowing that Hannah had not gone to bed, he got up, dressed in clean clothes, and walked softly on stocking feet to her side.

"Hannah." The gentleness of his voice only brought another barrage of tears. He handed her a clean handkerchief. She honked long and loud, swiped viciously at her streaming eyes, and told him to go back to bed.

She sent an elbow into his side. "Go away."

"Just tell me what's wrong, Hannah. I'll do anything, anything to make you stop crying. I've never known you to be like this."

"Go away. Just go!"

"No."

Almost she got away from him. She rose halfway, turned, but his hands caught her waist and brought her to him, close enough that she could smell the soap from his washing, the baking soda clean of his teeth.

"Tell me, Hannah." His words were spoken against her hair, so soft and dark and silky, they seemed to be liquid.

Almost she stayed in his arms, breathing in the smell of him, putting her arms around him, and sinking against his solid strength.

Then her pride reared its face, the alpha force of her existence, and she extracted herself, but not without a sense of loss, unacknowledged even to herself.

"I'm all right. Go back to bed. It's just been a long winter."

A lesser man than Jerry might have lost his patience and tried desperately to reclaim the moment, thinking selfishly of his own desire. But he let her go, stepped back, and recognized what had occurred. For the space of a few heartbeats, she had been his.

He knew time and patience were on his side.

Hannah's spirits were a constant worry now. She roamed the house, her eyes vacant with an unnamed hopelessness, a look that drove fear into him. He tried to draw her out by suggesting different things, but what could be accomplished on the prairie in the winter was limited.

He had heard of pioneer women who were unable to hold onto their sanity, some of them losing their reason and never getting it back, turning into mentally ill patients that had to be "put away," that awful phrase that meant they were incarcerated in an institution, a mental hospital.

This was a whole new challenge, and a fearful one. Jerry knew she was trying to beat the dark moments, but she seemed unable to rise above the clouds of darkness that came down on her head like a heavy fog.

Then she refused to eat. For one whole day, she drank only bitter black tea and sat staring straight ahead, her dark eyes boring holes into the wall of the house, her arms hanging by her sides, the rocker squeaking as she rocked. Her eyes remained dry. She didn't cook and she didn't wash dishes. The floor remained unswept and the laundry piled up in the washhouse.

Jerry knew it was time to do something, anything. He had no clear path, but he had to make an effort. To ride through the snow would take a huge effort. The closest telephone was at the Klasserman ranch, now the Timothy Weber home.

He didn't relish going there. The couple left him with an unsettled sense of questioning, a strange atmosphere he couldn't define.

He had to get help for Hannah. He knelt at her side, without touching her. "Hannah." Dull eyes shifted to his, then fell away.

"Listen, I'm going away. I'm riding to the Klasserman place to use the telephone, to get help for you. You need to see a doctor."

"I don't need a doctor."

"Yes, you do. You're going from bad to worse. You're not feeling well at all. This is so unlike you, to sit like this. You're not eating."

"I will when I'm hungry."

"You keep the fire going, Hannah. Please. I have to go."

"Don't leave me here alone."

"Then you'll have to come with me."

She shook her head. "It's too cold. Too far. A storm could come up."

"Then you'll have to stay here. We have no choice."

Hannah stared into space and resumed her rocking. Her eyes clouded over with a startling veil of despondency.

Jerry rode hard, without sparing King. He struggled to keep the fear at bay, kept assuring himself that Hannah would be all right, that it was only the midwinter blues.

It was hard going, but they had ridden through plenty of drifts, been on the open range in snow up to King's underside. As they neared the turnoff, Jerry sniffed, drew his eyebrows down in bewilderment. There was a definite smell, an odor hovering in the air, a smell like . . . burnt something. It smelled like wood smoke. The Webers must be burning their stoves very hot. He rode on, noticing the dense sheen in the atmosphere.

As he drew closer, up over the rise of land and around the curve where the clump of cottonwoods huddled together like ancient refugees, the smell became overpowering, a thick, cloying smell of burnt wood and . . .

He gasped! What had been the Klassermans' house was a pile of charred timbers and twisted metal roofing, the snow around the dwelling melted away by the inferno that it must have been. All that remained were the black, twisted pieces of metal roofing, with smoke reaching to the endless sky, a pall of gray whisked away by the everlasting prairie winds.

The expensive automobiles stood blackened and charred in the front, a testimony of mystery, the truth of Timothy and Lila's inability to escape.

King snorted with distaste. Jerry reined him in and dismounted with numb extremities, his mind unable to comprehend what his eyes were seeing before him.

CHAPTER 9

Jerry stood before the remains of the house, his head bowed, his hat in his hands, as he prayed for guidance and for the souls of the departed. He sensed his own mortality, the limits of his ability to change the horror of what had occurred, felt the power of an all-seeing, all-encompassing God who allowed calamities of this magnitude.

Why, Lord, why? He turned to the barn, where he heard the restless banging of horses, the frightened rattling of halters pulling on the chains that kept them in their stalls.

Jerry dropped King's reins, which dangled to the ground, a sign for the horse to stay on that spot, an obedience he had learned well. Quickly, Jerry ran to the door, lifted the metal latch, and let himself into the dim interior of the large structure.

The overpowering stench of ammonia made him cough. He drew a gloved hand across his face and coughed again. The horses rose on their hind legs and whinnied, their nostrils quivering. As he drew closer, they reached out with their noses, begging, clearly needing water, anything to reassure them that help was on the way. The manure was piled around them. They were without bedding of any kind, their wooden troughs torn and chewed.

He turned to find the watering trough dry. Sparrows flitted from the rafters, twittering anxiously. Mice scurried across the top boards of the stalls, all signs that no one had been in the barn for some time.

Jerry shivered unexpectedly, a sense of horror washing over him. When he heard a thin, wailing cry, he turned toward the sound immediately to find a small child sitting in a corner of the forebay, a quilt that had been white with a design of pink and blue sequins, a crib blanket, laying in an untidy heap beneath him. Or her.

Jerry went to the child, bent to lift him, noticed the filth, the thin, trembling body, the coat that had been worn for too long. The child smelled of its soiled diaper, the face dirty, streaked with dust and tears.

"*Ach*." It was all Jerry could think to say, an expression of profound dismay. He reached for the child and held him up, resisting the urge to gag. The child clung to Jerry, laid his head on his shoulder, his body molded to him as if he would never allow himself to be pulled away. He cried great, dry, wracking sobs, then became still, breathing faintly.

Clearly, one dilemma marched in right after another, but Jerry wasn't sure if this one would not prove to be his undoing. Such a mystery. What had happened? Why was the child here, without any sign of its parents? How could he get this child to safety in the cold?

First, the horses needed water. Then he'd have to get the child home. He tried to loosen his grip, crooning, telling the child he'd be all right, he needed to see to the horses. But he soon realized the folly of that thought.

He tucked the child by his side, then began filling the watering trough with water that gushed from the hydrant. One by one, he loosened the horses, who almost ran over him in their need for water.

He saw now that the horses were white Percherons. They were work horses, a common breed among the Amish with their substantial height and wide, deep chests like Belgians. Their muscles were heavy and they had massive legs with a spray of thick hair surrounding their hooves. Their necks were arched and they had well-molded faces and large brown eyes. These horses were of a fine breed, well taken care of until now.

As best he could, he forked hay with one hand, the child gripping his body like a little monkey. Jerry shook his head as he watched the starved horses tearing at the hay. There were eleven of them. Some were tied in stalls, others were milling around in what he thought must have formerly been an enclosure for the dry cows.

He stood surveying the barn. He'd done what he could, so now he must see to this child. He could not get help for Hannah. The telephone was unavailable, so there was nothing to do but ride home to her, carrying the bedraggled child that needed a bath, a change of clothing, and food of some kind.

He wrapped him in the soiled quilt as best he could, with the child straining to stay against him, screaming hysterically if he felt himself being pulled away. Working fast, Jerry wrapped him up, bits of hay and dirt clinging to the blanket. Then he hurried out of the barn, shuddering at the harsh scene of the smoking remains of the Klasserman house.

He shook his head to rid himself of mental images of what might have occurred. Riding home without help for Hannah was not the worst of this day that seemed shrouded in unreality. The air was cold, but the surrounding white of the pristine plains seemed almost surreal after the appalling sight he had left behind.

Jerry clutched the child to his chest with one hand as he held the reins in the other, allowing King to find his way home, as he had done when he rescued Hannah.

When he opened the door of the ranch house, he saw Hannah sitting in the same rocking chair and staring dully out the north window, precisely the way he had left her. She did not turn her head at his approach. The house was cold.

"Hannah." She didn't respond, wouldn't acknowledge his presence.

He held out the child wrapped in its filthy quilt.

She turned, halfway.

"The Klassermans' house burned to the ground. I found this child in the barn." Hannah blinked, sat up, and turned toward him. She rose to her feet, clawing at the edges of the quilt. Her lips moved and a whisper emerged. "*Siss unfaschtendich.*" *There is no sense.*

"I don't know how long he was out there."

She took him out of Jerry's arms, carried him to the sofa, and unwrapped the poor, filthy child, her face grim. "Put the kettle on," she ordered.

Quickly, Jerry set about building a fire as the child began his breathless wailing. Hannah carried him to the bathroom. The water pipes pinged and bumped in the wall as she turned on the hot water in the clawfoot bathtub. He heard her talking in soft, muted tones. The soiled clothing and quilt were hurled out through the bathroom door, followed by a clipped, "Burn these."

Then, "Oh, Jerry!"

Quickly, he went to the bathroom door. "What is it, Hannah?"

"It's . . . she's a girl!"

There was nothing to say, so Jerry just nodded.

"Go get the baking soda. Quick!"

Jerry obeyed.

The little girl screamed in pain as she was lowered into the warm, soapy water, her bottom raw with her own waste, and no one to change the poor child's diaper.

Hannah reached for the proffered baking soda, tears running down her face unchecked, her nose running, her lips trembling. "Bring those muslin sheets from the closet in my bedroom. Cut them into six or eight pieces, it doesn't matter. We need diapers. And oh, Jerry, bring me one of your tee shirts, the nicest one you have. Oh, and the talcum powder on my dresser."

Jerry felt very much like a husband as he collected the items, although he hesitated as he approached Hannah's bedroom. He felt like an intruder. He had no idea what talcum powder looked like, but picked up an oval, pink container with roses on the front that he guessed must hold powder. He handed it to her, and she reached for it without looking at him, her one hand cradling the child's head as she lay in the soothing bath.

"Poor, poor baby girl. Jerry, put about half a cup of oatmeal in a dish and pour some of the water from the teakettle over it."

Again, Jerry did as he was told, vaguely aware of the rumbling from his own stomach. He spread the muslin sheet on the table, found a scissors in the sewing machine cabinet, and began to cut diapers.

Hannah appeared, the child wrapped in a large towel, her face glowing from the heat in the bathroom, two safety pins clutched in one hand. She toweled the little girl dry, then leaned back and surveyed the face with the mop of brown hair, wet and curling, that lay against the clean scalp, the large, frightened eyes in her small oval face.

"Who is she, Jerry? Where did you find her?"

Jerry related the whole story as Hannah dried the small body. She beckoned for a square of muslin and turned her back to diaper the child, then sat back down to draw the much too large tee shirt over her, securing it at the neck with another safety pin.

Jerry couldn't help noticing what a capable mother she was. But then, she had been the oldest in her family which, he presumed, would have given her some skills in caring for children.

"I'm going to the kitchen to feed her some oatmeal." It was an open invitation for him to join her at the kitchen table so he did just that, settling himself in a chair and watching the way she balanced the child on one hip, stirring milk and molasses into the oatmeal with the other. She brought it to the table before sitting down, sliding the child expertly into her lap, a move so motherly, so fascinating that it conjured up moments of his own childhood, a time in his life he'd as soon forget.

Hannah bent her dark head, coaxing the little girl to try what was on the spoor. Timidly at first, then with more courage, the child ate small bites of the sweet, milky porridge.

"Tell me more," Hannah said. So he told her in detail about the grim specter of smoking debris, the heat-damaged cars, the thirsty horses, the poor child.

"But what happened? We can't just sit here with the child without trying to contact her family. We know their names. Surely the deed to the property is recorded somewhere here in North Dakota. The sale's transaction. Something. How did the child end up in the barn if both the parents were trapped in the house? Or were they kidnapped, robbed, their house set fire to by thieves? Horse thieves? No, I guess not. You said the horses were still in the barn. My word, Jerry, we have to do something!"

While Hannah was speaking she was eating the leftover oatmeal the child was unable to consume. Still talking in fast, clipped tones, she made a larger pot of oatmeal and left it to set up while she returned to the table.

"She looks a bit like Timothy. Do you suppose it is their child? Did he even speak of having had a child?" Her questions were hurled so fast that Jerry felt as if he had to dodge some of them, while they zinged overhead like a volley of shots fired from a rifle. Sometimes he shrugged. Other times he shook his head. But most of the time he admitted he did not know.

"But we can't keep her," Hannah concluded.

"Likely not, in the end."

"Oh, but we have her now, sweet, innocent angel that she is. Who would put a helpless baby in a barn in the dead of winter? I can't begin to imagine the trauma, the fear. What kept her from freezing?"

"There are a lot of horses in that barn. Percherons. Huge, white ones."

Hannah opened her eyes wide. "Is that what they are?" she asked.

Jerry nodded.

"This is too much. I can't handle any of this. All I know is the fact that this sweet baby is safe. Oh, Jerry, I never saw such a pitiful bottom. Blistered. So fiery red. It will take days and days to heal." She blushed, having spoken on a high note of emotion.

Hannah bent her head over the sleepy-eyed child, drew her head against her chest, and rocked back and forth, another move that made Jerry's heart ache with memories of his own mother.

"She's sleeping," Hannah said, awed by the drooping eyelids, the relaxed expression of bliss. "Get down a few of the sheep's wool comforters from the high shelf in the closet of the guest room."

Jerry hastened down the hallway, smiling and thinking what a good husband he was turning out to be. He found the comforters and met Hannah in the hallway as she whispered, "Spread them in my room in the corner, beside my bed. Get a clean sheet from the chest of drawers in the bathroom."

Again, he did as he was commanded, trying to spread everything straight, the corners tucked in, then stood back, allowing Hannah to pass him and gently lower the sleeping child. She nestled down contentedly, giving a soft little moan.

Hannah shooed Jerry out of the way before retrieving a blanket at the foot of her bed, covering the small, weary body with the folded warmth of the heavy coverlet. She stood back, crossed her arms, and sighed with contentment. "Oh my. All winter I'll have her to look after." And then she did the most unexpected thing. She felt for Jerry's right hand with her left and grasped it, held it.

Afraid to breathe, Jerry stood still, silently praying that she wouldn't let go.

"It's just so unreal. I was at the end of my rope. I'm sorry. I don't know why I let everything get to me so horribly. It must have been the . . . you know. That night." And she still held his hand.

"Let's go. She's sleeping so good." She pulled gently, drew her hand away from his, but stayed by his side until they reached the kitchen.

"I'm hungry. Do you want a dish of oatmeal?"

Too flummoxed to say anything, he spoke with his eyes, nodding his head. Still asking questions, Hannah put the kettle on, making plans, what she would sew, the good thick flannel for diapers, the flowered print mattered not a snitch, the cotton fabric in the lowest drawer of the bureau that her father had been given when he left home. They had brought it the whole way out here to the Dakota prairie, can you imagine?

She'd need socks, though, and shoes, eventually. Hannah wondered if she could walk or crawl. How old was she? Was she really the Webers' child? Who else could she be?

Jerry could only sit and listen as he tried to make sense of Hannah's complete transformation, going from a vacant, immobile figure in a chair, to this animated, bright-eyed, talkative woman.

He had been convinced she was desperately depressed, sick with some mysterious ailment of the mind. And now, the sight of this soiled, derelict child had plucked her out of her despondency and placed her into a whirlwind of planning and curiosity.

Had she been aware of holding his hand? Probably not. He thought for the thousandth time, he'd never understand women, and most certainly not Hannah.

They ate in comfortable silence until Hannah scraped the last of the oatmeal from her bowl, a flush already appearing in her pale face, and looked at him squarely, her eyes boring into his with an intensity that bordered on panic.

"But, Jerry. Eventually we'll have to give her back, right? We have to do the right thing and find her family and all, right?"

"Yes."

"How will we do it?"

"I'll ride into Pine and see if there was mail at the post office, check the sheriff's office for documents from the sale. Anything. There must be family who needs to be notified."

Hannah crossed her arms, rubbing her palms up and down her forearms. "It gives me the shivers," she said. "It's just so awful."

"I agree. It's too confusing to let your mind dwell on what could have happened."

The fire in the cook stove snapped and popped. A stick of wood fell. Outside, the wind howled in the dark of night, sending sprays of snow skimming against the windows, skittering across the wood siding to the north.

Hannah felt the smallness of the homestead, little black dots on a vast, expansive land that seemed to have no beginning and no end, a sea of cold, white, frozen snow. How easily they could be erased from marring this unspoiled land. Was it good that they were here, her and Jerry, and now this child? For the first time in her life, she felt a drawing back, almost like an infidelity, a thing gone wrong. To barge ahead without a doubt had always been her way. But, somehow, here tonight, there was a growing sense of trembling and wavering under a power that seemed out of her control.

Was she deserting ship? Forsaking her true courage and fortitude the way a loose woman left her husband on a whim? An infidelity, yes. In one sense, her god had been the homestead. Or its success, whichever way you looked at it.

Hannah was unaware of her own dark brooding, unaware of the way Jerry was intently watching the softening of her face, the myriad emotions that crisscrossed it like invisible pathways.

Suddenly, she shivered. "Sometimes I wonder how long we'll be able to stay here."

Jerry started. "Why do you say that?"

"I'm not sure. All that's happened, this string of calamities, it just . . . I don't know, sort of takes the wind from my sails or something. I feel as if the strength is gone from my ranching legs."

"You'll feel better once summer comes. Spring, I mean. You just have an extraordinary case of the winter blues."

"No, it's more than that."

Jerry waited.

"I read Abigail Jenkins's diary once . . ."

She did not continue. He watched her face, the heavy lids drooping, the sweep of dark lashes on her pale cheeks, the tense line of her full lips. One hand crept across the table, found a tea-cup, her forefinger and thumb tracing the handle over and over.

She got up and went to the cook stove to put the kettle on. She measured tea leaves into two heavy ironstone mugs. When the tea was ready, she brought both mugs to the table and set one down at his elbow. She took her seat across from him, stirred sugar into her tea, and sighed.

"I read Abigail Jenkins's diary once," she repeated.

He raised his eyebrows. "And?"

"Well, she was as tough and wiry as shoe leather, you know."

"I never knew her."

"No, I guess you wouldn't have. She died of pneumonia. Hod has never been the same. Anyway, she was brought out here as a young bride and barely survived the winters. It was the wind. The loneliness. She suffered. I never would have imagined that of her. She seemed as if she was made for the prairie, tough and resilient. Nothing fazed her. I always imagined I was exactly like her. Designed for solitude, for wide-open spaces. Laughing at the elements. Now, I'm not so sure. And yet, I'm afraid this feeling of not being sure is somehow wrong."

She suddenly burst out, clearly exasperated. "How do we know what is right and what is wrong?"

Jerry sipped his tea, picked a bit of tea leaf off his tongue. "We don't always know. We pray for guidance, then God allows us choices, and if they're the wrong ones, we keep going in that direction until we learn."

"How do you know that?"

"I don't. It's just something I heard a preacher say one time. We're human beings so we make mistakes. The biggest thing is that we care whether we do the right thing."

"That's important?"

"I think it is, yes."

Hannah held her mug in both hands, her fingers curled around it for comfort. "You think being here is the right thing?"

Before Jerry could answer, a thin wail from Hannah's bedroom shocked them both into action.

"She's crying!" Hannah said breathlessly, already on her way with Jerry close behind her.

Then Hannah was on her knees, asking what was wrong, touching the baby's forehead, checking her diaper, examining the safety pins. The thin cry turned into a wail, so Hannah scooped her up, blanket and all, and took her to the low, armless rocker where she rocked steadily, her head bent over the child, talking to her in a low voice. As the cries quieted, Jerry asked if perhaps she was used to having a bottle of milk at night.

The rocking stopped. "You know, she just might be. And I bet you anything there's still one of Eli's bottles . . . Oh no, our house burned down. I forgot. We don't have a baby bottle of any kind."

"Could we feed her more porridge?" Jerry asked.

"She's sleeping again. She might wake up repeatedly, with all she's been through."

And that was how they spent that first night with the child. Almost every hour, she awoke, crying out, cold and frightened.

Hannah was always there for her, so Jerry went back to sleep, knowing she would tend to the little girl's needs.

He awoke with a start, the sound of clattering from the kitchen yanking him out of a deep sleep. Thinking he'd overslept, he pulled his trousers on, buttoned his shirt sleepily, and wobbled bleary-eyed out to the kitchen.

"Sorry, Hannah. I overslept. I'll get the fire."

She stood poking at a piece of firewood that didn't want to settle between the grates, her black hair in a long braid down her back, a white flannel nightgown that was about three sizes too big trailing on the floor.

She thrust a forefinger toward the clock. Jerry saw the time, 3:15 a.m. "Oh, sorry," he said. "I'll go back to bed."

"No, you won't. The little one is hungry, the house is cold, and I need you to fix this fire so I can heat some water for her oatmeal. I haven't slept more than an hour at the most."

So, once again Jerry obeyed and felt so much like a good husband that he whistled low, his breath coming in happy little waves of song.

Who could have predicted this? Life was, indeed, the strangest thing. Lifted from the pit of gloom and helplessness to this newly restored, softer Hannah, was a blessing far beyond anything he deserved.

He whistled as he got the fire stirred up and going, put the kettle on, and took the canister of rolled oats from the pantry. Hannah brought the child to the table. The soft light of the kerosene lamp surrounded them, the kettle hummed, and the fire crackled as the wind moaned in the eaves.

Jerry watched as Hannah spooned the oatmeal into the child's mouth. She ate and ate, opening her little mouth to receive another spoonful, and another, on and on, until they both laughed, unsure if they should be feeding her so much. But they found out that hunger was her main problem, and after she ate a large portion, they tucked her in and dragged themselves wearily back to their own beds and feel into deep sleep until the morning light awakened both of them.

Jerry rode off the following morning, alerted the Jenkinses, and made the necessary telephone calls. He accompanied the sheriff to the scene of the fire, then returned on horseback with Hod and the boys, just before dark. Hannah had begun to worry.

They came stamping up on the porch, all big wet boots, heavy coats, and caps pulled low over their ears, ruddy faces sporting uneven stubble like corn fodder, their beards unkempt where they hadn't bothered to shave.

Hannah scolded and said Abigail would be having a fit. They laughed and teased Hannah good-naturedly, said she was a sight for sore eyes. Ken and Hank both accepted coffee, their faces chapped and red from the cold, teeth stained brown from the plug of tobacco that very seldom left the side of their mouths.

They gawked at the little girl, shook their heads, their eyes wide as Jerry gave his account of the day he'd ridden over to use the neighbors' telephone. Hod pursed his lips and squinted at the fading light in the west window.

"If the cars were gone, it would make more sense. But there's no explanation for findin' the kid in the barn. Where are her parents? Did they do it? You jest can't wrap yore head around it, seems like."

Hank said the sheriff and the fire company would figure it out. "That still don't say we'll find a home for the kid," Hod argued.

Hannah held her tightly, her arms wrapped around her possessively, her eyes dark with the challenge already forming in her mind. *Let them try to come take her away. Jerry had found her. She'd have died if he hadn't. She's mine.*

"Best not get too attached," Hod said, watching Hannah.

"I already have," Hannah answered.

Hod shook his head. "I'se afraid o' that. My Abby never got over the loss of her baby girl. Not right. She mourned that child to her last breath."

"How long does it usually take to find the next of kin?" Jerry asked.

"Depends. They'll make phone calls. Write letters. Iffn' they got a decent address that is. Where'd you say them folks was fron?"

"They said they were from Texas."

"Not if they was Mormon they wasn't. They's a whole cluster of 'em in an' around Salt Lake City. No, I don't reckon they was Mormon. Somepin' ain't right."

Hank said them horses looked like they come from the circus. Never saw such clodhoppers in his life. What would a horse like that be? May as well turn 'em loose.

Jerry laughed, his teeth white in his tanned face. Hannah noticed and thought of mint toothpaste and baking soda and cleanliness and the times he'd kissed her. She compared his clean teeth to the Jenkins boys, and remembered Clay. Almost, she had loved him.

She vaguely listened to the men, but was thinking of a name for her child. No child should be without a name. Sarah? Anna? Rachel? All fine old Amish names from the Bible. But this was her child, and she was a special one, found in a cold barn. Fate, or God, probably mostly God, had directed Jerry to that barn.

She would call her Jane. Jane. To match Jerry, both starting with a J. Jane Riehl. Now there was a nice name. Not too fancy, not too pretentious. Hannah held her close and planted a soft kiss on the curly brown hair, then laid her cheek against the spot she had kissed.

CHAPTER 10

THE LAST OF THE SNOW FELL FROM THE ROOF IN MUTED THUDS against the ground. A warm wind melted the icicles that hung from the porch roof like jagged teeth. The drifts of snow became smaller, lost their pure bluish-white shine, took on a dusty yellow and gray appearance as they melted into the wet, cold soil, mingling with the limp, brown grass.

Geese honked overhead, flying in perfect V formations, their calls plaintive, beckoning, the call of changing seasons, on their way to the shores of the big lakes to the north. Whistling swans flew higher, their high, piercing cries shattering the early morning stillness.

Hannah stopped on the porch step, laundry basket balanced on her hip, pausing to listen to the cries of the swans. She lifted her face to the beauty of their faraway, white forms, their outstretched necks propelled by the magnificent power of their huge, muscular wings.

She couldn't stand there too long. Janie would be waking soon. Since she had come into their house, life revolved around her. The washing was done while she slept. Floor scrubbing was hopeless with little feet dashing across the freshly scrubbed linoleum. Hannah would leave her pail and rag to crawl after her, catching her in a corner of the kitchen and showering her with kisses.

And now winter was sliding into spring, bringing warm weather. Hannah would be able to take Janie outdoors and allow her to run and absorb the sun's rays as she grew strong and healthy and happy.

The only dark cloud was the inevitability of the child's relatives coming to claim her. Every day Hannah told herself she would have to give up, to accept the appearance of a grandparent, an aunt, someone who would travel to North Dakota for the horses, and Jane.

The Jenkinses had taken the horses home. They kept them in a makeshift enclosure in their rusted sprawling shed. Hank threatened to turn them loose every day, but Hod exercised his common sense, saying what if the owners did return? Then what?

Hannah taught herself to sew small dresses, thick diapers, little undergarments, hunkered over the treadle sewing machine with knitted brows, her back aching with tension. She was determined to learn.

Letters from her mother began to arrive with regularity now that spring was on its way, informing her about life back on the Stoltzfuses' homestead. Hannah wished she wouldn't call the farm a homestead. *This* was their homestead. Her doubts about whether they belonged on the prairie had melted away with the snowdrifts.

The longhorns had come through the winter unscathed, only thinner and uglier than ever, dropping calves with the same unhurried belligerence that they did everything else, swinging their massive horns at anyone or anything that came close.

Nip and Tuck loved to antagonize the mothers with calves, bounding and yipping just out of reach of those menacing horns, till Jerry put a stop to it. He made them stay in their pen where they cried and begged until they learned their lesson, before they were hooked by an extraordinarily agile cow.

There was never an extra minute in the day for Hannah. She threw open windows, washed walls and furniture and bedding. She tore the beds apart and washed the frames, the rails, and the wooden slats that supported the mattresses. She polished mirrors, emptied drawers and wiped them with strong-scented pine soap that had been left behind from Rocher's hardware where she used to work.

She could never use the soap without thinking of the unhappy couple and their merchandise in a store that was called a hardware store, but had almost anything you could ever need. And now, they had moved back East to Baltimore, Maryland.

She wondered vaguely whether poor Harry was surviving the city. He had not wanted to return, but with a wife as miserably unhappy as Doris had been, he didn't have much choice. He did the right thing, giving his life for his wife, giving up what he loved most and taking her home where he knew she would be happy. Hannah hoped he was blessed every day. He was a good man and Lord knows, there weren't many of them.

Janie sat beside a drawer, pulling out handkerchiefs, scarves, anything colorful, putting them carefully on a pile and patting them with her soft little hands, saying, "Now, now."

She spoke quite a few words, so Hannah guessed she might be nearing 18 months old. Older than a year, but less than two.

Hannah was on the porch emptying a bucket of water when she spied the dark vehicle plowing through the mud, water, and slush, veering sharply in the back as the driver struggled to keep the car on the road, such as it was in spring.

Her heart beat once, flopped over, then rushed on. Blood pounded in her ears. They had come. Her first instinct was to run inside and grab Janie, hide her, tell a lie. She couldn't do this. Nausea rose, a hot bile in her throat, as the color drained from her face. Her mouth went dry and her nostrils dilated as her heart thumped.

She struggled for control, to regain a sense of composure. Janie was still playing happily in the bedroom. She checked her appearance, plucked a few stray hairs, adjusted the navy blue *dichly* on her head, then watched as the car slid to a stop in front of the house.

She drew in a long, steadying breath as the passenger door opened, and a white-haired lady dressed in a fashionable coat and hat stepped gracefully from the car. The driver emerged at the same time, a tall, older gentleman dressed in brown tweed, a hat on his head.

It had to be them. The grandparents.

She hoped Jerry was in the barn. She badly needed him to greet them. There were no other passengers in the car, which was shocking. These two aging people had come all this way on these back roads, driving a car that required skill on roads that were barely passable in some places.

They stood, looking uncertainly at the house. Hannah forced herself to go to the door, open it, and call out a greeting. Immediately, the couple's gazes relaxed, a smile appeared on the woman's face, and they made their way up the muddy path to the door.

Where was Jerry? Well, nothing to do but face this thing head on. She had known it was coming. She stood by the door, waiting until they were both on the porch, and then extended her hand. "How do you do?"

"We are both well, thank you." They shook Hannah's hand, the gentleman's grip firm, his blue eyes inquisitive but kind. His wife had a soft handshake, her round face showing no emotion, only a calm curiosity from colorless eyes behind a pair of gold-rimmed spectacles, as round as her face.

"You must be Hannah Riehl."

"Yes, I am."

Visibly relieved, the gentleman sighed, shook his head, and gave a small laugh. Before he could say more, Hannah stepped aside and ushered them in, closing the door behind them. The prairie wind still had a bite to it, as Hod would say.

"Please, sit down. Make yourselves comfortable."

They sat side by side, stiffly, their feet tucked in beneath them, their gloved hands in their laps. Tension hummed between them.

"We are Thomas and Evelyn Richards. We have journeyed here from Utah. Have you heard of Salt Lake City?"

Hannah's heart dropped as if it was falling into her stomach. The room spun as she struggled to breathe normally. She licked her dry lips and answered, "Yes."

Soft footsteps came down the hallway as Janie made a shy appearance, her thumb thrust securely in her mouth, her eyes large with fright.

Hannah leaned down and extended her hands. "Come."

The couple watched Janie intensely. "We are Lila's parents."

"I see."

"And this is . . .?"

Hannah was clinging to Janie, holding her too tightly. She wriggled, wanting down, but Hannah only pulled her closer. "We call her Janie. Do you know the story?"

Mr. Richards nodded. "Some of it. I don't know if we'll ever be able to sort out the truth from the lies."

Hannah nodded.

"Lila ran off with Timothy Weber when she was fourteen years old. They disappeared one night, and we heard nothing for close to six months. By then they were in Texas." He stopped, struggling to control his emotions.

His wife continued for him. "They were taken in by a wealthy rancher by the name of Caldwell. I have no idea why or how they ended up here in this . . ." She spread her hands.

Hannah smiled. "Most people find the prairie unattractive," she commented.

"I don't mean to say that, but it is isolated. We knew they had had a child and that they lived in North Dakota. And then, we were notified about the fire, the child, and their presumed deaths."

Mr. Richards took over. "They are believed to have perished in the fire. The chief of the fire company said there was a gold wedding band in the ashes. A ring. Why only one, was my question. Later, they found the other one.

"So, I suppose, no matter how hard we try and tell ourselves they could still be alive, we know they are not. Why the child was in the barn is a searing question to which we may never know the answer. We may have to live with this for the rest of our lives."

"She is our granddaughter," Evelyn Richards said softly.

"She doesn't look like Lila, does she?" Thomas whispered.

Hannah replied matter-of-factly, "We actually only met them once and had a nice visit. Lila had gone to lay down for a nap, so we only talked with her briefly. She was so young."

"Yes. Sixteen. So you see, we're heartbroken. Grief is a terrible thing. Especially in circumstances that are beyond our understanding. The whole thing is a mystery, a nightmare we have to live with. If only we could wake up and it would all be a bad dream." Thomas Richards would carry the mark of this tragedy to his death. Hannah bit her lip and pushed back the sympathy that welled up.

"Lila was disobedient. Madly in love with the much older Timothy Weber. We hope she had time to repent. She was always such a sweet, loving daughter, never caused us a moment's trouble, until she met Timothy."

Thomas Richards's piercing gaze fastened on Hannah. "You say you met them once. You were in their house? You sat and had a nice visit? Nothing strange?"

Hannah thought back to the day of the storm. She shook her head. "He seemed a bit arrogant, maybe. Over optimistic. We saw no child and he said his wife was napping, so perhaps she was putting the child to sleep."

"Why would he not have mentioned the child?"

"I have no idea."

Evelyn Richards began to weep, delicately bringing a lace handkerchief to her face. "Lila may have suffered at the hands of this man."

Thomas patted his wife to console her, his face gray with pain. "We have the child, dear," he said. Evelyn nodded.

So, it was final then. Hannah felt as if there was a stone in her chest instead of a beating heart. She told herself to have courage, to be strong enough not to break down visibly.

"So you do realize, Mrs. Riehl, that we are her legal guardians."

"Yes." Hannah's voice was a whisper.

"Your husband? Is he about?"

Hannah sat up to look out the window. "He was here earlier but I believe he rode out to check on the cows. It's calving season."

"Yes, of course."

"May I offer you a cup of tea?"

"No. No. We have a long drive ahead of us. We may as well not linger here."

Hannah sighed. She looked into Janie's face, clasping her shoulders, and saw the question in her eyes. "Do you want to go to your grandmother, Janie?" A sob in her voice. Quickly, she swallowed.

As long as Hannah lived, she would remember the look of absolute trust in Janie's round eyes before she slid off her lap and walked to her grandmother. She stood at her grandmother's knee like a little princess. So much grace, so much trust, Hannah thought.

Evelyn reached for her, and Janie went into her arms willingly. The lady's tears flowed, but a smile appeared through them like sunshine breaking through on a rainy day. She touched Janie's hair, her nose, her pert mouth. She murmured and stroked as

Janie sat staring at her intently. Thomas reached over to touch the brown curls, tears in his own eyes.

How strange, Hannah thought, that Janie accepts them both immediately. Perhaps God was in all of it, and, in her mother's words, it was simply "meant to be."

"I'll get her things," Hannah said quietly.

She cried while she packed the flannel diapers, the home-made dresses, and the little stockings. She had no shoes. Her coat was a stitched-together, made-over affair from one of Hannah's own, made without a pattern. She felt ashamed, then, of Janie's meager belongings, and her own inability to sew.

She heard the door open and close, voices. Jerry had come in. Viciously, she swiped at her tears, set her mouth in a determined line. She would not allow him to see how devastating this was. She had her pride to uphold. He'd seen her down too many times already.

She brought the cardboard box out of her bedroom, her face expressionless. Jerry was deep in conversation with the Richard-ses, so she set the box on the table beside the rocking chair and stood politely, her face a mask of self-control.

Jerry could supply no more information than Hannah had been able to, but Janie's grandparents were more than satisfied to be able to claim the child, a consolation they would have as they lived out their days.

They would find the birth certificate and call her by her given name. Janie would live in a Christian family with a group of caring adults around her and therefore, would never know of the tragedy in her past. Jerry and Hannah would never be known by her, never remembered, never longed for. Mercifully, she was too young to know.

And then, Hannah desperately wanted this to be over. She wanted them gone, with Janie, so she could begin to live her days without her and to see if she would be able to survive.

She handed Janie's coat to Evelyn, who began to insert the

little hands into the sleeves. That was when she reached for Hannah, a puzzled expression giving way to howls of protest.

Quickly Jerry picked her up, finished putting on her coat and scarf while Thomas and Evelyn stood there.

"Just go," Hannah said, tightly.

Her last memory of Janie was seeing her over Jerry's shoulder, both arms outstretched to Hannah, crying, "Mama. Mama!" until Hannah closed the door with more force than was absolutely necessary. She ran into her bedroom and threw herself on her bed, the pain eventually melting into heaving sobs and rivers of tears that soaked the quilt.

She heard Jerry return. Her bedroom door was firmly closed so he'd leave her alone. She listened for the sound of the car engine and thought there was always a chance they'd changed their minds, take pity on her and on Janie.

She knew they'd be good to Janie, knew she'd have a nice life. Knew too that this had all been inevitable, but all that was of small comfort.

Hannah had never realized the joy of caring for a child. She had not known she would ever feel this way. She had loved her siblings, but not the way she had loved Janie. It was all a mystery, this bond between a mother and her child.

She thought of children of her own and knew she wanted them now. It was a settling of her mind, the sure knowledge of motherhood. Well, one day at a time.

Spring was coming, so she'd stay busy. She'd bury herself in work, ride with Jerry when he rode out to deal with the longhorns, and eventually, time would heal, as it always does.

But first, she'd have to learn to control her emotions.

Supper that evening was a strained affair. Jerry tried to talk about Janie and her grandparents, but Hannah cut him off with a harsh word of rebuke.

And yet, he saw and understood Hannah's anger. She had never been angrier and more ill-mannered than she was now, living in the quiet house, a bleak space surrounded by four walls, devoid of Janie's happy chatter, the little feet that were like a musical cadence.

Where most women would have cried and spoken of their loss, allowing their husband's comforting arms to surround them, Hannah built a complex, efficient wall by the force of her own belligerence.

Nothing suited her. She made fun of the winter-toughened cows, despised the mules, said the wheat looked sparse, yelled at him for walking into the house with mud on his boots.

And never once did she mention Janie, the tragedy at the Webers', nothing. The final straw came a few weeks later when she blamed Jerry for the palomino's loss, saying it wouldn't have happened if he'd known anything about how the weather works on the prairie.

He listened to her senseless tirade, his back turned and his shoulders squared as he held very still. When he turned, Hannah recognized the fact that she had pushed him too far.

He stalked to her on swift, furious feet, grasped her shoulders with claw-like fingers, and shoved his face close to hers, so close she could see the small red veins that stood out on his nose.

"Stop it, Hannah! There is absolutely no truth in what you're saying. You were the one who wanted to go. That, Hannah, is your whole problem. Whatever happens in your life is always someone else's fault. Your father, your mother, and now me. It's time you grow up and take responsibility. If things continue like this, I'm going back to Lancaster County. I'm serious." He released her roughly enough that she had to take two steps back to keep her balance.

Her mouth opened in disbelief as she watched him yank open the door with much more force than was necessary, and disappear. It pleased her to know he wasn't quite a saint. He was a normal man, but at the same time she felt the most uncomfortable sensation she'd ever experienced. A deep sense of shame stung her cheeks. He may as well have slapped her.

What if what he said was true? That part about going back to Lancaster. So he did want to go back. Return to his homeland like the rest of them. Like whipped puppies. Well, she had news for him. He'd have to go alone.

She thought of Harry Rocher going back East to Baltimore, Maryland, a stifling seaport that teemed with people, heat, and humidity. Would he find peace and happiness there? She pictured him standing on the dock, watching the barges, feeding seagulls, returning to a home with a happy wife, visiting relatives.

Harry had done the right thing. Hannah knew his personal struggle and how difficult it had been for him to lay down his life for his wife, to love her the way Christ loved the church.

Her own father, pious and self-righteous, secure in his plain Amish way of life, could not do what Harry had done, and he a man of the world. There was the sticker. Being Amish was all right and good, a fact she could appreciate the longer she lived with Jerry. But you had to be careful. To take the title of being Amish as a passport to righteousness was a falsehood. "By their works ye shall know them."

But then, her mother had submitted, truly submitted in the way the Bible taught married women to do. No one would ever know the cost of her submission. But that had been right as well.

Jerry didn't know everything. He had no idea what her father had done. Her anger was her father's fault. How could she ever say that it wasn't? He had done wrong, not her. This thought, that had played over and over throughout her life, firmly embedded in the groove of her mind, spurred her into action. She lifted dishes and slammed them into the sink, breaking the handle off a cup, running water so hot she burned her fingers, adding far too much soap as she mumbled justifications to herself.

Jerry did not apologize. He merely went on his way, plowed the garden, spoke of the weather, the calves, the need for rain, as if that incident had never occurred. But it had! For Hannah, Jerry's temper and his threat stayed in her consciousness like a prickly burr, uncomfortable and sometimes making her miserable. It caused her to lower her eyes, unable to meet the forgiveness in his, as she clung to her sense of having been wronged.

The wheat grew, the roots absorbing the moisture the snows of winter had put into the prairie soil. The grass grew strong. The warm winds blew like a hushed promise of hope for the homesteaders that dotted the vast land, these clutches of buildings that housed the hardy souls of the Western prairie.

A month passed, then two. Every day the sun rose, a fiery orange ball of heat that promised a day exactly like the previous one. Heated winds blew, a drying, hope-sucking swoop from the west. There was an orange cast to the land, a yellow fog in the atmosphere, that wore down Hannah's resolve, working away at her determination like sandpaper on a rough piece of wood.

Surely not again. A drought this year would mean failure. An incomplete wheat crop, thin, bawling cattle, calves who trotted after their mothers as they roamed in larger and larger circles, tearing at the withered grass that gave way to a brittle lack of moisture.

The great metal fins on the windmill whirred and creaked, the bolts straining against the indestructible frame, the pump working feverishly to draw water from the stream far below the surface.

The moaning, hot wind clattered against the eaves, tore at the tin roof and the wooden siding, sent porch chairs skittering across the floor, dumping them off into the dust of the yard. Open windows afforded comfort, the air moving through the stifling house but carrying a fine silt of gray dust that lay over everything.

Dishes in cupboards had to be wiped clean with the corner of Hannah's apron, a swift dab for every tumbler or cup before it could be set on the table. Even then, they had to be placed upside down before they sat down to a meal.

They never spoke of the weather. There was nothing to say as long as Hannah clung tenaciously to her hope of rain.

All the washing Hannah hung on the line dried within the hour. She had to wrestle it all in as soon as possible or it would be torn from the clothes pins and hurled away by the wind.

Jerry and Hannah rode into the town of Pine for supplies, windblown and sunburned, King and the unruly quarter horse hitched to the spring wagon. Entering the town, Hannah asked Jerry to tie the horses. She was ashamed to drive down the main street with the exhausted team covered in white foam from the chafing harness on their wet bodies.

Rocher's Hardware had been bought by a man named Amos Henry, a hardworking man from Illinois. Rumors floated around the countryside. Supposedly, his wife had left with a cattle dealer and lived in luxury in California, leaving all the children behind with Amos. There were ten of them, all blond-haired and blue-eyed, devoted to their father and the success of the store.

Hod Jenkins said the man was a wonder. Never complained, never spoke of his wife. You could see his devotion to them kids, in Hod's words.

He'd added a room, filled it with tools and plowshares, harnesses and saddles, tractor parts, nails, screws, lariats, halters, everything a rancher might need.

The dry goods were all stacked neatly, bolts of cloth upright, sorted by color, the plaids and patterned fabric separate. Spools of thread, packets of needles, scissors and elastic, buttons and snaps, all of it was sorted in convenient bins within easy reach.

Hannah walked among the many items she would have liked to purchase, but she had no idea whether Jerry could afford them. The shining teakettle, the new soup ladle. She held both of them, rubbed her palms over each item and wondered at the shine. Like a mirror. She became aware of a presence at her elbow.

"Pretty, isn't it?"

Hannah turned and found a girl, shorter than she, with beautiful eyes like cornflowers, hair like new straw.

"It's called stainless steel," she informed Hannah.

CHAPTER 11

Her name was Margaret Henry, and Hannah learned she was the oldest daughter. She was a mother to her nine siblings, a sweet-natured girl of eighteen, eager to help Hannah with anything she might need.

"Call me Margie; everyone else does," she said, smiling happily, her eyes alight with curiosity and interest.

Hannah was aloof at first, which was her nature. She did not need friends, certainly not strangers, and she wished Margaret would go away and leave her alone. She answered Margaret's inquires with short nods or clipped words, which did nothing to deter the young woman's friendliness.

Hannah chose a packet of needles and a few black buttons to repair some articles of clothing. Then she ran a hand down the blue fabric that resembled the sky. She'd never buy it. She couldn't ask Jerry for money, and she certainly didn't have any of her own.

Margaret reached up to touch her white organdy covering. "That's nice," she said. Then, "Why do you wear it?"

Hannah desperately wanted her to leave, had no inclination to explain the Bible verse the Amish adopted to explain the reason for a woman's head being covered. "I don't know," she mumbled, her face flaming as she turned away to examine a packet of steel hairpins.

Margaret laughed, a high, sweet sound of delight. "You don't have to tell me," she said agreeably.

Hannah didn't reply, so Margaret offered nothing more, simply turned and left, leaving Hannah to herself, thankful for this moment without her presence.

Hannah knew she wasn't friend material. Girls and their blathering, their senseless tittering, stupid secrets, and howls of accompanying laughter, weren't anything she wanted or needed.

Jerry walked over to find her. "Get what you needed?" he asked. She nodded and they walked to the grocery section, where she purchased cornmeal, rolled oats, tea, coffee, brown sugar, salt, flour, baking soda, baking powder, and then asked Jerry if he wanted anything else.

He picked up a package of chocolate and some tin cans of fruit for making pies. "I'm hungry for chocolate cake," he said. Hannah avoided his eyes, nodding curtly.

Margaret watched and thought he was the most handsome man she'd ever seen. Putting up a hand to adjust her blond waves, she ran a hand over her hips to smooth the pleats in her skirt. His wife was a piece of lemon, now wasn't she?

When all of their purchases were grouped by the register, she began her curious interrogations again, a high pink color in her cheeks, those cornflower eyes darting repeatedly to Jerry's face while he kept up a lively banter with her. Well, let him, Hannah thought sourly. She was married to him.

"Yeah, Ma left," she was saying. "No heartache for us kids. She hated the West. Hated the town, all of it. Life was no fun with her around. To live with an unhappy person corrodes your own spirit. Like rust. Don't miss her at all. I did all the work anyhow, so I did. Now, is there anything else I can get you?"

She was looking straight at Jerry, her eyes bright with interest, her white teeth flashing in her face. He answered with a too-wide grin of his own, enjoying this exchange immensely.

A shot of unaccustomed jealousy liquidated quickly into ill manners. Hannah's eyes shot daggers of deep brown fury in Jerry's direction. "If you can tear yourself away, it's time to load up these groceries." Her words held all the warmth of an icicle during a blizzard.

Flustered, Jerry scrambled to retrieve the brown paper bags, picking one up too quickly. He broke his hold as a large piece of bag tore off.

"Oh. Here, I'll get you another one," Margaret said breathlessly. "It happens all the time."

Hannah's dark eyes bored into Margaret's blue eyes. "I'll bet," she said, followed by a derogatory snort.

But at the feed mill, she sat spellbound, her hands folded loosely in her lap, held captive by the men's talk. Lounging against the high wooden counter, one leg crossed over the other, their old Stetsons stained with perspiration, tall, short, round in the stomach, or stick thin, these men were all cut from the same cloth, their parents and grandparents staying on their homesteads, eking out the meager existence they seemed to love.

Nothing dampened these grizzled men's spirits. They thrived on difficulty. Monetary success was a concept they didn't understand. They measured with a different yard stick than the rest of the world. The prairie was their life. "Got into Grandpap's blood, and his pap before him. Ain't no other place to live, far's I'm concerned."

Hannah felt a deep respect and awe for these battered Stetsons. Their sunburned faces were like prunes, deep lines and crevices etched from brow to chin, a map of their lives. They lived on the land, gleaned from it what they could, raised a few scrawny longhorns. Success was an evening spent on the porch, a barn cat rubbing along the creaking hickory rocker, a dog at their feet, and the spectacular sunset their entertainment.

"If the wife became unhappy, wal, then, she'd have to go back East cause they shore weren't gonna leave the prairie nohow."

Today, the subject was the drought. Wasn't it always?

"Ain't rainin' this summer." Stated bluntly, with absolute conviction.

"Who said?"

"Aw, come on. We'll have us a few good soakin' thunderstorms. What're you talkin' about?"

Wads of tobacco shifted, streams of dark brown juice were aimed expertly at the copper spittoon in the corner. By the looks of the dried dribbles on the outside, plenty of misses had taken place.

Hannah swallowed.

"Nope." The first speaker leaned forward, removed his elbows from the high counter, uncrossed his legs, and went to thump a feed sack of grain to form a perch for himself. "No sir, I'm tellin' you. We had that yaller look about us, come spring. You get that, it's gonna be dry as Abraham's desert."

Jerry stood off to the side, taking in every word, but seldom speaking himself, listening to learn the knowledge of the plains.

"Any o' you ever hear more about that house fire out there where them Germans usta live?"

Most faces turned to Jerry. He nodded. "The grandparents of the young wife came to collect the little girl. They're from Utah, where Timothy Weber said he was from, so we know that part is true, but not much else."

"Them young people died though, for sure? In thet there fire?"

Jerry shrugged. "They think so. Found their wedding rings."

"They shoulda found more'n that. No body turns completely to ashes when they burn." Heads nodded in agreement.

"I still think there's somethin' afoot."

Bill Hawkins, an old bachelor that ran the biggest herd of longhorns, cleared his throat, spit a long stream of molasses-

colored liquid from his mouth, wiping his mouth on the cuff of
his sleeve before commencing with his point of view.

"What kinda people would leave their kid in a barn in the
dead of winter? They were a normal couple, weren't they? Come
out here, bought that property fair and square, with good intentions. Nobody burns up that fast."

Hannah recognized again the common sense of these prairie
dwellers. She had thought the same thing, often. Did a person
turn completely to ashes in a house fire? Or did someone place
those wedding rings on the floor to throw everyone off?

As if he read her thoughts, Bill continued. "Them fire company big shots don't know nothin'. They make a good calcula-
tion and guess the rest. Whatever suits 'em, is what they go by.
We got enough horse and cattle thieves around. Them white
Percherons was in somebody's sights, I'd say."

"They was all in the barn, though."

Hannah felt a jolt of excitement. There had been more than
eleven horses the day she'd been there. All those white horse
trailers. She sat up straight, opened her mouth to speak, and was
cut off by a short, stocky fellow who tipped his hat back on his
head, scratched his thatch of orange hair, replaced his hat and
lined up his four fingers to examine the wealth of dandruff he'd
scraped loose.

Rubbing his nails down the side of his oil-stained jeans, he
hacked loudly, cleared his throat and said that nobody knew
how many o' them oversized chunks o' horseflesh had been
there ta begin with.

"More than eleven." Hannah spoke without thinking. Jerry
turned his head sharply and looked at her. Hannah didn't look
back; she looked out to the general circle of men and went on,
her eyes like dark sapphires.

"It was a few months ago, early in the spring, when I rode
over to see if the people from Texas had moved in . . ."

"They wasn't from Texas," Bill Hawkins said.

Jerry corrected him. "The young couple was."

"Anyway," Hannah continued, "the place was crawling with white horse trailers. I didn't count them but there were definitely more than five. If there were two horses in each one, I'd say there were more than twenty horses."

"Thet barn ain't thet big."

"It wasn't. It isn't. They weren't all in the barn," Hannah said quickly.

"Hm. Ain't that somepin' to think about?" Bill Hawkins asked.

"Ah, you know how it goes. Don't matter what we think. Them there horse thieves is slicker'n greased pigs. How you ever gonna ketch 'em? One sheriff in two hunnert miles and they don't give a . . ."

Bob Daley glanced at Hannah, cleared his throat, and said, "Don't care." Hannah grinned good-naturedly and said he was right. She wanted to tell them about Lemuel Short but Jerry didn't know about that episode and she had no intention of telling him, either.

"Any high falutin' caravan o' white trailers movin' into the area like that is like the wasps to a cake o' honey. Them horse thieves probably had them pegged way back in Missouri, if they came from those parts."

Heads nodded. "That's fer shore."

"Yer right."

"Yeah, but to light that house. That's just goin' too far."

The conversation changed directions, turning to the growing of wheat, half a dozen different opinions crisscrossing the hot, dusty feed mill.

Jerry and Hannah stopped at the butcher shop for lard. A five-gallon tin would hold them over for a while.

Seated on the high wooden seat, Hannah felt rich, endowed with great wealth. Such a large amount of supplies was something. The ability to ride into town and purchase even more than was necessary was an indulgence that she could not have imagined for many years. She hoped she would never take it for granted and forget to realize the gift of provisions.

Hannah gazed at the land with unseeing eyes, her thoughts churning faster and faster. Was this the secret to the true homesteader then? What separated the greenhorns from the true pioneers? The ones who stayed. It was possible. Over and over, the folks who stayed lived through drought and hail and all kinds of calamities. They kept their homesteads, adapting their views and values to suit the environment and not someone else's version of success.

Worry did not fall into their vocabulary, posed no threat. If it didn't rain, they pulled their belts tighter and ate cornmeal mush and prairie hens. Here, success might be measured by the ability to weather whatever the Almighty handed you.

She didn't want to reveal her thoughts now, while Jerry was busy controlling the cranky quarter horse, reining in King, who wanted to run full out, which was the way he always ran when he was hitched to a spring wagon.

She might just keep the whole thing to herself. She wanted to ask Jerry how much money he still had in his bank account, but was too proud to ask. How did one ask for sky-blue dress fabric without giving him the notion that she was buying it to be attractive to him?

Which she definitely wasn't.

The wheat had turned from the brilliant, earth-toned green of spring to a drab, olive-hued, windblown mess, probably half the height it should have been. Hannah turned her head to keep from looking at it more than was absolutely necessary.

"Here we are," Jerry called out, his usual good humor evident. She didn't answer, just stepped off the spring wagon and began the trek to the house, carrying armloads of provisions. She couldn't tell him, but the solid weight of the food was a joy,

a feeling of luxury, a cared-for and appreciated gift of sustain-
ability in the face of another drought. The surge of happiness
she felt gave her strength.

She knew she should thank him that evening as they rested
on the porch after carrying buckets of water in an effort to save
their potatoes and pole beans.

"What do you think, Hannah? Is it worth lugging water?"
Jerry asked.

"Long as it doesn't rain," she answered.

"But the potatoes look half-dead."

"They always do. You can't compare Western potatoes with
what we were used to back East."

"Do you get any potatoes to dig?"

"Sometimes."

They fell silent as they listened to the sounds of the evening.
When the wind slowed for the night, the sounds of birds and
insects became easier to distinguish, the crickets and grasshoppers, the little dickeybirds and the evening whistles of the larks.
Hannah loved this time of day. The serenity of pure, empty skies
in several shades of lavender and pink, the blue fading to gray
before twilight followed the setting of the sun, that effortless
disappearance of amazing light and heat.

She thought of all the crow's-feet etched along the side of
these ranchers' eyes, imagined they squinted all day long from
beneath their filthy hat brims. Tentatively, she reached up to run
the tips of her fingers along her own eyes, the outer edges still
smooth. She lowered her hands quickly when Jerry looked her
way.

"So, what do you think, Hannah?" he asked.

"About what?"

"We are having another drought, whether we admit it or not.
I don't know if we can expect any wheat at all. Which means the
calves are our only source of income, and they're not too great
either."

"You heard the men."

Jerry looked at her. She was sitting on the porch floor, her knees drawn up, her skirts pulled taut down to her brown feet. Her arms rested on her knees, her neck long and graceful like a swan. Her hair had come loose from the heavy coil that lay on her neck and strands of it were blowing lightly in the evening breeze.

As black as midnight. Black as coal. His mind wandered, thinking of a different time, a different place, another girl with black hair. What had kept him from marrying her? Why had he walked away from Ruth Ebersol?

God's ways were far above his own, but sometimes the thought of being successful in business at home in Lancaster County, with a girl . . . no, a wife like Ruth, seemed like a bright beacon of rest, one he had missed entirely.

He wanted to go back home and resume a normal life.

"I heard them, yes."

"Well, what did you get out of what they were saying?"

"One thing's for sure. They don't look on droughts or . . ."

Jerry laughed ruefully. "Or anything at all with too much concern," he finished for her.

Hannah met his gaze, her eyes flashing. "Exactly! You do understand." In the depths of her eyes there was a spark or recognition that kept his eyes riveted on hers.

"Oh, Jerry. Don't you see? Today at the feed mill I found the reason why some people stay here in North Dakota and all the lands west of here, and others don't. It's so plain to me now, especially why our Amish neighbors went home. These people out here measure their time on earth in a completely different way than we do. They don't care about what we call success. They are happy, Jerry, happy with food on the table and a roof over their heads, enough wages to keep their clunker automobiles or trucks going. In other words, getting ahead, our version of it, with a large herd of cows and money in the bank, simply isn't important."

Jerry narrowed his eyes. "So you're saying to be a successful homesteader, you need to adopt a different attitude."

"Yes."

"You mean, a drought isn't so awful, as long as you're content with what you have."

"Right."

Jerry said nothing for a long while. Then he asked, "Would you be content here, like this, if we never had more than we have now? No church, no fellow Amish, no parents or relatives, simply this seclusion day in and day out?"

"Yes."

His heart sank. He didn't speak again. He simply rose, let himself in the house, and let the screen door flop behind him. Decidedly, the conversation had taken a new and different turn, and he needed time to think.

Hannah remained on the porch, her chin resting on her arms, now a bit miffed. That was unnecessary, Jerry cutting off the conversation like that. He just couldn't bear to think of staying here. He figured she'd break down yet. Well, she almost had.

But after today, she wasn't so sure. These old ranchers had something, an element of satisfaction, of peace, no matter what happened. They took it, made the best of it, enjoyed themselves with simple pleasures. Oh, the list went on and on.

She thought of her father, the manic fasting and praying, believing that God would come on his terms and bless him because he was a righteous man. Wasn't he misguided? Which one was God's way?

The ranchers gathered in a feed mill with total kinship, saying what they thought, accepting and accepted, easily doing the same with whatever life handed them, paragons of patience and contentment.

Her father had left Lancaster County because of the argumentative brethren who aired their highly esteemed opinions, took offense and held grudges, all in the name of Christ and his written word. Her father would not have wasted the time telling her these men were all unsaved heathens, and perhaps they were. But that part was up to God.

Hannah knew her own mind. These *ausrichy* (outsiders) displayed plenty of the fruits of the Spirit, in her view. They demanded nothing from God, appreciated plenty, and lived in peace and harmony, helping anyone who needed it. They would have starved, the whole Mose Detweiler family, if Hod and Abby had not given and kept on giving.

And so Hannah remained on the porch watching the pinpricks of white stars appear, one by one, then in clusters, then in numbers far beyond her ability to count. Nip and Tuck came from the barn, surprised to find her, shoving their wet noses in her face, then flopping down beside her.

"Phew! You smell. Have you been unearthing your treasures? Get away from me!" She shoved them aside with her foot. Killing prairie dogs and other rodents was play for these swift-moving dogs. They buried the excess, then retrieved it after it became putrid.

And still she lingered, her thoughts racing from one subject to another, questions left unanswered, new ideas like cartwheels cavorting through her mind. She couldn't expect Jerry to stay if he simply did not see things her way. Neither could she keep up her expectations of living together for the sake of enough money to keep the homestead.

Clearly, she was in over her head. To move to Lancaster now was simply not possible. He'd have to take her by force, kicking and biting like a wild horse!

As for that other. . . . She felt so tired so quickly, her thoughts dragging along like a hundred-pound weight, trying to reason her way out of it. Regret was suddenly very real. Why had she married Jerry on a whim? For money of course, when money was still important. After today, she'd have to be honest and somehow have the courage to tell him she would never return to Lancaster County and give him the option of leaving to go back by himself.

Jerry lay in his own bedroom with his own thoughts, trying to be reasonable. Mentally, he made a list. Number one: he was married to her, the girl of his dreams, who obviously had no normal love or desire for him. Number two: her goal in life was to stay on the prairie, especially after today. His goal was to leave this endless prairie, the dust and wind that shaved away at his goodwill and patience. Number three: today, she had come up with a whole new philosophy.

He was weary, bone-weary, in mind, body, and soul. Regret for the marriage became an insistent whine, which he tried to slap down like a mosquito, but he had to face it. He wished he'd never met her. That marriage certificate was binding by God and by man. Holy Matrimony. He turned his face to the wall.

He felt old, bitter, and hostile toward Hannah, a whole new, uneasy accumulation of thoughts and feelings. He couldn't pray in this state of mind. But he did tell God that he was in too deep and couldn't find a way out. So, he'd allow God to lead and go where He thought best, and if it was His will, he would stay. He would sacrifice his life for Hannah's love. But he did require Hannah's love, if it was meant to be.

The summer ended without rain. The wheat stayed short and never grew to a head. The dust blew between the limp plants and lay like volcanic ash. They worked together to put up enough hay to last through the winter before the worst of the drought. They never talked about the failed wheat crop, or the endless dust.

Just when Jerry thought things could not get worse, Hod Jenkins came by in his rusted, blue pickup truck in a cloud of dust, almost setting it on its nose, he hit the brakes so hard.

Hod strode up to the porch, brought his fist up, and banged on the screen door. He said they'd had a telephone call from Abby's sister that lived down Ventura way.

Hannah moved quickly from the table, opening the door to let him in, her eyes wide with dark apprehension.

Their food turned cold as Hod told them what Tessa had said. "There are horse thieves around. Seriously dangerous ones. Men who won't think twice about knockin' you off to git at yer horses. That King o' yourn . . ." Hod shook his head. "They's workin' at night. Hittin' every ranch from Ventura to Calvin. Gittin' closer by the day. She says even the sheriffs is afraid of 'em. Callin' in a buncha cops from the capital. Alls I'm sayin' is to keep watch at night. I dunno how yer gonna keep 'em from takin' yer horses, though. Iffen they do show up, uer better off lettin' 'em take 'em, I guess."

Hannah set down a mug of coffee in front of Hod with shaking hands, her face gone pale. Jerry's face looked grim, but he said nothing, allowing Hod to have his say.

"They'll ketch 'em, eventually. The thing is, will they git 'em fore they git this far? Hannah, now if they show up, don't you go doin' anything stupid. Stay in the house. Act like there ain't nobody around." He slurped his coffee and grimaced.

"An' they say there's a green tint to the east. Old timers used to say the grasshoppers is walkin'. Like the plagues of Egypt, mind you. Time'll tell, I guess."

CHAPTER 12

Aftter hod left in a cloud of dust, jerry sat in a kitchen chair dazed, as if all the vigor had gone out of him. He couldn't bring himself to look at Hannah. He didn't want her opinion just yet. He needed space to think. He drained the last of his coffee, stood, and walked out.

He was halfway to the barn when he heard his name being called in strident tones laced with the old belligerence. He stopped, turned.

"Come back in here!" Hannah shouted. It was about the last thing he wanted to do, but he knew ignoring her would only make things worse. He returned to the kitchen and sat down without meeting her gaze.

"You know you're acting like a coward. Like an ostrich! Or whichever animal it is that sticks its head in the sand when trouble comes along."

As irritating as a burr in his sock. "An ostrich is a bird."

"We have to talk," Hannah said, ignoring his correction.

"Go ahead."

"Don't *you* have anything to say?"

"No. Go ahead. Tell me what's on your mind."

Hannah sighed. "I wish you would go first, okay? You won't like what I have to say."

"Well, keep going. I want to hear it," Jerry urged, trying to sound like he meant it.

"All right. I know you want to go back to Lancaster. I don't. I want to stay here, away from all the people who know everything about everybody. After our afternoon at the feed mill, I feel like I finally have a grasp on what it takes to make it out here. And I love it so much."

"I know you do, Hannah. And if it means so much to you, we'll stay, for a while anyhow. But didn't you want to talk about the horse thieves? And the grasshoppers?"

"Oh, you can't listen to that Hod. He's always making this stuff up. I don't believe all his horse thief talk either."

Jerry's eyebrows shot up.

"Don't look at me like that!"

He shook his head. "It's good to have confidence, Hannah, but to be too confident after a warning like that can be extremely foolish."

Hannah snorted, that grating sound that said everyone was foolish except her. There were few things he actually disliked about her but that was definitely one of them. He wanted to bring up the subject of how long they would still be living in this manner, but he figured that wouldn't do him any good at this point, either.

Was he a coward? Quite likely. He preferred to think he was patient and understanding.

At first, they thought a hailstorm was brewing. The greenish cast to an otherwise cloudless day seemed the harbinger of a mighty storm.

Hannah was watering the garden while keeping an eye on the approaching strange weather, whatever it was. She dumped water from a tin bucket, watched the parched earth soak it up greedily, and noticed the healthy green of the plants, especially the beans. All the hard work had paid off. The bean runners climbed to the top of the poles. The beans were hanging thick and healthy. The cabbage heads were firm, if small, which meant they'd have sauerkraut this winter.

If the storm kept coming toward them, they would be able to quickly harvest an amazing amount of vegetables before it hit. Jerry would certainly be impressed. She'd show him that with a bit of hard work and good management they could beat the odds.

But, what was that odor? She straightened and sniffed the air. She turned her face in every direction, taking deep breaths through her nose. Strange, that smell.

Well, likely it was a dead animal somewhere. Nip and Tuck were always dragging some putrid carcass from their burying places. Thinking no more about it, she refilled the bucket and finished her watering. She went to the house to finish the breakfast dishes.

The hens were laying well, plenty of eggs every morning, a treat she appreciated as she cooked eggs to perfection, serving them with fried mush made from the newly purchased cornmeal. She thought of the ear corn they used to buy, roast in the cook stove oven, shell and grind for their cornmeal, thus saving a dollar or so, when her mother and Manny were still here. Every penny had meant the difference between hunger and eating a meal, even if it was just cornmeal mush eaten with a pinch of salt.

The strange smell permeated the house now. Hannah tried to ignore it, finishing the dishes with a puzzled expression before stepping out on the porch to sniff the air again.

Jerry came in from the barn, his eyes questioning. Hannah met his eyes, shrugged, and shook her head.

They sat together on the porch steps, side by side, pondering the stench and the green atmosphere, as if the air contained green dust. Jerry rose uneasily, searching the sky, the waving drought-sickened grass. He paced from one end of the porch to the other.

"Sit down!" Hannah growled. "You're making it worse than it is."

"I've just never seen anything like this. Something is so weird. Strange. I don't like the dust or the smell."

Suddenly, he turned sharply. "Hannah, you . . . could it be the grasshoppers?"

She gasped, sprang to her feet, shading the strong forenoon light with the downturned palm of her hand.

Oh, please no, she thought. She'd heard tales of millions of gnawing creatures walking, plague-like, through the land and destroying everything in their path. But that was years ago. This was now the 1930s, modern times. Somehow, the automobiles, tractors, all the newer inventions did not seem like they could coexist with the grasshoppers of old.

Jerry pointed a shaking finger. "What is it?"

Hannah stood staring in disbelief. A wall of greenish-brown, yellow, and black. A moving front of writhing, gnawing insects. Spellbound, they watched their approach, a descending cloud of unreality, like a bad dream holding them captive.

"We need to close windows," Jerry said, quietly, too calmly, as if he would be punished if he raised his voice.

"What about the barn?"

"We can't help that. Cracks in the eaves, under the door," Jerry replied.

"The hens? Nip and Tuck?"

Jerry leaped off the porch, raced to the barn to corral the flapping chickens. Hannah dashed after him. They shooed and yelled, Hannah screeching and flapping her apron, maudlin with fear, as the wall of grasshoppers advanced steadily.

Nip and Tuck were stuffed into their doghouse, the rubber flap closed securely with nails, before Hannah and Jerry turned and fled to the house, panting, slamming windows and doors, stuffing rags in every noticeable crack.

They heard a grinding, buzzing sound. The sound of countless jaws chewing grass, briars, weeds, each other. The dead insects rolled over and over until a sticky mass of body parts quickly putrefied in the sweltering, dust-infused sun.

Hannah felt a rising panic. She put both hands to her cheeks, her eyes wide. On they came, across the driveway, over the barn, scaling the walls like a million prehistoric creatures with oversized jaws, half flying, half leaping, grasping any available vegetation and completely mutilating it.

Hannah screamed, a long, hoarse, primal yell of fear and loathing. She screamed and screamed, stamped her feet and flapped her apron, as if her actions could put a stop to this disgusting onslaught of horrible creatures.

Quickly Jerry was at her side. "Come, Hannah. Don't watch." She was crying now, shaking like a leaf, begging Jerry to do something or they'd crawl in the house and over both of them. He pulled her away from the window, begging her not to watch. But she seemed powerless, mesmerized, her fingers spreading across her face, still peeping through them, wild-eyed with fear.

"Do something, Jerry. Please help me!" she screamed.

Jerry realized she was in danger of losing her sound reasoning, so completely was she consumed by her loathing of these large insects. It was a situation that was so out of her control that she felt powerless. And because she was such a fiercely determined person, he felt afraid for her.

He sat on the sofa, pulling her down, turning her face to his. He made her look at him until her eyes focused.

"Listen. Hannah, look at me. They can't get in. We're safe. Did you hear me? They'll walk over the house, but they can't get in. Hannah, look at me."

She was wild with revulsion. She clawed at his shoulders, broke free and ran to the door, tried to yank it open. He caught her just in time, hauled her back and held her.

Finally, when the grasshoppers reached the house and began their ascent up the north side, she shuddered and fell against him, sobbing, a desperate heaving of her body, choking, begging him to hold her.

The whole house was consumed by a grinding, sawing noise, the sound of millions of raspy legs and gossamer wings and devouring, ravenous mouths. Up from the ground they walked, up the wooden side, across the roof and down the other side, through the garden, leaving not even a tendril of green.

Jerry held Hannah, her face buried in his shirt, the stifling air inside the house causing them both to perspire freely. He could see the undersides of the insects, their bulging eyes, their high, crooked green legs and oversized jaws as they tried repeatedly to scale the slippery glass of the windows, falling back to be walked on or eaten by the grasshoppers who came behind them.

They fell down the chimney into the low embers of the cook stove, dropping by the hundreds and sizzling to their death. The chimney became clogged with grasshoppers. The stove began to send out a scent of burned insects, puffing out a sickening stench.

Hannah trembled, clung to him with all her strength. Putting his handkerchief over her face, he turned her head against his chest to hold her ears shut. It was like being in a vacuum, knowing the chewing insects were like a second skin, finding any crevice available and crawling through. They sat together, hardly breathing in the unbearable stench coming from the cook stove.

Jerry wiped the sweat from his forehead, felt it sliding down his back. He took an arm away to swipe at the soaked hair on his forehead, but quickly put it back around Hannah when she cried out in distress. "I can't. I can't," she kept saying over and over.

"Listen, Hannah. It'll be over soon. They'll stop coming eventually." He was seriously afraid for her. So impetuous, so angry, so sure of herself. Her breakdown after spending the night in the blizzard. And now this. He was afraid this was far worse.

She had been through so much, too much. An overwhelming need to protect her, to keep her safe from more disastrous situations, rose in him. If only he could take her back to safety, to the normal weather patterns, the hills and dales of the fertile valleys he loved so much. To keep her safe among friends and relatives. To take her to church and social events.

He chasteneth whom He loveth.

Deliberately, he drew her closer, his hand stroking her trembling back. Ah yes, he well knew the ways God chastened His children. He must love Hannah to put her through so much.

For the Lord looketh on the heart.

He saw in Hannah something worth redeeming or He would not allow all of this. Is this why I love her, then?

The grinding clatter of insects continued as they huddled together in the overheated, noxious house. The fumes from the stove were overpowering. Scratching, clawing, falling back, climbing over each other, killing one another—the march of the dreaded insects moved on.

Jerry sat up straight, listened as the rasping sounds lessened, then clearly faded. No grasshoppers out the north window, which meant the end had come and was on its way out.

"Hannah."

Her only response was a distinct tightening of her arms, her face burrowing deeper into his chest. "No, no, no, no."

He tried to release her arms, prying with all the strength he could muster, but her grip was like a vise, a panicked death grip.

"Hannah. Hannah. Let go. It's almost impossible to breathe in here."

"No, no, no."

He had to open windows, had to get away from the fumes coming from the cook stove. He wrestled her away from him with a strength born of desperation, shoving her onto the sofa where she collapsed, crying hysterically.

He tore open windows, gagged at the smell of dead grasshoppers strewn over everything, hanging body parts from window ledges, edges of siding, drooping from roof edges like cooked noodles. It was a grisly scene and there was a horrible, slimy stink where dead insects had been half-eaten by their peers.

He left Hannah and walked across the bare yard, stripped of any and all vegetation, a dry desert, a land cursed with the plague of Egypt come to visit them. He crunched across dead grasshoppers. Kicking them away, he gagged and swallowed the saliva that welled in his mouth, then gave into the nausea, leaned over, and threw up his half-digested breakfast.

First, unclog the chimney. He grabbed the wooden ladder from the tool shed and hurried to the house, setting it against the wall, climbing onto the porch roof, and from there onto the roof of the house.

Clogged, black with insects. It was a good chimney, made of creek stones and mortar. He'd simply burn them out, which is what he did, with paper and kerosene. Lighting a match on his thumbnail, he threw it in the cook stove. He was rewarded with a mighty whoosh, a roaring, crackling sound with clouds of smoke rolling out from under the stove lids.

Nothing to do about that. He'd have to help Hannah wash walls later. He swept the porch and steps, flicking his broom along the siding to rid the house of dead grasshoppers that clung to cracks in the walls.

The smoke in the kitchen was a better aroma than the sizzling insects. He heard the satisfying roar of the burning chimney, then searched for any stray insects before he went to urge

Hannah to sit up and notice her surroundings, to calm down and think of it as a bad dream.

Looking back, Jerry could remember the moment when Hannah's courage overrode her fear. Her disbelief and revulsion faded and normalcy returned. She followed him to the barn, to the creek, across the land to check on the cattle. She refused to stay alone. She asked him to stay in the house till the dishes were washed and she had tidied the house.

Often, her eyes would return to the horizon, searching for another wall of insects, her hands clenched into fists. There was no fight in her eyes, though.

Something had changed, but exactly what it was, Jerry couldn't say. She didn't sleep at night, but paced the floor, locked and re-locked the doors, until she passed into a stupor toward the morning hours. She begged him to stay with her, her pride and anger hidden away, erased by the memory of the crawling grasshoppers.

Finally, Jerry could not take the sleepless nights. He walked around the homestead in a fog of bewilderment, numb from lack of sleep, watching Hannah become even thinner, with a haunted look in her dark eyes.

He confronted her and told her simply that this could not continue. She lifted frightened eyes to his, like a child who knows they've done wrong, waiting for punishment.

"Hannah." His voice was kind and extremely gentle. "We're a married couple. If you don't want to be alone at night, why don't you sleep with me?"

"I don't sleep. I never sleep."

"We both hardly get our rest."

Hannah twisted her hands in her lap, chewed on her lower lip. "I have nightmares. The minute I close my eyes I see thousands of bulging eyes. . . . Jerry, I never saw grasshoppers that big. They were like monsters!"

"I know, Hannah, I know. It surprises me, though. You're so strong in the face of most things. Angry, charging through."

Hannah picked at a loose thread on her apron, her eyes downcast. "It was Janie." Jerry watched her face closely. "It was being lost in the storm, then Janie. It seems as if God must really have it in for me. As if He just can't think of more bad things to send my way. I know I'm a horrible person."

"No, you're not."

"You know I am. It's my father's fault. He brought me out here."

"Your father is dead, Hannah."

"So?"

"Your father did the best he could."

"No, he didn't. He was crazy."

"Forgiveness never comes easy. I know. And yes, he did put his family through more than most men would deem right. But it's done now, it's over. Your past is like water under a bridge. It's gone. Irretrievable. You'll never be able to change one moment of all that has happened. But you can change your remembering and the way you choose to cling to past wrongs. Let it go, Hannah."

For one second he thought she would soften, her eyes turning liquid with the thought of taking his advice. To try.

And then she sniffed, straightened her back, sat ramrod straight, and turned her head to gaze out of the window, her eyes seeing nothing. "I hate Lancaster County, you know."

"No, you don't. You are deeply ashamed of your past, to this day. Folks forget. They likely barely remember exactly what occurred, and if they do remember, it's bathed in the rosy light of forgiveness, which, you know, fixes a lot of bad memories."

Unconvinced, Hannah pouted.

At bedtime, she spent a long time in the bathroom, running water at regular intervals, opening and closing drawers.

He heard her brush her teeth until she surely must have nearly brushed all the enamel off! He waited.

Finally, she emerged, a long flannel nightgown draped to the floor and covering her body like a heavy curtain. Her arms were crossed and one hand went to hold onto the button at her throat, scraping it nervously as if to reassure herself that it was still there and closed firmly.

"I'll sleep with you."

Jerry blinked. His mouth went dry. Was this all there was to it, then? Those four words, stating her necessity, spoken in her exhausted, gravelly voice, surrounded by the ravaged, destroyed land.

She turned, like a tired ghost of herself, and walked into his bedroom.

Soundlessly, Jerry lifted himself from the bed, careful, quiet. In the light of dawn, she lay on her side, her dark hair spread across the white pillow, her heavy lashes like crescents on her pale cheeks, her breath coming in soft, slow puffs, a hand tucked beneath her cheek. He could have watched her all day.

He gathered up his clothes, tiptoed out, and silently entered the bathroom, checking his face in the mirror to see if his appearance had changed overnight. He blinked. Quick tears sprang to his eyes.

Overcome by emotion, he braced himself with the palms of his hands on the edge of the sink as his head sank to his chest. He squeezed his eyes shut, trying to keep the tears at bay. But in the end, he gave up and sobbed, praising God in a language that came from his heart, a reward for his patience, his bitter cup of self-denial.

So, God was right all along. His love for Hannah was real and not just infatuation or lust, not just a challenge, the winning of her a triumph, a victory. His heart sang praises as his spirits soared. He could live in this harsh land for the rest of his days with Hannah by his side, in spite of having so many misgivings. He would truly give his life for her, give up his own idea of how and where they should make a home. He would love her to the end of his days.

After the barn chores were finished, Jerry entered the house by the back door, removed his shoes, and washed up carefully. The house was strangely quiet, so he made very little noise.

The kitchen was empty, the cook stove cold. He tiptoed to the bedroom door but didn't have the heart to tap on it as he heard soft snores, like those of a sleeping child. Smiling to himself, he decided to forego breakfast rather than wake her. He knew he'd clatter around with the cook stove top and the frying pan, so he let himself out into the washhouse, put on his shoes, and went to the barn and sat.

He simply sat on a sawhorse, his legs stretched out in front of him, his arms crossed, and grinned. He didn't think of anything, and yet he thought of everything. His mind was filled with the wonder of Hannah. His wife.

Their future was in her hands. He was willing to stay. He could sacrifice everything, the companionship of friends and relatives, the ability to become financially successful, the privilege of attending his beloved church services with the brethren, all of it. He could be happy wherever Hannah was.

He went to the door, leaned an elbow on the doorjamb, and gazed at the devastated land. He shook his head in disbelief. Like a desert it was. Nothing remained. Not a stub of grass. Nothing. The garden was visible only by indentations where plants and rows had been. He thought of the potatoes.

They'd need rain before any form of vegetation would grow. The swarm of grasshoppers had been a few miles wide, roughly estimated, so the Jenkinses likely knew nothing of it yet.

The water tank had been choked with grasshoppers, turning the entire metal container into a slimy, tepid heap of stinking bodies. He'd merely kicked the whole thing over and turned away, unable to tolerate the smell of the half-dead, drowned, mutilated bodies of these oversized creatures.

They'd dried in the hot sun and crunched underfoot like cornflakes. He swallowed and shuddered. One of the worst experiences of his life, most certainly. Jerry wondered at the bullheadedness of that King Pharaoh in the Old Testament. That guy sure was stubborn. So many plagues, one right after another, and still he clung to his own way and kept God's children captive. He tried to imagine a sea of frogs coming hopping across the prairie, followed by a spell of darkness unlike anything anyone had ever seen. And even that wasn't the end of it. Jerry could not imagine what the children of Israel had endured before they could enter the Promised Land, and even then, things had never been perfect.

As they would not be with Hannah. He smiled, remembering. The way she described people, the narrow-minded suspicion with which she viewed every person she was not acquainted with. He laughed outright, thinking of the time they met Simon and Drucilla Rutgers in town. Simon was a good fellow, amiable, friendly to a fault. He ran a successful (for that area) cattle operation west of Pine. Simon was a short, wiry guy with a face like a good bulldog, sporting the unusual habit of spitting when he spoke.

Hannah hadn't been in his presence longer than a few seconds before she started glaring at him. She'd stepped back, crossed her arms, and watched in fascination as he sprayed spittle enthusiastically. Later, seated beside Jerry on the spring wagon, she'd started in immediately.

"What's wrong with him? He needs to wear a bib. Or carry a towel in his belt. Honestly, that face. He looks like he ran full tilt into the side of his barn."

Jerry's shoulders began to shake, even now. His nose burned and tears rose to the surface, again. He could never scold her. It was simply too funny. Hannah did not like people, which, of course, was the biggest reason she loved the plains so. *Ach, my Hannah*.

It was all part of who she was, and he loved even that about her, no matter if it was a fault, a shortcoming. He loved her for being herself, for hiding nothing in the exalted name of pride, the way most folks did. His Hannah didn't care one little bit what people thought of her. She said and did what suited her at the time.

The sun rose higher in the sky and the bare land glared like the balding head of an old, old man.

CHAPTER 13

SARAH SAT IN THE KITCHEN OF THE STONE FARMHOUSE IN LANCAS-ter County. She was alone, the old clock ticking rapidly from the high shelf above her, the spigot dripping slowly into the white, porcelain sink. She'd have to get her father to look at it.

She read and re-read Hannah's letter. It was a long one, which was unusual. Her letters normally consisted of a few paragraphs, mostly about the weather and nothing much of interest. She read it slowly, for the third time. She folded it carefully, put it back in the envelope, and held it to her heart.

The blizzard. Janie. The grasshoppers. *Ach, my Hannah.*

So much like Pharaoh of old. How long would God continue to chasten? She didn't mention Jerry once. Sarah shook her head, hoped for the best. She knew why she'd married him, and it certainly wasn't love. Mothers knew.

She wasn't convinced that Hannah was capable of staying in North Dakota too much longer now, but neither could she imagine a homecoming. *Oh my Hannah, my Hannah.* The source of worry, of constant prayer and longing, her heart tethered to Hannah's by the bond of motherhood, never able to fully sever it.

She folded her hands, bent her head, her lips moving in silent prayer.

When the dry late summer air took on the biting cold of autumn, Hannah and Jerry dug the potatoes from an unrelenting, heat-baked garden. Water from the house had been dumped on the potatoes by the bucketful and still it produced only a half-bushel of small, wrinkled potatoes with green tops where the searing sun had discolored them through the thin soil.

Hannah stood in the wind, her scarf tied securely around her head, looking at the potato harvest. She snorted. Picking up her bucket, she flounced off to the house, leaving Jerry to follow, lugging the half-bushel of potatoes.

She slammed plates on the table, scattered knives and forks, thumped down empty water glasses, and sliced bread with a rapid, sawing motion. She heated milk and threw in a couple of eggs. Then she sat, her arms crossed, staring at the floor.

Jerry knew this was not a time for questions. She looked at him, a frank, dark, incomprehensible stare. "What's the use?" she asked.

"The use?" he answered, dumbly.

"You know what I'm talking about."

"You mean the potatoes?"

"Of course." She kept looking at him, fixing him with her dark gaze. The kitchen darkened with her mood, expanding and contracting with unspoken words. The air became heavy with their breathing, the two of them alone with their own thoughts and feelings, unable to break through a barrier of pride.

Finally, Hannah spoke. "I don't know if I can manage another winter."

Jerry said nothing.

"I guess you know I've changed. The grasshoppers. I can't even . . ." Her voice faded, then stilled. "I mean, how many more calamities have to happen before I give up? I can't take another winter. You'll ride out to check the cattle and I'll never know if you'll return."

She stopped, her face reddening. "And, I want children. I've known since Janie left. I want a whole pile. And I . . . well, I remember Abby's impending birth too well. I'm not going to put myself through what my mother went through. I don't have that kind of faith to believe that God will see me through in this isolated place. With me, you never know what God's going to unleash. So, I figure, I'm about done."

"But, I thought you had it all figured out," Jerry said, so kindly.

"I'm not talking about money, success, or financial security. I'm letting go because I have to. How long does God have to let you know something isn't right before you finally get it?"

Jerry blinked, shrugging his shoulders. Everything was happening too fast. But then, this was Hannah, so surprises cropped up with no warning.

"I want to go home." The words were spoken in a flat monotone, as if she was telling herself, first. There was no question at the end, no self-pity. Only her blunt statement.

Bewildered, Jerry raised his shoulders, palms upturned from his outstretched hands. "Home? But what do you consider home?"

"Lancaster County."

"But . . ." Jerry was sputtering now, trying to wrap his head around the possibility she had just presented. "You just said recently . . ."

She cut him off. "I know what I said. I don't like Lancaster County. But it's the best alternative. I've weighed the options, and the scales are definitely tipping toward Lancaster, for one reason. With all I've experienced, I'm afraid to keep on trying. I don't have the courage. The determination, maybe, but not the courage. I can't take the winters with you gone. It's different now since I . . . uh . . . you know. Love you, or whatever."

Jerry watched her face. Her eyes found his and held. Slowly

he rose, his eyes fastened on hers. He reached for her, lifted her from her chair, and held her, his eyes drinking in the light in hers.

"You do love me, then?" he asked.

She stilled his words with her lips.

Much later, they sat around the supper table, dishes strewn everywhere, the cook stove turning cold, half-scraped pots and pans thrown in the sink, the fading light of evening settling across the house.

They talked, speaking freely with a new intimacy. Jerry felt reverent with this new and undeserved gift, everything he'd always longed for presented to him on a platter, almost more than he had ever prayed for. He told Hannah that he was willing to stay, willing to try again. Perhaps another year would be the opposite of this one.

She reminded him that the year after that could be exactly like this one. It was foolish, this glue-like adherence to the homestead.

"We've come so far, Hannah," Jerry protested.

"You have no heart for this place, so stop being false. You know you'd be happy to return." Spoken in the way only Hannah could convey feelings. He grimaced. She was looking right through him, her eyes like darts. He got away with nothing.

"All right. All right." He threw up his hands in mock surrender.

She laughed, that short, sharp bark he seldom heard.

Sobering, she told him what had helped her make this choice. "I could probably live here if it wasn't for our heritage. Our way of living, our lives entwined with people like ourselves. We have no one who truly understands us. I've come to the conclusion that family is important. So is community. Relatives, extended family. I don't miss people. I just miss my mother and Manny. I don't want to . . ." Here she faltered, then her eyes found his and stayed. "I want to be close to my mother when . . . you know, we have babies."

Jerry nodded and breathed deeply. "So, it seems as if we have plans to make and more work than we'll get done if we want to leave before the snow flies."

Her eyes shone. "Oh, Jerry," she breathed. "Now that we're going, I feel as if I can't stay in this house another day. I want to go now. This instant!"

"Not too long ago, you had it all figured out. What it would take to stay here. Remember?"

"I do. And I would turn into a real plains-woman if I had been born and raised here with the rest of these tough, old characters. Perhaps I've grown up. Who knows? I will always love North Dakota, the wide open spaces, grass, cattle, riding horseback, the isolation. But I want a whole houseful of children like Janie. That toddle around and fill the house with their funny words and well. . . . You know, Jerry. Janie was sent into my life to direct my path. It's strange, but she was. I'll never get over losing her."

She paused. A distasteful expression crossed her face. "I'll never get over the grasshoppers, either."

"No, you won't. But you know what I think? I think they may have finished what Janie started."

"Now don't you get all prophetic and spiritual," she said, eyeing him with a look that still held the old rebellion.

"*Hoi schrecka.*"

"Hoi what?" Hannah asked.

"*Hoi schrecka.* Grasshoppers."

"*Hoi schrecka* is German for grasshoppers? Literally, that's hay scarers."

Jerry's eyes turned gleeful, teasing. "Scared you straight into my arms. I love it. I pitied you, but it was extremely nice."

Hannah blushed, a beautiful infusion of color, the soft stroke of delicate pink. No one would be able to produce anything close, not even the most gifted artist, Jerry thought.

"I hope we won't always need a million grasshoppers to lead us," he said, laughing.

They got down to business then. Hannah produced a tablet with lined paper and wrote: mules, King, saddles, harnesses. She looked at Jerry, chewed the end of the pencil, and said that this didn't make sense.

"We can't send all these animals to Lancaster County if we don't know where we're going."

"This list is not our shipping list."

"Well, what else is it?"

"We're going to have to have a public auction if we want to go back before winter."

"You mean . . . ?" Hannah was incredulous. The thought of selling everything was staggering. For one moment, anxiety overtook her. The animals, the beloved land they had worked so hard to keep. What, exactly, was "making it" anyway? How did one go about measuring whether you were successful?

She hated that word suddenly. They had had a lot of small successes, and large ones, too. If their success was measured in dollars, then no, they weren't exactly well to do or anything even close to profitable. The house and barn had been built from the charitable contributions of the brethren in Lancaster, as well as the surrounding community of non-Amish. They had all proved to be caring far beyond anything Hannah or Sarah had ever expected.

So, there was that. They definitely would not have made it without help. They would have been forced to go back East. But how could one measure anything in the face of all they had been through? The list went on and on, a bitter tower built with incidents, layer after layer of hard, natural disasters, each one a monument of suffering, blocks that added to the whole shaping and forming of the past years.

Were they better for all of it, or worse?

"Hannah, you're not listening." Hannah started, blinked, and said she heard every word, but of course, she hadn't.

"It would cost too much, for one thing."

Hannah had no idea what he was talking about, but kept nodding and feigning agreement.

"Should we sell everything? House stuff? Furniture?" he asked.

Hannah considered. To part with these things was something she believed she could do. The heirlooms of the past, what they'd brought from Lancaster in the covered wagon, had burned in the fire. The rest of it? All replacements. Nothing Hannah had ever become attached to. But to return empty-handed, like immigrants from another country, was not something she relished. But would anyone have to know? It's not like everyone would be standing at her grandfather's farm waiting for them to arrive. Maybe they could slide back into Lancaster life without a lot of fuss.

"What do you think?" Jerry's question brought her back to the immediate problem. "If we sell everything, we had better get the public auction done as soon as possible. I don't want to be on a train in the middle of winter," Jerry said.

And so they sat, debating, making plans, batting problems back and forth, finding solutions in a sensible way. Hannah knew that her opinions mattered to Jerry, that she would never be like her spineless mother who had been hoodwinked into making that senseless journey, that ill-thought-out venture into the unknown, propelled by a man who seemed far inferior to her own husband.

Husband. That is what he was. He was a good man. He rose to any overriding problem, faced it squarely, and found a reasonable solution, with her help. He considered her advice.

She was suddenly humbled, a sensation she didn't like, so she said loudly, "Nobody is going to want those mules."

"Oh, now, come on, Hannah. They're good mules. The best. You'd be surprised how many of these ranchers still own a good pair of mules."

"Maybe. But no one has any money."

"Times will get better. We may not make much, but we'll be all right."

The day of the auction arrived, a biting wind and a steely sun bringing folks in heavy coats, hats flattened over red ears, women dressed in heavy socks and sensible boots, scarves and woolen overcoats.

Jerry had hired the florid auctioneer from the cattle sale in Pine, who arrived in a new truck, washed and gleaming like a wet bathtub, a silver bucking bronco mounted on the hood, a senseless ornament that raised Hannah's ire.

Fat little man. He could never get on a horse, let alone one that bucked. Why would you have something like that on your truck? She watched him strutting around like an under-sized bully, throwing his arms around and shouting orders. She decided he wouldn't get any tip from her. If Jerry wanted to give him extra money for his work, then that was up to him.

Many of the women came up to Hannah, their kind, wrinkled faces curious and alight with interest. One middle-aged woman, as tall as Hannah and almost as thin, met her face-to-face, her dark eyes boring into Hannah's with unabashed questioning.

"So, what gives?"

Hannah was on guard immediately. That was no way to greet anyone. Her eyes narrowed as her mouth stretched into a grim line that didn't contain a shadow of a smile. Coldly, she sniffed and said, "What do you mean?"

The woman waved an arm, taking in the homestead, the fur-niture in neat rows, the bedding and dishes, everything they had worked so hard to set in an orderly display so that the auctioneer could move up and down the rows in an efficient manner.

"Why? Why the auction?" the woman asked, her voice gravelly like a man's, her face lean and long with cheeks that resembled a burnt pumpkin pie, the kind that was pocked on top.

An intense dislike for this ill-mannered upstart rose in Hannah, but she squelched the fiery retort with all the effort she could muster. "We're going back home."

"Where's that at?"

"Pennsylvania."

Putting one fist to her hip, she cocked her head and squinted, giving a short, nasty guffaw. "Chickens! Turned chicken, didya? Grasshoppers gitya?"

Hannah's heart pounded furiously. She stood her ground, her eyes boring into the other woman's. "It's none of your business," she ground out, turning and walking away, her face cooled by the prairie wind.

There were other women who spoke in a kinder fashion, but mostly, Hannah was reminded over and over that to leave a homestead was a sign of weakness. These women had mostly been born and raised here. The prairie was in their blood. Their suffering and hardship was all a part of life.

As the day wore on, Hannah felt worse and worse, sinking into a darkness that threatened to overturn her resolve. According to these folks, she was a loser. Running home to her mother, waving the white flag of defeat and crying "Uncle! Uncle!"

Then, quite suddenly, a fierce gladness welled in her. No matter what they thought, she was looking forward to seeing her mother, her face like a beacon of light that beckoned and guided her home. And that was all right.

She went to stand beside Jerry. She needed the reassurance of touching his sleeve with hers. He looked over and gave her a small smile of recognition. "Everything all right?" he asked.

She nodded. His look affirmed his love in the midst of this crowd of weathered prairie dwellers.

Hannah watched the auctioneer on his block, fascinated by the amount of spittle that sprayed into the wind. He must have an endless source of hydration somewhere in that crimson face.

Jerry whispered, "We're getting fair prices."

"That's good," Hannah whispered back.

The auctioneer's voice was like wagon wheels rumbling across a wooden bridge. He spoke so fast that Hannah wasn't aware that an item had been sold until the gavel was smacked against the wooden partition in front of him.

After the trucks had been loaded and most items hauled away, Hod Jenkins came to stand with Hannah. Hank and Ken sidled up soon after, their eyes alight with a new interest.

"So, this is it then?"

Jerry nodded. "This is it."

"Must be hard for you, Hannah."

Hannah lowered her eyes, the toe of her shoe scuffing the dust at her feet. "It is."

"I imagine so."

"Hank here was wonderin', since you can't sell the homestead, we'll jest go to the courthouse or wherever, whatever it takes to take on the land and the buildings. He'll likely have to put in another ten years, but he's good with that. Right, Hank?"

Hank turned his head and directed a jet of dark brown tobacco juice into the dust with a wet smack. Hannah swallowed the nausea that welled up in her throat. "Yeah," he said, shifting the wad of soaked tobacco.

"Reckon he'll find hisself a woman, ifn' he ain't already done that, and this here ranch is better'n ours. He'll be well off afore he even starts."

"Yeah," Hank agreed. "Hannah got married to this guy, so I gotta start all over." He jerked a thumb in Jerry's direction, his wide grin revealing a row of yellow, tobacco-stained teeth like rotten corn. Hannah thought the mule's mouth looked better, even when it brayed! Hay was cleaner than that disgusting wad of tobacco.

Hod laughed. "You coulda had all my boys, Hannah. Every one of 'em was so sweet on you they thought up every reason they could fer ridin' over here. Like bees to honey, they was."

Hannah smiled, but didn't blush. She'd always known. And might have gone ahead and married Clay if it hadn't been for her mother. Hod prodded her with his elbow. "Yer not sayin' nothin."

Hannah smiled. Yes, she might have married Clay but she couldn't think of the disaster that would have amounted to. Young, headstrong, unable to put up with the "aw shucks" of the Jenkinses. They lived out their days with an ambling easiness, nothing riling them too much. If the roof leaked, there was always a bucket to catch the drips. If the fence was broken, it stayed that way. Mud, dust, manure. It was all tracked into the house. Weeds and tin cans and pecking chickens, mangy dogs and skulking cats . . . that was just their way of life.

The divide between the two cultures would have proved her undoing. Would she have been able to love anyone, back then? All the raw misfortune that had presented itself, over and over, had shaped her into who she was today.

Jerry liked to remind her that God puts us through the fire so all our impurities are melted away. We become a golden, shining vessel for His use. Well, she had plenty of dross left over but she guessed it must be true, if you looked at it the way Jerry did.

Hod looked at her. "Now that remark put ya to thinkin."

Hannah nodded, but had no words, no smart retort.

"Ah, likely jest as good this way. Clay an' Jen's happy. They couldn't be here today. Went to visit Jen's gramma over'n Montana somewheres."

"I was wondering where they were," Hannah remarked.

Hod smiled at her. "Wal, I'll tell ya right now. I've been pleased to have you folks fer neighbors all these years. Too bad about yer pa, Hannah. He was a good man, just a mite determined to do things his way. Out here in God's country, ya gotta listen to the old timers. They know what they's talkin' about. Seems as if yer pa had his own ideas, doin' things the way he did back East. But, like I said, he was a good man. Now yer ma, there's the salt o' the earth. Never knew a better woman. I'd a asked her to marry me, but I ain't near good enough. Besides, there's that religion thing. Don't hold with all them rules.

"But jest want to let you know, it's been a pleasure knowin' you folks. Hopefully, we'll do their place proud. Ya'll kin come back 'n visit, and likely Hank 'n his wife'll be livin' in the house, runnin' livestock of their own."

"It seems right that one of you will be living here," Hannah said. "I'm so glad the house won't be setting empty."

And she meant it.

After everyone had gone, the auctioneer went over the results of his day's work and Jerry paid him, along with a too-generous tip, in Hannah's opinion.

Hannah wouldn't talk to him for some time, simply sweeping the house in angry jerks, slamming things around until Jerry got the message that he'd done something wrong.

"All right, what is it? What did I do?" he asked, blocking her way to the near-empty pantry.

She wouldn't answer him then, but later she decided to clear the air and tell him about the auctioneer. She concluded her rant with a firm, "He didn't need a tip!"

"I disagree," Jerry said. "You can't look in someone's face and decide then and there that you don't like them. He's one of the best auctioneers I've ever seen. We were paid well for all our possessions. We have enough for a down payment on a small house when we return to Lancaster County."

Hannah was effectively silenced.

For one last time, she walked across the prairie, felt the absence of Nip and Tuck acutely. How many times had she thrown a stick and watched them rocket after it, dropping it at her feet, eyes shooting sparks, mouths wide, panting? Over and over. Hank and Ken had taken them home. She refused to even say goodbye. It was easier that way.

Her scarf was tied snugly beneath her chin, so she loosened it, held it by a corner, and swung her arms wide, feeling the rush of pure wind in her ears, the headscarf billowing out like the sail on a boat. She twirled on one foot, turning to all four directions, tried to inscribe on her heart the isolation, the wonder of being alone in this vast land. She wanted to capture the wind and the scent of the soil, remember the sight and sound of the undulating sea of grass, forever.

And then she was crying, sobbing with abandon, until her eyes felt swollen and her cheeks chafed with the cold and the runnels of tears. She knew her face was purple, discolored, ugly, but nothing mattered. She was who she was, and nothing would change that.

She whispered her goodbye, and her thanks to this great land that had, indeed, clasped her heart and held it with its awesome, indescribable power.

CHAPTER 14

CLUTCHING THEIR SATCHELS, SUITCASES AT THEIR FEET, JERRY AND Hannah stood by the old railroad station, the cold wind biting their faces with the first icy blast of winter's arrival. Many times in recent days Hannah had nearly changed her mind, nearly begged Jerry to return to the homestead. But that wind reminded her of all the reasons they were leaving and gave her the courage to face the unknown ahead of her.

Displaced, unanchored, a wanderer. Hannah acutely understood the true meaning of losing a home, of striking out in uncertainty, in spite of the fact that she was returning to her roots.

They heard the train, saw the billowing black smoke, long before it rattled and hissed into the station in a cloud of steam and charcoal-gray smoke.

A few bedraggled passengers stepped down. Men wheeled clattering carts of boxes, burlap bags, trunks, luggage of every description. They shouted directions to one another, lifted heavy containers on capable backs, and disappeared into the rail cars. They reappeared, issuing more commands.

Not much different from an anthill, Hannah thought sourly. And then, the conductor appeared on the lower step of the passenger car to their right. Jerry stooped to pick up the largest of their suitcases, nudged Hannah, and said softly, "Here we go."

She followed him, feeling utterly empty. Is this all it would be, then? Board this monstrous thing that smelled of coal gas and tar and rained sparks like the biblical brimstone, then sit in a miserable seat and gaze out a soot-streaked window, all the while crying inside until your heart felt as if it was melting away into nothing?

She arranged her face into a cold mask of indifference, sat as close to the window and as far away from him as possible, piercing the window glass with her hard, polished eyes that held back the torrent of regret, the sadness that rolled over her in waves of pain.

She had known leaving would not be easy. But she was ill-prepared for the onslaught of varied emotions that built up in her throat until she was unable to breathe properly.

Jerry knew to leave her alone. The joy of returning beat strongly in his chest. He knew no regrets. He had made the promise to stay, and would have done it, had Hannah not chosen otherwise.

The whistle sounded, that earsplitting scream Jerry loved. He leaned forward, past Hannah, watched the prairie begin to move, sliding away as the train picked up speed. His eyes shone with the challenge of returning, looking for a home, a small farm. They would find a place that was at a healthy distance from neighbors, away from prying eyes. He looked forward to this new chapter in his life with Hannah.

For miles, Hannah feigned sleep, sagged into a corner, and pouted like a disobedient schoolgirl. Jerry watched the landscape rolling past, and reached under the seat for the packet of cold meat sandwiches Hannah had prepared that morning.

She had refused to make breakfast, saying the cook stove was gone, so how could she? Bread and butter would have been fine, but he drank the last of the milk, wiped his mouth, and said nothing.

He knew the leaving would be hard, but this? Oh well, he was sure it wouldn't be the last time he'd have to face her stone-cold eyes and the disapproval of all he said and did. Especially the things he did. Her unhappiness was like two strong arms she used to pull him in, trying to drag him down with her. He had recognized this early on, so he knew the best way to handle it was to cheerfully ignore her until she got past the dark cloud hanging over her head.

Now, the sight of the sandwiches being unwrapped irked her. "It's not lunchtime," she hissed, her eyes sliding past him to the travelers in the seat beside her who were eyeing Jerry curiously.

"I'm hungry, so I'm going to eat."

She was hungry, too, but swallowed the saliva that rose in her mouth at the sight and smell of food.

"Want some?" He offered half of his sandwich to her, but she shrugged away from him. Hours later she still refused to eat, simply sagging in the corner of her seat and gazing out the window with dull eyes.

They were observed curiously by the passengers across the aisle, but Jerry had his back turned much of the time, his eyes barely leaving the window as he took in every sight, drinking in the scenery in spite of its sameness.

The train stopped at so many stations that Hannah lost track. People gathered belongings, spoke urgently, then hustled off the train, shoving children and crying babies ahead of them, begging pardon for the disruption.

Hannah glared at all of them, fat mothers that smelled like sour milk and howling red-faced babies, sticky-faced children that needed a good wash and a firm reprimand. When an overly friendly farmer leaned in to ask their destination, Jerry opened his mouth to answer but Hannah spoke quickly, telling him it was none of his business and he had food in his moustache.

He walked on but turned to look at her with a baleful,

whipped puppy expression before he exited the car. Hannah held his stare with her cold eyes until he disappeared.

She told Jerry they could have brought Nip and Tuck. Other folks brought animals. Why couldn't they? Jerry explained, patient as always. The journey was only part of it. They had no home yet and to expect her grandfather to take them in along with two rowdy dogs was too much.

Hannah harrumphed plenty about that. Who did he care about after all? Her or her grandfather? Finally, Jerry spoke firmly and told her she was being impossible. He knew this was not easy for her, and he felt her pain. But, come on!

If she was ashamed after that, she gave no indication. Jerry knew that giving up was an ordeal, a genuine misery for her. Most times he found it humorous, or at worst, tolerable. But even he had his limits.

They slept fitfully, cramped in uncomfortable positions, a cold draft seeping through the windows and sending shivers down their spines. Hannah's mood steadily worsened, until Jerry decided it was best just to ignore her completely.

Then trees appeared on the horizon. Vast forests of dark pine and bare-branched trees, miles and miles of them. Hannah reflected on all the firewood, the dwindling cottonwoods in the creek bottom. What would they have done when the last of them were chopped up and burned in the cook stove?

When the first mountain appeared in Northern Pennsylvania, a steep, gray, cold-looking monument covered with trees, rocks, shrubs, and brambles, Hannah sat up and turned to watch as the hills slid by, her eyes now open wide and alight with interest.

Suddenly, she said sharply, "We could live in the mountains." Jerry said nothing, knowing full well there were no mountains like this in Lancaster County. Hannah couldn't explain the overwhelming plenty of trees. On and on, everywhere, there were trees. Firewood to burn. Lumber for houses and barns and chicken sheds. Those trees represented warmth and shelter and safety. Her mind whirred.

So, why couldn't they buy acres and acres of this mountain land and set up a sawmill? They could sell lumber for anything anyone would need. They should have kept the mules. Nip and Tuck would have loved these mountains.

The train wound its way between the mountain ledges and along a cold, gray river flowing to who knew where. If mules were too light, they could always buy Belgians. Those heavy workhorses were what loggers used to drag out the wealth of these forests.

Her mind churned, making plans.

Their arrival at the Lancaster train station was like all other stops, without fanfare, the train gliding smoothly into the station. The city outside the window was a frozen, gray landscape of towers and bulky buildings set beside each other, brick and stone, concrete and painted lumber with windows like spying eyes. The air was gray, heavy with smoke and steam, gritty with soot.

When Hannah stepped off the train, there was an absence of oxygen, a suffocating stillness containing malice and suspicion. Her eyes searched the crowd of people herded together like cattle, but found no one she recognized.

Jerry prodded her elbow with his hand. "Keep moving, Hannah. There are other folks who want off the train." She jerked her arm away from his touch and glared at the conductor who ushered them into the milling crowd.

Her feet were swollen, stuffed into her old, stiff leather shoes. Her face felt greasy and filthy. Her shoulders ached with the weight of her satchels. She wished for wings—huge, flapping, capable bird wings—to lift her above the sordid gray roiling mess of humans, across the mountains, across rivers and plains, depositing her straight back to the lonesomeness of the homestead.

What had they done? What had possessed her to tell Jerry she couldn't survive another winter? She couldn't survive this, either.

They moved along with the crowd, propelled into the high-ceilinged, monstrous railroad station, alive with voices, calls, people shoving, never stopping their constant chatter. Her chest tightened, her breath came in short, heavy puffs.

Then she heard her name. Quickly, she turned her head to find her brother Manny wading through the sea of jostling, straining people. When he reached her, his dark eyes shone into hers. He clasped her extended hand with a teeth-jarring grip and said, "Hannah!"

He wrung Jerry's hand as warmly, saying his name as well. Then he surveyed them both, said marriage suited them, and grabbed a suitcase, pointing to the north entrance. "We'll talk later," he mouthed.

Hannah's mood lightened as she followed the black, broad-brimmed hat and wide shoulders of her brother's black coat. When they emerged from the station, there were still more than enough pedestrians, cars moving, and trucks blatting their horns at incompetent drivers squeezing their vehicles past them.

"Where's Mam?" The question had hovered on Hannah's lips the moment she spied Manny. He laughed. "Oh, you know our mother. She won't step into an automobile unless it's absolutely necessary. I think the train ride to return home aged her ten years. She just doesn't like speed."

"So, she's at home?"

"Yes. With enough food prepared to feed twenty people!"

Hannah laughed, that short, raucous burst of sound, then turned to smile at Jerry, who returned her smile wholeheartedly. So, there was joy in Hannah's return.

The drive from Lancaster was too long for Hannah. She felt

herself pushing her feet against the back of the front seat, willing the driver to drive faster.

The fields and woods were brown, or a drab, olive green. Corn fodder lay like colorless paper, yellowed and torn. Holsteins, sheep, goats, mules, horses of every description roamed pastures, pulled carriages, or plodded in standing fields of brown corn, drawing wooden wagons with rattling sides. Black-coated, straw-hatted men and scarved women were ripping off the dangling ears of corn with a swift movement of their wrists, before hurling the ears on the wagon.

Hannah watched, kept watching, turning sideways in her seat to keep an eye on people husking corn, an expression in her dark eyes that Jerry couldn't begin to decipher.

"Remember?" he asked, gently. She nodded.

In truth, she could feel the cold, the biting, wet air that stung her cheeks and tingled her nose. The satisfying whump of an ear of corn hitting the wagon bed and rattling off into the corner. The gentle Belgians standing in the rows, snacking on corn, moving forward obediently, stopping when necessary, the smell of harness leather, the dusty, drying fields, the exhilaration of being outside in the fields with someone you loved. Her father. In memory, that's who she was with. And he'd sing. He sang German songs on the slow *veiss* (tune) from the Ausbund, the hymnbook they used in church. He practiced over and over, then led singing in services the following Sunday. He had a strong voice, a good baritone to lead the congregation.

Hannah blinked and felt an unwanted lump in her throat. Once, her father had been someone. An honest, esteemed member of the Old Order Amish church, working the farm that had been his father's before him.

The old shame returned, the feeling of inadequacy, of not being enough. Well, she was married now. A woman in her own right. Had taken the name of Riehl. Was no longer a Detweiler.

Her thoughts churned like a spring creek swollen by torrents of rain. Could a name change her past, though?

When they arrived at her grandfather's farm, everything came rushing back, the unhappy time when her mother had given up in North Dakota and her subsequent return to Lancaster County. All a blur of misery.

The house was built of gray limestone, serviceable, sturdy, a monument of hard work and foresight. The trees flanking the house on either side were like sentinels, shading the structure from the heat of summer, heightening the spring glory with their tender red buds that lay scattered across the green lawn like nature's carpeting.

Hannah noticed the bulging corn crib, the corn husking already finished. That was Elam and Ben, likely. She wondered if their work ethic would rub off on Manny, who had learned the ways of the plains before moving back home among his German ancestors who lived to work hard, making every hour count.

The door was flung open and there was her mother. Hannah fumbled for the door handle, then flew to the porch, her feet barely touching the uneven cement sidewalks.

They clasped hands, looked long into each other's eyes, one as dark as the other. There was no hug, no outward display of emotion. That was the way of it. A sincere handclasp coupled with a long searching look, a checkpoint to gauge whether all was well.

Mother to daughter, and daughter to mother, strengthening the bond that would never be severed, no matter what life handed them. Hundreds of miles, trials almost more than could be borne, differences of opinion, verbal arguments, hurts and animosity—all of it only increased the mysterious bonds that held them.

"Hannah! *Ach*, Hannah. *Vie bisht*?"

Nodding, soft-eyed, Hannah replied, "*Goot. Goot.*"

What a mother wanted to hear. Everything was good. Good. Her daughter had married a nice man who would keep her happy and love her to the end of their days. Nothing would change that. A mother's hope is kept alive in the face of tumultuous adversity, always searching, longing to hear the good news, the love, in her daughter's union.

A clatter of men, handshaking, satchels and suitcases, the squeal from Eli and Mary, so tall, so grown-up. Her grandfather was bent and wizened, his dark eyes shedding tears. His hands were like tree branches, bent and gnarled, calloused, veins like tributaries of the strong river flowing from his heart. He still husked corn and could hitch up a mule with the best of them.

Sarah, her cheeks flushed, eyes bright with excitement, bent and swayed, moved from icebox to gas stove. A wonder, this gas stove, she said, between questions and exclamations, barely listening to what Hannah had to say.

She dished up mountains of mashed potatoes, shook the small saucepan with the browning butter till it hissed just right, then poured it over the creamy mound, watching to make sure it did not run over the sides of the service dishes.

She brought out a blue agate roaster and lifted the lid to produce a wealth of browned, steaming *roasht*, one of Hannah's favorite meals. One chicken went a long way if it was roasted, the gizzard, liver, and skin ground in a cast-iron meat grinder, the meat cut into bite-size pieces and mixed with cubed bread, celery, eggs, salt and pepper.

The smell was heavenly. Hannah bent over the steaming roaster and breathed deeply, then pinched a corner of the savory filling with thumb and forefinger and popped it into her mouth. She closed her eyes, savoring the wonderful flavor. "Nobody makes *roasht* like you, Mam," she sighed, reaching for more. Sarah slapped her hand playfully. "Fork, Hannah!"

There was thick, yellow gravy. Homemade dinner rolls, their tops golden and gleaming with butter. Lima beans. Canned green beans with *schpeck* (bacon). Chowchow, sweet pickles, and applesauce. Homemade noodles, rich and heavy, swimming in browned butter and parsley.

They all pulled up chairs, while Eli and Mary slid along the bench. Without spoken direction, they bowed their heads as one. The grandfather's lips moved in silent prayer, his eyes gleaming with unshed tears as he lifted his head and told everyone to help themselves.

Elam and Ben watched Hannah, each curious to see if she'd come to accept Jerry as more than a business partner. She was something, that Hannah. It had been hard to believe she'd married anyone. Both were convinced that Jerry couldn't be too smart. Or had Hannah seen the light, repented, and changed her selfish ways?

Hannah passed dishes, laughed, talked, and appeared happy, even glowing. But she never spoke to Jerry. As far as her uncles could tell, Jerry wasn't present at all.

When the cakes and pies, the cornstarch pudding, and canned pears and peaches were served, Jerry held his stomach and groaned. "I'll have to let this settle first."

Sarah, always eager to serve, immediately began pouring coffee, telling everyone to sit back and relax, let their food settle because, my goodness, they had all day.

The conversation turned to the plentiful food on the table. "In these hard years," Jerry said, shaking his head in bewilderment.

"Oh, I know," Sarah said. "I hope we never forget to give thanks."

The grandfather nodded, shook his spoon in the general direction. "You have to think about it, though. Everything on this table so far has been raised or grown on this farm. Potatoes, vegetables, eggs, chicken, butter. We farmers have had to tighten our belts some, with money not being worth what it once was. But, the times are changing with President Roosevelt at the helm. He'll get us out of this."

Elam and Ben nodded. "Farms are cheap. Interest is low at the banks. Now's your time, Jerry," Ben said.

Jerry looked at Hannah and shook his head. "Oh, I don't know for sure yet what we have in mind."

Ben thought, *You mean, what your wife has in mind*. But he didn't say it aloud.

Elam narrowed his eyes and looked at Hannah with a knowing wink. "She'll be ready for North Dakota in about a month," he predicted.

"You think?" Jerry's eyes twinkled. "Ask her."

"What do you say, Hannah?"

To Elam's surprise, Hannah faced him soberly and said, "I don't believe I'll ever go back."

Feigning surprise, Elam acted as if he would fall out of his chair. Calmly, Hannah said, "Stop it, Elam. I'm not joking."

"What gives?"

Jerry spoke for Hannah, giving a detailed account of the grasshoppers' march across their homestead, the burning of the Klassermans' house, Janie, the blizzards, everything. His arm stole along the back of Hannah's chair.

Elam listened, openmouthed. Ben detected the shifting of Hannah's weight, the almost imperceptible movement to lay her hand on Jerry's leg, the dropping of his arm to her shoulders.

Sarah shuddered, breathed, "Why didn't you tell us?"

Eli piped up, "What are locusts? I thought only King Pharaoh had locusts." Everyone laughed, but without mirth.

"The grasshoppers were the most horrible," Hannah said quietly. "I never had the heart, the real courage to stay after that. You know what the prairie looks like during a two-year drought? Well, this was much worse. Imagine not a blade of dead grass, not a shrub or a weed. And the smell was unbelievable."

Sarah shuddered. Mary twisted her face in disgust. Jerry said he'd left the final decision up to Hannah.

Her eyes alight, leaning forward, Hannah spread her hands to state her case. "In the end, does it really make sense? Just before the end, I had come to the conclusion that if you really want to be homesteader you have to lower your standards of what we consider success. Out there, success is measured in many more ways than simply how much money you make.

"If you lose too many calves, well, next year will be better. If it doesn't rain, it's a victory just to be able to 'git by.' They're not bothered by small hindrances because they're so easygoing. The biggest thing those ranchers have is settin' at the feed mill, measuring one natural calamity after another, seeing who weathered the longest drought, the worst storm, or whatever. There's a fierce loyalty to the prairie, a determination to live like their fathers before them. They can't imagine anything different.

"But us? Well, we know another way of life. This is in our blood. Although, I know it won't always be easy. In fact, until I saw Mam on the porch, I wasn't sure if I could be happy here again."

"Oh Hannah! Really?" Sarah's smile grew as she did her best to keep the tears from spilling over.

"I missed you terribly, Mam," Hannah said.

Sarah flung both hands over her face and left the table, ashamed to let her family see how much Hannah's words affected her.

After all she and Hannah had been through, every harsh word and rebellious shrug, the storming out of the house leaving Sarah to wrestle with her own bravado, her own fear of mishandling her wayward daughter who, by all appearances had simply hated her. Leaving Hannah in North Dakota had been as painful as losing one of her own limbs.

Sarah was a servant, someone whose own happiness sprang from bringing happiness to others. Her children, her husband, the acquaintances around her, all benefited from her deep inner kindness. She had been so afraid for Hannah. For Jerry. She knew full well Hannah didn't love Jerry. She knew, too, the reason for Hannah marrying him. But here they were, alive and well, with the kind of intimacy between them that only a mother could discern.

Surely God had heard all her begging, her prayers on their behalf. How often had she fallen on her knees in the middle of the night to pray for them? Times when sleep slipped out of her grasp, the terrors of the plains crashing and screaming around in her head until she thought she'd surely go mad. Leaving Hannah in North Dakota had been a torment, a punishment, the blame-taking wreaking havoc with her faith.

She was grateful to Hannah for keeping the blizzard, Janie, the scourge of insects from her, and so allowing her to live in peace, not knowing of their suffering.

Composed now, Sarah dished out more dessert, smiled, and refilled coffee cups, glad to hear the conversation had drifted to other topics.

"So Jerry, what do you have in mind as far as where you'll live and what you'll do to support your wife?" Elam asked, spooning an alarming amount of vanilla cornstarch pudding over a huge square of black walnut cake.

Jerry's eyes widened. He jutted his chin in the direction of Elam's pudding and cake. "Are you planning on eating all that by yourself?" he asked.

"You just be nice and mind your own business," Elam countered, lifting a spoon piled high with the sweet concoction.

Hannah smiled as she cut a large slice of peach pie. The sense of belonging that pervaded the kitchen was like a haven for her battered spirit. Here was the companionship of family, a knot tied with so many intricacies, impossible to be fully separated. Loosened, perhaps, frayed edges whipped by storms and every mischief of the mortal mind, but tied, inexplicably bound and reaching into the future.

CHAPTER 15

Aʟʟ ᴛʜᴀᴛ ɴᴇxᴛ ᴅᴀʏ, Hᴀɴɴᴀʜ ʀᴇʟᴀᴛᴇᴅ story after story, her mother listening spellbound, intermittently shaking her head, making soft, clucking noises of disbelief. Occasionally, Sarah would try to interject a thought, but words poured from her daughter like an overturned tumbler of water that ran dripping down over the tablecloth and onto the floor.

Finally, Hannah stopped, took her teacup to the white, porcelain sink, and asked if they shouldn't be doing a job, making dinner or something.

"No, not yet. We'll have bean soup and cheese for lunch. But, did you say this little Janie's parents both died in that fire?"

"They say so, but no one really knows. I think they did. The grandparents seem like really nice people. And Janie will never remember her own parents. She's too young, so that's a comfort I still have."

"Right." Then, "Oh, Hannah. I can't imagine all you've been through. You say the worst was the grasshoppers?"

"Yes. Without a doubt. But the winters! After being lost in a blizzard . . ." Hannah's voice drifted off. "Being lost in a blizzard is beyond suffering. The cold is only a small part of it. It's the feeling of being cut off from all you know. Every single thing we take for granted every day is removed and there you are, at the mercy of the howling, driving wind, the snow and ice and brutal cold. I almost lost my toes. Probably would have if Jerry hadn't known what to do."

"So, you and Jerry are in love?" Sarah asked her, emboldened by the conversation that had flowed so easily between them for hours now.

When there was no answer, Sarah knew she had struck the wrong chord. She slid a glance sideways at her daughter, whose eyes were lowered, her teeth worrying her lower lip.

"I guess. I don't know. How do you know if you love someone?"

"Oh, well, you just do."

"I'm not always a nice person."

Sarah laughed. "Nicer than you used to be."

"I would say he loves me, but he hasn't always been nice, either."

Sarah knew this was dangerous territory, so she said nothing. With Hannah, always being nice was an impossibility. She could only imagine the patience it required to live with her.

"But you are . . . I mean . . . you know . . ." Sarah reddened, then blushed so furiously that tears sprang to her eyes.

"Yes," Hannah mumbled, then quickly got up and disappeared behind the bathroom door.

They never spoke about Sarah's marriage after that. It was the way Sarah's mother had taught her; in some matters, things were best left unsaid.

A few weeks later, Jerry and Hannah had found a house. Hannah wanted to live in the mountains, a good distance from other Amish folks, and everyone else, for that matter. She had their whole logging operation already planned out. But after listening to Ben and Elam, Jerry decided that farming and milking cows was probably the best thing to do, especially since he had a good down payment ready for a nice farm.

He listened patiently, considered Hannah's opinion about logging, but knew that cutting trees and dragging logs was not his future. He had no interest in wrecking forests. Not now, and he doubted if he ever would.

They were lying in bed in the blue painted guest room with the high plastered ceiling, deep windowsills, and the ever-present smell of mothballs and cedar that infiltrated the room like a giant's breath. It was their only time for communicating with each other away from the rest of the family, so they often lay there murmuring together about their plans for the future. But this thing about logging and living in the mountains was starting to annoy Jerry; it was like a whining mosquito hovering in his ear whenever Hannah had a chance to be alone with him.

Patiently, he explained his view. Horses would not always be competitive, in logging. Caterpillars, those big yellow machines on tracks, could go where it was difficult for horses and drag out ten times the number of logs. But, if they wanted to stay Amish, then she'd have to think about what was reasonable.

"But I don't want to live on a flat farm surrounded by flat Amish neighbors and all their flat children," she hissed.

Jerry shook with the force of his silent laughter. "We can buy a hilly, rocky farm then."

"No. I don't want to milk cows. I hate cows." Hannah rolled onto her side, punched the feather pillow, huffed a few times, bounced up and down to settle herself, and refused to talk any more about it that night.

Jerry lay on his back, hands propped behind his head, and sighed. He watched the rectangles of gray light that marked both windows, traced the pattern of black branches across the window panes, listened to the sounds of traffic stopping and starting on Route 30, and thought about farming when his wife detested the mere thought of milking cows.

What kind of life would that be? Well, he'd wait. She was still a bit sore about losing the homestead in the West, so perhaps after she had the opportunity to listen to what members of her family had to say, she'd change her mind.

"I hate this smell!" Hannah said out loud.

"Shh. Someone will hear you."

"No one's going to hear," Hannah said, louder.

To keep her from knowing he was laughing, Jerry rolled on his side, as close to the edge as possible. When she found resistance, and had to give up, her rebellion knew no limits. It simply boiled out of her like an overfilled pot of rolled oats, hissing and foaming.

"I don't like the smell of mothballs, either," he said, quietly. Then, "Good night, Hannah."

He was wavering between consciousness and sleep when Hannah said, "Horses aren't going to be competitive with tractors, either."

When he didn't answer, she muttered, "You know that, too." He let her think he was sound asleep. It was easier than thinking of a soothing reply.

The woman was headstrong, self-willed, more determined than anyone he'd known. His thoughts drifted into prayer, not a plea of desperation, but only that God would bless their union. And he was thankful. Thankful for Hannah, thankful for her willingness to return, thankful for Lancaster County.

It snowed, but the storms were gentle, in spite of folks talking about the cold and the large drifts piled by the roadside. The absence of harsh winds and driving blizzards were an immense relief to Hannah, though she didn't mention it. No use letting anyone know she was glad to be here.

On Sunday morning, they rode to church with Ben. They had no carriage of their own, no horse, nothing. Everything had been sold.

Hannah sat in the back seat of the buggy dressed warmly in a heavy winter coat, a woolen shawl, scarf, and bonnet—all black. She had dressed with care, painfully aware of the scrutiny she would be under. A purple dress and cape, the cape pinned neatly to her dress, two pleats down the back, pinned to a V in front, her black apron pinned around her waist. She hoped she'd pass the inspection of curious eyes. She had no idea if anything had changed since she had traveled out West with her parents.

In spite of the austere way of dressing—modest, homemade, the same pattern used for every individual—she had been old enough to know there were ways of pinning a cape and choosing the sleeve length and the length of skirt and apron that set one apart from another.

The girls who were more concerned about fashion than obedience wore shorter dresses, combed and arranged their hair in attractive waves, and set their coverings back on their heads just far enough to set them apart, appearing stylish to their peers.

Vilt. See harriched net. How often had she heard her father say with frustration that she was wild, that she'd never listen? Her mother would nod solemnly, her mouth puckered into a self-righteous petunia. Her parents had always been strict, obeying the *ordnung* to the letter. Hannah had always had a distaste for her mother's severe wetting, *schträling*, the way she combed her hair and put it back. Her long, black tresses were always rolled like two worms and then pinned into a bun at the back of her head, each hairpin a single agony of its own.

Her covering had always been larger than most of her friends', the strings wide and tied below her chin in a *gehorsam* bow. Some of the older *rumschpring* girls had narrow covering strings tied loosely and laying on their chests.

The whole idea of fashion was frowned upon, but it was there nevertheless. Hannah figured as long as people were people doing the things they did, some of them more concerned about looking attractive than others, that was simply the way of it.

Well, she had no intention of walking into church services with an appearance that suited a pathetic Western hick. She knew her dress was not one of the most conservative, which suited her just fine.

To shake hands with a kitchen full of women she barely remembered, to have all those eyes following her, was the worst form of punishment she could think of. She held her head high and refused to give the ministers' wives the holy kiss that was expected. She wasn't about to touch anyone's lips, she didn't care if it was a requirement or not. That, of course, did not go unnoticed. Eyebrows were lifted or lowered, depending on the individual, but as a whole, Hannah had set herself apart, refusing to submit.

Tongues wagged. "*Vos iss lets mit sie? Hals schtark. Vie ihr Dat.* What's wrong with her? She's headstrong, just like her father."

Undeterred, Hannah took her place among the women, staring ahead, her large dark eyes hard. Bold.

"*Hott sie ken schema?* Has she no shame?"

She sat among the women, her back straight, showing no emotion. When babies cried and apologetic mothers pushed past her, she held her knees slightly aside to let them pass without lifting her head to meet curious eyes or smile.

After the three-hour service, she stood apart and refused to help prepare the long, low tables for lunch, telling herself it was unnecessary. That was the single girls' job, not hers. If they wanted to stay true to tradition, well, they could.

Jerry was obviously in his element. Hands tucked in his pockets, he greeted old friends, uncles, cousins, a genuine love shining from his eyes. To be among those acquaintances of his past was a blessing, an undeserved joy the Lord had provided, and his heart swelled with gratitude.

His eyes searched the room for Hannah but found no trace of his wife, which left him uneasy. When he took his place at the table, spread a slice of homemade bread with the soft *schmear kase* (cup cheese) he loved so much, his eyes were still searching the room for a glimpse of her.

They were invited to Uncle Ezra Stoltzfus's for supper. Jerry accepted gladly. He knew Ezra was one of the more successful dairymen even in times such as these, with depressed milk prices and cows that brought next to nothing at auction or at private sale. He wanted advice from a person of Ezra's experience.

He found Hannah standing alone against the rinse tubs in the washhouse, her arms crossed tightly, her expression keeping everyone at bay. He saw her dark, belligerent gaze, raised his eyebrows in question, and asked if she was ready to go.

She nodded quickly.

"Uncle Ezra invited us for supper," he said, just before she went to gather her things.

Without turning, her head moved from side to side. "No."

"Hannah. Please? I would love to visit with him."

"Then go visit with him. I won't go. I don't know them."

A smiling mother came into the washhouse surrounded by a group of small children and holding a crying baby. Jerry had no wish to press his argument with the woman present, so he turned, let himself out the door, and went to the barn to find his horse.

Hannah dressed herself in the thick black coat and woolen shawl, pulled her black scarf and bonnet severely over her head, thrust her hands into knitted mittens, and stood at the end of the sidewalk by the wire gate, waiting for Jerry.

She waited for a long time, her eyes scanning the parked buggies, the men hurrying to lead their horses to their own carriages, their thick *ivva reck* flapping in the cold, winter wind.

A voice beside her asked, "*Iss eya net an bei kumma?* Is he not appearing?" Hannah turned her face to meet the kind, watery eyes of an aging grandmother, stooped and bent, one gloved hand clasping the smooth handle of a cane. Behind her, an elderly husband smiled as he kept watch, protecting his wife from hidden spots of snow and ice.

Hannah smiled, a small quick spreading of her lips, to be courteous. "Doesn't look that way," she answered. She stepped aside to let them pass, her rubber boots sinking into the piled snow along the sidewalk. She watched as a middle-aged man brought a large, plodding horse hitched to a creaking, ancient carriage. The horse stood, its neck outstretched, waiting until the elderly man helped his wife into the buggy, tugging a bit, pushing at the right moment, years of practice making a smooth transition from the ground to the cast-iron step, and from there to the safety of the upholstered seat.

From the depth of her wide-brimmed bonnet, the old woman's eyes twinkled at Hannah. "You can't imagine this now, my dear, but this is how it goes when you're old." She chuckled, lifted the heavy lap robe and spread it across her legs. Her husband heaved himself into the buggy beside her, grunting with the effort, then took a long time to tuck the lap robe around his wife, while the middle-aged man stood patiently at the horse's head.

He looked a lot like Yoni Beiler, but Hannah wasn't sure, and had no intention of asking, either. She had no idea if the aging couple had lived in this church district so many years ago. That time seemed like another life, a dim, blurry memory viewed as if under water.

Hannah watched as the middle-aged man handed the reins to the driver and stepped back saying, "*Machets goot, Dat.* Stay well, Dad." The elderly man lifted the reins and clucked to his horse who leaned tiredly into his collar and moved off.

Hannah was seriously perturbed by now. She stamped her feet to warm her toes, clutched her shawl tightly around her chilled body, and glared at the barn. Someone should paint that thing. It looked scaly, like the loose skin on a diseased dog with mange. Maybe Reuben Detweiler couldn't afford to paint it. Hannah guessed that nobody painted their barn during the Depression. Well, times were getting better; she'd heard it on the train.

She sniffed with impatience. If Jerry didn't show up soon, she was going back into the washhouse. He could come looking for her.

She became aware that there was a ruckus from somewhere inside the barn. A horse must be acting up. Suddenly, men ran from the implement shed to the barn. She heard loud voices.

Never once did she imagine that Jerry would be in that barn, so she was not alarmed, only cold and impatient. But when her uncle Ben appeared, his face like a pale, waxen mask, his lips colorless, she knew something bad had happened.

His stricken eyes found her questioning eyes. "Hannah!" His voice sent shock waves through her body like sizzling, painful lightening.

"Han . . . Hannah. You have to be strong. Jer . . . Jer . . . Jerry was kicked in the . . . the chest by a horse."

Hannah reacted with disbelief, then a powerful urge rose in her to hit Ben, to pound him with her fists, hurt him and make him stop his childish stuttering. She felt the color draining from her face, her breathing becoming shallow, as if there was not enough oxygen in Lancaster County to keep her heart beating.

"Is he dead?" Incredulous now. He couldn't be dead. She had refused to visit his uncle. She'd told him no.

Wild-eyed boys raced past her to spread the news to the women. Hannah suppressed the urge to grab them and stop them from spreading gossip, untrue things.

"Take me to him," she ground out, between teeth that began chattering of their own accord.

She entered the barn, the poorly lit interior a harbinger of darkness and pain. Men stepped aside. Someone reached out to her. She slapped the hand away. She smelled hay, manure, leather, the rancid, sweetish odor of cows. Pigs snuffled. "*Bisht die Hannah?* Are you Hannah?" Kind words from constricted throats. Men kneeling over the prostrate form of her husband. His eyes were open, deep and dark. His face was ashen, so pale she thought he was already gone.

His breath was a painful gasping for air. A gurgling. Another gasp. Hannah fell to her knees, tore at the buttons of his white shirt. Someone had opened his coat, loosened the hooks and eyes of his vest, peeled away the *ivva reck*.

Hannah called his name in a strangled voice. "Jerry. Jerry." Her eyes were dry, her throat rasping.

He struggled to breathe. She opened his shirt with trembling fingers and lifted his undershirt. In the poor lighting, she could see the shape of a hoof in deep blood color, the skin around it already black, blue, purple. There wasn't much blood. No more than from an insignificant nick with a scissors. She told herself he'd be all right. She replaced his tee shirt and straightened.

"Did someone use the telephone?"

"Yes."

Her mother was there, then. Her grandfather. Ben and Elam. Jerry's brother David and his wife.

Sarah reached for her daughter but Hannah pushed her away. "Move! Everyone get away from him so he can breathe," she ordered.

From the back of the crowd, a head taller than any of the others, Dave King watched Hannah, saw her refusal to weep or accept her mother's comfort.

He knew whose horse had lashed out. He'd warned Jerry that morning not to tie his horse with Samuel Esh's stallion.

The ambulance from the Gordonville Fire Company arrived. Hannah stood aside, her large, dark eyes burning with bitter, unshed tears, her hands clutching the fringes of her black shawl.

Jerry's strangled scream of pain when they lifted him onto the stretcher was almost more than Hannah could bear, but she knew there was nothing they could do to prevent it.

She rode in the back of the wailing, careening vehicle. She took in every contour of Jerry's face. She memorized the heavy black bangs, the longish sweep of hair sweeping over his pale forehead, his lashes perfect.

She turned away when his struggle to breathe became too hard. She reached out a hand as if to help him, begged the attendant to do something, anything.

Wasn't there anything the medical professionals could do? White beds in rooms painted a sickly green color. Nurses hovering, doctors coming and going. Silence. Whispered conversations. So many questions. And, what was that giant, busy-haired Amish man doing in here? He was no relative.

Hannah crossed her arms and glared at him. He glared back, his colorless eyes cold and calculating, sizing her up. He stepped forward.

"I know you don't want me here but I saw it happen, so I'll need to answer some questions."

"Go to the police station then," Hannah said, coldly.

"I was there. The doctors need me."

Hannah turned away.

Jerry lingered for less than three days. In that time, Hannah never left his bedside, only sleeping fitfully a few minutes at a time. She refused to eat or drink until a nurse told her that if she wanted to stay strong, she'd have to at least start consuming something.

Sarah came and went, as did many other relatives, half of whom Hannah did not know. Stony-faced, pale, her large dark eyes as hard as polished coal, Hannah spoke curtly, repelled sympathy, and efficiently constructed a brick wall about herself, impenetrable, even to her own mother.

Alone at night, she spoke to Jerry. She smoothed his hair, ran her hands along the contours of his face. She told him she loved him. His eyes opened and closed. He strained to breathe. Sometimes his breathing stopped, then resumed in powerful hiccups, hard and fast.

Hannah knew he was in terrible pain, unbearable discomfort, hanging between life and death. Suspended on waves of pain, his heart struggled valiantly. The doctors said there was nothing they could do.

Hannah glared at helpful, well-meaning nurses, listened to concerned doctors, waving both nurses and doctors away with flaps of her hand or curt nods and short words. She wanted them to just be quiet and go away. Shut up. What does all this talking help? He was kicked in his heart and he's not going to make it. If you can't help him, leave me alone.

And they did.

She was alone with Jerry when he inhaled one last shuddering breath, then exhaled in a slow, faint rhythm. The rising and falling of his chest ceased. Complete and total silence.

Hannah sat like a stone, cold and immovable. Slowly she reached out to place one hand, then the other, on his chest. She bowed her head as a great obstruction rose in her throat, followed by a rasping, wrenching sob.

She had told him over and over she was sorry. Now she would spend the rest of her life unsure, wondering if he had heard her words. So many times she had said no to him, refused to budge even on trivial matters. Why?

No one understood Hannah's refusal to shed tears, at least in front of anyone. They called her cold, calculating, abnormal. Older women shook their heads, said it wasn't good. She'd have to be "put away" if she wasn't careful.

The homestead swarmed with well-meaning friends and neighbors descending on the house and barn with cakes and pies, buckets and mops, the men bringing teams of horses hitched to manure spreaders, shovels, and pitchforks. They cleaned and scoured, emptied the downstairs bedroom and cleaned it to a shine. The body arrived from the undertaker in town.

This was the ultimate test for Hannah. To remain dry-eyed while they clothed Jerry in white funeral garb and laid him in the plain, handmade casket, took superhuman effort.

She willed herself not to give way to the sobs in her throat. Over and over she steeled herself under the watchful eyes of her mother. After his hair had been combed and adjusted to Hannah's satisfaction, she stepped back, turned, and walked out of the room, her hands at her sides, her shoulders squared, her eyes brimming but not spilling over.

What had she done? She could have been loving and kind and submissive. Blindly, she walked through the washhouse door, the ache in her throat like a fiery boulder that threatened to steal her breath.

She ran into a hulking figure clothed in wool, rock solid, slamming the toe of her shoe against the leather toe of his shoe. She would have lost her balance had it not been for two paws that stopped her fall. Hannah was tall, but he was taller. His arms were like cables.

She tried to glare, but her eyes were glazed with tears. Defiance made her tears run over, leaving her gaze a mixture of pain and frustration, hurt and remorse, a look that would haunt Dave King for months. He uttered a useless apology.

She swung through the door and out into the wintry yard wearing only her black widow's dress and apron.

CHAPTER 16

As the long funeral procession wound its way along the road to the cemetery in Gordonville, the sun slid behind an increasing bank of clouds, casting gray shadows along wooden fences and sides of buildings. Black branches of trees huddled together in the still, cold air, as if waiting for the snow that would soon cover them.

The sound of steel-rimmed wheels on gravel roads melded with the dull *clop clop* of horses' hooves, the jingle of buckles and snaps, the creaking of leather. White puffs of steam came and went from the horses' nostrils as they tugged at restraining reins, held back to a slow trot to stay in an orderly procession.

Hannah sat in the back seat of the first buggy following the horse-drawn hearse. Her grandfather drove the team. Her mother sat beside her with Abigail. Manny followed, with Eli and Mary.

Hannah said nothing, her ironed, white handkerchief folded in her pocket. Her face was pale, lined with deep fatigue. Repeatedly, her mother tried to draw her out, to express herself, consolation flowing through her words. Sarah had been here in Hannah's place. She had mourned the loss of her husband. She had grieved to the point of ruining her health. A tragedy, they called it. But that didn't begin to describe the pain.

Sarah wanted to make this easier for Hannah somehow, but she had no way of knowing her senseless prattle was much the same as a burr in one's shoe.

Finally, Hannah grated hoarsely, "That's enough, Mam. Your grieving was different from mine."

Bewildered, Sarah set her mouth in a straight line and watched the horse's flapping neck rein the rest of the way. How could grieving be different, she wondered? Grief was grief, wasn't it? But Hannah knew the difference. Her mother grieved for the loss of one she loved more than her own life. She had loved deeply, dependent on her husband to flavor her days with his love.

Hannah's grief was saturated with remorse. That awful unspooling of unkind words, her unwillingness to obey, her defiance and anger, deeds of the flesh that she could never take back. There had been times that were okay, but too many times when things were not all right. Everything, just everything was complicated. She should never have gotten married.

With these thoughts buzzing in her head like angry wasps, Hannah's breathing became fast and shallow. Her head was bowed as she stepped from the buggy, and remained that way. Not once did Hannah lift her face or speak to anyone. Tears ran down Sarah's cheeks as the minister spoke. The young men shoveled chunks of frozen soil on top of Jerry's coffin as the voice of the second preacher droned on. After the German *lied* (song) was read in a quiet monotone, heads bowed in unison for a last silent prayer.

The crowd turned and dispersed. The horses and carriages were loosened and brought to the gate.

Back at the house, the funeral dinner was being prepared by appointed workers. Men straddled benches to mash vats of steaming cooked potatoes with handheld mashers, their wives hovering over them with salt and butter.

Roasts of beef that had simmered in the *eisa kessle*, the iron kettle, were taken up on wooden cutting boards and sliced. In a corner of the kitchen, workers rubbed quartered heads of cabbage across graters to create immense bowls of pepper slaw. Fresh sliced bread and apple butter was ready to be distributed across the tables.

A respectful, quiet hum of conversation rose and fell. The women who seasoned the grated cabbage rolled their eyes in the general direction of workers, then bowed their heads and shielded their lips with the protection of a palm held sideways.

"They say no one has seen her cry yet," Esther Zook hissed.

"Who?"

"Oh, that Hannah. You know."

"Oh, you mean his wife. Oh, I know. She's so cold. They say she didn't love him. Not right."

A forkful of pepper slaw was shoved under the speaker's nose. "Here. Taste this. What do you think? Vinegar? Sugar?"

Mary Miller made an awful face, puckering her mouth like the drawstring on a cloth purse. "No more vinegar. There's enough vinegar in there to pickle a pig!"

"Nah, Mary. Don't be so odd."

"Here, Suvilla. You taste it." Suvilla took a hearty chomp, waving a hand across her mouth as tears rose to the surface. "Too much vinegar! Who put it in?"

"More cabbage. The only thing to do."

"Hurry up. You'd think they'd be back from the *begräbniss* by now."

"Not if Eph Lapp has it."

"*Ach, ya*. He's so long-winded. They say Henner King's wedding, you know, he married Eva, didn't leave out till almost one o'clock."

A very heavy woman sailed over. "Shh! Quiet. They're back. Use a little respect now. Hush!" Noses wrinkled in the disappearing woman's wake, but there was a general air of respectful silence.

Hannah forced herself to eat a small amount of mashed potatoes and gravy, but all she could think of was how much Jerry would have enjoyed them. He'd often made them himself when she'd refused to do it.

A deep sense of shame turned her mouthful of creamy mashed potatoes to rancid slop. She laid down her fork and took out her handkerchief to wipe her mouth. A perfectly ironed square of white linen. Never used once, all day. A sense of accomplishment made her feel better.

She received kind words and handshakes stoically, nodding, murmuring *"denke,"* over and over without shedding tears, devoid of outward feeling.

She was achingly weary. Her knees buckled, her shoulders drooped. She watched the men and women clearing off the tables and carrying out the benches. She noticed the giant man, Dave King, carry benches like they were toothpicks. He grew a beard, which meant he was married. A young woman touched his arm. He bent his head to listen, then nodded. He disappeared. That must be his wife.

Later, when she thought she would collapse on a heap like melted butter, she saw him carry a chair over the row of remaining benches. When he reached her side, he placed the chair on the floor and left without saying anything. Gratefully, she slid onto the chair and sat with her hands folded in her lap.

Strange, the way that simple act of kindness immediately brought stinging tears to her eyes.

Hannah did not sleep at all that night. Over and over, scenes that brought a sickening remorse flashed before her eyes. Jerry had not kissed her good-night. He would have, but he knew she wasn't happy. How gladly would she milk cows with him now.

Her night was raw with regret, bitter with unshed tears. The loss of the homestead, all she had ever known all those years, blurred with the loss of Janie and the palomino, King, and now, Jerry, her husband of a little over a year.

Was that really all the time they'd had together? If she looked back, her sadness was like a jumble of impenetrable rocks, sharp and dangerous, useless to try to navigate. Boulders of mistakes and anger, bitterness and pride. A harsh landscape without mercy.

God did not have mercy on her. He showed her no love.

An empty calendar without numbers. A blank future that likely held nothing at all. An existence where she breathed, ate, slept, and tried to avoid questions and invitations from rude, nosy people she didn't like.

Wasn't there a verse somewhere in the Bible about wings of an eagle and waiting? *Okay, Lord, I'm sorry. I was not a nice person. If You'll forgive me, I'll do better. I need Your mercy. Badly.*

With that short and startling prayer, Hannah got out of bed, dressed, went down to the kitchen, and made three soft-boiled eggs and two pieces of toast with butter. She ate every mouthful. Then she got down the box of cornflakes, poured some in a bowl, and sugared them liberally, dumping milk over them. She ate every last bit. She felt fortified, courageous, and ready to face the future now that she knew God had forgiven her.

She coughed, blew her nose, adjusted her apron, filled a bucket with water, and proceeded to wash the living room floor on her hands and knees. That was where her mother found her at 6:00 a.m., her usual time to appear in her kitchen to prepare breakfast.

"Hannah?" A surprised question.

"Couldn't sleep," Hannah said over her shoulder, her right arm with the scrub cloth making rhythmic motions, great arcs of scrubbing across an already clean floor.

Sarah sank down onto a chair. "*Ach,* I was afraid of it. I

heard you turning. But I must admit, I fell asleep in spite of your suffering. I was so exhausted."

"It's all right."

"Is it?"

"Yes. It is."

Sarah considered trying again to draw Hannah out of her shell of suffering, but thought better of it. She'd talk when she was ready, and not a moment before.

The stodgy lawyer with the vest stretched across his stomach like the skin of a sausage harrumphed and twirled his moustache with the tips of his fat fingers (which also looked like sausages).

"What we have here is a fine example of forward thinking. Mr. Jeremiah Riehl has bequeathed all his possessions and worldly goods to his dear and beloved wife, Hannah Riehl. Which had all been sold at auction, is that correct?" More hacking and throat clearing.

"Yes," Hannah said levelly, swallowing and wondering what the poor man's breakfast had been to create all that phlegm.

He pinched the tip of his moustache and twirled, rolling the coarse gray hair into a twist, then releasing it, whereupon it quickly twirled back to its former waxen spiral. "So, we have an amount of ten thousand, nine hundred and eighty-four dollars to be bequeathed to Hannah Riehl on the date of, let me see . . ." More moustache twirling and attempted phlegm removal.

"Pardon me, ma'am. Pardon me. It's the bacon. Bacon at . . . well, you don't normally make a habit of dining at the eating establishments in the city. You plain folk live frugal lives. I respect that. Deeply admire that." Hannah nodded and willed him to bring this endless meeting to a close.

On the streets of Lancaster, she walked slowly beneath flourishing maple trees and read copper plaques. "Smith, Rembrandt and Heron." Another read "Dougherty" and still another, "Leek and Leek." All lawyers in this part of town. Brick sidewalks and ornate buildings with deep, wide windows.

Hannah was fascinated as she strolled along, drinking in the sights. She was awed at what men could accomplish with wood, brick, stone, and mortar. There were heaps of sooty slush, snow the color of chimney smoke, automobiles in gleaming shades of red, blue, or silver navigating the streets like beautiful brides-maids sailing down an aisle in all their finery.

There were mud-splattered trucks, horse-drawn delivery car-riages with names of businesses embossed in gold calligraphy on their sides. There was milk delivery and freshly baked bread from Emmaus Bakers.

She came to a swinging sign suspended from a horizontal pole fastened to the top of a window frame. ZIMMERMAN'S she read. Just that. Zimmerman's. She knew many Mennonites named Zimmerman. Then she spied the words, FINE DINING.

Now, what if she went inside and paid to have a full-course meal brought to her table? Would that be so awful? She shook her head. Jerry had been buried less than eight weeks, spring was on its way, and there was work to be done. So why should she loiter here, spending her money on unnecessary luxuries? She walked on, but not without a mounting sense of loss.

Hannah walked behind the drugstore to the hitching post where Manny waited in the carriage. She smiled to herself to find him draped across the seat, his straw hat over his face to shield his eyes, sound asleep. The horse looked as if he'd been taking a good snooze as well, standing on three legs with his nose almost touching the ground.

Hannah reached the buggy and shook it with all her strength. Manny's head wobbled on his shoulders, his straw hat sliding off his face. His eyes popped open, clouded with sleep and confu-sion, before he caught sight of her. "Hannah! Stop it!" he yelled in a hoarse voice, his throat constricted with sleep.

"Lazy, Manny. That's what you are!"

"It took you an awfully long time."

"Lawyers." Hannah untied old Dobs, got in the buggy, pulled steadily on the reins to back up, then turned right and began their trip out of the city to return home.

"I got my money. Or rather, our money. Mine and Jerry's," she said. Manny gave her a sharp look.

"What do you mean, Jerry's?"

"A part of me will always belong to the memory of our time together."

Manny nodded, understanding.

"How is it going with Marybelle?"

"I asked her to marry me on Sunday evening."

Hannah turned to look at him, sharply. "She agreed? She said yes?"

"Of course. We love each other very much."

Hannah bit her lip. She had been married but she could not fully comprehend the meaning of his words. What was love? How exactly did you know when you loved someone? And how did you measure love? Who knew the moment they changed from liking someone to loving them enough to want to marry them? It was Hannah's shameful secret. Could she ever ask her brother? She desperately wanted to ask him but a deep sense of embarrassment kept her from it. All she said was, "I'm happy for you, Manny."

"I'm sorry to tell you, after all you've been through."

"No, no. It's all right. You deserve to be happy, Manny. You do."

"Thanks."

There was nothing more to say, Hannah thought. Not now. *Perhaps someday I can ask someone the questions that tag along behind me like unwanted baggage. Someday.* Though what did it matter now? She had had her chance at marriage and love and now that part of her life was over. Besides, she had loved Jerry, she really had. Even if it didn't look or feel like the way other people experienced love.

"What will you do with your money?" Manny asked, slapping his grandfather's horse lightly with the reins he had taken over from Hannah. The only sign old Dobs had felt the slap of the leather reins was a flicking of his large ears, a few quickened steps, before returning to his usual plodding.

"I don't know yet. I don't want to stay at Doddy's."

"Why not?"

"I don't know."

But she did know. Their last night together ending in an argument, Jerry's searching good-night that met with her frigid silence. She hated the blue guest room, could barely tolerate sleeping there, in spite of falling into bed exhausted after a day of washing, ironing, housecleaning, and baking bread.

"You could clean houses for English ladies."

"Uh-uh. No."

"Why not?"

"Because."

Manny shrugged his shoulders, knowing that was the only reason he'd ever receive. So, he turned his head to the right, whistled softly, switched to humming, and back again.

Suddenly, Hannah asked if he liked it here in Lancaster County, her words without kindness. There was an accusatory note in her voice.

Instantly on the defensive, Manny said, "Sometimes."

"Why do you live here then?"

"Well, it's the sensible thing to do. I loved the West, like you, but it's a tough way to raise a family. The hardships . . ." His voice drifted off.

"Yes, but that hardship kept life interesting. Here, we sit in the middle of all this verdant growth, the tropical jungle of vegetation and lots of people, where it always rains when it should and everyone leads normal, secure, measured, ordinary lives, making money and having kids like rabbits. You do and say what is expected of you. You're put in a slot, like a cow in her stanchion. There are never any surprises or anything to appease your sense of adventure."

"Jerry's accident was a surprise . . . and a shock, Hannah."

"Well, that, yes." Ashamed, Hannah fell silent.

Manny did this to her. Always had. He made her feel humble and childish when he spoke the truth.

She watched the countryside, the white farmhouses and white barns, the green already appearing in low places, the pussy willows shooting green growth.

A promising spring, another season to plant, another summer to hoe and harrow, pull weeds and nurture with compost and manure. Another fall to harvest and another winter to start the process all over again.

She wouldn't do it. She would not conform to everyone's expectations. A fierce rebellion welled up within her, like a wild, growing algae in a clear pond, destroying common sense as it grew.

She'd return. Ask Hank to allow her to continue. He'd let her. She ached for the prairie in spring. The colors of the purple and lavender columbine. The patches of white daisies with hidden nests of prairie hen eggs. The crested wheat grass like swaying hula dancers from her geography book. She yearned to hear the myriad songs of the little brown dickeybirds, a flock of them like a spray of buckshot exploding across the waving grass.

She could smell the wet undergrowth, that sharp, pungent odor of moist soil decaying old growth, and bursts of brilliant new shoots appearing like magic.

How could she ever live without it? How could she manage life in Lancaster County without Jerry to keep her there?

At the supper table Hannah was pale and subdued. She pushed a chicken leg around on her plate, nibbled the canned corn on her spoon, took too many agitated sips of water from her tumbler, repeatedly clearing her throat. Her grandfather watched her closely, his kind eyes welling with moisture. He saw Sarah casting bewildered glances in Hannah's direction.

"Hannah, how did things go today?" Doddy asked.

She nodded too soon and too fast. "*Gute.*"

"So, your money is deposited in the First National Bank?"

"Yes."

"That's good, Hannah. I trust you will pray about God's will for your future, now that you have entered widowhood. What is the common saying? 'Take a year. Don't do anything rash. Take your time to see what unfolds.' When a person is grieving, they don't always make the best decisions."

Her face like a ceramic bowl, smooth, with no expression, Hannah looked at her grandfather. He recoiled inwardly. Her eyes were cold and hard.

"Do you have any plans made?" he asked.

"I want to go back!"

Sarah gasped audibly, speaking out of turn, completely unnerved as Hannah's words settled around the table. "But, Hannah, you can't!" her mother gasped.

The grandfather raised a hand, palm outward, to bring calm and quiet. The clock on the kitchen wall behind the table kept up its fierce ticking until it reached six o'clock, adding to the elevated tension that had wound its way into the room. Sarah's face registered wide-eyed panic. Manny's mouth hung open in unabashed disbelief. Mary leveled a look of disgust at Hannah, as only young girls can. Eli went on humming, chasing noodles around his dinner plate with the tip of his fork, thinking of the salamanders that lived in the stone spring house down by the creek.

Doddy Stoltzfus weighed each word before he spoke. When he finally aired his response, there was a bewildered hope in Hannah's eyes. "Hannah, you say you want to go back. I presume you are referring to returning to North Dakota. What makes you want to return?"

"The prairie in spring. The freedom of wide open spaces. Away from . . ." Hannah spread her hands, waving them in arcs in the air. "This. This claustrophobic county crawling with people."

To Hannah's great surprise, a smile spread across her grandfather's face, followed by a wide grin, then a loud guffaw of mirth. Sarah slanted an annoyed look at her aging father. For the first time in her life she thought he was becoming senile, unfit to hand out advice to her wayward daughter.

"Well, then, I imagine if you can't live in a county crawling with people, as you put it, we'll have to let you go. If this is what you truly want, then we'll put you back on the train with our blessing. *Herr saya.*"

Incredulous, Sarah sputtered words of rebuke. "*Dat, doo kannsht net.* You can't. We can't, any of us, go through this horrid ordeal one more time." A hard edge of hysteria crept into her voice. "Hannah, the prairie in springtime is a mirage. You know reality follows. Drought, fire, shriveled garden produce, the endless insanity-inducing winds." Sarah's eyes were wide with remembered agonies. She clutched one arm with the fingers of her opposite hand. She visibly trembled.

Hannah lifted her chin. "I love those winds."

Sarah rose halfway from her chair. She pointed a shaking finger in Hannah's direction. "If you go back out to North Dakota, you will do so completely against my will. I say, 'No,' and I mean no!"

Manny nodded in agreement with his mother. He placed a hand on Hannah's arm. "You are grieving, Hannah. You are missing Jerry more each day. That's what you're trying to escape. Your sorrow."

Hannah's eyes blazed with a black rebellion. She got up from her chair in one swift movement, the chair toppling over and hitting the floor with a crash. "Don't tell me what I can do and what I can't! None of you have the slightest idea what's wrong with me!"

She hurled her harsh words of accusation, her face crumpling like a child's, as grating sobs rose in her throat. Her eyes squeezed shut as the deep spring of her grief opened, the cache of denial she had allowed to fester and grow.

Hannah fled out of the room, away from her family. She threw herself on the bed in the blue guest room, her face crumpled, her eyes squeezed shut, as she cried heaving sobs and groans, emitting the deepest form of grief. She had no thoughts, only a sadness so profound it felt as if she was hurtling into a bottomless pit, a void completely empty of light.

Finally, she stilled. Thoughts entered her head, marching through in quick succession, like soldiers. She filtered truth from thoughts she knew were only an imitation of the real thing. Did she truly want to return to the homestead alone? In spring, yes. But not for any other reason. Not for blizzards or drought or, oh mercy, grasshoppers!

Without Jerry? No. Even with Jerry, if he were alive, probably not. It was living here in Lancaster County, always feeling like the odd person out and now the object of sympathy. The poor widow. The poor thing.

What no one knew was the fact that she had a substantial amount of money. And that she planned to use it to establish herself as a good, solid Amish frau with a business. She wasn't sure what kind of business, yet, but she'd figure it out.

Yes, Manny, I do miss Jerry. I miss him so much that I did want to escape. I thought I could flee, get away from my sorrow, my regret for all the times he was so loving and I was so mean. The flowers he brought. The limp bouquet of columbines. She shrank within herself remembering her snort and her words— "They're wilted." His hurt expression as he arranged them in a mason jar.

Jerry never pouted, never showed his hurt feelings. The man didn't have a selfish bone in his body. Jerry had been the best. Her tears began to flow again, a torrent of regret.

"Jerry, whatever it's worth to you now, wherever you are, I'm sorry. I loved you as much as one mean, selfish, hardhearted person could."

CHAPTER 17

THAT SPRING, THE FRESH DEW LAY ON THE LANCASTER COUNTY countryside, the air was still chill and bracing, and the first peas and onions were shooting from the depth of the rich, brown soil. Hannah was up and dressed, watching the road for the black station wagon.

She could have hitched up her grandfather's horse to the buggy, but she figured with all the miles she had to cover, it was worth hiring a driver. She told no one of her day's plans, giving her mother some offhand answer about going shopping.

She actually was going shopping, but not for groceries or fabric or anything of that sort. She had dreamt of Rocher's Hardware, a dream so vivid she could smell the fabric, the spools of thread, the dusty trays of buttons, and the paper sacks she handed to the women who came to buy necessities. She awoke that morning with her head full of plans, staring at the ceiling, her heart pounding with excitement.

She would be the first plain woman to have a dry goods store. She had plenty of experience with Harold and Doris Rocher in the town of Pine, North Dakota. Paid in flour, cornmeal, salt, and coffee, it was the single thing that had kept their family from starvation. That, and the prairie hens they cooked, salted, and gravied.

First, she needed her own place, which was what she was doing today. House shopping. The palms of her hands were wet with perspiration, her face felt flushed, and she chewed her thumbnails to the quick.

The driver's name was Jim Raudabaugh. He was a retired gentleman, short and portly, stuffed behind the black steering wheel like a sack of horse feed. His white hair stuck out from under his small gray fedora like porcupine quills, but his face was shaved and smooth, his eyes quick and bright. He viewed the world through rose-tinted spectacles, literally, perched on the end of his nose.

The minute she was seated in the car, he introduced himself, reaching across his ample stomach to shake her hand with his own.

"I'm Hannah. Hannah Riehl."

"Yes. Yes. The young widow. Please accept my deepest sympathy, Hannah. A tragedy. Tragedy. A man dying in his youth. Are there children?"

Hannah shook her head.

"That is good." He looked at her with so much watery-eyed sympathy that Hannah felt a burning in her nostrils, the beginning of tears in her eyes. *Bless this kindly man*, she thought.

"Now, where are we off to?" he asked, all business.

"Actually, I don't really know. I'm house hunting. I want to find a small place of my own."

He didn't need any more information. Hannah knew only too well that Amish drivers were the best source of carried news, and often gossip. Which, she supposed, was the Amish folks' fault, the way they rode along with their drivers, offering all sorts of interesting tidbits.

"Well, then, there's a place east of New Holland, on Route 23. But that would be a bit out of the way. Well, tell you what we'll do. We'll drive to Route 340 and follow it a ways. How's that?"

Hannah nodded.

The fields and forests were bursting with color, like a quilt pieced in a myriad of greens, with brown strips of plowed earth, white seagulls flapping behind plodding horses, the lavender and purple of the lilacs, the red and yellow of tulips bordering houses like fancy collars and cuffs.

Clematis climbed wooden arbors, waiting to burst into color. Hedges of forsythia sent forth brilliant green leaves after their yellow blossoms had dropped to the ground. Yes, there was beauty here—a cramped, cultivated sort of beauty, like the women in clothing catalogs with their faces painted and patted with powders and oils.

But the blue sky was above them, the clouds like puffs of cotton balls, pure and white and unfettered. The sun was as bright yellow here as it was in North Dakota, so that was something, wasn't it?

From that same sky and those clouds the rain would fall in spring and summer. In the autumn of the year the creeks would be running full. And winter would bring nitrogen in the form of snow, piling up on the fields with fresh cow and horse manure spread underneath. Here was a land that would blossom like a field of wildflowers. The climate, the soil, the work ethic of the many plain peoples who adhered to their farming practices, bringing trade and a constant influx of enterprising, hardworking folks who would live in prosperity their whole life long, and their children after them.

Hannah planned to be one of the prosperous entrepreneurs.

"So, you're searching for a small home on an acre of ground? Or maybe more than one acre?" the driver inquired politely as he broke in on Hannah's wandering thoughts.

"Well, what I have in mind is a small house, but I do need an addition, or a small garage for what I have in mind," she replied.

Jim was intensely curious, but something kept him from asking more questions.

The house along Route 23, just east of New Holland, was a small house built of cement blocks with a deep porch, immense posts holding up the wide roof, and a garage that was set at the end of the gravel driveway.

Hannah had a bad feeling about the house. Cement blocks were not warm or inviting, no matter if someone had slapped a coat of thick, white paint on the exterior. So, she shook her head no, and Jim backed obediently out of the driveway, turned right, and continued on his way.

The next house with a For Sale sign was along Hollander Road. The roof had a fairly steep pitch, with two of the cutest dormer windows she had ever seen sprouting from the shingles. It reminded her of a gingerbread house or a cabin in the woods—homey, cozy. It brought to mind evenings sitting in a comfortable chair with a gas lamp hissing softly above her, a coal fire in a small black stove, a braided rug, and a bowl of popcorn.

The wind could howl around that sturdy house and it would never budge. It was built of brick. The porch was deep and wide, with three windows facing the road. The front door was oak—wooden, solid, and homey.

Hannah's mouth went dry as her heart sped up. This was her house. There were boxwoods planted along the front, sheltering the porch like a green privacy fence. The yard was in need of a good cutting.

"Can we go inside?" she breathed.

Jim suspected this was a house that suited her as he observed her wide eyes. "Well, we'll have to see."

He grunted as he heaved himself from behind the steering wheel and again as he pulled himself to his feet. Hannah stayed in the car, thinking he might be acquainted with the occupants.

She held her breath as he went to the side door that was set lower against the house than the front porch. *Please, please, let someone be at home.* She was not aware that she was chewing down on her thumbnail until she tasted blood. Quickly, she lowered it and wrapped her apron around it.

Yes! The door was opened by an elderly lady in a flowered house dress. They spoke too long, then Jim turned toward the vehicle and motioned to Hannah with his hand.

Hannah fumbled for the door latch and stumbled out of the car, walking too fast, too eager, she knew, but there was no stopping. She extended a hand. "Hello. I'm Hannah Riehl."

The elderly woman peered up at her through round, gold-rimmed spectacles, her small blue eyes set in deep folds. Her nose looked like a tulip bulb, a veritable tributary of purple veins crossing it. Her mouth was small and puckered with the biggest mole Hannah had ever seen sprouting a growth of stiff hairs, like a tiny toothbrush.

"Good morning, my dear. A beautiful one it is, wouldn't you say?" she warbled, in a high, quivery voice.

"Yes. Yes it is."

"So, the man tells me you've come to see my house?"

Hannah nodded, her smile reaching too wide, her eyes going to the adorable little V-shaped roof above their heads. Just enough of a roof to keep the rain off someone who came calling.

"Well, then, I suppose I'll have to invite you in, right?" she chortled, stepping aside to allow them both to enter.

Hannah felt a stir of irritation as Jim, the driver, entered too. He really had no business accompanying them through these rooms, following her around like a nosy pig. Too curious. Did she have a choice, though, without displaying bad manners?

It was two steps up to the kitchen on the left. There were hooks to hang outerwear on the stoop just inside the door. The kitchen had white cupboards, a darling window above the sink with no panes on the lower ones, only two vertical panes on the top. It was bordered by a limp, flowered curtain, yellowed with age and faded by the sun.

The linoleum was black-and-white squares, waxed to a high gloss. The woodwork was sturdy, with routed lines and squares at the top corners with fancy circular grooves, all painted white. Good plaster walls and hardwood floors that were varnished like a mirror.

Hannah gasped audibly when she saw the open stairway with its elaborate bannister, the spindles carved into a complicated pattern that presented a line of perfect symmetry as they marched up the stairs. It was like a dollhouse, except large enough for real people!

A brick fireplace in the living room had a real fire crackling. There were two small bedrooms up under the eaves, with slanted ceilings and more hardwood floors. A bathroom at the top of the stairs had a white claw-foot bathtub, a small sink, a metal medicine cabinet with a mirror, a commode, gleaming stainless-steel toothbrush holder, towel racks—everything she could possibly need or want. A clever little linen closet was built into the hallway.

The thought that she might not be able to afford this house flitted through her mind suddenly, bringing with it a sharp blow of reality.

There was a bedroom downstairs and another small bathroom with only a sink and a commode, the fixtures in green. By this time, Hannah harbored a sinking feeling that she would never be able to purchase this sweet, homey dwelling. For one thing, she didn't deserve it. God knew she was not a nice person, so He only handed her one blow after another. Or let the devil do it. She was never quite sure.

She turned to go down the stairs to the basement, and almost pushed the driver, Jim, down ahead of her as she bumped squarely into him. The old irritation welled up. She couldn't stop herself from wishing he'd either move out of her way or fall down the steps. He'd bounce like a rubber ball, the fat thing.

The basement had gray cement block walls and a smooth concrete floor. Imagine, Hannah thought, being able to clean the basement with buckets of soapy water and a mop. Every farm-house she had ever lived in had a dirt basement floor, packed down and slimy with moisture. She hated having to go to the cellar for a jar of applesauce or peaches, imagining snakes and lizards and all sorts of wet creatures with beady eyes.

By the time Hannah reached the kitchen, she was filled with deep despair, wearing her self-doubt like a black mantle, all her anticipation squelched.

"I don't want to move, but the daughters won't allow me to live by myself. So they're packing me up to live with my Shir-ley. Not that she isn't a nice person, but I'll certainly miss my house." Her blue eyes became liquid with emotion. Dabbing at them with a wrinkled handkerchief she fished out of her apron pocked, she sniffed bravely, then stuffed it back.

"I don't need the money, but the girls do, so they told me not to take less than seven thousand. I'm not supposed to be show-ing this house to you, or telling you the price, but I'm still on my own two feet, breathing through my nose!"

She chortled and tapped her nose. "Or my mouth, when my sinuses act up. Unpredictable as the weather they are."

Jim giggled with appreciation, then cut it short when Hannah gave him a hard look that said, clear as day, *She's not talking to you.*

Seven thousand dollars. Her mind whirred like Harold Rocher's cash register. Could she build an addition for another thousand? Pay for fabric and sewing notions? There would be lawyer's fees for the sale of the house, hidden costs like taxes and so many other things, like shelves for her merchandise, and a counter. Well, first things first. She'd have to find a good car-penter. She could do without much furniture and she could bor-row the basic household supplies from her mother.

Hannah clenched and unclenched her hands, wishing for Jerry and his sound advice, his knowledge of business transactions. She hadn't known she depended on him, had always made him believe she was perfectly capable on her own.

Should she make a lesser offer? Return home and ask her grandfather? No. She wanted this house. The old lady's daughters wouldn't take less and she had more than ten thousand dollars. She was going to go ahead and take it.

"I'll take it," she said firmly, hiding her doubts.

"You will? For seven thousand?"

"Yes."

"But, you likely need to go to the bank. You'll need to be approved. Where's your husband?" Distrustful now, calculating.

"My husband was buried a few months ago. I'm a widow, and no, I don't need to make arrangements with the bank. I have the money."

"Oh, I'm sorry," the old lady said, her voice quivering. "I didn't mean to be rude. So you lost your husband so young? Oh, God have mercy. It's a horrible thing to have happened. And you so young. So young." She went to Hannah and clasped both of Hannah's hands in hers. Holding them, she looked up at Hannah with absolute sympathy.

"Call me Thelma. Thelma Johns. My husband was Richard, may he rest in peace."

Under normal circumstances, Hannah would have pulled her hands away from the old woman, but her mind was elsewhere, already considering when she'd move in, how she'd arrange her sparse belongings, what she'd absolutely need to purchase to get the store up and running.

Her grandfather, her mother, Manny, everyone had to see the house. They hitched up old Fred to the spring wagon and drove over to see it the following Thursday.

It was a perfect spring day. The sun shone like liquid gold, bathing everything in its glistening light. The trees burst with fluorescent green, new leaves unfolding with their newborn colors. Daffodils hung their spent, withered heads like deceased little men. Tulips drooped in faded colors, having spent their finery. But the roses were coming into bloom with the purple irises like bearded kings, showing off their intricate splendor.

New petunia plantings showed bits of pink. Geraniums transplanted from tin coffee cans pushed red blossoms. Yellow and orange dots of marigold heads surrounded symmetrical borders.

Hannah thought all of this was rather artificial beauty, but she supposed if she bought a house, she'd best get used to it and forget about wide open spaces dotted with lacy wildflowers, all dancing in one direction as if in concert, the untamable wind the conductor of the amazing concert.

As they turned onto Hollander Road, Hannah's stomach flipped a bit. She was nervous now, afraid of what her grandfather might say.

Surrounded by woods, down a low rise and around a bend, and there it was, even more charming than she had remembered.

The perfect little house.

An indescribable feeling of joy welled up in Hannah, leaving her breathless, her eyes shining with anticipation.

"Doddy," she called from the second seat. "Turn here. This is it."

He slowed Fred, turned expertly, and brought the horse to a stop. "*Vell*," he said.

"Why Hannah, it's a very nice house, like you said," her mother said, always kind, always supportive.

Manny smiled and nodded his approval. "I think it's worth what you paid for it."

"Thank you. Oh, I'm so glad you approve."

"Can we see the inside?" her mother asked.

"I'm sure we can, if Mrs. Johns is at home."

And so the tour began, led by Thelma, of course, who commenced a lengthy discussion of the house's origin, the happy times spent there with Richard and the girls, until Hannah thought she would fly to pieces with impatience.

"So, how do you plan on providing for yourself?" her grandfather asked once they were back in the spring wagon, Fred clopping clumsily down the road.

"I will be looking for someone to build an addition to the house where I plan to have a dry goods store," Hannah explained.

Her grandfather stared straight ahead without comment. Her mother turned in her seat, her elbow dangling over the back. "But, Hannah . . ."

"What?" Instantly defensive, Hannah brought her eyebrows down, a pinched look to her mouth.

"I don't know. Amish people don't have their own stores. Especially not, uh . . . women."

"So? I can be the first."

Doddy Stoltzfus wagged his head, his wide-brimmed straw hat lifting enough so he had to reach for the brim and tug it into place. "I wouldn't try it, Hannah. I'm sorry, but I doubt if old Ezra would approve of something like that."

"What does he have to do with it?"

Shocked, Sarah turned and said, "He's our bishop!" As if that finished it. She knew she was expected to submit. Total *gehorsamkeit*, unquestioning obedience.

It riled Hannah, this unswaying vigilance, this immediate stop to her plans. She wasn't giving up that easily. She had given up too much already. The homestead, Jerry, oh, just on and on. It wasn't fair. She had her heart set on her little venture. So what if she was the first one?

"You don't know what he'll say," Hannah said, thrusting her petulance like a wedge.

"I think I do," her grandfather said, shaking his head up and down, dislodging his straw hat again.

"I won't know for sure if I don't ask."

Sarah turned back to Hannah again. She spoke quietly. "Hannah, I wouldn't ask. You know what our *ordnung* is."

A slow burn began somewhere deep in Hannah's chest. This was precisely why she dreaded living back in Lancaster County. Everyone knew your business and handed out advice so freely and easily, taking for granted that you would bow down and live according to another man's wisdom.

She had no intention of giving up her dry goods store. Amish women sewed constantly. Through the worst of the Depression, clothes had worn thin, held together by patch upon patch as families made do with what they had. Or they used feed sacks, the cotton fabric dyed, washed, and sewn into clothing.

Now, with the money market lifting bit by bit and Teddy Roosevelt giving his famous speeches about not being fearful, folks would start buying more.

It was an opportunity. She would be supplying essentials to the community. The Amish women would not need to go to the city of Lancaster to purchase basic necessities. It was discouraged to be among the worldly, so what was worldlier than walking the streets of the city, past the bars, houses of ill repute, cars honking their horns, and men of the world calling out their insults?

No! She was not backing down. She wanted her own business. So she said nothing. And, riding in the back seat beside Manny, letting everyone believe she'd swallowed their refusal to allow her to continue with her plans, she went right on making her plans, choosing to ignore their words.

She didn't ask anyone for help in contacting an experienced carpenter to build the addition to her house, either. She merely talked to the neighbors down the road and asked to use their telephone. She called Jim Raudabaugh, the driver, and asked him a direct question. Who was the most trustworthy man to build the addition, she wanted to know? After many strange sounds coming from his mouth, hisses and clicks like a cornered snapping turtle, he finally came up with a name. Dave King. "He lives over along 340 below Leola," he told her.

Hannah had no idea who he was talking about, much less where he lived. When Jim offered to drive her to his house, she was short with him, saying it would be much cheaper to drive her grandfather's horse. Besides, she had to go speak with old Ezra King first.

So she said goodbye to Jim without thanking him or hiring him to take her in his car, leaving him to hang up the phone receiver and comforting himself with a sausage and ketchup sandwich. He admitted grudgingly that Hannah Riehl was not a very nice person, widowed or not.

Manny told her where the bishop lived, so one evening after supper, she told her mother she was going visiting, which she was. She knew Sarah would be gratified by the thought of Hannah becoming more social, which would keep her from asking questions.

Hannah goaded Fred to a fast trot, scaring him with a nip of the whip on his flapping old haunches. He was losing his winter coat, reddish brown hair flying through the air like snow. She spit them from her lips, snorted through her nose, wiped her eyes, and arrived at the bishop's farm covered in horse hair.

Nothing to do about it. She guessed if the bishop was old, he'd have seen many springs and more horses shedding their winter coats.

She tied Fred to the hitching rack by the wall of the white barn, brushed herself off as best she could, her black cape and apron patterned with stiff horse hair.

She turned to the house, evaluating its size and layout. Often the aging parents lived in an apartment built onto the original farmhouse with interior doors connecting the two, a perfect arrangement that allowed privacy but also handy access if one or the other family group was needed. She wondered if her life would have been much like this one had Jerry lived to be her husband to an old age.

Ah, Jerry. My husband. A shudder of grief. For the hundredth time she vowed never to marry again. Never. This time, she meant it. Firmly, staunchly. Written in stone. She simply did not need a man. She had loved Jerry. In her own selfish way, perhaps, but she had loved him as much as she knew how. And here she was, awash in missing him, as helpless as one of those hickory nut shells they used to set in the water at the creek's edge, watching the current take it, whirling it away, tumbling past rocks and eddies.

She hated having no control over her grief. It raised its head and looked her in the eye at the worst moments, without mercy. It pounded her with its fists, roughed her up and left her lying there, brutally accosted, beaten down and grasping the air for deliverance.

She blinked, straightened, shrugged off the melancholy cloud of sorrow, and decided to try the door at the end of the gleaming floor of the front porch. Since the younger folks were the farmers and the gable end of the house was turned toward the yard gate, she assumed the main part of the house was the first door. So, she'd go to the second door.

The evening sun slanted across the glossy gray paint of the porch floor, illuminating the freshly planted red geraniums, the tender green lawn in the background, the brown trunk of an oak tree. A bluebird was sitting on the clothes line, a portrait of peace and contentment.

CHAPTER 18

THE DOOR OPENED SOON AFTER HER SOFT TAPPING. A ROUND, BALD-
ing head appeared, encircled with wisps of snow-white hair, a
sparse white beard, and two small brown eyes as bright as a
sparrow's, almost hidden in folds of loose facial skin.

"*Kum yusht rei.* Come on in." The voice was surprisingly
light. His height was disconcerting. He was so tiny. Hannah felt
like an ox or a giraffe towering over this feathery wisp of a man,
who stepped gingerly aside to allow her entry.

"*Vy,* hello." This from the undersized, crooked little woman
who must be his wife. There were only a few wisps of white
hair visible from beneath the huge white covering. Her eyes
were bright with curiosity from behind small, gold-rimmed
spectacles.

Hannah tugged self-consciously at her own smaller, more
fashionable covering, and introduced herself.

"I thought so." Ezra King nodded his head in recognition.
"You are Jeremiah Riehl's widow."

"Yes, I am."

"*An shauty soch.* Such a shame."

"Yes."

"What brings you here?"

Hannah sat in the chair indicated by the petite, elderly wife, took a deep breath, and began, her hands clenched tightly in her lap. "I have purchased a house."

The white-haired old patriarch listened, his eyebrows elevated with kindness, a half smile playing around his mouth.

"I would like to build an addition to own and operate a fabric store."

There! It was out in the open, swimming in plain view in the lamp light. To ease the transition from hidden plan to open scrutiny, Hannah found herself babbling, explaining.

"My grandfather doesn't think I should do it. That's why I'm here. What is the difference? An Amish woman having her own business or having to walk the streets of Lancaster with all its *freuheita*? Would it not be better that the women stay among their own to purchase goods?"

The elderly bishop held two fingers to his lips, contemplating Hannah's argument. Nervously, Hannah twisted the hem of her apron. Finally, he spoke.

"Yes, I can see your point of view. But—and this is the thing—you would be introducing something new. The Amish have always been slow to change. We strive to keep things in a *demütich* way, humble. Would it represent a woman's meek and quiet spirit to be the owner of a store?"

"But . . ." Hannah began, devastated.

He held up a hand to quiet her. "I am not finished. I don't believe there is an Amish store run by a frau here in Lancaster County, and I would discourage such an undertaking. I would be glad to see you accept a no, based on the wife being a keeper at home, quiet, meek, subject to her husband.

"However, you have no husband, and you are expected to allow the church to pay for expenses in all *demut*."

"But, I don't want to do that," Hannah said, with all the force of her powerful nature. "Everyone would watch me, to see what I spend, where I go, what I wear. No, I won't do that."

The old bishop's eyes watched Hannah's face, but he gave no comment. Here was one who knew what she wanted, and didn't like anyone to stand in her way. He weighed with the scales of justice and fairness. If he firmly forbade it, he might not be making the best decision, owing to this woman's strong will. Determined as she appeared to be, to operate a store with that headstrong nature. . . . He wasn't sure.

"Why don't you let us sleep on this one?" he asked, still kindly.

"But I want to know."

"You will not be able to know this evening. I think it is a case that should be presented to the other ministers. We will take into account the fact that you are a widow intent on making her own way, and I will present your argument about Amish women on the streets of Lancaster.

"I hope you are aware, though, just how unusual your request is. Most women would be happy to bake pies or raise butchering hens, sell eggs, or work in a truck patch."

"I am not most women," Hannah replied.

Did she hear a soft, suppressed giggle from the bishop's tiny wife? Stooped over with her black cape falling over her shoulders, her angelic demeanor framed by the halo of her large white covering, she had squeaked out a bit of laughter.

The bishop smiled broadly, then laughed outright. He shook his head in disbelief. "No, you know, Anna . . ."

"Hannah."

"Oh, yes, you did say Hannah. I should say no to this thing. But I will present it to wise counsel, and we will come to a conclusion. Surely, you understand my concern. It simply is not always the best to allow a new thing, although I do appreciate your ambition. It could be a good thing if it stayed within reason and did not become a store filled with frivolous items the household could do without."

Hannah's words tumbled from her mouth in her haste to assure him of her utmost respect for his wishes.

They spoke, then, of the fine spring weather. He asked questions about North Dakota, and Hannah found herself portraying it in the truthful framework of her own suffering. She shared her intense desire to keep the homestead in the face of fierce adversity.

"Yes, yes," he said, his eyes bright with interest. "Your story is interesting. Often in this life we are so certain something is the will of God, and everything goes against us, until we see the truth of His will. For some, it is easily discerned. For others, sometimes never. When we suffer, it is because of God's love. He sees our wayward path and pulls us back, bit by bit. There is much happiness to be found in humbling ourselves under the mighty hand of God."

Hannah nodded.

"The grasshoppers were a mighty blessing, then," Hannah said, a trace of sarcasm adding a bite to her tone. The bishop laughed and Hannah snorted, a spark of understanding between them, igniting into a small flame of friendship.

Hannah rose to go, struggling to accept the outcome of her visit. She wanted to beg him to say yes, but knew it was beneath her dignity. So, she accepted his blessing and the warm handshake and let herself out the door.

She ground her teeth in disappointment, leaned forward to see the crossroad better in the waning light of evening, and went home and to bed. Unable to sleep, she lay on her back staring at the ceiling, the smell of mothballs as unendurable as always.

The thing was, you couldn't always be careful. Worrying constantly whether you were doing the will of God was exhausting. Did God really care that much about every little thing like having a store or getting a job, or butchering chickens to sell, or gathering eggs, or raising pigs?

He allows us to make our own choices, she thought firmly. Well, she was going to go ahead and see this Dave King about the addition. Perhaps he'd be busy and couldn't do it for a few months.

If Jerry was here, he would have soon had it completed. But Jerry wasn't here.

That deep sense of being separated from him, completely cut off, never again to touch him or hear him speak, pressed down on her heart until it became a physical ache, altering her normal pattern of breathing. She willed herself to remain calm, thankful for every good thing she did have. She had safety, a solid structure that housed her, more than enough food to eat, her mother, her siblings, weather that was like a glimpse of heaven. She'd survive all right. She had come through worse than most folks endured in a lifetime.

Mr. Jim Raudabaugh took her to the Dave King residence which, to Hannah's surprise, was not the usual white painted farm. A long driveway that turned into cornfields on either side, a plain white house with an L-shaped porch along the north and east sides, a yard that needed cutting, and no flowers. Not one flower bed. A small barn that was barely big enough to house two horses and a carriage.

Everything was in a perfect state of repair and it was clean enough. But . . . Hannah couldn't find the proper word to describe the place. Was it lonely? Neglected? Poor?

She didn't know, so she shrugged it off, stepped up on the peeling floorboards of the porch, and knocked.

"Just a minute," a male voice belted out.

Hannah waited. She waited so long she was becoming irritated and had actually turned to walk back down the steps, when the door was almost jerked off its hinges and a voice like a thunderclap bellowed, "What do you want?"

Taken aback, Hannah turned. His frame filled the doorway,

his curly head of hair reaching almost to the top of the door frame. For a moment, she lost her voice.

She'd seen this man somewhere before. "Uh . . . I . . . heard you're a carpenter." When he didn't reply, she cleared her throat and rushed on. "I . . . uh . . . bought a house on Hollander Road and I need an addition built."

The smell of burning meat was overpowering. Hannah blinked as blue smoke wafted through the screen door. "Step inside. I gotta turn my meat," he said.

She hesitated, unsure if she should pull open the wooden screen door, or if he wanted her to remain on the porch. "Come on in!" he yelled.

Hannah jumped. He was so loud. So huge and noisy. She did not like this Dave King at all, she decided.

She went in. The kitchen was sunny, with golden sunlight slanting through the window above the sink, dust mites spiraling above mountains of dirty dishes. The whole room was bathed in the blue light of smoke pouring out of the enormous cast-iron frying pan. His back was turned, his shoulders hunched, as he pried at a piece of beef that was vastly overheated.

He was almost as wide as his cook stove. The top of the stove seemed to be somewhere in the vicinity of his knees.

Finally, he turned.

"Push the pan away from the heat," Hannah said, without thinking.

"No. I'm hungry."

"Suit yourself."

They looked at each other. He towered above her, a hulk of a man with unkempt hair, strange yellow eyes, and a grim slash of a mouth.

He reminded Hannah of a moose.

"What do you want?"

"I told you."

"Yeah, guess you did. I'm busy. Can't do it."

"Why not?" Hannah asked.

"I just said."

"You don't have to yell at me. I'm not standing on the porch."

"Aren't you that widow? Anna or something?"

"Hannah."

"Yeah. I saw you before. You're the widow of Jeremiah Riehl. You lived out West. Let me get this meat. It's done. You want some?"

"No."

"You sure? I'll tell you what. If you wait a month or so, I'll see what you want done."

"I want an addition built onto my house."

"Oh yeah. You did say." He searched the cupboard for a clean plate but couldn't seem to find one. Then he turned to the sink, rattled around in the stack of dishes until he excavated a plate, held it under the cold water faucet, wiped it on his shirt, and speared the biggest steak Hannah had ever seen, flopping it on his plate.

She swallowed, thinking of that plate.

He waved in the general direction of the remaining chair. "Sit."

Hannah sat. She turned her head, her eyes taking in her surroundings. An old davenport with blankets and a pillow. His coat and hat thrown in a corner. The rug was mainly mud.

"Where's your wife and children?" Hannah blurted, never one to let good manners hold precedence over blatant curiosity.

"Don't you know?" His look was incredulous. His eyes turned dark, a greenish color like brackish water below tree roots in a drought. A bitter light illuminated his eyes, his mouth set in a hard line of control. "They all died."

"All? How many were there?"

"Just her. And two unborn babies. Twins. Her name was Leah." His voice grated now as it dragged over remembered pain. He blinked, his eyes focused as on a faraway scene, as if pictures played over in his mind. He shrugged and said it was the way of it. What're you gonna do?

For once, Hannah was speechless. Her throat constricted with jammed-up words that threatened to choke her. Suddenly, her eyes burned with unshed tears of shared pain. When she finally did find her voice, she said, "Right. Well, I'll be on my way. You'll let me know?"

He nodded, a forkful of half-cooked beefsteak on its way to his mouth.

Thelma Johns moved to her daughter Shirley's house about three weeks later. Hannah had ridden with them to a lawyer's office in the city of Lancaster to settle for the property. She fell thoroughly out of the good graces of the lawyer with her impertinence but was soothed by the gentle Shirley and deposited back at the Stoltzfus farm in a huff.

Hannah's family descended on her newly acquired house armed with brooms and pails, rags and soap, vinegar and baking soda and lemon juice.

Manny pushed the reel mower, Eli and Mary raked piles of sweet, succulent grass, running and bouncing and shouting in the early summer sunshine. Hannah washed windows upstairs, leaning out over the windowsill to tell the kids they were worse than wild calves.

Mary stopped, looked up at Hannah. Eli turned an expert cartwheel, righted himself, shook the grass from his hair, and grinned.

"Jump down on this pile of grass, Hannah!" he shouted.

"I guess not! You know you're both old enough to behave yourselves."

"We are behaving!" Mary shouted back.

The woods surrounding the little brick house resounded with the happy cries of the children. Doddy Stoltzfus smiled and smiled. His eyes twinkled at the children's antics as he applied a screwdriver to a loose hinge, and tapped a nail into a broken windowsill. He told Hannah he thought she had chosen wisely. The house was well-built.

Hannah shone with a new happiness at her grandfather's words. She felt validated, lifted above the sense of many failures that dogged her steps.

"Well done, Hannah," he'd said. But he did not approve of the dry goods store. That was only in the planning stages, so there was no sense in sniffing out other people's opinions. The bishop, bless the dear little man, held the ultimate decision.

Or did he? Hannah wasn't ready with an alternative plan if he batted down the whole idea. She knew she wasn't about to disobey openly, but she also wasn't planning on giving up. She would find a solution.

Her determination had served her well on the Dakota prairie, and it would serve her well here in Lancaster County, too.

What was wrong with a woman owning a dry goods store? In Proverbs, the husband praised his wife for her crafting skills, the selling of her wares in the marketplace. She even purchased an acre of land.

So, there you go. A woman had the right to some form of entrepreneurship, as long as it was decent, necessary items she was selling. And what was more sensible than plain broadcloth and cotton and denim for men's work trousers, buttons and snaps, and so on?

Thelma had left the overstuffed sofa, a brown monstrosity that Hannah eyed with a critical sniff. Shrugging her shoulders, she said she didn't know what else to put in the living room. She certainly wasn't going to buy a new sofa.

Sarah suggested covering it with one of her everyday quilts. But Hannah shook her head. "Quilts slide every which way. I hate a quilt on a couch." So, that was the end of that idea.

Sarah gave her the armless rocking chair, the table in the sunporch, and an extra chest of drawers. But the house looked barren. Unclothed. Cleaned and polished to a high shine, the floors glowed and the windows sparkled. The bathroom fixtures and mirrors shone. Yet there was no coziness, no warmth.

"It's the curtains," Mary trilled, after standing in the doorway of the living room to survey the clean, nearly empty room.

"Mam, do I have to hang green, roll-down window blinds?" Hannah asked.

"Yes, of course. That's our *ordnung*. You know that."

"If you want me to hang them from my window frames, you're going to have to buy them."

"No, that's your responsibility, Hannah. You're capable enough to take care of such matters."

So, she did. She obeyed her mother by going to the hardware store in the town of Intercourse with measurements carefully written on the back of a calendar page.

Manny helped her install them, which made the house look Amish, but did nothing for an aura of hominess.

The family helped her move in, with her meager belongings put in place in an hour or so. Sarah turned to Hannah, shook hands with her, and wished her the best in her *forehaltiss*. Her grandfather told her gravely to keep her door locked. Manny promised to bring Marybelle as soon as he could. Then they all climbed into the spring wagon and were gone down the road before Hannah had a chance to feel emotional.

So, here she was. All alone in the house of her dreams.

Silence reigned everywhere. The floors echoed when she walked. A faucet dripped. Windows creaked. The green blinds flapped in the open windows. She needed so many things. She had no refrigerator. And she had no idea where to go to use the telephone, or the number to call the Ice and Cold Storage Company for ice delivery. She needed a gas stove and a propane company. She needed a horse, a buggy, a harness, and a pen built into the small shed at the end of the drive. She needed more dishes, pots and pans, bedding, towels—just about everything.

Well, one day at a time.

She sat in the armless rocking chair, her hands clasped loosely in her lap. She felt that the rooms around her were enfolding her with a certain safety. The golden sunlight, the variety of green colors, the blue sky and the breezes that were gentle, the hidden trust that it would rain whenever they needed it, one season following another in order and sameness.

She had nothing to fear. That was something, wasn't it? Now, if the bishop would only hurry up with his answer, and if that Dave King wasn't too busy, she'd soon be on her way. Her first priority was getting a refrigerator. She'd have to find the nearest telephone.

She began her search by walking down the road until she came to a house similar to her own. There were children in the yard and a small, brown dog. When she walked up to them, they stopped playing and stood and stared at her with frightened eyes. The dog jumped up and down with the force of its high, yipping bark.

"Is your mother at home? May I speak to her?"

"No!"

Yip. Yip. Yip, yip, yip from the dog.

Hannah looked around, not quite knowing what she should do.

The screen door on the porch was flung open. A thin, pretty woman with blond hair to her shoulders appeared, calling out to Hannah. "Hello! You must be the new neighbor that moved into the Johns house."

"Yes. I am."

"It's nice to meet you. Come on up on the porch."

Hannah met her on the steps and noticed the friendliness that shone from her eyes. Their faces were level, with the blond-haired woman on the top step.

"I'm Diane Jones. My husband, Tom, is at work at Myers Refrigeration. The two children are . . ." she rolled her eyes, "Diane and Tommy Jr."

Hannah laughed. "We Amish often name kids after their parents, too."

"Well, my husband is a stickler for tradition."

They sat in the metal porch chairs, sizing each other up with practiced eyes. Hannah thought Diane was lovely, which caught her off guard. She almost never liked someone right off the bat. Diane thought Hannah could be a model, so tall and with that striking face. But there was something hidden in the depth of those black eyes that was unsettling.

The children clambered up onto the porch—blond, blue-eyed, perfect replicas of their mother. The dog sniffed Hannah's legs. She pulled them back behind the seat of the chair, as far as they would go, and resisted the impulse to push him away. She despised small, yappy dogs. This one was a terrier of some kind. The worst. She eyed him with a baleful look. He eyed her back. Why did small dogs do this to her? Hannah had no idea, but she had a premonition that he'd love to sink his sharp, little teeth into her ankle. She'd bet anything that the minute he saw her arriving with no children to control him, he'd growl, make a beeline for her, and yes, take a chomp out of her ankle.

"What's his name?" she asked, pulling her mouth into the semblance of a smile.

"He's Toto," the small boy lisped, picking the dog up to let him nuzzle his face. Hannah watched and swallowed, thinking the dog would probably give the small boy parasites.

"I came to use the telephone to call a refrigeration company. But I see you might be able to help me if your husband works at Myers."

"He does. Isn't that great?" Diane asked, clearly pleased to be of service to her new neighbor.

That problem was soon solved with Tom Jones delivering a used ice box, ice, and a second-hand stove. Before the week was up, she was equipped with a useful kitchen, all for the price of sixty-five dollars.

One evening, a horse and carriage slowed, then turned into her driveway. Hannah peered through the living room window and saw two somber-faced ministers wearing grave expressions.

She smoothed her hair, yanked her covering forward, and pinned it securely, hoping to convey a sense of *demut* (humbleness) and *gehorsamkeit* (obedience).

"*An schöena ovat*," one of them said, "such a pleasant evening."

"*Ya*," Hannah nodded, her shoulders hunched in an attempt to appear sorrowful. A bereft widow, in need of sympathy and approval.

She was told kindly that they had conferred among themselves about her proposal. Hannah's heart beat rapidly. Her head felt as if it might explode. She bit her lower lip and watched those serious faces with a sense of doom.

"It would be best if you gave up the idea," one minister began. "But, Ezra thought that if you promised to stay small and sell only the kind of fabric our women could use, and if you would be frugal in all of your dealings, we could allow it and see if you are capable of such a venture. However, you should have your grandfather, who is an esteemed elder with a good sense of business, to oversee your accounts on a regular basis, as women tend to become sidetracked where sums of money are concerned."

Gratefulness warred with irritation, but her face remained passive. She didn't ask about the addition and they didn't mention it, so she thanked them in the most humble manner she could manage. They made a few minutes of small talk about the weather, wished her the best in her new undertaking, and then left.

When the carriage had disappeared, Hannah's elation knew no bounds. She smiled, whirled across the polished floor, lifting her hands in thanksgiving. She was on her way!

A list started to form in her head. She needed that addition to her house, then she could stock the fabric, and she'd need to get a horse and buggy. She'd also need to have a stall built in the garage. Could she really afford it all?

Well, one step at a time.

CHAPTER 19

Dave King had his own opinion of where and how the addition should be built. He stood in the hot morning sun with his faded straw hat pulled low over his forehead, his white shirt stained with perspiration and about two sizes too small for his hulking shoulders.

"You don't want the addition on that side of the house. If you put it there, you'll never be able to enter your kitchen through the side door without going through the store. You won't like that."

A searing flame of rebellion shot through Hannah. "I guess I know what I'd like and what I won't."

He had the nerve to laugh at her. "You want to lock and unlock the door every time you go in and out?" he asked.

"I'll use the front door."

Their eyes met. The challenge sizzled between them like the angry buzzing of bees.

"Well, I guess that's it, then. I'm not building anything until you use some common sense."

With that, he strode to the car, spoke to the driver, and took off, leaving Hannah standing there with her mouth hanging open in disbelief. She was so angry she kicked the doorstep and banged her big toe. It hurt, but she didn't care.

She'd get Elam and Ben to help her. That big lummox wasn't going to set foot on her property, ever again.

She began to think about the side entrance, the row of hooks on the wall. The more she thought about it, the more the truth dawned on her. Dave King was right. Well, one thing for sure, he'd never have the opportunity to find out he was right. What did he care about? It was her own business. If she paid him, he was supposed to supply a building according to her wishes, not his.

A poor excuse of a carpenter, she decided. He should be farming like the rest of the Amish men his age.

Dave King showed up about a week later, standing in the rain on the stoop at the side entrance, his bulk shutting out the gray morning light. "Did you decide?" he asked by way of a greeting.

"No."

"Well, I thought of a solution. Why not put the store on the opposite end of the house?"

"No! That's not going to work. I won't go through my bedroom every time a customer shows up."

"You can sleep upstairs."

"Look, I don't need your services. My brothers can build what I need."

"What do you want?"

"Oh, come in out of the rain," she said, irritated at him standing there as if he wasn't aware that he was getting wet. She stepped back to allow him entry and watched to see if he'd take his shoes off. Of course, he didn't.

"Your shoes are wet," she said pointedly.

No answer. Of all the nerve! Rude. Ill-mannered. At least he could give her some sort of reply.

It seemed like he filled up the entire kitchen. Her house was very small with him standing there. She watched him as he turned his head from side to side, assessing, measuring, calculating.

He was actually not bad looking with those amber eyes and rounded nose. Actually, Hannah thought, with a good shave and a toothbrush, he might be attractive. But his size! And his curly hair. Like untamed wool.

"Your feet are wet."

He bent to look at his feet. "Not my feet. My shoes."

She felt scolded. She wasn't sure but she felt a blush creeping into her face. She sincerely hoped not.

"Why don't you go out the back with your store?" he asked suddenly.

"There's no door."

He shoved his face forward, much too close to hers. "That's what carpenters do. They cut doors where they want them."

She stepped back, feeling like a blushing school girl. Which infuriated her. "Is that right," she shot back, her dark eyes blazing.

He laughed, then. He had the gall to stand there and laugh at her!

"Come here," he said. He extended an arm, and looked out the window by the sink. She walked over as one hypnotized.

"Look. Here is where we will put your door, okay?"

Unbelievable! She felt that massive arm come up and his great, heavy hand came to rest on her shoulder. She was aware of his size, his nearness, his warmth. The scent of his shirt did not repulse her. Spicy. Some oddly comforting mix of lumber and summer and leather and fresh mown hay.

Hannah swayed, quickly righted herself. Her breathing all but stopped. She resisted the urge to turn and lay her head on that powerful chest and tell him she didn't want a store. She just wanted to go home with him and wash that pile of dirty dishes, sweep the mud out the door, and sleep in his bed.

All of this rushed through her head like a strong summer thunderstorm, leaving her deeply ashamed and berating herself internally with firm words of self-loathing.

Jerry was barely gone. With Jerry firmly in her mind replacing her thoughts, she crossed her arms and thought of stepping away, but didn't. Couldn't.

She'd never felt like this before. She was lonely, grieving, in sorrow. That was the only explanation that made any sense to her.

"See this window?" Dave was asking. "I'd put a door in here and a few steps down to the lower level and there's your store! Inexpensive. Easy. You'll want windows, though. Women need to see what they're buying." He grinned down at her.

Hannah almost wept with the depth of her feelings. When he stepped away from her, she felt disoriented, leaning against the countertop for support. When he let himself out, she found herself reaching out her hand to stop him. Why was he going home now?

She watched him as he stood in the backyard, his eyes taking in the length and the distance to the clothesline. Without thinking, she let herself out of the door and joined him, her arms crossed as if to protect her heart from galloping off without her permission.

"Shingles or metal roofing?" he asked.

"Which is cheaper?"

"Metal goes on quicker. Less labor. But shingles look nicer."

"How much ch . . . cheaper?" Oh, now she was stuttering. Ch . . . ch . . . like a baby chick!

"I'd say a hundred dollars, maybe more."

"That's a lot."

"I know. But you have shingles on this roof, so it won't look right if you use metal on the new section."

Hannah nodded. He was probably right. But, where was her irritation? She felt as if she had been cast into a whirlpool, spun around, over and under, and spewed out on dry land. Disoriented, dizzy, as if she needed a map to guide her, to tell her which road to take and how many miles there were to her destination.

What was her destination anyway?

Her eyes narrowed as she watched Dave King pace off the length and width, his boots coming down like thunderclaps. Pulling out a tablet, he scribbled notes with a yellow pencil, gazed across the backyard, and thought out loud, like she wasn't even there.

She wanted to jump up and down, wave her arms, let him know she was there standing on the lawn, in the rain. She felt a sob rise in her throat. The rain was falling so softly and gently, leaving grass and flower beds smelling so sweet. She had never known rain to have an odor. It was like liquid ambrosia, nectar from flowers.

Water dripped off his straw hat. He looked up and smiled at her. "Better get in out of the rain," he said.

Hannah turned to go. Yes, better get out of the rain.

Dave King followed her but stopped on the stoop, poked his head in the door and said, "I'll get a rough estimate for you sometime this week." Then he was gone.

Hannah watched the truck back up, turn around, and chug off through the rain. She began to cry, soft little whimpers and a runnel of tears that sprang from her eyes and dripped off her chin. She swiped at them, furiously, trying to make sense of her sudden and overwhelming change of feelings.

She was lonely. Too many changes in too short a time. Jerry's death too sudden. There was nothing left to do but sag into the armless rocker, her hands dangling down on each side, her head tilted toward the ceiling, seeing nothing.

Where had all of this come from? Something had to change before he brought back the estimate. But she knew she had never felt this way before. Not with Jerry. Not with Clay. A wave of humiliation swept through her. She felt pity for Jerry and a longing for him. He had already diminished, growing smaller and smaller, already moving away into the far reaches of her memory, if she were honest. Jerry's face had become shadowy, no longer clear.

Surely God had something to do with this. She had never been close to God, except when she called out to Him in desperate situations, of which there had been plenty.

If God was allowing Dave King to come into her life, He'd need to let her know somehow. Never devout, Hannah simply sat and stared, wondering how to pray, vaguely acknowledging a Higher Power, but without proper words to turn her thoughts into an actual prayer.

She tried, instead, to focus on her business. She hoped she'd have enough money to build the store and stock it with a decent amount of fabrics. She had no idea how to go about contacting the textile mills or a wholesale store. Surely there was one. If she could find Harold Rocher's address or telephone number, he could give her all sorts of useful information. But she would need a Baltimore, Maryland phone book. Getting his information would be like looking for the proverbial needle in a haystack.

Hannah sat and watched the rain, heard the musical patter and the gurgling of the downspout. She imagined the limp, withered green grass in the lawn taking in the droplets, the soil becoming moist. She envisioned happy little earthworms aerating the ground, tunneling through the mud and grass roots.

The leaves from the oak trees dripped with moisture. Green and velvety, as thick as a crocheted curtain, the leaves spoke of health and steady growth each year, the roots buried deep under the surface, taking in the nutrients and moisture that was supplied without fail.

She thought of the West, where there was little moisture. Rain failed. The brittle drought, the endless, searing days parched throats and left the cows searching endlessly for grass and water.

And still she had loved it.

Now, what to do with the rest of this day? She wondered how long Dave King would take to finish his estimate. She should have offered to help him with his dishes.

He did not return.

Two weeks. Hannah went to church with Manny. She worked in her house, arranging, cleaning. She baked bread and a pie. She helped a farmer pick cucumbers and green beans. For a half day of backbreaking labor, she received one dollar. It was enough. She returned the following day and picked bushels of lima beans and more green beans under a sultry, sweltering sun, the air thick and wet with humidity and portent.

Straightening her back, she scanned the thunderheads in the distance. They looked like piles of black sheep's wool, with gray, threatening sky stretched from one horizon to another, the sun erased by scudding clouds.

She didn't mind the approaching storm. She bent her back and continued grabbing the stubborn lima beans, ripping them from their stalks by the handfuls with her strong fingers. If she could finish this row, she'd likely make two dollars, enough to purchase the few groceries she'd need for the week.

As Bennie D. paid her, his eyes scanned the skies. He told her she'd better get on home.

Hannah knew she'd picked too long. She could smell the rain, sense the wind in the churning clouds. But she'd left her windows open so she'd risk the hike home. If she got soaked, it was better than her house getting soaked.

As soon as she was out of his sight, she ran, her arms pumping at her sides, her feet flying along the road. She could hear the oncoming wind like a freight train and feel the moisture being propelled by the wind.

The storm hit her about halfway home, the wind taking her breath away, the rain slashing its fury into her face. She winced at the brilliant lightning followed by a drumroll of thunder. Rain streamed down her face, pelted the top of her head. In a few seconds, she was soaked through her cotton dress.

The trees above her bent and swayed, lashed by the strength of the wind and rain. Her breath came in gasps. She heard the crunch of gravel behind her. Headlights pierced the barrage of rain like giant cat's eyes.

She slowed, unable to catch her breath, the water streaming down her face. The truck pulled up alongside her. The driver yelled at her, some watery garble she couldn't absorb, so she shook her head.

There was a blinding flash of lightning. Electricity sizzled through the atmosphere, followed by a horrendous thunderclap. She didn't hear the slam of the truck door as she continued marching through the torrential downpour, determined to make it home to close those windows.

Suddenly she was hauled back by two arms as thick and powerful as hawsers. She tried to scream, but only a hoarse, wet sound gurgled from her mouth. She was stuffed unceremoniously into a slippery upholstered truck seat, floundering and spluttering like a half-dead fish.

She wiped water from her eyes with the backs of both hands. Him!

"What's wrong with you?" His way of greeting.

Angrily, she glared at him with all the power of her black eyes, her face glistening, her hair a sleek, black cap. "I would have made it home," she stated forcefully.

Another blinding flash and a deep, reverberating roll of thunder. The windshield wipers were almost useless. A gust of wind rocked the truck. The air in the cab was heavy with moisture, stuffy with lack of oxygen, the driver hunched over the steering wheel, gripping it with both hands, his eyes searching for her house.

Hannah was dripping water over everything. When they turned into the driveway of her house, she nudged Dave King and told him she needed to get out. Her windows were open.

Her house was soaked. Water streamed through both kitchen windows, spraying through the screens as if someone held their thumb across the nozzle of a hose. She ran to the bathroom after yanking the windows shut, grabbed towels and proceeded to mop up the ever-widening puddles of water.

She yelped, remembered the upstairs, dashing up the stairs and clunking the windows shut, hard. Clattering back down for more towels, she saw him at the sink wringing out towels, twisting them with those arms like logs.

Between them, the house was wiped clean—windowsills, walls, and the floor. The bucket was emptied and the towels were placed in the wringer washer.

Dave King leaned against the kitchen counter, his straw hat pulled low over his eyes, his arms crossed, and told her that if she saw a storm coming out of the northwest, she should stay put. And keep her windows closed when she went away on a sultry summer day.

"You know, if your windows were open in your store, you'd have a bunch of ruined fabric," he finished.

That raised her ire. "I'm not that dumb. If the windows of my store were open, I'd be here," she said, loudly.

"Still, you need to respect these Lancaster County storms. They can come up pretty quick."

She scowled, thinking he had no idea what a real storm was, what kind of weather she had survived out West.

Outside, the rain had not let up. Sheets of wind-driven rain pummeled the window glass and pounded the roof. Rivers of water sluiced through the downspout, the gutters overflowing in a sloppy current that splashed along the front of the porch.

Lightning lit up the dark kitchen as jagged streaks snaked through the air, followed by claps of thunder like rifle shots. The wind howled. When hail began to bounce against the window panes and leap in the yard as if it was alive, Hannah had to admit to herself that it was a legit storm.

She ran to the living room door to watch the icy balls hit the lawn, bounce up, and fall back down in the watery grass.

She was aware of his presence behind her. She winced as the blue-white lightning illuminated the darkened house and endured the hard crack of thunder without showing the weakness she felt. She shivered.

"You're wet. Go change your clothes," he ordered.

Hannah went.

"I'll put on the tea kettle."

When Hannah emerged from her bedroom, she'd toweled her hair dry and was wearing a clean navy-blue dress with no apron. Her feet were encased in warm, black slippers. She was carrying her hairbrush, her hair a tousled, glossy mane spilling down her back. Tilting her head to the left, she began the slow task of removing the tangles, unselfconscious, watching the rain through the living room windows.

Dave watched her from his stance beside the kitchen stove. When she turned to say something mundane about the weather, he couldn't take his eyes off that tangled thicket of glossy black hair. He thought he'd been over those kinds of feelings. The loss of Lena and the babies was a heavy weight he carried around with him no matter how hard he tried to discard it. Grief and sorrow were like that. It took you to the depths of black loneliness and longing you'd never forget. After a few years, he'd honestly thought he would never feel the attraction necessary to become friends with another woman.

But there was something different about Hannah. She had given him quite a jolt the first time he met her. Later he decided he would do well to forget his initial attraction, given that attitude of hers. She was an angry, ill-mannered, brusque young woman; he didn't need that kind of challenge in his life.

He was too old to be swept in by a woman's looks alone. His mother had always said, "Choose your wife by considering whether she would make a good mother to your children." Hannah was anything but motherly.

Born the youngest in a family of twelve, Dave had known plenty of teasing, plenty of rough and tumble with a line of older brothers above him. He'd grown up kicking and pounding and running away from them. Now, there was not one of them who dared lift a hand to his massive strength.

He'd simply kept on growing and building muscle after the others had reached their full growth. And he didn't take any nonsense from anyone. Never had. It was his method of survival in a tribe of rowdy siblings.

He had fallen hard for Lena. Petite, soft-spoken, her hair like spun wheat, she was everything his brothers were not. He'd worried and prayed and was afraid for her frail body. When he took her to the hospital, there was nothing they could do to spare her or the babies. Too much infection.

He had entered a deep, dark place of intense suffering for a longer time than he cared to admit. He became obsessed with his work, the drawing of plans, the endless hard labor that became his saving grace.

Angry and blaming God, he retreated into a hermit-like existence until the kindly, old bishop came to visit him, his wife bringing his favorite dish of *schnitz un knepp*. They explained Lena's loss as a chastening and a polishing of a clay vessel that needed refinement.

After they had left, he wept most of the night, waking to a new day with the anger and self-pity banished forever by the kindly, old bishop's healing words. The death of Jesus on the cross for his sins became brighter and more real than it had ever been before.

And now, here was Hannah, like a sultry temptress. He couldn't be sure.

She turned, grimacing, as the hairbrush hit an especially large snarl. "Does it often rain like this? You'd think anything unfastened would be washed away."

He wanted to answer, but he couldn't. Not right away. He wanted to take the hairbrush away from her and run his hands through that luxurious mane of heavy black hair. Her large dark eyes were on his, waiting.

So powerful was his attraction to her, he had to gulp for air and was afraid he'd have a heart attack right there in her kitchen. "Uh . . . no. Well, yes, sometimes. But only in summer."

She finished with the brushing and reached back to grasp her heavy hair, expertly wrapping some sort of elastic band around it.

Then he had to put up with her nearness, the scent of her hair like spring rain and some tropical flower he couldn't name. His senses swam as he took a piece of tablet paper out of his pocket, pointing a finger to some numbers.

"Yes, yes." She nodded her head, agreeing, and sending off a fresh wave of floral scent.

"We can start in about ten days, weather permitting." All business now.

"And, what if the weather doesn't cooperate? I mean . . ." She spread her hands to indicate the downpour outside.

"Then it'll be later."

"And I'll be picking lima beans longer."

He laughed. "And getting caught in storms."

She smiled. Their gazes held. Both wondered if there could be love without pain.

Soon after Dave King left, the sun sank in a blaze of glory, illuminating every drop that hovered on blades of grass or beaded a gentle flower. The corn produced great yellow ears, every kernel filled in by the aid of the moisture that seeped up through the sturdy green stalks.

Hannah walked among the wet flowers and eyed the fields of healthy corn that grew like a miniature forest. She thought of her father.

She felt a growing sympathy that edged out her irritation and blame. No doubt that he'd imagined this for the prairie. Verdant growth for acres on end, spreading to the edge of the horizon. Life-giving rains, fat cattle that ambled among lush prairie broom grass, timothy, and all the other nutritious native grasses that grew wild, feeding his cattle at no cost to him.

He had traveled all that distance in faith believing that God would provide. Believing until it turned into human determination, eventually pushing him over the edge. The sadness of it clung to her in a new, claustrophobic way, until she no longer experienced the beauty of the glistening world around her.

Her mother. How had she endured? Well, it was in the past. She needed to move on. But that was difficult. What if she was to begin a friendship with Dave King? Would her irritation, her dislike of people, eventually pull them apart?

To explain his amber gaze was not possible. She could memorize, easily, the roundness of his nose, his full cheeks, his thick beard, and the indentation of the thin line of his mouth. So different from Jerry's features. No dark hair, dark eyes, the face she had come to know as well as her own.

All that wooly, curly hair. Hannah stepped up on the porch and sat on the wooden rocking chair her grandfather had given her, tucking her feet under her skirts to dry them. She gazed across the green lawn.

What would have been the outcome on the plains with rain like this? The wheat. Her father's corn crop. The cattle. Well, it wasn't the way of it. Not in the West. That was likely the reason it was so sparsely settled, whereas here, in this blessed valley, the soil and the climate drew people from every imaginable corner of the world. Immigrants from Ireland, Poland, Germany, Switzerland, the Netherlands. All sought a better life or religious freedom. Often both. Her own ancestors had arrived on some creaking, storm-tossed vessel, persecuted Swiss brethren who made their homes in Pennsylvania.

No, their homesteads. Some of these farms, most of them actually, had already been handed down for generations, and would remain in families for many more. So, a homestead could be anywhere folks chose to live, to prosper, to raise their families, live their lives in harmony with the folks around them.

Hannah smiled and tucked her feet into her skirts. This was her homestead. This adorable house with the kitchen cabinets painted white, and the hardwood flooring that shone from much polishing.

She loved every little corner, every clever closet tucked away throughout the house. She loved the curve of the railing that followed the stairway to the second floor and the built-in medicine cabinet and green tile in the bathroom.

Without Jerry, this would not have been possible. She laid her head on her propped-up knees and whispered a thank-you to her deceased husband.

Remorse was a terrible thing. That was the main reason she would have to stop her idiotic pull toward the carpenter. She would only become testy, irritated beyond control, and then she would speak harshly and be determined to have her own way.

She could never be a proper wife.

But still, he'd persuaded her to build the store where he thought best. That was something, after all.

CHAPTER 20

Hᴇ ᴛᴏʟᴅ ʜᴇʀ ᴛʜᴇ ᴘʀɪᴄᴇ, ᴡʜɪᴄʜ ᴡᴀs ꜰᴀʀ ʟᴇss ᴛʜᴀɴ sʜᴇ ᴀɴᴛɪᴄɪ-pated.

She hid her elation under lowered brows, pursed lips, and what she hoped was a professional look, the aura of a business woman. She asked, "Can't you do any better than that?"

"Hey, look here! I'm already scraping the bottom. Giving you discounts here and there, you being a widow and all."

The old irritation. "I'm not poor," she snapped.

"I didn't say you were. Just wanted to give you a good price."

"Well, I hate the label of 'poor widow.'"

He couldn't help wondering how she had any funds at all, having lived in North Dakota all that time. Her husband must have had some money, or else she certainly couldn't have afforded all this.

He wore a white, short-sleeved shirt, the muscles of his massive arms bulging from the too-tight sleeves, his neck rising from the open collar like the trunk of an oak. Buttons missing, a hole torn in the back, his trousers ripped, safety pins serving as buttons in more than one place.

She avoided his amber eyes, deciding she would not allow herself to drown in their unexplainable depths.

Hannah winced when the machine arrived and tore up her back yard like a scissors to cloth, digging the footer, leveling the ground, removing chunks of turf like slices of cake and tossing them aside. A truck wheezed in, a solid chunk of cement blocks was unloaded, and the concrete mixer put to work by the tug of a rope on the gasoline engine.

Dave King strode among the men and machines, clearly the lord of his own domain. Two Amish boys with clean-cut jaws, their straw hats tossed aside, bent their backs and laid block like pros, with quick, precise movements. Dave worked along with them, whistling and watching everything with a practiced eye.

Now, she needed to find a supplier of fabric, a wholesale company from which to order the goods she would need. She thought maybe the post office in New Holland might be the best place to begin, but she needed a ride there. She really needed a horse and buggy, but she wasn't sure she could afford one until the store was up and running.

Dave came to the back door. "I forgot to bring my water jug along. Mind if I get a drink?" he asked.

"Help yourself."

He drank like a camel and said he'd be back for more if it was all right with her. She nodded, then quickly blurted out her predicament. He listened, fastening his eyes on her face. "If you wait until Saturday morning, I'll come by and give you a lift."

She made the mistake of meeting his eyes, becoming consumed by the warm, golden light beneath the brim of his old, darkened straw hat with rawhide string tied around the crown.

The kitchen disappeared. She felt unanchored, thrust into a world without gravity, unsure of anything she had ever been or what she would ever be. Her self-assurance, the reliance on her armor of anger and irritation was dissolving like sugar in boiling water, leaving her stumbling for a foothold, grasping for something, anything to hold onto.

His voice broke the spell. "If you have nothing else planned."

"Planned? Planned?" She couldn't imagine what he meant.

"I'll take you to the post office. Didn't you need an address or a telephone number?"

"Oh, that. Yes. Yes, I do." She felt like a child caught stealing candy. Her face flamed with an unimaginable embarrassment like she had never felt before. Then, there was nothing else to do but save herself from feeling smaller and smaller, that hated inward cringing, the self-loathing that was like an uncomfortable burr in a woolen sock. She glared at his brown work shoes and told him gruffly that he had mud on his shoes. Couldn't he respect a woman's floor?

He let himself out but not without seeing her discomfort, a cynical smile playing around his mouth.

When the door closed behind him, she locked it. Then she sat on the brown davenport feeling so miserable she wanted to die. Not really die, but at least fall into a faint so she'd be temporarily free from these churning insecurities. He made her feel like a bumbling teenager, and when he left, she wanted him to come back immediately!

She was frightened by her lack of understanding. It couldn't be what folks described as falling in love. Or could it? She did not love Dave King. Didn't even like him. She had never been in love and had no plans to be.

Like a moth trapped in a spider web, she beat against the confines of her self-inflected prison, hurting herself in the process. Where to turn? Who to ask? Her mother? No, she couldn't ask her mother. She was, or had been, a married woman. How could she ever approach her own mother with such an unusual question?

She had, quite simply, no idea where to turn. Hannah had never had the kinds of friends who spoke of liking boys and how it felt to be in love. This could not be love. It was misery!

How would she ever be able to sit beside him in a buggy? Buggies were so narrow. You could barely keep six inches away from the person sitting beside you.

Hannah took a deep breath to steady herself. She tiptoed to the window to peer out, checking to see if he had gone back to work.

He wasn't there. Now where had he gone? How could he have disappeared so fast?

For the rest of the week, she considered calling a driver, walking all the way to the Jones residence to use their telephone to let him know she would not need to go to the post office.

She thought of hiding in a closet or in the basement so he'd think she wasn't at home. Or, she could always lock the door and crawl under her bed. He'd drive in, knock, and eventually leave again.

No, she was turning into a sniveling, wet dishrag, a person with no backbone. She'd just march right out to his buggy and ask him to leave. She had no need of his assistance.

She thumbed through the six dresses she owned. Red? Too showy. Purple? Oh, she couldn't wear either one. She was a widow, so if she was going to be seen in public, it had to be black. She was in mourning for the traditional year, the time allotted by the Amish *ordnung* to dress in black.

She washed and ironed her black dress, cape, and apron, then fell into an awful despair of indecision. Should she wear a cape, or not? He might think her too fancy if she went without it. If she wore one, she'd look as though she was dressed for church.

She washed and starched her best white covering, ironing it with utmost care, using a paring knife to pleat the gathers properly.

Picking lima beans was out of the question. All week, there was no sign of Dave King's carpenter crew, which drove Hannah to distraction until she remembered that he was building a dairy barn over close to Leola at the same time he had worked her addition into his schedule.

By Friday evening, she sat herself down calmly, hands folded in her lap, working on her resolve to remain aloof and in full control of all her senses. She'd speak primly like the sorrowful widow she was.

He would surely respect her. She would keep her eyes averted demurely, accepting his kindness for what it was, an offer to get her to the post office. After that was decided, the realization hit her like a sledgehammer. He had absolutely no interest in her. If he had any romantic inclinations he'd never be seen with her on the streets of New Holland.

Never. It would be breaking all the rules of tradition, of respect. Well.

Well, that was interesting. All this craziness of washing and ironing and starching and pleating for nothing.

A thin drizzle was falling Saturday morning, a mist with the sky a dome of milky gray. No trace of the sun. The air was humid, tainted with the smell of summer's end, aging beanstalks and wet, crumpled weeds hanging like scraggly fur by the roadside.

Hannah threw on an old navy blue dress, pinned her everyday apron around her waist without bothering to see if it was straight or if her *leblein*—the fold of cloth sewn on the waistline—was in the center. She didn't wash her hair and left the clean covering in the drawer for church. Instead, she wore the slightly yellowed one she wore most days. Now that she realized he had no romantic interest in her, she felt much freer. She'd get over her own nonsense soon enough. It was probably just exhaustion from grieving and all the excitement from buying the house and starting her business.

Untroubled, at ease, she met him at the stoop, smiled, and said she'd get her purse. Then she climbed into the buggy and sat with her hands in her lap.

"Ready?" He looked at her. In the dreary light of the rainy day with the humidity like a tropical rain forest, her skin glowed luminous, an olive hue to her tanned face. Her eyes were large and dark, her lips parted softly.

There was no avoiding touching him—his large frame took up most of the seat, leaving no gap between them. Her shoulder rested comfortably against his. Her leg touched the coarse texture of his denim trousers, but that was all right. No different than being seated beside Manny or Elam. Like a brother.

But he kept looking at her, even after they had pulled out on the road, the horse traveling at a fast clip through the gloom. Rain misted the horse's back like a glistening dew.

"Did your husband ever tell you that you are beautiful?" he asked suddenly, his voice low and gravelly, as if he had a sore throat.

Shocked, Hannah stared straight ahead, blinking rapidly. "Yes, he did. I think."

"You think? You don't know?"

"Yes, he did."

"You are beautiful."

She said nothing. Her mind had gone blank, as if an invisible eraser had wiped away any ability to speak or think. Now, how was she supposed to handle a situation like this?

"You've never had children?"

Stiffly, she told him they hadn't been married very long.

"Tell me about the West."

"It would take a long time to tell you about my life in North Dakota."

"Good. Then I'll come over this evening and we can talk about it."

"That wouldn't be proper."

"Why not?"

"Why would you? You have no interest in me."

"What makes you say that?

"You are going to New Holland. To town. If you . . . well, nothing."

"What?"

"Drive your horse. He's pulling toward the middle."

No more conversation was forthcoming. Her lips were sealed, as if padlocked. They drove into the town, tall brick buildings lining both sides of the street, automobiles parked on each side. Teal, blue, red, and silver trucks with metal racks or trucks with no racks at all. One gleaming vehicle contained one passenger wearing a white fedora and smoking a fat cigar, eyes half-closed in his wealthy insolence.

Hannah thought of the rusted out, dusty trucks of the West, wheezing and gasping, black smoke from overheated oil pans rolling behind them, loose wooden racks flapping like crows.

It took her a long time at the post office. The post master was a grizzled, stooped, and bent old man, his spectacles sliding down his nose with alarming regularity. His rheumy eyes examined her face as if he doubted her sincerity.

"Ball-ti-mer?"

"Yes, Baltimore. In Maryland."

He shook his head. "Big city."

"I know."

Shuffling to a back door, he returned with a dog-eared copy of telephone numbers from various states. Humming to himself, he pushed his glasses back up on his nose with an arthritic index finger.

Hannah shifted her weight from one foot to the other. She drummed on the countertop with her fingertips. She read every poster on the wall.

"You said Rocher, right?"

"Yes. Harold Rocher."

The humming resumed.

"If you'll let me . . ." Hannah began.

"No, no. I'm getting there. Rogers. Richard. Hmmm." Satisfied, he thumped the cover of the book and said, "Nope. Ain't no Rocher livin' in Bal-ti-mer."

"May I have a try?"

The bell above the door tinkled. It was Dave. Hannah looked up. "I'm going down a few blocks to the feed store. I'll be right back."

Hannah nodded.

"Look, I seriously need to locate this man. If you'll allow me to try . . ."

Reluctantly, the old post master handed over the book. Hannah found the Rocher's address and telephone number in a few minutes. She asked to use the telephone.

"Pay phone."

"That's all right. I need to contact this man."

Hannah dialed zero, spoke to an operator, and dropped the required amount of coins in the slot, waiting breathlessly until the third ring. She felt an unexpected rush of emotion when she heard Harry Rocher's compassionate voice. "Hello. Rocher's."

"Hello." Hannah swallowed, blinked back the moisture that filled her eyes. In a thick voice she said, "This is Hannah. Hannah Detweiler."

A pause. Then, "Hannah!" His voice took her back to his general store. Back to the scent of fabric and tools, coils of rope and plowshares and shovels, the dust, the blowing wind, the horse waiting in the shed till day's end. Then there was the long ride home across the blighted prairie clutching the staples that would keep her family alive, a bag of cornmeal and one of flour.

She bit her lip, blinked furiously, sniffed, and concentrated on a war bonds poster that said BUY U.S. BONDS.

"Hannah! Dear girl, how are you?"

"I'm fine. I'm living back in Lancaster County. I want to start up a dry goods store and I need information on wholesale companies," she said, her voice thick with unshed tears.

"You're back in Lancaster? That must have been hard. I know how much you loved that homestead. How's your mother?"

"She's good. She lives with her father, my grandfather."

"You know, we don't live so awfully far apart. My wife and I would love to come and look you up. Guess what I'm doing? Working in a restaurant as a chef!" His excitement rose above the static on the line. "I love it. Love it. In the evening, I walk down to the harbor, feed the gulls, and watch the water. It grows on you, Hannah. Human beings are resilient. We bounce back. Doris is a different person. Oh, you have no idea. She sings, the radio is always on, she dances and visits her parents every day. You know they're old. You know what I cook? Fish, scallops, shrimp in olive oil and garlic, lobster—all of the food that comes from the sea. I love it. I love it."

Hannah could barely get a word in edgewise to remind him about the information she needed.

"Oh yes, yes, of course. I'll send it to you. Still have it all. I'll put it in an envelope, one of those brown ones." And then he was on to more descriptions of his colorful life.

When Hannah finally placed the phone receiver back in its cradle, she had used up all of her dimes.

So, that was Harold Rocher's reward. He had given in, accepted his wife's unhappiness, and did something about it, even if it meant a huge sacrifice for him, leaving the place he truly loved.

She thanked the postmaster, who grunted in her general direction. Hannah thought he was too old to be a postmaster. Weren't there some kind of rules about that? Old grouch! He needed to go home, make himself a cup of tea, and cover his knees with a blanket.

She told Dave that the old guy at the post office had to be a hundred years old. He laughed, loosened the neck rope, and backed the carriage up by drawing gently on the reins and pushing against the shafts.

He asked if she was able to talk to the person she wanted to ask information from. Hannah nodded, watching the horse's ears.

He tried again to spark conversation. "The old guy not very efficient, huh?"

"Hmm-mm."

They rode back along Main Street, carefully avoiding parked cars and trucks as big as houses that bore down on them. The towering brick buildings were stacked together like bales of hay, wedged tight. Hannah fought the feeling of being smothered by too-tall buildings, an excess of motor vehicles and pedestrians, everyone moving, their faces expressionless, not making eye contact, as if actually meeting someone they knew would destroy their single-minded goal of keeping to their schedule.

She breathed deeply when the town slid away and open fields and forests met them in their natural state—green, brown, and a dull yellow.

Dave looked over at her. "You don't like the town?" he asked. "I heard you did not want to return to Pennsylvania."

A pinched, "You don't know."

He drove on whistling under his breath, watching the scenery to the right, wondering what had produced the bad mood of his passenger. He did want to stay for the evening and hear her story. He wanted to get to know her better, or at least try to understand her. There was no doubt, he was intrigued and captivated by her.

He did not try to keep a conversation going but merely drove his horse and ignored his glowering companion.

As they approached her house, she seemed to brighten a bit. She sat up straight as if the black mood had been left in New Holland at the post office. Until they reached the driveway.

"You can let me off and then leave. No need to turn in the drive." Her words were brittle and caustic.

Where Jerry would have agreed and gone on down the road thinking everything was all right and he'd bide his time, Dave put up an argument.

"You can snap out of it, Hannah. You have a lot of nerve getting all riled up by an old man who was doing the best he knew how. I didn't cause your bad mood and you're not taking it out on me."

Her mouth dropped open in surprise. She was not used to anyone standing up to her when she was in one of her black moods. She controlled her family with them. And she'd easily handled Jerry with them. When she was out of sorts, he made excuses for her and did anything he could to appease her. Only on a few occasions had he ever stood up to her. And here was this man, someone she barely knew, accusing her of wrongdoing, when it was all his fault.

His yellow gaze was not golden or warm and certainly did not cause her to go spinning off into a warm and lovely place of confusion. It was like a spark to gasoline. A clear, burning distaste for her behavior flickered from his amber scrutiny. A black blaze began in the depths of her own dark eyes. Without thinking she shot back, "Of course it's your fault!"

No one ever spoke to Dave King in that manner. Without giving her the benefit of an answer, he hauled back on the reins, the horse obediently lowering its haunches as it leaned against the britchment and pushed the carriage backward. A loosening of the reins in Dave's hands, a call to go forward with a hard tug to the left rein, and Hannah was conveyed unceremoniously to the stoop at the side of her house.

"Get out!"

Hannah got out. Stumbled out to be exact. She watched helplessly as he drove past her. She wanted to stamp her feet and yell at him to come back here right now because they had things to discuss. But it looked as if that would only make everything worse.

She didn't know whether she wanted him to leave or tie his horse. When she saw him climb down and unhitch—unhitch!—she was at a loss. What in the world? He had unhitched his horse, which meant he planned on a lengthy stay and not only an hour or so. In broad daylight! What if someone came?

Frantic now, she felt her knees weaken. Should she be afraid of this man? Embarrassed to be standing as if she had grown permanent roots down through the gravel, she kept her gaze on her shoe tops.

"Is your door locked?"

"No."

"Then I'll let myself in."

There was nothing to do but follow him in. He threw his hat on the table (didn't he know what clothes hooks were for?) and walked into the bathroom. He turned on the spigot and began soaping up, splashing water all the while.

Hannah did not know what to do. This big galumph marching into her house and using her bathroom as if he owned the place. Well, at least he washed. No one should ever drive a horse without washing their hands afterward.

He returned to find her standing by the table as if her one hand was nailed down on top. Her face was pale in the dreary afternoon light.

He pulled out a chair and sat down. As wide as the table. "All right, now. How was that mood my fault?" he asked.

"You're so dumb."

"Oh really. If I'm so dumb, you're sure you want me to go on with this addition?"

Not friendly. Not one word was meant to appease her, to make her feel better. She whirled away from the table, stomped down the hallway and was halfway to her bedroom, when she heard his footsteps like cast-iron pans thumping after her. Grasped firmly by his oversized hands, she was effectively stopped, then turned back toward the table, and not very gently.

"Just go on home," she breathed.

"Not until you tell me how this is my fault and why I am evidently extremely dense."

"Let me go!"

His hands fell away and immediately she felt their absence.

Her face was an open map of misery. He appeared calm, curious, settling slowly into his chair while Hannah collapsed into hers, her hands shaking.

Finally, she spoke. "All right, you asked, and I'll tell you how it is. If you drove to New Holland in broad daylight without caring at all if other Amish people saw us, it's obvious you have no interest in . . . in being my friend. Young widowers do not go sporting about town with widows their own age. You know that."

She could see he was amazed. Delighted, even. A broad grin creased his golden eyes, crow's-feet like combs on each side of his face, his smile spreading as he absorbed her words.

"So, you're upset that I'm not interested in you?"

"No. I mean, yes. Well, no. I just don't want people to talk. You know . . ."

"Well, I don't care what people say. Not now, not ever. I haven't in the past and I have no intention of beginning that bad habit. I live my life in the sight of God, trying to do what's right, and that's it.

"Am I interested in you? Should I be?" he finished. His eyebrows raised and his eyes were on her face.

He really should do something with that hair, Hannah was thinking. She kept her eyes somewhere along the top of his head, then let her eyelids fall, turning her gaze to her knees, which was the safest place with that look in his eyes.

He laughed outright. Reaching out, he touched her hand, then took it in his own. Her hands were not small, for a woman, but his engulfed hers like a baseball glove.

"Hannah, look at me."

When she did, the dark watching of her eyes melded with the amber search of his, creating a nameless space filled with light. She felt a complete knowing of his intentions, the goodness and depth of this man, the harmonious chord with the earth and its creatures, and God, above all. He would never need to mention his faith, or his love. It was all the same, forever.

After that, there were no words. The tug on her hand became an embrace as Hannah found herself held against that wide, deep chest, his arms holding her delicately as if he was cradling a small child.

He sighed. She felt his chest move, felt his breath on her hair. "Hannah, I am interested in you. You intrigue me. I want to know what makes you happy and sad and angry. But you know as well as I do that we both hold pain and fear. And you, it would seem, have a problem with telling the truth."

CHAPTER 21

THE LIGHT IN THE HOUSE SHONE OUT THROUGH THE RAIN. DAVE'S horse waited patiently in the shed. His ears flicked when two hands pulled on the window in the main house, lowering it against the falling rain. When nothing happened after that, he dozed off, to be awakened by two mice racing along the top pine board, squeaking, then tumbling off behind a few cardboard boxes.

Hannah and Dave sat at the kitchen table. Dave listened to her speak about North Dakota from her cache of memories. He watched her face, felt her sorrow, her joy, her helpless rage, every disaster and every disappointment that had seeped into her soul, creating who she had become. The only thing that bothered him was her senseless determination, the power she wielded by her own anger and selfishness, her family as compliant as bread dough.

As was his way, he told her this. A long silence followed. Then, "But I hated the thought of returning to Lancaster County."

"I know. And you were young. It's just that you and I getting together could be a full-on disaster! No one bosses me around. Lena was so mild, so meek in her spirit. And you . . ."

Suddenly, he asked why she'd married Jerry when her family returned to Pennsylvania. "His money," she answered. "The homestead couldn't go on without funds to start over after the drought."

"You didn't love him?"

Hannah turned her face away and shrugged her shoulders.

"That wasn't fair to him. Hannah, you use other folks for your own advantage."

"He wanted me. He agreed to everything. And he won me over, in the end."

"You loved him then?"

"I guess. I don't know. How can a person tell if they love someone?"

Dave was flummoxed, completely at a loss. Red flags of warning waved in the air, so real he could almost feel the breeze. He changed the subject, realizing that he needed time.

Together, they made a pot of chili with red kidney beans, ground beef, green peppers, and yellow onion. He added a can of corn, said he didn't like chili without it. She made a face, but he told her to try it. She'd probably never had it that way before.

He used a tablespoon to eat his chili. Hannah became worried that she may have underestimated the amount in the pot. He emptied all the soda crackers and ate a large bowl of applesauce. Taking out a pound of Lebanon bologna, he ate slice after slice on bread with mustard. Then he asked if she had pie or cake.

They washed and dried the dishes, side by side, talking about his interest in the construction world, how he got his start, and his plans for the future. She could see his incredible energy, his passion for his craft as she tried to understand his lack of interest in farming.

They parted late at night, each feeling the amiability between them, as well as the danger, the lack of trust. Did it make sense to try again after the flaws in their past? They circled, wary, their spirits eyeing one another, then moving back, yet drawn to each other by an invisible cord.

Hannah watched the mailbox for Harold's package almost as much as she watched Dave and his men as they erected the addition. It was amazing to watch the plate being bolted to the concrete that had been poured into the cement blocks. From there on it was like children building a house with Tinkertoys, except this was life-sized. Hammers swung, driving nails as if they were merely straight pins.

The roof was being put on the day her wholesale catalogs arrived. She left the package in the mailbox, not wanting Dave to see it. She wasn't talking to him, had avoided him all week. Allowing him to sit in her house and eat with her with all his oversized familiarity was going at breakneck speed down a steep, slippery slope. It would not happen again.

It was nice to feel her heart speed up as she remembered the feel of those massive arms being so careful of her. But there was always the memory of Jerry and her blatant mistreatment of him. Above all there was the humiliating truth that she didn't know what love was, or if she had ever been in love, or fallen in love—however you wanted to say it.

Very likely, if she were to marry Dave, it would be the same story. So it was safer, much safer, to stay away. He'd never asked her for a date, just sat in her house as big as a furnace and made himself at home. The amount of food he ate was alarming!

She thought of the size of her garden and the canning she would have to do. At least a hundred quarts of applesauce; perhaps a hundred and fifty. Would he eat an entire quart of canned peaches in one sitting?

Hannah snorted.

She worked on ordering supplies for her store with the help of her mother, who knew what type of fabrics the housewives would buy. Her grandfather kindly offered to finance some of her purchases, but Hannah waved him away. She was an independent woman, capable of managing her own affairs.

Ben and Elam worked on the shed in the back, converting it to a small horse barn, complete with a hydrant and underground water pipes from the new addition. They donated their old courting buggy, without a top, an open-seated, rattily old thing that suited Hannah just fine.

John Esh came to see what the addition was for, the nosy old thing. But then, she figured word would have to get around if she wanted any business, so she'd better train her thoughts along a more hospitable line. People like John Esh irked her so badly. Swaggering up to the carpenters with half the manure from his cow stable stuck to his cracked leather shoes, at least a week's growth of stubble on his cheeks. She was certain that the bulge on one side of his face wasn't a toothache. She'd been around too many tobacco-chomping ranchers to miss that wad of brown, juice-producing plug.

"Well, Davey!" he had boomed that day, his voice bringing her to the window immediately. It was as if he was announcing a hurricane!

Dave stopped his work and came over to him, pushing his hat to the back of his head, a huge grin on his face.

Hannah stepped back from the window. He liked this man. Well, good for him. Dave knocked on the back door and told her John had a horse for sale, a brown standard bred he'd sell for a hundred dollars.

Hannah drew down her eyebrows and said nothing for a while. Then, "Not without seeing him."

Smiling, Dave said, "I'll ask him to bring the horse over. He lives a few miles from here." Hannah nodded. When there was no returning smile, Dave went back to John, wondering why Hannah still intrigued him with that terrible attitude of hers.

Hannah's words were clipped, almost nonexistent as she negotiated the sale of the horse, a small, brown gelding with a white star on his forehead and one white foot.

John Esh began by touting the merits of his wonderful horse, smiling too much with that lopsided, swollen cheek. She told him the horse looked like a camel and surely needed to be wormed.

"Aw, come on. Now you're just driving a hard bargain, lady." His grin widened, eyes sparkling.

"I won't pay a hundred dollars. He's not worth it."

Taken aback, John Esh's smile puckered like a released rubber band, his mouth becoming pinched as a pained expression crossed his face. He made the usual mistake most folks made when they came in contact with her cold glare.

He smiled, wheedled, bowed, scraped, did anything to get back into her good graces, which had never been present to begin with. "I'll throw a harness in for a hundred."

"No doubt it won't be worth it, the way your shoes look."

John looked down at his offending shoes with beginnings of a fiery blush creeping up his neck.

In the end, she got her way. A horse, a harness that was perfectly serviceable, all for the frugal cost of one hundred dollars. She also got the boiling disapproval of Dave King, coupled with a vow to make restitution to that poor man, John Esh. She was planning on being the proprietor of a store? Well, he was having a talk with her.

Which he did, arriving unexpectedly on Saturday morning, his day off. He caught her off guard, downstairs cleaning the basement, wearing an old *dichly* over her uncombed hair that had not been washed for the better part of a week.

Dust swirled around her as she plied the coarse straw broom. A horrendous pounding on the side door propelled her up the steps, her heart racing, certain there was some emergency or calamity in the neighborhood.

Dave King.

She stopped and glared. "What?"

"Don't you ever use a normal good morning or hello?" he asked, his eyes not friendly, the brim of his straw hat serving to enhance his hostility. Almost, she shivered.

"Depends on who it is."

"So, I don't merit a greeting? Obviously, that poor John Esh didn't either." He pushed past her, threw his hat on a peg, went up the steps like a steaming locomotive and put the kettle on. Hannah followed, completely at a loss for words.

How dare he? She hadn't even invited him in. She certainly had not offered him a cup of tea, or whatever he had in mind with that teakettle. And he was angry! About John Esh.

She sat down. Then she remembered the dust in the cellar and got up and closed the door. She stood hesitantly, like a truant scholar, unsure what the teacher was going to say.

"Sit down."

She sat.

"You know, Hannah, if you are going to be operating a store, this simply is not going to work."

"What?"

"You don't like people. If you treat one customer the way you treated John Esh, word will get around and you won't have one person coming to buy your fabric. I don't care how nice it is or how low it's priced. You were rude, ill-mannered, ignorant, and downright mean. It's uncalled for."

Hannah leaped to her feet. "Out! Get out! It is none of your business how I choose to treat people."

Coolly, he looked at her in the brilliant morning sunlight that slanted in through the kitchen window, the snarls in her uncombed hair, the crooked *dichly*, the dust that had collected at the edge of each flaring nostril, turning them black. He took in her heaving chest and her steaming anger.

"Yes. It is. I'm working for you. I'm building your store. You are going to be out of business before you even begin. Take my advice, Hannah. Otherwise, your store is a lost cause."

"Get out of my kitchen!"

"No. The water isn't boiling and I'd like a cup of tea."

Emotions crashed and collided in Hannah's mind. She knew he was right. He also made her so mad that she wanted to punch him. Physically pound him with her fists. Helplessness fought with her anger and spilled over to quench his attraction. The sheer muscular size of the man, his arms and shoulders, his eyes and oh, just everything. She couldn't go marching out of his sight the way she'd done that once because that would mean he'd come after her and . . .

What she did do was slide back down into her chair. Thrusting her legs under the table, she crossed her arms while leaning against the chair back, adjusting her famous glare, her lips pulled in and pinched tightly together.

He got down two cups and found the tin canister of tea. Hannah had always been able to control those around her. Her inability to dominate Dave, to conquer him, tilted her whole world toward the steep slope of confusion. Even now, she scrambled to understand her thoughts.

What if she tried his way of dealing with people? Wouldn't it be a sort of protection? If the store failed, it wouldn't be her fault—it would be his, for convincing her to behave differently. It would be a kind of barrier against failure and disappointment. Of course, it would all be fake. She'd have to pretend to like people, which she really didn't—especially men.

Dave poured the tea and brought it to the table. He asked if there was pie. "It's nine o'clock. My break time."

"It's your day off. And I don't take a break."

He chose to ignore the winds off her iceberg. Going into the pantry, he lifted tops off containers until he found half of an apple pie. Yodeling with appreciation, he brought it to the table, going to the cupboard to find plates, a knife, and forks.

"Got any cheese? Apple pie is twice as good with cheese."

"I don't know."

"You don't know if you have cheese? Or you don't know if you like it with apple pie?

"Oh, shut up!"

He laughed. She liked the sound of his laugh. Like gravel rolling over stones. "You don't like me, either. Well, we'll just have to work on that."

He ate the entire remains of that pie plus the slice he'd set out for her, which she refused to touch. He ate almost a pound of Swiss cheese, and drank his tea in three gulps.

It was scary, his capacity for food!

He pushed the dishes away and crossed his arms on the table. She wished he wouldn't do that, the way his muscles bulged and all those blue veins ran up over his hands like trails.

"So," Dave asked. "Why do you dislike people like John Esh? The poor man. It was worse than seeing a cat play with a mouse, torturing it before the kill."

"It wasn't that bad," Hannah shot back.

"It sure was."

Hannah had no reply.

"It's un-Christian. The Lord tells us to love our neighbors as ourselves and you sure don't hate yourself."

"There you go, getting all preachy."

"You need to be preached to. You need to go to church and learn the ways of a Christian. Your attitude toward others is worldly. You're all about yourself, just like the world."

"You know, you aren't really being a good Christian yourself, sitting here numbering my faults like some sort of self-righteous Pharisee."

"You think?" He laughed again, the sound she had to admit she loved. "I guess you're right, Hannah. I'm just concerned about your business is all. Plus . . ." His voice became very deep, cross-grained with feeling. "I would love to spend the rest of my life with you. I'm not one to cover anything up for pride's sake. I say what I think and feel. You are so terribly attractive, but I'm afraid of your . . . well, Hannah, you're just not a nice person."

"Thanks!"

"I'm trying to figure out why."

Hannah took a deep breath. She avoided his eyes and shook her head. Then, "You try being shamed and humiliated, cast out of all you know at the tender age of twelve. Riding in an old spring wagon with a tarp thrown over its ribs, with two old worm-ridden horses, a *schputt*!

"People either made fun of us or pitied us. I had a ghost-like mother who floated above the wagon, never really present. A father who was crazy in the head. We were hungry, Dave. Hungry!"

For a long moment, he said nothing. The clock on the shelf ticked loudly. A drip from the faucet echoed through the silence.

Then he said, "Boo-hoo."

Thinking she hadn't heard right, she said, "What?!"

"I said, boo-hoo."

Furious, she spat out, "Now *you're* making fun of me!"

"Yes, I am. You're the shining example of someone who blames their parents for the not-so-nice person you are today. That was in the past. It's over. Get over it. Forgive and forget and move on. Live a life free from all that garbage. God allowed all that in your life, so evidently there is a purpose.

"You know, Hannah, did you ever think that all the cruel weather, hunger, drought, all that stuff you told me, could have been avoided if you would have obeyed your mother and come back home to Lancaster where she wanted you to be? Did you ever think about the children of Israel's wandering in the desert when they were led by Moses, a man of God? Same thing. God could have led them all in a straight shot to the Promised Land, but He led them through trials and awful crazy stuff to teach them lessons. If they refused to learn, they perished!

"If you never learn to move on and stop blaming that godly mother of yours, or your imperfect father, you'll never get any further than being in your own tight cocoon, spun by a web of your own making, a dark prison where you sit and glower at other people with hate-filled eyes like you did to John Esh."

She said nothing, running her forefinger around the rim of her teacup.

"It may be cruel to speak to you like this, but I have a strong hunch no one ever had the backbone to do it before. Am I right?"

"Jerry did, some."

"Bless Jerry's heart. He must have been a great guy."

"He was." What kept her from pouring her heart out, confessing her mistreatment of Jerry and her ongoing remorse? She knew Dave deserved to hear it from her. How did he know . . . ?

She blurted out, "How do you know my mother was godly? Still a saint?"

"I had a long talk with her at your husband's funeral. I wanted to marry her, except for her age."

Hannah's mouth dropped open. "My mother? But . . ."

"I would have, except for you."

She stared at him, uncomprehendingly. "What are you talking about?"

"I'm teasing." He reached across the table and draped his enormous hand over hers. "I wasn't interested in your mother the same way I am in you. But she did remind me of what Lena would have been like had she lived to your mother's age. Your mother's a good woman, Hannah. It wouldn't kill you to admit it."

Hannah pulled her hand away, returning it safely to her lap. He had no idea what her family was like, no idea what she'd been through. He barely knew her, and it was probably better to keep it that way.

The weekend was spent alone, the last cloying heat of August making Hannah even more miserable than she already was. All Dave had told her banged around in her head, giving her a tremendous, pounding headache until she put her fingers on either side of her head and groaned with the pain. She shed her clothes and went to lie down on her bed. But there wasn't even the whisper of a breeze, the curtains hanging stiff and straight, the air sultry with humidity.

She should have gone to church at Levi Stoltzfus's. Her mother would be disappointed by her absence. Manny would be searching the rows of women, eager to spot her face among them. But she hadn't felt up to dressing in her heavy black garments, with all the turmoil going on in her head, not to mention the steady weeping of her heart.

What if Dave's words were true? All that suffering, and all her fault? No, he hadn't said it that way. He'd merely stated the obvious. Could she have avoided it all? Of course, but she wanted the homestead. She had been determined to keep it. The truth was her life had also been enriched. The wind, the wide-open spaces, her communion with earth and sky. She'd come to know the weather patterns intimately, all as diverse as human faces.

She'd found reserves of strength and courage she could never have imagined. She'd loved and lost and yes, she had also learned. And here, her face burned with shame.

She had risen to her former level of dictator-like cruelty with her *grosfeelich* treatment of John Esh. Right in front of Dave.

Well, Dave didn't understand. It was all that manure on John Esh's shoes. That wad of tobacco in his cheek. Let Dave go and marry her mother. Hannah was certainly never going to be like Lena, the "perfect wife," his little angel. If that's what he wanted, he better keep looking. The man had no social graces himself. Every word out of his mouth served to put her in her place. It was like herding a good milk cow into a stanchion.

She tried to picture herself running the store, acting like she enjoyed people. She imagined John Esh coming into her store as she smiled sweetly and asked him to please wipe his feet. She could put a spittoon in her fabric shop. She could do it. Couldn't she?

She got up, shrugged into her dress, squinted into the mirror, and decided she looked old and mad and ugly. She pulled her mouth back into the caricature of a smile but felt she looked a lot like the witch in *Grimms' Fairy Tales*.

Why did he have to say that about her mother? He had said he was teasing, but she wasn't sure. Why wouldn't a man want a sweet, submissive, pushover wife instead of a mean-spirited, stubborn woman like Hannah? When she imagined her mother and Dave together she was taken captive by a fierce jealousy, one that made her want to slap them both.

Finally, when the heat became too oppressive, her thoughts as heavy as rocks, she dressed in her black Sunday garments, hitched up the brown gelding, and drove. She drove out to the Old Philadelphia Pike and turned right toward Bird-in-Hand, the small village where she believed her friend Priscilla had moved after marrying Abner Beiler.

She waved at oncoming teams, practicing the friendly gestures she had never much cared for. It felt fake, like she were pretending to be another person entirely. She allowed her eyes to glass over, giving her a sense of anonymity, as if she were a wax figure or a see-through spirit.

The sun beat down on the black bonnet that covered her head. Her black clothes grabbed at the fierce sun and held its heat to her skin. The horse (she still had to name him), a gallant, willing animal, kept up an even trot, the white foam that sprang from his sweating hide a testimony to her lack of a good washing before she had thrown the harness on his back.

Everywhere she looked there were farms or houses, sheds, automobiles, people in buggies. A black car roared past with a young boy hanging out of the window, his nose pinched between a thumb and forefinger, gesticulating, mimicking the smell of her, the horse and buggy, or both.

Hannah longed for a handful of ripe horse manure to stuff in his face, until she remembered she was pretending to be nice.

Well, what of it? She was only who she was—no more and no less—and thoughts couldn't hurt someone anyway, right? Could she help it if little boys like that made her want to retaliate? She wasn't a saint. She wasn't her mother, either. And she certainly wasn't Lena. If she was smart, she'd never give that arrogant Dave King the opportunity to compare the two of them.

She rode through the village of Bird-in-Hand, eyeing houses, going under the train tracks that ran over the arch of cement and stone bolstered by sturdy iron and tons of concrete, she hoped. She pulled on the right rein, on a whim, thinking she'd take a side road and find some shade to allow her horse a rest. Perhaps there'd be a passerby from time to time and she could inquire about Priscilla Beiler's whereabouts.

The horse slowed to a walk, then stood obediently beneath a canopy of maple branches with leaves like a heavy, green cloak, stirring faintly as if afraid to disturb the heat. Hannah loosened the neck rein on the horse, then fanned her face with her apron, finally wiping it across her neck and cheeks to dry her streaming perspiration. She scanned the hot, metallic sky for signs of a cooling thundershower, but there was none, not the slightest indication of relief.

There were no passersby, no one walking, not a buggy or a car in sight. She didn't want to knock on doors to make inquiries, so she drove home in the stifling heat, a strange melancholy settling over her shoulders.

It was odd, this being alone among so many people. She had always relished isolation, but that was different, in North Dakota. To be alone on a great and glorious prairie was to be one with nature and the earth and God—all the same thing.

Here, she was alone, while others walked or rode together, sat down together at mealtime, drinking and eating and sharing their lives.

She sighed and decided to name her horse Flapper for the way his loose haunches flapped when he ran. Flap for short. "I guess it's just you and me, Flap," she said, thinking she was glad for a companion who couldn't berate her, question her, tell her she was a bad Christian or how poorly she compared to other people.

CHAPTER 22

Hannah's store was open for business on the twentieth of September. She stood behind the counter, the green metal cash box below her on a shelf, a small, speckled composition book to tally the day's sales beside her.

The room was almost square with white painted shelves along every wall, and a wide counter down the center of the room. The windows along three sides allowed plenty of natural light to enter, illuminating the area where women would inspect the various bolds of plain and patterned *duchsach* with calculating eyes.

Buttons, thread, bias tape, rickrack, elastic, needles, straight pins, hooks, and eyes. The list was endless. Manny had made small wooden bins to hold the notions. He'd painted them blue and brought them one Friday evening, as a surprise.

Sarah donated her best pair of Wiss fabric-cutting scissors. Hannah refused, at first, saying, "No, no, Mam. Not your Wiss scissors." But she knew they would make her task easier.

She would sell scissors in the future, but stocking her shelves had taken almost the whole of her bank account. Harold Rocher had given her access to some of the best textile mills in the Northeastern United States, so she was set to make a profit.

Dave King had been paid in full, the check handed over to him without fanfare, her face a cold mask. She had spoken only what was absolutely necessary until his part of the deal was over. And that was how things stayed.

He went home shrugging his shoulders and telling himself she could take him the way he was or stay alone. She told herself she had had enough of being told off. He could wash his own dishes and live by himself. She'd never be sweet and submissive, and if she didn't like people, well, he wasn't going to dig up some deep psychological reason for it that would only make her feel worse.

She welcomed her first customer, Sadie Lapp, a thin-as-a-rail spinster with a nose like a parrot's beak and a squawk to match. She roamed the store with a condescending air, asked dozens of questions that Hannah answered politely, although with an air of stretched martyrdom. Sadie bought one yard of white covering organdy, holding on to every dollar as long as she possibly could, counting out her own change twice, then folding the coins in a tiny leather packet. She lifted her apron and rummaged in her pocket to make sure the purse was beneath the large men's handkerchief nestling there, which had been used and reused, if her horrendous, honking, nose-blowing was any indication.

The effort to stay amiable drained Hannah. She stood behind the counter, her arms feeling like dishrags as she took slow, easy breaths.

All forenoon, then, women arrived. Some were brought by their husbands. Others drove teams themselves. Babies were slung on hips, carried around by strong arms attached to muscular shoulders. Big women, some of them. Big and rangy and uglier than a mud fence. But friendly, openly excited about Hannah Riehl's store.

At first, the smile she plastered on her face felt awkward and every bit as fake as it was. But as customers commented on her nice selection and her cash box began to fill, a natural excitement lit up her countenance. Her cheeks turned pink, a rosy glow surrounding her as she dropped coins into the metal box and folded dollar bills carefully, laying them down neatly as she did so.

"Do you have quilting thread?"

"No snap buttons? The kind you sew on?"

"Where's the chambray?"

Each time, Hannah was able to help, showing them the item. If there was something she didn't have, she wrote it on a tablet, to be ordered immediately.

At the end of the day, she had a little over sixty dollars in her cash box. Sixty dollars was wealth far beyond her imagination. She needed to keep it stowed away. Most of the money would go back into buying inventory.

She was sweeping the floor when the door was pushed open barely wide enough to allow two small girls to enter the store. Wide-eyed, their cherubic faces were both frightened and adventurous. They slipped in like a soft breeze, then stood uncertainly, staring at her.

"Hello," Hannah said, setting her broom against a shelf.

"Good evening." They spoke in low, well-modulated voices, sounding much older than their size. Hannah was held in the grip of two pairs of very blue eyes.

"May I help you find something?" she asked.

"Our brother is sick with chicken pox." The oldest girl cleared her throat. "Our mam sent us to see if you have baking soda and Epsom salts." The words were spoken clearly, without the usual lisp of a child.

Hannah shook her head. "I'm sorry, but I don't have those things in my store. Only fabric and other things that are used for sewing clothes."

Hannah was pinned behind the counter with a clear blue gaze. "You should. Mothers need those things sometimes."

Hannah agreed quickly. What was it with these small children holding her directly responsible for her lack of wisdom? "I have both of those things in the house if your mother would like to borrow them."

"Yes, she would like to."

Hannah hurried to the medicine cabinet in the bathroom and came back with both items. The girls were rooted to the same spot, just inside the door, their feet as still as if someone had nailed them there.

"You can just take these containers. I have more. Then you can return them sometime later," she told them.

"I think that would not suit my mam. Please pour some in a small poke and we will pay for it with the money she gave us."

Feeling as if she was under some strict requirement from a judge to obey them, Hannah did as she was told, without argument. She charged them twenty-five cents, which the girl handed over without hesitation, staring up at Hannah with unwavering blue eyes.

"Thank you."

With that, the girls turned and left, leaving her with the distinct feeling that she had fallen short. What odd little girls.

Well, she had met all sorts of women today, starting with that first old maid, Sadie Lapp, and ending with the two little girls. She was bone-weary. Her shoulders ached with a deep dull throb and her neck was stiff. She leaned her head from side to side and worked her shoulders to loosen them, smiling at the ceiling.

Cash. She had all that cash. She would label her first day a success. What a turn her life had taken now.

She swept the floor, surveying her small store with a sense of satisfaction. She knew her job at the hardware store in Pine had been for a reason. She had never imagined that those days spent arranging shelves and cleaning for Doris were anything other than a necessity, a means of survival.

Like Harold, she, too, lived now in an area she had been fiercely opposed to, but she was learning that it was possible to become accustomed to another environment, another way of life entirely. Going to church, interacting with strangers—women of her own faith but strangers nevertheless—seeing her mother and siblings, living among a close-knit community held together by a patchwork of fields and crops, clusters of woods, ribbons of creeks, all crisscrossed with roads and dotted with towns. This area was a beehive of energy, swarming with all sorts of human beings, the exact opposite of the vast open land with only waving grasses and the wind for company, the air as clear and pure as she imagined Heaven's to be.

She shook her head to clear her thoughts, then let herself out the door to feed Flap. He nickered, welcoming her presence, shook his head up and down as if to remind her that it was high time for a feeding. She scratched his forehead and told him he was a faithful steed. Common looking as all get out, but faithful.

He needed a pasture, a small plot of grass to eat. A place to kick up his heels and get some exercise in between his jaunts on the road. She could do it. She would have to put in some posts, but she'd seen it done plenty of times. She'd watched the Jenkins boys dig holes and set posts. All she'd need were locust posts and a few rolls of barbed wire. That meant she needed to make a trip to the neighbors to use their telephone to call the sawmill and she'd need to go to Zimmerman's Hardware for the barbed wire. She wished she could talk to someone about the cost.

Would a hundred dollars be enough? She couldn't use the sixty she already had. That needed to be set aside for new inventory. For a moment, she wished for a partner to help with all these things, but then she stopped herself. All that bowing to someone else's will, negotiating every problem that presented itself . . . it simply wasn't worth it.

The cold winds of autumn were already rustling the brilliant fall foliage by the time Hannah began digging post holes. Her work at the store kept her from ordering the posts immediately and then the delivery took an abominably long time. She knew she could wait until spring, but in her own driven way, she began digging until her fingers were covered in painful blisters that popped, exposing the tender layer of skin beneath. Still, she kept digging, her fingers covered with white adhesive tape, setting posts with aching shoulders, tamping down the dirt around them with a heavy digging iron. Blood seeped from beneath the adhesive tape, mixing with dirt and perspiration, but she kept on working feverishly every evening as the daylight hours became less and less.

She fell into bed, exhausted. Her back and shoulders burned with fatigue, her fingers and the palms of her hands throbbed with pain. Far into the night she lay awake, turning miserably, trying her best to lay her hands in a comfortable position. She thought about the cash she had from her store and wished she had a dog. It would be extremely comforting to know that a good watchdog would alert her to any prowlers.

Every morning she turned her face into a smiling, friendly shine, washed the painful blisters, and applied fresh adhesive tape. She hid her pain and bit back the winces that came unbidden.

That evening, she stopped digging and stood surveying her accomplishments. She still had over half of them to go. The pain in her left hand was excruciating. The dull ache had turned into a biting, heated thumping that made her sit down, unwrap a strand of tape, and hold her hand up to the golden autumn sunset.

Her whole hand was grotesquely swollen now. Bewildered, she lowered it, clutching it with her right hand and trying to decide what she should do.

Slowly, she got to her feet, only to find a horse and buggy turning in her driveway. It stopped at the shed, the driver remaining seated. Hannah turned her back to pick up the shovel and digging iron, rolled the offending, bloodied adhesive tape into a clump of grass, and turned to make her way to the visitor. Was it someone needing something from the store?

When Dave King stepped out of the buggy, she thought he might turn it on its side with all his weight hanging on one side. Now what did he want?

Irritation did its best to quench her gladness at the sight of him. So, he had come. Her heart pounded. She willed her painful, swollen hand out of her thoughts and marched ahead, gamely carrying the digging iron and shovel.

"What are you trying to do?" Came right to the point, didn't he?

"What do you mean, trying? What does it look like?"

"Tell me you're not digging fence post holes!"

Closer now, setting her tools against the side of the shed, she faced him. She'd forgotten the warmth of his eyes and the line of wrinkles on the side of his face. Now what was she supposed to do as she was caught under the spell of his golden eyes?

"I am building a fence." She spoke firmly, expertly, hiding away any trace of quivering, her heart pounding in her throat.

"By yourself?" He flung this over his shoulder as he tied his horse to the steel ring on the side of the shed.

"Who else?"

"You should have asked me. I'd gladly help you."

"I can build a fence."

He walked over to the first post, grasped it with both hands, and shook it. It seemed fairly stable, or so it seemed to Hannah.

He said nothing and she asked no questions. They both let well enough alone. If he thought the fence posts inadequate, he kept it to himself. She was not about to ask what he thought, either.

"How have you been, Hannah?"

The wind played with the strands of loose hair, tossed the ends of her black scarf. She wore no coat although the air felt chilly now that the day was coming to an end. "All right."

"Store going well?"

"So far."

After that bit of mundane conversation, words eluded them. Both seemed unsure, stripped of their usual lack of inhibition. For one thing, Hannah felt weak with the pain of her hand, her head spinning as the throbbing worsened.

"I'm going inside."

"May I come with you?"

"Up to you." She stepped inside and sagged into a chair, hoping the shadowed kitchen would mask the extreme pain she was enduring. He stood awkwardly, unsure of his welcome.

Hannah knew it was not going to work. She was so close to tears that she blurted out, "My hand is infected, I think."

"Let me see."

She thrust out her painful hand, swollen and discolored. He moved away from the sink and took her hand in his. Turning it over he bent his head to examine it more closely. He emitted a low whistle.

"You know this could be dangerous, don't you?"

She nodded.

"Why did you keep on going with these blisters?"

"Because I wanted to finish the fence."

He shook his head and thought of pliant Lena, who would never have started such a project. She would have left all the physical labor to him while she sat down in the soft, sweet grass with the gold of autumn surrounding her. She would have admired him and he would have known he was deeply loved and respected for his masculine strength.

Here was another type of woman entirely. Should he help her with her badly infected hand, then leave and never return? All this circled around in his thoughts as he held her hand. Gruffly, he released her hand and said, "Wood ashes."

She shook her head. "I don't have any."

"Kerosene?"

She nodded yes.

So he soaked her hand in a dish of smelly kerosene, washed it with a mixture of homemade lye soap and boric acid, followed by a liberal dose of drawing salve, black, oily, and vile.

Hannah wrinkled her nose. She was close to tears watching his huge fingers with their fingernails the size of a small spoon, spreading the salve, tearing strips of fabric, and then winding them round and round her painful hand with so much care and precision. The thick curly head of hair above the hulking shoulders with yet another discolored, torn shirt, the perpetual scent of new lumber and soap . . .

"Thank you," she whispered.

He drew back and looked at her with a depth in his gaze, changing his eyes from gold to a deep, murky green that churned with strong feelings of . . . of what? What, exactly, was this?

Neither one understood. For one thing, they barely liked one another. He disapproved of her flagrant determination, her undermining of a man's strength. Her uncanny ability to make him feel worthless, the opposite of his first wife's adoration.

She could not bend him to her will the way she manipulated everyone else most of the time. There was nothing ordinary, nothing normal, between them. Yet, there was this unexplained draw toward one another.

Why did she occupy his thoughts most of the time? He knew it was foolhardy, this hitching up of his horse and driving to her house with no clear purpose. No speech, no prepared words to make his intent clear. You simply did not ask Hannah for a date. She'd laugh in his face and tell him no while enjoying his discomfiture.

She drew back, both of their thoughts driving a wedge between them.

"You know you'll have to repeat that in the morning," he stated, gruffly.

"Not kerosene."

"I'll bring you wood ashes."

"Aren't you going to church?"

"You will obviously not be going."

She nodded. The silence settled between them. Darkness crept over the kitchen. She got up, intent on lighting kerosene lamps, but could not strike a match.

"Here, let me do it."

She stepped aside. The soft yellow glow of the lamplight surrounded them, creating a coziness, a space where home and togetherness joined to form remembered evenings spent with loved ones.

Suddenly, Hannah spoke. "I'll need a fire before long. I wasn't sure if I wanted to bother with wood. I thought maybe I'd try coal. The only thing that keeps me from buying a coal stove is the thought of the harmful gas that can poison the air at night."

"Well, you can't dump a whole bucket of coal on a low fire and turn the damper too low. That's what causes it."

She pondered this. "So, you think wood is best?"

"Not really. With wood, you have the chimney to keep clean and sometimes there's a creosote problem. I'm thinking you wouldn't attempt climbing onto the roof to clean the chimney."

"Why not?"

"Because you might fall and break a leg. Or your back. Or worse, fall on your head and die."

Hannah snorted. Would he care? But she didn't ask.

The evening was turning into a ridiculous word play that didn't sufficiently provide a base for any meaningful conversation.

Finally, after a few self-conscious attempts at repeating bits of daily news and gossip, Dave asked if she didn't drink coffee or tea, or if she had lost the practice of offering some to visitors.

"Get it yourself."

Without answering, he got up to put the kettle on. He sank back into his chair and decided it was now or never. They were getting nowhere and he was afraid of confrontation or of stating his purpose—a state he had never experienced until he met Hannah.

"All right. The reason I came over tonight was to ask what you would say to beginning a regular, every Sunday evening courtship."

"I hate that word," Hannah blurted out.

"Well, friendship then. Relationship. Dating. Getting to know each other better. I don't care what you call it."

When there was no response from her, he let well enough alone and got up to get a few cups, the milk and sugar. He began opening cupboard doors as he searched for tea.

"Left," she directed him.

They sat with their steaming cups on the table. Dave pressed on. "I wasn't planning this, Hannah. But I can't get you out of my mind. So I figure we'll keep going with each other's company so we can find out if we want to get married some day. Isn't that what courtship is? What's wrong with that word?"

Hannah shrugged. "I don't know." Then, "I had an uncle who sang a silly song about froggie went a-courtin', and every time I hear that song I imagine a long-legged, slimy bullfrog like what Manny used to catch and throw at me."

Dave's laughter broke the restraint around them both.

"You're a prairie girl."

"I am. But I can't live there. I had to let the homestead go."

Dave shook his head, his heart in his eyes.

"It was the hardest thing I've ever done. To give up, let go, admit defeat, that was excruciating. I'm not sure if I'll ever get over it. I tell myself this is home, this is where I belong. Anywhere you have a home is your own personal space and you can be happy there. The store is a challenge, and it's fun to see if I can make a profit. But you wouldn't believe how tired I am at the end of the day from being nice to people. Smiling, you know. Helping people. It wears me down. All of this artificial smiling when I'd love to tell that Sadie Lapp to go home, wash under her arms, and eat a piece of cake to sweeten her up. It doesn't matter how hard I try. I just don't enjoy people."

Suddenly, she looked at him with an almost beseeching expression. "Do I always have to live here? I mean, I enjoy being close to my family, but I feel so . . . well, caged in."

"I thought you liked it here."

She pondered his statement, swirling her tea with a teaspoon, biting her lower lip. He could tell she was trying to say what she felt, but could not come to grips with her pride.

"Well, I do, I guess. But if I think of being here until I'm like Sadie Lapp, old and thin and tight and mean, well, I won't do it. You say you want to start a friendship. Does that mean here? No hope of ever moving somewhere, anywhere, where there are wide-open spaces and fewer people but decent weather? I mean, out West the weather is unpredictable. You can't win. Jerry did his best and he could have made it if anyone could have. But those grasshoppers were the final straw. It was the worst time of my life. And yet, it turned me toward Jerry, to . . ." Her voice drifted off.

Dave watched her face and wondered what the truth about that marriage had been. He didn't want that kind of marriage for himself. He was a builder, a carpenter by trade. It was all he knew. He had always planned to do that until the day he died. A few sentences out of her mouth and he was questioning his own vocation.

"I saw in the newspaper at the post office that folks are raising turkeys in Illinois. Amish people started a colony there. What is Illinois like, I wonder?" She spoke tentatively, gauging his reaction.

Dave watched her face. He saw the desperation of a captive suddenly grasping at a glimmer of hope, a ray of light illuminating her dark existence.

"You're serious."

"Of course. If I continue to wait on customers I'll become physically ill from the effort. It's just not me. It's not who I am. Look, this is how it is. I'm a loner. I don't need people and they don't need me. Call it what you want, I don't care. Perhaps I'm not a born-again Christian the way other people are. Sometimes I wonder if I need some spiritual conversion, but I can't be who I'm not. I have no desire to put on a false front so people accept me."

She launched into a vivid account of the two strange little girls and how she scuttled off to supply the items they requested. It was so unlike herself. She should have told them she didn't sell health remedies in a fabric store and to go home and stop bossing her around.

She finished with, "So, it's up to you. If you want me, this is what you get. Life has often handed me a bunch of sour grapes and I like to think I'm improving, year after year. But one thing I know. God knows me and He knows my heart. He gave me this nature so He'll have to help me as I go along."

Dave sat quietly, watching her as she finished her impassioned speech. Then, he got to his feet, found her hands, and tugged her upright. He held her hands, then released them and reached for her with both arms. He held her against his chest in a vice-like grip that took her breath away.

Lifting her chin, he gazed into her eyes in the soft glow of the kerosene lamp. He kissed her, sealing their commitment with the soft pressure of his lips on hers. He drew her closer still until Hannah was filled with the golden light of his love, a sensation that felt new and unexplored, promising a vast, sun-filled land of happiness.

CHAPTER 23

THEY WERE MARRIED IN A SMALL CEREMONY ON THE HOMESTEAD, her grandfather's farm. The stone house rang with *hochzeit velssa*, the traditional wedding songs. The tables were loaded with *roasht*, stewed sweet and sour celery, mashed potatoes, and gravy.

Some said Dave King wasted no time after he met that strange widow, Hannah Riehl, and her husband not long gone. Youthful spinsters pursed their lips, conceding to the loss of yet another available widower.

The more generous in spirit rejoiced with Dave, recognizing the aura of happiness surrounding the couple. Everyone could tell that he had met his match, the brooding Hannah no one really knew. It was a mystery. Who knew what went on in that dark head behind those penetrating eyes.

Sarah had never seen such loveliness and she cried for Hannah. Manny sat with Marybelle and counted the months until next November when she would become his bride. When the strawberries bloomed in spring, he would place his hand on hers and ask her to be his wife.

A week after Manny's wedding, Dave and Hannah moved to Illinois. He built low turkey barns on a vast area of almost three hundred acres of rolling grassland, and raised turkeys by the hundreds.

The farm was located in Central Illinois, close to the town of Falling Springs, with no neighbors in sight. An established Amish settlement, each family had the pioneering spirit, but in an area that had a far more hospitable climate than Hannah had experienced out West.

They paid less for their three hundred acres then they would have for a much smaller plot back in Lancaster County, and Hannah was able to sell her own house quickly and for a good price. They moved into the small, clapboard house. The sun shone and the winds of winter whistled around the corners like good-natured ghosts. Hannah sang and twirled, whistled and hummed her way through the days, embracing her husband and kissing him soundly at every opportunity. She fell in love deeply and thoroughly.

Hannah missed him when he was gone and threw herself into his arms when he returned. She noticed the colors in the winter sky, the deep blue shadows of the snow drifts, and told her husband she loved him every evening and every morning.

They held heated discussions. Dave was like a boulder, rock-solid and immovable. He made the decisions about the turkey barns, no matter how she railed against the idea. She pouted like a spoiled child, so he whistled his way through his days and ignored her, until she knew her silence wasn't going to change anything.

The first shipment of turkey poults arrived late that spring. Hannah stood in the middle of the sweet-smelling wood shavings and released them from their cardboard prisons, murmuring as she held them to her cheeks. Poor, frightened little birds, having to crouch in those awful cardboard boxes without food or water. She spent all day teaching the frightened poults how to find water and feed. The way they pecked at the wood shavings alarmed her.

Dave stood in the doorway, one elbow propped against the frame, watching her. "Hannah, they'll find the food when they get hungry enough," he told her.

"But, they're so dumb! If they don't stop eating these shavings, they'll die. It doesn't matter how many times I show them where to eat and drink, they forget immediately."

"Just let them go. They'll be all right."

The following morning, eleven turkey chicks lay on their backs with their legs like spindly wax flowers, their eyes closed. Dead. Hannah cried, becoming so upset that she blamed Dave for saying they'd be all right, when they obviously weren't.

Patiently, he explained that some of them would always die. Turkeys were not smart like young chicks were, which couldn't be helped.

He bought a team of Belgians and grew corn and hay, enjoying his days immensely. He wondered why he had thought he didn't like to farm, when this was so much better than moving around crowded Lancaster building things for people who were often too tightfisted to pay the amount his work was worth.

Sarah was born in summer, when the hay lay drying beneath the blazing sun. The old doctor held her upside down and spanked her bottom, until she let out a lusty wail of resentment. "This one's like her mother," he chortled to himself.

For hadn't Hannah led him on a merry chase, the likes of which the poor doctor had never experienced? Unconcerned about any prenatal care and refusing the appointments he made for her, he often had to drive out to their farm and then leave without seeing her. Not that he really minded. He enjoyed driving out to their idyllic little farm tucked between two rolling hills, a windbreak of chestnut and oak trees, and a few white pines. The barn was hip-roofed and painted red. The house was a small, two-story, like a square box with windows, a green shingled roof and green trim around every door and window. There was a row of hedges along the porch and everything was repaired, painted, and neat. There was a flower garden the size of most folk's truck patch!

Her mother came on the train, arriving on a sweltering August day. She smiled and cooed as she examined her namesake with glad, quiet eyes. She held her, unwrapped her, and said she was a beautiful child. That was high praise from Hannah's stoic mother.

Hannah refused to stay down. When Sarah was five days old, she swept the kitchen, dusted the furniture, and walked out to the turkey barns. She came back white-faced and limp, sat in the rocking chair, and didn't say much that whole afternoon.

Her mother brought news from home. Grandfather Stoltzfus was ailing. He was no longer able to do his everyday chores. Elam and Ben should both be looking for wives. She feared there was something wrong with them, the way they made no attempt to date or even appear interested. Hannah snorted and told her mother to get over it. They were bachelors!

After Sarah left, Hannah was relieved. Now she could do as she pleased, which was exactly what she proceeded to do. She could not stand the way her mother folded clothes, so she went to the baby's changing table and refolded every tiny article of clothing and all of the diapers.

Sarah was not an easy baby. Her stomach cramped. She bent double with spasms of pain, screaming and crying, her face as red as a beet, her eyes squeezed shut, her mouth like a foghorn emitting the most awful yells Hannah had ever heard. Surely there was some remedy, Dave asked, his face white with the sounds of his daughter screaming in pain.

Hadn't he had enough, going through the fear for Hannah and the unborn baby, remembering the agony of losing Lena and the twins? There was Hannah, waltzing through the months before Sarah was born, without a trace of concern. And now, this.

It was more than he could take. He stomped out of the house and stayed out. Hannah was furious! Well, if this was how he was going to be, there would be no more children.

Sarah screamed and yelled her way through the first three months of her life. Well-meaning visitors all recommended a different remedy.

Catnip tea. Chamomile. Comfrey. Massaging the baby's feet. Wrapping her around a table leg. Touch her elbows to her knees. Loosen those muscles. A bit of baking soda to sweeten her stomach. Hannah told Dave if she tried everything they recommended, the baby wouldn't survive.

Suddenly, Sarah stopped crying, looked around with her dark brown eyes, and noticed a ray of sunshine reflected from the colored leaves outside. She rolled over and played with her hands and that was it.

She sat by herself at five months, crawled at six months, and walked by herself at eight. If she was not allowed to have what she wanted, she threw herself on the floor and kicked with all her little might, yelling.

Hannah said she was a mess! Dave watched his wife's face, a small grin playing around his mouth, as he asked, "I wonder why?" Hannah smacked his arm as he reached out for her and pulled her onto his lap, kissing her. He loved her as never before.

Samuel was born the following year, a gentle child with Dave's curly hair already sprouting all over his head like a good stand of alfalfa. He was born at almost ten pounds, his wails normal, his naps long and undisturbed by any gastric churning of his tender digestive system.

A sturdy newborn, he was a quiet baby, content to lay on a blanket, his eyes watching the play of sunbeams through the window panes, waving his large hands in the air and kicking his chunky feet with toes like marbles.

For months, the parents could not decipher Samuel's eye color. Mud, Hannah said. The color of mud. Dave disagreed and said his eyes were the color of dark peppermint tea.

Sarah, who was pronouncing whole sentences by the time she was eighteen months old, kept peering over the side of the crib saying, "*Sayna mol. Sayna mol.* I want to see!"

Hannah kept house with strict discipline for herself. Wash on Monday and Thursday. Iron on Tuesday. Bake bread on Wednesday. Pies and cakes and more bread on Saturday. Clean all day Friday. Every day, morning and evening, she was in the turkey houses, checking the growing turkeys, cleaning waterers, making sure their feed was fresh and clean.

She didn't particularly like the fowl themselves. She often thought of them as stupid and dumb, without much sense, even for a bird. But to be among them, caring for them, was so much better than being among people. At least turkeys didn't judge her or expect her to be someone she wasn't.

She often wondered why she had even tried to be the owner of a dry goods store. She hoped Sadie Lapp was happy after her father purchased the house, the store—everything. So happy to be out of Lancaster County, she walked among the gentle hills of Illinois, a good ten miles to the closest Amish neighbor, adapting to the isolation so quickly that Dave told her he'd never met a person like her.

Hannah felt fulfilled in a way she had never thought possible. The anger still flared, the embers of that fire never quite extinguished. But her bitterness was gone. Its miserable grip on her past that had chafed like an open wound was healed, scabbed over until only a small, unsightly white scar remained.

She still struggled with feeling inadequate, that she was not good enough to pass the inspection of others. The first time they attended church services in the home of Abram and Edna Troyer was nothing short of a punishment.

She began the morning by snapping at Dave who was taking an inordinate amount of time in the bathroom. She slapped little Sarah's fingers when she reached into her oatmeal bowl with her hands, which only served to fill the house with her awful howls of self-pity, which set Samuel to crying.

Until they were seated in the buggy, Hannah was on edge, having rolled and re-rolled her hair so many times her scalp smarted. Her covering looked lopsided and smashed, the strings unable to be tied in a decent bow.

Sarah's dark hair had to be put into "bobbies," those fashionable little rolls of hair twisted around bendable pieces of lead that Dave had flattened with a hammer.

First, Hannah wetted Sarah's black hair, smoothing it down with both hands and plastering it against her scalp, which set up a round of indignant howls of protest. Hannah, already stressed beyond endurance by her inability to comb her own hair just right, reacted to her daughter's howls by a smart cuff on her shoulder. "Stop it, Sarah!" This only brought on more howls, which was the last straw.

"Dave!" He appeared from the bedroom door in his white shirt, buttoning it with his large fingers, an accomplishment Hannah never could figure out given the size of those thick appendages.

"Help me with this."

At her side, he asked what he should do. "Hold her chin so she can't move her head." Grimly, Dave did as he was instructed, gently holding Sarah's face in his giant palms, his daughter's howls increasing when she saw she was outnumbered. Hannah rolled her hair around the lead and doubled back. When he thought everything was finished and he was free to go, Hannah tilted the unhappy child's chin to bring her face close to her own as she focused on the two rolls of hair, unhooking one to start over.

"What in the world?" Dave erupted.

"Don't start, Dave," Hannah said in a low, threatening voice.

And so the morning continued, the ride to church strained with impatience and ill feelings. It was one thing to comb a child's hair in such nonsensical forms, quite another to think everything had to be perfect. At one point he'd asked her if she needed a carpenter's level!

At the Troyer's house, the women standing in a large circle in the kitchen where church services would be held were openly curious, kind-faced and offering to help with the baby. Little Sarah stood at her mother's side, eyeing the women with dark eyes.

Hannah managed to smile, shake hands, greet the women with respect, but mostly kept to herself, offering her friendship to no one.

A young mother named Sally Miller, short, rotund, and happy, spoke more to Hannah than any of the others. She invited Hannah to a quilting the following week, telling her to bring the children. Barbara, her oldest daughter, would love to watch them. Hannah smiled, said all the right things, and had absolutely no intention of going to any quilting. She'd rather swallow a tablespoon of vinegar!

A quilting was a stretched piece of fabric surrounded by a bunch of cackling biddies that all talked at once and no one listened. Hannah couldn't quilt, for one thing, pricking her fingers incessantly and knotting the thread until she had to cut the needle loose.

Sally felt as if she'd made a friend as she chattered happily to her husband about Hannah the whole way home. What a beautiful girl she was! Her little girl looked exactly like her. She remarked how nice Hannah was and how she looked forward to their friendship.

Hannah, on the other hand, slouched against the side of the buggy and told Dave that if Sally Miller thought she was going to a quilting, she had another think coming.

Dave raised his eyebrows and asked her why not? It would do her good to be among other women.

"If I want to hear a bunch of chatter, I can go out to the turkey barns. Same thing."

Samuel had fallen asleep on her lap. Sarah stood at Hannah's knees taking in the sights, the warm breeze laced with loose horse hair stirring her little bonnet strings.

They drove for miles, the steel wheels crunching on gravel roads, the ditches filled with rain water, dandelion, new grass, bluebells, and columbine. The landscape could only be described as beautiful, Hannah often thought. Mostly level, the land was covered with verdant grass, but enough woods and thickets to create an illusion of patchwork, shades of green so deep and brilliant they hurt Hannah's senses. Windy days, calm days, rain in the form of scattered showers, or hard, week-long clouds that dripped rain as if God had changed His mind about allowing another flood. Sunshine and beauty after the rain filled the land with millions of dew drops like costly diamonds.

Hannah loved Illinois. Here was the isolation she craved, with a compromising land that loved them back in the form of corn and hay, which Dave harvested and stored in the barn. He built a corn crib and filled it to the brim. He bought a herd of ten sheep.

He built fences, fertilized the grass, bought a few Herefords, and the farm was up and running. He marveled at the changes in his life, the contentment. He'd never imagined he wouldn't miss the pace of his carpentry, the dealing with people and the challenge of pleasing each customer.

Dave knew, though, that his wife was his biggest challenge. For sure. Her garden was immense, enough potatoes to last for three years, row after row of green beans and corn. Tomatoes enough for a shipment to a cannery.

Samuel was raised in the garden, sitting among plants like a little rabbit, playing with the cucumbers and beans. Sarah ran among the rows, covered with dirt, pulling out beanstalks with both hands wrapped tightly around the stalks, her heels digging into the soil, her eyes squeezed shut as she bit down her tongue and heaved and tugged, until Hannah spied her and yelled.

Her mother's voice was no threat to Sarah once she was on a mission. She kept tugging mightily, until she felt her mother's presence beside her, the whoosh of her hand and a firm whack on her skinny little bottom. "Stop it, Sarah!" Hannah exclaimed. "Those are not weeds. They're beans!"

"Weeds."

"No, they're not."

"No beans on here."

"There will be later. Leave them alone." And Hannah went back to her weeding. Sarah went back to pulling out the bean-stalks, determined to prove her mother wrong.

What to do with an *ungehorsam*, disobedient, child? They could administer all the discipline they wanted but Sarah went her own way, her eyes popping and snapping.

Dave smiled and said there wasn't much Hannah could do; she was her mother's daughter. He imagined Hannah had been the same, a real handful.

The harvest from the garden was a steady flow of vegetables, the blue agate canner on the top of the gas range in constant use, preserving beans, peas and corn, tomatoes, peppers and onions and squash, sliced and shredded into relishes and compotes so that Dave had to build more shelves in the cellar.

Hannah whitewashed the stone walls with a mixture of lime and water, swept the packed earth floor, lined the new shelves with folded paper, carried everything down cellar, and stood back to survey her horn of plenty.

Without being aware of it, the hunger from her past drove her like a slave master. Hannah worked with a ferocious intensity, cutting only the smallest amount from the red beet tops, shaking off the clinging soil from the smallest onions and braiding them together with the larger ones.

Every ear of corn was saved, down to the smallest nubbin, the tip of her paring knife gouging deep holes to extricate the fat worm that feasted on her corn.

The smallest potatoes were sorted, put in Mason jars, and cold-packed for fried potatoes. Late in the fall, she covered the celery and the carrots with mounds of garden soil, a layer of straw heaped around the cabbages that had not been shredded and packed in crocks for sauerkraut.

She hummed and whistled, talked to her children, moved around her kitchen with the speed of a small whirlwind. She grabbed her husband by his heavy shoulders and kissed him after eating an onion, breathing the tainted odor into his face. She laughed and ran for dear life when he growled and came after her, until Sarah shrieked, frightened by the thumping noise of her father's boots.

This was on a good day, when Dave counted his wife among the best women he had ever encountered. He loved her with a fierce passion and thanked God for directing their paths together, in spite of having endured pain and grief.

Sometimes the cloud would descend and cover Hannah like a gray shroud. All conversation would cease, her eyes turn dark, her face morose. He always tried to conjure up the past few days and what he had said or done to bring this on. But, more often than not, he came up empty-handed.

Then he'd go his way, avoiding her as much as possible, enduring the silent meals, the slamming of serving dishes containing half-cooked potatoes and lumpy gravy. She had to crawl out of her foul moods by herself, he soon learned.

And he did what he could to help. He'd take the children out to the barn to play while he did the chores. He made sure the wringer on the washing machine was oiled. He weeded the potatoes. From time to time, he lost his temper and told her she was acting worse than a sullen child and needed a good spanking. That only served to prolong the frigid silence, but he said it anyway.

He came to accept these times, but learned not to tiptoe around her, which was what she wanted. She wanted to control him. He knew that, somehow, he had failed her and this was her way of making his suffer for his shortcomings.

Mostly, however, the sun shone. There was laughter and love and plenty of hard work, a church and community surrounding them like a protective fence.

There was plenty of food. The skies turned gray and showered them with rain. The wind blew and dried the land. Bees hummed from plant to plant and butterflies winged their erratic way from one milkweed pod to the next. There were fat woodchucks in the fence rows, shy deer in the woods behind the barn.

Hannah often thought of the wolves and the coyotes, those lurking, shaggy enemies that had inhabited so many of her thoughts in those long winter months when the snow flew past the kitchen window, hurled by the endless, powerful prairie winds of winter. Sometimes she cringed, patted her full stomach, went down to the cellar and stood, breathing heavily to calm her remembered feelings of panic. The food was there and would stay there. She could always come here to this dank, moist, earthy place and find potatoes and turnips, carrots, and onions. Tears would push to the surface and spill over. Her hand would reach out to touch the smooth, glass jars, feeling the tops of the lids, checking to make sure they were sealed.

Then she would pick up a potato, run her fingers across the dry, dusty surface of its skin, and replace it carefully before turning to make her way back to the kitchen, feeling reassured.

"Have you ever been hungry?" she asked Dave one evening, adjusting her head on his shoulder as they lay together in bed, the children both tucked in for the night.

"Of course."

"No, I mean, hungry hungry. When you knew there might not be enough to go around. When you went to bed with an empty stomach?"

Dave considered her question. "No, never," he responded. "I have always had enough to eat. Maybe not what I wanted, but something to fill my stomach."

"It's not funny."

"I'm sure it's not."

There was a soft, comfortable silence. Dave stroked his wife's hair, that sleek, heavy mane he loved so much.

"I still shiver when I think of those winters on the prairie. I'll never forget them if I live to be a hundred years old."

"I would be happy to turn a hundred years old with you."

Silence. Then, "I'm not always nice."

"Doesn't matter. I love you." And he was asleep.

Hannah sighed, turning on her side. But sleep would not come. She knew what love was now. She'd figured it out, in her own way. Love was wanting to be with Dave. It was looking forward to mealtimes with him, craving the closeness of him, loving everything about him. The way he walked, the way he brushed his teeth and drank a glass of water. The way he ate a slice of bread in two gigantic gulps.

She felt his magnetic power, the physical pull of his strength. She felt less than him, conquered by him. She also had an emotional need that only he could fill. But this was her own knowledge, hidden away, never to be revealed.

Dave was no-nonsense, abrupt and businesslike, often leaving her scrambling for security, a sense of trust and belonging. When she felt her handhold on this safety crumble, the dark cloud would descend and she was far too proud to ask for the reassurance of his love.

Wasn't she Hannah? The proud, the powerful woman who didn't need a man to make her happy? And underneath that thin veneer, a week and needy person resided, longing for his time, his attention, his caring. He was her light, her cornerstone.

Well . . . God and Jesus Christ first, of course. That relationship was on better ground than it had ever been. But Hannah figured that Dave came a close second.

CHAPTER 24

Seasons came and went. They planted and harvested, lived in the cold of winter and the warmth of summer. The turkey poults grew and were sold for a good profit. They were fed on corn raised in the fertile, rolling earth. The sheep multiplied and were shorn by the traveling Scottish sheepshearers, the wool sold for another fair amount of cash. The cattle grew fat and lazy. The yearling calves were hauled off to the livestock auction, resulting in a good check that came in the mail a week later.

Hannah planted lilac bushes and forsythia in a long row along the north side of the yard. She planted tulips, irises, daffodils, climbing roses that made a bower along the porch posts on either side of the stone walkway. All spoke of her love of beauty, the appreciation of the finer things in life.

She mowed and trimmed her yard. She fretted about moles and dandelions. She raked every wisp of hay from the driveway after Dave had hauled in the day's work from the fields.

The barn grew. Dave built an annex to the simple framed structure, then added a silo to house corn silage for fattening the steers in winter. He built another corn crib and an implement shed.

Sarah and Samuel went to school when Sarah was seven and Samuel was almost six. Samuel brought home report cards that made Hannah proud. Sarah's were wrinkled and torn, streaked with mud or food stains, peppered with Bs and Cs. Notes from frustrated teachers almost always fluttered to the ground from between the fold of the report card.

Emma was born two years after Samuel, a winsome child with straight dark hair so much like her sister's. When Rudy arrived, they had their hands full once more, his screams and wails echoing through the house until Hannah thought she would surely lose her sanity. Unprepared, with Rudy still screeching at the top of his lungs, Suvilla was born less than a year later.

This was Hannah's personal North Dakota. Here was her biggest challenge. So, she took the bit in her mouth and rose to meet it with the same determination that she did everything else.

If loving Dave produced all of these little ones, then she guessed it was God's will, finally absorbing some of that spirituality for herself. If the baby cried and she got precious little sleep, well, then, so be it. She rose at five o'clock and drank cup after cup of scalding black coffee and did loads of laundry she hand-fed through the wringer she turned herself. She built a roaring fire to heat the *elsa kessle* of cold water to boiling, adding lye soap and stirring the whole load with a stick, after she filled the gasoline engine and yanked it to life with its cord.

She took pride in achieving the whitest whites, bed linens and underwear, socks and nighties as white as the pure winter snow. She washed diapers by the dozens, took pride in the way they hung straight, bringing them in to fold on the kitchen table and thinking how Abner Troyer's wife, Lydia, asked how she got her diapers to look like new. Hannah had cast a disgusted look at the stained, yellow diaper in Lydia's hand and told her flat out she didn't use enough soap or wash them long enough. And, her hot water was not hot enough.

Lydia pinned the diaper on her baby, blinked, and mumbled something about the soap she got from her mother-in-law. But Hannah knew better. Lydia was fat and lazy. She'd rather make doughnuts and eat them then do her washing. *That's what happens, Lydia*, she thought and sniffed indignantly as she moved off.

In some ways, Hannah remained the same, even as the years rolled by. She went to church faithfully, crowding into the buggy with her growing family every two weeks, except when one of the children became ill. She visited with the women of her church group, even laughed and smiled at the affairs of their community, the idle news and the gossip. But no matter how hard the young women tried to include her in their quiltings and Sunday evening suppers, she never went.

Dave wanted to go sometimes and told Hannah so. "Then go," she'd say. "Go ahead. I don't care." Sometimes he did, especially when the supper was held at the home of his favorite friend, Emanuel Stutzman.

They were both sheep farmers. Both enjoyed prosperity after the years of the Great Depression. Both enjoyed cattle auctions and a good game of checkers. Hannah couldn't stand Emanuel's wife. Thin, simpering, and just plain dumb, she'd bet Sarah was smarter at seven years old. For one thing, whoever heard of a name like Fronie? Maybe it wasn't her fault that her parents named her that, but she could come up with a more suitable nickname. If you didn't have the blues when you met her, you would afterward, the way she complained about everything from her tail bone to her sore eyes, her grouchy baby and her husband's foot odor. It was enough to make Hannah want to run out the door.

Dave suggested that Hannah could help her, perhaps give her some kindhearted, understanding tips about all her troubles. "She needs a good kick on her bottom, that's what," Hannah snorted. "Maybe if she'd do her work and quit rubbing that Watkin's salve over everything—her sore shoulder, her nostrils. You can smell the camphor before you see her!"

Dave didn't think it was funny. He told Hannah that her lack of compassion was frightening. He was afraid she'd have to pay for it someday, that God is not mocked.

"I don't pity people, no. The women especially. They need to get to work and quit their whining. Life is never easy. Get over it." And she pounded her bread dough and set it to rise.

Dave sat in the kitchen and watched his wife's strong shoulders, her muscular arms, and he thought, no, sometimes marriage wasn't easy. She made him angry with her refusal to socialize. He'd love to have a normal wife who would look forward to spending an evening giggling and talking, sharing recipes, trading fabric and buttons the way they did back home when he was a small boy. His mother loved a good game of Parcheesi and a round of Rook, becoming boisterous when they spent another evening with Roman Yoders.

So, if he would give his life for his wife, loving her the way Christ loved the church, did that mean he would always have to stay home, with no social life at all? He told Hannah that they were still young and he didn't want to stay at home all the time. This was after Emanuel told him to bring his family after the first snowfall. They would make homemade ice cream.

If there was anything Dave loved, it was hand-churned peanut butter ice cream. Hannah listened from the armless rocker, peering up at him with bleary eyes that were swollen and sleep-deprived, the tip of a diaper strung with other laundry from a line above the stove tickling her head. Suvilla threw a stream of milk across her shoulder, then arched her back and howled like a hyena.

She laid Suvilla calmly on the floor, stretched to her full height, looked Dave in the eye, and told him if he didn't shut up about Emanuel Stutzman and his ice cream freezer, she'd leave him.

"If you can't see farther than your own nose, all right then, go!" Dave answered, so angry he couldn't see straight.

They didn't go to the Stutzmans'. Hannah walked around the house thumping her heels, her chin in the air, and didn't speak. That was fine with Dave, who had no intention of bringing any warmth to the arctic atmosphere pervading the house.

Guilty about their own lack of forgiveness, they paid extra attention to the little ones, reading them stories and drawing pictures with them, without a word passing between Hannah and Dave.

The snow fell, the wind blew, the temperature dropped to below zero. But Dave stayed in the barn, determined to worry Hannah. She'd feel sorry for being so bullheaded.

Hannah clattered dishes and hoped Dave's toes would freeze. It was time he stopped being so selfish. Couldn't he see that she wasn't getting her rest, with Suvilla awake every two hours and not settling down for another hour? No, of course he couldn't. He was sound asleep, snoring like a truck without a muffler.

How could he? And a whole new set of self-pitying feelings took hold of her.

Who broke the silence then? They were never quite sure. They missed each other eventually, so one of them would comment on the weather, the sick ewe, the baby's cough. And, if there was a response, they knew they were on the way out of the silence, which was a huge relief. Laughter and conversation were restored and the good life resumed with stolen kisses and cuffs on the shoulder, fond, smoldering glances and little whirls of heady joy that neither one understood.

From time to time, Dave stood his ground and thundered an obstinate refusal to Sarah's incompetent plans. Things that made no sense. No, he would not build rabbit hutches on the north side of the barn, regardless of what she'd promised Sarah. Rabbits needed sunshine, especially morning sun.

Sarah whined and begged and balled her little fists, pounding his pants leg, whereupon she got a few spanks from his enormous, calloused hand and was told to go sit on the couch until she straightened up.

Hannah was furious but she was well-taught. For a mother to take the disobedient child's part was calling for heartache and sorrow. To turn children against their father was a slippery slope leading to disrespect, which led to more blatant disobedience. So she said nothing, although she thought she'd die of heart failure right then and there from all the belligerence churning in her chest.

He hadn't even heard her out. Rabbits did well on the north side of a building in summer, when the nights were cool and they were shaded from the day's heat. What did he know about rabbits? Probably nothing. She cried that evening when he told her she needed to speak with him about something like rabbit hutches before making any promises to Sarah. It wasn't fair to their daughter to punish her for her reactions.

Why did a husband's words mean so much, though? When Dave said what he thought, the words were heavy and became uncomfortably embedded in her conscience and stuck in her thoughts regardless of how often she told herself she didn't care what he thought. She cared an awful lot, no matter if she brushed it off or not. So, Sarah had no rabbits that summer.

When Suvilla stopped her incessant crying, Hannah thanked God with a grateful heart. She resumed her work with her usual bursts of energy, painted the porch floor with gray enamel paint, so shiny it looked wet. Dave built a porch swing and added an extra two by four to the ceiling joist, hanging the swing with sturdy hooks.

With the profusion of purple lilacs, the irises, and roses, Hannah's porch swing was her evening paradise, a vacation from her hard work and the constant childcare that consumed each day. She would sit, idly pushing the swing with one foot, an arm slung across the back, listening to the sounds of the robins' frenzied chirping as they settled themselves for the night.

She always hoped that Dave would join her, and often he did. She loved these warm evenings when the children played in the yard and the swing would groan under his bulk. They would talk, share their day, and make future plans. Hannah would reach over to straighten his collar, to lift a piece of hay from his beard, hoping he would capture her hand and hold it.

For Hannah did love her husband with an adoration that bordered on worship. Most of the time. But submitting to someone's will other than her own was a monumental task, one that drained her energy, often taking away the sunshine from her existence.

She wished someone would have told her the inordinate amount of giving up that was included in the headiness of romance. How many young girls were swept off their feet by the good looks of an ardent suitor, courted politely under the strict eyes of their parents, married in a godly ceremony that promised days of sunshine and rain? The minister could have included tornadoes and hurricanes and flash floods, in their case!

But she knew she'd do it all over again. Have all these babies, work on the farm with Dave. It was the challenge of a lifetime and, increasingly, a deep contentment and peace she could never really figure out.

She loved the farm and she loved Illinois.

When church services were announced to be held at Dave King's, Hannah felt the same lurch of excitement she always felt. Here were two weeks of *rishting,* preparation for services to be held in their home on a lovely Sunday in May. At least she hoped it would be lovely. Hannah had long planned the display of her flowers, her yard mowed, raked, and trimmed, flower beds without one weed, the soil hoed and loosened with fresh petunias planted in small clumps. The women would walk along the stone pathway to the house, thinking how Hannah was a talented frau, everything so neat and presentable, the growth of flowers amazing.

She washed walls, yanked beds apart, and cleaned the frames and slats with strong-smelling soap. She poured baking soda on mattresses, wiped the steel bedspring coils, washed quilts and blankets, sheets and pillow cases, hanging them on her sturdy wash line. She thanked God for Dave's clothesline poles, thinking she'd be able to hang a ton of clothes on those lines and the poles wouldn't even bend.

She polished windows with vinegar water and clean muslin cloths. She yanked dressers away from walls, upended chairs and small stands, threw articles of clothing from the drawers, and wiped them with the same odorous soap. Not a corner of a closet or drawer went uncleaned. Not a ladybug or a spider remained safe.

Hannah cleaned all day every day and made cold sandwiches for Dave at lunch time. She slapped bean soup on the table for supper. The children were put to bed early so Hannah could collapse on the couch for a moment, her shoulders aching, her lower back on fire with pain.

Dave told her he'd rub it with horse liniment, which brought a snort of mammoth proportions. Everyone stayed out of Hannah's way, even the unruly Sarah, who took pity on Suvilla with her wet diaper and her runny nose, standing in the middle of the kitchen and howling to herself with her mother nowhere about when they got home from school.

Sarah wiped Suvilla's nose, laid her on the floor, and changed her diaper. Then she gave her saltine crackers to eat, all the while glaring at her mother for being so negligent.

They had a colossal argument. Dave wanted to hold services in the house, spring weather being unpredictable the way it was. Hannah insisted on the barn. Why not? It would save him so much work not having to clear out the furniture before setting the long wooden benches in place.

"All you have to do is spread clean straw, sweep cobwebs, and we're ready. The weather is unseasonably warm, Dave."

"It is this week. It's May, Hannah. Anything can happen, and usually does."

"I've never seen a pessimist like you."

"Why can't you give up, Hannah?"

"Because, it doesn't make any sense. It's warm enough to hold the service in the barn. The bays are almost empty. I can take the food and dishes out on Saturday and the house will stay untouched."

"What if it turns cold and rainy? No, we're going to hold services in the house."

With that certain look—his nostrils slightly flared, his amber eyes wide, his temper like a boiling cauldron beneath his compressed lips—Hannah knew there would be no budging.

She tried anyway. The children were in bed and they felt free to state their minds, which soon drifted from the subject at hand to other accusations, darts of demeaning epithets, genuine mud-slinging, resulting in Dave slamming the screen door, breaking the latch, and Hannah crying great bursts of tears, awash in self-pity and burning rebellion.

Neither one admitted their lack of sleep the following morning. They spoke in clipped tones at the breakfast table, asking only what was absolutely necessary, a half-strangled reply from the other.

She kept on cleaning, mowed the yard, washed the porch, and baked twenty-six snitz pies from the dried apples she'd stored in the pantry over winter. She mixed the peanut butter with molasses, made cup cheese from the crumbles she'd prepared beforehand, and opened ten quarts of sweet pickles and six quarts of spiced red beets.

And still Dave did not give in. Church services would be held in the house. It was so completely against her wishes that it was like taking a mouthful of warmed, slimy cod liver oil.

Grimly, she helped him move furniture. She couldn't stand the sight of his unruly mop of hair. Every time she gave him a bowl haircut, he looked like a tulip bulb. She still hadn't figured out why his face looked so out of proportion.

When had she ever thought this man handsome? Certainly not now as he tugged red-faced at yet another heavy piece of furniture that could have stayed exactly where it was if he'd listened to her.

On Sunday morning the temperature on the John Deere thermometer tacked to the porch post had the mercury somewhere between 30 and 40 degrees. Hannah had tumbled out of bed at four o'clock, shivering, the floor cold to her bare feet.

Wide-eyed and startled into speech, she told Dave perhaps they should start a fire in the living room. Before daylight, Hannah heard a roar, like distant rolling thunder, except there was no let up.

From the porch, she saw the cold rain that slanted in from the east, driven by a stiff wind. The dawn was gray and eerie, the moaning of the wind like a correctional ghost admonishing her to be grateful for once in her life, for her husband's good judgment.

The irises hung their soggy heads in the driving rain. The roses lost their red petals in the harsh wind. The lilacs waved and nodded, thoroughly soaked and battered by the cold rain.

Women scuttled up the stone walkway, their black bonnets pulled well past their faces, clutching babies and small baskets containing diapers and milk bottles, raisins and saltines for cranky little ones. Not one of them noticed the perfectly trimmed yard, the groomed flower beds, or the profusion of flowers planted according to Hannah's exact specifications. Every one that stepped from the buggy into the lashing torrent had one objective and that was to get to the house as swiftly as possible.

A warm fire burned in the cooking range, another one in the living room. Women held out their hands to the warmth, appreciating that the service would be held in the cozy house. Hannah smiled and nodded and kept her secret. No one would ever pry the fact out of her that she had tried to make the service be held in the barn.

Unbelievable, this weather. It was May. But she seated the women, sat erect with Suvilla on her lap, her face carefully arranged to appear caring and friendly. She was more than glad she had listened to Dave.

The minister droned on for an unspeakably long time. Hannah mostly worried about the coffee and whether the cheese would be too runny to spread on the bread. If the pie crust was hard or reasonably flaky.

Long after the last song had been sung, the tables set and re-set, everyone cleared out and Hannah sagged with relief into the armless rocker. Dave came in and stood in front of her, grinning. "So Hannah, weren't you glad you listened to me?"

"Go away. Just go and stop bothering me." But she had to smile in spite of herself.

And so the lives of Dave and Hannah King progressed through the years. A total of ten children joined their family by the time Hannah reached the age of forty-three, each one loved and cherished in her own way.

Samuel and Rudy followed their father's ways, but none of his boys ever grew to his size or stature. He remained the giant father figure, but a fair and level-headed one.

Daniel, Ezra, and Noah were in a line, all looking up to *Dat* with respect and even reverence. Noah had the same wild, untamed mop of hair as his father, his amber eyes and large hands and feet.

With Hannah's temperament, he was a genuine troublemaker in school and in church, bloodying the nose of more than one boy older than himself. He swaggered, he spit, and went by the name of "Max." And yet, somehow, in spite of the thread of headstrong natures running between mother and father, they raised their brood in the Amish faith.

They all acted up as teenagers, bringing sleepless nights and humbling Hannah in a way that no horrific events of her lifetime ever had. The homestead in the West had been a constant chain of life's lessons, but not one of them served to smooth the rough edges of her personality the way her children did.

Sarah resisted all of her mother's advice. She pouted around the house and refused any form of discipline. She was quick to speak and quick to judge, the despair of Hannah's life until she decided, painfully, that we reap what we sow. It seemed her life was one constant flashback. Shot through with fiery remorse, Hannah begged forgiveness for her past and was rewarded with a spirit of humility, a sweetness in her nature of which she was quite unaware.

She went to quiltings and auctions, shook hands warmly and met people's gazes with friendly eyes and genuine caring. She stopped talking about innocent women who did not quite measure up to her standards.

Her hair turned gray. She threaded her hand through the crook of Dave's elbow as they stood by the woven wire fence, watching the baby lambs on a fine spring morning. All around them the earth bloomed. Dogwoods, redbuds, crab apple, cherry and apple blossoms opened and sang to God's glory. The woods were thick with new green leaves, burdock, plantain, dandelion, and thistle. Small creatures rattled the heavy plants and skittered away as the aging couple walked along the fence.

"Our homestead," Hannah whispered.

Dave patted the hand on his arm and turned his amber eyes on her dark ones. "Yes, Hannah. Our homestead. Our place here on earth. I have never regretted a minute of our union."

Hannah snorted. "Oh, come on, Dave."

"I still love you. Even more now that we're older. I'm serious."

She held the gaze that still caused her knees to turn liquid, the unspoken language of love that had carried them through the rough times as well as the joyous ones.

The spring breeze sighed as he bent to kiss her, his wrinkled eyes filling with tears of gratitude and appreciation for his beloved.

The sun slid behind the thick, green forest, casting an ethereal light on the undulating farmland, bathing the white farmhouse and the red barn in a golden glow.

Hannah laid her head on her husband's shoulder, saw the perfect morning glow over the farm, and whispered again, "My homestead. My home where contentment and love reign."

The End

GLOSSARY

Ach du lieva—Oh, my goodness

An schöena ovat—A nice evening

An shauty soch—A sad thing

Auhàèmlich—Something that is familiar or memorable; reminiscent of home

Ausbund—The book of old German hymns written by Amish ancestors imprisoned in Passau, Germany, for their Christian faith

Ausricha; ausra—Outsiders; "those people"

Auseriche leit—People outside the Amish church; people of the world

Aylend—A poor work ethic; unconcerned about work

Begräbniss—Burial

Bessa-grissa—Your conscience

Bisht die Hannah?—Are you, Hannah?

Bupp—Baby, in a pejorative sense; cry baby

Byshtant—God's "standing by"

Dat—Name used to address one's father

Dat, doo kannsht net—Dad, you can't do that

De lieve—Love

Demut—Humility

Demütich—Humble

Denke—Thank you

Der Gute Mann—The Good Man; that is, God

Der Herr—The Lord

Dichly—A triangle of cloth worn by women instead of a head covering

Die goot schtup—The guest bedroom

Doch-veggly—Literally, a "roof wagon," it refers to a buggy with a roof that a couple usually purchases after they are married, if they could afford one

Duchsach—Fabric

Dummheita—Foolishnes

Eisa kessle—Iron kettle

Englische leid—Those whose first language is English; anyone not Plain

Englisha mon—English man

Fa-sark—To take care of; look after

Frieda—Peace

Fadenkas—To judge a person

Fer-flucht—Cursed

Fer-late—Despair; loss of hope

Forehaltiss—Future plans

Fottgung—To succeed, as with a business

Freuheita—Freedoms

Freundshaft—A person's group of friends

Gaul—Horse

Gehorsam—Obedient

Gehorsamkeit—Obedience

Gel—Right; to agree with something another says

Goldicha fauda—The golden thread

Gottes furcht—Fear of God

Gottes saya—God's blessing

Grosfeelich—Proud

Gute—Good

hals schtark—determined

Heiliche Schrift—Holy Bible

Herr saya—God's blessing

Hesslich—Ugly

Himmlischer Vater. Meine Herre und mein Gott—Heavenly Father. My Lord and my God

Hochmut—Loose morals

Hochzeit velssa—Wedding songs

Hott sie ken schema?—Has she no shame?

Iss eya net an bei kumma?—Is he not appearing?

Ivva drettung—Overstepping set boundaries

Ivva reck—Overcoats

Ketch—Catch, as in a man who is "considered quite a *ketch*"

Kinnershpeil—Child's play

Knepp—Thick, floury dumplings

Kum yusht rei—Come on in

Leblein—A piece of fabric on the back of a dress; in modern times, it is a traditional sign that the woman is Amish

Lied—Song

Machets goot, Dat—Stay well, Dad

Maud—A girl who lived with other Amish families in a time of need. A helper, usually in the house, to the wife and mother in a family

Meine dochter—My daughter

Mensch—A person; used to stress the humanity of all people created by God

Mishting—Pooping; used when referring to animals

Mitt unser Herren Jesu Christus—With our Lord Jesus Christ

Mutterschprach—Mother tongue

Nein—No

Ordnung—Literally, "ordinary," or "discipline," it refers to an Amish community's agreed-upon rules for living, based on the Bible, particularly the New Testament. The *ordnung* can vary in small ways from community to community, reflecting the leaders' interpretations, local traditions, and historical practices.

Ponhaus—Scrapple

Roasht—Chicken filling

Rishting—Preparing

Roasht—A chicken and bread casserole

Rumschpringa—Literally, "running around." A time of relative freedom for adolescents, beginning at about age sixteen. The period ends when a youth is baptized and joins the church, after which the youth can marry.

Sayna mol—I want to see

Schenked und fagevva—To forgive

Schnitz un knepp—Dried apples cooked with chunks of home-cured ham and spices, with a covering of thick, floury dumplings called *knepp*

Schöene frau—Nice lady

Schputt—Mockery

Schrift—Scriptures

Schtrāling—Combing with a fine-toothed comb

Schnitz boy—Dried-apple pie

Schnitz und knepp—Dried apples cooked with chunks of home-cured ham and spices, with a covering of thick, floury dumplings called *knepp*

Schmear kase—Spreadable cheese for bread

Sei—His

Shick dich—Behave yourself

Shicklich—To present oneself properly and with good manners

Shtrubles—Fly-away hair

Ungehorsam—Disobedient

Unfaschtendich—A person not on a good spiritual foundation; something that doesn't make sense

Ungehorsam—Disobedient

Ungehorsamkeit—Disobedience

Unsaya—The unblessing

Vass gebt?—What gives

Vass geht au?—What's going on?

Vass in die velt?—What in the world?

Verboten—Forbidden

Vie bisht?—How are you?

Vie ihr Dat—Like her father

Vilt. See harriched net—Wild. She doesn't listen

Vissa adda unvissa—To know or not know

Voddogs — An everyday shirt or dress, patched again and again, then handed down to a younger child

Vonn glaynem uf — From childhood on; something about a person that has been since he or she was a child

Vos iss lets mit sie? — What is wrong with her?

Wasser bank — Dry sink

Wunderbar — Wonderful

Youngie ihr rumschpringas — The youths' running around

Yusht da vint — Just the wind

Zeit-lang — Homesick

OTHER BOOKS BY
LINDA BYLER

LIZZIE SEARCHES FOR LOVE SERIES

BOOK ONE

BOOK TWO

BOOK THREE

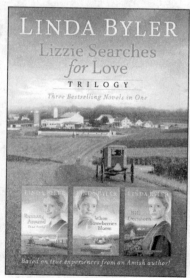

TRILOGY

COOKBOOK

Sadie's Montana Series

BOOK ONE

BOOK TWO

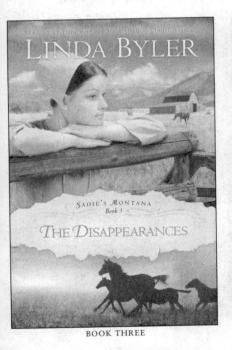

BOOK THREE

TRILOGY

LANCASTER BURNING SERIES

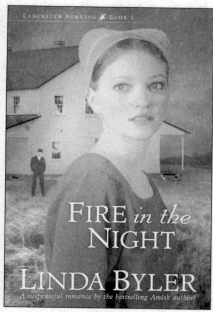

BOOK ONE

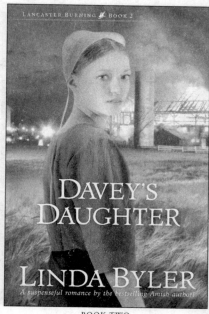

BOOK TWO

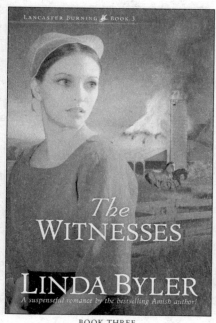

BOOK THREE

TRILOGY

HESTER'S HUNT FOR HOME SERIES

BOOK ONE

BOOK TWO

BOOK THREE

TRILOGY

The Dakota Series

The HOMESTEAD

An Amish romance set during the Great Depression

THE DAKOTA SERIES
BOOK 1

LINDA BYLER

BOOK ONE

HOPE *on the* PLAINS

THE DAKOTA SERIES
BOOK 2

LINDA BYLER

BOOK TWO

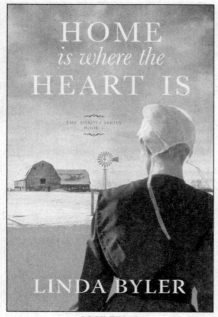

HOME *is where the* HEART IS

THE DAKOTA SERIES
BOOK 3

LINDA BYLER

BOOK THREE

"The authenticity of Byler's narrative shines on every page . . ." —*Publishers Weekly*

LINDA BYLER

The Dakota Series

TRILOGY

Three Spirited Novels by a Beloved Amish Writer

TRILOGY

CHRISTMAS NOVELLAS

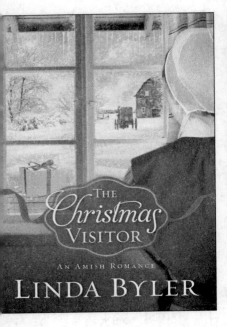

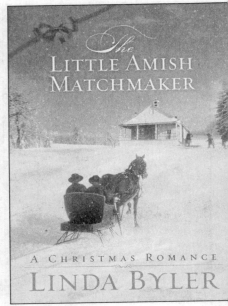

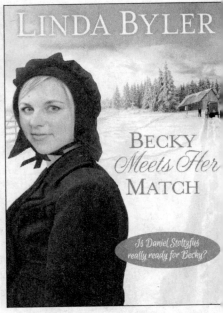

A Dog for CHRISTMAS

AN AMISH CHRISTMAS ROMANCE

LINDA BYLER

A Horse For ELSIE

AN AMISH CHRISTMAS ROMANCE

LINDA BYLER

LINDA BYLER

The More the Merrier

AN AMISH CHRISTMAS ROMANCE

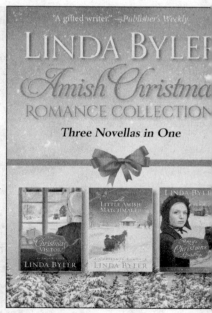

"A gifted writer." —Publisher's Weekly

LINDA BYLER

Amish Christmas

ROMANCE COLLECTION

Three Novellas in One

The Healing

A Second Chance

Hope Deferred

Buggy Spoke Series for Young Readers

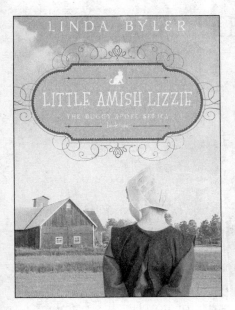

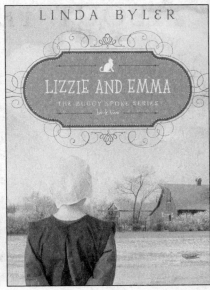

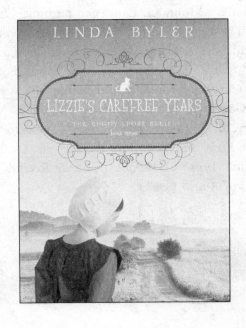

ABOUT THE AUTHOR

LINDA BYLER WAS RAISED IN AN AMISH FAMILY AND IS AN ACTIVE member of the Amish church today. Growing up, Linda loved to read and write. In fact, she still does. Linda is well-known within the Amish community as a columnist for a weekly Amish newspaper. She writes all her novels by hand in notebooks.

Linda is the author of six series of novels, all set among the Amish communities of North America: Lizzie Searches for Love, Sadie's Montana, Lancaster Burning, Hester's Hunt for Home, The Dakota Series, and the Buggy Spoke Series for younger readers. Her stand-alone novels include *The Healing*, *A Second Chance*, and *Hope Deferred*. Linda has also written several Christmas romances set among the Amish: *Mary's Christmas Goodbye*, *The Christmas Visitor*, *The Little Amish Matchmaker*, *Becky Meets Her Match*, *A Dog for Christmas*, *A Horse for Elsie*, and *The More the Merrier*. Linda has coauthored *Lizzie's Amish Cookbook: Favorite Recipes from Three Generations of Amish Cooks!*